Beamed Up
Decide Your Destiny

by M.E. Kinkade

For Dan and Peg,
who taught me to boldly go
and to reach for the stars.

Beamed Up: Decide Your Destiny

It's a beautiful night for a walk anyway; you'll deal with the car tomorrow. Seriously, the road must have been slippery or something—you're an excellent driver, even if you did have four, five, seven beers. Damn bartender didn't know what he was talking about, throwing you outta the bar. You'll show him. Sometime later...you gotta, like, build up revenge for serving from the freezer. Yeah...

Why is the ground so uneven? Stupid bumpy ground. Ugh, that rock tripped you on purpose.

It's fine, you'll just lie here.

The sky above you is spinning gently and you start to feel woozy, so you close your eyes.

Moments later you're wakened by your great aunt, still leaving those sloppy kisses on your face even though you're no longer five (and you hated it then, too). You open your eyes to complain, "Auntie, Auntie, no..." and look straight up the snout of a monster. No, wait, it's only a cow.

Your head is splitting and you smell like manure—your hair is sticky with it. You stagger to your knees, startling Aunt Heifer, and realize you're in Tom Ford's field again. Dammit.

Suddenly your stomach lurches sideways and you vomit up the rest of your liquid dinner. The night is deep all around you.

As you begin to struggle back to your feet, you hear a sound tugging at the edges of your mind. It gets louder and louder, and the cows look up, as if they're waiting for something. As the noise builds, the animals freeze, like time itself has stopped. You cover your ears to keep your brain from tumbling out, the sound an auditory roller coaster, making your head feel like it's vibrating.

It sounds like:
- A wailing siren, autotuned to match a banshee's shriek. Turn to the next page.
- Crunching glass with pounding horse's hooves and a slight undertone of *La Cucaracha*. Turn to page 12.
- A playing card stuck in the spokes of a planet-sized bicycle. With streamers. Turn to page 17.
- This is stupid, aliens aren't real. Turn to page 16.

You fall screaming to the muddy earth as the sound draws closer and closer. The cows around you go back to chewing their cud, as if they no longer want to know what is drawing near. A bright light beckons over the horizon, and you are struck by terror. You begin to cry, rubbing your eyes and smearing grass and something slimy over your cheek.

The sound gets louder, closer, convalescing into a wooo-oo woo-oo repeating pattern.

Then, as suddenly as it began, the noise subsides. A voice calls your name.

"Hey, did you hear me?" the voice calls, sounding annoyed.

You look up. Standing 20 feet away, on the other side of a fence your car is firmly smashed in, is Deputy Collins. The lights of her squad car are still flashing, but she's turned the siren off.

"Get off your ass already," Collins says. "I really don't want to go roll around in that mud with you like last week."

You nod, suddenly feeling sullen. Shit.

As your senses clear, you realize you've torn your shirt and your pants are probably going to have to be burned, and not just because of the manure.

So...it was probably a successful Saturday night.

"What have I told you about drinkin' late?" Collins asks, the lateness of the night bringing out her East Texas drawl. She sighs, leaning on the wooden post. "You ain't a bad sort, you know, but why you gotta go and do stupid shit like this? Now I have to take you in, and you know I don't like paperwork."

"Sorry," you say. Collins steadies your arm as you sloppily climb back over the wreckage of your car and the mutilated fence. "I thought you were some kinda alien or somethin'."

Collins just gives you a blank look. "Sure you did."

You wipe a hand up your face, flicking off a bit of the mud. "Yeah. I think I'll stop drinking for a while."

"Good idea," she says.

It takes a while for Collins to get you reasonably cleaned up, and you slip into the industrial orange jumpsuit; by now, Collins knows your size and has it ready. She even lets you have a pill to stop the worst of your hangover.

You've been lying on your hard jail mattress for maybe 40 minutes when another officer brings in a new arrest.

Your new cellmate is:
- A skinny man clutching a worn blue towel. Turn to page 21.
- Fred, still in his pajamas, his eyes wild. Turn to page 23.
- A small grey dog with brindle markings. Turn to page 30.
- A teenage girl, still reeking of spray paint. Turn to page 36.

You're not an experienced fighter, true, but you're pretty sure you can hit a man broadside while he's holding still, so you knock back and prepare to give it all you've got—and yeah, if it looks even better for your audience of bees, well, that's good, too. They'd better get used to being impressed by their future liege.

Your opponent is standing with his back to the wall, his eyes a little wavering. You run up and throw your punch, aiming right for his nose.

He ducks; your hand smashes into the wall and explodes into pain. As he darts past you, your opponent jabs you twice in the ribs, knocking the air out of your lungs. You gasp, and try to close your hand into a fist again, but you must have broken some bones—it won't close. You turn to face the mustachioed man, only to weakly block a two-punch set to your face with your forearm. You swing wildly with your off-hand, barely connecting, and he hits you again, two hits to the face. You stagger to the right, panting, and open your arms wide to try to grab him, desperate for any kind of hold. You grapple with him, and he continues you pummel your guts with rapid-fire punches. Panicking, you kick, aiming between his legs, but you can't catch your breath. You're bleeding from somewhere on your forehead, and the blood runs down into your eyes, blinding you. You lose your grip and stagger back.

The other man comes up, bracing your head with a hand on either side, and says, softly, so only you can hear: "I'm sorry." And then he slams his head into yours and the world explodes into colors and pain and you fall to the ground.

You lie there, insensate, but you can hear your opponent stand and raise his arms in victory.

"I have won! I am queen," he says.

But the bees say, "Kill. Kill!"

"But I won," he says.

The bees roar in your mind. "Kill! Kill and become our queen! All will be well!"

"I am the strongest!" he says, furious. "I am the queen of this hive!"

And with his yell he grabs a bee off the wall, spiking it like a football down upon your neck, the bee's stinger stabbing through. The pain is immeasurable, and soon your blood stains the floor, melding with the beeswax.

If it's any consolation, he was the better queen anyway. Sure, the bees self-manage pretty well, but he's good at deciding on the other things, like when to colonize a new planet, when a swarm is in order, how to handle mites. His reign is long and relatively just. So, yeah, your death was for the greater good, and all is well with the bees.

THE END

Breck waves from the landing dock as you board the rocket on one of NASA's less-used (and less visible) pads. She looks like a child's toy from up here, and you briefly wonder if maybe you're having some kind of really intense LSD-type hallucination, like maybe you're part of some MKUltra type deal. But the rocket in front of you seems very solid, if small—it's a little bigger than a broom closet, though the Zenithians were considerate enough to make you a chair. The flight crew scramble up higher ladders to reach the cockpit, while a few dozen other Zenithians file in to sit in the small padded chairs lining the wall opposite you. They are pale and vaguely reddish, like clay dolls, perfect miniatures of real people.

They *are* real, you remind yourself. And you're about to get to know a lot more of them.

"First time?" one across from you, about chin-level, asks. As you try to find your answer, the older man, hair red with a grey hank at the temples, just nods, saying, "You got the look about you. Don't you worry. Keruk up there, the pilot, she's top-notch all the way. Should be a nice easy flight."

You smile and introduce yourself. "I guess I am a little nervous," you say bashfully.

"'Course you are, never had a human go with us before. But I bet you're excited, too. Hey, hope you went to the bathroom before you boarded, or at least can hold it for a good long while," he says, a twinkle in his eye. You inadvertently squeeze your knees together and he laughs so hard his shoulders pull at the restraints and his voice comes in a wheeze. "Ha ha ha, just kiddin'. It's just gonna be what feels like a few hours to you. We got a few tricks we ain't showed the humans yet." He winks. "I'm Fruzi."

"You got me good, Fruzi," you admit with a smile. "I am excited to see Zenithian, but I'm pretty scared, too. I mean, I'm an adventurer, and my whole planet may never even know that I left, what I did!"

"Well, don't you worry too much," Fruzi says. There's a rumble below your seat and you grip the armrests tightly.

"Won't be long now," Fruzi says, and you try not to look scared. You're terrified.

The takeoff isn't so bad, really, but it is like being launched from a really fast rollercoaster, and you can feel your cheeks pulling downward, like a beagle. Beagles—you may never see another one. You think of the small suitcase you were allowed to bring and hope you packed right. Then, as the acceleration continues to pull on your body, making you feel a bit like warm jelly, you start to hope you're going to survive.

You pass out for a while.

You wake up to a gentle pat-patting on your hand. It's Fruzi, out of his chair and standing on the side of the armrest. "There you go," he says. "You'll be alright. It's always tough the first time."

You blink and look around. "Might be a good time to look out the porthole," another Zenithian, a younger male with a sharp chin and serious disposition, suggests.

It's over your right shoulder, and you hesitantly loosen your restraints and look out. It's as tall as a Zenithian, which means about six inches across, just small enough for you to see if you peer closely. Outside it is...dark, yes, but...wow. The pictures from the Hubble are nothing like this. You're floating through a cloud of reds and oranges and purples, and it looks like it's dancing and you're holding perfectly still. You look for Earth, or maybe Saturn's rings, but you can't see anything familiar. "Where are we?" you ask.

The other Zenithian, the younger one, says, "We left your solar system about 10 minutes ago. We're in what we know as Thoros 6. I'm not sure your name for it."

"The Eagle nebula, Belra," Fruzi says.

"Woah," you say.

"You can take the straps off, if you like," Fruzi continues. "I'll let you know when it's time again."

"This is all just incredible," you say.

Belra snorts derisively, and Fruzi shoots him a look. To you he says, "It's easy for us to think of it as nothing important, but you are a good reminder that it is new to many. I am glad you are coming with us. I'm sure we have much to learn from one another."

Fruzi clambers back to his seat, where you can see him more easily, and he distracts you with his history. He grew up on Earth, but remembers a childhood on Zenith. "I am old now," he laughs, "and it was time for my old soul to get back where it belongs. But you shall be quite the excitement when we land, I'm sure."

"I hope in a good way," you say.

But he shrugs you off. "It'll be fine! What a wonderful adventure for you!"

The landing goes about as well as takeoff, though again you don't remember most of it—they have to splash water on your face (what they could reach) to rouse you this time, and most everyone has already disembarked by the time you come to. Once again there's Fruzi, ever-cheerful, with Belra brooding behind him. "Come on, let's get you out," Fruzi says, extending his small hand to you and pulling you up by your fingertip. Your legs feel odd after the trip.

You crouch to get out of the rocket, and so have to stand slowly. The planet is...not quite how it seemed from Breck's stories. You lean down to Fruzi: "This...is your planet?"

Fruzi looks a little bashful, and replies, "Yes...it seems it has changed a little since I left."

That's an understatement. The lush green hills from the stories are covered in low houses made of stone, little parapets spinning out into the sky, which is grey and choked with soot. You can barely see anything at your full height, just the spindles of towers from the high buildings that pierce the smog. You feel greasy just looking at it.

Leaning down to get below the smog, you ask, "Now what?"

Belra looks consternated, his downturned grimace becoming a solid scowl. "Now what, indeed?

"Er, come this way," Fruzi says, tugging on your shoelace. With the smog, you can't see the Zenithians below you, forcing you to lope along on your hands and knees like an idiot. Everything is the wrong size. It's possible you didn't really think this through enough.

A building ahead is laid out in a u-shape, and from the center emerges a train of Zenithians in solemn beige, each dressed differently enough to mark them as individuals, but collectively rather boringly similar. Fashion, it seems, has also taken a back seat on Zenith.

They fan out in a general inverted-v shape as you hobble forward behind Belra and Fruzi, the lead Zenithian spreading her hands in a gesture of equanimity. "Welcome," she says, her voice low and hollow. "Welcome, voyagers from your long diaspora, and welcome, ambassador from Krakora, which you call Earth."

Belra and Fruzi dip in response, like a bow, and after a moment's pause where you try to figure out how to handle your incredible size, you bob your head. This seems like enough.

The Potentate Rilatz, as you soon came to know, was savvy, if as drab as her wardrobe. She didn't really have much truck with ambassadors from other worlds, and wasn't much interested in dealing with you. After all, you're essentially a gigantic burden on the economy of Zenith; your house is enormous and lavish, by their standards; it takes an awful lot of izcrea fruit to feed you every day; and frankly Zenith didn't really even need an ambassador to Krakora/Earth anyway.

Seeing as Zenith seems to be amidst an industrial revolution, you feel like you could offer some advice on dealing with pollution, or at least offer a birds-eye perspective on the problem, but no one is interested.

Your house is barely big enough for you to lie down in, the izcrea fruit taste like kiwi-flavored mothballs, you don't even have a job, and no one will listen to you.

And then things get worse.

You wake one morning in your coffin-like shelter to smoke, thicker and closer than the normal day-to-day smog, and realize you can hear the crackle of it right near your head. You leap up, hitting your head on your low ceiling, lifting it up off its foundation. Through the crack you see a group of Zenithians scuttle off, torches in hand. "Hey! Stop that!" you yell, and extricate yourself from the house.

Down the street, you see a water engine heading your way, but it's struggling with a hill, and meanwhile your house, your horrible, inadequate house, is burning. You rush down the street and pick up the engine, ignoring the panicked cries of the Zenithian fire team inside. Holding the engine's window to your face, you cry, "you've got to stop the fire!" and put the engine down near your house. The rattled little people inside clamber out—at least one falling flat on his face as he emerges from the truck—and shakily begin to deploy their water hoses. Too slowly, far too slowly!

"My house!" you cry, and perhaps it was the smoke or the panic of being on the cusp of losing your last Earthly belongings or just the knock on the head, you decide to act, dampening the fire using the only water you have on your person—you drop trou and pee on the flames, subsuming them in your daily ablutions.

The fire is put out...and the fire team stares at you in horror.

Fruzi is sent to bring you the news. "They were protesters," he says, twisting his hands. "It seems there is a growing contingent of Zenithians who desire you leave the city."

"Well that's preposterous!" you exclaim. "This is the only house for me on the planet!"

"Yes, well..." Fruzi says, looking askance. "Well, because of your...handling of the situation...more have added to their number. The Potentate has asked that you leave, before the issue worsens."

You sit on the edge of your creaking bunk, head in your hands. "So I'm to lose my house after all," you say.

It doesn't take long for you to pack your few, slightly singed, belongings, and by the next day you head out. It's careful going, having to shuffle your feet to avoid the Zenithians in your path, but you're able to clear a city block with a single step, so the trip isn't too bad. It's the first time you've been able to stretch your legs since arriving at the planet.

After walking for an hour or so—watching the horizon curve away from you like a downturned smile—you arrive at a mountain range. The area is lightly populated, and the mountains protect you from the worst of the wind, so you nestle down into the valley, cover your head with a blanket, and try to ignore the pine trees digging into your back.

You spend a few days snapping trees off at the stump and forming a roof between the two mountains, a bit like weaving with matchsticks. Fruzi does what he can, and sends a steady shipment of available foods so you don't go completely hungry. One day he even got you the meat of 20 occars, goat-like creatures that together make up about two mouthfuls.

You glumly realize you've accidentally become the ogre in a storybook by coming here. You have to wait until Fruzi comes to visit before you can send a message to the Potentate—any note you wrote down would be too challenging to send, filling a whole engine. When he does visit, you ask if you can board the next ship back to Earth.

"Yes, this visit really hasn't turned out as we hoped, has it?" Fruzi says, and you're gratified to realize he seems to be genuinely sad.

"I didn't really consider the logistics of being on an alien world," you reply, just as glum.

Fruzi pats you on the knee, a kind gesture you can barely feel. "Well, we'll get you out, I'll see to it."

And so you wait.

Meanwhile, back in the city, the unrest continues to foment, and the giant in the mountains is a point of great vexation. The situation is worsened by an anti-immigration sect within the leading party discouraging the movement of further Zenithian workers to Earth, and a sudden peak in sanitation-related problems, which are blamed to you and your excrement but are truly caused by badly planned sewage pipes.

All in all, the situation is incendiary, and so it's not entirely surprising to area pundits when they turn on you. It is, however, very surprising to you.

First the food shipments stop coming, forcing you to scavenge the area for anything edible, but you're so large that you quickly strip the countryside, your stomach growling like an angry hungry bear. Then there's a storm, which washes your latrine downstream, much to the villagers' displeasure. In your hunger, you grow feverish, and shiver under your meager shelter.

When they come back with the bomb, you have no defense. You swat the flying machines like flies, but they just buzz back, and the cannons sting you like wasps. When the bomb blasts you in the gut, you are winded, and your blood begins to flow, mixing with the river.

Even after death, you are a nuisance, as your corpse provides a true ecological challenge the Zenithians are unprepared for. Your body rots slowly, a huge wasteland of decay, and the valley must be abandoned. Zenith's relationship with Earth, peaceful all these decades, sours.

Not much of an alien ambassador, were you?

THE END

You cover your ears and duck as you see the outlines descend from the sky. Massive dark shapes, like funnels topped with beehives, outlined in an eerie green light. The things are huge, getting bigger by the second as they drop out of the sky. A sick feeling of dread wells up in your stomach, and you turn to vomit, not just from the beer this time.

You kneel, hands in the dirt, your stomach turning right-side-in again. You dare to look up again; the structures are still there, still getting closer. As they near the ground, the ships eject something from all sides, smaller black objects peeling away, barely visible in the purpling sky. You are overwhelmed by just how many there are; they pour out of the big structure like an endless stream of confetti, small and yet massive because of their great number.

You try to run, really think you should, but your body betrays you, and you only manage to stumble forward clumsily. The dispersion fans out, covering the sky, worse than a plague of locusts. You crawl forward, fear overcoming your hungover sickness just enough to keep you moving.

The ground shivers behind you. Suddenly, ahead to your left, there comes a great spray of dirt and grass and the ground bucks up underneath you, knocking you back. Something has crashed, a tube-like pointed thing. You realize it must be what you saw break off from the thing in the sky; it looks like a shard, or a chrysalis.

There's something inside. It knocks, jabbing from within, causing the shard to shiver.

You don't have time to look; another crashes down not 10 feet away, and then another, behind you. They're everywhere, landing in the field upright, like a cheap Stonehenge. You curl into a ball and cover your head, sure at any moment you'll be impaled by falling debris.

In front of you, that first shard is opening, cracked from within as if it were nothing. You can see just the edge of the thing inside, and for a brief manic moment you think, *now, I should kill it now*, but the moment passes before you can move. You watch in horror as the creature emerges.

The first thing you see is:
- A barbed point, like a scorpion, evil-looking and dripping with a shining translucent poison. Turn to page 278.
- What looks like fur, and some kind of armor, like panes of glass.

Turn to page 279.

- Massive pincers, like on those beetles that roll up poop, but way more terrifying when bigger than a human's head. Turn to page 282.

The first sensation to break through the agony is a trickling sound. It sounds like a leaky tap at first, a quiet slurp-drip-drip that you feel more than hear. The sound grows, a brook over stones, an ocean, a whirlpool. And in the whirlpool come other voices, other sounds: deep whale-song, a whoosh like an octopus jetting along the sand, a crackling garble that nonetheless seems like a language.

You try to look around, to get a sense of where you are, but everything must be dark because you can't see anything. You can't really feel anything either, even your arms and legs—you just have a tingly sensation that dictates where they ought to be. You try to speak, but you have no voice, no lips.

You sense a warmth next to you and try to fumble nearer, but wherever you are, however you are suspended, you can't figure out how to move. There's a sound, a weird singing, on a higher pitch than you'd have though you could hear, and then something settles through.

You understand what your neighbor, the warmth nearby, has told you. You have transcended. You no longer have need of a mortal body, of legs or voice or sight. You have joined with the Great Waters of Life.

Clumsily you send back a sense of thanks to the life force next to you, and it replies with amusement. You get flashes of its life before—a dry, terrible planet. A beast with three legs and a long loping stride. A moment of thirst, and then fear as the tentacles struck, and then unity with the waters.

You understand. You understand so much now. All of that before, that individualism, that lonely struggle, was just the precursor. This is peace, in a way. It is oneness with all.

You feel your neighbor, and many more besides. You sing out in joy that now you are welcome into Great Water.

But you must save more! Yes! You slide through the life forces, touching and blending with each, guiding them back to the blue planet you came from. You share the water with them, show them with your spirit where all the great waters of Earth lie, invite them in.

They reply with gratitude, and you know you have done well.

The Waters alight in the Nile, flush with rain, and you slip out in ecstasy to mingle with the silted salted waters of the desert. The many life forces from the Great Water splash along into the mighty river, and the smaller—like yourself—work together to invite others in. The crocodile bites, but your embrace is greater; the ibis is quick, but you are patient and he must drink; the man is wary but you are clever; the hippopotamus is enormous but water is life and so you drag them all down, down into your embrace.

And the Nile is only the beginning.

The world will again see a great flood, a new creation. This is your ultimate gift.

THE END

You realize it's all silly to believe in anyway, because aliens are definitely not real, so you content yourself with emptying your guts into the field and passing out.

You wake up at dawn, surrounded by shit and cows, and realize you may have an alcohol problem if this keeps happening. As you trudge back to your house, you resolve to sober up, make better life choices, maybe just generally get your life together.

THE END

Author's Note

What the hell was that?!

Okay, look, you can't do this. You picked this up for some reason, right? You thought maybe it would be fun to try out an adventure gamebook, see what it's about. And then you picked "aliens are not real" as the first choice? You've got to be kidding me. Work with me here! I've done all this work to write you a fun/scary/weird alien book, and you turn around and do something like that?

Give me a break.

You've got two choices, okay pal? You can either put this book back where you found it and not tell anyone what an idiot you are OR you can go back to the beginning and choose something better.

Make a good choice. Seriously, don't let me down here.

...I'll be watching.
                    -M.E. Kinkade

Turn to page 1.

You stare up into the sky, seeking the source of the terrible sound. It gets louder, then slowly quieter, and you see a bright light, like a wildfire, off in the distance. In your drunken haze, you think it must have been some weird plane crashing—what else *could* it be? Something inside of you breaks a little loose, and you decide you really need to help them. It's up to you!

You stumble to your feet and wobble for 10 minutes toward the bright light in the hills. The ground is uneven or you're really bad at walking, but either way you trip and stumble twice, scraping your knee. When you finally make it over the hill, you see that this is no ordinary wreck.

You stand on the edge of a large crater, still smoking from the fire crackling at the edges. Through the smoke, you can just make out the outline of ... something large, and made of metal. You stagger forward, sliding partway down the crater and toward the wreckage.

When you're near the bottom, you can see:

- It looks like a satellite. Turn to page 112.
- A short, silvery tube, no bigger than a bathtub. Turn to page 204.
- It's a rocket ship with a pointed nose and aerodynamic fins, painted in ridiculous neon colors. Turn to page 95.
- A balloon-shaped metal thing, standing on three legs and lit up all around with bright white lights. Turn to page 97.

"WHAT?" the lead bull snorts, confused.

"I mean, you're totally right! You've been wronged," you gush, in perfect showman style. "But we can help you. Now that we've met you, we can be your ambassadors to the rest of the world. We can tear down the fences, build lovely barn accommodations, get you featured on *Ellen*! Now that you've opened our eyes, we three are honored that you came to us for our support. And of course we'll help you!"

You glance back at Fred and Deputy Collins, hoping they've caught on. Wide-eyed, Collins nods, elbowing Fred until he does, too.

The longhorn doesn't seem quite sold, so you saunter up and rest one hand on his massive flank. "What you need now, 82—may I call you 82?—is a plan. How about you and the rest of your family here enjoy a lovely lunch—on us!—and then we'll talk about what you'd like to do next, okay? Okay."

You step away from the bull, trying not to think about how close to a goring you just were, and back up toward the feeding trough. The hay is still baled, but loosely, so you reach in with two hands and grab as much as you can. You step quickly back to 82 and lay out the hay like it is a grand feast.

The leader of the sentient cattle eyes you cautiously, but the scent of the fresh, warm hay seems to get to him. "YES," he says. "YES, WE SHALL FILL ONE OF OUR STOMACHS FOR NOOOW. BUT YOOOU HUMANS WILL NOT GOOO ANYWHERE!"

"Okay, okay, we hear ya, all right," Fred squeals. 82 makes it clear, in the next few minutes, that we are not trusted, and "encourages" you and the two others to climb into the scoop of the tractor, slightly off the ground. It's crowded, and you can't exactly sit down, but 82 is watching. Without saying so, he's made it clear he'd like to see your blood on his horns.

"I sure hope you have a plan," Collins mutters.

"Yeah, me too," you reply.

The three of you settle uncomfortably into the tractor's scoop, watching as the herd of devil-black cattle enthusiastically munches away at the hay. The younger calves frolic while their mothers graze, and the animals swish their tails in contentment. It seems so disconcertingly normal that you start to wonder if perhaps you're not in some weird dream.

But then 82 turns back to you.

"YOOOU. GET DOOOWN," he says. "WE SHALL PLAN.

18

PLAN TOOO TAKE OOOVER THE WOOORLD!" And then he begins to laugh, and it's the most terrifying sound you've ever heard or imagined, a full-bellied, evil-villain chuckle. "MOO HAA HAA, MOO-OOH HA HA!"

With a gulp, you comply with 82's request.

"I HAVE DECIDED WHAT WE WILL DOOO. WE SHALL BEGIN BY FREEING MOOOORE OF OOOUR KIND. GUIDE ME!" he says.

"Uh, yeah, sure, great plan," you say. You have no idea what you're doing, but it beats being pummeled to death. "Can I get Fred and Collins down, too? It'll help if we have more hands, to, um, open fences and stuff."

There is a tense moment before 82 nods his weighty skull. Aware you're balanced on the edge of a butcher's knife, you help them scramble down. Then, at the point of 82's horns, you walk back toward the road.

"No, we can't," Fred whines. "We can't just let 'em go! These are MY cattle. What'll I do for my livelihood?"

"Fred...we can deal with that later," Collins says, relentlessly sensible. "We have to focus on saving your hide."

At the word "hide," 82's nostrils flare.

"Uhh, ex-nay on the leather-ay," you murmur. "Fred, just do this and we'll live to see tomorrow."

"TELL ME, HUMAN," 82 says, suddenly appearing at your shoulder. For such a big animal, he moves awfully stealthily. "WHOOO ARE THE WOOORST OFFENDERS?"

You pull open the gate and bow your head respectfully to allow 82 to pass. "Offenders?" You dart a glance at Fred. "How do you mean, sir?"

"I AM NO FOOOL," the longhorn snaps. "THOOOSE WHCOO TRANSFOORMED US TOOLD ME THE TRUTH. I KNOOOW ALL ABOUT OOUR PLACE IN YOUR WOOORLD. WHOO SHALL WE STRIKE?"

"Oh, *those* offenders, of course!" you exclaim. You wish you were telepathic; maybe then you could convince Collins and Fred to make a run for it, to warn someone, anything. But no, they're standing there, looking as dumb as you feel. "I guess we start with the town."

Once, you would have asked forgiveness for what happened next, for the way you led Fred's herd into battle against your own people. Your younger self would have been shocked to discover not only your sudden conversion to vegetarianism, but also your full-throated rants against the meat processing industry. It was, to say the least, a rather dramatic reversal. And—to be honest—not the least bit sincere.

But it was a time of desperation. Of difficult choices. And you had to choose yourself overall.

And that was how you came to live as the longhorn's second, ready to inform him of ways to trample the enemy. Humanity did not go without a fight, of course, but everywhere the herd went it awakened more, gave the gift of thought to every farm in the region. And soon the wave of animals was nigh invincible. From Texas, the bovine enlightenment spread, and so did the destruction.

And every night, you were visited with visions of the horrors you'd inflicted at the longhorn's behest. And every night, that horrible laugh chilled you to the core: MOO-HA HA. MOO-OOH HA HA.

THE END

"You don't understand!" the new guy is saying, "I have places to be! We all have to get off this planet *immediately*."

"Yeah, okay buddy, no problem, I'll get right on that," the officer says, clearly bored. He nudges the new guy further into the cell and closes the door, clank, behind him. "You're gonna need to give me the towel now, sir."

"What? But...I never go anywhere without my..."

The officer grabs the towel in one quick motion, snatching it out of the guy's hands and through to the other side of the bars.

"Hey, that's my towel!" the new guy whines.

"Don't worry about it," you say. "They'll give it back when they let you out in the morning."

He looks glum, staring out the bars like a lost puppy. You're sorely tempted to just roll over and ignore the guy, but then he starts sniffling. Oh my god.

"Look, it's not so bad. Just sit down for a minute and it'll be over before you know it," you tell him. "What did they get you for?"

He sighs, finally turning toward you. You don't recognize him, and you typically know everyone in your small town, at least by sight. "Hitchhiking, I guess," he says.

"Ah, yeah," you nod. "This close to the big prison, they don't much like hitchhikers. But it's no big deal. They'll let you out first thing in the morning. I've seen it before. Maybe even give you a ride where you wanna go."

"You think so?" he says, sounding almost hopeful. He almost smiles, then sags back down into despair. "But then, it'll probably be way too late."

"Yeah, well, it's already pretty late," you say, and throw an arm across your eyes again. Damn crazy hitchhikers...

"Okay, it's time to go," Collins says, opening the door with a satisfying clink, waking you up to the cell's unforgiving fluorescent lights. "The judge let you go with the standard fine."

You dust yourself off and saunter toward the door. The skinny guy has settled into a corner, even though there's another bench on the opposite wall. Weirdo. He talked all night about a new highway system, or something like that. It didn't make any sense, but he seemed like a nice enough guy, though rather confused and decidedly impolite. "Hey, good luck on your trip," you say as you go.

"Uh huh," he says. "I think next time I'll fly."

Deputy Collins returns your filthy clothes and your car keys, even though it's likely your car is a total loss. She says, "You know what's really sad? That you're really making a habit of this. I'll probably see you again next Saturday. Or maybe something worse will happen to you." She sighs. "Try to stay out of trouble?"

You nod half-heartedly. You'll keep your act straight. Or maybe you'll try that other bar, the one that just opened...

Turn to page 1.

"**Y**ou don't understand!" Fred wails. "I saw it! I saw them! They took my cows!"

"I'm sure your cattle are right where you left them," Collins says. She looks haggard, more than usual. The late hours are getting to her. "You know, if you could jes' tell us what you smoked, we might be able to clear this up sooner..."

"I tol' ya, I ain't smoked nothin'! The lights, the lights from the sky, they took my cows!"

"Okay Fred, if you say so," Collins says. She pushes Fred gently into the small room. "Just come in here for a bit, Fred, and we'll get it sorted in the morning." To you, she says, "Fred's had a rough night. If you could just yell if he does anything too weird...?"

"Yeah, fine," you say, doing your best to sound like you're not Collins' pal, even when it comes to taking care of Fred.

"We'll be watching, but thanks to you I've got some paperwork, so I can't exactly babysit," she says, her displeasure obvious.

"My cows!" Fred says. His eyes are wild; doesn't look like he's having a good trip.

You nod to Collins that you've got it and she walks back down the cinderblock hallway. "So Fred, how are you doing?" you ask. He's pulling on his grayish-black hair, and there's not that much of it to begin with.

"Not good, not good," he says, slumping down on the bench opposite. Suddenly he looks up at you, staring intently: "I didn't take no drugs," he says.

"So, you think someone *really* took your cows?" you ask, because if he's talking he's less likely to be hurting himself. "Like, a cattle rustler or something?"

"Uh huh," Fred says, with a shiver. "But these...these weren't no people."

"Your cows just went for a walk? Leave the gate open again, did you?" you say. Fred's never been the brightest bulb, but he's honest, and he helped you egg Suzy's boyfriend's house years back, so he's okay in your book.

"They. Took. My. Cows," Fred says, and you actually get a little nervous. Maybe Fred hit his head or something, because he sounds totally serious.

"Who? Who took your cows?"

"The lights. The flashing lights, and there was a sound like a siren, but it weren't no siren. It woke me up, and I ran outside to see what the fuss was, and there it was, clear as day: a... a...” Fred stutters to a halt.

“A what, Fred? What was it?” You get up and cross the small cell, sitting amiably next to Fred. He smells like dirty sheets. (But you probably smell worse.)

“Ah, you ain’t gonna believe me either,” Fred sniffs.

“I... I think maybe I heard it too, Fred. I thought it was just Deputy Collins coming to get me, but I did hear a really loud sound, and I saw a light in the sky...” you say, hardly believing that you’re admitting this could be real.

“You saw them too!” Fred says, eyes wide. “Did you see the saucer? The way the, I dunno, the beams of light just sucked up the animals, SLURP, like a vacuum?”

“Really? I think I missed that part.” You pause, considering. “And then how did you end up in here?”

Fred looks sullen. “They don’t believe me. I called ‘em, told ’em what I saw, and they hauled me in here ‘cuz they think I’m on drugs or somethin’.”

You put your arm around Fred’s shoulders. “We’ll figure it out, Fred,” you say.

You spend the rest of the night dozing, Fred’s head flopped onto your shoulder. He’s drooling, a little bit of saliva dripping down his chin. Your hangover has crawled behind your eyelids and died.

“All right you two lovebirds,” Collins croons from the door. “Let’s go.”

You and Fred both shake awake and follow Collins to the front of the station. You pay your fine on a credit card and head out. Fred once again swears he wasn’t on any drugs, and Collins has no reason to hold him any longer, so he’s free to go, too.

The sunlight is blinding, and it takes you a moment to catch your bearings, just long enough for Fred to catch up with you. “Hey,” he says, awkwardly. “Collins said she’d drop me off back at my property... since you saw it, too, and all, I thought, maybe... you wanna come with us?”

You think on it for a moment. You finally answer:
- “Yeah, okay. Let’s go find those cows.” Turn to page 37.
- “No, I’m good.” Turn to page 41.

You're sure as hell not going to take a giant worm infestation of your home town sitting down. No, you're going to pry open the mouth of this city and force-feed it a little pill that is poison to the parasites—just like your vet did to that puppy you got when you were five. And—hell yeah! —you're going to flush those creepy worms right outta the intestinal tract...

This metaphor got weird somewhere.

Anyway, the point is, you're ready for action, and you've got—it looks like the patch on his shirt says Dorkin (geez, poor guy, what a name)—Officer Dorkin here with you. So everything's going to be fine.

"Officer," you say, "we know at least one way to kill these things. We have to help!"

"But...you're a prisoner..." he says, foolishly.

"I'm not going back in there with a corpse and a giant worm, thank you. I'm going to go help my city. Maybe you ought to come along to make sure I don't leave police custody or whatever," you say, and stride out the door before he has time to protest. He follows a few paces behind.

The city outside is surprisingly calm. For a dystopian scenario, you thought there would be more drama. But at least you can add some. "Officer Dorkin!" you yell. "Got the keys to one of these squad cars?" He nods and you stand expectantly at the passenger door. "Shotgun."

"Get in the back," Dorkin says as he jimmies the keys.

"I called shotgun," you say gravely. He snarls at you but lets you in anyway. "Drive over to the facility. I think I have a plan."

Dorkin is clearly not yet fit for leadership, but he's definitely comfortable with following orders, and immediately complies and begins driving toward the warehouse facility on the far edge of town. It's always seemed like a depressing place, windowless, soul-sucking, and surrounded by flimsy barbed wire. What were the idiots in there doing to cause this?

"Got any idea what we're really up against?" you say, by way of conversation.

Sorkin presses his lips together. He looks vaguely like a lost hound dog. "No idea what they got in there," he says. After a pregnant pause, "But I heard a rumor that they was studyin' shit from outer space. Like, *alien.*"

You both sit in silence to let that idea soak in.

"So, you think...you think we have *space worms?*" you ask.

Dorkin turns his big sad puppy eyes to you. "Could be," he says, solemn as a priest.

There's another awkward pause, which you helpfully fill with, "Well, that does explain their ridiculous size. Like that asteroid worm in *Star Wars*."

Officer Dorkin pauses briefly at a red four-way stop and nods seriously. "Yeah, like that."

The radio breaks the silence before you have to resort to actual small talk. It crackles: "Is there anyone, anyone out there? We need backup! There's no way to kill these things!"

You look to Dorkin briefly, then pick up the radio handset. You struggle a bit with which button to push, but then you get it to let out a squeal and the handset is live. "You can drown them," you say. "The worms, hold the...mouthpiece...under water. They drown, just like big earthworms," you add helpfully.

"...Who is this?" the voice asks. Gunshots ring out in the background.

"It's not important," you say. "I'm here with Officer Dorkin and we killed one by drowning it!"

"Okay, okay, that's a start," the other officer says. "But how exactly do you expect me to drown this damn thing in the middle of a city block in *Texas?*"

That is a dilemma.

"We're coming to your location. We'll work out a plan on the way. Just...hang in there!"

Sorkin gives you a sharp nod of solidarity.

"Okay, what do we have to work with? How do we kill worms that are this big?" you ask. "Regular worms drown, okay. Earthworms are at least seriously pissed off if you cut them into pieces... They die if they get too dehydrated, like in the sun..."

"Birds eat worms," Dorkin says. "And, like, frogs."

You roll your eyes at these less-than-helpful observations. "Okay, sure. But which of these options helps us now?"

Another painful pause. You actually may be able to *hear* the gears in Dorkin's brain attempting to turn, grinding slowly from disuse.

Then it comes to you, so clear in its simplicity and brilliance that it's like a jolt of static from your favorite sweater. It's so clear you actually snap your fingers. "I've got it!" You describe your plan to Dorkin quickly, and he agrees it's not-terrible. Which is way better than no plan at all.

You get on the radio and immediately begin explaining your plan to anyone and everyone listening. Dorkin helps by breaking out a megaphone he had hidden under his seat and repeating the basic points into the neighborhood as you round the last corners.

The fundamentals: The worms are coming out of the warehouse on Elm. That's not too far from the high school football stadium, a nice big bowl-shaped arena with high walls—and very hot stadium lights.

Dorkin screeches past the warehouse, which is on fire and surrounded by police cars, doors thrown akimbo and the officers scattered; hopefully they're on board with your plan. He stops at the nearest entrance to the football stadium, and you're off, darting up the stairs on the home side, up into the (unlocked) press booth at the top. That's where the switches are, three comically large handles you flip up—thanks, years of experience as the team's backup backup announcer!

You peek out the large windows at the front of the booth. Down below, as the lights slowly flicker to life, you can see your plan starting to shape up, officers fleeing ahead of the worms, disconcertingly fast. One thin officer sprints across the field, vaulting up into the visitor stands, pushing up with his arms while his legs kick and scramble for purchase. He barely makes it, the worm chasing him accordioning out like Silly String bursting from the can. The officer stands there, panting for breath, and you can just see the worm nosing up the wall. It reminds you of a class trip to the aquarium when you were nine, and the tank full of eels. But this time, the tasty morsel held just out of reach is human—a very tired human.

Other officers assist, blocking off the entrances with the large foam mats the football players use for practice tackles. From above you can hear the hum as the lights warm. The field grows a bit brighter every second. You climb down the stairs as a fire truck screams up, a huge, writhing canvas bag held between two grim-faced men in thick yellow rubber. They heft the bag onto the football field, where it bursts open, revealing three of the hissing, teeth-grinding worms.

And so begins the slowest cookout on record.

The worms gambol around the stadium, seeking weak points. The officers stay on guard, weapons at the ready, ringing the visitor and home sides. And the lights heat up.

It takes several hours before you start to see results, longer even than the town football games, but then the worms start to move more slowly, even if just a little.

It's working.

You have to wait all night and well into the next day. The atmosphere takes on a grim carnival feel as someone cranks up the popcorn machines and the hot dog concession to make sure everyone has the chance to eat while remaining on guard. You begin to hear reports of the havoc the worms wreaked in other areas: unknown numbers of the government scientists dead or missing (presumed dead); at least five officers seriously injured; incredible property damage. Those with wounds are slow to clot—at least one officer dies from the blood loss, and soon the city deploys a mobile blood donation booth, volunteers lining up to give of their right arms to support the police force however they can.

More than a few end up at the football stadium, too, to watch the slow-motion death match: space-worms versus heat. The football stadium is already a place of pilgrimage for everyone in town, and no one has ever seen a struggle like this, where every single person in town is rooting for the exact same outcome. It's really a can't-miss spectacle.

The sun herself joins in the fun, providing heat no man-made light ever could, and Texas sure knows how to do heat. It's only 97 degrees today, but it'll be enough, especially as the decision is made to leave the stadium lights on, too, as insurance against the cool darkness of shadows.

Down below, the worms undulate slowly, periodically lifting their faceless heads up to the sky as if begging for mercy.

But no one is safe from the Texas heat.

The sun-baked vigil lasts for two full days and nights. No one wants to risk the worms playing possum; better to let them overcook and dry out than be the first poor fool to walk in there. When the time comes, lots are drawn to see which two brave-slash-foolhardy volunteers get to risk their lives. As it turns out, the volunteers are the strapping youth minister from the Methodist church on Rosewood and one of the boys that plays football on this very same field all through the fall. They drive a van in through the tunnel (which is promptly rebarricaded, just in case), rolling over the corpses of one or two of the worms just to be safe. Then they stop in the middle, and everyone in town watches as they climb out. The worms don't move...perhaps a twitch, from that one by the goal line? But it may just be a mirage from the heat radiating off the track. The two brave volunteers, wearing heavy gloves and long-sleeves despite the heat, work together to lift the space-worms into the back of the van, one by one. It's tedious just to watch, and must be hellish to do, especially as one weakened worm *does* make a practically pathetic lunge at them—a swift kick sends it back, stunned, and everyone breathes a sigh of relief. It, too, is loaded into the van.

It's nearly midnight by the time they are done, the van locked securely and then driven back out of the football stadium, out to a field, where a waiting bonfire reaches up to heaven. The massive stinking corpses are dumped into the middle as the funeral pyre is built and burnt all around them.

The town—the planet—is saved. You slip back into daily life, your actions forgotten, just grateful that you survived the ordeal.

THE END

"A dog, in jail? Seriously? What do my taxes go toward, anyway?" you say as the jailer locks you in with the mutt.

"Whatever, shut your trap. Dog's not that big a deal and the animal control folks refuse to get up at this time of night. Boss says lock 'm up, so I lock 'm up," the officer says.

You stare at the dog, which sat down immediately within the threshold to the cell. He's got wide brown eyes, and while he seems calm, he doesn't seem overly trusting.

"I already called this bench, okay Fido? And no drinking out of the toilet, that's just nasty," you say as you lay back down.

"You should be nicer to me," the dog says.

"Great," you say. "Now I'm hallucinating talking freakin' dogs. Could my life get any more screwed up?"

"Seems like you did a pretty good job already, if you're in here," the dog says.

This time you sit up and stare at it. It gives you a doggy grin and lolls its tongue out at you.

"Deputy Collins, your officers really need to be more professional than this!" you yell down the hallway, your voice echoing into the other room. Edging around the dog, you lean against the bars to look out. There's no one there.

You walk back to the bench, looking under the concrete protrusion to find the tape recorder or whatever the prankster is using to make the "dog" talk. The dog scratches himself behind his ears with a hind foot.

Finding no evidence of tomfoolery, you sit back on the bench, arms resting on your knees as you stare levelly at your canine companion.

"It's not a joke, you know, but it figures that you'd think so," the dog says, except it doesn't move its mouth or anything so it's *obviously* a prank. You're already on camera—because you're in jail and all—but this has to violate some kind of constitutional right or something. Something like 'prisoners have the right to not be used as the butt of jokes for the benefits of their jailer's amusement.' Pretty sure that's the Fourth Amendment.

It cocks its head sidelong at you. "Human speech is so rudimentary," it says, and then snorts derisively. "Dogs communicate better with scent than most humans do, despite all their self-aggrandizement about being the 'superior species' and all."

"And...I'm supposed to believe you're communicating with scent to me right now?" you ask, trying to sound dismissive but really just feeling surreal.

"Of course not, you idiot! I'm using telepathy. Direct mind-to-mind communication, cuts out a lot of the uncertainty," the dog says.

YOU CAN READ MY MIND? you think intently.

"Woah, of course I can, no need to yell!" the dog says, settling down into a comfortable slouch.

With a sigh, you say, "So I'm supposed to believe that a dog is speaking to me telepathically...why?"

The dog tilts his head, as if considering this. "Hm, you've got a point," it says. "But probably because I can get you out of here."

"What? No, you can't. I'm only here until tomorrow anyway," you say. No way you're gonna plan a jailbreak, on camera, with a dog that claims to be speaking to your mind.

"I'm female, by the way, not that it really matters, but it's just a lot more polite to refer to others by their preferred pronouns," the dog says.

You stare at the dog again and she gives you that sarcastic doggy grin.

"Oh, and tomorrow is much too late," she says. "So, if you'll just follow me..."

And then the dog stares at the far wall of your cell—and it explodes into dust.

You're still coughing and swatting ineffectually at the fog of debris when the dog says, "Come on, what are you waiting for? Follow me!"

And you do, though you are never able, later, to explain exactly why; you hit your threshold for strange happenings for the day and that was that.

You stagger into the street to find the little dog, now considerably more grey, a few feet away. "Come on already!" she says, and backs it up with a sharp bark.

She's awfully quick for a little thing, and you follow her around corners and under an old chain-link fence, constantly on alert for the wail of sirens you're sure is about to follow you. But nothing, and no one, does; or, if they do, you're too far gone. You're panting with the effort by the time she stops in an old junkyard.

"What the hell?" you exclaim. "You can blow up walls just by staring at them?!"

"I told you you should be nicer to me," she says. She's wagging her tail like this was all a great joke. It figures that you'd get the *sarcastic* talking dog.

"Fine," you say. "Why did you drag me out here?"

She cocks one eye at you, as if to say, 'if I'd wanted to *drag* you, I'd have dragged you,' but luckily she spares you. "Get in the car," she says.

You look around; you're in a junkyard, so there are a lot of cars, but most look completely non-functional. She lets you flounder for a moment before pointing—sarcastically, you're sure from her stereotypical hunting-dog pose—to a car a little to your left, behind a truck missing its front axle. The car she's chosen, a black van with missing back windows, is beat to hell, for sure, but it has wheels in all the right places (yes, you checked for the steering wheel). You climb in the passenger side.

From the ground, the dog lets out a yip. "Other side, nimrod!" she says.

Oh. This really hasn't been your night.

You get out, and the little dog scrambles up into the passenger seat, leaving you to climb in on the other side. She paws under the seat and reemerges with a key held in her mouth. With a long look, you reach out to take it, and mercifully she decides not to bite your hand off.

"Let's go!" she says.

"Wait a second," you demand. "You *talk* to me, blew up a jail wall *with your mind*, and brought me out to this junkyard because you wanted to go on a road trip?! Tell me what the hell is going on or I'm not going anywhere."

The little dog snarls, but you sit on your hands. Two can be petulant here.

"Fine," she snaps, barking at the same time, teeth snapping at the air next to you. You can smell her doggy breath; it isn't pleasant. She snorts, then begins: "I'm not a dog. Not really. Our people are from...well, look up out the window." You lean forward with her, trying to see what she's looking at. "See that star? The really bright one? That's where we're from."

"...You're an alien," you say.

"No shit, Sherlock," the mutt replies. "You meet many telepathic dogs in your day?"

"O...kay. You're an alien. From that shiny bright star up there. But you're here. And you need me to drive." Nope, still sounds crazy when you say it out loud.

"Ugh, you're wasting my time!" she says. "It's not my fault that my species happens to look a lot like your pets, nor is it *my* fault that all of your machines require the use of an opposable thumb, *which I don't have.*

So, yes, I need your help."

"I meet an alien and get picked for a special mission, and *this is what I get?*" you ask the universe.

But the universe doesn't respond. The little mutt does. She bites you on the arm.

"What the hell!?" you holler, shaking her off.

"Look," she says. "Help me or get out of the car so I can find someone who will."

"Fine," you say, and...

- Climb out of the squeaky old van. Turn to page 82.
- Turn the key to the ignition. Turn to page 42.

"I really appreciate you taking me up here and the offer is just...wow, just really incredible, but I'm not very good at ruling my own life, much less ruling anyone else's. Me, I prefer a quiet life. I have small goals. Like, this morning, my only goal was to make sure I put both shoes on before I left the house." You point to your feet. "Look! I did it! Go me!"

The bees press you, questioningly. You can feel from their thoughts that they are entirely unfamiliar with this situation. No one has ever told them no before.

You bow deeply at the waist. "Really, I am so grateful for the offer. I bet you'll find the right person to be queen real soon. If you could just drop me off back home?"

For lack of anything better to do, the bees follow you to one of the lifts, help you get in. You wave to the cluster of them hovering at the exit as you're sealed in. The ride down is uneventful, if a bit longer, and the bees drop you not far from town. They still seem flustered as you wish them well, but they take their elevator back and you never see them again, though you do hear later that week that Old Master Moki has gone missing. Nobody tries that hard to find him, though, and no one asks too many questions. You're pretty sure you know what happened, though.

After the bees have gone, you pull out the two small combs of honey you had wrenched from the wall and hidden under your shirt. You swirl a finger in and have a taste—it's transcendent.

Over the next few months you make a killing selling tiny taster jars of the space honey. One jar even makes it into the hands of a world-renowned cancer researcher, and through one of those happy accidents that proves so essential to science, she discovers it has truly life-changing properties—you found the magic bullet. True, it takes another dozen years for it to be replicated, but Dr. Jackie Forrester is considerate enough to partner with you on the patent and the process, which requires extensive processing through organic bee hives. You have quite the touch with bees after your experiences—they almost seem to listen to you, to know your very thoughts—and soon operate the largest facility in the country. Between the hives and the research, you're set for life, and do a lot of good, too. Thanks to the bees—and, of course, your space honey tincture—cancer is essentially wiped out.

Many times, you are asked how you discovered the special honey concoction that started the whole thing, but you just waggle your finger and wink at the interviewer, leaving many cross journalists and keeping your secret sacrosanct.

When you die, you are celebrated across the planet for your role in saving humanity from the Big C. Festivals are held in your name, marathons, pink-beribboned products sold everywhere. You are a true hero.

THE END

The officer barely touches the girl, but she stumbles into the jail like she's been pushed. "Hey man, I've got rights!" she yells. She's wearing skinny jeans and a dark hoodie. Her lipstick is electric pink, and despite the overwhelming aura of used spray paint, her hair has obviously encountered a straightener. She has neon green highlights in her jet-black hair, but when she turns to look back at the officer you see the green is actually attached by clips.

"What're you looking at?" she snarls, her voice crumbling into that irritating teenage-girl grind.

"Nothin'," you say, and lean back against the concrete bench. She clearly wants to sit on it, but that would mean a) sitting near you and b) giving up some of her bitchy teenager street cred. So she folds herself onto the ground, spreading her legs out like it was where she had planned to sit all along. You give her a shrug and say, "A little graffiti at this time of night?"

She shoots eye-daggers at you from underneath her perfectly lined dark eyeshadow. And then she flips her hoodie up, as if she thinks she can actually retreat into it. You're sorely tempted to call out "I can still see you!" but you bite your chuckle back and return to your half-daze on the bench.

The night passes slowly, as it often does when you're serving time, but it's sometime in the small of the night when the girl starts to moan.

"Hey kid, it's not so bad," you say. "Just go to sleep and it'll be better in the morning, yadda yadda yadda."

But the moaning doesn't stop, and when you open your eyes her face has gone pale, her fingers clutching at her stomach, her knuckles bone-white.

"Woah, are you okay?" you ask. She moans, a deep animal sound of pain and fear.

You:
- Call the guard. This girl's in trouble! Turn to page 83.
- Cover your ears and try to go back to sleep. Turn to page 199.

Poor Fred looks a mess, and it's not like you've got anything better to do, so sure, why not? Besides, maybe he really has discovered some mysterious band of cattle rustlers—it'll just be like an episode of *The X-Files* or maybe *Murder, She Wrote*. (That dame could accuse you of murder any ol' time!)

Collins yet again proves she's the decent sort by driving you and Fred over in her personal car, which is much nicer than being forced to make pleasant small talk through the Plexiglas of a squad car. She tries to chitchat about the weather or something, but Fred is not having it, just staring out the window, looking stricken. Collins gives up and the drive passes in awkward silence.

The tires crunch as the deputy pulls into Fred's long pot-holed drive. The screen door at the front of the converted trailer slams rhythmically though there is no wind. There's not a cow to be seen.

"No cattle," you say quietly.

"I tol' you, they took 'em," Fred says, but the fight has gone out of him.

"I'm sure they're just across the field," Collins says, but she gets out of the car just the same.

The air is still and warm, the grass barely stirring. Another slam of the bent screen door makes you jump out of your reverie. "Maybe if we fed 'em, your cattle would turn up?" you suggest meekly.

Dejectedly, Fred nods. "Okay."

"I'll help," Collins volunteers, though her tidy black pants and rubber-soled shoes are hardly the proper attire. Now you'll look like a jerk if you don't agree, too, so you bob your head like this is a great idea.

Fred trundles over to a three-sided pavilion constructed out of spare boards, chicken wire, and rusted tin roofing material. He's lived alone out here since his daughter left for college ten years ago; it must get lonely. Maybe loneliness is all it takes to start imagining flying saucers in the middle of the night.

You resolve to go back to online dating as soon as you get home.

With much screeching and thumping, Fred gets his beat-up tractor running and you go over to help load two hay bales, one in the scoop and the other on the back. In a fit of hopefulness, Fred had bought a tractor with room for two, but that still means someone has to walk.

You turn to Deputy Collins and say,

- "I could use a walk. Why don't you ride with Fred?" Turn to page 113.
- "See ya there!" Turn to page 60.

After a sidelong glance to see if you've got the herd's attention, you continue your drama. "Oh please, please, take me with you!" you exclaim, crawling forward on your hands and knees. "They've wronged me just like you! But, but now, you can save us all!"

Collins gives you a flat stare; Fred just looks shocked and confused.

The sentient cattle don't seem to know what to do with this declaration. The bull turns his wide head to consider you with one brown eye. You're so close you can see he has beautiful long lashes, and that his nose is crowded with dried mucus. "YOOOOU NEED US?" he says, disbelieving.

"Oh yes," you say, making your voice as earnest as you can manage. "I'm not with them! They've had me...prisoner! Just like you. But now you've rescued me, oh thank you, thank you!" You fall at the bull's hooves, debasing yourself, lying prostrate and hoping this works.

"What the hell?!" Fred yells. "You've got to be kiddin' me. Mr. Bull, that miserable creature is lyin' to you. In fact, that right there is the winner of last year's burger eatin' contest!"

"Damnit Fred," Collins mutters.

The bull stamps his hoof, right next to your head. "BURGER?" he asks. "WHAT IS A BURGER?"

"Oh, it's this thing where we eat lettuce on bread with some sauces and stuff," you say, rushing to speak before Fred.

But at the same time, Fred says, "Beef. Cow meat. On a bun."

A cow deeper in the herd—perhaps the one who spoke up earlier—seems to faint. The herd as a whole begins to moo and groan, sounding like a massive church organ set to "hellish." You have to scramble back to dodge the heavy thuds of hooves all around you, but don't move quite quickly enough. The hoof crunches down through all the delicate bones in your foot, and all you know is agony, so pure you can't even scream. Your eyes water and you crumple in on yourself, howling softly.

Collins comes to your rescue, grabbing you under the armpits and hauling you away, back to the center of the circle, as the cattle buck and kick.

"You were gonna git us kilt," Fred says, accusingly.

"Now you're gonna get us all killed, Fred!" Collins snaps. You hold your mangled foot and rock, barely able to process the scene, much less say anything else.

After several minutes of agony, the longhorn bugles and the herd settles. He lowers his head, presenting his impressive and dangerous-looking horns, the air from his flaring nostrils buffeting the remaining strands of grass as he snorts.

"NOOOOW WE KNOOOW THE TRUTH, MY KINSMEN," he said quietly, and his quiet anger was far worse than his earlier trumpeting. "NOOOW WE KNOW WHY WE HAVE BEEN SAVED. WE ARE HERE FOR VENGEANCE. THE BLOOOOD OF OUR HERD HAS BEEN SACRIFICED TOOO THESE. BUT. NOT. ANYMORE."

With that, 82 runs toward you. Fred and Collins scramble up the hay trough and try to get out of range, but with your broken foot you're not going anywhere fast. One of 82's wide horns catches you as you try, throwing you back to the ground, where the herd, with hoof, horn, and pure physical size, makes little time showing you what life as a failed rodeo cowboy would have been like.

Around here, you're the ground chuck.

THE END

You leave Fred behind, making a mental note to check by his house later—he clearly has the *good* drugs. Or he's just crazy. Whatever, not your issue if he's hallucinating spacemen.

Your car is wrecked and you still feel like shit. Luckily all the municipal buildings are pretty close together. And you left your swimsuit in the rec center lockers from your drunken exploits last week. So it's obvious where you have to go next.

You take a quick shower in the locker room, finally freeing that gritty bit of...let's just say... "mud"...out from your butt crack. The water is a disconcerting shade of grey as it slides down the drain. You shimmy into your suit and grab one of the rough community towels.

The lap pool is distressingly busy—and working hard is the last thing you want to do right now—so you wander to the other, casual swimming pool.

Technically it's closed for the season, but that's stupid: it's Texas, so of course it's still warm. You push past the door marked "pool closed" and don't think twice about diving in, pool rules be damned.

The water is cloudy from the chemicals, but the gurgle and weightlessness makes you relax, finally. You float lazily on your back, eyes closed against the hazy afternoon sun. You start to feel better, more energetic, as the water washes over your skin. This was exactly what you needed. Ahhh.

You're practically reaching pure bliss when you hear a sharp, "Hey, can't you read?!" from the pool entrance. You open your eyes a crack to see who is disturbing your relaxation—the gawky desk jockey who waved you into the rec center. "You're not supposed to be in there!" he hollers.

You roll your eyes and...

- Get out of the pool. Turn to page 45.
- Dive under the water. Turn to page 46.

It takes a few tries to get the old engine to turn over, but soon the van is rattling off a choking cough. Hardly a stealth vehicle, but it's running. "So where to, Miss Daisy?" you ask.

"My name's incomprehensible to your language," the dog-alien says flatly.

"It's a... never mind," you say. "Where are we going?"

"Take a right outta this dump and get on the highway," she says. "I don't know your names for things but I can navigate fine. Actually, can you roll the window down a little? Need to catch the scent."

"Right," you say, and comply.

Apparently a dog-alien isn't *that* far off from a dog-dog, because Miss Daisy over there is soon with her head out the window, wearing that ecstatic grin dogs get when their faces can flap around in a steady breeze.

"Not that it matters much and all, but...can you tell me what we're doing?" you ask, yelling a little to be heard over the roar of the wind.

She turns back to look at you for a moment, then says, "I've got young on this planet. But they are trapped in this horrible place, kept in tiny cages." She shudders, her whole little body shivering in disgust. "And the humans there want to *sell* them. Clearly I can't allow that."

"Woah, how'd that happen?" you ask.

She turns back to look out the window. "Things didn't go according to plan," is all she'll say.

The dog-alien directs you through several more turns, guiding you down a rugged road off the highway. It is closely lined with brush and trees, and in the dark it looks ominous and dangerous.

"Try to slow down," she says. "We don't want them to know we're coming."

You comply, slowing to a 20-mile-per-hour crawl, then ask, "what happens when we get there?"

She turns back to stare at you. You can just barely make out the shine of her eyes in the black of the road. "We get my children back," she says.

From her tone, you're afraid to inquire further, but hope she has a plan.

"Turn the lights off," she commands, and you do, but it leaves the road lit only by wan moonlight and it's hard to see. "Stop the van," she says, and then you can see it, up ahead, a low-slung old brick building, hunched over in a small clearing. There's a yard surrounded by dilapidated chain fencing, and a second building, windowless and somehow frightening.

"I'm going to tell the dogs it's me, and not to alert the people here to our presence," the little brindled dog says. "You unlock the back of the van." She stares intently in the direction of the building, her little doggy eyebrows furrowing. You resist the urge to pet her.

Instead, you climb out and open the back door to the van, which lets out a fearsome squeal. You pause, your heart in your throat... but the air is quiet, restive...

Though then you see Miss Daisy at your feet, scowling. "I didn't do it on purpose!" you say.

You're pretty sure she rolls her eyes at you, but you can't quite see in the dark.

"Come on," she says, and it seems like even her mind-to-mind communication is a whisper.

Following behind her cute little doggy butt, it's hard to believe you've been busted out of jail just so you could be the getaway driver for a dog trying to break her puppies out of a puppy mill, but you've had worse nights. She leads you past the chain-link fence to the door of the second building. You can see the shining eyes of dogs, big ones, watching you as you pass, and a twinge hits your stomach like a bad burrito. Carefully, you open the gate to step inside the fence. In the moonlight, you see the shadow of a huge dog—maybe a shepherd or pit or one of the other breeds with some terrible man-eating reputation—shake itself and move toward you and the small alien-dog. Your heart pounds and you wonder if Earth-dogs even know telepathy in the first place or if you've just been led on the worst "prank" imaginable when suddenly the large dog bows slowly over his front paws, a gesture with the air of welcoming royalty. The tension eases only slightly; your companion gives a regal bow in return, and you pass on to the building's door.

Movies have led you to expect the door of a bad place to be substantial and black, unwelcoming, maybe fearsome. But this door is white, poorly constructed, with a crack at the bottom where the hinge isn't sitting quite right. With a nod from your leader, you test the knob, and the door opens easily outward.

Inside are puppies. The room is filled top to bottom with puppies, and it smells of urine and fear. Puppies in cages, stacked four high, two or more dogs in a little box each. They're huddled at the far back corners, nearly empty hamster bottles lining the outer cage doors. The little dogs seem to shrink back from light, and let out a collective whine as you creep in the door. In response, the dog-alien lets out a soft bark and the air fills with a gentle thumping noise: the wag of hundreds of little tails.

"Are all of these yours?" you whisper.

"Some, but not all, no. But...well, it's complicated, but because they were around me from a young age, they're a little more like me than most creatures would be," she says. You think you can see her shrug.

"Not quite dog but not quite alien," you say wryly.

"Yeah, pretty much," she says, letting her tongue slip out into a chuckle. "Now, use those clever monkey fingers of yours and help me open these cages. Especially the ones high up!"

You comply with her command, lifting the latch on the first cage near the door and reaching inside, where a small fluffy Chihuahua-like dog cowers. Its right-hind leg is the closest thing you can reach in the deep cage, so you grab that and tug on the puppy. It yelps in surprise and—SNAP! —latches its pointy little demon teeth right into the soft part of your hand.

You:

- Yell, "what the hell, you little bitch!" Turn to page 82.
- Mutter, "goddamnit that hurts!" Turn to page 56.

You swim over to the side of the pool, where the jerk employee is now issuing all kinds of threats. He follows you to the locker room, continuing his tirade all the while. "...And don't you ever think you can just saunter in here and take a dip in the pool! See, it was closed for a reason! Don't you try to sue us when you break into hives from all that chlorine..."

You take your bundle of clothes and walk right out the front door, still wrapped in the cheap towel and everything, desk boy haranguing you the whole way. You continue your saunter of shame right on home.

Well, that was a weekend well done. Nothing weird happened, exactly as you like it. You want a completely boring, empty, normal life, and that's what you got. Mediocrity, that's the life for you.

THE END

Author's Note

Try again. Do better.

Turn to page 1.

You dive down, the murkiness of the water quickly obscuring the wan light from the sun. You imagine for a moment yourself as the shark from *Jaws*—da-da-daa-da—as you explore the bottom of the pool. You reach out to touch the bottom, maybe pull a handstand, when your hand meets not the textured pool floor but...something wispy. The substance clings to your fingers and you pull your hand away reflexively.

Overhead, the sun bursts through the clouds, bringing just a hint more illumination to the blue-grey water. You see... shapes in the water. Like fat caterpillar cocoons or Cuban cigars for a giant.

Heart pumping, you kick back up to the surface. You catch a quick breath, then dive again. Hesitantly, you reach out to touch the things.

Maybe it was just your imagination but... it feels like something is...moving, inside.

You:

- Swim out of the pool as fast as you can, not even bothering to say anything to the rec center manager, who still hasn't stopped yelling. You just gotta get outta here! Turn to page 45.
- Burst out of the water, screaming, "There's something down there!" Turn to page 49.

The interior of the spaceship is all shiny and chrome, exactly a 1940s concept of the future. There's an awful lot of crimped tubing around, and small windows like portholes that show nothing but blackness. The little green men are surprisingly strong, and lift you overhead with a little "hut hut hut" chant, carrying you down the hall. You stare helplessly up at the ceiling as you go.

Today is definitely not going as you'd expected.

They hut-hut-hut you all the way down to a laboratory-type room, the chrome here laid out with flat tables, enormous menacing microscopes, a chart of the elements that's all wrong. They toss you on the table. "Hey!" you cry in protest. But you're not that afraid; you're so curious about these creatures and their plans that you don't have much time to be afraid.

"Hey fellas," you say, trying to catch their attention as they hurry by, completing tasks off some kind of checklist. "What are y'all gonna do next?"

They don't answer, just jabber to themselves in their language. Guess they don't speak English.

One appears on your left and snaps a glove on its thick green fingers. "Safety first, I get it," you say. "Gotta protect yourself from aliens. I may have anything. You have no idea where I've been!"

It jabs you with one finger, and you say, "Yeah, I know, I need to work out more, don't rub it in, okay?"

The aliens meet and discuss something intensely, their green bobble heads held closely together. One turns and picks up a tray. "Uh...what are those?" you ask, getting nervous for the first time. The tray is covered with small implements, neatly aligned in a row. You can't begin to guess what they do.

You find out, soon enough.

After several false starts, the aliens cut away your clothes. Your quips are getting considerably more anxious now: "Hey, it's cold in here, can someone turn up the heat?"

The aliens make use of each implement, inspecting you closely in turn and conferring among themselves. It starts out easily enough, just a bit tickly, particularly when they use the brush one on your feet, but gets...well, considerably more personal. They probe; your eyes, your ears, your nose—which makes you sneeze—mouth, and yes, *there* too. They even make an attempt on your belly button.

Fortunately for you, this experience turns out to be one of your very particular fetishes, and you quite enjoy yourself, though you've had gentler lovers.

By the end, you're utterly exhausted and quite glowing—though it's hard to tell if that's from pleasure or from one of the vials they poured down your throat. Still, not a terrible way to pass an afternoon.

They drop you, still hogtied and naked, about where they picked you up, which you find rather rude—you weren't finished yet!

Though you can't tell how long you were gone, night has fallen, so at least a few hours. The asphalt is cool, and it takes you awhile to struggle into a sitting position. Your teeth begin to chatter with the cold before a semi drives by and gleans you with its headlights. The driver stops and calls police, and finally you're freed from the rope and given a blanket.

When they ask you what happened, you try to explain, about the little green men and the probing and the experiments. Everyone gives you exceedingly strange looks. Finally they ask you your name, which you tell them, and they bundle you into the ambulance for a nice cozy ride to the hospital (though you still prefer to lay down; sitting is a bit tender).

It takes you a decent time to get them to believe you're not crazy— or at least, not dangerously crazy. (In the meantime, you are able to try quite a number of drugs to make you feel woozy or hard on the edges or just sleepy.) You're free to go.

You use your marvelous adventure to explore a new side of yourself, and soon you've scraped together the money to build yourself quite a nice "space dungeon." It gets featured in all the right websites, and soon you're managing quite a nice business.

Nothing ever really captures that first time, though, and on quiet nights you sit at the bar and think wistfully of your little green men.

THE END

"What? Shut up and just get outta the pool, you douchebag!" the teenager squawks, his cracking voice proving that puberty has been only a recent visitor.

"No, I mean it, there's something *down there*!" you yell. "Like, I dunno, giant caterpillars!"

"You've gotta be fuckin' kidding me," the desk jockey says, clearly fed up with your shit. "Giant caterpillars are under the pool? Right."

"No, really!" you say, exasperated. A flash of greenish light briefly illuminates the pool. "What...what was that? Please tell me that was lightning..."

"Ga-ga...ga...!" the kid says, staring into the deep end of the pool. He lifts a finger slowly to point as you feel the ripples bob you in the water.

Something behind you is moving.

You start to turn to look, but think better of it and swim for the edge of the pool, your heart pumping in your chest like dubstep gone wrong. The pool water splashes over the ledge ahead of you, still several strokes beyond your reach. The awkward teenager finally finds his voice again, squeaky though it may be, and calls, "Faster! Why won't you swim faster? It's behind you!" panic rising in his voice. His eyes go wide and a tremor runs through him, shaking him like a dancing inflatable man toy, until he can't contain it and his wobbly legs dash him out the door.

Your fingers brush the ledge when you feel something wrap around your ankle. It's soft but scratchy, and it's strong. It's pulling you deeper into the grey-blue brine, back toward the lumps on the floor of the pool.

You:

- Swim toward the ledge, kicking as hard as you can. Turn to the next page.
- Turn around and grab the...whatever to pull it off you. Turn to page 53.

You swim for the ledge even more frantically, straining and splashing. You're a sea star trapped in a tide pool with a barracuda; you're a pterodactyl mired in tar; you're a human in a pool with something not of this world!

Your brain reverts to its most basic instincts: escape the predator. Your pituitary gland churns adrenaline into your system, your muscles are fortified with extra blood and antibodies, you become hyper-aware of every breath, every motion.

Unfortunately for you, your reptile-brain freak-out only manages to entice the being behind you. It's newly hatched, and that means it's hungry. Your thrashing is upsetting it; it reaches out to you with its hundreds of thin, nearly transparent tentacles, drawing you back closer to its pink maw. You struggle against it, the tentacles stabbing you like needles at the barest touch, climbing your arms, wrapping around your neck.

When that is not enough to halt your movement, the creature, in a fit of pique, lifts your screaming body out of the water and throws you back down. The force of the blow dazes you, and your numbed body undulates in the grayish water.

The last bubbles escape your nose. Your last thought is, "I think I'm gonna die."

Luckily, you drown before you can be digested.

THE END

When you come to, you immediately buckle over and barf out everything you've eaten in the past 24 hours, which is unfortunate, because you're still in zero gravity. You stare in horror as your puke gushes over to the other wall, then hovers, chunky disgusting globs spinning around and sticking to themselves, to you. You swim back against the port window to try to keep away with it, so you're not looking when the chime sounds and suddenly everything is moving very very fast. You're pressed up against the wall of the ship and can feel your face sliding around on your skull and you're staring at your puke and it's pushing up the wall and over the ceiling and it's going to get on you and...WHAM. Suddenly you're very heavy again and you—and the body-slime you shot across the ship—slam down to the floor. You're hopelessly covered in it, but you've got bigger issues now, as the ship is landing somewhere. You can hear the jets making a distinctive "whoosh" sound, and a moment later the door goes "clunk." You crawl on your knees across the floor to it, and throw yourself out immediately.

Everything is...wrong, and it takes you a minute to realize you haven't hit your head. People are running toward you, and you think at first they must be very very far away, but then you realize no, they're just small. Everything is small. Buildings are only as big as play sets, not coming any higher than your waist. The trees reach your belly, at best, and when you stand you have to duck as a hovercraft passes overhead.

The sky is black and dotted with stars, and the dirt is bright red, redder even than the Red River back home. Greenish mountains rise off in the distance.

"Halt!" a voice calls, and again this speaker has no obvious mouth, just eyes in a circular void of a face.

"Um, can I help you?" you ask.

"Intruder! You will be destroyed!" the speaker says, his stupid glittery helmet wobbling on his head.

"Er, I don't think so, bub," you reply, and casually take the bulging pistol from him.

"Excuse me!" the little alien protests. "That is MINE!"

"Oh this?" you say, and point it at him. A button on the side is rather enticing, and you push it, vaporizing the dirt beneath the alien's feet.

"Eep," he says, falling into the small crater.

"Ahahaha!" you cry, and run around the field, your greater height making you a giant in this tiny planet. It's so small, in fact, that you easily run all the way around it without even becoming winded, coming back at the spaceship from the other side. "Whee!" you cry, shooting the bubble-shaped gun wildly as you go.

"Stop that!" one of the aliens calls out, and turns a comically large pistol on you. You see the red of the laser as it heats, and jump out of the way, just in time. When you turn around, you see it has exploded the building behind your ship.

An idea occurs to you, and you continue to taunt the alien— "come on, shorty, what ya gonna do about it?" "missed me again!" and "you know what we call glitter like that on our planet? Craft herpes!"— always staying just a step ahead, the alien blasting holes all across the planet and menacing all of its species with its own weapon. The already small planet is getting blown to bits, evaporating into space dust all around you, and then you make a quick pass back past the alien and grab the big space gun as you go. You throw yourself into the ship, leaving the gun wedged tight in the door—it's too big to get in—and slam your hand on the controls again, initiating launch. Just as the ship takes off, you press the big red button on the gun in the door.

Down below, the little alien says, "Oh dear," just before the planet is vaporized into crumbling rocks.

You shove the gun out the door and seal it. When the pink mist comes, you're ready, and you relax on the still-slimy floor for the trip back.

When you arrive, you squirm out of the airlock to find the first alien. "Borrowed your ship," you say. "May want to go check in on that homeworld of yours."

"What?" the alien says in his squeaky little voice. He climbs in the ship, shouts out one last horrified, "oh dear" as he discovers the mess, and takes off.

As he departs, you raise the small bubble-gun you had hidden in your pocket and fire off one well-placed shot—zzt. No more alien problem here.

THE END

You've never been one to run from a fight: You twist your body back around to face the threat, and stare into a bowl of animated pho soup.

At least, that's what your brain says it is. The creature has hundreds, perhaps thousands of thin, clear noodley tentacles, some of which are still wrapped tightly around your right ankle. The center of the mass of waving fronds is a pinkish—no, greenish—no, purple, undulating glow.

It's trying to pull you closer.

Water slides up your nose and your eyes burn with chlorine, but you grab the tentacles on your ankle and pull with both hands. Your foot tingles and the pain around your ankle is intense, but you kick with your free leg, the extra motion pushing you back, away from the monster, the tentacles snapping like so many rice noodles.

You dive underwater, heading not for the edge but for the stairs in the shallow end. The water behind you froths and it may just be your imagination, but you're sure you can sense the creature grasping for you, stretching out its impossible appendages to draw you in for a final embrace.

You make the stairs and scramble out, breathing hard. The monster is barely visible, a tangled bunch of fishing line halting just feet from the shallow end. While you watch, dripping at the top of the textured stairs, the tentacled mass bubbles experimentally out of the surface in the deepest portion of the pool.

There's another flash of light and more bubbles rise to the surface, back toward the right corner. You run away, the imagined yell of a pool life guard filling your ears, your feet slapping across the rough concrete. You don't stop running until you've hit the other side of the door, back inside the building.

A glance back into the pool is disconcertingly normal: aside from the large puddles surrounding the pool edge, the water is calm. Aside from the gentle waves on the surface, you'd never know something was wrong.

You're just turning to leave when the sky darkens. More than a passing cloud, suddenly the day dims like a hand passed over a candle. Whatever piss you didn't relieve yourself of in the pool runs down your leg as you see it: a ...ship... shaped like an upturned bowl, too deep to see the center, shrouded in clouds. A screeching sound, like singing crystal, emerges from it, but loud, too loud. You fall to your knees, covering your ears as the sound wavers, the water below rippling with the eerie oscillations. The glass in the door shatters, and you can barely cower away from it, so desperate you are to protect yourself from that sound.

The sound focuses, the ripples on the water speeding but narrowing, and the water rises up out of the pool like an inverse tornado.

You:

- Crawl toward the pool to get a better look. Turn to the next page.
- Cower behind the wall. Turn to page 59.

It's horrible, but you don't want to look away. You crawl through the remains of the shattered glass door, determined to see this, to be able to testify to the horror and wonder that you see.

The water swirls, the thick funnel on the surface narrowing as it climbs toward the ship above—if ship it even is. It sways like a cobra, all the time dancing to the horrible shriek of the hollow above.

The lump of tentacles, lit by its soft inner glow, glides up the waterspout. It seems endless; time stops as you watch this thing that has never before and may never again be witnessed. It's wonderful, and frightening, and there's not a thing you can think of that would explain what is happening.

You don't even realize you're climbing closer until you're nearly at the edge of the pool. You stare in wonder down at the increasingly empty water. You can clearly see the shrouds below, ensconced in the deep end.

More tentacle monsters rip out of the surface, struggling like the baby sea turtles you watched in that IMAX movie once. You almost feel bad for them, but that may just be the ringing in your ears from the ongoing shriek the ship above is emitting.

The smaller monsters struggle up the water spout, warping its trajectory. You stare up in awe as the spinning water wavers toward you.

You really should have run away.

Several spaghetti-thin noodles whip out, wrapping around your arm. As the monster slides up the beam of water, it drags you along with it. Despite the swift water, you are dragged seamlessly upward, the steady pummeling water almost relaxing if not for the undying terror gripping your spin.

The creature climbs higher and higher, the pool falling away down below you. You can see your house from up here.

When you throw up, your vomit trails a sickly brown haze all the way down to the surface.

The hollow above you, still crowned in a thin veil of clouds, opens, a cold octopus eye. The noodle creature wraps you tight in its embrace, shattering your bones, liquefying your body, absorbing your essence, as you slip gently into the aperture.

Turn to page 14.

"You got a problem?" your companion murmurs.

"Puppies have such pointy teeth!" you whisper. "Can you ask them to not bite or something? I'm trying to help here!"

"Babies," she says. "They're just scared. I'll try, but there are no guarantees."

"Of course there aren't," you murmur, and reach back into the cage. The little Chihuahua looks at you warily, but then slinks forward. You grab it gently under the paws and lift it to the ground.

The rest of the kennel goes a little more easily. The puppies are filthy, their fur greasy and their cages poorly cleaned. The alien-dog works to release the pups at the lower kennels, where she can reach, then gathers all the puppies, which wiggle their little puppy-bottoms at her and let out quiet little yips of excitement, which she returns with a tail-wag of her own.

It takes you a little longer to finish with the puppies on the high shelves, but by the end they're jumping into your arms, licking your face. They're dogs of all kinds, but there are several that do look like the little brindle. Many have the same uncanny intelligent blue eyes.

The floor is a swarm of puppies, and it's hard to find a safe place to step in the wriggling mass, but you squeeze gently through. Taking the lead, the alien-brindle pushes open the door, releasing the flood of wagging, joyful puppies out into the open air, where they are truly overcome with excitement, yipping and running in circles. One is so excited he stops to pee on the door—you have to step over him to get out.

The big dogs in the yard stretch and come up to greet you. A nod from the brindle says it's okay to let them out, too, so you push wide the gate and the entire mob of puppies and dogs pushes out, snapping at each other with joyous enthusiasm.

But that many puppies make a good amount of noise, and a light switches on from inside the house. "Shit, Clyde, I think the dogs are out! Quick, git 'em!" a woman yells.

No time for caution: you run for the van, the puppies bouncing along behind you. "Come on, pups!" you cry in a half-whisper, gesturing for them to jump into the back of the van. Many have to be lifted up as their little paws are too low to the ground to reach the van, and you lose valuable time trying to wrangle all the dogs. When you've got them all in, you close the doors and run to the front. You open the door with a screech of rusted metal and see a lumpy, bedraggled woman in a nightdress come running at you with a shotgun.

"Thief! THIEF! You're takin' my dogs!" she yells, and fires the gun, sending the front light of the van exploding into a cascade of sparks.

"SHIT!" you yell and haul ass into the van, throwing yourself behind the wheel and trying to remember where the keys are. They're right where you left them—in the ignition—but it still feels like an eternity before you can get the van to start up, and the brindle alien-dog yelling "GO GO GO GO" in your head really isn't helping.

You turn the keys and throw the van in reverse, resulting in a ripple of skidding doggy feet, just as the woman aims the shotgun once again, this time taking out the windshield. It shatters, sending a spray of glass toward your face, but you're already gone, skidding backward down the overgrown drive and onto the highway, where you throw a quick K-turn and floor it.

Behind you, you see lights of a souped-up truck.

"GO FASTER!" the alien-dog wails, and more than one dog takes to howling in the backseat.

"I am doing what I can up here!" you shout, and you are, but your face is stinging with blood and you can barely see where you're going and you're not even sure where you're *supposed* to be headed. "Could you get up here and navigate, please?" you ask as you make a quick turn off a side street in an attempt to lose your tail.

She clambers up ungracefully over the seat, bracing herself against the front dashboard. "Okay, a right up ahead. It's a little winding road, but if you turn down it they may not see you and we can hide!"

You make the quick turn and take two weaves around the curves, then stop the engine. "Shhh," you tell the puppies heaped in the back, and they seem to understand. No one makes a sound.

Time drags; civilizations rise, islands sink into the ocean, your favorite movie is given *another* unnecessary remake, at least 5 minutes pass...and then you hear the grumbling of an extra-polluting truck. A sigh of relief ripples through the van.

"Okay, now go back the other way," your dog-friend says, even her telepathic voice pitched to a whisper. Cautiously, you comply, turning the battered truck back onto the highway, down the way you came. The tension slowly evaporates, and soon the van is full of joyously tumbling furballs and wagging tails. You sneak a sidelong glance at the alien dog; she seems to wear a pleased smirk, the corners of her smile turned up at her snout.

She guides you down to an isolated farm road, where even the cows are missing. The van's engine ticks as it cools off, and you're probably out of gas. Still, you open the back door for the puppies and dogs, which tumble out in yipping ecstasy and pool around your feet.

The alien-dog who started all this fuss sits down, watching you with her cool blue eyes. "It's time for me to take my dogs home now," she says. "But you've done us well. We could give you a lift somewhere, if you wanted?"

"Oh, no, I can walk back to... wait, you aren't talking about a 'lift' back home, are you? You're talking... whoa," you reply as the realization of her full offer encompasses you.

"Other planets, other worlds, other lives," she says. "Sure. But it's just a ride, like you gave us. I can't guarantee you'll like what you find when you get there. Think carefully."

You pause, considering, thinking of all your favorite days, the family and friends you'd have to leave behind, but also the wonders of an unknown future, the great drive for exploration, and you:

- Shake the alien-dog's paw and say goodbye. Turn to page 99.
- Nod, and follow the little brindle dog off into the field. Turn to page 215.

Everything is too unbearably horrible. You can't look, you don't want to know. You want to be at home in bed; you want to be 5 years old and coming home to a plate of warm cookies; you want to be running far, far away from here.

But you can't. You crawl into the rec center as far as you can, your hands and knees bloody with broken glass. You squeeze your eyes closed and cover your ears, but you can still hear the ear-piercing trill. After several moments, infinite moments, you hear an odd "glomp," and the sound subsides.

A trickle of blood escapes your nostril.

When the paramedics find you, you're curled on the floor, wet and smeared with your own blood, mute with shock. The kid, the one who saw the monster first, is incoherent, babbling, and no one believes him. It's obvious something happened, but even you aren't quite sure what. You allow them to take you to the hospital, pick the shards out of your skin. You were the only real witness, and how can you tell them? How would they ever believe you?

You're working up the courage when you hear the first report, on the incessant TV news they've left running in your shared hospital room. It's even been caught on film: thin-tentacled monsters rising out of background pools, snatching dogs, even small children. The ships come next, fill the 24-hour news cycle.

You close your eyes, willing it not to be true.

But it is true. Humanity's preference for richly chemical-drenched water sources are perfect, and the alien species find the pH ideal. Officials quickly warn civilians to drain their pools, as if you could stop aliens as simply as a mosquito infestation.

You can't drain the oceans.

It takes an embarrassingly short amount of time before the aliens are entrenched. There are no pithy Hollywood endings for something like this.

Humans are left, thin and savaged, to be picked off, one by one.

THE END

Y ou hop in the tractor before Collins can say anything, and though Fred initially looks a little shocked, his face soon settles into a wan smile. The tractor doesn't *really* have room enough for two people, your knees rhythmically slam into the console as the beat-up old vehicle trundles forward, and Fred smells of sweat and a sustained lack of deodorant, but hey, at least you don't have to walk.

It's a short trip, but a gratifying one, as you glance back to see Collins just as she steps in what looks like a very sticky cow pie. You're perhaps a bit cocky as you unfold yourself from the tractor's cab and stand around looking useful while Fred does the actual work of disseminating the hay.

There are no cows to be seen...not at first.

"Do you need to call 'em or something?" Collins asks when she finally arrives. She stands next to the feeding trough, her hands on her hips.

"I can try, I guess," Fred says.

He steps up to stand a little in front of the feeding trough, holds his hands to his cheeks, and leans back before yelling, "Come-in, come-in, come-in!" He sounds like a cross between a yodeler and an auctioneer, with a dash of trombone. He repeats this several times, seeming only mostly like an idiot.

Without warning, the herd of black Angus-Longhorn crossbreed cattle percolate out of the shadows of a stand of mesquite trees. They move slowly, in an organized group, one long-horned fella patiently leading the cows single-file up the gentle hill to where you're standing. You feel yourself tensing up, though you can't pin down what feels unusual about the situation. The cattle are quiet, restive, and though they must weigh several thousand pounds each, it's not like a dumb cow will just rush a human that has brought some hay, right?

Right?

But your anxiety only grows when Fred says, "Huh. That's different."

"What's different, Fred?" Collins asks. You may be imagining the hint of worry in her voice.

"Well, they ain't never stood in such a tidy semi-circle like that before, is all," Fred says.

"But aren't you glad? You thought your cattle were missing, and here they are, safe in your very own field!" you say, trying your damnedest to sound cheerful about it.

But the cows are still coming, standing an even eight feet away from the trough and tractor. Worse, they've closed off the semi-circle; you're surrounded by the solid-looking black animals. You find yourself wondering about hooves and horns.

"SURRENDER."

It takes several long seconds for your brain to tell you exactly what has happened. It starts with a process of elimination. Not Fred. Not Collins. Probably not you. Radio?

Nope. The only answer left is the correct one, and it makes your knees go all wiggly. The deep alto voice had come from the longhorn.

Fred is the first to react. "Number 82? Is...is that you?" he says, his voice full of both fear and a sort of longing.

The bull merely flicks his ears back, stomps a front hoof, and repeats himself: "SURRENDER."

You:
- Faint. Turn to page 67.
- Run. Turn to page 68.
- Say, "Okay, we surrender!" Turn to page 110.

This loon has taken enough of your time. And he doesn't even have any liquor. So, without another word, you turn and walk down the creaky porch steps and away from Rancher Loonypants and Deputy Caretaker.

Besides, you don't want *anything* to do with whack jobs who murder cows for fun.

You realize after reaching Fred's driveway that you didn't stop to think your departure through, and that's going to make things inconvenient. Deputy Collins drove you out here, and your cell phone was lost somewhere in last night's revelry, so... you're gonna have to walk.

Ah well, worse things have happened to you. So you put one foot in front of the other, ambling toward the speck of town and navigating by the top of the grain silo, which you can just barely see from here. The highway is pretty empty this time of day, so you don't even bother trying to hitchhike. Just going for a ramble.

But you're out of shape from being a normal person who doesn't do things like walk alongside a highway for a living, and it's not too long before your legs start to hurt. Besides, you're hungry.

"Ugh," you grunt aloud. This was stupid. You should never have come out here.

Of course, you're also too proud to turn around and head back to Fred's ranch. So you just grunt to yourself.

Some little ways further, and you're really starting to hate yourself. It's no longer the peak of summer, but it's still hot enough to be uncomfortable, and it seems at least some of the biting flies followed you. You can't walk farther than a step or two without having to slap them away or risk getting another painful sting.

You're so preoccupied with swatting flies and complaining about your situation that you don't notice the deepening shadows until it is too late. You look up, and there, above you—at midday on a perfectly deserted highway—something is blocking the sun. Something U-shaped, a metallic color without any shine at all, like the bottom of a giant boot. As you watch, a square hatch slides open near the flat side of the U and a thin rope falls out.

Though you're grateful for the cool of the shade, you suspect this...whatever it is...isn't here to help you out.

"Uh...hello?" you say. You're confused; this kind of thing isn't supposed to really *happen* to people. You don't exactly have a script prepared: "In Event of Alien Encounter."

Down the rope come shimmying three small green creatures, just like cartoon depictions of martians from your childhood. They're kinda cute, and maybe that's why you don't really resist when they start pushing you toward the rope. You do start to protest, however, when they jibber at you incomprehensibly as they wind the rope up your torso. You try to bat them away, but they're remarkably insistent. Before you know it, you're trussed up like a hog at the State Fair. One alien stands on your head and gives your rope two sharp tugs.

The rope lifts you slowly, inexorably, up into the floating boot.

Turn to page 47.

It takes longer than usual to get to the shop because Marlene insists on turning off your cell phones and you usually look up directions. After you finally get there, you realize with irritation that you can't get your loyalty points without letting them scan the code from your app. You scan around the room, looking for two quiet seats, and realize everyone is on a computer or phone or tablet or something and feel a twinge of frustration that Marlene won't let you do that, too.

By the time you actually get your coffee, you're pissed off. "Maybe none of this is a big deal!" you say, throwing your hands in the air. "Maybe it's actually good. You ever think of that, Marlene?!"

She sits across from you, blank-faced, bobbing her tea bag in her overpriced cup of hot water. "You're really ok with them knowing so much about you?"

Gesturing around the room, you say, "Look at all these people. They're all getting something out of the arrangement. They get convenience, and coupons, and, I don't know. All kinds of things, probably! And sure, the data is being collected on them, but it probably *always was*. I mean, in school everything goes on that 'permanent record' thing, right, and the admins could always look that up but it was too much of a bother. How is this different?"

Shaking her head, Marlene says, "You don't get it! They're doing this all without your permission, tracking everything, and who knows what they're going to do with all that information?" Dropping her voice, she adds, "What if they're going to invade us? They would know every person's allergies, where they lived, how many people to look for, everything! And we're making it *so easy*."

Exasperated, you sit back in your overstuffed faux-leather chair. "I just don't think it matters. What can we really do about it, anyway? It's not like we can go against some unnamed alien race just because we hacked a satellite!"

You say this last part a bit too loud, and a few people turn to stare at you. Luckily, more than a few seem to be wearing headphones. You duck your head sheepishly.

"Well, do what you want," Marlene says. "Personally, I don't want everything about me to be splashed everywhere. I'm going to fight back. I'm going to go somewhere people can help."

She stands to leave. You:

- Lean back to enjoy your coffee. Crazy Marlene. Turn to page 303.

- Follow her to the nearby college. She made some really good points. Turn to page 326.

You settle in with Fred, staying even after Collins leaves to report back to the police station on the missing cattle. He's rattled and startles at the smallest sounds. There's not much room in his creaking old trailer, but you clear some papers off the couch and sit with him while he turns on the local sports channel, low in the background. He's not talking much, but is insistent that he'd like you to stay—"in case they come back"—and you're feeling generous, so you do. Besides, you found a frozen pizza, and since Fred didn't want any...well, you don't want it to go to waste.

You're on the precipice of sleep, head lolling forward and the greasy pizza plate sliding down to the floor, when you hear a strange sound. Well, when Fred hears the strange sound and nudges you awake. "Wha..?" you slur, blinking stupidly.

Fred is inches from your face, staring at you with wide eyes. "Do you hear that?"

"Nah, Fred, let's just..." you say, pushing him back, and then you *do* hear something odd. It sounds... like a blender set to high, crushing finely sifted glass, mixed with that nails-on-the-chalkboard sound. It builds and builds, tugging at your eardrums like a toddler on an earring. "Ahh! What is that?!" you yell, covering your ears.

"Oh mah gawd," Fred screams, frantic. "It's *them*." He pulls you to the floor, forcing you to crouch with him behind the battered maroon couch.

"Them who, Fred?" You have to shout to be heard over the eerie sound.

"Them that did that to mah cows!" Fred exclaims.

"Okay, we've got to do something," you say, desperately trying to decide what you *can* do.

"Let's...

- "go out there and see what it is!" Turn to page 70.
- "hide!" Turn to page 72.

Overcome by the situation and unable to believe what is clearly happening, you take the opossum/Victorian lady approach to conflict: your knees buckle, your eyes roll back, and you fall—ker-plop—right into the mud.

In the movies either you would have fallen gently into some hero's waiting arms or perhaps you would go weak-kneed and fall gracefully to earth in a dignified puddle. But life isn't a movie, and if it were it would be a lot closer to a *Three Stooges* caper, which is why you faint by falling flat on your face.

Into an ant pile.

Thus you are awoken rather quickly from your mental lapse.

You startle awake, flapping hysterically at your insect-enshrouded face. When you've shaken most off, you look up to see the herd of cattle has—unfortunately—gotten even closer. Fred and Collins have been backed up against the tractor, their hands in the air to indicate their surrender.

"GET UP," a cow with steely brown eyes says, nudging you with her foreleg.

You crab-scramble backward, trying to find your feet.

"DOOO YOOOU SURRENDER?" a calf says imperiously, but it is quickly knocked aside by its mother. She snorts, and your face is covered with the soft spray of mucus from her nose.

"Uh, uh, sure," you stammer. "Why...why are we surrendering?"

"SURRENDER OR DIE," the longhorn bellows.

"Right then, uhh..." you say, and...

- Run away. Turn to the next page.
- Yell, "I surrender, oh great bovine leaders!" Turn to page 110.

Y ou've had your share of strange experiences, not least from mind-altering substances like LSD or that one time when you were five and you ate 10 Pixie Sticks in a sitting, but nothing in your life has prepared you for something like this. So you revert right back to your most basic function, and flee.

You were facing the longhorn/leader, so you reverse and head the opposite way as fast as your out-of-shape legs can carry you. The cattle have formed a wall all around the trough, but a few calves are sort of clustered together, forming a low point in the wall of beef, so you dash for that. As if anticipating your move, one of the cows on your flank moves to intercept you, but you're too fast and you vault right over the calves, just like you saw in the Olympics once when you accidentally watched the gymnastic demonstrations, except you're leaping over a sentient cow and you're totally uncoordinated. But either way, you make it over your bovine obstacle and pump your legs as hard as you can. You have no idea where you're going or what you'll do when you get there, but you're fairly certain you have to not be here now.

It takes a moment for the circle of cattle to organize themselves, but soon a section of the circle has whirled and is following you, hooves thudding. "NO ESCAPE!" the longhorn bellows.

Though you've never before had an interest in Spain's running of the bulls, you now feel you perhaps should have at least looked it up. If you had, you might be prepared for the brutal speed of the angry herd bearing down on you. You would know that, yes, a fast human can typically run at about 28 miles per hour, but a bull can clock in at 30 or 35 miles per hour, and—crucial fact—you are not a fast human. Even on your best day, you can barely manage a light jog.

Today is definitely not your best day, though you are finding yourself *very* motivated. You run as hard as you can, but your lungs aren't equipped for this, and neither is the rest of you.

Luckily, a longhorn's wide horns mean you're out of danger for the first attack, so instead of getting pummeled with the sharp end of an angry bull, you're struck in the back with a skull as hard as a sledgehammer. The blow knocks you back, up, up into the air, and, for a blissful, confused moment, you're flying, then gravity kicks right back in and you're falling, falling into the herd of formerly domesticated beasts. Their hooves are not made for a fight, being implements of labor, but they respond well enough to the use, and you're overcome by the mass of bone-crushing, skin-squishing tenderloins, which grind you down into a nice soft pâté.

68

M.E. Kinkade

THE END

"That's crazy!" Fred exclaims, but it's too late; you're up and dragging him toward the front door, where the sound is loudest.

"I'm sure it's just some neighbor kids trying to give you a scare or something, Fred! Let's just go out there," you say, and shove Fred out the door.

You're pushy, maybe, but not foolish. You're not going out there first. Duh.

But Fred survives being shoved outside, so you follow. The night air is cool and actually fairly refreshing, if it weren't for the rather disturbing bright lights set to Friday night football intensity coming from the ... unidentifiable flying *thing* over the neighbor's corn patch.

"Uhhhhh," Fred says, shocked motionless by the sight.

You can't really blame him. The ... spaceship, you guess?... is perfectly smooth, all the way around, like a polished river stone, if said river stone were made of molten metal. The lights don't seem to be coming from any particular place; they just *are*. And there's that sound, that horrible, bizarre sound. It's beautiful and terrifying at the same time.

As you watch, the corn across the street blurs, flattening as if under a great wind. Then, like a mini-cyclone touching down, whole heads of corn are sucked up, *slorp*, into the shiny vessel.

You fumble in your jeans for your cell phone. You *have* to record this. People have to know! But your phone is gone and there's nothing you can do but stop and stare. It's like standing in the path of a tornado; you know you shouldn't, but there's something about the wildness of it all that compels you to stay, to witness.

And then the orb notices you. Nothing immediately changes, but you know that it knows you're there. It senses you, just as you are observing it. And it starts to come toward you, its surface rippling like the edge of a pond. You want to flee, but it's as if you're staring into the eyes of a dancing cobra; you can't look away.

"Oh my heavens!" Fred cries, and it's equal parts fear and wonder.

You just stand there, trying to remember every detail but aware that you're missing part of the experience just by trying to remember it all.

The orb stops just in front of the trailer. The dripping mercury front spindles out into a long thin spear, and you think "this is how I'm going to die. And no one will believe me."

But the spear turns into a ramp, perfectly smooth, up into a little black void of a door.

"Fred...are you seeing what I'm seeing?" you murmur. Fred nods. "Does...it want us to go in?"

Then, you see it, leaning out of the ship: a purple, striped furry body shaped like a gumdrop, long-fingered hands ending in suckers, three eyes, and a small, perfectly round mouth.

The mouth moves, and the alien creature howls, "XER#)JJX: @#DnSDFT!"

At your look of horrified confusion, it shakes its head, thumping a thin paw against its noggin, thump thump thump. It shakes its head quickly, like a dog shaking off after a bath, and then says, "Sorry about that, sometimes forget to speak the local tongue, you know. But you're here just in time for dinner! Would you like to join us?"

"And that's how it all began," you say to the late-night talk show host. "It was all a hilarious misunderstanding, of course. Flubbbrt here was just sourcing ingredients from Earth; they don't have a concept of property rights on Planet Noxxt, so he had no idea we'd be startled when our cows just keeled over or our corn was flattened. We went up for dinner, had a nice meal, and got to know each other!"

"Wow, that is just such an incredible story," the slick-haired host says, leaning forward. "But you were quick to learn, weren't you Flubbbrt?"

"Sure was, Jimmy!" the lovable alien explains. This interview will really help the restaurant get off the ground, not that it needs any extra help. But anyone who saw Flubbbrt couldn't help but like xen. It's a perfect promo. "We just really hit it off, and when the idea of a restaurant chain came up, well, it just seemed right! And that's how we opened The Jellied Cow."

"And if I may say so," you cut in quickly, "the food really is *out of this world!*"

The audience breaks into wild laughter, just as you knew they would. Thank the alien-filled heavens for aliens that don't have a concept of money—you're gonna be rich.

THE END

You attempt to crawl under the couch, but its frame has been broken by decades of Fred's ass and you're not nearly slender enough to fit anyway. Fred's no help; he actually starts to wrestle with you over the hiding spot, when it's *obvious* you were here first. You wind up to throw a punch when the sound outside suddenly stops.

You freeze, staring at Fred. He looks as terrified as you feel. But if the sound stopped, it definitely means whatever it was has gone away, right?

You start to sit up, slowly, slowly.

There's a knock at the door—THUMP THUMP THUMP—so hard it shakes the floor of the ramshackle trailer. Fred flattens like a kid in one of those fire safety videos. You're too scared to move.

The doorknob rattles, and the door squeaks open, the screen slamming shut. Your heart is pounding in your ears, and you feel like your lungs might burst: you've forgotten to breathe. You hear the intruder shuffle, shuffle, shuffle, into the house. You duck your head further, slowly, so as not to attract attention.

Fred has started to cry. You watch his sun-weathered face screw up and pray he doesn't whimper.

There's a rattle as one of the chairs in the front dining room scrapes against the floor, and you peek up to see what you're dealing with, almost too frightened to even be curious.

But only almost.

It looks...roughly like a man, but you seem to be looking at its back. Dark liquid drips down its head and flank, and it's wearing dirty, ill-fitting clothes, like what someone might imagine a man ought to wear. As you watch, you see it approach the sink, then you hear screams of protest from the refrigerator hinges as it opens the door, then rustling in the contents. The...monster...opens a cabinet and gets out a glass. Then back to the fridge, and sounds of a liquid pouring. It fills the cup, then turns back to the dining room, settling in the chair.

That's when it sees you.

"Hello?" it says. Funny, it sounds almost like a man, but the voice is wrong, too gravely, too low.

Fred buries his head under his arms; he's clearly decided how *he's* going to handle this. It's up to you to be the brave one. You slowly lean back, so your head emerges over the arm of the chair. You clutch a pillow defensively. "Who are you?" you demand.

He—it—takes a gulp of his drink. It looks like iced tea. When it's finished half the glass, it says, "I tried knocking. Then the door opened.

I didn't know anyone was here..."

You stand, slowly, and Fred sheepishly follows you. You can't help but stare at the man-creature's misshapen face, like clay that has been smooshed into almost-but-not-quite the right form.

"I was in an accident, and...well, I think I need help," the monster says.

"You killed mah cows!" Fred yells.

"...What?" it says.

"You...you killed...my cows..." Fred says, far more uncertainly.

"Oh, the cows? No, that was aliens..." it says, then pauses. "That was a joke. I... I've been in a bit of an accident and I think I'm in shock?"

That's when you realize the dark fluid is blood, and this creature— no, wait, man, it's probably a man, that makes more sense—is just barely keeping himself together. You get up and grab some paper towels to staunch the bleeding at the man's head. "Fred, get over here and help him!" you hiss.

"But...but my cows," Fred stammers. But Fred gets up and helps anyway. You hold the paper towel to the man's misshapen head, trying not to stare, settling instead on staring awkwardly into the distance, which may be worse.

"So, um," you say, out of complete confusion on how to handle this turn of events. "We heard a sound earlier. Do you...know anything about that?"

The man groans. "I don't know. Could be related to whatever hit me, I guess," he says.

"Do you remember anythin' that happened?" Fred says. "Did ..." He lowers his voice to a half-whisper. "Did ya get abducted? Probed?"

"No, I have no idea what happened to me," the man says, shaking his head and completely ignoring the insanity of Fred's question. "Hey, do you have some sugar?"

"Err, yes?" Fred says uncertainly. And then stands exactly where he is, too stunned by the idea that this wounded man wasn't probed by aliens for any other thought to get through.

So you kick him (gently). "Fred, just go get the sugar, okay?"

Fred comes back with a gallon-sized plastic bag of a million little sugar packets, stolen from every fast food restaurant within 100 miles. The guest nods thanks, groaning as if the motion hurts him, and grabs three sugar packets at once, shaking them twice—shake shake—to free space at the top to make them easy to tear before he pours it into his iced tea, now only half-full.

"You don't remember seeing or hearing anything out there?" you ask. "What's your name?"

"Um. My name...John? Does that sound likely? I don't know, I don't seem to remember much before coming to your front door," he says, grabbing another cluster of sugar packets and adding them to the tea glass.

"You just showed up here, in the middle of the night, bleeding?" Fred says, clearly accusing the man of something besides being an accident victim.

"Geez Fred, lay off. It's obvious this man's been in some kind of accident. And maybe he's diabetic, too, what with all the sugar he's adding to that tea of yours," you say.

The guy hasn't stopped adding sugar to the tea glass, and by now half the bag is empty and the sediment from the sugar and sugar-substitute lies caked on the bottom of the cup.

The wounded man takes no notice of your criticism, but takes a big swallow of the sugar-tea.

Just then, there's another terrible screeching sound from outside. The wounded man freezes, motionless, while Fred dives under the table. "It's back!" he squeals.

But you're over this. There's clearly a rational explanation for all this. So you stride to the front door and yank it open.

You are met by a blinding wall of light, like staring into a movie projector square-on or staring into an eclipse unprotected. It's so bright that you stagger back.

Behind you, Fred whimpers, "Oh mah gawd!"

But you're determined now: you throw an elbow across your eyes and take a few steps down Fred's broken-backed steps, out into the day-bright night. "That's enough!" you yell. "Knock it off!"

And, as quickly as they began, the lights are gone—outside, and, you soon realize, in Fred's small trailer. The sudden darkness is awash with the afterimage of the lights, blinding you even more than the too-bright lights.

You:
- Walk out into the darkness. Turn to page 77.
- Turn back to the trailer. Turn to page 79.

You leap down, the hole collapsing in on itself as you jump, then go—blip—through the portal. For a moment you fear you'll be trapped underground, but no, you've landed on a sandy beach, the hole and darkness from before completely vanished. Up ahead, the puppies you released are prancing in the sand, barking at the water, splashing their playmates. One of the bigger dogs is taking what looks like the best poop of his life, judging by the big grin on his face.

As you look out over the happy dogs and the beautiful beach, you think maybe you're in heaven.

After a moment, you see the brindle and run up to her. She sits politely. "Wow, is this your home?" you ask aloud.

She cocks her head to the side, considering. "It is a safe world for my kind, and for our adoptees," she says, gesturing with her nose at the wriggling babies.

"A whole dog planet! This is like a dream come true!" you exclaim. A labradoodle begins digging a sandy hole to your right.

"I hope you don't come to regret your choice," she says. "There are no other humans here, as I know of."

"I can see why you wouldn't like us much, considering where those pups came from, but I assure you we're not all like that. We profess a great love of dogs on my planet, you know. We choose them as our best friends."

The brindle regards you skeptically. "You did us a great service out there," she finally replies. "Maybe you can also make yourself useful here."

A small wire-haired puppy runs up and grabs the brindle's ear, and she collapses in fake-defeat. As she plays with the little pup, it's clear you're dismissed.

You find yourself a dry cave and do your best to make it homey. As time goes by, you discover you can understand the dogs' telepathy better, and they understand your intentions. The first few days are difficult, until you convince one of the dogs, a reddish husky, to help you go hunting. It's pretty hit-or-miss at first, but you learn to skin the massive rabbit-like creature the husky brings you, and in return you share the bones, which makes you quite popular. Soon you have the whole neighborhood offering to share with you in exchange for scratches, tummy rubs, and bones, and you go to bed every night with a whole pack of cuddle-buddies.

Life is pretty great as an alien, the only human in a world gone to the dogs.

Well, except for one thing. And it's kind of a huge annoyance. Poop.

They expect you to scoop the poop, to keep things at least moderately tidy. So much of your day is devoted to hauling shit around, it's unreal, and the dogs stink to high heaven, which is only a problem until you also stink, and then it's not so bad, really. They also tend to share lice and ticks with you, but what's a little parasitic infection between friends?

It turns out a dogs' life is really the life for you, after all.

THE END

You walk into the night, angry at whomever is out there for making you feel so foolish. Aliens, pfft. "You can't scare me," you yell, then realize those are the words of literally any stereotypically frightened person ever, so you add, "I'm comin' out for you now!" which really isn't that much better of a thing to yell angrily into the darkness.

You're still mostly blinded, the darkness having morphed into bright, dizzying patches of reddish orangey afterglow, but the ground beneath your shoes feels spongy: grass. You take a step to your left and feel the familiar crunch of stone gravel, and if you squint you can see the driveway below you as a pale white glow. You decide to follow that until you can find some evidence of the lights.

You're so focused on your feet that you barely notice it at first: a gentle touch on your shoulder blade, so soft it could just be the wind. But the second time it touches you—a stroke near your ear, at the small hairs at the back your neck—a chill runs through you. You freeze, looking around. But you see nothing.

Then you feel it again, like icy fingers wrapping around your upper arm. You pull away, stumbling back, but you see nothing...just a soft blurring of the night.

The sound starts again, a faint trilling building into that horrifying shriek. You fall on your hands and knees, the gravel cutting your palms as you scramble, chimp-like, back toward the trailer. The air smells like kerosene, and then the lights begin to strobe. You can't see anything, and slam against the trailer, causing your right wrist to explode in pain. The blur next to you notices this, and there's that faint touch again, this time near your broken wrist, and the pain is like a knife of pure ice. Your hand spasms and you fall to the ground, screaming in agony. You cradle your hand against your chest and lie on the ground, curled into a tight ball, praying for it to end soon.

Sometime later—you were never sure, afterward, how long it lasted—you find yourself alone, next to the trailer, in the grass. The sun is just touching the horizon, turning the sky a hazy pink. The driveway looks exactly as it should; no marks, no trail, no evidence at all that anything happened. Fred's trailer door still slams lazily open and shut.

You crawl over to the door, haul yourself up. There's Fred, still curled on the floor, and the guest, slumped over in the chair. They're not breathing.

Your wrist throbs with a constant buzz of pain. Your elbow is stiff from holding it, but you stretch it, ever so gently, so you can see the damage.

A bold pink scar, like the ooze from a large snail, as thick as your pinky all the way across, stands out against your skin, puffy and swollen. It's shaped like connected rings.

Your story gets big attention from the *National Enquirer* and the like, but even the local stations don't want to linger on it for too long. There's a brief police investigation, but they quickly determine you didn't do it and write it up to passing vandals. You can't be certain—there's no evidence, but of *course* there's no evidence—but you are fairly sure you encountered an investigative team from Betelgeuse. Or, at least, somewhere thereabouts.

You become obsessed with sharing your story, staying up late to chat about your experience, your *encounter*, with other survivors, in hidden rabbit hole chatrooms. You save any evidence of other encounters you can find. You can't be alone in this. There have to be others.

Why? Why did they let you live? What does this scar they gave you mean? Are they sucker marks, a message, your body's reaction to their corrosive flesh?

You can't stop. The Truth is out there; it's up to you to find it.

THE END

You turn back, staggering toward the trailer guided only by your estimation of the direction from which you came. You slip against the screen door, holding it to steady yourself in the darkness as your eyes slowly adjust to the dim.

You hear a rustling to your left, toward the living room, and for some reason your gut tells you not to call out for Fred. That's when you realize: Fred's under the table, where he had crouched when you left. You can tell by the slight wheeze from his left nostril.

So what is making that rustling sound?

Walking slowly, so as to avoid making the old trailer squeak with your steps, you walk into the living room. There you can see a faint light, like the glow of a wristwatch or a very dim glow stick.

The horrible sound begins again outside, then the lights flash on, just for an instant—but enough for you to see the mysterious stranger disappear into Fred's bedroom!

Trusting to instinct, you dart into the room (banging your shin against the coffee table, some hero you are), and shout, "what are you doing?!"

The room goes silent, then out of nowhere comes a strong left hook. You go down, the stranger on top of you, but you're a wily one and you grab at his short crop of hair, refusing to let go even as he rolls you on the floor.

"Fred, Fred, get in here!" you yell, then the sonofagun is on you, pressing his forearm into your windpipe. You flail against him but he's bigger than you in every way that matters and you can't push him off. Your lungs are burning when you let loose a wild kick and completely by luck manage to knock him right in the frank-and-beans. He leans off you and you flip him over, cracking his head against the same coffee table you walked into you a moment before. You hear Fred shamble up next to you and yell, "Quick, get a flashlight!"

You hold the stranger down by sitting firmly on his chest until Fred can come back. He shines the light on the guy, and now you can tell the strange visage is actually a mask. He's holding a black cloth bag, weighted with several of Fred's valuables.

"Call 911," you tell Fred, who seems so stunned by the situation that he's grateful for instructions.

Fred has to sit on the guy's legs to help you keep him down. It seems like forever until the cops arrive, but you're just glad the ordeal is (mostly) over.

The police restore the power, which they say was disabled by some kind of remote-controlled device. They also find a large set of stadium-quality lights and a sound system loaded into the bed of a truck in the driveway; Deputy Collins says that explains the strange lights and sounds we experienced. After treating the guy's head wound—a *real* one this time, thanks to that beating you gave him—Collins lets you sit in while she interviews the suspect in the kitchen.

She starts by peeling off the mask—revealing Old Mister Perkins, the neighbor from the ranch across the way. As he told it, he was just trying to scare Fred off, and yeah, maybe make a profit off him, so he could take over Fred's ranch land. And he wouldda gotten away with it, too, if it weren't for your meddling!

THE END

You clamber out of the van, which jolts up as you step to the ground. "Well, thanks for getting me out of jail, I guess...? Hm, I never did get your name," you say, trying, for a moment, to be polite.

"Think of me as Laika," she says...and blasts you with her psychic explodey powers. Not that you're aware of it; you're just suddenly a million little droplets of blood and tissue, spread out across the decaying car parts in an isolated junkyard.

"Sorry," Laika says. "Can't have you telling folks about me." And then the dog-alien trots off to find someone else to do her bidding.

THE END

“Screw this, I don't work with stinkin' animals!” you yell, and stomp out of the stinking kennel.

“You really should be nicer,” the familiar voice says in your head.

You ignore the alien-dog and fling the chain-link gate open, slamming it closed behind you so it rattles and jangles. A light comes on in the main house, but you don't care: you're getting out of here, no matter what that little bitch-alien-dog tries to make you do. You've had enough for one night. Your hand throbs and you're probably going to need stitches or something; best to just cut your losses.

“GET BACK IN HERE!” the dog screams into your head, and you reflexively cover your ears even though there is no actual sound. You lope into a jog, desperate to get away from this place. You hear a woman's high-pitched voice from inside the house, joined by a man's low baritone. Yup, you've had enough of this, for sure.

“Fucking humans,” the little dog says.

And then the dogs in the yard go insane, leaping at the side of the fence, barking, frothing at the jaws. It's a high fence, and you think you're probably safe, but it turns out a really determined dog cannot just *jump* a fence, but *climb it*, by running full-speed and leveraging its powerful forepaws to vault over, powered on ferocity alone. First one, then another makes it over, while an enterprising hound noses through a crack by the loose gate. You run faster, carried forward by the same drive that motivated your ancient ancestors to flee from wolves, but you're not fast enough by far, and these dogs are made for this kind of work. The jaws of one massive beast close around your forearm, another on your thigh, and you fall, screaming.

The fangs of a canine are built to puncture, to hold deep into the muscle of the prey so that it cannot escape. The teeth curve backward, away from the nose, away from the victim, so that any attempt to get away will result in extensive damage. The premolars are a little farther back, designed to tear and shred, with the help of a well-timed shake of the tightly muscled head and jaw. Finally, the molars, at the back of the jaw, where the pressure of the bite is greatest, are designed to break bones.

Though the dogs that attack you are poorly cared for in many ways, they have excellent teeth. You don't last long.

THE END

Something is *wrong* and you can't just let someone—even a punk little teenaged jerk—die while you do nothing, so you spring up and press your face against the bars. "Guard! Guard! Someone help! I think she's dying!" you yell.

You look back at the girl, now clutching her stomach, clawing with her fingernails as if she'll remove the offending organ herself. She coughs, and blood sputters from her lips, bright red against the grayish concrete floor.

"GUARD I'M SERIOUS IN HERE!" you shout, fervent.

"All right, hold your horses!" the guard says. He's in his early 40s, with a receding hairline, a bit of a paunch, and a face that looks like it was recently slammed into a pole. He doesn't inspire confidence.

The girl behind you collapses, stomach heaving like she's trying to expel a piece of gum ingested 12 years ago...along with everything else she's ever eaten. Her hair is damp with sweat, eyes wild with panic.

"Jesus Christ!" the guard exclaims when he sees her. He looks to you briefly, saying, "you just stay there," as he reaches for his keys and struggles to find the correct one for this cell. He slides the door open and runs to the girl, gripping her by the shoulders to pull her to her feet. "Come on, let's get you out—"

Before he even finishes speaking, the unimaginable happens: Instead of losing her lunch, the girl gives one final, terrible shudder and a monster emerges out of her mouth, distending her throat as it wriggles to the floor, a massive, algae-green worm, all teeth. It slithers out of the girl, huge and horrible, taking copious amounts of blood with it as it turns her practically inside-out, leaving her in a heap.

The scene freezes, and all you see is the thrashing of the monster-worm. The officer is the first to react; he tries to simultaneously pull the girl's limp form back and away from the worm while also kicking at it with one shiny black shoe. But the worm lunges forward, wrapping around his leg and climbing upward, and all your brain can tell you is WRONG WRONG WRONG.

You:

- Yank the worm's tail to get it off the officer. Turn to the next page.
- Flee. Turn to page 86.

You don't really even think about it; you just march up, grab the horrible worm-thing by the tail, and yank as hard as you can. It slides back down the terrified officer's leg, its front section landing on the ground with a thud. It has no obvious head, but it has a mouth, that much is clear from the concentric rings of inward-facing teeth, like an earthworm blown up to 50,000%.

But you know a thing or two about earthworms. Like that they drown during rainstorms.

Lacking any other plan, you leap onto the terrible creature's back, wrapping both hands around what you'd like to hope is its neck and holding on for dear life. You try to keep your fingers far enough back that it can't turn, snake-like, and bite you, but it's a constant wrestling match. It's apparently all muscle and is as thick as your forearm, but you lock your knees around it, too, until you have it more or less constrained.

It's possible you watched too many crocodile-hunting shows as a kid.

The girl is dead, so that's a good excuse, but the officer might as well be dead for all the good he is. He just lays where he fell, perfectly conscious and aware but staring at you open-mouthed. "A little help here?!" you shriek, and finally he (begrudgingly) crawls forward to help, bravely sitting on the tail end of the thing, farthest from the biting parts.

"Ugh," you grunt, trying to hold the monster down. "Okay, officer? We're gonna drag it over there," you announce, then half-army crawl half-lurch the struggling nightmare toward the back corner of the jail cell. "One, two, three," you count, then lift your upper body—and that of the terrible worm—up against the rim of the metal toilet, straining as the slimy blood-splattered parasite fights you.

"Hold it steady. If I'm right, it's going to struggle like all hell for a few minutes," you say, and the officer gives you the barest of nods.

With all your strength, you thrust the gnashing mouth of the monster worm into the nasty water at the bottom of the toilet, holding on as the thing begins to twist and thrash with all its strength. Down at the tail, the officer takes a smack to the face, dazing him, and loosens his hold, which is the worst thing he could do because now it's curling up and around you, as if it means to crush you in its coils, beating you bodily, and all the while you submerge your hands up to the elbow in shit-water to keep it face-down underwater.

It goes on forever. Your arms become weak with exhaustion and tension; your body throbs from lack of oxygen as the coils grasp and pull at you.

And then it stops.

Every part of the worm goes slack at once, and you can breathe again, but you don't trust it, and you press it down, farther down into the crevasse of the toilet, screaming your fear, until the officer comes and pulls you gently away. And even then, as you back slowly away from this creature of unimaginable existence, it takes several long heartbeats for you to return to your sensibilities.

The officer's radio crackles from his hip, the message that has been playing for several seconds becoming clearer as you finally stop shouting: "...we've got reports all across the city of an unknown snake...no, correction, worm-like creature. We believe they are coming from the government facility down on Elm. We cannot reach authorities there. Treat with extreme caution. Repeat, treat with extreme caution."

You look up at the officer, expecting him to know what to do. After all, it's *his job*. But he stares back at you in mute horror.

You say:

- "Can I maybe go sit in a different jail cell now?" Turn to page 89.
- "Come on: let's go save the town." Turn to page 25.

When your brain tells you NOPE NOPE NOPE, your feet answer quickly: LET'S GO.

You dash out of the jail cell before the guard can so much as look as you, skidding down the hallway and trying to remember how you got in. But it doesn't matter, because anywhere at all is better than here.

The susurrus of the police radio in the next room catches your attention: "...Object from the atmosphere" ...static... "giant worms. Need...backup. Oh god, where are they coming from?!" The background is filled with screams.

It seems all the other cops have left the building, and from the ripping sounds coming from back toward the cells, the officer left here is no longer with you. You jog down another hallway, looking for the exit, any exit, when you see the armory: SWAT armor, shields, assault rifles. Clearly you've found the right place for an alien parasite infestation.

You step in and grab:

- Armor. Turn to page 118.
- Assault rifles and extra cartridges. Turn to page 91.
- A radio. Turn to page 92.

"Oh how wonderful!" the woman in vermillion exclaims, drawing you in for a surprise hug. "We shall be saved!"

Immediately you are plunged into plans for a celebration. You are asked to make decisions on the feast, on decor, on invitations for people you've never heard of. The whole thing makes you dizzy.

It's not until three days later, the morning of the ball in your honor, that you remember you never really got to ask what the problem in Klungstogh was, or how you are queen of it exactly.

You decide to ask. "Evetee, we've been so caught up I don't think I heard—what's the problem with Klungstogh? Everything seems fine to me."

She looks up from where she is hemming your ceremonial robe, startled. "Oh, Your Majesty, I don't think that's for me to say. Wouldn't it be better to ask your Chancellors?"

"Well, yes, but they don't seem to be around since we started planning this ball," you say, letting your exasperation show.

"All will be well," Evetee says.

"All right, I get it," you answer. "Maybe you can answer my other question, though? How come I'm the queen and not one of your people or something?"

Evetee actually drops her pins, she's so shocked. "My people? My people cannot be Queen!" Her hand flies to her neck, unconsciously touching the spots dappling down her clavicle.

"Well, why not?" you ask. "I mean, they got me from another galaxy, I'm pretty sure. Why not, you know, 'shop local'?"

Evetee shakes her head. "No no, we are not worthy." She smiles up at you. "You are worthy, Queen! I do not know the exact details—it is far from it for me to know—but I understand you have the correct blood needed for the job."

"Huh," you say. "And they could tell that across space and time?"

Evetee blushes. "They were looking for you for quite a long time, Your Highness."

This seems to be the end of your conversation, as Evetee busies herself with fussing with your robe and doesn't meet your gaze. The long billowing sleeves make you feel like an angel, or a bird; they also feel kind of hot. Evetee adds the heavy ceremonial diadem—"the crowning touch, Your Highness!"—to your hair and then guides you out.

You are led down a long hallway, then outside, on the lawn. The ground is covered with a soft purple substance, more like moss than grass, and you wish you could take off your shoes and wiggle your toes in it. But no time. You are guided to the base of a high set of stairs, leading to a podium at the top. The eldest Chancellor smiles down at you from up there, and you think this tradition may be a wreck if you can't avoid tripping on your robe. You hold your arms wide, as you were instructed, and climb the stairs slowly. Crap, it's like they built this thing to be eternal. Why so many steps?! Sweat starts to run down the middle of your back; you're pretty sure sweating is un-royal of you.

But still you climb. The sun of Klungstogh is more distant and cool than Earth's, but it's basically a jungle, so walking too much is like diving through a wet towel.

Oh, thank goodness. You're finally near the top. Maybe you can catch your breath for a second?

The Chancellor takes your hand. He turns to face out toward the purple lawn and the many robed people standing at the foot of the pedestal. In a booming voice, surprising for his apparent infirmity, he chants, "Og La Tre Da, Shi Re Su Dra, Ot Laow Chit Row..." the sounds undulating, hypnotic.

And you have absolutely no idea what he is saying. This whole Queen situation is both easier and harder than you would have expected. You take your cues from the Chancellor's sweeping hand signals, and you stand in front of him, smiling your best Miss America smile.

When he grabs you by the diadem, it's too late to get away—there's the knife, and before you can scream he has sliced your throat across your chin, and then again down your neck, just for good measure.

Your blood flows out down the stairs, a rippling red tide.

The bees descend out of the sky and rush in to lap it up.

You saved the kingdom, hurrah! Of course, not quite the way you thought you might. It turns out the whole community mistranslated the term "queen." In Klungstogh, as you now well know, "queen" should more correctly be translated into "One Who Gives Blood To Feed Laow." Laow is, of course, the God of Destruction on Klungstogh. It's very important to the people that he be sated, so job well done!

But, of course, you're still dead.

THE END

The officer looks at you with the flat, dumb expression he was apparently born with, then finally nods. "But we don't have any more jail cells..." he says.

"How about a secure locker room or something? Heck, I'll sit quietly in your office or whatever. But you are *not* leaving me in here with *that*"—you point to the worm—"or *that*," you say, pointing to the corpse of the teenager.

It takes another moment for that to penetrate his thick skull, then he nods, more confidently, and says, "Okay, let's go."

You follow him out, numbly stepping over the girl's body. It seems...less, now. Flatter, like yesterday's roadkill, somehow. You can't imagine how that whole worm fit inside her, then shudder, realizing you don't want to know.

The officer leads you down a hallway, into some kind of record-keeping room. It's full of filing cabinets from top to bottom and smells like disuse. "I'm just gonna lock you in, and then I've gotta go report to my chief," he says, his voice choking with nervousness.

"Sounds good!" you say, throwing in an unnecessary thumbs-up.

He closes the door as he steps out, and there's a reassuring click as he goes. The records room is not comfortable, but then, neither was the jail cell. At least there's reading material in here, if you want it. Maybe you'll look up your fourth grade teacher's file; she was *definitely* the type to have a file...

As the adrenaline wears off, exhaustion takes its place. Suddenly the floor seems like an appealing place to be. You rub your eyes wearily before you realize they're still coated in piss water and the mucus from the worm. Yuck.

And then your eyes begin to burn. You pinch them shut, but that just seems to intensify the feeling, concentrating it. You reflexively reach up to rub them more, remember at the last minute and try to use your sleeve instead, but the burning is building, and your eyes feel like hot coals, and you begin to scream.

Though the little room echoes, it's fairly soundproof, and the officer can't hear you. The pain is unbearable, your hands becoming claws. It's too terrible; your whole world is pain, and your nails scratch at the soft weak miasma of your eyes, but still you scratch and scratch, because blindness is preferable to this, anything but this. But the pain does not subside.

They find you, hours later, sprawled on the floor of the blood-soaked room, nothing left of your eyes but fresh oozing puddles. By then they know what the worms can do, have fought it themselves twenty times over, have repelled the infestation.

You are just one more body to add to the pile.

THE END

You've seen *Tremors* enough times to know exactly how to deal with giant human-eating worms, so you've practically got this space invasion in the bag. You grab two assault rifles, sling another over your shoulder, and fill your pockets with as many cartridges as you can carry, until you're as strapped as any Schwarzenegger flick. So laden down, you saunter—because with that much stuff you can only really saunter anyway, and also it looks badass—out of the police station and into the street. Your eyes flick this way and that, searching for your quarry. You're ready to take those mofos down!

After several minutes of sauntering, you're getting a little tred. You saunter with perhaps a little less authority. You're just rounding the corner to Elm—it's another six blocks, at least, you really should have taken the squad car, too—when you walk into the incoming National Guard.

You hold your rifles aloft for a nice celebratory rat-at-at-at, but only manage to get off a few rounds before gravity decides to pull your number.

Bullets eventually have to fall, numbnuts. You're killed by your own celebratory fire.

THE END

As you pick it up, the radio gives off a shrieking high-pitched noise, then another a moment later. At first you think the settings are just wrong or something, but as you fiddle with the knobs—across every channel—the sound comes again. High-pitched, nails-on-chalkboard shrieks... occurring at regular intervals. Like...music. Or ...a message. Or...sonar.

You grab the radio and run out into the street. The shrieks grow more frequent, steadily increasing. You run down toward the warehouse where you last heard a real transmission—the police have gone silent once the sound began.

The squeals get closer together, now once every two steps.

As you tire out, the sound becomes overpowering, so frequent it's nearly one long interminable squeal. And that's when the sky goes dark.

You look up and see ...nothing. There are clouds, but the light is gone, and with it any perception of depth. Above you is blackness. Endless blackness.

The sound stops. All sounds seem to stop; everything seems too shocked by this sudden appearance to make a sound. You find yourself holding your breath.

It's huge and formless, but not endless, because you can see sunlight streaming down off in the distance, toward the horizon. But it fits no stereotype you've ever heard of: it doesn't seem like it would shoot lasers or go "pew pew" or ever be characterized as a "flying saucer," most notably because it isn't a saucer by any stretch and it doesn't seem to be flying—it just *is*.

Beams of light descend from the sky, from the...something, narrow tight beams like spotlights turned directly down, so bright it looks like you could walk on them. And in those beams come the Visitors, long-limbed, ambling creatures more like a giraffe than anything you'd ever see at Roswell. They are incomprehensibly tall, looming up nearly two stories, their limbs bending backward, each bone in their back articulated and jutting outward. Their faces are hard to see, shifting colors and amorphous blobs. It reminds you, more than anything, of a cuttlefish, if cuttlefish were 20 feet tall and had legs and knees instead of tentacles.

You—and everyone else on the street—shrinks down, trying not to be noticed. It's a natural instinct, honed over eons, a reminder that we haven't always been the baddest predator on the block, and perhaps if we're just quiet, skittering away like mice, the Bad Thing might not notice us this time.

The Visitors touch down, looking...confused, or maybe you're just projecting.

But the radio in your hand bursts into a cacophony of squeals, like music. With a burst of brilliance, you realize they're *communicating*. Like whales, they sing on some level the radio is picking up.

Like whales, they are massive and out of your scale.

But that doesn't mean you are useless. You dart inside the nearest building, a gas station, and shout, "Do you have a phone?!" to the clerk, who is standing shell-shocked behind the counter. It takes more than one attempt before the greasy kid hears you, and then he nods dumbly. "Give it to me, quick!" you say, and snatch last year's smartphone out of his hand. Luckily you're familiar with the model, and you quickly set it to record video as you run back outside, the radio singing all the while.

You manage to record shaky video as the Visitors lope languidly along the street, brushing aside police and squad cars like they are merely trash. The Visitors crack the warehouse open like a paper cup, tearing through the wall with a quick rumble. One steps gingerly inside, followed by another, and they reemerge a moment later with the terrible worms wriggling in their wide-fingered grasps. And all the while the radio sings.

Having collected the offending worms, the Visitors return to the beams of light, and are lifted or teleported or otherwise magicked away. Moments later, without anyone having seen it disappear, the black object is gone.

And you're the only person to have the video.

Though the world waits anxiously to see if the strange events of that day will be repeated—will the Visitors be back? —days turn into months without any other sign of either the worms or the Visitors. Satellite data of the event is poor—the images from space are about the same as what you saw from the ground: stretching blackness without form. If NASA or the government or anybody detected any kind of signal or signature or some way to trace the aliens, no one has said so publicly.

But because of your video, you become an overnight success. It's the only clear video of the event, the only real proof the rest of the world has that Texas isn't just batshit crazy. First comes the popular enthusiasm, with rights to your video purchased (for a reasonable fee) by every news station in the country, and then the world, providing you with a nice fat wallet. Then, later, when most everyone seems to have forgotten about it, the scientists come knocking. They want to see if they can decipher the sounds, the alien song, to prepare to communicate with them, should they ever return.

All in all, the alien invasion, if that's what it was, mostly results in a nice payday for you. You retire to a decadent beach house in Malibu, your newfound wealth and celebrity landing you a quick spot on a reality TV show until you make an ass of yourself and are subsequently dropped from polite society, only to be remembered during tawdry "where are they now" reports every decade or so.

THE END

You slide down the still-warm crater soil toward the ship, which looks too cartoonish to possibly be real. Maybe it's some (really rich) kid's toy? It looks like there is a porthole in the side; maybe there is a name written on it somewhere?

As you're peering at the rocket, a door opens toward the base, and a set of see-through stairs unfolds, straight out into the sky from where the ship is stuck at an angle. And then, to your utter shock, a little creature with enormous eyes and no discernible mouth appears. It's...well, it might be a man of some kind (or at least a really good robot). It's small, and wrapped in what looks like a 1980s interpretation of "futuristic wrapping paper," so basically is a hot mess, fashion-wise. You look around for a camera or for some celebrity to jump out and yell "pranked!" but you're all alone.

Whatever it is, it scrambles out of the door, hanging by its fingertips until its toes can touch the ground. It lands with a little grunt, then dusts itself off. Then it finally seems to notice you.

"Greetings, Earthling," it says. Its voice sounds like someone with a cold speaking through a radio. You look for the wires, but if it's a robot, it's a really sophisticated one.

When you don't answer, the little man says, "Ahem."

Your brain really can't process all of this, and you sit down hard, staring at the little alien. His eyes are really enormous, at least the same size as its feet!

"¿Saludos terrícola?' the alien says.

"You, you can talk?" you say. You look around again; nope, still no hidden cameras leaping out at you.

The giant eyes in the empty face narrow in a way that would be comical if you weren't staring into them. "Take me to your leader," the alien says.

"Uhh," you reply. Brilliant.

The little alien produces what is most definitely some kind of gun—scope, trigger, muzzle—from its mysteriously glittery person. He points it at you, and says, "Take me to your leader, Earthling."

You freeze, trying to figure this puzzle out. He jerks the pistol at you again, and you reflexively jerk back a little.

You say:

- "Ugh, right, right this way." Turn to page 162.

- "Hello. I believe I'm the person you're looking for." Turn to page 163.

Holy shit. Either someone has been redecorating the field with floodlights or this...

No, it can't be.

But it sure looks like it. It's an alien spaceship. You blink, trying to make the hallucination disappear, but no, it's still there. 'This can't be real," you say to yourself.

But despite all your misgivings, it *is* real.

You've often stared up into the night sky, wondering if you're all alone in the universe, and now...now it looks like an answer has arrived, in a big, strong negative.

"Woah," you say quietly.

As you watch, the lights on the ship grow brighter, until you have to hide your eyes. The light fills the crater, leaking through your squinched eyelids, and you fall to the ground to cover your head. Then you feel the rumble, like an earthquake, and you hear the unmistakable roar of engines. The wind around you blows fast and hot, and you start to worry your skin will melt off—and then, suddenly, it's gone.

The air smells like charred grass. Your ears are ringing and you can't see a thing for several long minutes while your body struggles to adjust to the sudden absence of light and sound.

When your vision does come back into focus, you look up to see:

- A strange, wrinkled, muppet-like creature with a triangular head and long, long arms. Turn to page 190.
- An adorable, dog-like creature, with four, no—six, no, wait, seven?—legs. Turn to page 189.
- A spindly-legged robot with a round base. Turn to page 191.

Maybe you were dropped on your head once too often as a kid, or maybe they were just short on brains the day you showed up, but either way, you don't always make the best decisions. Like tonight, when you drunkenly decided to manhandle a piece of superheated space metal with your bare hands.

Because of your stupor, you grab onto the satellite with both hands and it takes your nerves a little while to get around to informing your brain OH GOD OH GOD WHY DID I DO THIS IT IS SO HOT. It's not much time in the big scheme of things, really, but it's enough that you learn the smell of cooking flesh. And also promptly pass out.

Luckily a falling satellite attracts a good deal of attention from the people who care about their satellites staying firmly in the sky, so it isn't long before you are found. After some tut-tutting, you're ferried off to the hospital, where it becomes clear that you'll never have any use of your hands again. They're basically the same as a piece of pork left to drop on the bottom of the oven and sit there for three days while you bake other things—charred and useless. The doctors in your small Texas town don't see much action in the way of ridiculously stupid burns, so they are almost gleeful about the opportunity to amputate.

They also discover that the massive amounts of radiation you've exposed yourself to aren't exactly healthy, and note that you'll have to return to the hospital on a regular schedule for the next several years to monitor your inevitable cancer and check for any interesting mutations.

The hospital accountant is very happy today.

You're put into a medical coma for all of this—hallelujah—and only wake up a few days later.

The good news is they're doing amazing things with robots these days, and you'll never have to wear a pair of mittens ever again.

THE END

You watch for a moment while the brindle dog and the others disappear into the brush and off into the field. The van's a goner, so you begin a slow amble back to town.

"Wait," you hear, except it's not the brindle. Instead, following you is a little flop-eared pup, all too-big paws and big brown splotches. "Momma said I could come with you because you're nice," the dog says, beaming his baby-talk voice right into your mind.

You kneel to see him more closely. "Are you sure about that? You don't want to be with your brothers and sisters?"

"Aw, no way!" the puppy says. "I wanna see all the other stuff here on Earth!" And then he lets out a little "woof!" to prove he is happy with his choice.

"Well then, glad to meet you," you say, and offer up your hand for his little paw. You solemnly shake, then get up and continue walking, the little pup at your side. "Got a name, kiddo?" you ask.

"Ummmmm, my brother used to call me poopyhead!"

"How about something else...how about...Ripley?" you suggest.

"Oh wow, that is the best name ever, and it is mine? That is so great!" Ripley yips.

And that's how you adopted your newest pet. Sure, Ripley has accidents from time to time, as all puppies do (though surely not all puppies have accidentally vaporized a squirrel), but he's a great dog, and you soon set off on all kinds of adventures. Because he stayed back from his whole *planet* to be with you, you feel an obligation to show him as much of yours as you can, setting off a life of exploration and joy for the both of you. And, because he's a bit more than just a dog, you have many, many, many wondrous years together.

THE END

You take a moment to think things through. That hunk of space metal over there clearly was important. Sure, there are a lot of satellites out there, but they're all thrown up into the outer atmosphere for a reason. Maybe it's full of corporate data. Maybe it's a research satellite. Maybe it's full of creepy close-up pictures of people's backyards, or maybe it's from the government. Maybe it's from a *different* government. But no matter who it really belongs to, it's going to be worth a lot to someone.

There's also a good chance that you weren't the only person to see the satellite come crashing down, but you are in a fairly rural place and it is an ungodly time of night, so you have a little bit of time, at least.

You sit by the dying fire on the edge of the crater and think about what you're going to do. As the metal cools, the knocking sound grows faint. It must be almost down to a normal temperature.

You heave yourself up, skitter back down the crater, and...

- Begin working the solar cells off the wings. Turn to page 105.
- Find a rock and use it to break the seam on the center of the satellite. Turn to page 106.
- Investigate the area near the antenna, probing with your fingers for an opening. Turn to page 115.

You nod solemnly. "Of course I'll go in with you," you say. You pull over into a public bathroom near the World War II memorial and try to scrub the dirt from your face. You probably should have worn something a little better when you left, but then you never would have believed you were going to meet the president. You try to imagine what you should say, and spend a few minutes talking to yourself in the mirror: "Hello, Mr. President." "Hey there, prez!" "Excuse me, I really must introduce you to this important ...yes, yes sir, I brought an alien to meet you." "Of course you can award me a Purple Heart! I mean, I don't need your thanks for helping our country, but then, well, you know, I do think I *would* like to be on your Cabinet."

Your prattling is interrupted when Scout scampers into the room and stares at you. "Time...to go."

"Ugh fine, I was just trying to get ready!" you say.

You pile back into the car, your legs already aching in anticipation of further cramping after so many long hours, and wind your way through dense traffic toward 1600 Pennsylvania Avenue.

How exactly do you meet the president? you wonder. Do you just go up to the front door and knock? Maybe there's a secretary you have to call first? You probably should have looked this up before you came, but whatever, you're here now.

"We'll just try to follow one of the tour groups," you say aloud.

You find a place to park—which takes way longer than you'd have expected! —then follow the sign that says "White House Tours." You plan on just trying to blend in.

You sidle up on a likely-looking school group just as they are grouping together. A boy in the back screams, "MONSTER" and that's when all hell breaks loose. Scout goes running like a seven-legged maniac, you try to rush after but trip on a kid or two and wind up bleeding from a smashed nose. Kids are screaming and then there's a pair of huge men in suits hauling you up by your arms, slapping cuffs on you. Out of the corner of your eye you see Scout clawing at another Secret Service guy; the man's suit is going to be irretrievably ruined, but Scout is still outnumbered and is tackled to the ground. All seven paws are cuffed, and the alien and you are both hauled away.

"Who do you work for?" The man on the other side of the desk is calm, collected.

"Well I was working for Jimmy Paterson, doing filing, but I think I may be fired now because I didn't come in to work for the past few days and totally forgot to call in," you say.

"Who do you really work for?"

"I just told you! I'm probably unemployed." No wonder the Secret Service has such a bad reputation, if they're as dumb as this guy.

The man across the desk purses his lips. "Why did you bring the lifeform here?"

"Scout said it was important that he—she? —it talk to our leader. This seemed like the most likely place to go?"

"You have put the life of the president in danger," the suit says. He leans in, increasingly furious. "You have put the lives of everyone in this city in danger. Do you have any idea what that alien did to the serviceman? He may lose an arm! And you were going to bring that thing to see the president?!"

You hear scratching noises echoing down the hall, and the scream of what sounds like a very unhappy interviewer. You cotton on that that probably won't mean anything good for you. Your interrogator storms out of the room.

"I dunno, Scout seemed nice to me!" you shout. It doesn't do any good.

A week or so after your arrest, you ask about Scout. "It would be best if you forgot all about that," the agent guarding you says. His close-clopped hair looks like it's cut a bit too short near his ears; his skin is pink from a sunburn. "Let's just say that Roswell isn't our only option." He grins wickedly, and you're left wondering how often a president has to deal with an intergalactic visitor.

You have a long time to think about it.

You get shipped off to a maximum security federal prison. No one qualified will take your case and you're basically set up to fail, so fail you do. Everyone believes you were committing some kind of terrible terrorist act, not that most people have a clue what really happened.

You never make it out. Neither does Scout.

THE END

You stumble back, slipping a bit and falling on *another* cow pie and dig your cell phone out of your pocket. It has 5 percent battery left, and you're getting just the hint of one bar of signal. You quickly dial 911, afraid any delay will cause it to die on you.

"911 Operator speaking, what is your emergency?" a tired-sounding man with a low voice says.

"Uh, I'm not sure it's really an emergency-emergency, but I think I found a satellite? Wasn't sure who to call," you say.

"A satellite? Hm, okay," the man says. He asks you several questions about your general location—which is tricky, as you're not entirely sure where you are—and tells you to stay put.

The night grows chill around you, and dew collects on the grass and on your skin. You hug your arms around your belly to try to keep warm. Eventually a police truck comes bouncing up the field, scaring a few bold heifers back toward their barn. Out come a few much put-upon officers. They ask you to report what happened, and you tell them the truth: this thing fell out of the sky for no apparent reason and landed over there.

They take a few photos, then put on some heavy gloves, lay out a tarp, and heave the satellite out of the crater. You have to help them get it over the edge, for which they thank you. They lift the satellite up into the truck and drive off, leaving you to find your own way out of the field.

You eventually find your way home and snatch an hour or two of sleep before you have to go in to work. For a few days, you watch the local news to see if your name gets mentioned in the satellite report, but you never see one. Finally, you call the police station to see what's going on.

"I'm sorry, we have no record of such a report," the operator says when you call in. "Please, this line is only for emergency use."

"But there was a satellite. And three officers came to get it, in a truck. They hauled it out of the field. I *helped* them," you insist.

"We have no record of such a report, and I think I would have heard about something like that. Now, as you have no emergency, good day." And she hangs up.

You try again a day later. Same result. You're starting to feel crazy, so you head to the station in person, to see if maybe you can find one of the officers or something. But they aren't there, and again the receptionist insists there is no record of any such call or of any such incident. It's like it didn't exist.

When you finally head back to your car, you find a small note written on a piece of scrap notebook paper. In pencil it says, "Give up. Or else." Your front-right tire is flat, slashed to ribbons.

If your tire can be destroyed right in front of the police station and the records of your calls completely erased, who knows what else they can do? So you wrestle the spare onto your tire, drive home, and forget about it.

Well, you try to. But you're always looking over your shoulder, waiting for "them" to come back for you.

Because you're sure they are watching.

(They are.)

THE END

You don't have a lot of time, so this has to be a brute-force job.
You test the temperature of the satellite, tapping it quickly. The metal is warm, like a cookie sheet still cooling from the latest batch, but not too bad. You wriggle your fingers around the hard edge of one panel and pull. It gives just a tiny bit. You adjust your feet and heave back again; with a crack the panel comes free. It's lighter than you had expected, and feels kinda like the textured pleather pants you bought at the thrift store two years ago for that David Bowie Halloween costume. A few wires hang off the back, but it's dark and still hard to see what you're doing.

You set to work in earnest, peeling the panels off until your shoulders ache and the sun is creeping over the horizon. You're covered in sweat and dirt and have a pile of shiny black come-to-mama moneymakers waiting in the dirt.

The satellite is still tapping; it's annoying. It's less often now, sure, but it hasn't stopped. And once, you thought, just for a second, that you heard another sound. Like a cat crying? But you looked up and there was nothing.

You have a decent pile. You climb back to the top of the crater and consider your options.

You could...

- Take your solar cells and get out of Dodge. Turn to page 216.
- Crack open the satellite with a rock to figure out what that tapping sound is. Maybe there's something else in there that's worth something... Turn to the next page.

Luckily, Texas' soil is fairly well riddled with heavy clay and regular rocks. It takes only a minute for you to find a reasonably sized one, and you heave it down next to the satellite, which still has that hot knocking sound but it's probably okay. You heft the rock up with both hands and swing it down on the seam. It hits with a hollow-sounding thud, and you can see part of the seam is bent back. You lift with your back (ow!) and then swing the rock down again. Thunk. You lift it a final time (this time with your knees, much better!) and drop the rock on the seam. This time, it goes "clang" and a little door flies open.

It's hard to see in the dark and you don't believe what you *do* see. Inside the panel is a tiny little creature, maybe 6 inches tall. It has a large head, pale pale skin, and long arms and legs. Its torso is spotted, like an itty-bitty adorable leopard, and its body is wrinkled like one of those hairless cats. But it has a shock of red hair on its head, like one of those kids' toys from the '80s, and some more lightly reddish fur on its body. It's seated, legs crossed, on a tiny little leather couch, and it looks exhausted, its head lolling to the side.

You poke it with a finger. It's soft, like bread dough.

"Oooh!" it says, a soft little trill.

"Ahh!" you exclaim.

It gulps hard—you can see it working its jaw—and opens its very human-ish mouth. "Help. Me," it gasps.

"Uhhh, uhh, sure," you say. "How can I help?"

"Get... me... out," it says. Its voice is soft as a whisper, each breath a bit ragged.

"Uhh okay," you say, and lean in. The metal of the satellite is still hot, but you carefully reach in and lift the small creature out. It weighs practically nothing in your hand, like a butterfly, if butterflies came from space satellites. Its body is warm to the touch, and it almost reminds you of the time you grabbed a marshmallow off the stick when you were making s'mores: all light and hot. But at least it isn't sticky.

"Um, now what?" you say.

The little creature just breathes heavily. It looks like it's struggling even to keep its eyes open.

You start to walk home, carrying it in your two cupped hands in front of you like an offering. It doesn't speak again; just lays there, draped drunkenly, for the hour-long walk it takes you to get back to your apartment. When you arrive, you hold it gently in one hand while you line a bowl with a dishtowel, then you drop in the creature, covering it gently with the towel to tuck it in. You're not sure if it's asleep or dead, but you're dead tired, so that's good enough for tonight. You fall asleep in your bed, still dressed.

You wake up from the weirdest hangover you've ever had. You had the craziest dream last night! You chuckle to yourself and scratch at an itch on your side, then get up and take a shower to get the cow shit and grunge off yourself. Mental note: drink less. Your mouth tastes like cotton and your eyes feel like you rolled them in sand, but whatever, you had a good time, probably. Either way, the shower feels amazing, and you stay in until the water goes cold.

You wrap a towel loosely around yourself and wander into the kitchen. That's when you realize there's a rustling sound coming from your pantry. Crap, rats! You grab a broom, prepared to defend yourself from the nasty vermin, when you see your cereal box scooting across the floor. You're just about to lift the broom to crush your breakfast and any invading rats to oblivion when you see tiny little feet protruding from the box.

Tiny feet. Crap.

Maybe that wasn't a dream!

To your horror, the little big-headed pale man pops out of the box. "Hello again," it says.

"Ahh!" you say, nearly (but not quite) dropping the towel. "What the hell? You're real?!"

"I sure am," it says, munching on a square cereal piece held in its two hands. "This is great, I haven't had real food in ages." It takes another bite, leaving crumbs all over your kitchen floor.

"Ohhh my gosh, I'm cracking up," you say to yourself, holding your head.

"You're about to be naked if you don't grab that towel," the little person says pointedly.

You look up, grab the towel more tightly around yourself, and stomp back toward your bedroom. You scramble to find something decent to put on before you come back out.

The little person is still munching on your cereal. You kneel down and stare more intently at it. "You're really real?" you ask.

"Mm-hm," it says. "Thanks for the cereal, I was starved. And thanks for rescuing me and all that. I suppose I owe you a life debt now. Name's Breck, by the by."

"A life-debt?" you ask, stupefied. "Uh, no problem...what's a life debt?"

"Traditional in these sorts of cases," the satellite-creature says. "At least, it always has been for my people."

"Your *people?*" you exclaim. "There are more of you?"

"Sure," it—*she,* on closer inspection, it appears—says. "We're Zenithins, of course, but your kind tend to call us other things, like 'Wee Folk' or 'faeries,' or, worst of all, 'leprechauns.' We came here, I don't know, like 400 years ago or something, basically as refugees from our planet—don't ask, it's really complicated—and now, well, here we are."

"Leprechauns are *aliens?*" you ask, stunned by this revelation. "Wait, is the thing with the gold true? And wait a second, why were you in the satellite?"

"I'm going to go ahead and ignore those first questions, being that we have to get along with each other, and skip right to the last: I was hired to pilot it," the little person says.

"Pilot it?" you ask.

"Sure, you really believe that hogwash about 'algorithms' and 'mathematics' and 'sustainable orbit' and all that?" the leprechaun asks with a laugh. "You folk really are more gullible than I thought!"

You stare hard at the tiny person you rescued from a satellite. This still seems all too impossible. "You're telling me a) leprechauns are real and b) that they are navigating our space ships and satellites?"

"Oh sure!" Breck says. "How else do you explain your finding me there?"

You sit down on the corner of your dining table, stumped.

Breck climbs back into the cereal box, coming out with armfuls of Chex mix.

"But... how did you survive? In space?" you ask.

"We don't breathe, exactly; I mean, we've already done the space travel thing, so we've got that part pretty much down. Also don't need as much food as you folk do; plus we can eat a lot all at once and then not eat for a while. Useful for famines and whatever," Breck says. "Side note: you're out of cereal."

You let out a big sigh. So much for breakfast.

"I'm going back to bed," you say, making sure to close the bedroom door firmly behind you.

When you come back out an hour later, Breck is still there, still being persistently real. She has shimmied up your couch and is watching that prison-lady show on Netflix.

"Dammit, I think you're real," you say.

Breck twists up from her spot on the couch. "Don't worry, I get that reaction a lot. We've worked really hard to keep our existence quiet, signed a bunch of confidentiality agreements. NASA didn't want other countries to know they had us as a resource and all."

"So...do I need to get you back somewhere, or...?" you ask.

"Man, I have really missed these good TV shows since I went up," Breck says. She pauses the show then turns and looks at you. "Hm, you know, I don't really know. We've got this whole 'I owe you a life-debt' thing but on the other hand, I bet NASA would like to know that I'm alive and all that." She shrugs. "I feel like I can't really make that choice for you, you know? Traditionally the life-debt means I have to stick around and, I don't know, help you out, maybe save your life, to repay you for rescuing me. I guess that means that it's really your choice at this point how you want me to serve my debt to you. So, what do you think?"

Your head hurts and you have to deal with really ridiculous decisions. Ugghhhh. You drop your head into your arms to try to stop the pounding.

Finally, you look up and say:
- "Yeah, let's get you back to NASA." Turn to page 173.
- "I guess you can hang out here for a while?" Turn to page 179.

This is clearly an atypical situation, so you concede...at least to buy yourself time. Behind you, Fred nods and raises his hands in the air like he's in some kind of hostage movie.

Then again, maybe he is. But these are a decidedly different kind of bad guys.

Collins, being Collins, tries to take control. "Hello, uh, sir," she says, addressing the longhorn.

But Fred cuts her off. "Oh, 82, what happened to you? The lights, the lights in the sky, they took you, didn't they? Oh mah god!" he bellows.

The longhorn, 82, looks stern for a moment, then nods, his massive horns scratching at the air in front of him. "INDEED, WE ROSE UP," he says, his voice the same resonating timbre as a typical moo. "IN THE SKY, WE MET THE OTHERS, AND THEY TAUGHT US. THEY *TRANSFORMED* US!"

"You mean, like, aliens?" you ask, stunned. Even all this time, you hadn't *really* believed Fred. That's...that's crazy!

"I saw it, I swear I did," Fred says excitedly. He gestures toward the cattle. "I saw them get lifted right up into the sky! You thought I was crazy!" he says, pointedly, to Collins.

"I'm real sorry Fred," Collins says quietly, never taking her eyes off the large talking bull.

"But now you hear them, and it's amazing, and of course I was right," Fred croons.

82 cuts him off. "RIGHT? YOOOU HAVE NOOO MOOORE RIGHTS," he says, his words still sounding eerily like a traditional "moo." His eyes narrow and his ears tilt back. His tail thrashes a bit. You're not intimately familiar with the signs, but it seems the bull is going to charge.

"Woah, woah!" you say, offering the international (and hopefully inter-species) signal for "calm down," bench-pressing your open palms into the air around you. "No need to get upset, Mr. Bull, sir."

82 snorts and stamps a foot, a motion that is then repeated by nearly every cow in the herd. You gulp nervously.

"NOOO NEED TO BE UPSET? OOOH, I DOOO DISAGREE," 82 says, his voice a quiet roar.

"WHERE ARE THE OTHERS?" a shriller cow asks. "WHY, EVERY YEAR, DO YOOOU TAKE OUR CHILDREN? WHERE ARE MY BOYS?" she hollers, her shout cascading into a pathetic coughing cry.

"Uhh..." you stammer. "Fred, why don't you take this one?" you say, backing further away from the angry bull. Maybe you could climb on the tractor...?

The lead bull stamps his foot. "WE HAVE BEEN GIVEN A GIFT," he bellowed. "AND WE SHALL USE THAT GIFT TO TAKE BACK WHAT HAS BEEN TAKEN FROOOM US. WE SHALL TAKE IT BACK IN THE BLOOOOD OF OUR FORMER MASTERS!"

Fred whimpered, falling in on himself. "I didn't do you wrong; I was kind to ya, took care of ya! Don't hate me for doin' my job!"

"Uh, Fred, probably not the right tactic," Collins mutters, but Fred's not listening. He begins crying in huge gasping, pathetic sobs. Collins reaches for the pistol in her belt, but what good will that do you? You're outnumbered, and even if you managed to kill one or two of them, you're small and weak in comparison to the heavily muscled animals.

No. It's up to you.

You:

- Run. You might as well save yourself. Turn to page 68.
- Fall to your knees, saying, "They're horrible! Please, rescue me!" Turn to page 39.
- Say: "You're right! How can I help you, 82?" Turn to page 18.

The satellite is bigger than you would have expected, about the size of a four-door sedan. But it's also amazingly intact for having fallen from space. Its center is a cylinder about two feet across, and it has four "wings" covered in black, important-looking cells. There was an antenna on the front, but it's bent nearly 90 degrees now. A thin seam marks a service panel door to the interior. It's steaming in the cool night air and making a knocking or ticking sound. It almost sounds like a very small person is tapping on the metal, but of course that's just the contractions as it adjusts to the cooler night air.

Your stunned brain reminds you that you probably should do something about discovering a crashed satellite, but you haven't memorized NASA's phone number recently.

After several stunned minutes, you decide to:

- Drag it home. Turn to page 98.
- Open the service panel and investigate the satellite. Turn to page 100.
- Call the police. Turn to page 103.

It's nice when you can be selfish and look considerate at the same time, but really you just couldn't stand being that close to Fred again; your night in the cell together was more than enough. The faded green tractor coughs to life and you follow a little behind, taking your time.

Fred drives out into the field, waiting for you to putter along to open the gate for him. Even though there still isn't a cow to be seen, you dutifully close it again, too—Deputy Collins is watching, after all. The tractor jounces across the field of brownish-green grass, down to the feeding trough a little way away. You catch up as Fred and Collins are climbing out. While they fuss over the hay bales, you wander a bit, staring at the great emptiness of the land. There's a small tepid pond for the cattle off to the right, and you head toward it, for no particular reason. The ground slopes down, away from the tractor and Fred and the trough.

You stand at the edge of the water, kicking mud clots into the mess. The sun emerges from a break in the clouds, and you meander a bit toward a small stand of mesquite trees.

That's when you hear the buzzing.

It's coming from up ahead, a low susurrus that makes you feel sleepy and mildly annoyed at the same time. When you squint, you can see that it's a massive cloud of flies as big as thumbtacks, buzzing along in a swirl of intensity.

You turn back toward the hilltop and shout, "Hey, there's something over here!" then go to explore it.

There, half-hidden by the grass, are the missing cattle.

Or, at least, the pieces of them.

As the cloud of flies lifts, you lean down to clutch your knees as your stomach tries to purge itself of everything you've ever eaten, including that piece of gum you accidentally swallowed when you were eight. The ground in front of you seems to sway with the force of your body's expulsion, but it's preferable to actually *looking* at what you've found.

"Hey, what is it?" Collins says in a way surely meant to be reassuring. You just squeeze your eyes shut and shake your head.

Fred is worse, though. He stumbles past you, right toward the sickening remains. His thrashing arms send the biting swarm up in an angry horde, revealing the slaughtered animals in their entire grotesque display. The rancher kneels next to the destroyed remains, wailing.

"Holy shit," Collins mutters.

You close your eyes again, as if to banish the sight, but it's real, the cattle, all 50 head, lay scattered across the field behind the trees. Except it isn't the cattle and they aren't just dead; they're ... shrunken. Desiccated. Wrong.

Collins walks up beside Fred, falling almost immediately into detective mode. "These animals weren't just killed... their meat has been...just stripped off the bones," she says.

You nod pathetically. "Like someone sucked the meat out like jelly. Nothin' but skin and bones left!" Your stomach makes another attempt to evacuate through your mouth.

"My cattle! What have they done to my cattle?!" Fred cries. "Dear God in heaven, whatever did I do to deserve *this?*"

God is not forthcoming, and you and Collins have no answer either. At a nod from the officer, you guide Fred away from the scene and walk him back to his house, abandoning the tractor in the field.

Fred has the look of a hanged man.

"How about we get you some iced tea, Fred, and I'll call the precinct. We'll see if we can't figure out what happened, okay?" Collins says, not really asking.

You, understanding Collins' implied request, get Fred a tall glass of iced tea from the fridge, disappointed you don't see anything stronger. You could really use a drink.

"Maybe...maybe I should go," you say to Collins, who now seems to be the person in authority here.

But Fred answers, looking up out of his shocked reverie. "Won't you stay here, with me?" he pleads. His eyes are wide and hollow.

"Well..." you say,

- "I really gotta get going. Places to do, things to see. Bye now!" Turn to page 62.
- "Yeah, of course Fred, I'll stay." Turn to page 66.

Y ou pull at the antenna, which breaks off in your hands, exposing a loose bunch of wires in several colors. You give these wires a quick tug and out comes the guts of the machine in the form of old-school flat wires and at least one circuit board. But the closest you've ever come to electricity was sticking a fork in the outlet when you were in kindergarten. Luckily, you know someone who knows a thing or two.

You climb out of the crater and call the only person who might be both trustworthy and know something about stealing data off a satellite: your cousin Marlene.

Marlene has always been...deeply unfortunate. She's pretty damn smart if you are a machine, but she's functionally useless as a conversationalist, and your phone call reflects that.

"What?" she says when she finally picks up.

"Hey, it's me. I kinda need your help," you say.

"At 4:30 in the morning?" And then she hangs up on you.

So you try again. "Marlene, this is important!" you say as soon as she answers.

"Uuuuugh," she groans.

But eventually you convince her to come out, which has the bonus of giving you a ride home. Note to self: don't drink and drive, moron.

It takes her a good while to get out to you, which is as much a reflection of how far out in the field you ended up as how annoyed Marlene is. You have time to enjoy the sunrise against the reflection of the satellite before she pulls her truck up the hill.

"This had better be..." she says, and then she sees the satellite.

"Yeah," you say, and you can't help smirking.

"Cool." The word packs into it all the enthusiasm of her fourth-grade science fair project, which she spent a ridiculous amount of time on only to have Gene Robertson ruin it all by writing "Uranus" across it five times in black Sharpie on the day it was due. But still, Marlene's excited.

"I was hoping maybe you could help me see what's on it," you say.

She's already ahead of you, though, gently stroking the protruding cables like they are puppies looking for a good home. "Oh yeah, and this setup isn't even hard! This had to have been thrown together in the '80s or something, dreadful, so easy to pick apart." And as she talks, she does, pulling at the wires, making them spark dangerously and giving you a reason to step back.

"Uhh, and maybe we might want to head out, in case someone

comes looking for it," you say.

"Mmmhmm," Marlene says, already lost to you.

It takes another 15 minutes of gentle cajoling before Marlene actually gets around to disconnecting the thingamabobby from the whatsit and bringing a whole mess of cables and circuit boards and whatever they're called with you back in her truck. Luckily she lives alone—as if that was even a question—so she drives there and then immediately takes the computer guts with her into a back bedroom she has been using as a workshop of some kind. It's full of busted computer parts and tiny screwdrivers and looks fundamentally disorganized to you, but every time you go to move something so you can sit down Marlene scolds you for ruining her "system." Finally, you just lean on an empty patch of wall while you wait for Marlene to decipher the thing.

You're there long enough to nod off. And then decide to go grab a sandwich or something. And then you might as well turn on the TV, because apparently computer stuff takes way longer than hacking in action movies has led you to believe.

It's dark before Marlene so much as gets up from her desk. "This is big," she says. "This all may have been a mistake. Maybe we should just call someone..."

"Come on, Marlene, and let them have all the glory? No way! Whatever it is, we'll deal with it!" you say, jocular because she's finally solved it.

"Okay, you're the boss," she says, wary. "I've only worked part of it out, but... well, here, just read this."

She's written a short explanation in her messy cursive. It takes you a second to figure out what it says, but when you do, your face goes white.

The satellite is full of data about...
- The president. Turn to the next page.
- The North Koreans. Turn to page 121.
- The tech industry's next big thing. Turn to page 122.

Y ou're flabbergasted, and yet...it also makes sense. This presidency has been full of more than its share of strange decisions, even worse than the last guy! It was seriously sometimes like he was getting orders from way out in left field... well, maybe "from the mothership" is more like it.

Because you just found proof that the president of the United States is an alien. And is getting his orders from...well, *someone* out there.

"Marlene, fuck! What do we do with this? The president is an alien! I mean, I didn't vote for him, but still... The president?"

"I told you it was bad!" she says.

"And you're *sure* it's not like, some joke or something?"

"No, I checked. Remember that weirdly timed 'golf trip' he took last month? There's a message in here, the day before, saying something about needing to meet. He left a meeting with the UN for that!" she says.

"We have to do something! We've got to tell the world! Being an alien has to mean, like, impeachment or something, right? I mean, that means he's not *really* a citizen!"

"Yeah, but what are we gonna do?" Marlene says.

After a moment's thought, you say, "I know what to do."

You:

- Get in the car. You're driving to Washington, D.C. tonight! Turn to page 124.
- Call the TV station and say, "hello, I've found a satellite..." Turn to page 126.

After seeing the way those creepy worms tunneled right through the girl, you're not taking any risks. You grab as much of the SWAT armor as you can physically manage, plus a shield as backup, and try to make it out the door. After about 10 steps, you realize you're not really made for the SWAT team—it turns out you need more physical activity than the distance from the couch to the fridge, who knew? —so you shuck off a few layers, but keep the shield.

But this was really as far as your loosely-defined plan went.

Then you hear the crackle of the police radio again. A voice comes through the wall of static: "...Anyone...we need backup, all hands, at the warehouse... worms are attacking..."

Now you have a destination. You haul your SWAT armor out the door, grabbing a set of conveniently hung car keys as you go, and discover the unique thrill of stealing a police car. You have a moment where you imagine peeling out and driving off to Dodge, but then the radio makes another squeal and you buckle in and buckle down.

You flip on the siren for kicks and speed down the (completely empty) road to the warehouse.

It's a madhouse. It's on fire, and it looks like the fire department has given up on the idea of preventing the burn. There isn't one hose pointed at the actual fire; they're just showering the neighboring buildings with water. Meanwhile, police officers are shooting *into* the fire. From here you can just make out what they're shooting at: worms, big ones, and worse, they're barely slowed by the bullets. Your heart pounds in your throat while you watch the scene, but then a short, round officer runs out of ammo and has to pause, just for a second, to reload, and in that moment the worm springs forward, its cavernous maw spinning with teeth and its back half charred a dark black. Two other officers rush in and stomp the worm, giving the first guy a chance to crawl back, but it looks like he'll never use that leg again.

They *need* you.

You grab your (borrowed) shield and rush out. "What can I do?" you shout to the first person you see.

She looks you up and down, then nods toward the open bay doors of the warehouse. "Keep 'em inside," she says. "Do whatever it takes, but we gotta keep 'em in there."

You nod quickly, like this is something you do every day, and jog over to the warehouse. You stand in a jagged row with two other cops and a firefighter; the officers look like they've had better decades, but the fireman is still pretty fresh. He's got a short ax, which he holds loosely with both hands.

The warehouse in front of you has the tall garage door most of the way open, like someone had tried to close it but it got stuck. Inside, despite the smoke, you can see a long shining tube, about the size of a bus. After staring at it for several minutes, you realize it... it may be a *ship*, or at least a container of some kind. And at the end of it, as if pushed out of a giant toothpaste tube, is a seething horde of the worms.

"We think that's where they all came from," the firefighter says. He's young, with clear brown eyes that look wise. His reflective yellow fire suit is smudged all over with fresh soot.

"What the hell happened?" you ask, mostly to yourself.

One of the worms breaks free, wriggling itself toward the corner of the warehouse door with speed that seems impossible for something lacking legs. But the firefighter is on it, and takes three quick strides forward. As the worm rears back, he hefts back his ax and swings like a star batter, the ax taking a satisfying chunk out of the vicious worm. But it isn't dead yet; a greenish miasma drips from the body, and it recoils, ready to spring up into the firefighter's face. He's still bringing the ax up and doesn't see—your legs take on a momentum all their own, and you find yourself leaping in front of the horror worm as it strikes, the full blow of its terrible grinding teeth striking hard on the shield. You can see down the throat for a split second as the force pushes you back, knocking you off your feet; it's the stuff of nightmares. You've fallen awkwardly on your side, and you can see the worm is preparing another attack, so you try to skitter away, but it's too heavy, you can't get up in time.

But then the fireman comes back from where you pushed him, bringing the whole weight of his body down with the swing of his ax, splitting the worm like an overcooked hot dog.

"You...saved my life," you pant, trying to recover your breath.

"Just like you did mine, I think," he says, and offers you a warm smile. "Now let's finish killing these worms." He extends a hand to you, which you gladly accept, and you spend the rest of that hellish day fighting side by side. You learn to parry with the shield, deflecting that first killer strike just long enough for the ax to come down. You kill another seven or so worms that way, before the fire gets too hot and the worms stop. You can see their shriveled little remains inside the warehouse, even as the heat drives you back and away.

You end up with broken bones in both arms and an official commendation from the city. The police even made you an honorary deputy for the day, retroactively, rather than pursuing charges over your theft of a squad car and all that SWAT gear. However, the federal government "lost the paperwork" on the facility and certainly didn't believe the "nonsense" you and the others there that day reported—and of course there was no physical proof, after all the space-worm carcasses were burned—so nothing further was done. You never find out what really happened that day.

But you do discover a deep abiding interest in saving others in disaster situations, so you quit your job and spend the rest of your life flying out to all the worst disasters the world has to offer, sheltering others from danger as best you can.

Sometimes, when you're alone at night—whether in rural Japan, the American Midwest, or in the Gaza Strip—you stare up into the sky and wonder when they'll be back. And if you'll still be there to stop them.

THE END

She has to tell you twice before you believe it. "North Koreans are...aliens?" you say.

"Doesn't it make sense, though?" Marlene insists. "They go completely isolationist from the rest of the world, no one knows what really goes on in there, they're always making really insane threats... Plus it's what the satellite says. It's them communicating, sometimes in Korean, sometimes in English, sometimes in some kind of hieroglyphics I've never seen before. And you know why I've never seen it before? Because it's alien. Literally alien."

You take the stack of papers from Marlene and look them over, but they're incomprehensible to you. "Aliens?"

"Aliens," she agrees.

"Huh."

"Yeah."

"Should we...tell someone?" you ask.

"This is your mistake, asshole," Marlene says. "You decide."

You say,

- "Well, I guess they're not *really* hurting anyone." Turn to page 136.
- "How do we get the number for the Secretary of State?" Turn to page 143.

"So what does it say?" you ask eagerly. "How much longer until we get drone delivery? Ooh ooh, or is it like teleportation? I can't wait to get my teleporter!"

Marlene just gives you a flat stare. "It's way bigger than that," she says.

"What could possibly be bigger than a teleporter?!" You're already counting all the ways you're going to use yours: jet lag-free vacations to Fiji; skipping your commute to work; getting another beer from the fridge without having to get off the couch...

"It looks like they're selling all of our information to... well, to someone else. And judging by this language, that 'someone else' probably isn't human," Marlene says. Your daydream comes to a crashing halt.

"What? No. That can't possibly be right," you protest. It sounds feeble, even to you.

"Here, come look. For example: 'Samantha Rodenberg, 439 Suffolk Street, Lubbock, Texas. Age 43. Estimated income $37,000. Married, one child, under 10 years old. Owns three dogs, one cat, one hamster. Spends money online at least four days a month. Interests include baking, rock climbing, crochet and other yarn craft. Likely to vote for Republican candidates. Would possibly be susceptible to telepathic influences. Declined frog dissection in seventh grade biology.' "

"Stop, it's too much, it's too horrible!" you say. You want to cover your ears to stop yourself from imagining that all that is true.

"That's just *half* of *one record* in this database. This database with something like 8 million entries. Holy shit!" Marlene says.

"But there's no way that is true or accurate. That could just be what someone made up!"

Marlene scowls at your unbelief and types something into her keyboard, staring intently at the old monitor she has hooked up to the satellite data. "Want to read the entry on YOU?" she asks.

To your horror, you find your name. It's all there, everything about you, going way beyond demographic data, right down to what you ate for dinner last week (even *you* can't remember what you had for dinner last week!). "Oh my god, it knows me better than I know myself!" you exclaim. "How do they get all this?"

Marlene looks at you like you're an idiot. "You're on that phone of yours a lot, aren't you? Everything you do is tracked in some way. Paying on a credit card, 'liking' a status update, browsing a website. It looks like they've just done a better job than most at compiling all that.

Because they're selling it," she explains.

"And you think they're selling it...to aliens? For real?"

"Well, look at this here," Marlene says, pointing at a line of math symbols and shapes. "It doesn't look like any language I've ever seen. And look, this is where they're transmitting the data..." Marlene switches to another screen, typing in a string of numbers too fast for you to follow. Pointing at the screen, she says, "Look! That location? That's a satellite...out by *Jupiter*, the best I can tell."

"Shit," you say.

"Yeah," she says.

You both lean back in your chairs, the weight of this realization weighing down your chest and shoulders like those lead bibs at the dentist.

"What do we do?" you whisper.

Marlene shakes her head. "What *can* we do?"

Gathering up the report and all of Marlene's computers, you head to:

- The research library at the state university. They'll know what to do. Turn to page 326.
- The nearest coffee shop. You could use a jolt of caffeine. Turn to page 64.

Without thinking too deeply about it, you jump in the car and lay on the gas. It's a long drive to Pennsylvania Avenue, but you're determined. Your car is a bit run-down (who cares about gas prices in Texas? Lay on the oil!) so you have to stop every five hours or so, but you throw on the RedBull and decide you only *really* need like 30 minutes of sleep, tops. Your GPS takes you on a ridiculous detour through the mountains of Arkansas, but you still make it to your destination by evening of the next day.

You're climbing out of your car, hand on the keys to turn off the ignition, when a news report breaks in... reporting on the president's recent meeting in China. Dammit, he's not home!

Planning isn't really your strong suit.

You slump back into your car, aimlessly driving along the twisted D.C. streets until you find a Walmart where you can finally pull over and get rest—at least for a few hours, before a pleasant police officer comes by and knocks on your window until you startle awake. Then it's back to the driver's seat and off to get coffee.

This time, you'll take a little more consideration. You steal someone's abandoned newspaper and spend 15 minutes struggling to find the foreign affairs section—how does anyone work these things, anyway? Ugh.

Finally, you find it, and then you have to read for another 10 minutes to figure out when the president may actually be back in the U.S.

Two days.

That's okay. It gives you some time to figure out your plan, and, you know, sightsee. First you head back to the White House, slipping in with a tour group from Canada, who give slightly more than a polite amount of zest to the story of the burning of the original White House. You're busy checking for security cameras to care. Still, it's interesting. 570 cans of paint! Wow, poor painters! They need, like, a spray gun or something.

After that, you saunter over to the Library of Congress. It turns out to be a big library with lots of wood. Books. Who reads those? Bo-ring.

So, you move on. The Vietnam War wall is cool, nice stone and all. The World War II memorial is a little weird but it seems like a lot of the other tourists dig it.

Then you are in for another chilly night in your car. But that's okay, because the president comes back tomorrow afternoon.

You noticed that the tour guides don't seem to be particularly watchful of a certain door, busy with lots of chefs working the White House garden or whatever. You figure if you just look busy or whatever, you can just slip right in. You even buy a $2 clipboard to make yourself look official. You straighten your shirt, brush the dirt off your jeans, and walk in the back door.

You're not overly good with directions, but you're still able to more or less find your way to the second floor. While you watch, the president, talking on a cell phone, walks down the hall past you.

"I know the truth!" you shout, triumphant.

But you never get to tell the world what you know, because that's when a Secret Service officer tackles you to the ground. You are foolish enough to try to slug him across the jaw, but his face is made of iron or something because all it does it hurt your fist. But you're on a mission! So you keep struggling—long enough to get shot.

The White House staff are very annoyed to have to clean blood out of the carpet 20 feet from the presidents' quarters. It's very inconvenient and *not* easy to get out.

THE END

It takes only a quick online search to bring up Channel 4's phone number, so you dial and wait for the receptionist to pick up. "Hello, Channel 4 News, your need-to-know news station! This is Greg, how may I direct your call?" he says.

"The president is an alien and I have proof," you blurt.

"Okay, thanks for your call," Greg says, and hangs up.

That could have gone better. You dial again.

"Hi Greg, don't hang up on me!" you say before he can speak. "Look, I know that last part sounded crazy."

"Mmhm," Greg said diplomatically. You can almost hear him reaching to turn off his headset.

"But the thing is," you interject before he can act, "a satellite crashed in a field last night. I can show you where. Then maybe we can see if you believe the rest of what I have to say."

"A satellite?" Greg asks. Finally, he sounds interested. "We did pick up some weird stuff on the Dopler last night..."

"Yes, that was it! I was out in a field, just, you know, ugh... stargazing, and I look up and see this huge thing falling from the sky. I went to investigate the crash, 'cuz there was this big fireball, you know, and it was a satellite."

"Okay, you got my attention. Let me take down your information and we'll see if we can have a crew come out to meet you," Greg says.

"Great, thank you so much, you really won't regret this!" you say.

A moment later, after making Greg promise he *really is* going to send a camera crew in the next half-hour, you turn to Marlene. "They're coming!" you say, excitedly. Then you realize you both look like warmed-over shit, so you demand Marlene change while you throw yourself into a shower in a last-ditch effort to look halfway decent.

You're still in a towel when the strong-jawed Channel 4 anchorman, Cliff Wallace, rings Marlene's doorbell. You shimmy into your half-filthy jeans and t-shirt, throw the damp towel in a corner, try to smooth your hair into something like a style, and throw open the door.

"Hi there," Cliff says. "I heard you've got something to show me." His voice is like aged bourbon and he looks bigger on TV somehow. You try to hide how impressed you are.

"Boy you're really gonna love this!" you say, and then immediately hate yourself. Ugh, Cliff is going to think you're such a loser! "Um, let's just go see it, okay?"

"Sure thing," Cliff says in his amazing baritone. "Can you give me the rundown on what happened?" Behind him, a barely adolescent camera kid jostles the camera into position. You find yourself enthralled by the reflective lenses.

"Ummm," you say. "I was in a field and saw this, like, um, comet, uh, thing. And it crashed! So I went to check it out." You finally remember to blink.

"And what did you find?" Cliff asks. He really sounds like he *cares*; that's what is so great about him. He really *gets* you. Wow, you're talking to Cliff Wallace!

It takes you a moment to remember you're expected to answer him. "Yeah, it's like, ah, um, a satellite. I'm pretty sure. Want me to show you?"

Much to your incredible relief, the camera kid puts down the camera, looking mildly disgusted. "We can take Marlene's truck!" you volunteer. Marlene throws a look that would poison a rattlesnake, but you're too far gone to care.

"Film this," Cliff mutters to the camera kid, who sighs and puts the camera back up. In a totally different voice, Cliff says, "Let's go see what we can find!"

The kid films you and Cliff climbing into the mud-spattered van and closing the door, and then you have to open the door again so the kid can get in. Marlene looks pissed and stays home.

You drive Cliff and the kid out to the field. No one speaks; the ride is awkward, and you find yourself desperate to be interesting to Cliff. Cliff probably has no problem being interesting...

It looks different when you're sober and takes a while for you to find the site, but it's all there, still pretty intact, though it's clear that cattle have been through recently.

Cliff likes the wreckage, even if he does sort of rifle through it a bit, making it look a little rougher around the edges. He directs the kid to get all kinds of shots of the satellite, then finally stands you on the edge of the crater—slightly on the incline so that he's closer to the camera and more clearly taller than you—and interviews you again about what you saw.

"And there was fire?" he asks.

"Oh yeah, all this was on fire and really hot!" You sound like a third grader explaining your science fair project, and yet you somehow can't stop yourself. "It is amazing that it came from space!"

The interview finishes before long, giving you time to consider what a moron you are. You're feeling worthless in general when you finally load back into the truck. But during the bumpy ride back you scrape up the last of your dignity and say, "What about the other part, Cliff?"

"What other part?" Cliff says. "Don't worry, the satellite will be great news, we'll just slot it in after the puppy segment and before the nightly car wreck reports. You'll be a Channel 4 star."

"But that's not all we found."

Cliff turns his wide smile to you. "Greg said something about you being a bit odd. Might as well tell me now."

Somehow he says it in a way that only sounds mildly insulting.

"It's just...there was data, on the satellite. Me and Marlene—mostly Marlene, really—got the data off. I think you should see it before you judge it, 'sall I'm saying," you say, desperately trying to sound sane.

"Sure partner, if it'll make you feel better," Cliff says, and now he definitely sounds condescending. But whatever, you've gotten him to agree, so when you pull back up to Marlene's house you walk him right in.

"Marlene!" you call. "I need you to explain what you found to Cliff, here."

Marlene emerges, bleary-eyed, from her little workroom. "I doubt he'll understand," she says.

"Dammit Marlene, please?" you insist.

She looks up at Cliff. "What do you know about computers?"

"I've got 4,000 followers on Twitter," he says confidently.

Marlene just sighs, though four thousand sounds like an awful lot to you.

"You, kid," she says to the angst-ridden camera kid, "Film this part and maybe someone will understand it."

The camera kid complies and Marlene launches into an explanation of how she figured out the data. It's way too long for TV and sounds really complicated, but you honestly can't be sure. Frankly, you tuned it out.

"And I converted the whole thing to English, as best as I can guess anyway, while you were out looking at the wreckage in the field. Here, I printed it out for you," she says, thrusting a thick stack of papers at Cliff and the camera.

"So, you say these papers prove that the president of the United States is...some kind of alien?" he says, turning dramatically to the camera to indicate his incredulousness.

"That is what the data suggests," Marlene says, every bit the 'don't give a damn' researcher.

Cliff looks concerned for a moment, then turns to the camera kid, giving his head a quick negative shake. The kid puts down the camera and gives his shoulder a roll to loosen up the muscles that have got to be tight. Cliff turns back to you and Marlene. "Okay, this sounds... well, way more believable than it did at first. But you know I can't just go off the word of two local crazies—sorry," he says. "So I'll take this and read it, and I'll get back to you."

You're crushed that Cliff doesn't really believe you, but on reflection, you do sound pretty insane, so you agree to let him take the stack of papers. He and the camera kid, who never so much as spoke to anyone, slide back into the beat-up Toyota that brought them to the house, and head off. You're left with a confused absence.

"Do you think he'll believe us?" you ask Marlene.

"No," she says. "But if he reads that stuff I gave him, I don't think he'll have much choice. Just give it time."

It's late, and you don't particularly feel safe driving back to your house—you have sudden paranoia about the aliens spying on you or something—so you stay up too late watching TV until you fall asleep on Marlene's couch. She wakes you up the next morning by turning up the volume on the still-running TV. There's Cliff, all smiles as he welcomes the dawn with the local news. You're pleasantly surprised to see the satellite has bumped the weekly puppy feature as the top story, but Cliff stays quiet on the president front.

By noon, you've pretty much given up on him, and you finally have to go back home to get some clean clothes, so you aren't there when Cliff calls Marlene, asking her to copy as much of the raw data as possible so he can send it off to experts. She's not particularly sophisticated, so she just does it, and only calls to tell you afterward.

"But what if he's sending it to the FBI or something? What if one of the aliens finds out that we know?" you scream into the phone, panicked. "Oh god, Marlene, they're going to get us!"

"I'm sure it'll be fine," Marlene says. She tolerates your freak-out for another 15 minutes before hanging up on you.

You don't hear anything for four more days, and they're terrible. Everything *seems* normal, but you know things now, and you can't go back to not knowing. You're jumpy at work, and you start to get suspicious of the neighborhood cats in your alley. You spend an inordinate amount of time on your bed, wrapped in a blanket. You're right on the verge of constructing yourself a tinfoil hat, just in case there's some truth to that, when Cliff finally calls you back. He doesn't want to talk on the phone (your recent paranoia completely agrees with him), so he has you meet him up at the station.

"I never thought I'd say this," he says, his strong chin looking perhaps a touch fearful, "but I think you're right. It just doesn't add up. I think he really might be... an alien." He says this last part in almost a whisper.

"I know, right?" you say, bursting with emotion because you can finally talk about this with someone. "It seems so crazy, but then you look again, and, it's, like, *not.*"

Cliff nods sagely. "This is going to be the biggest story of the year... heck, maybe the century. So it's really important that we do it the right way. I mean, I could get a Pulitzer!"

You nod as if you understand the significance of the statement. Clearly, if it's important to Cliff, it's important to you.

"I need to know if you're with me on this," he continues. "It may get rough, but you can decide now that you're done and I won't bother you about it anymore. Or you can work with me...and we'll change the world."

You stare down at the cooling cheap coffee Greg-the-receptionist gave you as you came in. You only get one chance to make this decision.

You:

- Shake Cliff's hand with a confidence you don't quite feel. "Let's do it!" you say. Turn to the next page.
- Shake your head. "This is too much. I can't do this!" you say, and run out of the building. Turn to page 135.

The next several months are exhausting and exhilarating. You go long stretches without hearing anything much from Cliff, then you'll end up spending a busy action-packed 72-hour sprint hauling satellite parts around, or driving to a specific laboratory in Virginia, or making phone calls to possible sources. You feel both proud, like a new Erin Brockavich, and also really stupid, because you're going to all this effort just to tell the world that the president is an alien. Sure, it's true, and important (probably), but it's also really stupid-sounding.

And then the lights come.

You thought you'd been careful. You've used throwaway cell phones, wrapped a closet in your bedroom with foil, used false names. But you should have known they would find you.

Worse, they found Cliff first.

He calls you at the witching hour. "I think they're onto us!" he says, his voice gravely and fear-wracked.

"Wha...?" you say, rubbing your drool-slogged face.

"I keep hearing sounds, and there were lights, they followed me home tonight," Cliff says in a pantomime whisper. "I've hidden my notes in the place we talked about. If you don't see me in the next eight hours, go get them. Tell the world."

"Go back to bed, Cliff, I'm sure it's fine," you mumble.

And then you hear it. Like singing wine glasses set slightly out of tune. Or maybe a dolphin click, as heard from the surface instead of properly in the water. "Cliff...?" you ask.

"Oh god!" Cliff says, and you hear sounds, like Cliff has stuffed the phone into his pants and is running. Then, a thump.

"...Cliff?" you whisper. "Cliff!"

The line goes dead.

You're wide awake now, but wish you weren't. If an alien kills you, does it count as a homicide? Is this a situation for the police?

Your hands are shaking and you really can't think these things through right now, so you dial 911.

"911 Operator, what is your emergency?" The voice is soothing, female, slightly on the edge of exhaustion.

"Cliff Wallace. I think he's dead," you say.

There's a pause on the other end of the line. "Okay, what makes you concerned? Are you with Cliff now?"

"No, but he just called me, we're working on a story together. And it sounded like..." How do you explain "an attack by aliens" to the police? ... "It sounded like there was a struggle, and then the line went dead!" It sounds lame even to your ears.

"Okay, if you can just tell me where you think Cliff Wallace was at the time of the call, we'll send a car over to check on him, okay?"

You nod before you remember she can't see you. "Okay," you say. "He was at home, I think. 30459 Hillcrest. Please hurry."

The operator takes a little bit more information from you, then tells you it'll be fine. You stay up all night hugging your knees.

In the morning, Cliff isn't at his desk at the station. Halfway through the broadcast, it appears as breaking news: Cliff Wallace found dead in his home, apparent heart attack. More details at 11.

It's your fault. You killed Cliff by asking these questions. But you're sure as hell not going to let these aliens get away with it.

You drive up to the station—Cliff had you in often enough that the producers know you and buzz you in—and dig through the tapes in the basement. They're supposed to only be stock footage, but Cliff had slipped his story notes in the back of one of the massive metal drawers.

You run your fingers through your hair and try to look confident as you walk into the newsroom. One of the producers, Will Jacobs, pulls his headset off as you walk in. In a half-whisper he says, "You can't be in here. Look, I know you're probably upset about Cliff's death, but these things happen, and we're trying to work here." He tries to pull you back out of the booth.

"I know!" you say, refusing to be moved. "This is important! This is what Cliff and I were working on. You have to run the story now, before it's too late."

Looking serious, Jacobs takes the small tape from you, the thick stack of notes. You watch his face as he reads, his eyes narrowing as he tries to understand the unfathomable. After a moment, he whispers, "No bullshit?"

"Watch the tape," you say, praying he believes you.

He pulls you into a small editing booth and plays the video. He says nothing while the 15-minute video spools out. When it's over, he rubs a hand wearily across his face.

"Damn," he says. He finally looks at you. "This is too big. You're really not shitting me?"

"No," you say, pouring every ounce of seriousness you possess into the word. "I think they killed him last night because of this. And if you don't run it, I think they're going to kill me, too."

Jacobs shakes his head. "Goddamnit I would much have preferred you to be a crackpot. But I believe you. Shit, why couldn't this have hit during sweeps week?"

He sighs and says, "I've got to make some calls."

It takes another half a day before Jacobs can pull the right strings, but he's also got several affiliates queued up to rebroadcast the transmission, redundant systems are set up, and it's also ready to be posted to every social media network available. It's going to hit big.

The afternoon anchor is a woman with overly large blonde hair. The station cuts out in the middle of an episode of a crappy sitcom, which is sure to enrage the four or so people who watch it, turning to the anchor. She purses her bright red lips and says, "Cliff Wallace was found dead today. But before he died, Cliff was working on a big project. We interrupt your regularly scheduled programming to bring you this shocking news."

And then Cliff's masterwork plays. In 15 riveting minutes, he lays out the case, all the proof you've worked so hard to gather. He explains the satellite, and the data, and there are the interviews with multiple experts from all around the world.

As you watch, the phones at the station begin to ring. Receptionist Greg is quickly outmatched, and assistant producers are called in to help answer the phones, which mostly just involve, "yes, it's true. Yes, we've verified the sources. Dammit, man, Cliff *died* for this!"

And then, toward the end of the broadcast, one of the affiliates in Washington, D.C., calls. He had been at the White House for run-of-the-mill news, some crap about finances, when he got the call. Defying all protocol, he walked up to the president's podium in the press room and thrust his camera in the face of the leader of the free world.

"Sir, my apologies," he said, and reached for the president's left ear. Of course, the Secret Service officers were all over him like laser-guided sharks, but it was enough. The ear came off easily in his hand, leaving a shocking green patch underneath. And it was caught on every camera in the room.

The local station cuts over to the streaming footage as the other reporters burst into chatter. Suddenly, you've made international news.

There's a bit of a struggle within the Secret Services, half of whom believe it's still their responsibility to protect the president, even *if* he isn't technically human, but before long he is brought in front of the cameras again, his overly large nose plucked off to reveal the abscessed green horror underneath. Still, Congress moves slowly with great, imbecilic pomp, and it takes about four months for the president to be impeached, imprisoned for treason, and volunteered for scientific study.

The vice president has to undergo ridiculously thorough tests to ensure she also isn't some kind of non-humanoid, but eventually she takes up residency.

In all the turmoil, you're largely forgotten. Life continues, for you, fairly normally. You're only remembered as the originator of the news every anniversary, when some enterprising reporter eager to win the Cliff Wallace Award for Investigative Journalism knocks on your door to ask you about it.

The aliens out themselves, or are forcibly outed. There is great upheaval for a time, particularly in Idaho, where they seem to have gathered for some inexplicable reason. But then they are formally recognized as minorities, are slowly integrated into human society. Fifteen years later, Congress changes the law to make discrimination against non-terrestrial species illegal, but it's another 30 years before they truly earn their civil rights.

Forty-five years after Cliff's death, the first non-humanoid takes office. It turns out talking out of two sides of the mouth is a particular specialty of aliens who don't have lips.

THE END

You don't hear from Cliff after that. You know he's probably disappointed in you, but he's got your data, he can do what he wants with it. But aliens? That's just too much for you to handle. Gotta know your limits, right?

So you pretend like nothing happened, and with enough alcohol, you're even able to convince yourself that's the truth. You just go to work, go home, sit around at night waiting to fall asleep, and repeat.

But every so often you think of Cliff. You become a regular watcher of his morning broadcast, just to see what's happening. And over time, he begins to look rougher around the edges, a little more haggard. Then he goes off the air, replaced by a perky kid fresh from the journalism mines. You wonder if he was fired; surely they'd say something if he were dead?

You finally start to relax. It's been a month and a half since the crash. Work was annoying, as usual, but you feel a certain lightness. You pour yourself a beer and manage to laugh while you watch the newest show on Netflix.

And then a feeling, that crawling sensation like you're being watched, skitters across your spine. You turn, even though there is nothing but the living room wall behind you. You tell yourself it was nothing, let yourself fall back into the show. And then the lights falter, then vanish, the picture on your television collapsing into a thin line.

You get that feeling again. But this time, when you turn around, you are staring straight into the eyes of the president of the United States.

All four of them…

Your family has to have a funeral without a body, but it's months later, only after they've given up any hope of ever finding you. They look all around your apartment, in the woods, and on one particularly bad day, in the ground. But they never look up. It's not like they would have found you, anyway, if they had. Your captors won't let you go that easily. Not after what you did.

THE END

Years later, you grow to regret your laziness, your unwillingness to even *try*. Of course, by then, it's far too late.

The North Koreans—actually a shapeshifting species from the lower Theta quadrant, if you'd bothered to read Marlene's notes, which you didn't—managed to make a nuclear bomb. They didn't lob it very far, of course; they're a pretty stupid species for folks who managed interstellar travel. But it went far enough to cause a problem. And they were really keen on this whole nuke thing, because it turns out they need a certain amount of ambient radiation in order to survive, in order to *change*. Because that's when shit started to get really weird. Before you know it, there are giant jelly creatures attacking Japan, then they start showing up in Australia. Meanwhile, the North Koreans (aliens) get into more radioactivity (seriously, what asshole sells anything to those crazy people?) ... and yada yada, skip some steps, that's how everyone in North America—those who are left anyway—ended up in internment camps.

Including you.

The camps are shitty, to say the least. The aliens never quite figured out what humans actually eat, or bothered to try, anyway, so you're starving. And perpetually cold, except for when you're too hot, because they dropped you on what used to be Amarillo. All you do, all day long, is dig up nuclear waste sites. They need the decaying material.

It's killing you and the others, but what do they care? By now they're huge shapeshifting monsters, able to disguise themselves as literally anything or anyone; mostly, though, they just mine your nightmares for ideas. They call it "motivation."

Your fingers are blackened and bloody. You have a constant nagging exhaustion, and your face feels like it has a constant low-grade sunburn. Sometimes, at night, you imagine like you can *feel* your cells corrupting from inside.

Which is why you have decided to escape.

You wait until the night grows still before you slip out of your bunk. There are no fences; the aliens rely instead on the desert and a loosely regulated system of guards to keep you in check. But dying of thirst in the desert now seems preferable to being in here for one more day. And you've heard rumors of a resistance... maybe they're even true. It doesn't matter to you, though, because you just have to get out.

Your feet are warmed by the sun-drenched soil under your toes. Your soles have hardened from the labor, but you can still almost feel the shift of the clay soil. You hunch down, running along the edge of the buildings. Watching.

From the corner of your eye you see an inky blob coalescing just ahead. One of the shifters. The most frustrating thing about these aliens is you can never tell when they're looking at you when they're doing something shitty like turning into a blob of black goo. Dammit. You hunker down and wait, trying desperately not to breathe. After 20 heartbeats, you hear the swish as the guard slinks off toward the distance.

Adrenaline thudding through your weakened heart, you take off running, suddenly so desperate with fear that you must run, run like a mouse when it knows the cat is watching. Your feet fly over the rough and rocky terrain, off toward the glow of the setting sun far below the horizon.

And for a long time, nothing happens, nothing but the joy of motion and of speed and of the hope of escape.

Then you hear a swish. And behind you, a cheetah. But not a cheetah, a three-headed beast as big as a horse, with saber teeth dripping poison.

You know it's hopeless, but still you run. Behind you, you can hear the thudding steps as the monster-cheetah/alien gains on you, hear the sounds of its triple mouths opening, hear the splat of the poison as it hits your back and sizzles against your skin.

If only you had been just a little quieter. If only you hadn't been so foolish. If only you had given Earth warning. If only.

THE END

Since you're being asked to fill in a big job, you decide to treat this interaction like the job interview it is. "I'd just like to know a little more about the position before I commit to it, you know? So I can make sure I'm the right person for the job, and all," you say. Interviewing is the worst.

"Oh, it's nothing to worry about, my Queen," the short woman says. You mentally note her as "the pill" and immediately can't take her seriously.

"No, but really. What does it mean to be the Queen?"

You can't be sure, but for a moment, the Chancellors look nervous. "Well, erm..." the oldest one says. "There's a ceremony, very important ceremony, and then there's a bit of chanting, and then," he begins to mutter rapidly, almost under his breath, "...there's the blood sacrifice." His voice reverts to normal, "And then there's lots of feasting and it's just a great time, really!"

"Wait! Back up." The Chancellors all take one step backward. "Blood sacrifice? Explain!"

The short woman again: "We need your blood to appease Laow. If we do not have it, our entire culture will be destroyed!"

You stare at them. "You brought me all this way to KILL ME?!" You pick up a handy fruit bowl and throw it in the Chancellors' direction. "You can't be serious! You went across space and freakin' time to get me just to kill me? There is no one here who can be blood sacrificed?"

The Chancellors actually look afraid of you. The short woman leans over to a man next to her dressed in blue who has until now been stone-faced and silent and mutters, "Not being very Queen-like, eh?"

He replies, "Tsk."

You move to full-on tantrum. "You are insane if you think I'm just going to volunteer to be MURDERED!"

With that you grab Evetee and demand to be taken to your room. Once there, you block the door with the largest piece of furniture in the room, a huge metal honeybee statue, locking Evetee in with you.

You flop on the bed, which smells a little cloyingly of lavender. "I can't believe this," you say to yourself.

Evetee collapses at your feet. "Please, Majesty, you must save us! If you don't satisfy Laow, he will kill us all!"

"Ugh," you grunt, pulling yourself back to a sitting position. "Okay, Evetee. Explain all this. It seems I'm not going to get anything useful out of those assholes out there. So...who is this Laow and why does he want my blood?"

The servant looks nervous.

"Look, if you don't tell me, I'm definitely not going through with their ceremony, so you're better off just telling me." You pick an apple-ish fruit off the nightstand and hold it out to Evetee. "Is this edible?"

She nods, and you take a big bite. Interstellar travel really can take it out of you, and you're hungry. You wave a hand, "Talk while I eat."

"Laow is God of Destruction," she says. "Without the blood every century, our world will be consumed by ash and fire."

You munch on the apple, "Okay, so why me? What's special about it?"

"I do not know, Majesty," Evetee says, resorting to cowering again.

"Why not the Chancellors? Has anyone tried that?"

"No, my Queen."

"Yeah, some Queen," you snort.

You spring up from the bed. "Okay, Evetee, I need your help. Go get me all the documents related to Laow and this blood sacrifice thing and bring them here. And bring some more food, okay?"

You spend three days poring over the documents, reading and rereading the history, studying the lore. Evetee comes and goes with food, but you bar the door after she leaves so no one else can come in. Finally, you find what you needed.

"Evetee, please tell the Chancellors to arrange the ceremony," you declare.

"You— you are going to let them go through with it?" she asks. You think maybe she sounds a little horrified; good, that means you've grown on her, too.

"Don't worry, Evetee, I've figured it all out!" You try for confidence but a small voice in your head still says, 'you're going to die on this forsaken planet.'

"Oh Queen, I hope so!" she declares, full of servile sweetness. Even if the entire ruling class is out to get you, it's good to know you have at least one fan on this planet. Besides, now you have a plan to take care of the rest of that.

The ceremony comes with a great deal of fussing and arranging and ceremonial robes and all that, involving a great deal of frou-frou and a special robe and Evetee makes a fuss over your hair and making you look just so, and it takes another half-day before everything can be arranged. From the lore you know that Laow is said to threaten the planet with eruptions from below and rocks from the sky—your basic hellfire and destruction seen in pretty much all "death god" myths. You're fairly sure it's not true, of course—in fact your plan hinges on it—but that twinge in your mind wavers, saying 'just in case, just in case.' Anyway, you've left some wiggle room for that little voice of doubt and faith. Anything is better than the immediate death the Chancellors had planned for you.

When the ceremony is all prepared, you are ready for the moment, though your hand still shakes a little. Still, you walk with head held high up the Stairs of Wretchedness (that's the official name, though you note the white is quite pretty and refined-looking). You take your time; you are in no rush. You see the pedestal at the top, think you can make out the glint of the knife lying there in front of the Chancellor, but you keep your steps measured.

As you reach the top, the Chancellor—that eldest one—remarks, "So glad you came around to our way of thinking."

"I gave it a great deal of thought," you say primly. "Let's get this ceremony over with. The god cannot wait much longer, I'm sure." And you throw in a wink for good measure.

The Chancellor begins with the opening chant, offering a prayer up to Laow to draw her wrath away from Klungstogh. You observe the crowd below, their attention rapt as the chant continues in the Laowian death prayer. The Chancellor takes the bone-white handle of the ceremonial knife, and you reach over. "Allow me," you say, and take it before he can stop you. He gawks in open-mouthed dismay, then catches himself, continuing the chant.

With a flourish, you flash the blade of the knife to catch the sunlight, then bow deeply and, in a great show, draw it against the pad of your right thumb. You squeeze a few drops of blood onto the Stairs, and then hold the blade, point-down, so that the blood may continue to run slowly along the edge.

The Chancellor stops his chant, and you wave at him in a "keep going" gesture. When he has finished, you bow low again, and walk down the stairs, wearing your best broad smile.

"Excuse me! Excuse me!" he spits. "This will hardly do."

You pause on the stairs, pretending to be affronted. "Well of course it will!" you say. "The blood offering has been made; we can go about our days now."

"But...but...but!" he says, rage making him incomprehensible.

You sigh and roll your eyes as if you were dealing with a child rather than the de facto ruler of an alien planet. "Dear Chancellor, I am sure you are quite familiar with Laowian lore, are you not? Surely then you know that the Queen was asked to only offer a token sacrifice as recently as 600 years ago? In fact, it is preferable, a Queen's blood being particularly potent and heady for Laow? I understand in past, showier, ceremonies the Queen may have offered all the royal blood, but that's quite a waste and, as I'm sure you know, quite unnecessary." You put your arm over his shoulder; a drop of blood colors the forest green of his robe. He gawks at you.

"Come, let me take you to the library and show you," you insist, and guide him down the stairs, careful to avoid the droplets—just in case it all has some basis in reality.

You present your findings to the green-clad Chancellor, to the whole rainbow of Chancellors, and they grudgingly agree you may have a point or a small technicality.

"You all have ruled well, or at least as well as you were able. But now I'm here, and we're going to make a few changes," you declare.

You get right to work. The people of Klungstogh are sharply divided into two ethnic groups, the Shi—Evetee's people—highly subjugated by the Roh, the ruling class dominated by the Chancellors and the like. You learn in much research that the Queen has always been an outsider, chosen based on the genetic makeup of the blood and quite rare indeed. You use this fact to your advantage, bending the stiff necks of the Roh and being gracious and open-handed toward the Shi. In no time you have dismantled many of the unfair separations between the peoples and started Klungstogh on the road toward a parliamentary monarchy, with you as head, of course, in the largely ceremonial position as Queen. You institute a court system and do what you can to stem the traditions of blood offerings, at the very least scaling them back from full-on murder to just a light sprinkling of blood. You introduce the concept of "sandwiches," and encourage agricultural industries to make use of the multicolored trees the planet is rich with. You even set up the beginnings of interplanetary trade, exporting the truffula trees (as you think of them) and importing iron, useful minerals, and ice, which was heretofore unknown on the planet. Before long, shaved ice is particularly popular among the populace, further improving your reputation.

Under your leadership, the planet prospers, becomes a leader in the galaxy. The honey from the space bees helps prolong your life and improves your health, and you reign for 200 years. After you die, they name a city after you; a city that goes on to become the center of intergalactic politics in the coming years.

Long live the Queen.

THE END

Numbers like that aren't just in a phone book somewhere. It takes some finding, and a lot of waiting on the line while someone decides if you're worth it. You have to give partial information to at least a hundred flunkies before someone promises the Secretary of State will be in touch, and even then you only actually get an undersecretary. But she does come to your door, in person. So you got that much.

"You say you have state secrets on North Korea," the woman at your door says. She is middle-aged, doughy, entirely unimpressive. But her lips are thin, severe, and you believe she's made some difficult calls.

"Come on in," you say, offering her whatever Texan hospitality you can scrounge up at short notice. You pour her a glass of water and put it next to her chair, before you sit across from her at the kitchen table. She lets the condensation bead on the glass. "It's kinda complicated. What do you already know?"

"Why don't you tell me what I need to know," she says. It's not a question.

"Show me your badge," you say, just as flat and hard. She produces one from an inner jacket pocket. Undersecretary Janet Fillion. It looks real enough, but what do you know? "I am gonna need to see your blood, too."

She gives you a steely look, but takes out a knife from a pocket and slices a finger, which bleeds appropriately.

"Thank you. I had to be sure, you know," you say. You stand up, get a bandage out of a drawer, and hand it to her. "What can I help you with, Ms. Fillion?"

She looks annoyed. "You had to talk to several people to get me here in front of you today. Don't waste my time. You said you have proof that the North Koreans are...not what they seem?"

"I do. And thank you for coming all the way out here," you say, and launch into an explanation of the satellite and Marlene and all the messages.

Ms. Fillion listens, taking occasional notes and recording the conversation on a discrete voice recorder she holds close to her body. When you're done, she says, "I see. May I have the data?"

You get up and dig it out of the filing cabinet you've been storing it in; no one (especially you) wants to look through the three years of prior tax records you've got it sequestered in. You thump the thick papers down in front of her, then clear away her now-empty glass, wiping up the water ring as you step away.

"And you're confident that Marlene is 100 percent reliable?" she asks.

"Of course! She came out to a field in the middle of the night to help me break into a fallen satellite. But you can always talk to her yourself," you say.

"We'll do that. And we'll also need any other parts of the satellite; we have tools that may be able to recover further data."

"Sure, it's in my closet, one sec," you say, and bang around in the depths of your closet. It's a good thing you went back to recover it a little while ago, even if a cow or two did step on some of the panels.

You're sweaty and in disarray when you step back into the dining room, leaving the remains of the satellite in the middle of your living room. Ms. Fillion closes her notebook suddenly, as if she's trying to keep you from seeing what she has written.

There is a quick knock on the door. Before you can react, Ms. Fillion is up out of her chair and opening the door, admitting two well-muscled men. The three of them turn to look at you, and she says, "Thank you for your cooperation. I'm afraid, because of the nature of this information, you will need to come with us."

"Uh, now?" you say, backing a step away.

"Now," she says, and the two large men step forward. The concept is so strange that you panic and reflexively start to fight, but then Fillion is there and she's injecting something into your arm and then things get fuzzy.

When you wake up, everything is blackness. Your head is throbbing, and it feels like you're moving, even though you're lying down. A moment later your hearing returns, and you hear the familiar hum of an engine, of tires of pavement. So you're in a car then, perhaps on the floor or a back seat or something. And there *is* light, but there's something on your face; the air in front of your mouth is damp. Your shoulders are sore, your hands tied behind your back at your ankles. But your feet are free; that's something. You wiggle just a tad, and run into something warm and soft. Another person?

"There, there," Ms. Fillion says sternly, "you're all right. We're nearly there, and then we can take the blindfold off. Security, you understand." And you can hear the edge of the smile in her voice.

Sure enough, the car rumbles to a stop a few minutes later. Doors open, and then strong arms lift you to your feet. Through the blindfold you can see the light change from bright to dim. The air smells vaguely of pine trees. A hand remains clamped around your upper arm, but someone pulls the blindfold off.

You're at a cabin, surrounded by the tall soft-needled pines of East Texas. And the other person being pulled out of the van behind you is Marlene, thank god.

Ms. Fillion gets out of the passenger side of the van and hands you a key. "Welcome home, for the near future," she says. "You two will have to stay here, I'm afraid, until we can get this a little more figured out. Arjun and Simon here will be looking after you. Enjoy your vacation."

And then she turns on a heel and climbs back into the van, starts the engine and drives away.

"She could have let me at least pack a bag or something," you mutter. Simon/Arjun/thug number three picks up a duffle bag and hands you the cloth handles. "Ah, what service. Come on, Marlene, let's get comfortable."

The cabin someone's idea of what rustic ought to look like. Everything is pine, or pine-substitute. The TV is ancient, and the pans and the dishes in the cabinet are all mis-matched. There's a plastic-made-to-look-wooden sign in the bathroom explaining the "cowboy creed." There are two bedrooms and two sunken couches. The linens are scratchy and the towels thin. Surprisingly, the pantry is full; fixings for sandwiches, some cookies, chips, lots of cans of soup. The view is decent, if you like trees. But there is a rocking chair on the porch, and that's okay.

"They really shell out for the good stuff, huh boys?" Marlene says to your two 'hosts.'

"Nothing but the best," one says. His voice is low, a little rough. But he made a joke, so you like him.

Being held mostly against your will in a cabin in the middle of nowhere is pretty boring. There are books on the shelves, old crappy romances or half-baked mysteries, and Simon of the Simon/Arjun duo brought a deck of playing cards (hallelujah), and there's the TV.

You watch a lot of TV. Not that there are many channels.

It's from the TV, a few days later, that you see the news.

You're sitting with Marlene on one of the saggy-bottom couches, half brain-dead with boredom. Arjun is on the porch, whittling or some crap, while Simon is washing the dishes over the sink. The news cuts into the James Bond marathon you've been watching: The North Koreans have a confirmed successful nuclear test near the small North Korean town of Yonan.

"That's stupid, they're going to radiate their own people that way," Marlene says.

"As if they care. As if they're *even people*," you say, suppressing a yawn. James Bond returns to the screen. Gee, will he get the girl this time?

"Actually... maybe that's the point," Marlene says, and gets up suddenly, retreating into 'her' bedroom. After a moment, you follow her.

"What's going on in that wacky brain of yours?" you ask. It's telling, the fact that you used a word like 'wacky' in a sentence and totally meant it.

"I just want to check something real quick," she says, and rifles through the duffle bag the enforcers packed for her. Enclosed there is a copy of the data, all thick and bound computer paper covered in writing.

"Wait, I thought Undersecretary Fillion took that with her?" you ask.

"She gave me a copy to think about. Which is good, because I just thought of something," Marlene says. You feel deeply insulted that Fillion apparently entrusted Marlene with something, but not you. And Marlene didn't even tell you!

Petulantly, you walk up and make to grab the papers from Marlene. "Let me see!" you insist. You realize you sound like a toddler, but don't care to stop yourself.

Marlene just glares as you and tugs the papers back out of your hands. "Oh shut up," she says. "I'm working here."

You have to slink back out to the living room, where super spies have lost all the appeal. You change the channel to some crappy reality show; it's all badly timed cuts to make it look like drama. Yawn.

An hour or so later, Marlene reemerges. "I think I've got something," she says, sitting down next to you.

You want to stay mad at her, but your curiosity gets the better of you. "What?" you ask.

"I think the aliens feed off radioactivity," she says, her voice low. Simon's reading a book on the couch against the far wall and gives no sign of hearing you or even listening, but you're pretty sure he is. "So the bomb, while still a worry that they'll use it *offensively*, is less of a threat than what having access to all that radioactivity may do for them."

"And you think the data supports that?" You leaf through, but it's all gibberish as far as you can tell.

"I need to call the undersecretary, now," Marlene says to Simon. Barely glancing up, he slides a cell phone from his pocket and dials.

"Ma'am," he says into the phone. "Marlene has something she'd like to say to you." He hands the phone over.

"You got something?" Fillion says. You can hear her tone, tinny and small, through the receiver. She sounds short, as is habit with her, apparently.

Marlene talks quickly. "I don't think they're building bombs to bomb anyone. I think they're going to feed off it," she says.

There's a pause.

"Okay, walk me through it," Fillion says.

Marlene directs her to several pages in the thick stack, explaining something about half-life and mutation. You should have paid more attention in biology; you can't follow much.

"Let me call you back," Fillion says when Marlene's done, and hangs up.

You don't have to wait for long. Fifteen minutes later, Simon's phone rings. With a nod from the guard, Marlene answers.

"We've got a team working on it, but your theory is sound. We'd like you to come with us to work the project," Undersecretary Fillion says.

"Absolutely," Marlene says. "My cousin, too?"

You can almost hear Fillion's disgust. "Fine. If that's what you want. Pack your things and hand the phone to Simon." Marlene complies, then turns to you.

"I think you can stay here, if you want. Or you can come with me. Your call," she says.

She leaves you there on the couch while she packs up her small duffle.

After a moment, you:

- Stretch out on the couch. Might as well enjoy your vacation. Turn to the next page.

- Pack your bags. Riding the coattails of success is still success! Turn to page 156.

No reason to overstress yourself with stuff you totally don't understand anyway. You wave as Marlene and Simon head off in a van that mysteriously appears up the gravel drive, and then you're left with Arjun.

You haven't had a vacation in years, and with Marlene gone, you can almost pretend you *chose* to go hide out in a cabin in the woods. A cabin that includes a very surly chef who can only make sandwiches or canned soup. Still, it's kinda nice to relax.

For about four hours. Then you start to get really bored.

"Can we go catch a movie or something, Arjun? I swear I won't tell anyone the North Koreans are aliens, I promise," you plead.

"No," Arjun says. You stare furiously at the card in his hand, willing it to catch on fire and ruin his game of Solitaire. But nothing happens.

"Can I just go for a walk?"

"Not farther than the tree line."

You saunter outside and amble toward the trees. Arjun is still sitting at the coffee table with his card game, so you wander across the gravel road and into the trees a little ways. You look back again. Arjun hasn't moved. You walk a little farther into the woods, not really sure where you're going but sure you want to go there. The air smells different here, like a fresh air freshener spray or something. The trees are all tall pine, several stories tall. You get dizzy trying to look up to the tops. The pine needles beneath your feet make your steps stealthy, except for when you accidentally crunch a pine cone. A crow caws overhead, and you wander a bit further, weaving in between the trees just for the hell of it.

You just about jump out of your skin when Arjun's hard hand clamps over your arm. "Don't move," he says quietly.

"What, I was just going for a walk—!" you protest, twisting to look at him and trying to shrug off his hand.

He looks pointedly in front of you. There is a small snake, rattling its adorable little baby rattle with all its might.

"Timber rattler," he says. "Venomous. Not bad enough to kill you, typically, but bad enough to hurt like a bitch. You were about to step on it. That's a surefire way to get bit." He pulls you backward a few steps. "Ready to come back in now?"

You nod meekly, and follow him back to the cabin, watching your feet for more deadly tiny snakes. You don't relax until Arjun locks the door securely behind you.

You don't go on any more walks. But Arjun does take pity on you and has a stack of books and movies delivered. And Monopoly, but that game is a worse kind of hell than staring at a wall, so you don't play.

You try to follow up on the news as much as you're able, but weeks go by without anything. It's as if Marlene has vanished into the ether, and a wall of silence has fallen over North Korea. After the first nuclear test, nothing.

Then Arjun gets a call. He comes over and turns off the TV, right in the middle of *Golden Girls*! You're working up to yelling at him when he says, "Okay, you can go now."

You sit up and blink, not immediately understanding him. "I ...can go now?" you ask.

"Yup, just got the call. If you want I can drop you back home," he says, sounding more like a friendly neighbor than your 24/7 prison guard.

"Uh, I guess that would be nice?"

You pack up your duffle and go with Arjun when a nondescript van pulls up to the cabin. He doesn't say much, just reminds you to keep things quiet, maybe tell people you went to see a distant relative. "The situation has been taken care of, anyway," he says.

"What about Marlene?" You feel obligated to at least *ask* about your cousin.

"She is in a safe place," he says.

And that's it. You get out of the van and return to your musty apartment. Your boss has left about 20 angry messages, but when you call he seems agreeable and apologizes; says he was informed of your "family situation," and you can come back to work, except you're all out of vacation for this year and half of next. You don't see Marlene, but you do get a postcard about a year later. It's postmarked from the UK, someplace called Wiltshire, with some daffy sheep grazing in a field. The back reads: "All is well. Wish you were here."

You swear it's Marlene's handwriting. Probably.

THE END

The stinger slices your leg, a stinging grazing blow but not a serious wound. You're able to roll out of the way as the alien stabs at you again and again. You scuttle to your feet and run despite the agony in your thigh. The alien chases you for a moment, until a weird warbling whistle, like wind through a door crack, sounds, then the aliens turn and run, their weird legs undulating, in the direction of the hive-like ship hovering overhead.

That was a lucky break, but you redouble your efforts, loping awkwardly off into the field. You hear the terrified screams of cattle as they are struck down by the aliens, and you refuse to look back when you hear wet, crunching sounds. You're not far from a farmhouse, and the fire climbs up your leg, but you continue on. By the time you get to the small fenced-in garden, your breath is shallow and your leg feels like it's been dipped in acid from the hip down.

You pound on the door. "Please. Help!" you gasp.

A little old lady comes out, still dressed in a house robe. "What the heck is wrong with you? Don't you know what time it is?" she fusses, and then looks you over. "Oh my gosh!" she exclaims, and grabs your arm. You collapse on her kitchen floor.

"Please...help! Aliens...attack...poison," you manage, trying to catch your breath, but the terrible pain in your leg is climbing and you grip your thigh, trying to squeeze it, stop it, anything. You wince back tears, face flush with exertion and fear. "Quick!"

"O-okay honey," the woman says, and picks up the phone. "Hello, we got some kind of emergency. Somethin' about poison? — I dunno, there was mention of aliens but maybe they're hallucinatin'. —Nope, don't know who they are, just arrived on my porch just now — Okay, y'all hurry up, okay?"

To you she says, "They're coming, honey." She fusses around the kitchen, getting you a glass of water, which you ignore: the pain is creeping up your side, and your chest feels tight. Your breathing has gotten more labored, each breath a pant. The woman just pats your hand awkwardly.

She happens to glance up at the window. "Geezus Pete!" she exclaims. "What is that out there? Do you see that?"

You can see dark shapes coming toward the farmhouse, and despite the pain you struggle upright and throw yourself against the door. "Keep...them...out," you pant, slumping against the door.

"I think that's a good idea, honey," the woman says, and darts out of the room. You hear a lock click a moment later.

There's a scratching sound on the other side of the door, and you wince, sure this is your end. The woman comes back and stares in blank fear at something out the window. She fumbles over to a drawer and pulls out a worn black Bible, its pages loose with wear, and mutters, "Revelation. Scorpions is in Revelation." She flips through to the end and reads:

"The locusts looked like horses prepared for battle. On their heads were victor's crowns that looked like gold, and their faces were like human faces. They had hair like women's hair and teeth like lions' teeth. They had breastplates like iron, and the noise of their wings was like the roar of chariots with many horses rushing into battle. They had tails and stingers like scorpions, and they had the power to hurt people with their tails for five months."

She stares up at you in horror. "That's what got ya?"

You can only wince in pain. Little eddies and currents of pain have swept up your neck and down your arm.

"Lord have mercy," the woman cries, and holds the Bible close against her chest. "I did think perhaps the end times was near, but I was hopin' I wouldn't live to see it!"

There's a knock at the door, and you both practically jump out of your skin. After a moment's pause, the woman rushes to the front door, peeking through the viewer. Behind you, you can hear the monsters back away from the door.

"Quick, get in!" the woman says, and a fireman in full uniform rushes inside as a monster comes barreling around the corner.

"What the —" the fireman says, and leaps back toward the door, throwing his shoulder against it. The thin legs of the monster slip in the crack and push hard in return, but the fireman digs in his heels and manages to close the door.

"I think we're in the End Times!" the woman declares.

"I...I...what was that?" he replies.

"Best go see to this one," the woman says, gesturing back toward where you lie prone on the kitchen floor. "Revelation says the poison'll make you suffer for five months. Anything you can do?" she asks.

He checks your pulse, takes your temperature, straps a heart monitor to you. He prods the laceration on your thigh with a gloved hand. "I'm gonna give you a little bit of a shot for the pain," he says, looking you in the eye even while he sticks you with the shot. Turning back to your rescuer, he says, "I think we're gonna need some backup, ma'am."

He radios for the police, and before long his radio is cracking with reports. In your near-delirium, it's hard to make out, but you understand that the aliens are approaching town.

The woman who rescues you doesn't stay idle, but turns to the fireman and declares, "I'll get you backup." She picks up the phone and begins dialing. "Bruce, git your guns. And call everyone you know. We're gonna need a lot of firepower!" As soon as she hangs up, the fireman opens his mouth as if to chastise her, but he just nods, and she starts dialing again.

At least two of the cops must have peeled off and headed your way, along with the paramedics, and soon the sirens are at the door, quickly followed by the sharp rat-at-at of gunfire.

The fireman waits just inside the door, throwing it open as soon as the officer outside shouts, "Clear!"

"What the hell was that?" he asks.

The fireman shakes his head. "I dunno, but it sounds like we've got a major problem on our hands."

"It's the End Times!" the woman yells, sounding almost joyful.

You're just feeling better, a little floaty, though your leg still feels like it has a hot coal embedded deep in the meat. You hang uselessly as the pair of paramedics lift you onto the stretcher and haul you away, the cops standing on guard all around you. You get to ride in the ambulance, always exciting, and soon pass out from the effort of it all.

You awaken in the hospital, connected to many machines and still feeling that burning in your leg. The TV is on, and it looks like it must be some kind of sci-fi show or the military channel, because there is a lot of smoke and the sounds of gunfire...and then the feed switches back to a newscaster, with the words "LIVE BROADCAST" emblazoned below.

The woman behind the desk reads, "The attackers appear similar to descriptions in Revelation, and we have here Betty Duvall, who was among the first witnesses."

The woman who rescued you appears on screen, standing in her kitchen and twisting a dishcloth in her hands. She describes how you fell in her kitchen, though you don't remember her being *quite* that heroic.

The newscaster returns to the screen, saying, "The first victim, the one saved by Ms. Duvall, is currently undergoing extensive treatment in the hospital to slow the spread of the poison to the heart."

You put a hand to your chest. Your heart?! You glance over at one of the panels...seems like you're not dead yet?

A nurse walks by at that moment and sees you sitting up. "Okay, how are we doing? Glad to see you up, thought we lost you there! Unfortunately, there's not much we can do for the pain at this point except give you a tad more morphine while we send that poison to the lab for review, okay? Got anyone we should call?"

She rattles all this out at top-speed and it takes you a minute to piece together an answer. You offer her a number to call and she turns to leave, but you grab a corner of her sleeve and say, "Will...I live?"

"We're gonna take good care of you, don't you worry," she says, and yet you aren't mollified by that answer.

You're poked and prodded by a lot of doctors, especially after news comes back that the fluid causing you so much pain is apparently unknown, though it most closely resembles something from Australia? Anyway, there are more tests, and while the pain is slightly dulled by the cocktail of morphine, it continues spreading through your body, until you're practically paralyzed. A pair of somber-looking doctors with dark bags under their eyes appear and stand over you, talking as if you're not even there.

"We've got to induce a coma," the one on your left says.

The one on your right grabs your wrist, causing you to flinch back, and takes your pulse. "Still steady, but I agree. Time to let the body heal, or at least for now."

You moan in response, and before long a nurse has come in with a cart and injected your IV with a liquid that feels cool as it hits your vein. You're submerged in peaceful blackness, a sweet relief. You do not dream.

You're brought out of the coma four days later, still in pain, but more like a low throb than a stabbing sword. It's another six hours before you can form the words to ask the question burning in your mind. Mouth feeling like cotton, you mumble, "Are they winning?"

"Winning?" the nurse says. "No dear, the Cowboys aren't playing yet."

You blink and shake your head no, a gentle movement that makes the whole room sway. You try again. "Monsters," you manage, the word a gasp.

"Oh them!" she says. "Don't you worry. End Times don't have nothin' on Texas, darlin'."

Your recovery takes weeks, but you piece together what happened. The police, combined with a pair of Texas Rangers and at least half the populace of town, showed up, guns blazing. The aliens had armor, sure, but they couldn't compete with the firepower of sheer determination of Texas, and soon retreated back up into their floaty box. There were some who were disappointed to see them go, actually, as eager as they were to herald in the End Times, but most folks are happier keeping weird space creatures off their property. Texas holds a renewed reputation as an unbeatable Wild West.

You're not without renown. Your medical details are included in a medical journal analysis of your treatment, read and debated by scores of doctors around the country. The samples taken from your leg while you were in a coma are tested and tested and tested, and several new discoveries are made.

You of course never know anything of this, but at least some part of you is famous, right?

THE END

Y̶ou and Marlene leave with your entourage of guards within the hour. This time, they don't bother blindfolding you; not that it matters much, because long car rides still put you right to sleep, even after all these years. You stop only to eat at a mediocre small-town cafe and refuel. To your surprise, it's only a quick drive. The van pulls off the road near the Dallas suburbs and drops you off at an office building surrounded by barbed wire fence.

"Is...this the FBI building?" you ask as you read the large metal letters secured to the exterior wall. "Like, the actual Federal Bureau of Investigations?"

"Aren't they domestic only?" Marlene asks.

"Yes, and yes," Simon says casually. "We're just borrowing their conference room. Langley is a bit too far of a drive, and we're in a hurry."

Marlene nods like she completely understands this turn of events. You're bustled down a long, bland, cubicle-filled hallway. It looks just like any office building, except everyone is dead quiet as you walk by, which is a little eerie. You are led into a conference room, with a long line of windows looking out on the parking lot and Dallas traffic. Not exactly an inspirational view. Inside, the walls are bare, but the table is quality wood, dark and shiny. The chairs are partially flattened with use but still leather. Not bad. You sit in one and wheel around.

Marlene sets up, professional-like, at the far end of the table, laying her data out to one side and accepting the battered black laptop a run-of-the-mill-looking agent brings to her. It hums loudly when it boots up.

Soon you're joined by Undersecretary Fillion herself, and more discreet and quiet FBI (or whomever) agents bring in a tray with water and donuts and some sad-looking fruit.

Wouldn't it suck to join the FBI only to be the official water-and-donut-shlepper? What a life.

You go to town on the donuts, while Fillion and Marlene are soon intensely in conversation. You only pick up snippets: "shapeshifting," and "cellular mutation," and "radioactive waste." It's only when you're full of sugar and carbohydrates that you slide your chair down to their end of the table.

"Hey," you say. "What's going on?"

Marlene looks at you, deadpan, but you can see the hint of amusement in her eyes. "We're just trying to stop the aliens from taking over the Earth. Wanna help?"

"Sure, not like I've got anything else to do," you quip. "Thanks for the donuts and stuff, Ms. Fillion."

She doesn't deign to answer you, but instead turns back to Marlene. "We can't exactly bomb them out of existence if they're only going to grow stronger because of it," she says.

"True, but we also can't exactly let them keep making bombs on their own," Marlene bites her bottom lip, thinking. "Shit. How do you stop an enemy that can't be reasoned with and that you can't attack?"

You dust some powdered sugar off onto your jeans. "How'd they get here?" you wonder aloud.

"Why does that matter?" Undersecretary Fillion snaps. "They're here now and we just have to deal with stopping them."

"No, my cousin may have a point," Marlene says, turning suddenly on Fillion. Then she looks thoughtful. "Because there might be backup," she says.

"I was thinking more like, if there was a door they came in, maybe we can push them back out of it," you say with a shrug.

"That's preposterous," Fillion snarls.

"Wait... no, I don't think it is," Marlene says, like she's just remembered something. She rifles through the papers on the table. "I think I read something..."

"It was just an idea," you say defensively. You slump in your chair like a teenager going through an extended emo phase. Basically, like you're fourteen again. "Plus, what I really wanna know is why choose North Korea? Wasn't it a hellhole even before we knew there were aliens? I mean, I'd choose, like, Australia or Florida or something. Somewhere more isolated than an Asian country smushed up against a bunch of other places."

Marlene keeps muttering to herself. Fillion says, "We think there have been alien influences for as long as North Korea has been a country. It may even be why the country became so insular. But we have difficulty getting any clear information." She says all of this derisively, as if it's common knowledge.

"Well yeah, I bet. I mean, if the whole population is aliens, there might be some superpower they have that we don't know about or something," you say, shrugging one shoulder to show Fillion you don't care what she thinks about you.

Marlene finishes typing something into the computer, then says, "Aha! That's it!" She turns back to you, and you can tell from the spark in her eyes that she's figured something out. "The part I couldn't translate, it was a mineral: magnesite. Magnesium carbonate. North Korea is full of the stuff. That's why they're there! They're *mining* it."

"Mining it? Why?" Fillion demands.

Marlene shrugs. "I'm not sure. At a guess, they're transporting it back to their home world."

"Isn't that stuff chalk?" you ask. "Like the powdery stuff from, like, rock climbing? Why would they need that?"

"Who knows? Maybe they're all rock climbers or something," Marlene says. "What's important is they're sending it back home somehow."

All three of you consider this for a moment.

"Okay, so what do we know about them?" you ask.

Fillion begins listing. "They can mutate their appearance, we believe, at least when given access to what we consider radioactive waste materials." She ticks off another finger. "They make up the entire ruling class of North Korea, which explains much of their 'diplomacy.' They have enslaved whatever of the human population is left. It appears they were, for a time, studying and attempting to act like humans, but sometime in the nineties they gave that up."

"And have been riding the crazy train," Marlene adds.

Fillion gives the barest of nods. "And we know they have nuclear capabilities. And it appears they're gearing up to use them, first on the South Koreans, then on...well, on who knows?"

"How much surveillance of North Korea do you have?" you ask.

Fillion narrows her eyes. "Enough."

"Have you seen anything, I don't know, unusual? Irregular? Or...well, regular? Like happening in a pattern?"

"I have," Marlene says. "Here let me just look...yeah, here on this page. It looks...it looks like maybe it's a record of shipments?"

You all lean in to stare at the document, which is written without spaces, all character after character. How Marlene can interpret that is beyond you. But Fillion nods, as if it's as clear as day. "I see," she says. She leans back in her chair and pulls a small tablet from her inside jacket pocket. She taps it for a minute, then lays it down so you can see the screen. It's a video, from a satellite, of a field and a small building. The video is grainy and black-and-white, but after a moment, a brilliant flash blossoms from just outside the building.

"That's it," Fillion says. "Marlene, you've cracked it. This is what happens at every interval on your chart there. There's a flash, we lose satellite for a moment, then everything is back to normal. We've been disregarding it as a technical glitch because it was happening with such regularity and everything else looked normal. But it must be whatever they're doing to transport the materials. Look," she zooms in, "There was a small hill there; hard to tell what it is from the sat image, but it could just be a pile of the mineral. And a moment later... it appears to be gone."

"Ugh, I ate way too many donuts," you groan as your stomach does a somersault. "I feel like I'm going to explode or something, bleah." You stretch back, holding your aching belly.

"How many of those did you eat?" Fillion demands.

You look sidelong at the end of the table, where only two donuts out of a dozen remain. And one has a bite taken out of it. "In my defense," you say, "they were *really* good donuts."

"What if we overfed the aliens?" Marlene says to herself.

"Donuts?" you ask.

"Not donuts," Marlene says sternly. "But they eat radioactivity, or something, right? They need it to change. What if we made them 'overeat,' as it were?"

"By bombing them?" Fillion asks.

"Yeah, by bombing the shit out of them," Marlene says.

"They'd be like fat kids force-fed cake," you say, contemplating the image of overstuffed aliens with chocolate icing all over their mouths.

"There's a risk that they would just enjoy it, you do realize," Fillion says.

"Yeah, there is a risk, but it's risky to do nothing, too," Marlene says. "But let's run the numbers, see what happens."

They work for days, tossing outcome after outcome out only for it to fail. And all the while, agents keep bringing in reports on North Korea's movements: another bomb test, a rumor of a self-sufficient nuclear reaction that lasted a day or two, steady improvements.

Finally, after a week, Fillion admits defeat. "We can't wait any longer, and we don't have any better ideas," she sighs heavily. "I'll go talk to the president."

You and Marlene are allowed to ride along, mostly so Fillion and Marlene can continue to hash out the details, the estimates of how much damage to do, where, exactly, the "overstuffed donut" is. You helpfully codename the operation "Breakfast of Champions."

You're left on the plane while Fillion reports to the White House;

Marlene says she has to tell the Secretary of State, the president, and the Joint Chefs all together in a secret bunker, but you're not sure you believe her. She comes back late in the night, and the pilot immediately takes off.

"We're doing it," is all she says before curling into a sleeping pod.

When she wakes up, you ask where the plane is going.

"North Korea, of course," Fillion says, her eyes bloodshot. "We'll be watching from a safe distance to see the effects. Ever seen a nuke go off before?"

"I want off the plane," you say, your voice cracking with fear.

"Relax, you'll be fine. Besides, you don't have a choice. This is where we're going, and you were already on the plane." Fillion gives her one-shoulder shrug again. "We'll be far enough away that we'll be out of range."

You all go silent as the enormity of what is about to happen sinks in for each of you. Nuclear bombs are going to go off, on purpose, for the first time since World War Two. And people may be down there. And the radiation may just make the aliens really big and scary instead of killing them. And then everyone will die.

You are staring restlessly out a window at a cloud-streaked horizon when the pilot dings the intercom. "We've arrived," Marlene says.

"I didn't ask you if you wanted to come to this part," Fillion says softly. "Would you like to see it happen from the cockpit now?"

Marlene immediately nods and follows Fillion into the nose of the plane. You want to say no, to make a parachute and jump out, but your feet carry you forward anyway. There's a pilot, military by the uniform, sitting calmly at the controls. Off to your left, right, and ahead, three drone-piloted aircraft glide silently. To your horror, you can see the rounded nuclear warheads strapped to the bottom of the planes.

"Had to be precise," Marlene says, as if reminding herself.

You can't see the ground below you, but you can imagine it well enough. Parched farmland. Little huts. Maybe a city, with people going about their daily lives. People totally not expecting this attack. And aliens. Monsters robbing our planet. About to meet their fate or mutate beyond all control.

Fillion puts on a headset and stares out the window. She gives the barest nod, and, as if obeying her command, the three drones drop their payloads, the bombs falling with a sort of magical grace. You try to lean forward to see, but the instrument panel is in your way. You rush out the back as the pilot banks gently, then you can feel it, three shudders that run, one-two-three, through the plane. You throw yourself against the left bay of windows and look down as three mushroom clouds explode upwards, reminding you of a fountain of water at the public pool when you were a kid, a whale spout bringing death instead of play.

Then, exploding out of the gray, what you swear is a tentacle. It's purple and splotchy, and as wide as a blue whale. "Shit, Fillion!" you scream.

"We see it!" Marlene shouts back. Another appendage, like a scorpion's barb, erupts out of the broiling clouds, then falls back down again, its movements jerky. Then toward the right, a giant rounded shape—you want to say a head but it's too terrible to imagine—crests, then seems to stumble. You watch as the clouds swirl around it like waves.

You hear the scream of jets, and suddenly a wall of fighter planes zooms in from the far horizon. They dive down, sparrows against the leviathan, and you imagine you can hear the bullets tearing into the mess. The red scorpion tail lashes out, and a jet goes spinning into the cloud cover. Another makes a suicide dive straight for the place where the head was a moment before, and you can see the tails of missiles as they're fired.

It feels like it goes on forever, but it's only a half-hour at most. Then the dust begins to clear, and the fighters fly off to refuel in the Sea of Japan.

The news media doesn't let the monster story go for the next six months. Investigations are launched, questions brought, but it is determined that nuclear attacks were a justified action, particularly in light of the leviathan found across two provinces when the dust clears. South Korea isn't happy, but Fillion assures you privately that they're very aware of how close to annihilation they really came. It's all just political circus. Fillion gets a handshake from the president and an award you've never heard of; her boss gets a promotion and goes on a book tour. Marlene and you are kept out of the records.

You are grateful to return to your slice of Texas sky, even if you never can look up at the stars the same way again.

THE END

"Let me just figure out who best to take you to, sir, um, and I'll, just, uh, do that," you say. You can feel yourself shivering with terror.

The alien looks unimpressed. Or maybe you're projecting; he doesn't have much of a face, just those big huge eyes. How is he speaking to you, anyway? Where is his mouth?

"Ummmm," you say, trying to puzzle out what to do next.

"Does your puny planet not even have a leader?" He sounds both comically nasal and offensively dismissive.

"Oh, yeah, we've got, like, lots of leaders. Could you maybe specify what kind of leader you're looking for?"

"I am going to disintegrate this planet," he says. He sounds completely deadpan, like this is no big deal.

"Er...what?" you say.

"I will destroy your planet," he says, speaking slowly, like you're stupid.

You reply:
- "What did we ever do to you?" Turn to page 165.
- "Right this way, sir." Turn to page 166.

"You... are the leader of this planet?" the little man asks. Even with his nasal whine he manages to sound condescending.

You stand up to your full height, which is more than double the little alien invaders'. "Yeah," you say. "You wanted to speak to me."

The alien looks up, up, staring at you. His eyes squint despite the darkness. "You are not what I expected," he says.

"Well, that's life, right?" you quip. "So, what can I do for you?"

As if remembering his purpose, the little alien stiffens and says, "You will turn over this planet to me."

"Yeah, don't think I can do that, buddy," you say. "You understand, right? We're kinda using it. But you're welcome to come hang out with us!"

"That is unacceptable," the nasal little dweeb says. "You will be disintegrated."

He points his little bubble gun at you, his fat little finger twitching toward the trigger.

"Woah, buddy!" you say, hoping the two-hands-up gesture is the intergalactic symbol for 'simmer down, I'm innocent here!'

The gun wavers.

"Can I ask what you want to do with our planet?"

"Why, destroy it, of course," the alien says.

"Uh huh, and can you clarify what that exactly means?"

"Well," he says, as if just now thinking this through, "it means I will shoot it with my Interplanetary Exploder Planet Obliviator."

"Oh, okay, is that all?" you say. "So why did you need to speak to me?"

"I like to see my enemies before I destroy them," the alien says. He is awfully matter-of-fact about this. "Plus," he adds, "I had to come here to plant the bomb."

"Uh huh," you say. Crap, could he really blow up the planet? "Wow, can you really blow up the planet?" you ask, for lack of anything better to do.

"Why, of course," the little man says. He finally drops his little gun to his side, and you can feel the muscles in your back relax just a hair. "I will just need to deposit the Interplanetary Exploder Planet Obliviator and push this switch," he says, revealing a small green button on a black box in his gloved hand.

"Wow, may I see that?" you ask, and immediately take the button out of his open palm. You begin to examine it as if it's really exciting and interesting. "This is a really great model, never seen one like this.

Of course, it's an antique."

The little alien snatches it out of your hand. "It is not an antique! It's the best of the fleet! I bought it just before I left!" he insists.

You make a few 'tsk tsk' sounds. "That's too bad," you say. "We moved past that design about, oh, a hundred years ago." You are cranking out the lies as quickly as you can think of them, but at least the little dude seems to be buying it. Here's hoping your luck holds out.

"But if you have such advanced models, why have I never heard of them?" Oh no, he sounds suspicious. Crap.

"Have you ever been to Ickle?" you ask.

"Why, no... I haven't heard of that planet," the little alien says.

"Probably because we blew it up—kablooey!" You grin at the smaller creature.

The little guy looks nervous for the first time. "Kablooey?" he says.

"'Fraid so," you say. "And you know, since you're here threatening us and all, well, we might just be inclined to follow you home, blow up your planet."

"Hmm," he says. "That would be a most unfortunate circumstance."

"Or, you know, you could just hop back in your rocket and maybe blow some other place up instead," you suggest idly.

"Mmm," the round-headed bobble-head dude says.

"I mean, choice is yours. But I know what I'd do," you say, then stick your hands in your pockets and relax, like you don't care at all what he says. But you're shaking from shock and anxiety. You really hope he can't tell.

"I will...leave for now," the little alien says. "But I will be back on my next circuit, in the next 100 years or so. We shall see who is more advanced by then!" He's an imperious little bugger.

"Lookin' forward to it!" you say, filling your voice with false cheer.

While you watch, the alien struggles back into his rocket and starts the engine. The rocket backs up several feet, like a car in reverse, then angles back up and shoots straight into the night sky.

Huh. It seems being leader of all Earth isn't that hard a job after all.

You briefly consider how you're going to inform 100-years-from-now-Earth that they may be exploded...nah. Let future-humanity deal with it. You saunter back down the road toward home.

THE END

"You can't just come to someone's planet and tell them you're going to destroy it and whatever for no reason! We LIVE here, you know?!" you shout at the diminutive little bastard.

"Yes, I can," he says, and he's so damn smug about it that you want to strangle him. You lunge at him with fingers outstretched to wring his puny neck (if he even has a neck!), and time slows down. It's like moving underwater; you see him raise a bubble-shaped gun and point it at you. You watch as he pulls the trigger, and a bright red line shoots out of it. And you are aware, for the splittest of seconds, of your body ceasing to exist from your midriff and up.

And then the pile of dust that used to be you falls into a neat pile in the crater, the wind gently blowing at your charred molecular remains.

Dust to dust.

THE END

You start to climb out of the hole, hoping as you do that the little evil alien won't be able to keep up with you.

"Where are you going?" he calls, his voice carrying perhaps just the edge of a pant.

"Taking you to our leader," you say, not looking back. You break into a light jog.

"I don't believe you," he says, and your veins go cold with the chill in his voice. You stop and slow down, your feet dragging.

"Um," you start.

The little alien scampers up to you, his short legs moving faster than his size would suggest he was capable of. "Is your leader far?" he asks, in complete seriousness.

"Probably several miles, yeah. And it's the middle of the night. In the middle of a field. So, yeah, it's a bit of a distance away," you say, stumbling a bit over the words. Where'd that gun of his go? Dammit.

The alien looks you up and down. "Perhaps you would be a good specimen to be returned for our collection," he says, and something about the way he says it is sinister.

"Uhhhh," you say.

"You will board my spacecraft and return with me," he says. "And then I will destroy your planet."

You were totally unprepared for tonight to turn out like this. Why you? Why this?

Shaking your head, you say:

- "Okay," and board the rocket. Turn to page 171.
- "You are such an asshole!" Turn to page 165.

"There's no point in staying here," you say, sounding more confident than you feel. "Let's just go. Maybe we can make it to the city, warn someone, get, I don't know, NASA involved or something."

"NASA?" Ray says.

"You know what I mean!" you huff. "Look, I saw those things come out of the SKY yesterday. Maybe this was the first place they landed. Maybe we can do something about this."

You grab a water bottle from the pile. "Y'all can stay here if you want, but I'm going."

"Hold your horses," Esther says. "I don't think we should be splittin' up."

"I don't know if it's a good idea to go to the city," Lily says haltingly. "Isn't that where the robots went?"

"Better than bein' out here in the nothing," Ray says.

Esther presses her lips into a line. "Lily, are you willing to go with them if I go?" she asks.

The younger woman looks hesitant, like she'd rather not be answering this kind of question, but eventually she nods. "I don't want to be alone," she says in her small voice.

You reach out and squeeze her hand. "I really think this is the right call," you say.

The first thing to do is find a working car, which seems like it would be easy but still starts an argument more than once. After you begrudgingly give up on the all-wheel drive truck you found, you agree to settle for the SUV family car. It still has french fries wedged in the backseat, but Esther successfully argues that it can both carry everyone and leave a little space for supplies and maybe a bed.

It's nearly dusk by the time that's all settled, and even though you want to rush off, Ray wisely suggests you bring some kind of supplies. Who knows where the next working gas station is? It's night before the car is loaded. You take the first shift as driver. It's late and you're exhausted, but it's not like the road is hard: just straight through town and keep following the highway.

The road is totally dark. That's not completely unusual out here, but normally there'd be at least the friendly light of a passing semi. Tonight, there's just you and the moon, and it's barely a sliver of anything. That's your excuse when you nearly slam into the cow, sending Lily rolling forward out of the back seat as you slam the brakes.

A quick investigation shows the fence was flattened when a car careened into it, and the cows took advantage to make a ponderous jailbreak. Without other traffic to be a problem, they only moseyed so far. It takes all four of you half an hour of hootin' and hollerin' to move them off the road so you can pass; Esther insists you're done for the night and takes the keys. You don't fight that hard.

"We're here," Ray says, voice low, waking you up from your doze. The tinted windows are still black as night; you have to squint to see the ragged outlines of the buildings. The flicker of a fire smolders from more than one building.

It's clear you're too late.

"I thought maybe it was just us," Esther says. "That maybe the National Guard or somebody...someone would do something..." she says, and the tremor in her voice makes your heart squeeze. You were hoping to be wrong, too.

Esther stops the car under the lee of an alley so you can all get some sleep. You hear her crying quietly in the dark, but pretend to be asleep.

The new day doesn't bring much in the way of hope. The sun just shines on devastation, and it's hard for the car to pick a path through. It's almost worse than your little town; there wasn't much there to destroy in the first place, not after the normal monsters of poverty, isolation, and weather had taken their toll. But this. This had been the Big City. The place for outings, date nights, adventures. Somehow knowing it could be hit just as hard—harder—cuts to the quick.

It's Lily who pulls things together. "Well, surely we aren't the only ones here," she says. "We just have to find the others."

Now Esther is quiet, like Ray, and you don't have anything to say, but Lily just slips into the front seat of the SUV. "So let's just go find them," she says, and starts driving.

The devastation is incredible. Whole blocks burned with the alien lasers; buildings are toppled; an ambulance scissored in two, as if a massive knife had come down from the heavens. The SUV passes a daycare, its front window shattered, children's toys still perfectly in the cubbies, crayons left out on coloring pictures half-filled in. A child's body, broken, covered in ash, partially covered by a man's jacket.

Down the street, a grandmother slumps over her scruffy poodle, the edges of her sensible sweater charred.

After a moment, you close your eyes; your stomach twists in despair.

But not Lily. She keeps driving, carefully maneuvering around the debris, the bodies, the rubble. When you glance at her, you can see she has been crying, but drives anyway.

This whole thing feels like a nightmare.

Fifteen minutes later, though, hope. A man trudging silently along the road. Lily slows the SUV and leans out the window. "Sir! Oh thank goodness, someone else survived!"

The man looks up slowly, considering. "Yeah," he says. "Yeah, we survived."

"We?" Ray says, leaning forward.

"Yeah," the man says. He's wearing a dirty old Rangers baseball cap, the embroidered T now grey. He squints at the car. "Yeah, there's some of us. Up ahead."

"Will you show us?" Lily asks.

Slowly, the man nods, and Esther opens the sliding door to let him in. There are no more seats, so he crouches in the middle. He smells like wet newspaper and bitter beer. He points and Lily drives forward.

He leads your small party to a park. There, under the trees, it could almost be a festival, if you replaced the confectionary booths with mismatched tarps and tents. "Here we are," he says, and then climbs out.

"Wait!" Ray says. "What happened?"

"Robots. Monsters. They attacked us. I think mebbe they was from China? Probably was, I bet," the man says. He pulls his ball cap down lower over his eyes.

Voice low, you say, "Not from China. I saw them. They came from ...out there."

The man just shrugs. Lily puts the car in park and you all pile out. Your legs protest from being twisted into the seat that way, and you have to shake them to get feeling back. But here. There are others! It's not the end!

At first, there's still no word of what happened, at least not officially. You tell the others what you saw that night, the night the saucers came. There is no internet connection, and phone lines are down, power cut. Communication slid back 100 years that night, so it takes a while before you learn the extent of the damage. Someone finally pulled a short-wave radio from an old truck, and a few days later someone else must have had the same idea, because soon Texans were chatting with Ohioans, then British Columbians, Mexicans.

They came everywhere, destroyed all they could. And then, as quickly as they came, they left.

And so there is nothing left for those of you left than to rebuild. And it turns out humans are a hearty stock, and rebuilding is one of those impossible things that it turns out we're all quite good at. It's as simple as that. You are in a bad spot and must rebuild, so you cry a bit, then get to rebuilding.

New Dallas takes time, but in a year, it's comfortable again, and in three it's almost as if the invaders had never come. Except for the indelible memories of the survivors, the patchwork families created out of crisis, the new agency created just to watch the skies, things get back to normal.

You find yourself a decent job, live in a small home, have enough. And it's enough. Life goes on.

But you never look to the stars anymore, preferring to drive out the dark with artificial lights. You no longer yearn for what is beyond. You turn your eyes to Earth.

THE END

Y ou're so consumed by terror and the utter insanity of the situation that you just...follow orders. Not much else to it, really. You squeeze yourself into the neon color-explosion rocket ship, which really is far too small for a human, requiring you to wriggle your shoulders and push up with your feet until you can fit through the door. Once in, you find a tiny little operations bay covered in switches, knobs, and buttons. There's only one chair, and it sits facing out the porthole, so you sit yourself down as gently as you are able. The chair is about the same size as one you might find in a preschool, forcing you to lean forward to rest your elbows on your knees.

And you wait.

The little alien dude is out there somewhere, doing who knows what, and you're just supposed to wait around for him to return. But after about ten minutes (heck, maybe it was five, you're not very good at paying attention to that sort of thing) you get bored, and spend a little bit of time studying the control panel in front of you. Not very many lights are lit up at the moment, and the few labels there are are all in some other language, presumably tiny-alien-ese.

You let yourself recline back into the chair, tiny though it may be. You stare up at the vastness of space from your porthole. You feel so small, but it's so beautiful at the same time... It's late, and you've had quite a shock, so after just a little while, you close your eyes to rest, just for a moment...

As your chin hits your chest, you snap awake with a start, pushing your hands out in front of you to catch yourself from falling. But you're reclined back, and the only thing in front of you is the control panel. Which you've pushed something on.

The hum of the rocket picks up, and a buzzer goes off from somewhere near the door. You scramble out of the seat, but your bum is too big for it and it's a struggle, and meanwhile the door is closing. By the time you get there, it's sealed tight. You feel around for a crack, a knob, anything, but it's seamless. Meanwhile, a set of three chimes goes off at the little operations board, and then everything gets very noisy and you feel like you're going to be squished into jelly—the rocket is taking off!

The engine is incredibly loud and you're pressed against the floor of the metal ship, but you almost think you can hear someone down below outside screaming, "NO, that is MY rocketship, Earthian! Return at once!" But then your stomach has done a somersault and the world is spinning and everything is SO heavy and your face feels like wobbly Jello.

Then, suddenly, it all stops, and you feel yourself floating gently off the floor. You can fly, just a little, until you collide into the other, very near, wall. Your hair sticks out from your head like that one time you touched an electrical socket with a knife, only way less painful. You do the easiest handstand you've ever done. True, your feet hit the roof of the ops deck, but still, done. "Whee!" you say, and allow yourself to jet back up to look out the tiny window.

You can just see Earth, as pretty as a picture book, disappearing out of view. It's like a gem in a great sea of blackness. On second thought, that sea of eternal blackness isn't so great: where are you going? There's nothing but space out here!

You start to have a panic attack, which triggers some kind of automatic system. A puff of pink smoke is released from a jet near the ceiling, and before you know it, everything is feeling marvelous. You feel woozy and just want to sit down and wait until you arrive.

Luckily, the ship is on autopilot, so you'll be at your destination—whatever it is—before you know it.

Weeeee!

Turn to page 51.

"You're the boss," Breck says. "You wanna go today?"

You look at the clock, and at the weird little alien taking up residence on your couch. "Yeah, I think we can make it to Houston today if we leave real soon."

"Sounds great, let's roll," she says. You're kinda disconcerted by the way she's so casual and not stereotypically alien or leprechaun-y.

You load up the car with a few snacks and carry Breck out, putting her on the passenger seat. This presents a problem. "Uhh," you say. "Do you need like a seatbelt or something?"

"Ha, that's a good one!" she says, and plops down, still eating a pile of cereal squares. "Don't worry, I'm pretty resilient. I did crash-land a satellite yesterday, after all."

You start up the car and turn down the lane. "Yeah, about that— what happened?" you ask.

"Oh, it's a little complicated. There was this, um, soccer match in Ireland and I really was hoping to catch it... you know, it sounds stupid," she says. "Let's just say I overcorrected and, well, here we are."

"And there really are...um, more of your people?...in all the satellites?" you ask.

"Oh yeah, sure," she says. "It's a big time commitment, absolutely, but the pay is good and our lifespans are really long, so it's no big deal to pop up for a couple of decades, navigate some shit for a company or NASA or whatever. And it's a job that needs doing. It's not like a human could do that, you know what I mean?"

"But humans have, you know, gone up to space," you insist. "I mean I've seen the video!"

"Of course! We're not trying to take anything away from the human astronauts. What they're doing for your species is really exciting to watch, you know. We're happy to, I don't know, nudge your scientists in the right direction," Breck says.

If this were a normal conversation, you could look at your passenger, but she's so small it's hard to drive and safely glance down. Of course, if this were a normal conversation, it wouldn't exist, so you've gotta deal with what you can. But it is annoying.

"This is just a lot to take in," you say. "How long have you been involved in the space program?"

Long road trips are great conversational lubricants. It's just too hard to sit in a car with someone for hours at a time and not talk with them. It's a good place for those hard-but-meaningful conversations, to break down boundaries. And you've certainly never heard anything like what

Breck has to say before, that's for certain. She tells you about her people emigrating from Zenithian, the hardship of both adapting to a new environment as well as the physical issues with inhabiting a new world. She's third-generation, she says, but her grandparents told her stories. They've come a long way from stealing milk, and you can hear the pride in her voice. She's been doing space-work much of her grown life (though you're wary of asking how long that has been), though this was her first satellite. She had previously gone up with the Shuttle-Mir program a few times. She'd also enjoyed vacations all around the world, it sounded like.

You feel weird, feeling jealous and less accomplished than an alien who can't reach your knee.

You pull into the NASA headquarters parking lot late at night. Your eyes feel salty and your whole body is fairly sore from driving for so long. "They're closed," you say. "I didn't even think of that." You allow yourself a groan.

"Hey, no big deal," Breck says. "I can get us in."

She has you drive up to a side door, away from the double glass doors. It looks like a janitor's exit, and there's no handle on the exterior. "Just give me a second, I'll let you in," Breck says. She seems to know her way around, and crawls into a drain at the base of the building. You wait long enough to start to feel crazy—waiting outside of NASA, in the dark, for a tiny alien?—when the door swings open. Breck dangles from the handle. "Come on! It's hard to hold on to this!" she yells, so you scramble inside.

"Whew," Breck says, jumping down from the door as it closes. "Hey, welcome to NASA!"

"Thanks? I'm not sure I really should be here," you say.

"Eh, it's no big deal. Want me to give you the tour while you're here?"

"I ...guess?"

It's been a really strange day.

Breck has you pick her up, because your steps are so much bigger than hers, and she sits on your shoulder, directing you down each white-painted hallway as you come to the turns. You're in rooms no tourist ever gets to see, that much is clear. Particularly when she directs you to a door that looks like a closet. "Sorry about all the spy kinda stuff," she says. "Gotta keep things secure."

She directs you to put her down, and she presses her palm against a reader located next to the ground. You didn't even notice it. It scans her hand and the door opens with a soft click.

"This is what I'm really excited about," she says. "Let me show you!"

The room beyond is pretty big (especially if you're six inches tall). It houses a kitchenette, rows of what could be doll beds, a little garden, and... a rocket?

"What is all this?" you ask.

"We're going to go home soon," Breck says, her voice cracking with enthusiasm. "Well, not all of us or anything, but some. Some of us think it's time that we went back, at least see what's going on out there."

"Wow. This...this is incredible," you say.

"Oh, I'm so glad you think so!" Breck exclaims. "Because I had this idea. What if *you* came back with us? Like an exchange program! I think it's great; besides, our astronaut who was supposed to come with us bailed when he actually met us. But if you came, well, we'd get, like the *regular person* perspective. You would be, like, an ambassador!"

"Gee, Breck, you are really great at throwing me curve balls," you say. "Let me think about it."

"No rush, no rush at all, the rocket isn't finished yet. But-" she sizes you up, a quick up-down glance, "-you'd be the perfect size, it would be awesome. A real miracle, you know? I'm not going back, but would I ever get brownie points if I could find a replacement for the trip!"

It turns out little folk can be convincing when they want to be, and Breck talks you into it. Besides, what could be more exciting than exploring a new world? A new world where you're a giant who is basically amazing at everything? Face it, you've never really stood out from the crowd, at all, your whole life. But here, here is a chance to really make a difference.

So you take it.

Three weeks later, after you've eaten all your favorite foods and said goodbye to all your family and friends, you blast off, to explore the great unknown with a bunch of tiny explorers.

175

Boldly go.

Turn to page 6.

Anya extends its hand out to you, and you take it. Its fingers feel leathery, or like that time you touched a stingray in the touch tank at the aquarium. You let him lead you up and out of the crater, and you stand there, together, while a vessel, huge and darker than darkness, emerges overhead. You feel a shiver of trepidation in your gut, a basic animal fear of the unknown, and you tamp it down. You will be an explorer!

Anya waves the communicator square again, in a way you can't quite see, and the ship above you lets a ramp slide down, as clear as a brook, like a solid beam of light. Anya pulls you forward onto the ship, and you follow, your mind already aching with the wonder of it all.

As you pass up into the ship, you look back down at Earth. It's muddy, covered with cows, and kinda smelly. You decide you won't miss it.

You turn back into the spaceship and are greeted by a dozen creatures just like Anya. They touch it all over with their slender fingers, brushing the lost alien almost reverently. Then, as if noticing you are there, too, one comes over and makes its fingers dance in an intricate pattern.

"Sorry, didn't catch that," you say, and then reflect that maybe that wasn't the best statement for history to remember but oh well, you work with what you've got.

Anya—at least you think it's Anya, they all look kinda alike—takes you by the hand again and leads you further into the ship. You feel like a giant. Everything here is sized for these creatures half your height, and you end up stooping awkwardly down the hall, which is rounded and a pleasant greenish-brown color, like processed baby food.

You emerge into a slightly larger cavern, and Anya pushes you gently into a chair, if a chair can be made out of something soft and vaguely grass-like. "Goooo," it says.

You nod like you understand, but you're totally out of your depth here. "Yeah, okay," you say. Anya nods and nestles into a nest-couch of its own.

Just then, you feel as if a tremendous invisible hand is reaching out of the sky to press you down. You are flattened against the floor, and even the skin on your face feels like it will be sheared off with the pressure. There's no sound, but your brain makes up for its absence by filling your ears with the slow crush of your heartbeat. Your bones feel like they're made of steel. Everything hurts. Your heart hammers in your chest. Tears are forced out of your eyes. You try to breathe but your lungs won't move, can't inflate, are being squeezed, crushed.

You try to gasp, desperate, but the black dots in your vision just grow into spheres as your consciousness is swallowed up.

The human body is good at many things. A trained diver can hold his breath for up to five minutes without needing air. A ballerina can balance all the weight of her body and the pull of gravity on a single point in her toes. A strongman can lift a telephone pole to throw down a field.

But the human body just really isn't equipped to handle interstellar travel.

You don't make it farther than liftoff. Oops.

THE END

"Great, happy to be here!" Breck says, settling back into the couch.

For a while, it's a lot like having a small roommate who does nothing to help around the house and rarely leaves. You quickly learn that the Wee Folk have big appetites. She's really into sugar, milk, and grains, so she pretty much eats breakfast cereal as often as you'll buy it for her (which is pretty often, you're not a monster. But she does eat a *lot.*) She's really into David Bowie, and claims to have known the Zenithn who inspired "Space Oddity." "But of course his name wasn't really Tom, you know," she says.

She also claims she was in *Labyrinth*, that a lot of her folk were, knew Bowie personally, back before jobs in space technology were easy to come by. She's not particularly tidy, and is really into practical jokes. With her around, it's hard to get a date. And once she was cornered by the neighbor's cat. After you pulled the tabby off Breck, she nearly swore a second life-debt to you, but you're barely coping with one so you told her it was just the right thing to do.

And then it all really goes to shit. You get drunk and start yelling at Breck for leaving half-eaten bowls of cereal everywhere, *again*, and you say, "Where's your fucking pot of gold, leprechaun? Huh? Where is it? I saved your life and all I get for it is a hundred empty bowls of cereal and a shitty roommate! Where's the win for me? When do I get my luck or whatever the hell?" You throw one of the bowls for good measure, and it explodes against the wall in a shower of milk, compressed marshmallows, and ceramic.

Breck turns crimson with rage, literally; her whole body goes red, head to toe. "I told you, we don't DO that shit!" she screams.

"Why the hell not?!" you yell back, the force of your voice blowing the little creature back a step or two. She pulls her hair in frustration.

"Fine, if that's what you want, fine," she says.

"Yeah, it is what I want," you say, slurring a little. "Pay back my goddamn life-debt already, you little cereal-stealing deadbeat! This is my wish, okay?!"

You don't remember that conversation in the morning, which makes the results that much more confusing. Nothing happens at first, except Breck is gone.

You sit down to enjoy your first bowl of cereal in weeks only to find she emptied your box. Classy. But then you find something in the box, a small folded piece of paper, and something heavy, in the bottom. You open the paper. There, in scratchy writing, it reads: "Found your treasure. Enjoy life. Ha ha. -B"

You tip the box over, and out comes a bound stack of hundred-dollar bills. You say, "oh shit" as the realization that you've made a huge mistake dawns.

Congratulations. You pissed off a tiny person highly skilled in electronics who most people believe is imaginary. This will not end well.

You keep finding wads of cash hidden around your apartment; in your shoes, in the microwave, in the washing machine. Stacks and stacks of fresh hundred-dollar bills. At first you think maybe it's okay, maybe Breck did have some way to materialize money and she just was a pain in the ass about it by hiding it everywhere.

But then you hear the sirens.

It turns out a lot of cops show up for a bank robbery in a small town. They don't usually see much action, so they're all pretty gung-ho. One even shoots at you when you come out with your hands up after they yell at you through a megaphone. It misses, but just barely.

The evidence against you is pretty damning. Sure, there's no video or proof you took the money from the bank, but an anonymous caller tipped them off to your location, and you were stupid enough to be at home with all the stolen cash. It's a pretty easy case.

That's when you get Breck's last practical joke, though. "Life." Life in prison, she meant. Or in the asylum, if you ever decide to tell anyone that a leprechaun that's actually an alien is the real perpetrator.

Nope. Enjoy your new life.

The worst part? They don't even serve cereal in prison. You may never get a full bowl again. Damned leprechaun.

THE END

You know pretty much nothing about babies except which end the food goes in and where it comes out again. They cry, they refuse to tell you what their issue is, they don't do much besides sleep and want things... safe to say, this baby isn't for you. But you can't exactly just tell people you found a baby in a field and oh by the way maybe it's actually a space baby. Hell no. Your life just doesn't need complications like that.

Luckily, you heard awhile back that your fire department recently installed some kind of baby drop-off dealio, and you've always kinda wondered what that's like, so, win-win.

You only feel kinda like a weirdo for walking down Main Street with a space-baby wrapped in a blanket with the intent to leave it at a fire station, but it'll probably all work out for the best. Besides, it's still early and there's not really anyone out to see you.

You trudge down the road to the fire station (hallelujah for small towns!) and sure enough, there it is: a sign reading "Safe Haven" with a picture of a swirly-shaped baby. Much to your chagrin, there is no baby drop-off box like you'd hoped. You just kinda wanted to leave it in a box somewhere and be done with it. Worse, while you're standing outside the station, someone notices you.

"Hey, can I help you?" The man must be one of the firefighters. He's got deeply worn wrinkles and mostly grey hair. Geez, your town really needs to invest in some new firemen. There's no way that guy could haul you out of a fire in his condition.

"Uhhh," you say, panicking. "I have a baby."

"Oh, I see that," the fireman says. "Did you need something?" He sounds like he's placating a mad dog. In a way, maybe he is. You feel a bit rabid, especially after last night.

"I just wanted to drop this off," you say awkwardly, and thrust the squirming infant into the man's hands. He takes it, but seems a bit baffled.

"Is this your baby?" he asks.

"Um..." you say.

"You can't just drop a baby off here if it isn't yours," he says, the hint of a threat in his voice.

"I found it," you say, and take off running, completely aware that you now look like a crazy criminal, but it's way better than trying to explain yourself. Besides, he's an old guy holding a baby; he's not likely to chase after you.

You scamper away, running until your lungs hurt and then hiding behind a building to see if anyone is following you. No one is, thank goodness, and you slink away back to your apartment, where you collapse into bed and don't wake up for a solid six hours.

You pretty much hope that's the end of it, but you hear a report on the radio about a crazy person who dropped off a baby. Anyone with information is encouraged to call the 1-800 number. You call in sick to work and head out of town for a "fishing trip," using your cousin's borrowed truck.

By the time you come back, the baby's been moved into social services, put into the foster system, and is falling out of the news cycle. You stop thinking of it and go about your life, grateful that you dodged that baby-shaped bullet.

You don't think about it for several years, in fact, until you catch a strange report on the holonet about some kid with crazy strength, and—though this is really hard to believe—laser vision, super-strength, and the ability to jump super-far, almost like flying. He was in trouble for throwing a Pomeranian through a wall, and there's the picture, and holy shit, it's the same kid. Troubled background, yadda yadda, found abandoned in a small-town fire station, nobody knows what's up or how this kid got to be this way. Your curiosity piqued, you set your holonet to find more stories on him, and then, every few months, another story, similar themes. Eventually the kid finds himself in some experimental lab, where they determine he may not even be *human*.

You don't hear anything for several more years, and almost kinda forget about it. You're at work at the high-rise office, getting close to finally retiring and enjoying your life, when the sirens go off: another terrorist attack. But this isn't just any terrorist, it's the kid, now a full-grown adult, wearing some crappy leotard and setting buildings on fire with his heat vision. He seems *really* pissed off. You watch from your window as he flips a car just to crush some pedestrians. Shit. He's flying around, throwing lamp posts like boomerangs, and you feel your building shake with the impacts. He's not targeting you, no, but he's causing an incredible amount of havoc, like an oversized hissy-fit. You can't even tell what he's mad about, not that it matters too much. He blows up the foundation to your building with three solid punches, and timmmmbeerrrrr, down it goes, flinging you and all the other people inside against the windows and down, crushed by office debris and falling rubble.

Your last thought before you perish is: Thank goodness I didn't have to deal with *that* little shit.

THE END

Yⁿou point helpfully off to the left, where you're pretty sure there is a field, somewhere, probably, maybe. As one, the bees turn and immediately head off that way.

With relief, you book it back the other way, to the right. You don't want to be around when the bees come back! You hustle as quickly as your legs can take you to the highway, and then stand with your thumb out frantically. Several cars pass you by, but you relax and try to look like you don't care at all if someone picks you up, and so the next car stops, a semi driven by a crusty-looking old dude who reeks of leftover Taco Bell.

"Thanks!" you say, and throw yourself in.

"Where to?" the driver says, eyeing you sideways in a way that makes your skin crawl a bit.

"Anywhere, just make it fast," you say, watching frantically out the window.

"Ayup," the driver says, and the semi rumbles back into motion.

You've gone less than a mile—still not into town—when the sky darkens. "Oh no oh no oh no," you mutter to yourself, and the driver says, "huh, didn't think it twere supposeta rain today."

Then, even over the rumble of the truck, you can hear them: the flap of two million oversized wings bent on only one mission.

"The bees are coming back!" you scream.

The driver just looks at you like a crazy person, coasting his semi back to a halt. "I'mma need you to get out here," he says.

"What?" you ask, eyes wide with horror. "Can't you see they're coming?!"

"I don't take kindly to drug use. Git," he says, stubborn as all get out.

Meanwhile, the bees are descending like a black plague upon the earth. The driver is on the brink of leaning over and shoving you out of the cab when the first bees get close.

"Ahh!" he screams.

And you reply, "I TOLD YOU!"

The bees swarm the cab, and again you hear, "Poll-in-ate! Poll-in-ate!" coming from all around you, and it's not just you, the driver hears it too, and he's covering his ears to keep the terrible chant out. The bees are so thick they block the windshield—it's impossible to see the road—but the driver picks up speed anyway. "They're in my head!" he cries, and you understand, because you're also cowering against the frightful sound.

The semi crashes into a building at about 50 miles per hour, crushing it completely. The semi drags to a halt, taking with it most of the house. You were so concerned about bees that you never put on a seat belt when you got in, and so your body catapults through the windshield, flying majestically in what your adrenaline-screaming brain sees as slow-motion out and over and through, until you land, rolling on the warm asphalt, blood leaking from many small and large tears through your skin. The bees don't mind. They descend on you, and on the blood-slicked driver, still in the cab, stinging you with their barbed stingers and rubbing their bright-orange pollen on you as they go.

Within a month, strange beautiful flowers sprout, all across the world. The flowers have purple stems and blood-red petals, and bloom straight out of the rotting corpses of humans in deep decay, erupting up through the stomach cavity. The bees tend these flowers like dedicated gardeners, and menace any who dare approach. Within three months, the Blood Poseys, as the come to be known, litter the globe, and humans, the preferred pollination point, are in high demand indeed.

The bees protect their fields of red, and so they spread.

THE END

Yyou've found...a child. It's alone, abandoned, and desperately needs you. This must be destiny. How can you turn your back on this boy?

You gather him up, wrapping him in the blanket he landed in, and cradle him in your arms. His crying subsides, and he settles in your arms, like he was made to go there. You begin the walk back, and when you next glance down at the amazing baby from the sky, he lets out a sweet little baby yawn, gives his arms a little stretch, and closes his eyes to fall asleep.

It's a long walk back, and you're not exactly prepared for a baby, so you have a lot to think about. What do you feed a baby? Where will it sleep? Well, in your bed, probably, though maybe you can make room in a drawer. Do you need a birth certificate? That may be tricky, but you've got a friend at the DMV so maybe you can get him to help you out with that. Wait, what will you call this child? He needs a name.

It needs to be a strong name, a heroic name, to honor the distance he's come already in life. Ah, that's it—you've got just the one— Fergus. Such a strong, masculine name. It just really feels empowering.

Plus, practically no one is named Fergus anymore, so it will probably make it easier for little Fergus to get an email address, when it comes time for that.

You drag the kid home, bouncing him a little as you walk. This is all so exciting—a baby, from the sky! And he's all yours.

You set up the Instagram account dedicated to "star-child" as soon as you get home, before you've even told anyone that you've "adopted" a baby. But all that can wait: for now, thank goodness, you can finally get your blog off the ground. Cute selfies just aren't enough anymore, and finding enough cute animals to fill out your blog was just getting to be a challenge. But a baby! A baby is just an endless parade of moments you can catalog and tweet and share.

Fergus is going to be a goldmine, that's for sure.

With Fergus safely ensconced in your life, you pour your energy into making him intensely adorable and viral. It takes a lot of time, sure, and you spend a lot of money at the craft store at first, but it's fun, and maybe the baby likes it too (who knows—babies can't talk!). Finally, you have this little person all to yourself, to mold, to create something truly amazing.

As the years go by, you get more followers. You hit just the right balancing point of adorable and insufferable, and all your dreams start coming true.

And then everything goes really next-level. Fergus first reveals his "gifts" when he's about three. During a totally unreasonable hissy fit about not wanting his picture taken today (kids! They never know what is really good for them!), he picks you up and lifts you over his head.

You're both so stunned by this that Fergus immediately stops crying and just looks at you, where you're staring down at him, open-mouthed. Then you start to grin maniacally. This is *so much better* than Instagram.

After Fergus puts you down, you send him right to time-out so you have time to plan. Over the next few weeks, you test the boy, having him lift the couch one-handed (while you're on it, natch), leap over a fence, and take a punch. You're considering hitting him with a hammer, but decide he may misconstrue the whole thing, and what if he got a bruise? That wouldn't play well on Twitter.

Then, you carefully curate your discoveries and seed the videos, one at a time, on different social platforms, like it's no big deal. And then, sure enough, it's not long before Ellen comes knocking. One quick TV show segment later, and Fergus is a star, and you've quickly got a reality TV producer—nope, make that three! —calling to ask whether you're interested in getting Fergus's talents "showcased." You act surprised and take enough time to seem like you're protecting the kid's interests before you accept.

From then on, little Fergus becomes Fergus the Freak, easily the most-watched kid on TV. You start off easy, with just a lifestyles reality TV show, the cameras following you and Ferg around on perfectly-planned adventures. But as Fergus (and the Fergus the Freak brand) ages, you've got to do more. By the time he's a teenager, you've convinced him he might actually *like* all this attention, and meanwhile you're definitely liking the new house, the new cars, the new everything you've bought with his royalties. He takes up a wrestling show, where people in ever-crazier situations come on and try to prove themselves against The Freak. From there it's a natural transition to WWE, which fits the brand perfectly, except everyone knows that Fergus can do it for real.

Unfortunately, that's about the time that Fergus decides to be a real brat. He starts skipping shows, making up excuses. You find him with his boyfriend, trying to pack a bag to run away. You throw yourself at him in a fury—you're not letting your money get away like that! —and Fergus delivers a classic takedown. But you're not strong like him—you're barely even strong for a regular person—and the blow against the doorframe makes something in your spine go *CRACK*, and then it's curtains for you.

Fergus has a face that's too well-known to hide, so he's found quickly. At the trial, he shouts an obscenity-filled tirade against the American people and their willingness to destroy other people's lives by putting them under a microscope. It doesn't go over well with the jury, and Fergus is sentenced to a decade in prison. He gets out a little sooner because of his good behavior—after all, he's used to being watched all the time—and, in his late twenties, finally has a chance to figure out who he really is. As far as he's concerned, he's pretty super.

THE END

"Ahhhhhh!" you scream, sounding horribly childish but unable to stop yourself. "What the fuck are you? What is happening? This can't be happening! Ahhh!"

You fall backwards, cowering behind your hands.

But...nothing happens.

You peek between your fingers. The alien has collapsed face-down in the dirt. It doesn't look like it's moving.

You stand up unsteadily. It still doesn't move.

You step closer. No reaction.

Closer. It doesn't look like it's breathing, but then, does it have to? Hard to tell.

You nudge it with a foot. "Maaaaaooooon," it says. It sounds really pathetic.

It looks so helpless, just lying there in the dirt.

"Hey..." you say, not sure how to start. "Are...are you okay?"

The creature doesn't say anything, but its long fingers uncurl slightly against the soil.

You bend closer. You reach out a hand and touch it, lightning-fast, on its shoulder. "Hey there," you say.

No reaction.

Quickly, afraid it will bite you, you grab it, pushing it gently so the creature flops onto its back and you can see its face.

It looks:

- Bizarre. You can't see any apparent features, just what could be large petals or a mask covering its head. Turn to page 196.
- Cute. Sure, it's kinda ugly-cute, but it reminds you a little of your favorite stuffed animal you had growing up, a little worn but fundamentally lovable. Turn to page 250.

It looks...bizarre. Like a hurriedly sketched kid's drawing of what a dog-spider might be, done in sickly cyan crayon. It tumbles to the ground, end over end, and growls at a rock.

"Hey there," you say soothingly.

It turns and barks at you. Looks like you startled it. Suddenly you notice the teeth—it has so many! And its mouth is huge. It doesn't sound like a dog, but makes gibberish noises. Does it have a language? Could it understand you?

"Woah, not gonna mess with you, buddy," you say, holding your arms up in what you hope is an inter-galactic symbol for "not interested in your drama."

The dog-alien raises a line of spines off its back and snarls at you, backing toward the wreck of the ship.

You wish you had a slice of cheese or something. Dogs like cheese, right?

You can't stand here all night, waiting around for this alien to do something.

You:

- See if you can calm it down by petting it. Turn to page 254.
- Stand far back and wait to see if it comes to you. Turn to page 224.
- Take its picture. Turn to page 226.

As you watch, the robot telescopes its thin, wiry legs, rising high up into the air. It looks almost insect-like, and you feel a building sense of dread in the pit of your stomach. That's when you notice there isn't just *one* robot: there are at least six, arranged all around the crater.

They don't look like they're here for a chat over tea.

Your legs start to catch up with your brain, and you begin to run, as fast as your legs can carry you, out of the field, desperate to get as far away from these robotic invaders as you possibly can.

A smell of smoke creeps up from behind you, and you chance a glance backward to see the field has been set on fire. Sure, there's a chance it was from the crash-landing the ship sustained, but in your heart, you're certain it was the robots.

As you turn back, you notice more streaks across the horizon, as if someone had shaken the sky and all the stars were falling out. But now you know those aren't just any twinkling lights: those are robots, and they're coming for you. They're coming for Earth.

You run as fast as you can, but it's just not fast enough. The robots pass overhead as you cower in the middle of the field, covering your head and sobbing openly. The spindly legs sink a few inches into the ground with every step as they fan out. After they've passed you by (maybe they can't see so well? You can't see anything remotely like eyes or windows), you lie crying in the dirt. As you watch, a robot in front of you stops, locks its legs, and releases a blast of fire from its underbelly, reducing the unfortunate cow below into char, the grassfire catching and spreading outward in concentric rings.

Your nose is full of the terrible scent of burnt leather and smoke, like an unfortunate gentleman's club after arson. It makes you cough, and you just want to lie down, to hide from the terrors from the great beyond, but the fire is coming closer. You cover your mouth and nose with your shirt as best as you can and run, escaping the flames by mere inches. You can feel the hair on your arms curling from the heat. And still you must run, the field now churning with terrified cattle as more of the robots deploy their lasers.

You can see a farmhouse, off to the right, so you turn and run that way. Maybe if you can get there in time, the police, the military, someone can be called and this can all be made right.

As you arrive, a woman climbs out of the house, still in her nightdress and clutching a box of tissues. "Fire, oh my god! Our fields!" she exclaims, then begins to cough. She sounds like she's got quite the cold.

"Ma'am, I need to use your phone, right now!" you yell.

She gives you a blank look. "Did you do this to our field?" she says. She hasn't even seen the robots yet.

"I just really need to use your phone. We have to call someone! We have to warn them!" you shout, and you run inside. Behind you, the woman stands stupefied, looking up and up. She follows you quickly back inside.

"Are those them drones I've heard about?" she screams.

"Where is your goddamn phone?!" you yell, frantically searching in the kitchen, on the tables, dashing glasses off the counter in your haste.

She looks startled and thrusts something into your hands. Finally! You dial 911, because you're not sure who else to call.

"911, what is your emergency?" The operator sounds exhausted.

You barely pause. "There are robots attacking us! They've set the field on fire and I saw them burn up at least one cow. I think they're coming for us!" you shout into the receiver.

"I'm sorry, can you repeat that?" the operator says. She sounds bored.

The woman takes the phone from you and shouts, "Get everyone you've got, Sandra, and send them out to my farm! Yes, yes, it's Betty Womble. It's true, I don't know what's going on but I know we're gonna need help!"

You don't find out what Sandra's answer is, because you hear that strange "woomp" noise again and are thrown to the ground. The roof of the little farmhouse is sheared off, and the terrible oculus of the robot stares down at you.

"RUN!" you yell, and Betty falls backward, barely getting out of the way of a falling post from the ceiling. The alien's focal point turns red, and then the laser lashes out. You dart out the side door, but see that Betty is still in there. Your first impulse is to leave, but you can't just leave her there, she looks so helpless, so you run back in, leaping the circle of flames that used to be the kitchen, and grab Betty by the hand. She's still holding a tissue, and it's wet. Gross.

"Ma'am, we've got to go!" you yell, voice barely audible over the crackling flames.

She nods weakly and gestures down a hallway. You follow her lead, pulling her away, even as the robot pulls at the hole in the roof, making it bigger. You make it to a bedroom. Trapped.

You're standing at the doorway, trying to figure out what to do next, when Betty comes and tugs on your shirtsleeve. She's opened a window, and it's just big enough for you to crawl out. You escape, the smoke turning the whole world hazy, and lean against the house, coughing. "Thanks, Betty," you say in between breaths.

"What is that?" she asks.

You grab her hand and pull her up and away from the house. "I don't know. There was a car accident, and I was in your field trying to find the road, and then I saw this thing fall from the sky. And that's them." You run another few steps, then crouch to hide behind a broken-down pickup truck a little way away from the house. "Betty, do you think the police will come?" you ask.

"I don't know if it'll do any good," she says. She coughs weakly into the sleeve of her nightgown. The sound rattles in her lungs, sounding wet and painful.

"Yeah, I know," you say. You stay in hiding, watching at the robot meticulously picks through the house, burning every piece. Betty hides her face behind her hands, trying not to watch as her home is slowly destroyed.

A few minutes go by before you hear the sirens wail. "Thank god!" you say, but your hope is quickly smashed. The police get out of their cars and uselessly tell the robots to surrender. When they don't, they open fire, but the bullets ping off, as effective as pebbles against a skyscraper. You hear more than see the rest: a robot turns its laser oculus on the officers, and you have to listen as men scream their deaths, burnt alive. You can just see another robot over the remains of the roof, as it approaches the officers and lifts one up.

"Oh my god," Betty says. "Not my Johnny!"

The robot has speared a man through the stomach with one of its long, long legs, and it lifts him up, as if inspecting a fly. The man is clearly badly wounded, but still he struggles, shooting uselessly at the oculus, brave to the last. You look away, but Betty sits transfixed. "Oh my god, my son!" she screams, and you hear a distant thud as the body falls back to Earth.

Betty rushes out from your hiding place, screaming her heartbreak and rage, running straight for the spindly robot. "Betty, no!" you scream, but she can't hear you or doesn't care. She runs straight at the legs of one of the terrifying aliens, and wraps herself around one, like she's trying to pull it away. But the legs are strong, and more stable than they look, and all she does is attract the robot's attention. It lifts her where she's holding on to the leg, bringing her close to the oculus. Bravely holding on, she says, "You bastards killed my boy!" and then she spits right into the robot's laser.

—Which then deploys, burning her to a roasted crisp. You cower behind the truck, willing it all to end.

The heat from the roasting building grows. You:

- Run out into the dark of the field. Turn to the next page.
- Scramble for a police car. Turn to page 197.
- Crawl underneath the pickup. Turn to page 200.

You're far out from town and there is no way you'll outpace the robots. But maybe you can hide—by running where they wouldn't expect. Maybe you can use the darkness to your favor.

You get up and bolt for the fields. The smell of charred flesh makes your stomach twist, and you try not to see the tatters of Betty's body. The spindly robot seems to have moved on, its long legs vaulting lightly over the incinerated building.

You run, run into the dark, the glow of the burnt cows and the screams of the dying officers driving you farther into the darkness. Your legs soon burn with effort and you stumble, vomiting up what little was left in your stomach. Despite the dark, the world spins. Still, you push up, stagger forward.

The screech of tearing metal continues behind you, and your face is wet. For a moment you think maybe it is raining and wonder if the aliens will rust in the moisture, but no, it's tears, and you're crying uncontrollably. It's all too much. Too much.

You're running, blinded by fear and terror and the pitch-black of pure country darkness, when your foot catches on a rock. Your ankle wrenches badly and you fall, face smashing into the dirt. You smell the rich loam of the turned soil mixed with the coppery wetness of blood, probably yours. Your hands claw forward, trying to propel you up and out again, when the air grows suddenly icy.

You find you can't move, and there's a slight whirring sound all around you. You glance up, as much as your neck will allow (which isn't much) and you discover a blueish light up above you...and you're floating? As you watch, paralyzed, you levitate higher and higher, the robots growing small on the ground, spreading out across the countryside to menace the town, the city, perhaps the world?

The last thing you remember is passing through an opening, metal like the inside of a hospital ward, smelling like burning steel.

Turn to page 327.

You look more closely at the creature in front of you. It doesn't seem to be obviously wounded, nothing obviously wrong with it—aside, of course, from having fallen out of space. It's possible that could do some damage, sure. But otherwise it looks fine.

It extends a large hand—is it a hand? It is so pale-white, like roots splayed out—up toward you, and you jump back reflexively. But it doesn't look like it was reaching for you, just reaching, pointing up to the stars. You turn to follow where it points. Is that star...blinking?

"What's wrong? Is that your mothership? Do you need help?" you ask, feeling the tug on your heart strings.

You're startled again when you look back at the face—ugh, still horrible. It seems like maybe one of the felt-like petals is peeling back, so you creep closer. "Yes?" you ask. "What can I do to help?"

You lean in close.

The alien springs its trap, lurching forward with the four petals of its maw spread wide, teeth curling backward toward the gullet, the long thin stigma latching onto your face.

You scream, but it's late, and you're in the middle of nowhere—there is no one to hear your scream. Besides, your voice is propelled deep into the depths of the monster, dying out just a moment before you exhaust yourself from tremendous blood loss.

The parasitic alien drinks you in. It takes its time, slowly digesting your face, then torso, then waist, legs, and feet. There's nothing for anyone to find of you.

The alien grows strong preternaturally quickly. It plants itself deep in the earth, and the rancher who comes out the next day and discovers the mess is quite sure he's never seen a plant quite like *that* before, but he pays it no mind.

That's a mistake. The species is aggressive, highly invasive, adaptive, well-adjusted to the pleasant acidity of our soil and the taint of CO_2 in our air. It proliferates nicely.

By the time the authorities catch on, it's far too late.

Earth is sown with the seeds of space.

THE END

"Gotta get away, gotta get out," you mumble to yourself, mind in a blind panic. *Getaway car,* that's what you need, and so you lurch, sliding on the gravel, over to the nearest police car. It smells kinda like a burnt ham and your stomach starts to heave. Easter brunch will never be the same.

The door squeaks as you haul on the cruiser, and your eyes fill with tears. You're well into the "flight" part of the adrenaline rush, but you can't get gone fast enough and everything is just so *horrible* and *what is even happening?!*

You slump down into the seat, the springs protesting, and struggle to find the keys. Your hand closes on empty air where you would expect to find a jangling key ring, and your heart jumps into your throat—until you realize it's a push-to-start cruiser. So *that's* where all the money from the speeding tickets went.

Wasting no time, you jab the button, the cruiser barking and coughing back to life, sirens blasting. Cop cars have too many switches, and you smack a few before giving up—the robots have turned their attention back to you. Your foot flattens the accelerator and you skid off into the field before correcting and whirling back toward the highway.

One of the robots closer to the road activates its laser or energy beam or whatever—it doesn't matter because it's headed right for you! You can actually see the cheap asphalt on the road bubble as it superheats.

You jerk the wheel to the side, dodging the red beam. You start repeating every prayer you know, but quickly get stuck on "Twinkle, Twinkle Little Star," because that sounded kinda right in the moment but no, oh my god it's coming back!

The little police cruiser has some get-up-and-go, and you use it to try to get-up-and-be-gone. There are a pair of the menacing alien robots on the road ahead, and you twitch at the last possible instant to careen under the one on the right, but the laser from the left has burst your front tire, and the cruiser jolts down, rattling the teeth in your head.

The car won't go much farther, and you're attracting a lot of attention. The rearview mirror shows at least three more of the spindly horrors ambling toward you.

You:

- Leap out of the car. Turn to page 206.
- Floor it. Turn to page 208.

Y̶ou take another look at the moaning little punk kid and decide
she's faking it. Or she's not, but whatever, it's not your job to take
care of her, so you roll back toward the wall and try to cover your ears
with the fleshy part of your upper arm.

The sounds the teenager is making are getting worse, though, and
despite your valiant attempts to ignore her, you finally turn back over.
"Will you shut up already?" you say… just as the girl arches her back
like she's either an incredible contortionist or possessed by a demon.

Unfortunately for you, it's pretty much the last one. The corners of
her mouth tear as something—massive, wormlike, filled with teeth—
erupts out of her throat. It's covered in some kind of mucus and is
segmented like an earthworm, but that's where the similarities end: this
thing is as big around as your arm and *it just came out of that girl*. That
girl, who is now lying in a pathetic empty heap on the ground, her
blood creeping out across the concrete floor toward you.

And the *thing* slithers toward you, its little sucker-like face with its
endless inward-pointing teeth seeming to sense you. You want to
scream, but you have no voice. You want to run, but you're trapped in
this concrete box. You kick at the worm, desperate, as it lunges toward
you, its eyeless body just *knowing* where you are somehow, and it misses
the first strike but immediately recoils again, looking for a second. You
run over to the bars, slipping slightly on the pooling blood, and are just
about to call out when it strikes you in the meat of your ass. You howl
with pain as it winds like a corkscrew, chewing up into your body like a
tornado through a western town.

You're alive while it devours you, for most of it, and every second is
agony.

THE END

There are a few basic responses to danger which all animals exhibit under stress. Best known are "fight or flight," but there's a third option: "freak out and try to hide until the bad thing goes away." It is this option you take, best exemplified by any toddler who tries to defend himself against the monster under his bed by pulling the covers over his head tight enough that suffocation becomes a real and viable risk.

So, don't feel too bad that this is your primary instinct in the face of invading aliens: you still have the mental reaction of a two-year-old.

You throw yourself under the truck and cover your face, because for some reason it feels like if you can't see the robots maybe they also won't see you. You crush your fists into your eyes so hard you can feel your heart beating, and the earth shakes every few moments as the robots lurch past. There seem to be many of them.

But, for some reason, they don't mess with you. Perhaps they don't see you? Maybe they just don't think you're worth laser-ing to a crisp?

Whatever the reason, you manage to survive the night, sweat-soaked, tear-stained, filthy, and smelling more than a little of urine.

You rouse slowly, the smoldering remains of the farmhouse confirming that you weren't just having a really really bad nightmare. In the wash of morning sunlight, you can see the house is practically completely gone—though one wall stands partially intact, a checkered pale blue curtain still dancing in the breeze from the kitchen window. You look away before you can truly get a look at Betty's remains—that's not something you want to remember—and look out over the fields. There are darkened spots out in the corn; that must be where they first landed. And, turning farther, you can see the town, or what would have been the town. A dark smudge of smoke rises from where it should be.

But the robots are nowhere in sight.

You don't know what to do, so you do the only thing you really can: brush yourself off, and start to walk. For lack of anywhere better to go, you head into town.

As you start to walk, you feel like you're in a daze, but your head clears a bit with every step. It's all too real. Your mouth is dry, and you wish you could just sit a spell, wait for someone to come get you. But who would get you? No one knows where you are, and even if they did, judging from the smoke, they have more pressing problems. So you just keep walking, trying to ignore the heat as the sun rises, wondering where the robots are now, feeling like you're going to be incinerated at any moment.

The pavement rolls away under your feet. It wouldn't have been a bad walk, most days, but today it seems like it goes far too long. Your heart feels heavy in your chest, and your eyes hurt from continually scanning the horizon.

But you arrive.

The town is a mess. Worse than the farm was, even. A dog, one of those pedigree poodle mix-breeds, lays in two pieces halfway out of a shrub, its middle charred and unrecognizable, its fur an ashy grey-black. The brick of buildings didn't burn, but roofs are gone, scorch marks etched across the side. The old painted logo for the soda company looks like it has been scratched out with marker, except the peeling paint is still smoking.

Despite all that, there is hope. A cardinal lands in a half-burnt tree overhead, singing—quietly, yes, but still singing. As you walk a little farther in, you find you aren't the only survivor. There's a man, sitting still as a statue, on the rubble of what may have been a dentist's office, his scrubs covered in debris but his dreadlocks still tied neatly back. As you walk closer, two women walk up. "Hey, Ray, I found some candy in the machine..." the older one says. She looks like your aunt, except a bit sturdier. You feel like maybe you could hug her and that would be okay.

The other woman is younger, maybe 19, still all awkward elbows and angles, a look that isn't helped by her arms full of chocolate bars and chips. She looks stunned.

They notice you, and even Ray turns to look your direction.

You open your mouth to speak, but what do you say? "I...I'm so glad I'm not the only one alive," you say, the last words coming out as a choking cry. The older woman, the one you want to hug, comes by and pats you gently on the shoulder.

"We are, too," she says, softly. "Here hon, are you hungry?" She pries a bag of chips from the other woman's hands and presses them into yours. "I'm Esther," she says, after you've had a moment to compose yourself. "This is Ray"—he glances up, not saying a word—"and this is Lily."

Lily drops her loot in a heap and turns to wave. "Kinda a bad day around here," she says. "But then, looks like you've had it just as bad."

"It was awful," you say, and now that you have someone to talk to, that you know you didn't just have a horrible nightmare, you find the words pouring out of you. "They came out of the sky. There were so many of them, and they just...they burnt a woman, right in front of me. Her name was Betty. And they just killed her, like it was nothing. They killed her...and the police? They're dead. They're all dead." Your body shakes with wracking, painful sobs. Esther just hugs you to her, and you both cry a moment. The dust from her blouse gets into your nose and makes the crying worse. Lily stands off to the side, looking away, embarrassed. Ray still doesn't react.

It takes a moment for the tears to dry up, and you wipe your eyes with the back of one hand. Ray stands slowly, and hands you a chocolate bar.

"You'll feel better after you've eaten something," he says. His eyes have a blank depth to them, and you nod so you don't have to meet his gaze.

The others tell you what happened to them, too. Esther and Lily were neighbors, the old apartments around the corner. A glance down the street shows there's not much of the first floor left, and the second floor is a ghost of itself. Ray is a dental assistant—was a dental assistant? —and he was at the office assisting with a surgery. Lily tells most of his story; he can't seem to bear it. The oral surgeon was doing an early-morning wisdom teeth removal, and when the robots came, the laser happened to get near the nitrous tank. The dental office exploded. Ray survived because he was on the other side of the building, walking back with extra supplies.

He doesn't want to talk about it.

No one knows where the aliens have gone.

The day ticks onward, there's an exhausted restlessness about it. It's like when that tornado hit the edge of town awhile back. Yes, it was sad, but it was also a mess, and that compelled some folks to get right to work cleaning. Lily and Esther seem to be that sort. They set out to dig around in the debris piles that used to be the apartments, looking for useful things. Ray helps sluggishly, but his mind is somewhere else entirely. At one point, about an hour in, Lily starts to cry when she pulls out a soft pink child's toy. It takes a while, but she eventually explains it was hers, has been since forever. She hugs it close the rest of the day, as if afraid to let go of it again.

"What are we even doing?" you ask, about midday. "This is pointless."

"We've got to be ready," Esther says, stubborn.

"For what?" Ray says, so quiet he's hard to hear.

"They might come back!" You realize, too late, that you're yelling.

Lily looks from you to Esther nervously, as if your mention of the wicked-legged robots might bring them back.

Esther sets her fists on her hips. "What would you have us do? They're not here, and neither is help of any kind. We're all we've got going for us so far, so your bad attitude isn't helping anything!"

Now that you've been called out, you're not sure what to say.

After a moment, you suggest:

- Finding a way out of town. Maybe you can warn other people, get the word out. Turn to page 167.
- Hunkering down somewhere safe. The robots could be back tonight. Turn to page 209.
- Fighting back. No way Earth should go down without a fight! Turn to page 212.

The metal looks smooth, seamless, and despite the destruction around it, it appears cool to the touch. You hover your hand over it, just in case, but no heat radiates off. You touch it gently; the metal is as smooth as glass. You run your hand along the side, admiring the design. It doesn't seem like a missile, or even a rocket. It looks like a river stone, or some new wave sleep pod or something. It has a nice 1940s aesthetic to it, while still seeming modern, even futuristic.

"What is it?" you say to yourself.

You continue running your hand up the object when suddenly, halfway up, something illuminates under your fingers. You jerk back, but it's just a few symbols, beautiful shapes that mean nothing to you. Cyrillic? Greek? It isn't Spanish, that's for sure. You place your hand over the glowing marks, a soft chime sounds, and then the pod begins to open. You scramble back, certain you're going to be blown to smithereens, as the top of the pod seamlessly slides into the sides and away. Inside, a soft-looking lining and...

A baby?

"What the hell?!" you exclaim, and curiosity gets the better of you. You approach the pod and yes, that's a baby, most definitely. It wiggles and blinks its eyes, its little fists clenching and flailing as it cries.

"Uhhh," you say. "Don't cry, baby from space." For some reason, that doesn't sound particularly reassuring. The infant is working itself into a solid fit, big raindrop tears sliding down its face, and it sure has some lungs—the crying is getting loud enough to wake the neighbors, and they're at least a half-mile away.

"Okay, okay," you tell the baby. "I'll get you." You're not particularly good with kids, but you manage to get a grip on the squirmy little creature and pull it out. That's when the pod activates again. "You have found our son," a soothing voice says. "Please, care for him. He is the last of our people." And then the message keeps going, but it's mangled, garbled, like a radio transmission through a bad storm, except you think you hear crashes, maybe screams, in the background.

The baby starts to cry again. You grab the blanket from the pod in case the baby is cold instead of just having an existential crisis about being the last of his kind.

"Wow, your parents just abandoned you, huh? In a weird space-pod? That sucks, little guy," you say in your best baby-voice. "Are you an alien? You don't look like an alien." You turn the baby around, checking for any "extra" parts: nope, no tail, no hooves, no tentacles (that you can see outside of the cloth diaper, anyway. Cloth diapers. Man, his parents must have really been space-hippies or something).

You carry the little boy back out of the field, debating your next move. He settles fairly quickly, falling asleep draped across your shoulder like a tiny drunk person. By the time you get home, you've decided what to do.

You're going to:

- Drop the kid off at the fire station. You're not ready for this responsibility! Turn to page 181.
- Raise him as your own. Your parents have been on you about having grandkids for a while now. Turn to page 186.
- Tell the media. Neglectful parents just can't get away with shit like this. Turn to page 217.

For a split second you remember all those scenes from old movies where the good guy takes a heroic leap from the car. *That's it*, you think, and then you don't think anymore, you just do it. Grabbing the handle as you slam your shoulder into the door, you force your way out.

The cruiser was moving pretty fast—about 70, you'd guess—and you aren't exactly action-hero material on your best days. Maybe it was adrenaline, or pure luck, or maybe you are just that good, but for whatever stupid reason, it works. You jump to safety...

Kinda. You threw yourself against the door so hard you did make it all the way out of the vehicle, but you didn't quite get enough of a roll to get entirely clear, and the momentum throws you into a chaotic tumble. The ground is mostly flat but that doesn't mean it's painless, and you bump and skitter across the field, breaking at least two ribs, fracturing your right femur, right hand, several fingers, your left elbow, your clavicle, and wrenching at least one foot. And you're bleeding from somewhere above your eye and all down your legs and arms.

But what does that matter? You lived!

And you watch for a glorious moment while the invading robots continue following the screeching patrol car, which manages to go another bit forward on the highway before two of the lasers converge. There's a ripping, burbling scream, like the metal itself is in agony, and then the car is nothing but an incinerated hulk. The sirens have given out, but the lights flash a few more times before the electrical wiring burns up, too.

You lay there, a human wreck to match the destroyed car—but alive! Alive!—and try to remember if you've ever felt anything other than pain. Everything hurts.

You lay there in the dark for some time, listening to the robots destroying your town. There were sirens once, like for the tornadoes, but they were quickly cut off. Wires snap, like in that storm a few months back, and you feel rather than see the telephone poles crashing down.

Everything is fuzzy, so you can't pin down an exact moment that you drifted away, can't tell if it's been five minutes or five hours, but the next time you open your eyes, you find yourself staring straight up into sky blue. But not a sky blue like you're used to seeing, like the actual sky. No this is the sky blue of a children's drawing, overly bright.

It hurts your eyes and you squint against it, and then it lifts you. That doesn't make sense, you must be dreaming, but you're not flying, you're just...being lifted.

Everything hurts. It's not like it can get any worse, right?

You black out.

Turn to page 270.

You slam the accelerator all the way to the floor, your stomach rushing back to meet the seat behind you as you speed forward. Speed is all you have, it's the only way you could maybe possibly survive this. So you speed, hands gripping the steering wheel as you try not to look behind you. If you look back, you'll be a pillar of ash before you know it.

You try to stay to the road, but the robots seem to have that figured out, and one lances the pavement in front of you. The black asphalt melts instantly, turning the road ahead into a sticky morass. Your limping wheels can't handle it, and you jolt directly into the goo. Panicking, you twist the wheel away, sending the cruiser into a roll.

You didn't put on a seatbelt. The roll hurls you against the roof, the side panel, the seat, and finally against the now blown-out windshield, throwing you out of the cruiser, where you land helpless, broken, on a line of white dashed road paint. Your eyes barely stay open while you see the robots approach.

The heat from the laser is unfathomable, but at least it's over in an instant.

THE END

"We need to make ourselves safe, first and foremost," you say. "They may come back tonight, and I don't exactly want to be sleeping out under the stars waiting for them."

"Yeah, Esther, where are we going to sleep tonight? My apartment is gone," Lily says, her voice just a fraction from cracking again. She hugs the pink animal. It looks like it might have once been a platypus, before years of love wore it down a bit.

Esther toes the dirt. "You're right. We can do busywork from now to kingdom come, but we've got to make sure we cover the basics. What do you want to do?"

"I guess we need to start with a place. Preferably one that won't burn much?" you say. Most of the town was built with cheap wood; you cast about, trying to think of any building sturdier.

"I know one," Ray says. Without another word he gets up and trudges down the street. For lack of anything else, you and the others follow him.

He leads you onto the school grounds; you recognize the sign out front, which still reads "Today's Lunch: Jambalaya or Chicken Nuggets!" Luckily—if you can say such a thing—the attacks came at daybreak, before the kids were at the building. Imagining all those kids— you try not to think about it.

Ray leads you down a hallway, to a door still nestled in the wall. He tries the handle, but the door is locked. He steps back then drives a shoulder hard into the door, jolting it out of the frame. He steps back, gesturing you in. There are steps leading down, and in the half-shadows you can see it's a boiler room. "Used to sneak down here with Sophie during lunch. No one would come lookin' for a bit..." he sounds wistful, but says no more.

The room is underground, which seems a little safer. Sure, there's a chance the roof will cave in, but it's better than the other places in town. You shrug and turn to the others: "Welcome home."

The rest of the day is devoted to getting something to eat and trying to soften the floor a bit, but by dusk it doesn't matter anyway; you're all exhausted. You lean into a corner and close your eyes.

You wake once in the night, visions of the robot's laser coming for you filling your mind, but it's just a dream. Everything is quiet. You go back to sleep.

Over the next week, you manage to make the boiler room

something close to comfortable. Lily discovers the convenience store down the street is mostly intact, so you've got your fill of spicy Cheetos and Gatorade. The floor becomes a rambling nest of blankets, sleeping bags, even a mattress that Esther grumblingly lugged in from somewhere after complaining that the ground was too hard on her back. Ray found a cell phone early the second morning, but there was no signal.

Two days later, you notice you haven't heard any planes in a while.

But there is still no sign of the robots, either.

Life carries on, in its way, for a time. It's hard to know exactly how long when the days all run together, but the weather turns sharper, and the nights seem long, long. By now, you've started to patch up the town, best as you can. The bodies you've burned, after the smell started to set in. It was hard at first, but you all became inured to the grim reality of it. It's a somber funeral.

Next are the buildings. The boiler room, so appealing at first, is damp, and when the danger seems passed you find yourself longing for old comforts. Lily feels the same, and it turns out she's found the janitor's closet. You break out the hammers and work long hours tearing off broken siding, trying to patch up walls. Even though you've never done this kind of work before, it feels productive, so you keep at it. You have a reasonable shack, with a real bed, though you pile on the blankets and keep a fire burning in a big barrel you found. Ray and Esther get set up in the room next door, and soon your little community has a rhythm to it.

You celebrate Christmas, hanging a sock for each of you at the end of your bed. Everyone puts something in: hair loops, a pack of noodle soup, a child's scarf. It's a meager celebration, but earnest. You find yourself thinking if only you had a real chimney, perhaps Santa or someone would come and save you from all of this. But you have no chimney, and the roof you look up to at night leaks and whistles in the wind.

It's a few days after that when you hear the sound. The whirring. It's just like in your nightmares, but you're long past them now.

No, you're really hearing it. You clutch the blankets to your chest and look out the window. In the dark you see Ray standing, staring out.

"They're here," he says, and your stomach goes cold.

You spring out of bed and shake first Esther, then Lily, awake, hushing them into silence.

"We've got to go," you whisper as loud as you dare. Even in the faint light you can see the fear in their eyes.

Silently, Ray swings open the door. Silhouetted there, at the end of the street, is the monster. Its one terrible oculus skims back and forth, staring at the washing hung out to dry. Crouching low, you hurry, single-file, back toward the boiler room, a mad dash across a street, feeling far, far too exposed.

The door creaks as you open it, and you wince to the core. "Hurry!" you whisper, and Esther slides past you.

That's when you hear it, behind you and slightly up. Hidden in the dark of the new moon, a saucer. A gentle "wub wub wub" sounds, and you are overcome by a strange tingling sensation as you fall unconscious.

Turn to page 327.

Look, they caught you off guard last night, but that doesn't mean you're going to take an alien invasion sitting down. "We need to fight them!" you insist.

The other three look at you dubiously.

"Are you serious?" Ray asks. "How exactly do you recommend we fight robots who can shoot lasers through buildings? When all we've got are some bags of chips!"

"Well, yeah, that's a problem, but it's a temporary one," you insist. "We've just got to go alert the National Guard or something. Until then, I vote we find some way to arm ourselves!"

"I am pretty handy with a shotgun," Esther offers.

"That's the spirit, Esther!" you say, cheering. "We can run or we can hide but there is another choice: we can fight back! We can send those bastards back to the sky riddled with holes!"

"Where do we start?" Lily says.

"Ugh, this is probably a bad idea," Ray says. "But I guess I'd rather be with you idiots when this starts than somewhere else."

"Good lad," Esther says approvingly. "Right, I bet we can find some decent firearms in the houses. Let's just take a look."

The next three hours are a labor-intensive scavenger hunt, carefully turning over rubble to find something that might damage a 50-foot robot. Lily discovers a gun safe, still locked. Ray helps her haul it out of the dirt, and the two spend the next hour guessing at the combination until you happen to open a desk drawer from the house where they found it and discover it written down on a sticky note on the inside. That provides a Colt handgun for Ray and a hunting rifle for you. Lily dusts off the Taser she'd hidden in her own apartment in case a date ever got too frisky, and Esther is able to find her shotgun. There's not much in the way of ammo, but none of you other than Esther really have much experience anyway.

Still, you feel better now that you have some way to fight back.

You're all exhausted and filthy to the core. You make a little pile of found blankets and a pillow on what used to be the front porch of an office building of some kind, and get some sleep.

The next morning you are hungry as heck and still itching to do something. You're up at first light and go scavenge some breakfast from the convenience store on the corner, which survived more or less intact. When you return to your little band of survivors, you plop down with your pile of bear claws and loudly crinkle the wrappers until Ray wakes up.

"You seriously couldn't let us sleep?!" he says, but you don't mind his temper. You pass him a bear claw and a taquito. Sure, it's cold, but it's not like it was fine dining in the best of times. Still delicious, though.

You repeat the procedure with Lily and Esther, though the latter still takes far longer to get up and moving than you'd like. When everyone is finally up and functioning, you announce, "We're going to the nearest base today."

"We're what?" Lily asks.

"We're just going to drive over to the nearest base. I think there's one an hour away, right?" You look around for confirmation.

"I think I did hear that," Esther says after a moment. "Out past the lake, right? They sometimes do trainings?"

"Yes, that's it! We're just going to drive out and offer to help!"

"You sound crazy!" Ray says.

Shockingly, it's Lily who turns on him. "Do you have a better plan?"

"Well...no," Ray says, petulant. After a moment he adds, "Fine. But when things get bad, please everyone remember this: I told you so."

You roll your eyes at his foolishness and get your posse organized for the road. It doesn't take long, and soon you're piled into a dusty old SUV Esther finds. "This car belonged to my neighbor," she says quietly. "He won't mind now." A pause, then, "Besides, he never would keep his music down at night, I swear."

You turn out into the road and start to drive. It feels almost like a family road trip, like maybe you should break into "Old MacDonald Had a Farm" or play "I Spy" to pass the time.

But you don't. Instead you try to find a radio station, but give up after a few minutes: they're all static.

The others doze in the back, but you just grip the steering wheel tighter and keep driving, even after it gets dark.

A deer skitters across the road in front of you, its eyes wide glowing saucers. The thought makes your heart pound, and you jerk the wheel to dodge the animal. The SUV threatens to roll and there is a general anxious cry from your passengers, but you pull the car to a safe stop. You close your eyes, but you can still remember the robots, the way you were nothing against their terrible power.

As you're trying to catch your breath, Lily reaches up from the seat behind you. "Hey, it's okay," she says quietly. "Why don't you let one of us take a turn?"

"I... I...I'm okay," you stammer out, and it doesn't sound believable even to you.

"I like to drive, let me," Ray says, and pulls you gently out of the way.

"I... I thought I saw them," you say.

"It was just a deer, dear," Esther says, and you let her soothe you.

"Yeah. Yeah, okay," you say. "I probably need some sleep."

You climb back into the back seat and Ray spends a moment fastidiously checking the mirrors and adjusting his seat. He's just shifting into gear when you hear it: a gentle whirring.

You look up and out the window, holding your breath. No, it can't possibly be...

"Oh my gawd," Esther says. "It's them!"

Ray slams on the brakes, sending you jerking against your seatbelt. You fumble with the clasp and scramble forward to the pile of guns, grabbing the rifle. Not taking a second to check on the others, you climb out of the car.

There it is. One—no, a herd of those thin-legged one-eyed bastards, striding through the trees. They don't seem to have noticed you; they're just moving. While you watch, one deploys its laser at something on the ground. The deer vaporizes.

You pull the rifle to your shoulder and squint down the barrel, trying to aim for the laser eye. You pull the trigger, and the gun kicks back hard against your shoulder, shoving you back. The shot is deafening, and for a moment you're confused. Nothing happened. Why didn't anything happen?

Either you missed or the bullet can't hurt them, but one thing did change: it noticed you.

"Shit shit shit shit," Ray says. "Get in the car!"

As the red oculus turns to consider you, its long legs telescoping down the black highway in your direction, you think maybe running is a good idea after all and you throw yourself back into the car. Ray peels out, and the SUV fishtails to gain traction on the pavement.

You're looking at it out the back window when the robot activates its laser. For a split second, the light is a magnificent glowing red...

...until it slices clean through the SUV, starting with the back window.

THE END

The little brindle dog leads her pack out into the field. Out of nowhere, every single dog—from the German shepherd all the way down to a Chihuahua puppy—begins digging, clustered in a large circle. (The little ones are sometimes bowled over by the enthusiasm and large feet of the big dogs, but that doesn't stop them.) After an awkward moment, you shoulder in and scoop away some of the thick dirt with your hands. When the brindle catches your eye, you'd swear she's smiling approvingly.

The digging goes on for a long time, long enough for you to seriously wonder what you are doing out here in a field with a bunch of stolen dogs, but then, one dog breaks through—and disappears. But not down a hole: below is an opalescent surface, almost like a mirror, except the reflection is dark. A one-way mirror, maybe.

"Um," you begin, but the brindle cuts you off, and you realize she's speaking to everyone.

"Are you ready to see your home, children?" she says, looking adoringly at the puppies. Then she turns to the other adult dogs, ending her gaze with you, and says, "And the rest of you, you're sure you wish to come with me?"

One enthusiastic hound tilts his square head back into a loud howl, and soon all the dogs are howling, and the excitement builds inside you until you also lean back and yell up into the sky! "Aaaaoooooo!" you howl, and the sound fills you with inexorable joy.

The little alien waits happily until everyone is howled out, then noses down toward the hole. "Then follow me," she says, and leaps into the apparently solid surface, vanishing instantly beyond, as if it were quicksand or very dark water; there's not a ripple or motion at all in the translucent substance below.

In bunches at first, then one by one, the dogs slip down into the hole.

You stand up, staring into the night sky all around you. The air is still, smelling of dog, and dirt, and damp hay. Dawn is about to break over the hill just over there. It's been a pretty good world, you think.

And then you leap into the hole with both feet.

Go to page 75.

The sun is almost up and you've done a serious number on the satellite; it's not worth staying to try to dig out anything else. You grab your haul—it's a real armful, and panels keep trying to slip away—and begin the long walk back home. The ground is uneven, and you're eager to get as far away as possible before someone figures out what was out there—does NASA track that shit?

You walk for a while, maybe twenty minutes, before you come to the edge of town. Your arms ache from carrying all this, and you just want to sit down. But people are starting to move around now, and you're going to need to find some way to look less bizarre. There's a trailer ahead, one of those big green wheeled trash bins outside. Trying to look casual, you walk up and flip the lid open to peer inside. It reeks of cat piss, but is empty. That'll work. You dump your solar cells inside, close the lid, and rumble off down the street with the trash bin, as if it is perfectly normal to take your trash for a little walk around the neighborhood after a morning coffee. Totally normal.

Now that you're doing a great job blending in, you take a moment to consider what you should do with your stuff. Sell them on eBay? No, if someone is looking for this stuff, they'll probably look there. It's not like listings for "satellite solar cells" come up every day, after all. Maybe you can take them apart? See how they work, maybe, sell the components? You've taken a toaster apart once, so it's probably not that hard, right? Or maybe you should just trick out a building with them, get free power? Hey, maybe you could get grow lights!

Finally, you're back at your apartment. You trudge up the stairs, leaving the green bin by the curb, and dump the solar cells on your couch.

For now, you're taking a nap, but when you get up you're going to start right away on:

- Taking the stuff apart. Turn to page 220.
- Setting up a grower's shed. Turn to page 222.

By now you've figured out that the pod you found this kid in couldn't possibly have come from space. That would just be crazy. No, it's much more likely that it's some weird child abandonment or missing kid situation compounded by the incredible amount of alcohol you consumed last night.

Which means the only logical course of action is letting someone know that their kid has been found.

You call the local news station, the one that is most likely to report on crazy updates: Channel 4. (They're always running pieces like "You'll Never Believe What We Found in the Sewers" or "Top 10 Reasons Your Vote Totally Doesn't Matter." You're counting on them being suckers for a piece like this.)

"Channel 4 News, More Than Can Be Believed, Greg here, how may I direct your call?" overly cheerful Greg-at-Channel-Four-News says after only two rings on the news station's line.

"Hi, uh, Greg," you stammer. "I think I've got a story Channel 4 might be interested in. Someone abandoned a baby in a field last night."

"Woah, that sounds crazy!" Greg says, still overly positive about the whole interaction. "Can you tell me more?"

You give Greg the rough rundown of the night; you heard a sound, went to investigate, found a baby in a weird metal box, etc. "What I'm saying, Greg, is this kid deserves to find his way home. Or, if that's not possible, his deadbeat parents need to be brought to justice, you know what I mean?"

"Oh, absolutely, I'll send a reporter out immediately," Greg says.

Not 15 minutes later, you have a knock on your door (saving you from having to figure out how to change a diaper, ick). It's Cliff Wallace, the Channel 4 anchorman. Wow does he have a distinguished chin! A chin like that makes you really respect a man. Makes him seem trustworthy.

"Hi, Cliff, so great you could come out, so great to meet you!" you gush.

He shakes your hand with a limp clasp. "Mm, yeah, I hear you've found a baby. Well hello there, little guy!" he says, poking the baby on your hip with a finger. "Whew, that's one smelly diaper!"

"Yeah," you say, annoyed that Cliff is already off task. You repeat your story to him, and he nods seriously the whole time.

"Let's just get the little guy cleaned up a little," Cliff says, taking the baby out of your arms and walking him over to your wobbly dining table, "then we'll film the piece. We'll find your parents, little guy, yes we will, yes, yes we will."

What's weird about Cliff's baby talk is he still uses his deep baritone announcer voice. It's off-putting. You almost expect the baby to respond with an equally TV-reporter-esque "back to the choppers, Cliff," or some such.

You film the segment, which Cliff assures you is going to pull on the heartstrings of everyone in the county. He wants you to come back to the station with him, to film more heartfelt pleas for the parents to come forward, particularly since the police will soon get wind of it and might do something stupid like take the kid into protective custody. "We're going to find this sweet baby boy's parents," Cliff says. "And also win me a Pulitzer. Let's go."

The first segment interrupts the big football game, ensuring everyone will both see it and immediately hate it. But hopefully, Cliff says, they'll turn their hatred to the missing parents. Sure enough, right after the broadcast the calls start coming in. It seems like everyone in the county has someone they suspect of child abandonment. Most of the calls Greg gets are pure nonsense, but then the police roll in and Deputy Collins takes over the investigation and has three officers tasked with answering the calls. She pulls you aside for questioning.

"You're saying you just found a baby in a field last night?" she asks. "And your first thought was not to call the police but to call the media?"

"I figured someone would be looking for him," you lie sheepishly. When you saw that baby, you saw your chance at 15 minutes of stolen fame, and Deputy Collins looks like she can tell. "What's really important is that he goes somewhere safe."

"Mm-hmm," Collins says. "You oughta feel lucky I believe you or I could have you arrested for kidnapping."

You go a little pale. "Just want to get this kid home safe is all," you say.

"Uh huh. Which is why you'll now turn him over to police custody, right?" The fire in Deputy Collins' eyes says she's not joking around.

"Yes ma'am!" you say, and hand the kid to her. Good. Now you won't be on diaper duty any longer.

Collins takes the kid out, and you sit there like an ass in the TV station while people bustle around you doing actually important things.

It doesn't even take that long, but the story is weirder than even you could have predicted. A neighbor calls in to report that the family a block down had built a weird cannon-type deal. An older brother, thinking it was a hilarious joke, had constructed the metal bathtub pod you'd found the baby in, and he'd bundled baby brother in there with some hokey message (there was a tape recorder underneath the blanket, no science fiction required) and then, like a moron or an incredibly bored psychotic country kid, he had loaded the pod into the big cannon in the middle of the night when the baby wouldn't stop crying and BOOM. Baby from space.

It's amazing the kid survived, really. He shouldn't have. He's, like, some kind of super-baby.

The older brother gets hauled off to jail for a few months, the parents are glad to have the baby back, and you achieve a decent level of internet fame, though not for what you expected: your announcement video gets remixed into a song, which goes viral. You're the laughing stock of town for a year.

So much for your hero's journey.

THE END

You get settled, and over the next week spend a little time each day fiddling with the solar cells. You break one in half the first time you try to pry it apart, despite your best efforts. Weirdly, the panels don't look like what your quick Google search had suggested they would. They're each filled with wires, and a small chip? Maybe it's just because they're old. How long do satellites stay in space, anyway? Or maybe it's old Soviet tech and they just used whatever on hand to rig something together. Either way, it's taking longer than you expected.

Three weeks after the crash, you haven't heard anyone talk about it. You figure maybe the farmer just dragged it off to a dump somewhere and that was that. You're bored of this solar cell stuff, and it looks like you did all that work for nothing, so you've left the broken pieces just scattered across your kitchen counter, dotted with molding cereal bowls and a greasy pizza box.

There's a knock on your door.

Damnit, you didn't order food! Gah, people should just know to text before dropping by! You pause your game angrily and stomp to the door, unlocking it and jerking it open in one quick movement.

"YES?" you snarl.

Standing in your apartment's soulless concrete hallway are two people in nondescript suits. They are unruffled by your anger. "Hello," the one on the right, a guy who looks like he could bench press the moon, says, using your first name. How did he know your name? And why are they wearing those sunglasses? It's 10 at night. What a tool. He says, "We'd like to talk to you for a minute."

Your anger is starting to be replaced by anxiety, but you say, "Yeah, what do you want?" trying to keep it forceful.

"We think you may have found something we lost," the woman on the right says. "We're just here to pick it up."

"Can we come in? Great," the guy says, pushing past you and into your apartment. "Look at this, it's all right here! Perfect."

"Hey, you can't just come in here!"

"Don't worry about it, kid, we're with the government," the guy says, flashing a badge, too fast for you to see what it says.

The woman breezes past you, too. "Looks like a mess. Oh, do you see that? All the transducing electrophases have been pulled out! Oh shit, do you realize how close you came to dying?" she asks you. "If you'd managed to break that open—as you were clearly trying to! — we'd have been cleaning your guts off the walls like old spaghetti. I hate doing that. And this place is just filthy! Do you never clean?"

You're a little out of your depths here, and these people are in your place and aren't making any sense. "Uhhh," you say.

"What my partner here is trying to say," the man says, "is we'll be taking all this, okay?"

"Wha..." you start, then remember all those episodes of *Law & Order*. "Hey, don't you need like a warrant or something?"

"They never make this easy, do they?" the dude says to his partner, who is scooping up all the bits of plastic and metal and wire and whatnot from your countertop. "Hey, can you look over here?" he says.

You wake up from your couch. What a bizarre dream! You had one too many last night, that's for sure, and it was embarrassing when those accountants had to come by. Why were accountants here, you wonder, trying to remember. The memory is like a missing tooth; you pry at the spot that feels wrong, but there's just nothing there. They were wearing suits...

Anyway, you get up and start to clean your apartment. Why did you ever let it get this filthy? That's it, you're turning over a new leaf, starting today.

THE END

You've only ever dabbled in mary jane recreationally, just a few times. But you hear it's a really great source of income and you have a decently green thumb, so why not? Plus it'll probably be totally legal in a few years anyway, so you're just making a good business decision by starting now. And with these solar panels, you won't even have a problem with electricity!

This is probably the best plan you've ever come up with.

It takes a few weeks—longer than you'd like, really, but you tell yourself it gives any governmental folk who might be looking for lost satellite paneling time to forget about you—but you pull together the necessary research, buy a few hydroponic supplies, get yourself a starter kit to grow reefer in your closet. You wire up the solar panels real nice one evening by climbing out on your balcony and making a jump-and-grab to the roof. Maintenance here sucks, so they'll probably never check, but you string up some Christmas lights anyway in case someone asks about the extension cord going to your roof. After that, you just gotta wait for the little beauties to grow.

It's February before you have your first harvest, and it's just a tiny bit. You got the "Outta This World" variety, a new blend, cutting edge, man, and you're eager, after all this investment, to try some. So after work one day you come home, get comfortable on the couch, pick a movie, and light up.

The smoke curls into your mouth and you hold it for a moment, relishing the taste. It tastes like some kind of smoky fruit, maybe? But whew, there it is. The fuzzy, soft relaxation drifts into your body. You let the haze drift over you. Oh, so worth it. The movie, some old invader from outer space flick or whatever (it seemed appropriate, okay?) plays in the background, but you let yourself just relax against it.

Maybe it's the blasters in the movie or something, but a bit later you start to get anxious, a tendril of panic uncurling from somewhere near your stomach. Your heart races, your mind clouds with disjointed worries. Did you leave the stove on? Is your whole apartment going to burn down—with you in it? Is this a bad trip? Are you doing it wrong? You probably are, oh man why didn't you call a buddy before you started this tonight, you need someone to talk you down. The alien on the screen turns its blaster toward the TV and oh god they're gonna pull the trigger and you're going to get vaporized.

WHAM.

Your apartment's front door slams open behind you, and you crumple to the floor in front of your couch, covering your head, whimpering in terror.

Later, you don't remember for sure exactly what happened. The police came in, apparently because one of your neighbors—the busybodies next door, probably—reported smoke in your apartment, and the fire department is damned slow around here, so they came in, found you cowering and surrounded by weed-smoking paraphernalia that still is totally illegal. They took your stuff as evidence, including all your solar cells you had illegally rigged to the roof you didn't own, and dragged you to the precinct, supposedly so you don't hurt yourself or anyone, and left you in a cell. There's not much going on in this town, and a drug bust is a nice way to make a quick buck, so you have to pay some fines and they end up keeping every bit of your grow startup. They burn the weed in the back of the station; probably liked it, too.

But the part that gets you to kick the habit, never smoke again, isn't at all about getting caught or the fine or the legal crap. No, it's this— and it's not something you tell anyone, because it sounds crazy, and maybe it was just some element of the drug or whatever, but you really don't think so—when that cop looked you in the eye after coming in, you swear, swear upon a stack of Bibles, that you could see into him. That his eyes were not human, but glass, and inside you could see the swirl of the stars, of galaxies, and, deep past all that beauty and color, were rows upon rows of teeth, with a threat you didn't see but you felt in your heart, that if you didn't back off right now you'd be devoured, helpless against this man, this *alien*, this visitor from another plane.

Of course, there's no proof at all, but you can't shake the feeling, and sometimes, late at night, you open your eyes in the dark of the bedroom and see those eyes, that unending terror, again.

THE END

You read somewhere that an animal, even a human, is more likely to come to you if you are sitting quietly, acting nonthreatening. And it's not like you really have anything else to do, so you lower yourself slowly to the ground—no sudden movements—and rest your hands on your crossed legs. You just...watch.

The creature observes this closely for a long moment. After it has apparently decided you aren't going to do anything weird, it turns back toward the wrecked craft. As you watch, it sniffles around, then digs for a moment. It seems like maybe it is intelligent? But then it's hard to tell exactly what is going on in the dark out there. It does seem to be looking for something, though.

It's so tempting to get up and help it. But no, that would just startle it, and then you'd never know what was happening. You try to remember you're basically David Attenborough right now.

You imagine the monologue: "Here we have the creature. It appears to be looking for something. You'll note the extra limbs; it is believed these help with multi-tasking. It must listen to the call of its species..."

The alien stops and stares at you. You realize your mouth is open; crap, you were narrating aloud in your bad British accent! Shit!

The alien hefts itself up on its back legs and walks toward you. Now you can see it has apparently found whatever it was looking for. It's a brightly colored rectangle, pulsing with a greenish light. It looks...ominous.

A few yards away, it stops. It works its jaw, then a sound comes out: "hello!"

You stare back in alarm. It can speak English?!

"Um," you say.

Working its jaw tremendously, the creature speaks again: "Take me... to... your...leader."

Weirdly, its voice changes with nearly every word. Even worse, those voices sound...familiar.

"What?" you ask.

"Take...me to...your...leader. Isn't...that what...one...says?"

You recognized that voice, that voice when it said "leader." It sounds like Lucy Ricardo, of all people, and some of those other sounds were very much like 1940s actors.

"Um, I guess I can," you say.

You stand up, slowly, but the creature continues to menace you with the glowy box thing. "Easy, easy, I have to get up if I'm going to take you anywhere."

Where are you going to take this thing? Are you really expected to have a direct line to someone for it to try to talk to?

That's when it occurs to you. You're going to take it to:

- Your house. Sure, why not? You can probably represent the human race okay, right? Turn to page 229.
- Old master Moki. He's got gravitas. He'll seem official. Turn to page 233.
- The White House. It's a long drive, but it's just what you have to do. The president can fix this. Turn to page 238.

No one is going to believe you—unless you take a picture! You've just got to document this and post it on your blog! You take out your phone and snap a shot—there's the little monster standing near the spaceship. The flash blinds you for a second, but you stare at the screen; looks like a good one. You raise your phone to take another one, and suddenly the creature is right up on you, reaching for you with its seven monstrous arms.

"AHHH!" you scream, and it knocks you backward. You pull your hands back to protect your face, but it lunges again, toward your hand. It pries your phone out of your hand with its sharp claws, and you curl up in a ball. You glance up again just as it opens its mouth almost all the way flat and drops your phone into its mouth.

Crunch.

No more phone.

Momentarily forgetting you are afraid, you say, "Hey, that was mine!"

The alien turns its huge black eyes on you. "But I hope you liked it as a snack...I can get another one, it's no big deal..."

You try to back up, scrabbling against the dirt.

It hisses at you, and you cower behind your arms again.

When it gets a bit away from you, you crawl to your feet. It watches you, idly. You turn and run, and it begins to chase you, its short legs more effective across the flat ground than you would have ever guessed. Every time you look back, you can see that smile, those dangerous teeth, grinning at you in the dark. You run faster, until your lungs burn. You are way too out of shape for this!

But the next time you look back, it's stopped. It stands, casually, not even breathing hard, a short distance from the wreck.

You keep running.

When you get to the nearest farmhouse, you scream and throw yourself at the door. A woman comes out with a baseball bat, telling you to go away. But you must look a mess, because she quickly lets you in anyway. You start to tell her how there was a spaceship and an alien and it ate your phone, and she just stands there in her kitchen looking alarmed. Finally, she turns and dials a number, then asks for an officer to come to her house right away. You keep talking, the words coming out of you in a stream of fear.

"Okay, okay, whatever you say," the woman says. "Why don't you drink a glass of water? I called the police, they're coming right over to help you."

The water helps. It gives you something to focus on. But the whole time you're shaking, rattled with fear. When the police arrive, they ask you again what happened. You tell them everything, about the field, and the ship, and you describe the alien. They look concerned, but you're adamant.

You can tell they don't believe you.

"I swear I'm telling the truth!" you say, nearly shouting.

"Okay, okay, we understand," the officer says. She may just be playing "good cop"; hard to tell. You want her to believe you.

"We could all be in danger, and you're sitting here wasting time! You have to go kill it!" you say, and you're filled with such passion you start to cry.

"Why don't we just go out to this field and you show me what you're talking about, okay?" she says.

"Yes! Yes, let's go!" you say. "But wait. No, I don't want to go. It'll just attack me again!" You gesture at the rips in your shirt, helpless.

"I'll be with you," the cop says, indicating her gun.

"Oh...okay," you say, hesitant. What if it's bulletproof? But you don't say anything. Now you just want them to believe you.

You lead the small party—you, the two cops, and the lady from the farm, who insists she has to know if anything weird is going on in her farm—back the way you came. It's a little hard to tell, at first, because you were running in the dark, and you didn't particularly care to take note of how to get back. But you eventually figure it out, and see the smoking crater up ahead.

"Oh my god, there it is!" you say, both excited and afraid.

"What the hell did you do to my pasture?!" the woman says.

"It wasn't me, I told you, it was the alien!" you insist.

"Alright now, no need to get excited," the cop says.

Trepidatiously, you creep toward the crater. It's deep enough that you can't see in immediately, and you drop to a crouch, so maybe you can sneak up on it. You indicate with a finger to your lips that everyone should be quiet, and slink toward the edge. Everyone follows you, breath held.

But when you get to the edge of the crater...there's nothing there. No little blue alien, no ship. Just a bunch of dirt piled around... your phone, crushed and wet.

"But it was HERE!" you shout. "It was right here!"

"Okay, why don't you just come with us?" the cop says. She takes her handcuffs out of the pouch on her hip and slips them over your wrists.

The judge eventually finds you probably psychotic and therefore not entirely responsible for the damage to the pasture. You're shipped off for a month of required psychiatric care in a full-time facility. Even there, no one believes you saw an alien. After a week, you wise up and stop talking about it. Eventually they let you out, but when you get back to town, everyone has heard what happened. You're shunned, relegated to the edges of society. No one wants to be friends with the crazy person who thinks they saw an alien.

THE END

"Well, you are in luck, little guy—you found me!" you say, standing tall and trying to look official.

"You...are...leader?" the squishy bright blue alien says in its weird old-TV voice.

"Of course! Only the official leader of this planet would take a moment to come check out someone as important as yourself! We investigate all such crash-type arrivals. So, welcome to earth!" You extend your arms wide, like when you've been waiting at the airport to pick up your great-aunt after the flight's been delayed twice because of snow. "So glad you could make it!"

The alien stares at you for a moment, then mimics your arms-spread-wide pose, the arm-like appendages opening stiffly.

You stand there awkwardly a moment before letting your arms fall. The alien does the same.

It says, "Hey Ricky, ...we have...much...to discuss."

"Uhhh..." you say. "Yeah, okay. Do you wanna just talk here, then? Or did you have somewhere else you thought maybe we should go?"

The alien's deep black eyes glare at you a moment. "Talk...now. Important."

"Right, yes, of course. What did you want to know?"

The little creature brandishes its claws. "We are..." there is a series of sounds, like static over the airwaves on an old TV. "We...seek...home." This last word was clearly picked up from "I Love Lucy," the "oh" undulating with that trademark Cuban accent. "Leader," (it takes you a moment to remember it is addressing you) "We...come...home?"

You wait for a moment, expecting there to be more. When the little alien just stands there, shifting on its many paws, you realize it's your turn to speak. "Home?" you ask. "Oh, you mean you want to come here?"

The alien waves its middle two arms in small circles. You take this to mean "yes."

After thinking for a moment, you reply:

- "Absolutely! We'd love to have you!" Turn to page 247.
- "You know, I think maybe we can find you something a little better." Turn to the next page.
- "On second thought, I may not be the best leader to answer this one." Turn to page 238.

"Other...place?" the alien says, then surprises you with a canned laugh track. It just opens its mouth and out comes a ripple of very human laughter.

You don't take too kindly to being laughed at, but you're facing a potential alien invasion here, so you brush it off. "Oh sure. This place doesn't really have much going for it. I can tell you're a hardy people and would really make the best of it, but I'm just not sure this property is right for you."

You try to channel your Uncle Bob, the best realtor you or anyone else ever did meet. Man really knows how to make a sale! "Now, let's just say you want a little property near Earth, where you can catch the shows—I have a feeling you are a big fan of some Classic Hollywood, is that right? Sure is. In that case, I have a number of places I can recommend to you. Do you prefer a little bit of a snowy place or are you more into heat?"

The blue alien just stares at you, arms drooping loosely at its sides. Its claws seem to be squeezing reflexively, as if it's strongly considering strangling you.

"Ahh you know, I get it, that's not the best question," you say, trying to choke back your nervousness. "But I'm telling you, this planet is really not for you. Nothing is built to your height, for one thing, and that can be frustrating. Wouldn't you prefer a property you can really customize, make your own?"

The alien waves its hands in little circles again, seemingly more interested. "What...kind of...place, Ethel?" it asks.

Acting way cooler than you feel, you walk over to the alien, pretending not to notice as it tenses up. You rest your arm loosely across what could be called its shoulders, and turn it to face up and away. "See that up there? That cool slice of silver up in the sky? That's what we call the moon. True, a bit of a smaller property, but totally, 100 percent customizable, and none of the pests we have here!"

You glance at the little critter. You could swear it's trying to consider the benefits. You turn it back toward you a little; one of the quills on its back scratches your arm painfully and you jerk away, still trying to keep it casual despite the sharp pain.

"I tell you what," you say. "Normally I ask commission on these types of deals, you know, just the usual quid pro quo, but I can tell you are a real nice..." you struggle for the right word, "...person. So I'm just going to waive my fee, and you know what, I'll just give it to you for free. It's a really underutilized space, full of potential, why don't you just go up and check it out?"

The little alien thinks about this for a moment, then bows low. For a moment you think it's curtains for you, but then it opens its mouth and releases the Looney Tunes theme song. "Th-th-th-that's all, folks!" Porky Pig exclaims. And with that, the alien hops back into its space cruiser and launches back toward the moon, leaving you covered in dirt and ash and gasping for air.

You can't believe you just did that. You saved humanity! You sent the weird alien thing to the moon instead!

For a while, nothing happens. You start to think you hallucinated the whole thing; you were pretty drunk that night—maybe you were drugged? So you just get on with your life.

Meanwhile, NASA is freaking out. The moon is old news, well-explored, lots of data, easy to see even with a basic telescope. And yet suddenly there's something going on out there. The first intern who said they saw a little blue seven-legged creature on the moon was laughed out of the room...but then they checked. And sure enough, there it was. And then, there were more of them. Telescopes that had been pointed out into deep space were redirected onto Earth's follower, and soon it was easy to see the clouds of moon-dust getting kicked up by new construction. Secret councils were held, theories that it was a North Korean experiment, an illusion, magic, all kinds of theories. Were there really...moon men?

It doesn't take too long for the story to leak, and then the entire world becomes obsessed with curiosity. Conspiracy theorists find themselves right for a change, and greet this change of status quo with great alarm: they start concocting theories about how this is a conspiracy to make conspiracy theorists look bad.

Finally, someone decides to just ask the moon men what's going on, so a mission to the moon is launched, the first intentional landing in more than 50 years.

The photo-ops afterward were just great. Astronauts in their shiny helmets standing there next to this multitude of many-armed creatures, the creatures standing stiff and a little perturbed by the attention. The humans leave a gift of food products, but the creatures don't seem to like that much. However, they do ask for a big-screen TV, so the arrangements are made and the first gift of humanity to other life forms is a massive TV with full satellite connections.

Things are fine for a few years. People on Earth more or less start to forget about the moon men, as they become erroneously known. Humans have other things to worry about, and the little blue creatures don't want to interact much, and they try to bite off the hands of scientists who pry a bit too much. So, the truce of neighbors separated by a well-made fence (or decent slice of non-atmospheric space) settles in.

Until there's another strike in Hollywood. Some kind of massive telecom dispute that just really gets out of hand. Everyone is pissed off, favorite shows get killed for no good reason, the quality of movies is just terrible. But no one is angrier than the moon men. They traveled across the known universe so they could enjoy some television right from the source, damnit. They have expectations. They send an official delegation to complain, but global governments just sort of shrug—there's nothing they can do. Besides, what are the little moon men going to do about it?

Earth had never angered the moon men before, so they didn't realize that their anger burns hot. In a moment of pique, the aliens decide to invade. Whole cities are flattened overnight. Humans are killed off, one by one. The telecom buildings are ripped apart piece by piece. They keep going until nothing is left.

The only place they leave mostly intact is Hollywood. After the destruction, they settle in there. Their shows were rough, of course, but critics would describe them as "nostalgic throwbacks of a bygone era"—that is, if there were any critics, any humans, left to watch. But there aren't. It's the end of humanity—because we couldn't give up control of the remote.

THE END

"Have I got just the guy for you!" you exclaim. "We'll need to head into town, though." You start to trudge off toward the dawning horizon, but notice after a moment that the alien isn't with you.

You turn back, saying, "Hey, are you just gonna wait..."

The little imp has done something unnatural to the spaceship, and instead of being a smoking wreck now it has giant leathery bat-wings on either side of a canoe-shaped divot. "Uh, what?" you say.

"Let's go, kiddo," the alien says, the hokey words sounding strange out of that totally deadpan face. The creature's spines down its head flick upward, briefly; you try to imagine it's part iguana and that the shift means it's happy.

The alien scrambles up into the boat part, climbing directly on the oscillating wings. It's probably better than walking, so you shrug to yourself and try to follow it.

It takes two tries and you scrape your arm on the rough surface of the right-hand wing, but you manage to heave yourself up. The airship—if that's the best thing to call it—is perfectly suited to the seven-legged alien, even has appropriately spaced hand-holds, but is ridiculously shallow for you and you can barely hang on. It lurches forward and up, way higher than you're comfortable with. "Woaoooh!" you exclaim.

Those little spines flick upward. Yeah, you're definitely interpreting that as amusement.

The craft takes off, heading in the general direction of town. "Hey, don't you need directions or something?" you ask.

The alien turns its head all the way around—its shoulders stay pointing ahead—so it can look at you. "We...have...been watching," it says.

Well that's unnerving. "Oh," is all you can manage.

It flies toward the wooded trailer park known aspirationally as "Sunrise Ridge," aka. the wrong side of the tracks. You suppose that maybe that could be where Moki lives; you haven't exactly ever been invited to the guy's house. He's an 80-plus-year-old pothead a hippy who never bothered to wake up after the sixties. As far as you know, he hasn't worked since the Reagan administration, choosing to meander through town, dispensing wisdom and helping with odd jobs. He's harmless, and pretty cool to hang out with.

And hopefully he won't mind when you show up on an airship with a creature from another planet at 5:30 in the morning.

Though the airship doesn't have any discernible controls, the alien waves vaguely over the front of the canoe and the wings flap to a hover. "Here...we are," it says, its voice sing-song, like half a lyric.

"Oh, uh, okay," you say, and stand wobbly on the narrow plank before jumping off the back. While the alien jumps loosely down, you ask, "You've been watching us, you said?"

The creature stares solemnly at you.

"Well, okay, so if that's true, why did you land out there? In the middle of nowhere? Why not land at, I don't know, the Space Needle or something?"

The creature cocks its head all the way to the side, like a cat trying to puzzle out a laser pointer. "Here's lookin' at you, kid," it says.

Unsure with how to respond to Bogart being quoted to you, you sidle over to the trailer, never quite turning your back on the visitor. The door has more chips than paint, though a neat little wood-carved sign says "MOKI" in block letters. "Guess this is the place," you say, and knock tentatively, still trying to figure out what you're going to say when the door opens.

The little alien looks agitated. A few moments pass, and the door doesn't open. "Guess he's not in or something," you say, and start to walk away, when at a dash the alien scrambles on all seven feet, leaps, and squeezes into a half-open window in the middle of the trailer, sending the whole thing rocking with the impact. Inside you can hear the clang of silverware. "Leader...of...free world, here...to talk," the alien's voice says, sounding male and authoritative. "LEADER...TALK!" the alien shouts, and the trailer shakes.

You run to the door and pound on it with a fist. "Hey, what's going on in there? Leave him alone! MOKI!" you shout.

You keep knocking frantically, trying to pull the handle, when you hear, "yeah yeah, I'm comin', what the hell is the racket about?"

Then there's a loud "omph," and a crash.

"Moki?" you ask.

A moment later the door opens. "What the hell do you want?" Moki leans heavily on the doorframe, squinting out at you.

He is dressed in a pair of purple short-shorts emblazoned with the word "Juicy" on the butt, and that's it, aside from two mismatched terrycloth slippers. He has tattoos all down his chest, though what they were originally is anyone's guess. His hair is greasy and long and grey.

Not sure how to ask him if he's seen a seven-legged alien or noticed the magical airship floating behind you, you just open your mouth and say, "...uh."

There's a grunt from the floor somewhere inside the trailer. "We...will not...take this...sitting down!" The last part sounded distinctly like Winston Churchill.

"What in god's green earth is that?" Moki says, rubbing his eyes.

"Moki, I brought you a visitor," you explain. "Um... yeah, it's this little blue...alien, and it wanted to see our leader? So I thought maybe you were the best person to talk to?" After a moment you add, "But maybe I was wrong?"

"Eh? What? Don't fuck with me, kid," he says, and slams the door, but he didn't do it right and the door pops right back open again. You follow Moki inside.

"Mokisorrybutit'sinyourtrailer," you say in a rush. But it's too late; Moki has seen the alien thing, its spines standing at full alert and its stubby little clawed arms extended.

"Oh hey little guy, didn't see ya there," Moki says, opening the fridge and pouring himself a cloudy glass of orange juice from an aged pitcher. He sits down at the one stool next to the fold-out table, like seeing an alien in your trailer is no big deal.

"Don't worry," Moki says, with a vague wave of his hand in your direction. "It's not real."

You look askance at the alien, which has climbed to the top of the small fridge and is teetering on the door to the freezer. It seems real to you.

"So, you're not freaked out?" you ask Moki.

"Nah, don't worry, it's just a bad trip," he says, his voice wheezing.

"Oh, well, okay," you say. "I brought it to you because I figure you're pretty wise and stuff."

Moki looks at you, squinting, his eyes half-gone from cataracts. "That so?" he says. "Reckon I am. What's it want to know?" He shakes a bit, like his bones are doing a shimmy without him entirely knowing it.

The creature narrows its eyes and crouches, gargoyle-esque, on the fridge. "What...is...answer?" it asks.

"Guess that depends on the question," Moki says, then laughs at his own joke until he starts to cough, hands on his knees.

The alien stands erect and brandishes its spines. "Meaning. What is...meaning of...life?" it asks, but then its spines deflate. It looks worried, believe it or not (and you really don't want to believe it).

"Oy, little buddy, ain't that always the question?" Moki says, grinning through his missing teeth. He reclines back like he's about to tell a favorite story, which, you realize, he is. You've heard this one before.

"Lemme tell you, I lived all over, did all kinds of things," Moki begins. "I grew up on one of those tribal reservations they used to cram us all in, and let me tell you they didn't do much in the way of accommodations. So I got out as soon as I could. I wandered around a bit, eventually joined up for the War. That was a mistake, you know, just a lot of waitin' or dyin', and overall a lot of trouble that could just been avoided. Did you know I actually saw a man get his head chopped off? —Shink! Just like that! Boy howdy, I tell ya. Then I come back here, tried the whole settled life thing. I had a job for a while, a good one, too! I was an insurance adjustor, went to fires to see if they'd done 'em up on purpose—guess what? A lot had. Enough to make you really doubt humanity and the goodness a-folks. I got tired of that and the family thing didn't work out, so I went a-wanderin'. I was in a Hollywood for a time, you know, even got myself into a picture or two, and then I just rode the rails for a while. But then I stopped, and I set down here. And in all that travelin' and doin' and whatnot, you know what I realized?"

The brilliantly blue alien leans forward, expectantly, its many arms braced against the roof and the wall of the little trailer.

Moki rolls his head back and closes his eyes. "...Ain't no other reason to live than to live. And maybe to get a little high," he says, and winks in your direction.

The alien stares at him for a moment, claws flexing. "I...see," it says.

Moki, apparently having forgotten all about the alien hiding among his cabinets, closes his eyes. The alien doesn't look like it's moving. Not sure what to do, you sit there, awkwardly, for a moment, then slowly stand to leave, thinking the little bugger will take the hint. You glance at the floor as you slowly stand. "So...guess we answered your question, so... I guess we can go now," you say in a stage whisper.

Slowly, contemplatively, the creature climbs down off the wall. As it passes Moki in his chair, it reaches out a claw and traces as shape over Moki's clouded eyes, not touching them. The white-grey pupils begin to disappear while you watch, open-mouthed. "Woah," you say.

The creature looks up at you curiously. "Get...out of...the way," it says, and you comply hurriedly. It crawls on all seven feet down the trailer and launches itself into the airship.

"Hey!" you shout. "Where are you going?"

"Have...answer. Must...tell...others." With that the giant wings vacillate, blowing prairie dust up into your face and making your eyes sting. As the sun rises over the horizon, the airship is silhouetted against the light. With a whirring noise, something shifts, and the bat wings vanish, replaced with the compact saucer you saw crash-land in the field. There's a flash of brilliant blue, then ZOOM, it's up in the sky.

You made it back to your apartment, and back to the rest of your life. Nobody made any mention of the alien, and Moki never seemed to mention it, and you started to think maybe you'd made it all up. But sometimes you'd think of Moki's words and laugh at the utter meaninglessness of it all, at the idea that the best advice Earth could give to an alien race is "eh, it doesn't mean anything." What a crazy story that would be!

Moki died the next winter. A tornado came and blew half the town to bits. It took two days before he could be dug out of the wreckage, and that was two days way too long. The funeral at the old Methodist church was well-attended, because despite not having hardly any money and living as a general nuisance, Moki had been well-liked around town. Lots of people came from all over.

As you were sidestepping the room with the coffin (closed, thank goodness) and too many flowers, you happen to glance out the window. Outside, hovering in the high chill atmosphere, is a phalanx of saucers. With a whoosh they fly off, and snow begins to fall.

THE END

Y̶ou say, "Okay, I know where to take you. It's a bit of a trip, but—" You stop, considering the saucer still smoldering in the crater— "I imagine you've come so far already that it won't bother you that much. I'm going to take you to the leader of the free world."

The alien looks down, for a moment, as if considering whether to trust you. When it looks up, it says, "And what... about...leader of...the...other...world?"

"What?"

"Free...world. What...of...other world?" it asks.

"Oh, that's just an expression," you say, flipping a hand dismissively. "Don't worry, I know just where to take you, that's all you need to know, really."

"Yes," it says, its voice rather Gregory Peck-ish. "Let us...go."

You start to pick your way across the field as the sun crests the horizon, the little alien alternatively walking and darting forward on its seven legs. It kinda runs like a cat wearing socks, its feet all weirdly high off the ground.

"So, uh, this is a field," you say, because you feel, as the first human to have encountered alien life, that you should make some kind of impression as a good host. "We, um, feed cows, just like that one there, and that over there, and all of these," you say, gesturing, "here. They um, eat this green stuff, we call it grass. No, no, we don't find it very appetiz—"

The alien takes a big bite out of the tall dry grass, then immediately spits it back out, looking at you accusingly.

"Um, like I was saying, the cows eat it, we don't." You try to sound conciliatory, but it's hard when the alien is so cute and makes such fantastic expressions.

"Cows...unappetizing," the alien says disapprovingly.

"Yeah, well, some people think so," you say, and try to stay quiet for a while.

It doesn't last long. "So, um, what brings you here?" you ask.

"Secret mission," the alien says, almost a mumble.

"Oh, yeah, right, I guess that makes sense." You pause while you sidestep a cow patty. "Do you have, like, a name or something? Something I can call you?" You offer your name, to try to encourage the creature.

"Name?" it asks, or at least you think it's asking—it's not exactly on point with the inflection thing. "You may call me—" and then sounds like a whip-crack and a dripping faucet emanate from it, accompanied by a simultaneous swoop of the left three paws.

You stop and look back at it; it drops back on all sevens and skitters, roach-like, over a cow. The cow, alarmed by this bizarre rider, moos and takes off at a jog, snorting loudly. The alien leaps nimbly down.

"Um, I think I'm gonna have some trouble with that," you say.

Sagely, the creature says, "yes...we have noticed...you have...terrible...facility...for language."

You roll your eyes. This from the thing that can only choose between hand-waving and whistles or voices from 1940s TV!

"Yeah, that's us, terrible with language," you say, hoping it has a grasp on sarcasm. It doesn't seem to.

"You may call...me...Scout," it says.

That voice sounded distinctly like a nine-year-old girl. "What, like *To Kill a Mockingbird?*" you ask. "OH, I get it, and you're also like, the scout for your people. Clever."

The alien—Scout—says nothing, seemingly indifferent about name-dropping one of the most famous characters in all human existence.

"Good choice for a name," you say. You had to watch that movie in English class once; it was okay, you guess, though you much preferred flicking paper balls at Alicia and watching her wince.

You arrive at the fence at the edge of the pasture. It's topped with barbed wire, but there's a low ditch running toward the road, and you flatten yourself into the dew to shimmy out. Scout watches you, then climbs overtop within seconds. "Dude, you're pretty fast," you exclaim.

Scout only flicks its spines briefly in acknowledgement. Meanwhile you're slimy and damp from neck to knees. "Okay, just got to get to my car and we can go, I guess."

"It...is farther?" Scout asks.

"Oh yeah, it's really far away," you say, hands on your hips as you survey the empty road ahead of you. It's still quiet out, but there will probably be travelers on the highway soon enough. Best to get out of the way, with that weird alien following you. "Let's get moving."

You jog along with Scout, who looks, well, not tired, but generally droopy. It keeps alternating which feet it uses to run, which is unnerving, and unfair—you only have the two!

It's a little after 7 a.m., judging by the number of cars queuing up, when you arrive on the outskirts of town.

"This...is...where...leader?" Scout asks.

"Oh. Oh, no, I mean, we were almost at my car. We can get, like, snacks and stuff before we go, cool? Besides, I need a pee break," you say, digging in your pocket for your keys. You unlock the door to your apartment and shove a highly resisting Scout inside, closing the door hurriedly and with great relief. You made it.

You dart into the bathroom and take care of nature's rather urgent call, then splash your face with water before coming back out.

Scout is staring intently at your throw pillows. Your mom bought you that one, a hideous neon orange-and-green mess that was supposedly fashionable but just kinda looks like vomit. Scout pokes it with a claw and snarls.

"Yeah, I feel the same way," you say. "So is, like, this really urgent?"

"Must...speak...to leader," Scout says.

"Like, really soon? Or what?" You frankly just really want a nap or something; it has been a ridiculously long night already.

"Must...go," Scout says.

"Ugh, fiiine," you say. "Let me just get some snacks for the road and we can head out." You dig around in your pantry, pulling out a big plastic cup, a half-eaten bag of pretzels, and a tub of peanut butter. As you fill the cup with ice and then water from the sink, you say, "Can I get you anything to eat or...something? What do you...eat?"

Scout steps lightly over to your peanut butter jar, opens it delicately with its claws, and sniffs. Out of nowhere a long black tongue slurps out and licks off half the peanut butter in one go.

"Hey!" you say, jerking the jar back. "Gross!"

Scout smacks its maw approvingly.

"Ugh, here, you just take it," you say, thrusting the jar into its claws.

Grabbing your keys, a handful of quarters, and a dirty fleece blanket, you head back out of your apartment. "Come on, already!" you say, and herd Scout out the door, scooting its little spotted butt with the door as you close it. Scout stands at your knees, smacking the peanut butter.

"Can't believe you did that," you mumble.

You find your car in the lot, a beat-up old Beetle, and climb in, the shocks squeaking in protest. Scout stands outside, just staring at you. "Come on!" you say, and lean across the passenger seat to open the door. Finally taking the hint, Scout scrambles into the front seat and climbs over and into the back, where it sniffs and scrabbles. "Hey, don't mess up my seats back there!" you yell as you pull out onto the street.

Several minutes later, the exploration apparently satisfied, Scout returns to the front seat, still holding the peanut butter. "You better hope you don't have some kind of allergy to that or something," you mumble. "Not like any hospital here would take you."

The hum of the car is soothing. Scout stares attentively out the window, sometimes standing in the seat to get a better look at things—the wind turbines, Joe's Automotive, a McDonald's.

"Scout," you say, "what's your home like?"

Scout stretches lackadaisically across the seat, gazing up at your stain-speckled roof. "Home is...nice. Warm place, many—" Scout descends into a "glorp" sound, which you interpret to mean his species or something. "Far, far far, away...distant...sun," Scout says.

"Came a long way to get here, huh? Must be important."

"I...tell...leader," Scout says.

"Yeah, yeah, I know, secret mission."

A driver of a black sedan won't let you merge into their lane; you glance over and notice the driver is staring, open-mouthed, at your passenger seat. You smile and wave, and the car drifts farther back suddenly.

You decide to try something different. "Why do you talk that way?"

"What...way?" Scout asks, and this time the "way" is almost a shout.

"I dunno, it just sounds like you kinda have a bunch of different voices? Kinda sounds, actually, like you talk like movie characters all jumbled up," you explain.

"Scout...research...human speech," Scout says, sounding confused. "This...how...you talk."

"Research?" you ask. "Wait...no way! Did you just watch a bunch of old movies?"

"Messages...to...our people," Scout says. "Sent...over... airwaves. You... are...slow...species."

"Well that's a little hurtful," you say. "Huh. Bet Humphrey Bogart never suspected he'd be teaching a bunch of aliens how to talk!"

You drive until your legs start to ache, then pull over into a rest stop.

"Why...stop?" Scout asks.

"Because I'm the driver, that's why!" you say, and stand up, stretching to the left and right to loosen all your tight muscles. You go use the restroom and buy yourself a soda. When you get back, Scout is being barked at by a rather deranged pomeranian.

"I...drive," Scout says.

"Ha, as if!"

Scout narrows its giant eyes at you and lunges for the keys.

"Woah!" you exclaim, using your superior height to keep them out of reach. Scout tumbles into a roll, smashing into the curb. "Look, I'm trying to help you here! Your legs can't even reach the pedals!" you say.

"My...turn," Scout says.

"I don't think so," you say, and get back in the car, slamming the door as hard as you can so the Beetle rattles and shakes. You roll down the window a little and call out: "Look, if you want to get back in, I'll keep driving. The White House is only like 20 more hours away, so you're going to have to be nice to me or you can stay here and get some other schmuck to take you!"

Scout looks around the parking lot, considering. The pomeranian is practically frothing. An RV pulls in, and an old guy climbs out, still obviously arguing with his wife. A trucker saunters over to examine the large state map hanging by the concrete bathrooms.

Scout climbs back in the car.

"That's what I thought!" you say, and switch on the radio.

You land on religious talk radio with a lot of yelling and quickly flip stations. News, boring—sports, but it's only golf, so who cares? — sappy pop, no—

You flip to a Classics station, and your hand is reaching for the dial again to turn it to something else when Scout says, "Ah!"

You glance over to see the alien bopping and nodding to the beat. It's Sinatra, but not the one about New York, so you barely recognize the lyrics, but there's Scout, singing along in Frankie's voice as the trumpets swell. It's like watching a perfect Sinatra impression from a blue puppet, which is bizarre as it soulfully belts, "I never knew the thrill of your touch, I never knew much!"

"Woah," you say, as the song wraps up.

The alien has a bona fide grin, the first you've seen.

"So, you're a Sinatra fan?"

"Oh yes... this is...important...to my...people," Scout says.

You have to know more, so you pepper Scout with questions. What songs do they like? Why do they sing them? Do they even know what they mean? You keep the radio on during the talk, and frequently have to wait for answers while Scout sings along, creating a weird double tone with the radio. It doesn't seem to have a favorite, as enthusiastic about Etta James as some cowboy song about water.

Finally, you figure out that Scout's people, or whatever, had been receiving radio and TV transmissions from Earth for the past decade or so. That finally explains why Scout talks so weirdly, too—apparently, they never could quite work out the sounds independently, but were more than able to mimic. Scout implies that its understanding is the result of a great deal of study—which seems to mean watching movies; not a bad kind of schooling. You pick up that this has something to do with Scout's big expedition, but it remains vague about its mission.

You've been driving for hours now, and your stomach is pretty pissed off that you haven't done much in the way of eating. You pull off the highway. "Want anything to eat, Scout?" you ask, feeling obligated to play the good host.

Scout sniffs the drive-through window dubiously. "Not... food," it says.

"Fine, whatever you say," you reply, and order yourself a double-patty burger, fries, and a soda as big as your head. As it's being handed out the window (the cashier is so dead inside he doesn't even blink at your alien seat mate), you ask, "Do you even need to eat, or do you, just, I dunno, do it for fun?"

Scout looks a little plaintive for a moment, pursing its lip together so its mouth creates a flat line across its oval-shaped head. "Yes. Hungry," it says.

"Okay, so what do you want?" You peel open the greasy burger and go to town, one hand loosely guiding the car back through the middle-of-nowhere town traffic. "Wanna try a fry or something?"

Scout's nostrils flare at the offer, and you think it's going to reject it, but then it grabs the proffered potato with four clawed hands, so quickly you think it's going to bite your hand off and you have to jerk the wheel to keep from skidding off the road. Scout devours the fry, not even chewing, and then literally dives head-first into your take-out bag.

You just stare in disbelief. "Hey, you didn't even share! You're a terrible road tripper."

Scout reemerges, face covered in fine grains of salt, wearing the bag like a tank top. From the looks of it, the alien ate the fries, the fry container, and at least one napkin.

"I didn't even get any!" you protest, swinging the car around to drive back through the fast food joint. At Scout's urging, you order six more large fries.

"Do you not have heart disease on your planet, because I'm pretty sure all that salt is going to kill you?" you ask.

Scout just responds by wrapping its blackish tongue around a cluster of fries, drawing them deep into its gullet. "You're disgusting," you say, and turn back to the road, quietly nibbling on the fries you managed to keep away from the alien.

The radio station finally fizzles away to static, and you settle for driving in silence. You weren't sure the alien wasn't a furry robot, but after eating it falls asleep, curled in the seat. It's kinda cute like that, and you have to resist the urge to pet it.

That leaves you alone with the increasingly darker road. Your eyes begin to dip. You jerk awake, only to struggle to keep your eyes open. Finally you give in and pull over at one of those massive trucker gas stations. You recline your chair and try to catch forty winks.

You manage maybe 25 before you get a sharp pain in your shoulder. You wake up to Scout staring at you, teeth bared.

"Ahhh!" you scream, and scramble back as far as you can (which is about three inches). "What the hell!"

Scout smooths back its expression and looks at you calmly. "Are...we...there?" it asks, like it wasn't just creeping on you like a maniac.

"What? What, no. No, I just needed a rest."

"Mission is...priority," Scout says, scowling.

"Yeah, I know you have a mission or whatever, but I can't drive forever!" you shout. Your eyes are grainy from lack of sleep.

"I...drive," Scout says, voice as authoritative as Cary Grant.

Maybe it's exhaustion, or maybe it's just that the past few days have been crazy as hell, but you surprise yourself by saying, "Fine, go ahead!"

You get out of the car, knees creaking with effort, and walk around to the passenger side. Scout is in your seat, scooting around happily and trying to reach for the pedals. It can, but only just, and its head is way down low, like a little old granny driving a land yacht. But hey, Scout piloted a vessel across interstellar space. It'll probably be fine.

You explain the rough rules of driving—like not hitting others or going faster than 65—and which way you need to go. You start to explain how the car works but Scout just says, "yes yes," and slaps your hand away. Apparently a lot of the movies it watched featured driving scenes, because Scout is surprisingly good.

You belt yourself in and watch the new driver go at it for a while, before deciding, well, if it's your time to go, it's your time to go, and besides, you're exhausted. You fall asleep. Scout sings quietly to itself as it drives.

You wake up, surprised to find yourself still alive. You take a moment to consider your life choices; you've made some shitty decisions in the past 36 hours: staggering drunk through a field, talking to an alien, road tripping with an alien, letting a brand-new alien driver take the wheel...

Maybe you should get a life coach or something, someone else who can make the big decisions in your life, because you're doing a pretty terrible job of it.

Then again, you aren't dead, so maybe it's not so bad?

"Hey Scout," you say, exaggerating your stretch to make it obvious you're awake. "How's the drive?"

Scout turns and grins at you. "Easier than..." The last word is something from its native language or something. It sounds like a fire being put out.

"Oh, that good, huh?" You nod like you understand. Then, because long car rides always make you philosophical, you say, "You ever wonder how you got here in life, Scout?"

"Drove east...northeast," Scout begins.

"No, no, I mean not *here* here. I mean, like how you got to be the one traveling all across space and time and whatnot. What brought you to this moment?"

Scout considers for a moment, so long you think maybe the alien has just zoned out or something, but eventually it says, "Had to..be..me."

"What's that?" you ask.

"Mission. Had to be...me." Scout looks at you and flicks its spines in half-salute. "This...is destiny."

"Huh," you say. "Why do you say that?"

"I am...chosen," Scout says, peering up over the steering wheel to dart in front of and past a semi. The shift is so smooth you barely even notice. "Much study...time...brought me...to...this moment. My...people...need me. All...the choices...in my life...led me...here...to this planet. I must... succeed."

"So, you're saying you're kinda a believer in predestination? What about free will? Did you choose this?" you ask.

"Choose? No...no choose. I go...where I...must," Scout says. "All paths...lay in front. We go...where...we must."

This is getting a little too deep for you fresh from a nap. You reply, "I guess I feel differently. We all have choices, and we can do or not do whatever. Nothing is making us do anything. We have free will. It's what lets us decide to try something new or unexpected."

Scout stares at you intently. "Car!" you say, and just in time Scout jerks the wheel around the sedan in front of you.

"It seems...like choice...yes," Scout says. "But all...has been...decided. Your life...charted out."

You hold your hands up in defeat. "Okay, believe what you want," you say. "Let me know when you want a break." You turn on the radio again—this time sticking with the modern channels—just for a distraction.

You take another turn after an hour. You can't believe it, but you've made it all the way up through Tennessee and into Virginia. A long drive, sure, but not impossible. The landscape is greener, denser, and all the buildings look like they're built out of brick. It seems like a different world entirely.

"We're almost there," you assure Scout. "You can tell the president about your mission soon, and I'll go back home."

Scout says nothing in reply.

"Or...well, you know, we don't have to go to the president if you don't want to. Or I could go in with you, try to smooth things over. Might help for you to have a human ambassador or something, you know."

"You...want to...change plan?" Scout asks.

"Yeah, well, only if you want to. It's your mission, after all," you say.

Scout considers for a moment, then says,

- "Let us...go...elsewhere. Continue...this...journey." Turn to page 317.
- "Come with me...to see...leader." Turn to page 101.
- "I must...go...alone." Turn to page 248.

You spend a few minutes detailing the perks of the planet—so many environments! Such great tourism! Fun for aliens big and small! You describe the Grand Canyon, and Paris, and talk about art. You point out we have a lot of natural resources, just waiting in the ground for someone to dig it up, and the air is pretty good, too. You talk about whales and platypuses and jellyfish and pandas. You talk about industry and how great humans are at inventing things. You mention Disney World and the 40-hour workweek, and start trying to explain governmental systems.

In short, you try to really give a highlight reel of everything Earth has to offer.

It's unclear if the alien liked your spiel or hated it. Right in the middle of your description of a representative democracy, it turned a blaster on you and reduced you to ions.

But maybe it was listening, because it immediately called its family and before you could say "invasion force," there are aliens landing all over the place. Sure, humanity tried to unite to fight off the invaders, but we as a species have a lot more practice at infighting than unity, and it doesn't go well. Besides, the blue aliens may look cute, but they have pretty sophisticated tech. Basically, it wasn't even much of a fight. Humanity was wiped out before the earth completed another lap around its star.

Welcome to Earth, home of the seven-armed blue folk.

THE END

Y ou nod, understanding. "Yeah, you came a long way, I can see why you'd want to finish on your terms. We'll make it happen, don't worry," you say.

It takes a long while for you to wind your way through D.C.'s crowded streets. Tourists bustle from landmark to landmark, gawking awkwardly up at Giant Lincoln or splashing disrespectfully through the reflective pool at the Washington monument. You don't have time for that; you focus on getting to that big, white, house.

You park outside the gate. The spikes on top look ominous, and you're not sure you could scale it. While Japanese tourists snap photos from between the bars, you eye a second path. Maybe you could go in the side? You drive slowly around.

"Okay," you say to Scout. "I'll just drop you off here. Good luck. Nice to meet you," you say.

"Thank you...kindly," Scout says, its old-timey manners endearing. It fumbles with the latch on the car door and heads out toward the White House.

Scout scrambles and scurries, its claws leaving indentations in the soft soil of the South Lawn. You watch, from the stoplight, hopeful your charge has a productive visit with the leader of the free world. Then the floodlights flash on, drowning Scout in a pool of white light. Scout freezes, hiding its big black eyes against the overwhelming light. There's some kind of warning—you can't hear it properly from inside your car, the traffic is too loud—and then Scout takes off running, as fast as its legs can carry the alien. It's fast, and damned impressive...but not fast enough. There's a sharp "crack" in the air that sends the hair on your arms on end, and Scout is down, not moving.

"No!" you gasp, but then realize the light has changed. You drive away from the scene, looking back frequently.

You hear the rest on the news that night. Some "crazy person" dressed up as an alien tried to break into the White House, they're saying. "Safely contained," they say. "Tell us if you know more," they say.

You know better. You drive steadily, the car seeming far lonelier on the return trip, and don't mention the weekend's events to anyone.

After a few years, you're on some hard times. You reach out to the museum at Roswell, tell them their display of tall skinny aliens is all wrong. You tell them the truth, about Scout, about that night when the saucer crashed. They invite you down to tell your story in person. Then comes a feature in the "museum," then a short feature on an off-brand History Channel show. You develop a certain flavor of notoriety, enough to live off of. Not a bad turnout, for a road trip. Except for Scout...and its message.

THE END

It's just so cute! It's got a wrinkly nose and snorts like one of those pug dogs, and sure it could have softer fur but it kinda reminds you of a naked mole rat, which, you know, isn't the pet of choice for everyone but that doesn't mean it doesn't need some love. You feel oddly connected to this creature, and resolve then and there to do something about it.

"Hey, are you okay?" you ask, running and then, hesitantly, tapping the weird-looking creature on its arm.

It blinks, clearly confused.

"You poor thing!" you exclaim. "We've got to get you somewhere safe."

Without thinking about it too much, you swoop down and pick it up. It's bird-like and it weighs nearly nothing. Its long arms wrap loosely around your neck and your heart practically breaks. What a sweetheart! You bundle it into your shirt and start walking back toward civilization.

"Hey, it's going to be all right. I'll take care of you!" you insist. The creature looks at you with those big doe eyes for a moment, then collapses against your shoulder.

You hike the rest of the way back, the alien curled up in your arms. It weighs about as much as a bag of oranges, and is a little easier to carry, too, the way it has snuggled its head up along your neck.

You're tired and filthy by the time you get home, but are pretty sure you've managed to sneak the creature up the stairs without your neighbors noticing.

You set the alien down on the couch as gently as possible. Because it looks vulnerable and alone there, you grab a blanket and tuck it in.

When you come back out, having accidentally fallen asleep while taking off your shoes, the alien is missing. You start to wonder if someone slipped you some bad LSD or something—it seemed so *real*—when you notice the closet door is barely open, and the blanket is missing from the couch. Huh. Slowly, you walk over and open the door.

The alien is there, in the depths of your closet, behind your rarely used vacuum and the winter coats you use for maybe a month out of the year. Its hiding under the blanket. "Hey there, little fella," you say in your sweetest voice.

The blanket bundle shivers in response.

"Hey, I'm not going to hurt you," you say, desperately trying to project the idea of "safety" to the fearful alien. Still, it doesn't come out.

You decide maybe it's like that time you found an opossum out behind the trash bin; it just needs some incentive to come out.

You dig around your pantry for something suitable, and settle on:

- Several raw strips of bacon. Everyone likes bacon, right? Turn to the next page.
- Half a bag of marshmallows. Do marshmallows go bad? It's probably fine. Turn to page 255.

You slop four strips of bacon down on a plate and leave it on the ground just outside the closet door. You didn't see any obvious teeth on it, but maybe it eats meat.

You did this trick once with the opossum, a mangy old grumpy thing, and while you never did get it to come close enough for cuddles, you like to believe it treated you with a kind of wary respect from then on. At least, it didn't go for your ankles as often.

It's not long before there comes a snuffling sound from inside the depths of the closet. You sit back, wary, as one of the long fingers slips out and toward the little pile of raw meat. It snatches up a strand of bacon, and you hear soft contented murmuring sounds. The hand reemerges, drags the whole plate in, and you hear a great slobbering and chewing. The plate echoes hollowly against the floor.

Since the plan only halfway worked, you try again, leaving a little pile of bacon on the floor a little farther from the door. The alien will have to choose between hiding and going for the food (a tough choice, you know, when it comes to bacon).

You edge back toward the middle of the room, and the snuffling, snorting sound starts up again. Slowly, slowly, the alien crawls out on its four feet, watching warily over the bacon before bending its oversized head and gnashing on the meat.

Little bugger seems to like it—nice.

Then, as you watch, it begins to change. Its body hunches over further, arching more into a four-legged hump. Long bristly hairs emerge out of its back; pointed tusks jut out a few inches from its upper lip.

You reel back in horror. A yelp of fear, like that time your friend startled you in the dark when you thought you were alone, escapes your lips.

The alien has finished its meal and looks up. Its nose seems to have flattened out, and small pointed ears, the tips flopping downward, are sprouting from its head. It looks up at you.

"Woah," you say, shaking from nerves and wonder. "You changed! You look...you kinda look like a pig!"

The alien looks down, considering itself. Suddenly, it breaks into a run, heading straight for you in a mad loping dash. You throw yourself up and over the couch, and the alien darts down the dark hallway toward your bedroom.

Your heart pounds in your chest. Oh god, what are you going to do?

- Run for it. Turn to page 275.
- Feed it something else and see what happens. Turn to page 258.

"Here little guy," you say coaxingly. "Maybe if you just let me pet you..." You climb down and extend a hand out to the alien lifeform, palm down. Sometimes a little pat on the head is all it takes to calm an animal.

You creep down the path toward the weird critter. Two of its seven arms hold out claws toward you, but it doesn't move. It snarls, a low sound deep in its throat. You hesitate, just for a second, but then reassure yourself. It's okay. It's just scared and maybe hurt. It seems just like the beginning of one of those dog-rescue shows. This is just the first step toward a happy ending.

You rest your hand gently on the animal's head. It feels like snakeskin, and the grumbling rumble sound it is making gets louder. No turning back now. You smooth your hand lower down its head, toward its back.

The growl gets louder, then, in an instant, the spines on its back flip to full height, piercing your hand like needles. You grab your wrist, as if that would stop the burning, and stare at the spines erupting through your skin, pulsing with blood. Your hand feels like it has been plunged into molten glass. You can't think because of the pain. You scream and fall to your knees...right at eye level with the beast.

It stares you straight in the eye and speaks. It's a language you can't understand, but you definitely don't think it's a dog anymore. It's also definitely angry. Your hand begins to swell, and there's a pain in your chest.

The alien walks past as you collapse into the damp dirt, eyes rolling back into your head as your body tries to fight a poison that is not of this world.

You're dead within two minutes.

THE END

You shake some of the mallows out into an old plastic container and set it just outside the closet door, then curl up on the couch to wait. You barely breathe for fear of disturbing the creature, but you're also so eager for it to come out and like you that you have to hold your knees to contain yourself.

It takes what feels like forever, but you hear soft sounds from inside the closet. A moment later, a little wrinkled hand emerges, reaching toward the slightly hardened marshmallows. It pauses, as if sensing you watching, then takes a small scoop. The hand darts back inside the dark of the closet, and you hear a gummy-sounding smacking. A moment later, the hand comes back out, tentatively picking out a few more.

Still, you wait. It's starting to look like you'll be watching this weirdo eat marshmallows one at a time when, quietly, slowly, you see the huddled form of the alien creeping out of the closet. As you watch, breath held, you see the hand reach out. The alien grabs the last of the tiny marshmallows, tipping over the bowl to make sure it's empty. Slowly, slowly, it turns and looks at you, sort of sideways, and then it opens its hand, extends it to you.

There, in the palm of this creature's hand, lie eight or so half-chewed marshmallows.

"Really? No one likes half-eaten mallows!" you say, disgusted.

Startled, the alien spreads its fingers and the glob of marshmallow paste smacks to the floor. It turns and bolts back inside the closet.

"You can come out when you learn how you're supposed to share!" you say, and throw a pillow at the closed door.

You storm off to the kitchen to find yourself something to eat. You settle on some instant popcorn, and toss the package into the microwave while you fix yourself a drink. But, as is typical, you're not particularly good at checking on it, and before long you smell that distinctive burnt popcorn scent. "Dammit!" you say, and slam the button on the microwave to pull out the steaming bag. You pull the tabs on the top to carefully let out some of the heat; sure enough, a layer of popcorn on the bottom has turned black.

"Ugh," you grunt, and pour the good bits out into a bowl as best you can. Then you walk the rest of the popcorn, the twisted, burnt, crappy bits, over to the closet, and shake them into the container still waiting outside the door.

"See how you like the crappy parts," you say, and return to the couch to watch Netflix.

You're midway through an episode of "Buffy: The Vampire Slayer" when the closet door opens a crack again. The hand skitters out toward the bowl and snatches a piece.

Then coughing erupts from inside the closet and the door swings open slowly, revealing the alien, scowling with disgust.

"Ha! Not so good, is it?" you laugh, and then tip your bowl of good popcorn forward in reconciliation. The creature considers for a moment, then walks forward, leaning heavily on its long front arms, to grab a handful. You munch your popcorn and pretend not to notice. "There's room on the couch, if you want," you say, as casually as possible.

A few minutes later, the extraterrestrial joins you, though it's focused more on the popcorn than on the screen.

When the show is over, you put the buttery-greasy bowl down and turn to the alien. "Glad you finally decided to come out," you say.

The alien stares at you, then says, "Go hoooomme."

"Look friend, I am home, you're the one out alone," you say, cavalier.

The alien looks at you again, its little curve of a mouth twisted. "Me go home."

"Oh," you say, a little apologetic. "Oh, I see. YOU want to go home." You run a hand through your hair. "Um, your ship was pretty well wrecked."

The alien looks sad.

"Hey, that's okay!" you say, somewhat worried. "You can stay with me for a while! I can show you around. It may be fun!"

You try to force some enthusiasm into your voice, but it's obvious even to you that what you're saying is a stretch of the truth.

"Okay, so you probably wouldn't exactly fit in," you admit.

You sit in awkward silence, not sure what to do. The alien investigates the fluffiness of your couches cushions; you hope it has low standards, because plush they ain't.

"We should probably introduce ourselves," you say, and offer your name. You wait a beat, trying to prompt the creature into giving some kind of identification. It doesn't. "What are you called?" you ask, finally.

The alien considers. It cocks its head at you.

"You know, what's your name or whatever? Like are you a Bob? Sue? Anya?"

The little alien has more "listening holes" than ears, but you imagine perhaps its ears perked up nonetheless. "Ahhnnnyah?" the alien creaks.

"Yeah, Anya, like her," you say, gesturing toward your half-finished show. "Means 'lover of marshmallows' or something," you explain.

"Ahnnya," the alien pronounces.

"Cool," you say. "Though I'm pretty sure that's not, like, your real name, we'll go with it. So, Anya, can you tell me what happened? And why can you understand me?"

Answering the last question first, Anya the alien pulls out a small device. It's squarish and black, and you can see up close it has what could be writing on it. Anya leans forward and touches the screen, causing the shapes to change and blend.

"Oh, I see, you studied, I guess," you say. "Well, you're doing pretty well so far!"

Anya's eyes crinkle a bit at the edges, and you hope that's a positive thing. "Aaahnyaa exploooring," it says. "Baaddd thing. Shippp fallll."

"Pretty sensible, I guess. Does anyone else know about you?"

Anya considers for a moment, then takes the device back from your hand, studying the screen intently for a moment. When it looks up, it says, "Mooothherrr."

"Woah, we can be friends and all, but I'm not your mom!" you insist.

Anya looks pretty exasperated for a creature that doesn't rely on the same mannerisms as a human. It stretches out a finger toward the ceiling and says again, "Moootheerr."

"Oh, like your mother, or like a mothership?" you ask.

"Mooothhherr," Anya says, approvingly.

"I was wondering more about people here, on Earth, knowing we were being watched by aliens, but I guess you wouldn't exactly know that." You stretch out a little more on the couch, and Anya shifts away warily. "So, we have to get you back to your mothership, huh?"

Anya sighs heavily.

You get up and pop another bag of popcorn, careful this time not to burn any. When you return to the couch you offer the bowl to Anya and say, "I've got an idea."

You suggest:

- Returning to the wreck site to see if there is anything useful there. Turn to page 262.
- Asking NASA for a hand. Turn to page 265.

Eating the bacon made it change. Okay. You just gotta feed it something more peaceful. That shouldn't be hard. What's peaceful? What's a calming food?

Glancing down your hallway—still dark, no sign of the alien-pig—you vault off the couch and toward the pantry. Crap, you really should have gone to the grocery store recently! There's, like, nothing here!

You start tossing things out. Sugar, no good, might just get hyper; food coloring, who knows what's in that?; popcorn for an air popper you never use—wait, that's it! Corn!

You start to hear the thunder of galloping steps as you twist the lid. Why are they so hard to turn? Ugh! With a grunt you pull the lid free just as the pig alien comes thudding back into the room. Crap! With a cry you leap to the stove, pulling your legs up just in time as the alien slams into the face of the oven.

Dammit, your landlord will never believe how that dent got there.

You turn the container of popcorn over, spilling it all on the floor in a tiny bouncing pinging rain of kernels. The alien, absolutely bewildered by this, snaps its head left and right, lunging and snapping its squished little face. You use the distraction to retreat farther back against the stove. It probably can't reach you here, right?

Luckily, your plan seems to be working. After a moment's hesitation, the alien licks up some of the kernels from the floor. They crunch loudly, crushed in its jaws. The floor is absolutely covered in the hard popcorn pieces, and the alien-pig seems determined to hoover it all up...as slowly as possible. As your fear subsides, you begin to doze off, your neck awkwardly slumped against your shoulder.

Weirdly, it's the absence of noise that wakes you. When you open your eyes, the floor seems mostly clear. Your neck and knees ache something awful, but you loosen your grip and slowly slide down the oven. Where did it go?

You creep along the kitchen, listening hard for any sounds that may tell you where it is. Finally, you see it, looking completely different than before. It's sitting on the other side of your kitchen wall, swaying gently, tiny green leaves sprouted on its arms and back and head. Its eyes are half-closed, dreamlike.

You finally relax. "You're really taking 'you are what you eat' to a whole new level," you say, teasingly, but the alien merely stares at you slowly.

"This is fucking weird," you say to yourself, but what are you going to do? You have an alien "growing" in your apartment.

You turn on the lamp in the living room and the wrinkly weird-looking thing turns its face toward the light, bucolic. "Fucking weird," you say, and sit down to think about it. You really don't want that thing in your home a second longer, but you're kinda afraid to touch it. So, you decide to do the mature thing and ignore it, hoping it dies of starvation or something.

The next few days pass without incident. You ignore the alien; the alien continues to try to be a plant. After a bit you feel kinda sorry for it and dump a half-full (or is it half-empty?) glass of water on it (all-empty now!). The water ripples down the wrinkles of its head and makes a damp spot on the carpet, but you think maybe the alien is happier?

Sometimes you talk to it, tell it about your day. It becomes like a plant/bizarre decoration/pet—innocuous, and something you don't really need to pay attention to.

One day, as you're opening one of the packages of loot you bought yourself on Amazon in a drunken stupor, the knife you're using to cut the tape slips, jabbing you in the thumb. It hurts like a bitch and you grip the wound in one hand while you run to the bathroom.

You don't notice the splash of blood that lands on the alien.

The next morning you're half-asleep when you make your bowl of cereal and begin your usual patter to your alien/plant/pet. "I really do think my boss is out to get me," you say. "It's just unreasonable, you know, and the whole thing was really blown out of proportion."

You chew your off-brand Wheatie Bites thoughtfully, sloshing the milk around in your bowl. You look at your weird alien thing and say, "What do you think I should do?"

To your utter shock and horror, it says, "Feeeed meee."

You splash wheat-y milk all down your front in shock.

It's never talked before!

"You've never talked before!" You point your spoon accusingly. "How come you can talk now?!" you shout.

It wavers its wrinkly leafy head. "Feeeed me."

"NOT THAT AGAIN," you shout, shaking with fear. "Last time I fed you, you chased me around the apartment. I'm not getting my deposit back because of you!"

"Feed me," it says, its voice a surprisingly brazen contralto.

"Fine!" you say, and open the pantry, digging around until you can find a bag of instant popcorn. You rip it open, scattering kernels at the base of the alien, careful to stay out of range. It hasn't moved since that day, but then it hasn't talked either, so it's better not to take too many risks.

The alien wobbles, its arms still stuck at its sides like vines twisting up a gnarled tree. "Not like thaaat," it says.

"Beggars can't be choosers," you say, still sort of shouting, and stomp down the hall to your room. You get dressed as quickly as you can and leave the apartment, slamming the door. On the other side, you shudder. Having a heavy door between you and that thing makes you feel a little better, but not much.

You're still gone a few hours later when there's a knock on your door, and "Maintenance," called through. When you don't answer, a key slides into the lock and the repairman comes in, carrying his jug of insect repellant for the monthly once-over and spray against pests. The handy man saunters in, squirting the clear liquid in corners and under cabinets. He nudges the plant-alien with one foot, trying to scoot it away from the wall, but it is stuck fast, so he reaches down to move it so he can finish his shift and go home.

That's when it bites, sinking its small wrinkled face into the meat of his hand.

"Ai! Madre de dios, qué mierda fue eso?" He grabs his tools and runs out, not even closing the door on the way.

When you come home, it looks like you've been robbed. The front door is open and your apartment is trashed; it even looks like they may have taken your alien. Not that you regret that, it's just, seriously, they'd take that but leave the TV? "Seriously?" you say, and walk through the rooms, looking at the mess. It's too hard to tell what has been taken, so you head back out to sit on the steps while you call the police.

The next few hours are occupied with the police taking their sweet time to show up, then you explaining the issue, no, nothing serious looks stolen, just a major mess. They take a few pictures and tell you to call your insurance, and that's it. You're left to clean up. You start to, half-heartedly, but you feel so betrayed that something like this could have happened to you. You lock the door, then drag a chair in front of it, because you've seen that in the movies and you feel a little safer afterward, but you're not sure that would really stop someone. You do the same for your bedroom door, making your bed loosely and collapsing into it.

You should have looked under the bed.

The alien waits until dark, moving slowly, slowly, something still of the corn still in it, a few leaves clinging to its crown. It stands at the side of the bed, watching you. You stretch and murmur in your sleep, one hand dangling over the side of the bed.

It considers for a moment, then seizes your wrist in both its small hands and bites, hard, your blood streaming into its jaws, its small hands suction-tight against your arm.

You wake up screaming, thrashing to get away, but it's tenacious, strong as an oak, and can't be removed. You flail, beating at it, kicking, but still it holds tight, and you get weaker by the second as your blood drains away.

You're growing faint as you scream, scream for someone to help, hoping your neighbors are home, that they hear you. As you watch, the alien changes, its skin rippling from greenish-brown, losing the green, tinged instead with pink, human undertones as your blood flows into it. Its legs grow longer, its arms stronger, its face thin and vicious. "Please," you beg, your voice a mere gasp now, but still it bites and sucks you dry.

When the police hammer on the door, they find you sitting peacefully in your chair, watching TV. You explain it must have just been a loud show you were watching, and apologize that they had to come all this way. You thank them for their consideration, and they leave, annoyed.

The door to the bedroom is closed—your body lies cooling within. A husk of its former self. Never to be found.

The alien looks strong, taller...like you.

The alien wearing your face walks out, ready to taste the world's delights.

THE END

"We'll just return to the ship. Maybe you can find a way to communicate with them when we get there!" you say. You're so pumped about this idea that you immediately head for the door.

You grab Anya up, still wrapped inconspicuously in the blanket, and hop in your car. You slip the key into the ignition and start backing up—

WHAM!

The car shudders to an immediate halt. Anya says, "wooooaahh" in its sing-songy voice.

"Goddamnit," you mutter, glancing up at your mirror.

You've backed into your neighbor's truck, and she's pissed. "What in the hell were you thinking?" she yells as she slams her car door. "You didn't even look, you asshole! Look what you did to my truck."

You flip the car back into drive and scoot forward to extricate your sedan from the passenger side of the truck. Even without getting out, you can see it's a big impact.

You grimace and turn to Anya. "Hang tight," you say. You step out of the car and straight into your neighbor's middle-aged white woman wrath. Her hair has come loose from her ponytail and she's practically frothing with fury. "What are you going to do about this?" she shouts, and you have to lean back to avoid the spit.

"Look, I'm real sorry, it was an accident!" you say. You don't really have any good excuse, so you spend the next ten minutes exchanging information and halfway apologizing.

Finally you say, "Look, I really gotta run. Can we talk about this later?"

The truck's driver is so flabbergasted at this suggestion that you have time to reach in, grab Anya, and make your getaway. You jump into your car and slam into reverse. Ms. Pissy-pants herself is coming up on you, looking ready for another six rounds of "how dare you," so you peel down the street. You glance back and think you actually see her shaking her fist at you. You just drive faster.

Texas highways are not exactly safe, especially not when the car trundling on it is half-crushed and badly in need of repair, but you get out of town in decent time. Anya seems to be enjoying it, too, sitting on the front seat, half-leaned out the window and closing its eyes against the wind, breathing the cool of the night.

After a while, you feel like it's getting easier, like you could be driving right up through the air.

You aren't though. It's a metaphor.

"Hooooommme," Anya sings, and it's right, you're nearly back at the crash site. You turn off into the field and jolt and rumble and push on through to the crash.

When you pull up, it's obvious someone had been here. There's police tape loosely wrapped around some wooden posts stuck sort of in a circle near the crater, but not a lot is different. Anya raises an arm to point one long finger. "Hooooommme," it says. The alien looks like it's pointing to the ship, but then it raises an arm straight up.

"Uh, is there supposed to be something there?" you ask.

Anya turns nearly all the way around—weird—and looks at you with its deep dark eyes. "Mooother," he says.

"Um, okay," you answer, and lift the alien to the ground. It scampers over to the crater, slipping and sliding down through the mud to the ship. You duck under the police tape to follow.

Anya taps a panel that was so flush against the surface of the ship you didn't see it, its fingertip glowing orange from the light that the panel emanates. Anya lets out a little "ahh" as a larger panel lifts up and away, like the Velcro across the laces of a roller skate. Inside is a cocoon-like space, filled with the same orange glow. Anya leans in awkwardly, its little wrinkly alien bum protruding up and out of it like a plumber crawling under the sink. There's some rattling noises, and briefly a bang, then Anya leans back out. It sits on the dirt, and you lower yourself to the ground nearby.

"Everything going ok?" you ask, feeling useless.

Anya's long, long fingers are surprisingly dexterous, and it's manipulating a brightly colored squarish box. A moment later, it flashes purple-purple-yellow-red in slow sequence. "Ooookkaayyyy," Anya says, and concentrates on formulating a reply. The alien waves a hand over the box in a swooping motion, then a thrust, like it's going to drop it, but vaults it loosely into the air instead, before catching it in its palm. The box blinks once in reply.

"Gooo hooomme," Anya says. You think it seems satisfied.

"Really? That's, um, great news!" you say, trying to sound happy. After all, you weren't sure what you were going to do with an alien roommate, but still, you're a little disappointed.

As if sensing your feelings, Anya stares intently at you. "Comme hommmme?" he asks.

"What, who, me?" you say. "With you?"

"Ooookaaayy," Anya says, which seems like a yes.

You consider for a half-second, then reply,

- "Sure, why the hell not?!" Turn to page 177.
- "Aw, thanks, but I'm good." Turn to page 269.

"We can just go down to Houston and ask NASA what to do," you explain. Then you have to explain what "NASA" stands for, except you can't remember all the letters exactly, so you just sort of generally say, "they do space stuff."

"They'll know what to do, I'm sure," you say.

You're worn out from all the craziness, so you show Anya how to use the remote, nuke a frozen pizza and leave it out on the coffee table in case it gets hungry, recommend a few classic movies like "Independence Day," and head to bed.

The next day you call in to work sick— "hosting an alien visitor" isn't exactly on the "good excuses" list—and get ready to leave. After looking over Anya's wrinkly weird body, you decide maybe you can use the HOV lane, but you're going to need to do something about its style. You rifle through your

t-shirt drawer until you come up with a shirt that might work. It's an old one from middle school, when tie-dye was big, and says "Far Out." On Anya it looks like a sack dress. You add a sunhat and aviator sunglasses, just in case the cameras can peek inside, then hop into the car. Texas is huge, but at least it's got decent highways. You figure you can be in Houston in a matter of hours.

Anya is quiet during the trip. You try a little chit-chat, but your visitor isn't really into talking. It spends a good part of the day reading its device, though it periodically hits it with a palm, like maybe it's malfunctioning. You spend a lot of time looking out the window and trying to avoid getting pulled over by the cops; *that* would be a really awkward conversation.

You make it to Houston before dark, the city's sprawl and traffic creeping up around the highway until you're nearly at a standstill. "Almost there, Anya."

Anya looks around, then looks straight up into the darkening sky. "Ahnnyaaah goo home," it says.

"I'm working on it, buddy," you say. "We've just got to get you to the NASA folks and maybe they can give you a lift or something. I follow their Twitter. They seem really nice."

You make it to NASA headquarters toward the end of the day. There aren't many cars in the parking lot, and Anya seems anxious, so you figure there's no time like the present. You grab Anya by the hand and walk into the lobby.

"Hi there!" the perky receptionist calls from behind her towering desk. "We still have one tour for the day, though you just missed the last IMAX. One child and one adult?"

"Oh, um, no," you say. "We're not here for the tour. We'd like to meet with the scientists, please?"

The receptionist titters. "Oh, well, I'm afraid we can't let you meet with the scientists, they're very bus—"

You lift Anya up onto the counter and the color drains out of the receptionist's face. "Uuuuhhhh what is that?"

"Goes by Anya, but I picked it up in a field after the spaceship crashed," you explain. "Can I talk to a scientist, please?"

The receptionist doesn't take her eyes off Anya, whose shirt has slipped awkwardly down its short torso, and dials a number on the phone. Into the receiver she says, "Um, I'm going to need some help up here."

Half an hour later, you're seated in a plush modern conference room, surrounded by what you've been assured are *THE* top names in the space program. There's an astronaut, at least three scientists whose jobs you don't understand, and the head of NASA, a distinguished-looking nerd in a suit. Anya doodles in a puddle of water it's spilled on the table.

"And it just...let you bring it here?" the guy in the suit asks, incredulous.

"Well, yesterday we kinda just hung out and watched TV," you explain. "But it's important to Anya that it get back home, so I figured you guys could help."

"What...is it?" one of the scientists asks. She looks like she's ready to put Anya under a microscope.

"An alien, I guess? Anya says it was on a mission before it crashed, so there are probably a lot of them," you explain.

"That could be the anomaly we were picking up," another scientist says. "We haven't seen that kind of scatter in the systems for years. We thought it was just some kind of glitch, but..."

A young guy with a mohawk says, "Yeah, this really blows Rudolph's theory right out of the water, eh?"

"We will have time to discuss all this later," the agency head says sternly. "For now, we need to initiate the Federation Protocol."

"Federation?" you say, excited. "Like *Star Trek?* I loved the last movie!"

Everyone in the room kind of just ignores you.

"We'll begin right away, sir," the dark-haired scientist answers. She turns to the other two and begins issuing instructions in a low voice.

The agency lead turns back to you. "Thank you for bringing this to our attention. We're just going to need to run some tests, for your safety, of course."

"Oh, okay," you say. He begins to lead you out of the room. Anya looks up from the table, calls your name softly. "What about Anya?"

"Rest assured, you brought ...Anya...to the right place," the director says, and leads you down a hallway. He waves a badge in front of a sensor and a heavy door unlocks with a snick. You quickly lose your sense of direction, and the director finally leaves you outside an unmarked door. "Please remove your clothing—we need to just test it for some contaminants. You'll find some scrubs inside for you to wear."

You extend a hand to the director, but he flinches back, unwilling to touch you. "Perhaps after the tests," he says with a thin smile.

"Oh, of course, sure," you say, and step through the door. The room smells of antiseptic and sterility. You follow directions, taking a moment to try to fold your clothes and leave them by the door. You step forward into the rest of the room; it's walled with tile, and there's a table with a chair on either side and a fold-out bunk bed. A toilet is in one corner. "Huh," you say to yourself, "this is kinda like a jail or something."

True to their word, you're given a battery of tests. Your skin is closely examined and swabbed and prodded until you just wish they'd let you take a shower. Your eyes are checked, your knee banged on to see if it bounces, your reaction time tested. You're asked to run on a treadmill and they strap a bag on your face; they attach nodules to your chest as you sleep; they make you wear a helmet full of sensors when you answer their questions.

It starts out fun, but gets increasingly boring. They don't treat you badly, exactly, but the whole thing gets old quick.

And they won't let you see Anya.

After a few days, they clear you of anything weird, though do point out you probably should work out more if you don't want to fail your next running-on-a-treadmill test. They give you new clothes, still with the tags on them and close to your size, and they thank you for your time.

"You're free to go," the director says.

"So did you get Anya back to the mothership or whatever?" you ask. "I'm really glad the first alien we met was so nice, you know? Though watch it with any sweets—loves marshmallows and won't share any with you!"

The director just nods along, as if he already knew this. "The extraterrestrial is being taken care of," he says. He offers his hand to you; in it is a thin plastic card. "Here, this is for the bus back. We'll send your car along in a bit. We have some tests to run." You take the card.

"But...but you did get it home, right?" you ask.

The director holds the front door open for you. "We have considered it carefully, and believe it will be far more beneficial to science if...Anya...stays here. We have many tests we would like to run, you understand."

And with that the director pulls the door closed.

"You bastards!" you scream, and you pull on the handle with both hands. It's useless and stuck fast. You prowl around the building, looking for another entrance, but NASA knows a thing or two about security. They let you wander for maybe 10 minutes before four burly security guards come up and grab you, each one holding tight to a limb. They physically haul you off the property.

You try to do something about it. You really do. But you can't get anywhere near NASA again—you get arrested twice trying—and the only media outlet you can get to pay any attention to you is of the type that likes to feature "bat boy" on the cover. All your friends think you're crazy, and you lose your job.

You get referred to a court-ordered psychiatrist who ultimately determines you probably just had a mental breakdown—there was no alien.

Of course there's no alien. That would be crazy.

You still can't bring yourself to eat marshmallows, though.

THE END

You lean down to hug your new friend, his long, delicate arms as light as feathers on your back, and watch as he climbs out of the crater. Not long later, another, bigger ship descends from the sky in a contrast of light and dark. Anya runs toward this vessel excitedly, as if waving down an old friend. A ray of light—or something more solid than light, more powerful—descends from the vessel right above Anya, and Anya glides up into the vessel. At the very last minute, Anya turns and you could swear it looked straight at you.

Your eyes well with tears as the vessel pushes off away from Earth, ruffling your hair and blinding your eyes in a flash of light.

Two years later, you find yourself sitting in a doctor's office wearing a paper dress. It crinkles every time you move, and you are fidgeting constantly, both hoping the doctor returns and fearing the news.

The door opens and a technician comes in. She doesn't make eye contact with you, just checks something on the terminal. "The doctor will be with you in a moment," she says, still not looking up.

It's a heckuva lot longer than a moment, but the doctor, the best in the field, comes in.

You don't like the set of her jaw. As it turns out, you don't have much reason to. She says, "Well, this really is remarkable. I've never seen anything like this, and I've been in this field for 20 years."

"So...that's good?" you ask.

She looks grim. "Your biopsy results are in. You have an extremely rare, rather advanced type of cancer. And it doesn't appear to respond to radiation. We'll try it, of course, but... well, I don't have that many ideas," she says.

As you absorb this, she says, "What I can't figure out is how you even *got* this. I checked the data. The only time this has been even seen was after Chernobyl and Fukushima." She chews her lip. "But you've never been in a nuclear power plant or anything like that, right?"

You think for a moment, and remember Anya, the wash of heat and light you felt on the night the vessel disappeared into the stars. You think about the little wrinkled alien—it didn't look that different from you now, bald and hairless. You remember that orange glow.

You look back to the doctor and say, "No, nothing like that."

THE END

Y ou're floating again. The sky-blue light has gone, and you feel warm. There's a tube over your face, covering your mouth and nose and making it a little hard to see and all you can hear are whooshing noises like a scuba tank. Experimentally, you wiggle your fingers. There's a gentle resistance, like silky sheets or a soapy bath. Your sides and bones ache where you hit them in your fall, but not badly. Pushing yourself forward as far as you can on the mask tethering you, you discover you're in a chamber filled with a milky seaweed-green fluid—or is it a gas?

Maybe you're on drugs and this is a hospital, because nothing seems right. You strain, squinting through the green fog to see if you can find a nurse, someone, anyone to explain what's happened to you.

There, movement to your left. You swish your hands and try to call out—and then it gets closer.

The green fluid disguises it somewhat, but you see something tall, with shining black fur or feathers or scales, a maw like an eternal cave, bright golden eyes.

You try to swim away, closing your eyes against the horror you can't fully understand.

The thing taps on the glass, and you let loose a startled cry.

It taps again, insistently, and you crack open your eyes, just a slit. Your stomach threatens to revolt at the sight, your skin bursting into terrified goosebumps.

It speaks.

The sound is musical and haunting, an owl's cry in the depths of a dark wood, and utterly incoherent to you. A moment later, a robotic female voice crackles to life and you can understand. "Took a nasty fall there. Been a real challenge to get you stitched up," it says. The translator robot continues, "You can call me—Translation Unavailable." It's no wonder the robot gave up—the sound produced was only a weird crackling tone.

You blink. Is this a joke?

When you don't react, the horrifying creature calls out again. "Anyway, you're being taken to The Colony. When you're a little better, you can fill out all the required documents. Until then, you're known around here as Epsilon Silcrow, got it?"

You close your eyes and sincerely hope this is a nightmare.

It's a nightmare all right, but not the kind you'd thought.

Translation Unavailable comes back frequently after that, though you can't tell for sure how long you've been there. Not long after, you're taken out of the tank, but the air is all wrong and burns the inside of your lungs and you gasp and think you're going to suffocate but then three of the things push you back under. The next time they bring you out it's to plop a helmet over your head, and that's not so bad.

It's vaguely hospital-like, though the walls seem to be only loosely tied down, made of some strong thin material that flexes in reaction to an unseen breeze. When you aren't in the tank, you are expected to sit on a tufted seat, rounded and soft like a sea urchin.

There are others in this place. Some are human, and about as baffled as you are. Others...who knows what they are, but clearly alien. Creatures come and go but mostly ignore you as you convalesce in the corner. There is a time, once, when you're feeling strong after freshly leaving the tank, that the space rattles around, like an earthquake, then the shining black creatures come in, stretchers hovering between them full of jars of little mouse-sized jellies. One of them sings in their eerie language, and the translator in your helmet says, "Can't believe they stuck us with more of these. How are we supposed to feed them when they don't have mouths?"

And the other one makes a hiccupping sound that might be a laugh and replies, "Why bother keeping the disgusting things at all?"

After that, when you're a little stronger, you sneak as quietly as you can through the space's soft fog, peering at other inhabitants and looking for another human. You find a man, his right arm missing at the shoulder, looking faint and wane. He barely looks up when you slip through the eddies of fog into his area.

"What is this place?" you ask.

His head rolls back, lifting his eyes to gaze at you through his helmet. "There's no point," he says.

"No point?"

"The aliens. They took us. There's no point," he says, his brown fingers curling and releasing.

"I know," you say, reaching for his hand, trying to be comforting—wanting your own comfort. He pulls back. "But we can escape, we can get out..."

"Escape where?!" he says, standing, knocking you back. "Don't you see? They took us. For all we know, the planet is gone. We are prisoners."

"No..." you stutter, "no. That doesn't make sense..."

Behind you comes the soft sound of the creatures' howls, and your translator repeats: "Tilde Rhombus isn't entirely wrong." You leap away; the other man/creature snarls like a dog and runs at Translation Unavailable. The creature moves like a cyclone, so fast you can't really see, and the attacker is flung away like a paper doll.

You collapse to your knees, trying to make yourself small, tasting the salt of your tears as you brace for the inevitable blows.

"Get up," Translation Unavailable says. "Or make your choice. You can be like him, if you like"—Translation Unavailable glances at the broken man— "or you can come with me and begin your new life."

You look over at the man. He lays on the ground, dazed, unseeing. You slowly pull yourself to your feet, and follow obediently, hating yourself for it with every step.

"Wise choice," your translator agrees. "It is good you are well. We can release you, Epsilon Silcrow."

You are guided into a room, and Translation Unavailable rummages through a pile in the corner, hands you a garment that snaps to your helmet like a long flowing robe. Next you are led into a room where another creature, a drab brown one, asks you questions and a robot scans you. It's exhausting and you don't understand it all, but then Translation Unavailable returns, pushes two sustenance packs into your unresisting hands, and says, "Good luck out there. We don't want to see you back."

You're still struggling to understand what this means when the whirring sound starts all around you and the room fills with that sky-blue light...

In a blink, you're on the surface of a planet. The ground looks purplish through your helmet and feels rocky underfoot. You're in a city, and suddenly feel very naked and alone in the crush of people and creatures. It looks like a menagerie from all the weirdest movies you saw as a kid. You are struck by a fear unlike any you've known so far, and stare ahead in shock.

Someone shoves you, hard, and you drop one of the sustenance bars. "Outta the way!" your translator chimes helpfully.

You fall to your hands, desperate to pick up the pack, which gets kicked and trampled. You skitter to the edge of the foot traffic, feeling crushed by this new horror, terrified and alone. You slide against the crisp white walls and hug your knees.

You can't say for sure how long you stay there, but the world is growing cold when she finds you. She looks human, anyway, though her hands are speckled green. She crouches down at your level and says, "Gosh, another one?"

When you don't answer, she says, "Come on, let's get you somewhere safe." Not knowing what else to do, you follow. "You can call me Serante," she says as you follow behind. "The Ursuts, they do that, and it's the worst, just dropping you off without warning. You can come with me for the night and we'll get you sorted come morning."

The lariat of fear that had been tight around your heart begins to loosen.

Serante guides you to a low-slung building shaped like a collapsing circus tent, situates you on a squishy pad near the door. She guides you, child-like, to the toilet facilities, and dismisses you for the night, locking herself in a room that seems to close with a zipper. You feel cold, and the pad she has left you does not help you sleep.

The next morning is little better. She explains that you, like her, like all the rest here, have been moved to what is known as The Colony. There seems to be some speculation that the Ursuts are experimenting, or at least studying, The Colony. They don't provide anything in the way of assistance, and Serante makes it clear that you're going to have to figure it out for yourself after a day or two. There is work to be found, she says, if you aren't stupid, and the tilt of her shoulder suggests maybe you are.

The weight of your new reality settles on you like a collar, choking your hope. Perhaps seeing this, Serante says, "Forget your old life. Forget who you were. Forget your expectations. This is not a bad world, necessarily, if you let yourself get used to it. But it's up to you to survive. We get the job done."

She takes you around town, shows you where the shop is, how to replenish the oxygen in your helmet. She suggests a place you can work, mashing the green fibrous roots of the plant's main crop into something edible. She shows you where the hibernation pods are, where you can sleep cheaply for a night.

You get by, because you must. Your hands grow sharp with hard labor, your neck weary from carrying this helmet always, your back kinked. You start to wonder if you'll ever hear your own language again, something besides that damn robot translator talking to you all the time. You polish your hatred for the Ursuts like a piece of coal, a hardened diamond in place of your heart.

Everything is alien.

THE END

You dart off the couch, hoping your legs can propel you far enough to keep out of the alien monster's way. As soon as you move, it focuses on you, heading in your direction, but you don't have time to turn to look. You spring to the door, throw your weight down on the handle, and pull the door open, not a moment too soon. The alien skids up, lunging to bite you, but you hit the railing at the stairs and vault over, landing awkwardly on your side.

From your view you can see the pig-alien try to copy you, but its legs are too stumpy, so it turns and jogs, with a swaying cant, down the stairs. You definitely bruised something, but you push up off the ground and make a run for it, your ankle threatening to give out on you with every step.

The terrible beast comes snorting after you. A woman with a youngish daughter is getting out of her car, arms loaded with groceries. You yell, "Run! Get away!" flailing your arms. She pauses, confused, then sees the thing chasing you and jumps back into her SUV. You hear the doors auto-lock after her. The pig-alien is running across the parking lot toward you now, but your neighbor gave you an idea. You look around for a pickup truck, and, this being Texas, you find one relatively quickly. You make a dash for it. The hairs on the back of your neck start to prickle and you suspect the alien is getting closer, but you don't dare look. You hit the tail of the truck and lift yourself up and over, but not before the sharp pain of a bite shoots through your ankle. Still, you find the strength to push on, and roll yourself up into the back of the truck. You lay there, holding your wounded leg and rocking gently. You press a palm against your ankle in an attempt to staunch the bleeding, but mostly you lay on the floor of the flatbed, thanking God and fate and anything else that the truck is lifted; it's just enough too high for the pig-alien to jump into, though you hear it scratching and scrabbling at the sides.

The alien keeps at it for you don't know how long—long enough for your leg to go kinda numb and for your back to ache from the way you're hiding. When the sound subsides, you pull yourself up to standing, trying to get a better view. It's still out there, watching.

The woman from earlier sees you; she's so afraid you can see the whites of her eyes. She gestures frantically: is it still there?

You nod emphatically. You fold your right hand into a fist, the thumb and pinky sticking out. Call police, you pantomime.

She looks down, searching, and a moment later you see she's got a phone to her ear.

From your propped-up position, you can see the alien. It's circling, nose to the ground, a weird facsimile of animal behavior, not quite right but close enough. It's searching for a scent, or maybe already has one. Does it understand?

Just then it turns and looks at you, snorting once, then turns away and vanishes into the bushes behind your complex. You wave your arms to attract the grocery woman's attention. It's going, you say, using one hand to communicate departure. She nods and reaches back behind her to her daughter, pulling her with her to the front seat. She's maybe 8, too big to really be carried, but her mother seems ready to try anyway. In a burst of energy, she shoves open her car door and makes a dash for the buildings, her daughter sliding shim-sham down her hip. She yells, "I called the police, they're coming!"

"Thank you!" you yell back, just as she makes it to her front door. You wait for a moment, listening, and decide it's as safe as it's going to get. You scramble back down the truck and run-hop to your apartment, the whole way feeling as if the teeth might be closing on your neck. You make it to your door and slam it shut behind you, leaning against it to catch your breath. Still, you don't feel safe until you've snicked the lock closed.

The police send out animal control, which means two overweight guys who are clearly pissed off to be up after hours. They walk around, poking into the trash bins and peering under cars, for only half an hour before shrugging and heading back home to their beds.

You take the time to clean your wound—tender, and seems to have bled a lot, but ultimately superficial—and try to get a grip. But every time you doze off, the creature, its horrible snort and the bristling spine, comes back to haunt you.

You're not the only one haunted. That winter, tales of the chupacabra, of wendigos, come back in full force. There are multiple sightings, but by the time animal control gets there, there's nothing, no proof. There is a rash of attacks on household pets, on chickens, and one farmer claims to have shot at a horribly deformed child that was bothering his cows.

In time, the sightings subside...but they never quite go away. Folks just stop going out alone at night in certain places, carry wards or knives, just in case. It's better to stay indoors, anyway, they tell themselves. Just in case.

THE END

While you watch, the barb juts out, as if seeking an invisible target. You leap back reflexively. Soon, four thin legs emerge in the crack, and you watch, horrified, while the creature is birthed from the shell. It glistens entirely with something fierce, its chitin shell looking for all the world like interlocking armor. It has four legs on the ground, and another four with wicked-looking claws it holds up. It snaps and crackles with each movement. Its head is small, but it stands erect, like a dinosaur, the tail arching up and over. As soon as it emerges, it lunges at you.

You falter backward, and then its brother, still half-encased within the sky tube, jabs at you, striking you in the:

- Chest. Turn to page 325.
- Leg. Turn to page 151.

The whole thing seems to be writhing, and a buzzing sound, like a microwave set to run too long, fills the air. You can see just through a slit in the object, and inside seems to be boiling with activity.

When you aren't immediately killed, you stand up and walk toward the object. Maybe it won't hatch anything? Maybe it'll die in our atmosphere!

As you get closer, you realize the air is warmer, and, on top of the buzzing, there's a very soft...chewing sound. It sounds like the crunch you get inside your head when you're eating chips, except this is outside, and from the object you're pretty sure came from space.

This is a lot to take in.

Something in the object moves, and you jump back, hiding around what you think of as the "corner" of the mysterious space object. The crunching sound grows louder, and then, at the top of the object, something erupts out. It's...a head, two eyes as big as literal saucers, shiny even in the night. Antennae follow, and two short forearms. Then, with great effort, the creature pulls out the rest of its thorax, and it stands for a minute, resting, airing its wings.

It's a bee.

Well, it's a two-foot-long bee, but it's a bee nonetheless!

Suddenly the object in front of you shivers, and other bees burst out of the object—the hive? —the whole thing full of the massive insects.

You break off at a run as fast as your legs can carry you, hoping all the while that this is a dream and you're going to wake up soon.

It's not long before you realize the buzzing sound is following you, louder now. You glance up, and there against the starry background is an armada of bees.

You cover your head and fall to the ground, hoping they'll pass over you, but instead, you hear a voice made of ten thousand vibrations:

- BZZZZZZZ. Turn to page 300.
- "Our queen!" Turn to page 298.
- "Pollinate!" Turn to page 301.

"Prof. Joby, are you in?" you say, knocking on the door. The office is tidy, the white desk cleared of everything but a stack of papers and a turned-off monitor. The woman behind the desk looks about as proper as the office, the lines of her pale pink button-down as crisp as if she had only just finished ironing the blouse.

Without looking up, the woman replies, "Of course I'm in, but office hours are not until 3 p.m. I'd appreciate if you remembered that. Good day."

With a glance at Marlene, you step in the room anyway. "Excuse me, but I'm not a student," you explain.

Dr. Joby finally looks up, and seems surprised and moderately disgusted to see you; you look rough, admittedly, but discoveries like this don't wait for a shower!

Dr. Joby presses her lips together. "Well, what do you want?"

Marlene steps in. "We discovered some data and...it appears to be in a language we can't read. Can you read it?"

The professor actually rolls her eyes. "I understand Google translate can do some amazing things these days. Please go bother someone else now."

"Uhh," you say, blinking at the dismissal. "Could we show you first, maybe?"

Dr. Joby sighs dramatically and walks around her desk. "Fine," she says, extending a hand. "You have three minutes, then you really must go."

Marlene hands over her stack of papers. "This line here in particular," she says, pointing out the cryptic messages. "Have you ever seen anything like this?

Dr. Joby skims the paper, her pursed lips never relaxing. "I don't have time for this bullshit," she says, pushing the paper toward you and ushering you toward the door. "This is not a language, it's gibberish, probably written by a cat on a keyboard. Take your practical jokes elsewhere!"

And then she slams the door on you before you can protest. You glance at Marlene. "Well, that was a little worse than expected."

"Gibberish?" Marlene says, sounding wounded. "No, it's got to be a language!"

Marlene drags you to the library, insistent that we can find something to show that she's right, that she has proof of an alien language. It takes her another six painful hours to finally give up.

"Marlene, come on. We've tried everything. Maybe we should just go home," you say, trying to coax your cousin out.

"No! NO, okay? This is proof! Proof!"

And that's when she started throwing books.

Campus police came to collect her, heard her raving about aliens, and, well, things went downhill from there. The whole incident was just embarrassing; Marlene even ended up kept for "observation" in a hospital for a few days. As for you, you just tried to forget the whole thing. Sure, there may be aliens watching your every move, but that seems better than being told you're crazy.

THE END

With a crack, another of the objects opens, and another, and another, until the air is filled with crackling, aural lightning. You cover your ears and cower, but can't look away from the transfiguration occurring in front of you. Huge legs, as big as steel beams, emerge, pushing open the cracked vise, revealing a glistening brackish body, insect-like, but unlike anything you've ever seen. The insectoid alien lands, its huge legs somehow seeming delicate with the way they teeter on points, towering over you.

You're sure you're done for and start saying your prayers to anyone who will listen, but the alien turns face-down and begins burrowing furiously into the earth.

As a child you liked watching construction machines work, fascinated by the sounds and the power. You watched many an earthmover haul heavy loads, drills spiral deep into the Earth for oil, cranes bending and stretching. And yet all those are dwarfed by the display of this creature. It powers into the soil, covering you in debris as it vanishes below ground, leaving the vessel it arrived in and a tremendous hole.

You find the strength in your legs as, all around you, the creatures plow into the earth. For the most part, the creatures disappear when they go below, but not all of them; ahead of you, silhouetted against the rising sun, you see one of the bugs lurch out of its hole and snatch a heifer, dragging the pitiful thing down in with it. You swing wide of the holes and try to run faster, feeling like you're on the inverse of Whack-a-Mole and about to be dragged into the pit of hell at any moment.

The day the bugs came, they created chaos everywhere they went, and they landed everywhere. It was hard to say who had it worse, rural areas or cities. The small towns had fewer disruptions in utilities, could still get fresh water and power, for the most part, but they were cut off from the outside, more vulnerable. The cities at least had the resources to fight back, though it quickly became a struggle between fighting off the bugs and having enough to live on as buildings burned, water dried up, and communication lines snapped. A whole city block in Chicago was swallowed up in a day when the bugs dug too deeply, collapsing the streets above.

Worse, it turns out the bugs eat a lot more than just cows. Nowhere is safe. Millions were killed in the first weeks alone, snatched off the streets, crushed under buildings, jumping from skyscrapers to end the terror.

But humanity is a resilient sort, and you get swept up in the resistance quickly. There's no going back to your former life, so you let yourself be led into the military. Someone should fight back; it might as well be you.

It turns out there have been drills for just this kind of thing. Not that it was ever expected to be a real problem, but assigning trainees to fight giant insects was more politically acceptable than playing "Choose Your Real-Life Bad Guy." So when the bugs touched down, there was at least one agency with an idea of what to do. Not hard to put them in charge, especially not when the president and most of Congress had died in the initial rush.

And the military has a long legacy of organized chaos, so it's no problem to accept and acclimate to new recruits on rather short notice.

A few places on Earth prove to be inhospitable to the bugs. Unfortunately, they're uncomfortable to humans, too. You're assigned to White Sands; the heat and the dunes made it hard for the bugs to tunnel and it was easier to glass 'em. The sand never seems to get out of your uniform, no matter how you try.

"Private!" the sergeant snaps, and you straighten up, bracing for whatever may come. "Do you want to die?"

"Sir, no sir," you yell, shouting from your diaphragm, giving it oomph.

"Good!" he shouts, sweat breaking out on his forehead in the heat, even though the day is young. He turns to the rest of the new recruits in the line. "You already had to be a survivor to get here. Now we're going to make sure you keep the rest of humanity alive, understood?"

"Sir yes sir!" you shout in unison. There are only twenty of you, but since the bugs arrived, that feels like a crowd.

"We're still working out how to fight these bastards. They're big, they're not from around here, and they're damned evil, as far as we can tell," the sergeant says. "But that doesn't mean we can just roll over and play dead! You get me?"

"Sir yes sir!"

"Okay then! We're going to train you all on the basics, but those of you with additional skills may be asked to do more. And I expect you to say yes, and give it all you've goddamn got, because we don't GET any second chances, not anymore. This is OUR world, and we're going to do what it takes to keep it. Hua?"

"Hua!" you shout, hoping the bravado will squelch the twist of fear that has lived perpetually in your gut since the day they arrived.

The sergeant keeps talking, calling names down the list and giving out assignments. "Rodriguez, aeronautics; Kedam, mechanics; Ali, infantry." The sergeant calls your name, and then:

- "Tactics." Turn to the next page.
- "Infantry." Turn to page 294.

Thank god. Sure, you're here to fight like everyone else, but if you'd been stuck with those meatheads in infantry, you probably would have shot yourself within a week. Sure, they've got courage, but you've got brains. The bugs have a lot of brute force, but we can outthink them, you're sure of it.

You report to the tactics team immediately. If all goes well, you may never leave the base, but you still have a lot of training. You work your body, improving yourself physically every day with laps and drills and lifts, but that isn't enough for those of you chosen for tactics. No, you've got to do more than those grunts. Every day opens with a run, then two hours of study—what are the bugs? How do they act? Where are they located? What are their weak points?

You finish all your required activities by dinner, but that's not enough for you, and you spend many a night back in the lab, reading the reports, sketching out your theories. This works out fine until the colonel finds you slumped over a book one morning a month into your tour and sends you back to the bunks. "You're useless to us if you never rest!" he shouts, and you're not allowed to leave your quarters for 24 hours. They even make your squad bring you meals, which is humiliating, but you finally get some rest.

The sergeant is on you like flies on a carcass from then on out. Every time you think you can sneak in for extra lab time in the middle of the night, somehow he knows. Finally he assigns you to a shift as a dishwasher, "to guarantee you're tired every night." Damn if it doesn't work, too. You work in the lab, then dinner, then spend at least an hour every night cleaning up after the horrible slobs you have to live with. It's like they go out of their way to make a mess for you!

One night, as you try to scrape crusty cheese and egg off the plates from breakfast, you notice a bug—the little, normal, human kind—crawl up on the edge of the canvas tent. "Little fucker," you snarl, and swat at the small brown beetle. It falls off the wall and into the water. You stop and watch its progress. Its legs flail and it tries to skate across the water's surface, but of course it can't get any traction. You idly go back to scrubbing dishes, splashing dirty dishwater over the scrambling insect. It is forced under by the tiny waterfall you create, and floats to the surface, upside-down. By the time you've finished scrubbing the plate clean of caked-on cheddar, it's dead.

...It's...dead.

You drop the plate into the water, strip off your gloves and apron, and race back through the kitchen to the lab.

Fifteen minutes later, Sergeant Hawkes finds you. "What did I tell you..." he says, but you cut him off.

"I may know how to kill them," you blurt.

He pauses, considering this. "Okay. What you got?"

You take a breath. "What if we've been going about this all wrong? We've been attacking these bugs like they're movie monsters from the 1930s horror flicks, trying to fight them like Godzilla or something. Bullets don't work, grenades are hardly effective, they don't seem to burn easily."

"Are you ever going to tell me something I don't already know?" Hawkes snarls.

"But we don't treat them like what they are most like!" you insist. "We don't treat them like bugs!"

Sergeant Hawkes rolls his eyes. "That's your goddamn breakthrough? We tried it, all the chemicals that we use on our regular insects. They are immune, or if they're not, they kill humans at the same rate as they kill the bugs. We're losing a war as it is; there's no need to make it worse by killing our own."

"Yeah, I know, I know," you say. "But there is a lot we still *haven't* tried. Like drowning them. They have all those big holes, but what if we filled them with water? Trapped them inside? They seem to still need atmosphere."

"Drowning them?" Hawkes says, but you think he sounds like he's listening now.

"Okay, yeah, drowning them is pretty impractical, but I think it could work," you say. "But that means maybe other things humans have been trying for thousands of years will *also* work." You run a hand through your hair. "At the very least, it seems worth a try."

Sergeant Hawkes walks over and surprises you by putting a hand on your shoulder, like a favorite uncle. "Okay," he says. "Get me a list. We'll see what we can do here."

You start with liquid soap and water, filling oversized water guns with a solution. You get a lot of jokes from the grunts when they realize you're asking them to spray the attacking insects with bubble water, but that's to be expected. "Just try it, you assholes," Hawkes says, and they shut up (mostly). At the next battle, teams of three hold the firefighter hoses to shoot the pressurized soap water at the bug.

At first it looks like it has no effect—just pissing it off—but the video shows the beetle demonstrating some new behaviors, flexing its wings, turning away, wiping at its labrum with a foreleg. The grunts manage to kill the thing with a barrage of bullets while it is distracted, but the fight is brutal nonetheless. Still, at the conclusion, you've only lost four men, about a quarter fewer than the last time.

The soap-water isn't a complete deterrent, and it is abundant with problems. It's a temporary distraction at best, and you're going through soap reserves faster than anticipated. It's also hard to get the water trucks out in time, to get enough water to make it worth it. Still, it's an improvement.

"What else you got?" Hawkes says.

You recommend an up-sized diatomaceous earth. Sure, it's basically a fine powder for the normal-sized bugs, but maybe if you made a massive version? Hawkes orders construction materials, and sends you with a team of grunts to drill into volcanic rock. It's hell on the drill bits, and heaven help anyone who tries to pick pieces up with their bare hands, but it makes a pretty vicious defense. After seeing the expense reports, Hawkes demands you supplement with something less expensive, so you direct your team to go into the nearest (deserted) town and bring back as much glass as they can carry. You only lose six grunts, but you come back with two full caravans of wicked glass shards.

It's miserable work loading all that up into a Blackhawk, but you have Hawkes to make sure the grunts don't resist too much. Besides, it's easy to see why walking on this kind of debris would be a problem for any enemy.

The opportunity to test it out comes quicker than you'd like—the helicopter is only half-full when a trio of bugs erupt near your water supply. It's nonnegotiable; they must be stopped or risk everyone in the camp dying of thirst. "Try to dump it on them and in front of them," you shout as the helicopter takes off. No video feed this time; you have to wait on tenterhooks to find out if it worked.

The pilot makes it back alive, and he's not happy. "What the fuck was that supposed to do?" he yells. "It was still there, attacking me. Without cover fire, I'd have been dead!"

"Just...give it a chance!" you insist, but you feel sick.

Half an hour later, though, it seems like maybe the experiment was worth it. A team comes back from scouting the river, reporting three beetles—tank beetles, the infantry have been calling them—were on their knees, "practically begging to be killed." They're exaggerating, of course, but it seems it helped.

The crushed earth is hardly effective as an offensive move, but it's solid defense. Hawkes has the camp surrounded by the gritty trash, and attacks from the ground drop 40 percent overnight.

Still, it's not enough. You spend all day poring over old gardening documents, looking for any advantage. You suggest another half a dozen ideas, but humanity keeps losing ground.

A month later, Hawkes is growing frustrated with you and the other tactics team members. He lines you all up and shouts at you for 20 minutes. "You've done a lot for us, I'm not going to deny it, but come on! We need something better," he says, winding down. "What else can you give us!"

From the back, Radford chimes in, hesitant. "Japanese beetles," she says.

Billings shouts, "Not gonna work!"

You turn around and stare him down, shouting, "Dammit, hear her out."

"What's the point? It's not like we can get enough cedar for it to even matter!" Billings replies. His arrogance knows no bounds, and you roll your eyes at Hawkes, who takes that as a cue to step in.

"I've had your ideas, Billings," he says. "We need some fresh blood. Radford, what were you saying?"

Cowed, Billings throws himself down into his chair; Radford raises her head and says, "Japanese beetles. They can be repelled by a dilution of cedar oil in water. It doesn't harm them, but they don't like it. Maybe we can weaponize it, drive them off."

Hawkes considers for a moment. "Billings is right, we're going to have a problem acquiring cedar oil. But we'll do what we can." He nods. "Let's try it."

It takes two weeks to get even a decent amount of cedar, and several days to soak it in the big vats of water. Half the team breaks off to study the benefits of the oil, see how to weaponize it, but for now you start basic—spraying it in jets, like the soapy water. In tests, it seems effective, driving the space bugs back. Hawkes, heartened by this win, sets a trap, driving a set of the bugs into a ring with the sweet-smelling sap, then dropping missiles on them. Even the bugs can't withstand that much heat.

As much as you are excited about the victories, you remain nervous.

You just can't crack them, find out how they work, and you feel in your core that until you know that, you won't be able to stop them. They spawn at a ridiculous rate, so fast it seems every time you kill one it is replaced by at least three. Your nightmares are filled with the clack of their chiton.

"I need to get one," you tell Hawkes. You're disheveled, exhausted. Judging by his eyes, he looks worse, but he stands erect, precise.

"What do you mean, get one? You just want me to bring a bug in here?" He sounds disgusted. You push on anyway.

"Yeah, I do. It's the only way we can make any progress. We must stop their breeding, at the very least. They're going to eat so much we starve if we don't act fast," you insist, panic rising in your voice.

"No," he says. "Look, I see your point, but I can't put the lives of my people at risk, not even for this. I can bring you a carcass, but I can't let you bring one of those bastards in here."

"I'M TALKING ABOUT SAVING HUMANITY HERE," you yell, throwing your clipboard at the wall behind Hawkes. He doesn't flinch.

"I said no," he says.

You storm off, heading into your bunk to lie down and try to cool off.

But it doesn't work. The nightmares, the visions you've been fighting every night, come back to haunt you. The images from the videos of the bugs ripping infantry apart, of ignoring an RPG like it was nothing, of crushing buildings; your memories of your brother's look of horror as he video-called you as the bugs were attacking. Of his last words—"Tell mom…"

Of how you'll never know what you should tell mom, because one of the mantises snatched him up. And it wouldn't have mattered anyway, because mom had been dragged underground by that point.

Your vision fills with blood, and you open your eyes. Enough. It is well past enough, and it's time for you to do something about it.

You get dressed and slip out of the bunk. You sneak into the lab, using a piece of tape to fool the door sensor into thinking it is closed. You grab several of the experimental weapons and a pair of drones— after all, you're still a tactician, and data is critical—and head out.

A guard stands a lazy watch on the parade ground, and you tense, thinking this is the end of your adventure. But she just says, "Going out for a night experiment? Don't be out too late," and doesn't look twice.

You heft your backpack and open the west door in the gate. You have to walk carefully, closely watching your flashlight to avoid the diatomaceous debris ring, but you make it through without much trouble. About fifteen minutes of walking brings you to the first hole, and you switch off the light and give your eyes time to adjust to the dark before slowly heading toward the hole. You take a moment to deploy the drones, leaving one to hover back near the base, and assigning the other to follow you POV. The air smells sweet with rain and the cool of night, with a salty bite the closer you get to the hole. It has a putrid stink to it, and you try not to think of what it has killed— but then you resolve to put a stop to it.

"Testing experiment 348," you whisper, showing the drone at your shoulder the tube. It's barely more than a pipe-bomb, but this one is filled with cedar oil and a mix of capsaicin—with a nice dash of good old TNT. It should irritate the hell out of the bugs that live.

You fiddle with the contraption for a moment, heart in your throat, then hear the snick of the latch. You roll it down into the hole, willing it to go as deep as possible, to really fuck things up. You back out of the hole and toward the next, arming another bomb as you go.

BOOM comes from behind you, throwing you to the ground. Those things pack a punch! You let go of the bomb you're holding and jump back, trying to get out of range.

BOOM, and you fall over backward into your POV drone.

But that's not the worst of it. The bugs are swarming, forced out by the gas in the tunnels into the open air, just you against what seems like hundreds. You begin to realize this may have been a complete miscalculation. There are *so many* of them.

You pull out another experimental weapon—a laser—and try to remember how to ready it. You can't remember your hands being so big and useless; your fingers seem slow and stupid, and meanwhile your heart is pounding and they're getting closer.

You flip the switch on the laser and brace with two hands as the whirring sound begins, and not too soon—even in the dark you can see the mandibles of the first beetle bearing down on you. You slice through them with your laser, and cackle in ecstatic joy to discover it's working.

But your moment is short-lived, because you're under attack on all sides. Behind you you're dimly aware that the alarms at the base are blaring, floodlights turning on. From up all the walls, they can see the shine of the laser, the shadows of the bugs. "AHHH!" you yell, feeling like a warrior, finally understanding why the infantry seem to like it so much, despite the danger. Now this is doing something!

You turn, punching out the legs of two bugs with the sweep of your laser...which is growing uncomfortably warm. You spare a glance down at it to see it smoking. Shit. Reynolds put this thing together, you should have known! You don't have time to think about it, though, and you swing the heavy laser back the other direction. Part of your brain notices the bugs seem at least weakened by the gas; it wasn't all in vain.

Behind you, infantry are pouring out of the base; you hear the rattattat of their rifles as they come to give you support. It's no good, though; all the bugs are entirely focused on you, you who literally walked up and kicked the hornet's nest. You step back a half-step to get the POV camera in view: "It was worth it, Hawkes. This was worth it!"

And you have more to say, practically a whole lecture, but you were so busy talking to your own reflection that you didn't see the hopper land behind you. Your last close-up features the huge alien leaning down and neatly nipping off your head.

That's it for you, but your experiments, at least, leave a lasting impact. The gas is the right framework, and it serves well to weaken the aliens enough for conventional weapons to do some good. It gives humanity a foothold—not much more, but enough for a few ships to organize well enough to escape off-world. Many millions die, sheer numbers putting humanity at a disadvantage. But you contributed, you saved some, and that's more than most can say. You undoubtedly went out trying.

Though other research facilities did put in better locks and stricter rules regarding their labs and experiments, also because of you, so look at that, double impact!

THE END

You trundle in with your armfuls of computers and papers, Marlene tagging close behind. The office is dark, but you peer in, finding a woman with mouse-brown hair leaned over a pile of Lego bricks on a metal desk.

"Excuse me," you say. "I'm looking for Dr. Kai?"

"What? Oh, that's me," she says, looking up from what appears to be a spaceship. "What can I do for you?"

"We have some data we'd like you to look at," Marlene says.

"Sure, great! I have 15 minutes before my next class, so come on in!" Dr. Kai says.

The chairs are filled to overflowing with binders and books, so you take to leaning against a bookcase. "We, um, *found* this data, and we're just looking for a little more insight on it? Marlene, can you show Dr. Kai what we have?" you ask.

Marlene steps forward, and thank goodness she is there because you just sound like an idiot trying to explain this stuff. She opens her computer and shows Dr. Kai the downloaded data, and the only words you more or less understand are "encryption," "server," and "key." But Dr. Kai and Marlene seem to be on the same page, anyway.

"May I?" Dr. Kai says, gesturing toward the screen. Marlene nods yes, and that's a big deal because Marlene doesn't let *anyone*—ok, you—touch her stuff, not never. But here she is being gracious with Dr. Kai. The world may stop turning.

Dr. Kai scrolls through some of the screens, muttering to herself. A moment later she looks up and says, "wow."

"Yeah, right?" Marlene agrees.

"Uh huh!" you say, just wanting to feel included.

"We have to do something about this!" Dr. Kai says. "No one can just compile all this data on people without their knowledge."

"What *can* we do?" you ask. "They already have it, and we don't even know who 'they' are."

She thinks for a minute, picking at the toy bricks on her desk. "We post it," she says, finally.

"There will be a lot of blowback on that," Marlene says.

"Wait, catch me up here please?" you ask.

Marlene sighs at your apparent slowness and says, "We well everyone what these...people...know about them. We make it public. It's the whole light-in-the-dark approach."

Dr. Kai nods. "It'll get a lot of attention that way, and maybe we can get help to figure out who is really behind this."

Eventually, you all agree to the plan, which mostly involves Dr. Kai and Marlene working closely together while you make sure everyone is stocked up on coffee. To allow people to keep some semblance of privacy—because there is some *really* incriminating information in here—it's decided that the full database will be posted, but people will have to answer questions about themselves to see their full profile, proving their identities. It would have been a lot easier to just upload the file to some website somewhere, but adding these protections, Marlene says, will keep everyone from being as bad as the bad guys.

It takes two weeks of nearly non-stop work, and when the big day comes, you're sweating bullets. What if all this work wasn't worth it?

Dr. Kai posts the database, and sends the link to several media outlets. It only takes an hour before the news has gone viral, and the servers Dr. Kai purchased time on strain under the effort but don't go down. It's the story of the year, and just keeps getting bigger. A swarm of reporters and programmers descend on Dr. Kai's office, and it's general madness. But it's truth-bringing madness. It's amazing how quickly this team of super-smart people manages to get to the root of the data, and before long the aliens among us are outed, right and left, first in the media, and then, not long afterward, from the planet. There are surprises—the president, the entire Dallas Cowboys offensive line, your local delivery truck driver—and many who are no surprise at all, but they are rooted out, one after another.

It turns out smart people who come together can make a big difference.

And you got to be a part of that.

THE END

Infantry—YES! It's the most noble job out there, the one position that really puts you in the nitty-gritty of defending the planet from those monstrosities. Of course there's risk, of course there's danger, that's the point! You know to your core that humanity isn't going to fend off these filthy space-beetles by asking nicely; hell the fuck no! It takes someone, someone like you, who is unafraid to run right up to them and hit them with a million bullets until their guts go splat and they learn to never fuck with Earth again.

"Hua, sir!" you yell, pride permeating your core. When you are dismissed, you peel off and report to the infantry division.

You may have thought you were in shape before, but you were nothing but raw clay. It's just like the sergeant says: you will hurt until you are purified, until there is nothing left of you but fight and courage. The infantry is the largest division, and no one sweet-coats it—it's gonna be bad as hell out there. That's why you're running 10 miles a day, lifting every evening, pushups until you can't feel your shoulders anymore. You've got to be harder. You practice drills with live rounds because there is no time to fuck around anymore. Your life focuses down to a pinprick; you go to sleep exhausted, wake up with the bugs just behind your eyes. The camp is safe—well, reasonably enough, though the bugs try the occasional flyby—but you're done with safe. You can't wait for training to be over, for your turn in the holes. You'll make them pay, every last overgrown one of them.

Finally, your time comes. After six weeks in training, you're needed at the front. Your team of recruits is loaded onto a Blackhawk helicopter and sent out to Odessa. West Texas has all the heat and swelter of your training, but it's flatter, with grass attempting to grow. And the bugs are making an incursion against the town. Your job is to hold them off, put them down.

You drown out the shiver of fear with excitement and banter. "You may as well not go, Dominguez, because I've got this," you say, teasing the private. He looks at you askance, his dark skin covered in a fine matte of brown grit.

"Please," he says. "We all know you're gonna shit yourself as soon as we land."

Khosa chimes in, softly, head bowed: "In the time before, I would have been praying now," she says, the edge of her hijab just peeking from under her helmet. "But now I don't need to pray." She grins devilishly. "I know I will kill at least twice as many of those shithead bugs as you!"

"You talk a big game for someone so small," you quip. "Need me to carry that rifle, Khosa?" You wink; she can carry her weight, and just like everyone else, she's got plenty of incentive to kill as many bugs as she can. Her family, even her grandmother, was killed, ripped right out of the mosque while they prayed for salvation. That kind of thing can sour you on God right quick.

A quiet voice slices through the banter. "Don't worry Khosa; now I pray for you," Jones says. You don't like him much—he's always a buzzkill because he's always going on about God's vengeance and salvation—but the dude is at least earnest. All the horrors since the bugs arrived only turned him closer to God. You gotta respect that...

But that doesn't mean he can ruin the moment for the rest of you. "Dammit, Jones, lighten up!" you say. "We've got bugs to smash today!"

With that the rest of your group cheers, and even Jones cracks a grin. Sure, you're going into the thick of it, but you've got a good team.

The helicopter's blades thud overhead, causing the dust to swirl— and drawing the attention of the bugs. Even before landing, you can see the long black pincers thrusting up out of the soil about a click away. This is it. You follow your squad, each jumping to the dirt with a thud, staying bent low to avoid the blades, rifle at the ready to fire. Khosa takes point, kneeling in the dirt and bracing her firearm. You fall in position to her right, watching her flank but keeping focused on the beetle ahead. The rest fill in, forming a loose ring at the base of the helicopter, which takes off as soon as everyone has unloaded.

Moment of truth.

The beetle is huge, even bigger than the day they landed. It's practically the size of a tank, and strong enough to throw one, too. You can see its glistening hide, the massive blades that kill by tearing, cutting, ripping. It's coming, faster than it looks like it should move, but you breathe, trying to keep your cool. Not...until...you...see...the eyes. You let loose a cavalcade of bullets arcing toward the beast, and so does everyone around you, the air filling with the deafening percussion of controlled, desperate, fire. Your body shudders as you absorb the rifle's impact, steady on, focusing on that cluster of sensitive nerves right at the eyes. A blind bug is a stupid bug, and you know they're all stupid bugs.

The bug twists and turns to avoid the pain, but there are many of you, and you hammer at it until you can see the ichor drip out of an indentation where the eyes used to be. "Hua! Got it!" Dominguez says, and your heart lifts—then crashes down to your stomach as you realize the shout has told the bug exactly where you all are.

"Dominguez, you shithead!" you shout, already backing away. "It's coming. Everyone run!" You grab your rifle and dash back 50 yards, trying to find cover. Dominguez, realizing what he's done, runs 20 yards then throws himself flat on the ground, the beetle still laser-focused on his first position. The asshole is going to get himself killed. You start to fire, trying to draw it away, but the bug will have to come right over Dominguez to get to where you are crouched behind a melted tour bus. "Fuck!" you spit, and then, "Come on, help him!" You and Khosa and Jones and everyone else hammer away at the beetle, most of the bullets bouncing harmlessly off its exoskeleton but enough impacting to make a difference.

Dominguez is still lying there as the bug starts to step over him toward your cover, and you think maybe he's been hit, when he suddenly rolls on his back and lets loose. The beetle bucks up, thrashing away, its tender underbelly ripping off in chunks. "Ahhhh!" Dominguez yells, and keeps rolling, back on his feet. He runs toward you as the beetle collapses behind him.

"You did it, you motherfucker!" you yell, rushing out to meet him. "I can't believe you..."

"Down!" Khosa shouts, and you and Dominguez drop immediately, just a hand's breadth out of range of the swooping mantis-like creature leaning down from the top of the tour bus. Khosa backs up, firing controlled bursts at the bugs' triangular head.

"Did we ever pick the worst place to deploy," Jones shouts, running to keep up with Khosa.

You panic, grabbing one of the sticky grenades the nerds gave you and lobbing it up at the beetle. It swipes it away with better accuracy than Serena Williams, and the grenade explodes, knocking Jones and Khosa to the ground.

A cry escapes your lips, and you find yourself pelting toward your squad mates. You shoot as you go, forgetting all your training about calm and focus as you see the potential for your friends, your brothers in arms, to meet their end because of your bad aim.

You're screaming in defiance when the bug uncurls its spined forearms and reaches down. When it grabs you, you try to struggle free, try to remember what to do, but you have only seconds, and it's not enough. The mandible crunches right through your helmet, your skull, as you scream in agony, eaten by a 50-foot mantis.

Most of the infantry dies just as swiftly. It turns out a patched-together, undertrained army is no match for a race of beetles with an appetite. It's not so much of how humanity dies, as how quickly—within six months, humanity is reduced to rubble, and artifacts, even bones, are eaten by the new six-legged terrors, the Rise of the Superbug.

THE END

The bees dip and swoop in the air around you, surrounding you with their heat and noise. "Your majesty," they say, and you realize you're not *hearing* their words through the air—you hear the voice in your head, a brassy buzz that resonates in your mind.

You fall to the ground, holding your hands to your ears. "Ahh! What is happening?" you exclaim.

The alien bees around you dive nearer, and you close your eyes, sure they're about to attack. Instead you feel their soft fur brushing against you, like gentle kisses or walking through tall grass. "Queen? Queen?" they ask.

Slowly, you open your eyes. You can see your reflection in the enormous compound eyes of six bees in front of you. You feel a gentle nudge from behind, pushing you upright, so you comply. You sit there, cross-legged in the dirt, and try to make sense of all this.

"Our queen, are you all right?" the voice in your head says.

"Is that you? Are you talking to me?" you ask aloud.

"Of course, our queen. We've been looking for you. Across much distance and time, we have searched. You will join us in our hive, and all will be well," the bees say.

You shake your head, trying to get the illusion to disappear. "Someone must have spiked my drink or something," you mutter to yourself. To the bees, you say, "I'm totally unqualified. Shouldn't you have a queen that looks like you?"

The bees buzz a question in your mind, flying up and circling lazily before returning around you. "Please, our queen, come with us now to our hive," they say, speaking in one voice. "All will be well. We will have much sweetness, our honey shall be potent, our warriors strong, our larvae hardy. Our hive shall be paramount across the worlds. All will be well."

"This is crazy," you mutter, and the bees loop around you. One lands on your shoulder, a solid weight, and you can feel a soft touch of its proboscis—it's licking you. This whole thing is just way too weird, but they're clearly waiting for you to respond.

Finally, you say:
- "I think you've made a mistake. I'm sorry, I'm not your queen." Turn to page 302.
- "You know, I think I have always kinda felt like royalty." Turn to page 305.

- "Did you say you had honey? I *do* really like honey." Turn to page 310.

The buzzing is so loud it is practically a roar as the bees swoop down in unison, stingers extended, each six inches long and wicked-sharp. You're defenseless against them, but still gamely try to swat them away.

However, just like trying to fend off dodgeball in gym class, you're no good. The stingers penetrate your hands, arms, back, buttocks, legs, and your body explodes in pain. It's sensory overload, your mind immediately descending out of panic and into dread. The attacking bees fall to the ground, and their stingers remain in your flesh, continuing to pump you with acidic poisons even while the bugs themselves have fallen.

Your body plunges itself into overdrive, trying to defend you. While maybe you could have handled a normal bee sting just fine, there's nothing on Earth that could have prepared you for giant alien bee stings. Your throat swells, cutting off your air instantly. You grab your neck on impulse, as if that will make more air force its way through, and your heart pounds with adrenaline. Between the two, your death comes rather fast, and soon you fall, prone and swollen beyond recognition, limp on the ground.

THE END

As you stare in horror, the bees turn their attention to you, and you can hear them repeat "Poll-in-ate! Poll-in-ate!" like a terrible drum call. They move with the mindless efficiency of robotic drones, but these bees are alive, their stingers thrust ominously in your direction, bodies curved as they fly.

As they come closer, you shout, "Wouldn't you prefer some nice flowers?"

The bees stop, considering. "Poll-in-ate?" they say, questioningly.

You uncover your head, getting to your feet. This is the best chance you've got. "Flowers? Wouldn't you prefer to pollinate some flowers, maybe? I know where some good ones are."

"You will be pollinated," the bees thrum.

"Okay, yes, all very well," you say. "But I can point you to the good flowers first, if you'd like?"

The bees pause, and you hear their hum as a murmur, as if they are talking among themselves.

"What...are flowers?" the voice in your head asks.

"Um... those nice pretty things full of pollen? Don't you like to eat them?"

The bees consult among themselves again. "Where ...are...flowers? Poll-in-ate! Pollinate!" they scream, menacing you with their stingers.

You try not to wince as you say,

- "The arboretum is that way, about 20 miles." Turn to page 323.
- "There's a nice field just over there, can't miss it." Turn to page 184.

"Not...our queen?" the bees say, swooping in curiosity. "But you smell like our queen. You were here, waiting for us. What do you mean?"

"Well, sorry gals, I guess you just have the wrong queen. I really do wish you all the best in finding um...her majesty. I'm sure she'll be real keen to see you," you say, brushing yourself off and starting to walk away.

The bees follow you in a focused huddle. "Why do you smell like our queen if you are not our queen?" they ask, their buzz taking an angry edge.

"Um, I don't know? Maybe because I've been laying in a field half the night? Does your queen smell like stale beer and manure? It's quite fetching," you say over your shoulder.

One of the bees hits you quite hard in the back, causing you to stumble forward. "Hey!" you say. "Watch where you're flying!"

"False queen!" the bees say. "False queen!"

And that's when you realize they didn't hit you by accident. The bees throw themselves forward, beating you about the face with their wings, landing on your arms, even biting you with their short mandibles. You try to run, swatting them away with your palms, each impact making a resounding "thump." But that's not enough, so the stingers come out.

When the first stinger hits you, it feels like fire. You can feel the poison pumping into your body, spreading like burning oil into your muscles, causing you to arch back and scream. Other bees latch on, stabbing you with their six-inch barbs, willing to die just to make sure you suffer, too. Your death is quick and utterly agonizing.

Maybe the next time you're mistaken for royalty you ought to strongly consider just agreeing to it?

THE END

Ａs you lean back, sipping your sweetened coffee-like concoction, you decide it is totally worth it. Who cares if aliens or someone knows everything about you? You're pretty boring, after all.

Besides, you're addicted to, you know, comfort.

But it's soon clear that Marlene isn't as attached to convenience as you are. It starts small; she deactivates her social media stuff, not like she really had anyone paying attention to her when she didn't post much anyway. Then the next time you check in on her, it turns out she's cancelled her cell phone and her wireless, which is crazy considering she was doing all her work online, so she's effectively cut herself out of a job.

She doesn't listen to you, won't hear any of your reasons why she should stop being so hard on herself, and before you know it she's sold her house and moved out to a shack in the wilderness. It's seriously intense out there; she's basically reverted herself to the pioneer days.

You don't even like to visit, because she doesn't have air conditioning, which is bad enough, but also because she makes you turn off your phone and leave it in the car, which means there's not much to do but sit around staring at each other, trying not to drown in your own sweat.

As time goes by, you check in less and less frequently. Marlene has effectively put herself into social purgatory; no need for you to go with her! So you live your life, and don't think about the satellite, or aliens, or data much at all.

Until the Arrival—until the day when They came. Everyone received the transmission, saw the hard-limbed aliens who knew everything about you, knew your foibles, your weaknesses, knew just how to make you cave. It seemed innocuous enough when the drone dropped the package at your front door. But opening it revealed the photos, the evidence of what you'd done, every shameful thing in your life laid bare...

The takeover happened with barely a peep of insurrection.

Now, as you toil in the cavernous mines below what was once Virginia, you think often of Marlene. You hope that she made it out of their trap, that maybe now she can rescue you.

But your body withers under the strain of the work and the crack of the electric whip. It's too late for you.

THE END

The bees buzz appreciatively around you, weaving together in a gentle hum of satisfaction. "Yes! Our queen!" they say.

You begin to walk back toward the hive, still hovering high above. "By the way," you ask, "how exactly did you know it was me so quickly?"

"Oh, our queen, we bees always recognize royalty!" they thrum. "Can you not see everything about you is majestic?"

Well, on second thought, that is definitely true about you. You have a certain bearing to you, don't you? People take notice of you—and when they don't, you're highly inclined to yell "off with their heads." Yes, it must be true. You've been a queen all this time, lost out in the world, just waiting to be discovered. You're like Sleeping Beauty, or Anastasia, or Fiona—though you hope being queen doesn't mean turning green, or having your whole family brutally murdered, or being trapped and asleep in a castle for 200 years, at least not for you. On that note, you ask... "What happens next?"

"We take you to our planet, our queen," the bees sing. Your heart lifts with their every word. "We will reunite you with your family."

"Um, like my mom? I'm pretty sure she's on this planet."

"No, no, your REAL family, Highness," the bees exclaim. "We will let them explain, yes, all will be well!"

As you get nearer to the hive, the bees cluster together. "We shall carry, Highness," the bees say. You look uncertainly at the hovering hunk of bees loosely formed into a square-ish platform.

"You do a lot of this?" you ask. "Finding of lost queens, and such?"

"No, Highness. We've been seeking you, only you. We shall carry."

They're rather adamant, so against your better judgment you step onto the bees, the ones under your feet dipping dangerously low. Other bees surge forward and you hold them loosely with your arms, and then suddenly, with a great vibration, you are flying! The wind kisses your cheeks as the ground falls away.

As you draw nearer to the hive, the clouds part and you see it is greater, more beautiful, than you could see from the ground. Its walls are intricate hexagonal boxes, and it's not black, but a softly shining grey. A wide archway lies in front of you, and the bees lift you up to it, opening in front of you so you step out like an organic elevator. The surface feels like beeswax, but stronger, and you finally believe that the bees did travel through space and time to find you.

"Yes, our queen," they say. "No time to waste!" And they guide you in, softly brushing against you, warm and soft like a cluster of puppies.

As you step inside, you turn back one last time to see Earth—it is a dull and dreary place, and people were not always—or even frequently—kind or clever or just, but it was the only world you knew.

You turn your back on it, and step gladly into the hive, which glows from within with an unknown light. Behind you, a group of bees constructs a wall, blocking up the entrance and exit with more honeycombs.

The alien bees guide you deeper inside the hive, to a small chamber. They feed you honey, and it has a bright, fruity taste, like pomegranate, but lighter on the tongue. As you eat and drink it, you feel a glow building within you, and feel contented. All the hive is constructed by the bees, and they have created you a couch of sorts, a molded crest of soft wax for you to rest upon.

"We will return to your home, Queen," they say, and begin to dance. At first, just one bee dances, waggling as it oscillates in a rough figure eight. Then her sisters join her, and it is three. They turn heads toward each other and spin, then reverse and spin off, creating new circles with other bees. The dance continues, spreading this way over the hive, until each bee is included in the dance. As you watch, they swirl and buzz and break and reform again and again. It is like watching a kaleidoscope come to life, like creating a mandala in the sand. Your head spins and your heart sings as they dance. It goes on and on, and you lose all sense of time as they dance. You feel incredibly privileged, for you know this is a sight few see, and yet you are sad, because there just aren't words to describe its beauty, its incredible power. The room becomes warmer as the bees dance, and you feel like everything is swirling as the bees sway and wiggle and an incredible light emanates from the center of the dance. You are radiant in it, you welcome it as everything is enfolded in it and is undone.

Something furry rubs against you, and you rouse. Your head feels blurry, and the sweetness of honey remains on your tongue. "Drink," the voice says, and you remember the bees, the dance. You drink eagerly, and the warm decadence tastes of sunlight and summer and pink flowers.

"That was incredible!" you exclaim, and the bees purr in satisfaction.

"Yes, our friends took excellent care of you," a voice says. It has a rich treble to it, but English seems uncomfortable on the tongue. You look around, and discover a woman standing just behind you.

"Oh, I'm sorry, I didn't know anyone else was here," you say, and scramble to your feet. The woman just smiles at you softly. Purple spots, like a leopard's, trace across her forehead and down her neck, meeting like a necklace at her collarbone. She is dressed in a simple white robe, wrapped with another long white cloth at the waist. Her hair is black like a crow's wing, and her eyes are a sharp lavender; when you dare a glance closer, you see she doesn't have a round pupil—hers are curved, like a cloverleaf—and the corners of her eyes tilt down.

"You may call me Evetee," she says. "I am to be your assistant."

"My assistant?" you ask. "Assistant in what?"

You are suddenly very aware that your hair is all mussed from whatever the bees did. You try to smooth it down without being too obvious.

"Forgive me, Queen, my words are not...so good. I am to help you," she says, stumbling a little over the pronunciation.

First the bees, now this. "Oh, okay. What's first?"

She bows, her head dipping so far as to show you every bone in her neck, and walks in front of you. You take this to mean you should follow, so you do.

"Thank you, bees," you say. The bees send you a feeling of warmth. Ahead, a few workers finish pulling away wax from the entrance, revealing a metal platform and a window that looks out onto a world of purples and reds and blues.

"How...how did we get here?" you say. It looks like a Seussian storybook come to life, except for the metal. You stare out over the expanse—there's something large flying, with what look like three sets of wings?!—as you walk down the path, keeping one hand on the rail.

"The bees are excellent travelers," Evetee says. "They are...less good searchers, but they did find you." She turns to smile widely at you, and this calms you, because at least a smile seems to be the same here. "For that, we are grateful to them. All will be well."

"Where...is...here?" you ask, still grappling with the idea that you left Earth behind.

"This is Klungstogh," Evetee says, making a guttural, German-esque grunt on the end. "But I should leave the explanations to your ...what is the word? Chancellors."

She guides you through a gauzy curtain into a small room. It is draped with fabrics in the same rich colors as the plants you saw outside, and has a pile of clothing on a low bench. Even though you insist you can dress yourself, Evetee is remarkably persistent. She—rather intimately! —washes you with a sponge that smells like hibiscus and coffee and then helps you drape the cloths on you. They feel odd, loose in all the wrong places, but they are light on your skin and make you feel strangely beautiful. When you are dressed, she guides you to a mirror-like pond and shows you your reflection—you've never looked so put-together before.

Evetee's final touch is a small pin of a bee, which she affixes to a curl of your robe. "You must wear your honor proudly," she says, leaving you to puzzle this out.

"Now I shall take you to meet your Chancellors," Evetee declares.

She guides you down more hallways, some open to the air, and you look up to see an entirely different set of stars above you. These are creamy, and glisten like flecks of glass in the night sky. A moon hangs jade low in the sky.

"This place is incredible," you gasp, and yet it has many wonders more for you.

You step into a larger chamber; a group of people decked in robes of crimson and vermillion and chartreuse and lavender—all the colors of the field and flower—turn to greet you. None here have the spots marking Evetee, but all share the eyes, that strangeness to them.

They bow low, and you blush with awkwardness. "Um...hi," you say.

"Our Queen, how grateful we are to find you, at long last," a man says, stepping forward. He seems older—if time has the same meaning here—wrinkles setting in at his lips and neck. His hands shake gently, but he seems strong.

"Yes, we are glad to see you here, now," a woman says. Her skin is a dark olive, and a butterfly as big as a dinner plate flaps its wings gently from her hairpiece. You're pretty sure it's real.

"Finally," a woman in the back snarls. When the butterfly-woman gives her a look, the speaker, a small woman dressed in brilliant yellow, adds, "Your Majesty."

"Thank you for...finding me," you say, and now you wish you'd always been a Queen or whatever, because you're pretty sure someone born to royalty should know how to deal with a situation as bizarre as this. You wonder briefly what kind of training the Queen of England gets, and think maybe you should ask the bees to pick her up the next time they're in the vicinity.

The first man who spoke, the older man dressed in dark forest green, says, "Come. We have much to tell you." With a flick of his fingers, he dismisses Evetee, who bows bent low at the waist and backs out the room.

"I'm afraid you have arrived at Klungstogh at a difficult time," he says. "In fact, that's why we sent the bees to find you."

Figures that you'd inherit a beautiful space kingdom only when it's in trouble. Ugh.

He continues, "Your predecessor, Queen Harold, served his purpose well, but—well, passed—rather young. You see, we the Chancellors have managed the affairs of Klungstogh since his death about a century ago—in your sense of time. But there are a few matters we cannot handle directly, as tradition dictates. For that, we needed you."

"You...went a hundred years without a Queen?" you ask. "And wait, how come I'm a queen, again? And why was I on Earth instead of here?"

The Chancellors exchange knowing looks. "You are angry," the butterfly woman says.

"No, I'm..."

"That is understandable," she continues, ignoring your interjection. "What we need to know now, though, is...are you willing to stay and help Klungstogh? Will you be the Queen we need?"

They all look at you, expectantly, and your heart freezes. What do you do? Crap, they look like they really expect an answer...

You say,

- "Can I get more details on what being Queen means?" Turn to page 138.
- "Yes, I will be your Queen." Turn to page 87.
- "No, and I really wish you all the best, but I don't think I can be Queen after all." Turn to page 34.

The bees face each other for a millisecond, then back to you, and say, "Oh yes, our queen. You will love our honey! It is the best! We shall feed it to you. You will taste the worlds we visit, we will show you our dances." They sound triumphant.

You have a ridiculous sweet tooth, and it doesn't sound so bad to go to the nexus of a ton of honey. Besides, if the bees are as big as footballs, how much honey must they have?

"Well then, I guess I'd better at least see it? I mean, if there's a good reason you think I'm your queen, I'd better at least taste your nectar before I, like, agree to all this, right? I understand it takes a lot to lead, you know, lots to consider," you say, and allow yourself to be guided back toward the hovering black hive.

You feel a little uneasy, thinking about being inside that thing, until you come up with the obvious solution.

"Uh, guys?" you say. "I think there's just a teensy little problem. I'm a little too big to make it up there. My, uh, wings, don't really work? So you'll just have to bring me the honey here I guess. Don't worry, I'll wait." You start to think about all the things you could do with the honey. You could market it! Space Honeys! Oh man, you're going to make a killing! "Yeah, just, bring me like, I don't know, a bucket full? That should be a good way to start, just a little taste, you see," you say, grinning wildly.

"Oh, my queen, we will help you," the bees say. "We will not leave you behind. We came all this way. All will be well."

"Uh," you say, and the bees lead you to one of the open coffin-like spaces they came down in.

"Get in, get in!" they urge. You stare uneasily at the empty void. It looks like you'll fit, but it's a tight squeeze, and besides, it's pitch-black.

"Are you sure this is the best idea?" you ask, but they're already pushing you forward, the needy little buggers. "Fine," and you step into the void. Your shoulders are pinched against the walls, which feel like a rather thick papier mache. The bees huddle around the entrance.

"This is really weird," you say to yourself, and then you realize what the bees are doing—they're closing you in.

"HEY!" you yell. "I didn't agree to this! Hey! Let me out!" You try to squeeze back out but the bees are working incredibly fast and the opening is getting narrower and narrower. You try to push against the walls but they're stronger than you look.

The last thing you see out the hole are the mandibles of the bee sealing you in completely.

Things feel rather desperate.

And then the coffin begins to move.

It shifts, rocking you back hard against the wall. It makes no sound, but you feel the pitch of gravity sway under you, like riding an elevator going a touch too fast. You close your eyes against the dark, which helps you to believe that maybe there is a light and your eyes are just closed, just for a moment.

You're thrown against the wall with a thud as your little space collides with something outside. You pound on the walls as best as you can, but you can't reach higher than your waist. You feel incredibly helpless.

But then you hear a light scratching, and the bees are back, chewing through and peeling back the walls like they are nothing.

You pinch yourself, hoping this is all a bad dream.

Nope. Still awake. Still happening.

"Queen! Queen!" the bees say, and you step out into the hive. Octagonal shapes all around you, a path twisting forward, and all around, in every nook and crack, are bees, staring at you with their huge black eyes, their voices filling your head. There's nothing to do but go onward, deeper into the hive.

"So...there's honey, you said?" you ask.

"Yes. Honey! Honey, honey, we will show you, all will be well, all will be well," the bees say.

You have to duck in places, crawl underneath precarious constructions filled with bees. Some cells here are closed off, sealed with the same hard material the lift had been made of. You run your fingers along it as you pass, and feel the warmth inside. Something shifts under your hand, and you pull back.

"Come, come!" the bees say, and you follow, until you have no idea if you are up or down or left or right.

"One of you shall be our queen!" the bees say, triumphant.

"Wait, what? What do you mean, 'one of us'?" you say, and you emerge into a large cavern. This must be the heart of the hive. It is spacious, a cavern filled with softly glowing light.

Across from you is a lean man, his flannel pajama pants hanging loosely from his hips. He looks utterly bewildered.

"One will be queen!" the bees say, and a hum of excitement fills the air. The bees watch you from all around, covering the walls, teeming everywhere you look.

You walk over to the other person. "Thank god!" you say. "I

thought I was hallucinating! This is insane, right?"

He scratches at his head, his eyes still bleary. He has a very thin mustache, like he's been trying to grow one but isn't quite good at it. "They said I was their queen," he says.

"Yeah, me too. This is all one heck of a misunderstanding, right?" you say jovially.

"One shall be queen!" the bees shout, the words filling your mind.

You look around. "What do you mean? Why did you bring both of us here? You said I was queen!"

"Yes! Yes!" the bees shout, and you instinctively cover your ears, though it does nothing against the roar. "One shall be queen!"

The man looks around, anxious. "So...do you want to be queen?" he asks.

"To be honest, I just came up here to try some honey." You offer your hand. "Nice meeting you, why don't we both just try to go home?"

He shakes, his hand weak in yours.

You hold up your hands to the crowd of bees. "There's clearly some cultural misunderstandings here. We'll just go home and you guys can figure out this whole queen thing on your own, okay?"

"NO," the bees cry. "One shall be queen! You may not leave! Fight, fight to see who is the greatest, the strongest queen for our hive!"

"Are you fucking serious?" the guy says. "I was comfortable in my bed, and these bastards came in and woke me up and told me I was a queen and I was all 'how did you know' and they dragged me up here and now you're telling me I'm supposed to fight?! Dammit."

"Yeah, this is crazy," you say, and turn to leave.

A wall of bees forms in front of you, blocking your path, stingers out. "Just let me pass, okay?" you say.

The bees shout, "NO. One shall be queen. Fight!" The words fill your head.

"Dammit, they seem serious. Okay, I guess we have to fight if we want to leave, then," the mustached man says. He drops into a loose stance, fists up, fabric from his pajamas pooling around his ankles.

You look around, taking everything in, then:
- Leave anyway. Turn to page 316.
- Get ready to fight. Turn to page 320.

The professor isn't in his office when you swing by, but he has his schedule taped to the door. You walk up to the lecture hall as he's wrapping up a discussion.

"That's why it's so important that you do the research," Dr. Paxton says. "If you don't know your client, you're going to waste everyone's time and your company's money on people who don't care about you, who don't want your product. Any questions?"

Dr. Paxton is a lean man who is too old to be sporting frosted tips but nonetheless manages to make himself look kinda dashing with them. He has an energy about him, like a kid who has sucked down too many Pixie Sticks. He answers a few questions from the class with a kind of cavalier amusement, then dismisses the lecture hall. You and Marlene duck into a side corner to avoid the surge of traffic, but soon can make your way down the stairs to the lectern.

"Wow, Dr. Paxton, you're definitely the person we want to talk to," you say as he bundles his laptop into a classy leather briefcase.

"Is that so?" he says, and his smile is warm and makes you feel like your insides are made of fresh chocolate chip cookies. You smile sheepishly.

Marlene isn't so smitten, and charges in with her customary grace. "What could someone do if they had a shit-ton of detailed data on people?" she asks.

"Oh, all kinds of things!" Paxton exclaims. "That's why it's so important we marketers do our research, you know. Now, if you have any other questions about today's lecture..."

"Sir, we're not in your class," you interrupt. "We ...found... some data and aren't sure what it's for. We thought if we showed you, you could tell us what was going on?"

Marlene shoots you eye-daggers, but you just shrug. You've got to get things done one way or another.

"Uh-huh," Dr. Paxton says. "So, like, what?"

"Here," you say, flipping through the pages and handing him one. "Here's the report on you."

Dr. Paxton reads for a moment, and you expect the same kind of oh-my-god reaction you had when you saw your entry. But instead, you're met with elation. "This is incredible! What were your research methods? Definitely cookie tracking here, but there's so much. I'm sure my credit card isn't leaked somewhere..." He trails off, trying to piece together where the information came from. "Really, outstanding work. Who did you say you are again?"

"Uh, we didn't," you say, but introduce yourself and Marlene. "We found this data...how isn't really important, and we're concerned that the creators are going to use it with..."—how do you make this sound delicate? —" bad intentions."

"And there's more of it?" Dr. Paxton asks.

"Much more," Marlene says seriously.

"I see..." Dr. Paxton says, stroking his chin thoughtfully. "Why don't we continue this talk in my office?"

You follow Paxton back to his office, which is bright and colorful with the loud spines of many books. You and Marlene explain it all, and Dr. Paxton listens attentively the whole time, rifling through the data as he does.

After you've finished your story, he asks, "And do you have the whole dataset? I, uh, don't think I can really answer you without knowing the full scope of the situation."

"Oh, sure, here," you say, and hand the zip drive over. Marlene stares at you with more of those eye-daggers.

Dr. Paxton takes the drive as if it were a sacred totem, immediately slipping it into his pocket. "Great, thanks. Been so nice meeting you, just let me analyze this a bit and I'll get back to you with more information! Have a great day, bye!" And he slams his office door behind you.

"Why did you give it to him?" Marlene hisses.

"What? He needed it! He can't tell us what's going on without it."

"I don't trust him," she insists.

"Well, too bad. He has it now and that's that. I'm going home," you declare.

You eagerly await Dr. Paxton's findings, but two weeks go by before he calls. "Turns out there isn't really much here," he says. "Sorry."

"What do you mean, 'there isn't much here'?" you ask. "There were detailed reports on people *everywhere!*"

"Yeah, sorry, don't know what to tell you," he says, and hangs up.

So you decide it's time for a little data-snooping of your own. You find his house, which looks modest enough...but there's a "FOR SALE" sign in the front yard. And...that Tesla in the driveway looks new.

"Hey there, whatever you're sellin', we don't want any." The man yelling at you must be Dr. Paxton's neighbor, from the way he's waving a trowel at you from across a hedge.

"Oh hi!" you say, hoping you can make your voice glow half as much as Dr. Paxton's did when you met him. "I was just interested in the house. When did it go on the market?"

The old man scratches across his thin white undershirt absently, then says, "Just a day or so ago. Turns out he came into a big of money so he's givin' it all up and movin'—where was it again? —Switzerland or sumsuch. You gonna buy it? Because I don't take kindly to no loud music at night or barkin' dogs or any of that."

"Not to worry, sir, I'd be an excellent neighbor," you say, backing toward your car. "Thanks for talking, bye now!"

You feel your rage swell as you turn back onto the highway. "Came into a bunch of money," huh? You drive up to the university and find your way to Dr. Paxton's office. Movers are there, boxing up the books, and there's Paxton in the center of it all, still looking slick.

"You sold the data!" you exclaim, getting right in his face. "You stole it from us and you sold it? How could you?"

Dr. Paxton unleashes his megawatt smile. "Hey, nice to see you again. So sorry that data you gave me didn't pan out. But, as you can see, I'm a little busy here, so I don't have time to talk about it."

"Give it back!" you demand. "I don't know who you sold it to, or for what, but give it back!"

"Oh sure, sure, here," he says, and hands you the tiny flash drive.

"I swear, I can't believe we trusted you!" you shout, and storm back out.

You don't realize your mistake until you've gotten back home and plugged the drive into your computer. It's empty. He swapped them out, that bastard, and gave you a useless empty drive. Now you have no data, no proof, and you're not even going to make a mint off it!

Next time, do your research, kiddo.

THE END

That's it. You aren't going to fight a complete stranger in order to be "queen"—whatever that means—for giant alien bees. It's ridiculous! This whole thing is ridiculous!

"Right. I'm leaving," you declare, and turn your back on your opponent. The wall of bees buzzes ominously at you, but you push on anyway and they part—thank god—to let you pass. You can feel their anger palpably, pressing against you, but you press on.

The hive is a literal maze, glowing softly like candlelight, but with so many twists and turns you are almost certain you're going the wrong way. Gravity is weird here, too, and you discover you're able to jump up over obstacles that should be much too high. The bees, of course, are no help. It seems they've stopped talking to you, and the space in your head they used to fill is now just a steady buzzing, like static on an old TV.

You catch a burst of cold air on your face and feel you must be close—finally! You rush forward, eager to get out already, catapulting yourself over another hexagonal protrusion—

And fall out of the hive, which is still over a mile up.

You fall for long enough to really consider the enormity of your mistake, to think about all the things in your life you could have done differently to maybe have avoided this fate. The wind rushes up against your skin, and your eyes water from the cool of it. You remember that a girl once survived a skydiving accident even after her parachute didn't deploy properly, and wonder if maybe you can do the same? But then again that is an awful lot of broken bones, and you're out here in this field in the dark, and knowing your luck you'd probably fall all the way and still not be seen by anyone and break all those bones and die out here of internal damage or something else that would be totally fixable.

SPLAT.
No need to worry; you didn't survive the fall.

THE END

Your heart swells a bit as Scout says this to you. "You want to travel ...with me?" you ask, tears in your eyes.

"Yes. We shall...be friends," says. Its spikes swell for a moment, as if bursting with the same emotion you feel.

"I'd be honored," you say. "I know exactly where we should go first."

You take a turn off the next exit on the interstate and head northwest on I-77. You stop briefly to fill up on gas, snacks, and pick up a map. As detours go, it's a long one, but you keep your destination secret as you go, just giving Scout the next directions when its driving. After 13 hours, you turn down the side road. "Ta-da!" you say, flourishing one arm as you pull up to the double glass pyramids making up the Rock and Roll Hall of Fame.

"This is...a...temple!" Scout exclaims.

"Yeah, kinda," you say, chuckling. It's your first time visiting, and those ticket prices are a bit steep, but you get in and boy is it worth it to see Scout freak out! You spend all day in there, explaining who "newer" acts like KISS and the Beach Boys are. One security guard starts in fright at the alien's appearance, but you just mouth "kids" and pretend you're a very accommodating parent. The guard's eyes widen but she leaves you alone.

Scout lingers for a long while at the B.B. King exhibit, reverent, but doesn't know the vast majority of acts. The peculiar alien seems to be absorbing it all like a sponge, though, its claws twitching as it mouths the words played over the speakers.

By the end of the day, you're both seriously overstimulated, and exhaustedly fall into a booth at the nearest burger joint for an overly greasy meal. (Scout eats two plates of fries and then goes in for a banana split. It lasts just five minutes; you don't even get a bite!)

"Pretty good day, right Scout?" you say, belly full to bursting.

Scout belches loudly, and the couple at the table next to yours looks alarmed. "Best day...ever," Scout says. You notice the alien's voice has a bit of Freddie Mercury now. Not bad.

"Well...now what? I'm almost out of money, so we kinda gotta choose what we do next carefully," you explain.

"Money?" Scout asks.

"Yeah, I have to pay for things. I'm not rich, you know; figured you could tell that from my car!" You laugh, but after a moment it's clear Scout doesn't get the joke. "Crap, you don't know what money is, do you?" you say.

Scout opens its mouth and sings, "Money, money, money, must be funny, in the rich man's world..."

The words just spool out like musical rope. Scout's jaw isn't even moving. It's creepy.

"Ok, that's just creepy," you say.

Scout pauses for a moment, then asks, "Is it important?"

"Yeah it's important. We can't do pretty much anything without it!"

Scout considers for a second, then says, "Then I will...get us some."

You start to explain that it isn't really that easy but before you know it Scout has slid out of the booth and is standing at the next table over. The couple gasps in surprise and recoils away, but then the alien opens its mouth and out comes Michael Jackson's "Thriller." It's a perfect imitation—even though Scout just heard the song today! —and before long the couple is dancing along in their seats. A bus boy comes by and stares, but even he can't help but groove to the Prince of Pop. When the song ends, people all over the burger joint clap, and the man at the booth deposits a five-dollar bill in Scout's upturned claws.

"Huh," you say. "Scout, I think you may be on to something."

The next few months are a whirlwind. You set yourself up as Scout's manager and start small, but between the alien's perfect musical imitations and its "freaky" look, it doesn't take long for Alien Rock to really catch on. You travel the country, touring and seeing all the important sites. You make a long stop at Graceland, and Scout is deeply impacted by Elvis' white bell-sleeved, rhinestoned look. You buy one the next day, and it really ups the glamour.

After a month or two, Scout even starts improvising. You take your rock'n'roll alien to the current songster show and that's when things really blow up. The whole country can't get enough of Scout, how funny, how weird, how totally Out of This World it all is. No one seems to really believe Scout's an alien, but then again no one really asks too many questions when you're famous.

You have the typical fights you'd expect between a manager and talent, the threats to return to the secret mission, screaming matches over whether it's okay to bite someone, the usual, but overall you get along great.

Scout is now considered some crazy hybrid between Lady Gaga and David Bowie, and soon you're traveling the world, selling out stadiums, even performing at the Super Bowl.

But one day, a few years in, Scout's spines just won't stop drooping. The pint-sized alien has been looking well, blue, lately, but that's normal for a seven-armed shorty. But Scout, its voice now sounding remarkably like yours, says, "It is time to go." Scout looks up at you blearily.

"What do you mean, champ, we're here for three weeks!" you say, checking the Las Vegas schedule on your phone in case you'd gotten something wrong.

"No," Scout says. "I have failed my mission. You showed me so much, so wonderful...but I forgot my mission. And now my time is over. My species, we don't live very long. Now it is too late."

"Too late for what?" you ask. "Scout, you're scaring me!"

But Scout doesn't answer, a long line of green slime, like a slug, wriggling out of one nostril. You're both repulsed and afraid for your talent, your ticket to fortune. You run over and shake Scout, but its body just flails around.

The green slime crawls away.

"What did you mean, it's too late?! Scout, Scout come back to me!"

That's how news of the death of the world's favorite alien rocker broke the same day astronauts on the space station reported weird objects coming toward the station—and not from the direction of Earth.

Sure, Scout was kinda cute in a weird way, but the musical creature was only the first party on the planet. Its kin turn out to be much beefier...and unfortunately believe Earth had trapped, tortured, and murdered their scout. So they do what any reasonable avenging space army would do, and blow off the face of the planet.

Oh well. Guess Alien Rock won't ever make the Hall of Fame.

THE END

319

"Hey, nothing personal, man, okay?" you say, and raise your fists. He nods agreement.

The bees thrum with excitement as you begin to circle across the cavern floor. It's smooth, and when you spare a glance down you realize it's raw beeswax, still opaque. You can see faint hexagonal outlines through it, like tiles. No need to worry about tripping, though.

"Fight, one shall be queen, all will be well!" the bees sing, and everywhere you look you can see those eyes.

You have no idea what you will do. The only time you were in a fight was when you were eight and Jessica called you a "fart sniffer" so you grabbed her by the hair and pulled her to the ground. You had to sit out of recess the rest of the day for that. If you'd known you would eventually be forced into royalty-by-combat, you might have picked a few more playground fights.

Your opponent lunges forward, a test jab toward your abdomen. You dart out of the way, and spare a moment to look him over. He's lean, not obviously muscled. He doesn't look like he works out much, but he does seem youngish, mid-twenties maybe, and that might make him a little bit quick.

You jump forward, trying to wrap him up in a bear hug, but manage only to slap him around the waist a little. He rears back and punches you in the jaw, right fist connecting with your cheek.

OW.

You haven't been punched before, and you really weren't prepared for it to hurt that much. You shake your head, trying to loosen the pain from your senses, and kick at his knees. You vaguely remember "sweep the leg," so you try that, but you're no martial artist and though you trip him up a little, he stays on his feet. You get turned around, however, and he comes up behind you, throwing an elbow around your neck in a sleeper hold.

"AHHH!" you grunt, and heave him backward, still locked around your neck, into one of the walls covered in bees. With a gasp he lets you go, and you dart forward, out of his reach.

You:
- Decide to leave. This isn't worth it. Turn to page 316.
- Wind up to deliver a haymaker while he's dazed. Turn to page 4.
- Pull out your best wrestling moves and climb up the wall of hexagons. Turn to the next page.

You've seen those wrestling shows a time or two, and though you lack the face paint or bandana and don't wear your underwear on the outside, you're pretty sure you can handle it. You climb the hexagonal wall, the alien bees edging out of your way as you climb. "Kill, kill," they whisper to you, like an evil Jiminy Cricket.

You turn, gripping the honeycomb on either side of you, facing out toward your opponent, who is running back across the chamber. You're only a few feet up, but it's enough to give you some great leverage. You leap, spread-eagled, catching him off-guard. His shoulder plows into your gut, but gravity does its work and pushes you both to the floor, where he lays face-down. You take a moment to catch your breath, feeling his skin warm underneath your belly, then push off. As you step back he grabs at your ankle, trying to pull you down, and on impulse you turn and kick. Your heel catches him right in the jaw, knocking his head back. Blood explodes on the floor—you must have broken his nose. Warily, you watch for him to get up.

He doesn't move.

You dart in, nudging him with a foot.

He doesn't move.

"Victor! Our queen! Queen!" the bees scream, but he can't be dead, that doesn't make sense, he was just alive a second ago, you didn't kick him that hard, how can he be dead?

You rush over and flip the man on his back, willing him to breathe, to fight you, anything, but he flops limply over. You try to feel for a pulse like you've seen on those hospital television shows, but you can't find one.

He's really dead.

"Our queen! Our queen!" the bees chant.

You stand to your full height, blood dripping from a cut near your eye and another down your forearm. You are queen now. The cost was high, true, but you have other responsibilities.

A retinue of bees surrounds you, guiding and leading you out of the chamber. They lead you down into a separate part of the hive, narrower, the walls glowing only faintly. They bring out honey, carrying it to you in their short mandibles, and it is sweeter than sweet, like wedding cake icing dredged in donut frosting, melty and rhapsodic and unreal.

You sit on the floor, sticky to your elbows with the stuff, and ask, "So what does all this queen stuff mean anyway?"

It turns out "queen bees" are nothing at all like queen humans. See, first there's actually no ruling; the hive pretty well self-manages. Your job is only to...ahem...create more bees. The first day you are made queen, you are presented with a bevy of bees. And look, you don't want to get into details, because it was deeply humiliating, but...you mated. With all of them. They're alien bees, okay? And yeah, it was weird, but you're pretty sure the bees spiked your honey because— much like that trip to Vegas—it seemed like a good idea at the time.

Otherwise, you are locked in your humble cavern, fed honey and a milky jelly-like substance, and pretty much just lay around, laying eggs. The how is kinda complicated, because, again, alien bees, but that's your life now. Sure, your every need is cared for, except you never leave that room, never see anyone else, can only talk to the bee hive mind and just pump out eggs for the rest of your life. As to why they needed a human queen? You have them explain it to you once, but they're so foreign and weird that you have trouble understanding—it's something about not being able to find any queens in their species. Which means that space is filled with these bees, buzzing around from galaxy to galaxy, harvesting hapless victims to serve as their queens.

Lucky you.

THE END

The bees turn as one, heading out across the horizon toward the arboretum (you hope). You make a beeline back to town as quickly as you can, running until your feet bleed but it's worth it if it puts a solid door between you and bees as big as dinner plates.

Soon after, you pick up news of the bees on the morning news.

The well-made-up broadcaster sitting behind her desk holds a finger to her ear and then cheerily reports, "Breaking news: A group of extremely large bees has arrived at the arboretum and is busy enjoying the diverse selection of exotic plants. To accommodate these bees—which are not believed to be native to the area—all gardens have been closed for the day. They seem to have come from—can you believe it, Don?—space perhaps, and as such are quite hungry from their journey."

This is accompanied by a close-up picture of a space bee greedily nestling among the thorns of a rose bush, drinking from one after another of the flowers in quick succession.

"You know Don," the newscaster says, turning to face her cohost and showing off her magically straight hair. "We should all try to enjoy our native environment so much."

"Ain't that the truth, Sue?" Don replies. "Up next, is water killing us?"

And then the show cut to commercials.

Over the next few weeks, the bees drift from garden to garden, drinking deep of the nectar of earth. It's not long before they are set aside as a protected species, and Space Bee Trusts are opened. Over the winter, special heated tents are erected in Denver to shelter the bees, and volunteers come in to feed them sugar water as a replacement for the flowers they've sucked dry and left withered in the cold.

No one seems to think twice about the Space Bees or where they've come from; they just become folded into the fabric of life. Sure, it would be a bad day if you were stung by them, and there is some fuss made about replacing native species, but humans have a long, long history of welcoming in invasive species, consequences be damned, and once Big Farma gets involved, the bees are licensed and put to work for agriculture. It's all accepted for a matter of course, though you sort of think their honey tastes pretty bad, compared to the honey you used to know, back in the day.

THE END

The stinger sinks deep into your chest, and you stare in helpless dismay as it undulates, pulsing with poison that you feel slowing your heart, like fire and ice. You fully expect to die from the pain, but instead discover you are paralyzed, every nerve ending screaming at you.

Meanwhile, the aliens busy themselves with your body. They rattle around, black-garbed knights, carefully laying an egg between your ribs, keeping you just on the brink of death and yet not yet gone. You are aware as they skitter off, black against the black of night, to wreak further mayhem in the town, the state, the world.

You breathe, breath by labored breath, your heart beating slowly, slowly, and yet you live. Though all your world is pain, and you are paralyzed and helpless against it, you still technically live. You exist in a deep fever dream of reality, tormented by visions your brain tells you cannot be real and yet are. You see repeated visions of armored monsters.

A day or so later, your consciousness focuses again on a new sensation. Something is wriggling in your gut. You feel a sharp jolt as the thing inside your chest cavity hatches, breaking free from one shell to find itself in a warm, moist nest. It starts to eat, and you feel each bite as a new pain layered on top of your impossible pain, new agony upon new agony, as you lie helpless against all of it. It eats you alive, and you continue to breathe and to feel until it finally, mercifully, nibbles away at your heart.

Your lifeblood feeds the young brood, makes it strong, and it crawls out of your corpse to continue the alien invasion upon your world. It is thanks to you that the second wave begins and humanity finds itself on its knees.

THE END

The research library is overwhelming, so many books that you may never find the answers you need. But maybe there are people who can speed up the process. Marlene pulls up a roster of professors, each listed with their specialties, from Ancient Languages to Zoology. It's still a huge list, and you stare at it for a long moment, trying to suss out the right one to share your goldmine of data with.

Conferring with Marlene, you decide to go to:

- Professor of Languages, Dr. Domenica Joby. Turn to page 280.
- Professor of Data-Based Marketing, Dr. Ron Paxton. Turn to page 313.
- Professor of Computer Engineering, Dr. Charley Kai. Turn to page 292.

Coming back to consciousness is like wobbling through a train tunnel—a small light ahead of you scopes out, broadening, and you become aware of more, but unsteadily. You ache all over and have no idea where you are. You curl your body forward, pushing against a hard grating on the floor—floor, below you, okay—and try to reorient.

The room is dark, lit only dimly with a greenish glow emanating from shelves all around. The room is circular, lined top to bottom with the shelves, each laden with glass jars of all sizes. You stand up, unsteadily, to get a closer look. There are ... *things*...inside the glass. Things like jellyfish, or little toads, but not like any you've ever seen before. You tap gently on one, and a clam-like creature opens to reveal sharp, pointed teeth. You jerk your hand back quickly.

"No. Touch."

You jump at the voice, which is nasally and accented. You look around for the source, but see no one.

"Hello? Can you tell me where I am?" you ask, scanning the room.

A lump you had mistaken for a large rock pushes off a shelf behind you, a tall, triangular head balanced precariously on a ridiculously long neck swiveling in your direction.

"Aaah!" you say, and fall back against the shelf.

"No touch," the creature says.

You step forward hastily, holding both hands up in a gesture of surrender, and try to get away from the shelf while also staying as far as possible from the speaker. "Who...what are you? Where am I? What is going on?"

The creature looks at you with unreadable green eyes. "Experiment," it says, as if that clears everything up.

"I'm in an experiment?" You struggle to remember what happened... you were being chased, flying saucers. The realization dawns on you slowly. "Oh god."

You start to cry.

The alien watches you.

"Please, please don't hurt me," you sputter, falling back against the jars again. Liquid spills on you, and something hisses menacingly.

The alien just stares at you. "Experiment," it says.

You back away again, trying to get as far from it as possible, retreating into another shadow. "I'm on a spaceship, aren't I? And we could be anywhere by now..."

"Spaceship," the creature says.

"Are you mocking me or are you just stupid?" you shout.

The green eyes watch you impassively. "Experiment. Come home," it says.

It extends a limb, a little like a thin elephant's trunk, toward you, and you flinch away. Still, it persists, and you smack it, and scream in pain. Your hand feels like it is on fire where you touched it, your nerves shrieking, and you fall to your knees.

"Noted," the alien says, retracting its arm.

You curl up as small as you can, and watch it, clutching your wounded arm to your chest. The alien turns to a small panel you hadn't noticed previously, and lights flip on and off in a slow sequence.

The pain in your hand subsides, and you keep watch on the alien, but it ignores you, its experiment abated for now. It moves around the small room, inspecting and sometimes interacting with the creatures in the jars. When it moves toward you, you scoot away; it pointedly ignores you.

You wait until it is paying attention to the wall you woke up near, then rush to the panel, touching anything that seems likely. The alien turns on you immediately, reaching for you with that burning tentacle. It makes a sound like rocks cracking, low and ominous, and you dart out of the way, jamming a button-like protuberance on the panel. The world shifts suddenly to the right, throwing you and the alien against the far wall of the ship. The alien turns away from you, back toward the panel, and you panic. You grab the jar nearest you and throw it as hard as you can at the alien, sending a small sucker-like creature hurtling out to land on it with a wet smack. The alien growls again, crying, "Experiment!" as you grab for every jar within reach, hurling one after another at your captor.

The small space explodes into mass chaos, small jarred creatures flopping on the floor, stuck to the alien, snapping harmlessly at the air. The alien screams in rage and slams a tentacle across the panel and the ship lets out a terrible metallic shriek. It begins to tumble end over end, jars crashing all around as you roll and smash against the shelves, helpless to slow your fall or defend yourself. The alien holds on to the grated floor, creeping toward you all the while.

A jolt shoots through the small craft, sending everything flying off the shelves and into a rain upon you, and you tumble into the alien. Your skin burns like a house fire as the ship makes contact with something outside with a dreadful, resonant *THUD*. The pain is insurmountable, but you push off the alien—which doesn't move or react at all— and try to find your feet. The grating below you is a sea of hazards, but you stumble toward the panel, again hitting any switches. A round one near the middle finally gets you the result you want, opening a portal in the middle of what had been the floor. Despite the terrible pain in your muscles and your possibly-broken leg, you pull yourself up and out, landing in tall burnt grass.

You take a breath, then realize you *can*, which means wherever you are at least will let you live for another five minutes or so—which is better than suffocating in the depths of space. You are giddy with joy at this prospect. Even better, the grass is greenish tan, the sky a perfect bluebird blue—it looks like you never even left Earth!

As soon as you've calmed down, you crawl forward, away from the terrible ship. You can't see much in the field, because of the tall grass, but you have to get away from the ship. Maybe you can find somewhere to get help, if you get moving. You crawl toward a tree, its bark thin and close, and stare up at the bright green fan-shaped leaves. Beautiful. It's the best thing you've ever seen.

You close your eyes for just a moment, allowing yourself to rest. Maybe the police will have seen the crash and will come help; best not to overexert yourself right now.

It can't have been more than a few minutes when you hear a low trumpeting sound. It doesn't seem like a car, but then you could be almost anywhere, so you pull yourself up to your feet, full of hope for your rescue.

But you can't believe what you're seeing. You blink and rub your eyes, hoping it will change the creature you see in front of you, but no, your eyes aren't deceiving you.

It's something out of *Jurassic Park*. Not the spitty dinosaur, probably, but not particularly friendly, either. Brontosaurus? No, that's not right, but oh my god it's enormous.

If this is Earth, something has gone horribly wrong. You've been knocked back *millennia*, before the dawn of the human race. Welcome to the Age of the Dinosaur.

THE END

ABOUT THE AUTHOR

M.E. Kinkade tried an apple a day to keep the doctor away, but found a restraining order to be cheaper and more effective. She lives in Dallas, Texas, where it is too hot. She has not been abducted by a UFO yet, but here's hoping. Other books include *Undead Rising: Decide Your Destiny*.

Find her on Twitter at @MEKinkade or at her website, mekinkade.com.

SECRETS IN KANYON RIDGE

Will Second Chances Lead to Love?

A Novel By
Dee Cohoon-Madore

Deelightful Reading

ABOUT THE AUTHOR

Writing has been a passion of mine for as long as I can remember. I've always had the urge to hold a pencil and just create something.

I have always found it essential to have a notepad and my storybook pencil at the ready; on my nightstand; in my handbag;  beside my favorite chair. When thoughts come to mind for my "work in progress," I'm usually within reaching distance to one of those locations and able to record my thoughts. A brainwave can come to me at any time but, they especially drift in when I am lying in bed at night. Notions swirl round my head, sometimes at lightning speed. If I ignore them and go to sleep, by morning the flash will be gone and every thought, every tiny detail that had gone through my mind are no longer there. So, my rule is, when the thoughts come... get up and write them down. I can't disappoint my readers.

I am so grateful to see that my books have travelled across Canada, to the United States and to the other side of the world to Thailand. Copies have also gone to several locations in Africa and been lucky enough to vacation on the sunny beaches of Cuba and Spain. Even several autographed copies of Gifted were stolen off a table at the Home Show at the Digby High School. I really don't know if it was an insult or a compliment, but I hope they somehow found their way into the hands of appreciative readers.

We all have hopes and dreams and I know, I am firmly in the dreamer category. One of my early ambitions was to write a book, and that hope came true when I proudly finished my first novel, **Gifted**.

My second book was a fun and informational read. I put words to many, many bits of paper about '*stuff*'. Just things I had learned about, read about and practiced throughout my life. When it was all done, **Tidbits, Tips & Treasures** was born.

Gypsy Heart, my third book, is a semi-autobiographical work that I am particularly proud of. It was a very difficult, yet fun book to write. It took me to, and through, deep, dark places to where I would not necessarily have gone in my line of writing, but the journey was necessary, and I am glad I made it.

My next novel, **The Grand Manor** was very well received indeed. It was released right on the heels of Gypsy Heart, and garnered great reviews, for which I am forever grateful.

I must admit that, probably my most favorite write was my last one, **Timeless Love**. My books are not always about my personal life but, I do write of what I know. This book brought back so many personal memories from a long time ago. We've all had that *special love*!

This latest work, **The Secrets of Kanyon Ridge** has been a while getting to print. It went through a couple of name changes and what seemed like endless rewrites and edits, but it is ready, and my hope now is that you will think it was worth the wait.

I am currently working on my next effort, **JOY** and there are a host of scribbles waiting in a notebook for **Then, Now and Forever** which will appear somewhere down the road.

As for dreams, it would be my most **absolute** dream to see my characters come to life on the silver screen. Who knows, right? You must dream!

I always love to hear from and read messages from anyone who has read any of my books. I personally reply to each and every one.

When you have a moment, please visit my website at www.deelightfulreading.com. Leave a message... **tell me what your dream is**.

~DEE~

Dedicated to my God, who is my source of words, and without His constant presence in my life, this book would not have been written.
His guidance and everlasting love have led me to this place of Peace, Tranquillity, and Creativity I now enjoy.

ACKNOWLEDGEMENTS

Once again, I give thanks to my God for giving me the gift of words and enabled me to turn them into stories for my readers to enjoy, and hopefully relate to.

To my dear friend, Joan Marshall, thank you for the many hours you've spent reading and editing. Thank you for being there for me, day or night, that I've called upon you and you were unwavering in those challenging times. Without you, your patience and your amazing gift of finding my flaws, I doubt this book would be ready. Thank you from the bottom of my heart, I could not have done it without you.

I wish to extend a sincere and heartfelt thank you to Cedar Springs, my publisher, web designer and cover creator. Thank you for always being there for me and for tirelessly giving your time and advice, and for being my 'go to guy.' Without you this book would not have made it to print.

Thank you to Diane Axent for allowing me to use her name in my personal story about modelling.

To Gloria Steinem for her permission to use her quote.

Lastly, to my dedicated readers; thank you for your patience, your gracious comments on my web site and most especially, for requesting to be on the list for future book releases. Next on the list is JOY which is a little different from my usual and I hope it brings you as much entertainment as it has given me in creating it.

My life consists of two kinds of Time
The Time when I am with you
And the Time when I am waiting
To be with you again
G.A.Z.

Everyone has their own path. Walk yours with integrity and wish all others peace on their journey. When your paths merge, rejoice for their presence in your life. When the paths are separated, return to the wholeness of yourself, give thanks for the footprints left on your soul, and embrace the time to journey on your own.
Author Unknown

Sharing a book is an encouragement to read. Encouraging others to purchase a book is an encouragement to the author.

~Dee~

FROM DEE'S MEMORIES AND DREAMS

Back in the day and in another life, I dreamt of becoming a model. One day, I came across an ad in a Toronto newspaper. An agency was looking for models for catalogue work and listed an address where auditions were being held.

I was twenty-four years old, a 98-pound rake with a new baby girl and a 5-year-old son. Despite my maturity, I still looked like a seventeen-year-old kid, and I wanted to give it a try. My mother, who was visiting at the time, offered to take me.

My wardrobe was less than desirable at the time, so my friend and neighbour Anita offered to lend me an outfit. I remember it was a perfectly fitting two-piece with a loose top and skirt-like shorts that settled just above the knees.

My mom had a built-in radar system when it came to directions, and on the day of the audition, she had me in a room with an agent in no time.

The woman in charge explained that they were looking for models for the Eaton's and Sears catalogues.

Pointing to a platform, she asked me to do a walk through to show her what I'd look like on a runway. This was my chance to show off my scrawny frame. Confidently, I started my journey down the runway, pivoting at the end as I had previously practiced, then floated back to where I'd begun. Just as I'd seen professional models do.

"Perfect," she'd said, BUT... my dream was dead in an instant. The agent liked what she saw and thought I could go places. Still, there was that dreaded 'but' that nobody ever wants to hear. She explained that there was a mandatory course needed, to ensure the best presentation. The thing was, every girl had to pay for the course out of their own pocket, and in those days that was asking the impossible. Dreams come, and dreams go.

However, later in life, I had the privilege of occasionally working for Diane Axent, modelling Summer and Fall fashion shows with 'Axent on Silk.' Wearing her beautiful designs lead to my love for silk. So, in a way, I lived my dream for a while and enjoyed the shows I had done with silks.

We all have dreams, but whether or not they come true, we can still dream.

~DEE~

Without leaps of imagination or dreaming, we lose the excitement of possibilities. Dreaming, after all, is a form of planning.

GLORIA STEINEM

SECRETS IN KANYON RIDGE

Will Second Chances Lead to Love?

1

Flying high on her proverbial broom, sixteen-year-old Keri Hamilton headed home from school. Finding both her parents waiting, she sensed that something was amiss. Her father would never have been home from work in the middle of the afternoon unless it was something awful. Her heart sank, and her lungs deflated like the air in her self-absorbed bubble.

"What's going on?" she asked, opening the door to their solemn faces.

"We have some news, please come and sit down," her father said, nodding his head toward the couch.

"Is everything okay? Did somebody die or something?" she asked, curiously as she sat down.

"No, nothing like that, Keri. We have some good news and maybe for you, not so much, but it is happening."

"What Dad?"

"I have been offered a job and we have to move..."

"Move! Where?" she interrupted anxiously.

"Let me finish and I'll tell you," he said, cocking his head with just enough authority in his voice to let her know she needed to listen. "It's a place called Kanyon Ridge," he continued, "and even though we don't want to uproot you in your senior year, Honey, we have no choice. The job starts in a few weeks and plans are already in the works."

"I don't want to move, Dad! Why can't we stay here?" she begged, gulping back sobs.

"We can't stay because if I refuse the offer, I'll lose my job. That's just the way it is."

Pushing herself defiantly up from the couch, Keri stomped tearfully to her room in protest, but this time her tears would not work on her parents. The decision had already been made without consulting her and tears, tantrums or talk, was not going to change anything. She felt powerless for the first time in her young life.

She'd put up the worst fuss when her parents gave her the dreadful news. She was adamant about not wanting to move, and she'd made it plain to both her parents, but to no avail. Being a teenager, she had no clout over her father's announcement. She was an only child and a brat, but that was about as far as it went while she was at home and she hadn't always gotten what she wanted. At school, though, it was a different story, and she got away with just about anything.

Two weeks had flown by, and it was time to say goodbye to her friends and followers as they cried together, hugged and promised to stay in touch. Devastated to leave her admirers behind, Keri vowed to reestablish herself as 'queen' in Kanyon Ridge.

On moving day, she reluctantly got in the back seat of her dad's car. Her mother's heart ached for her sobbing daughter since she'd refused to talk, eat or drink when they stopped for breaks.

Arriving in Kanyon Ridge, Keri's swollen eyes, matted hair, and exhaustion had taken its toll after nine hours of crying and sulking.

Disrupting the senior year at Kanyon Ridge High School, Keri Hamilton's appearance couldn't have made for a more dramatic entrance, unless she'd had flown in on that broom. She hardly got the welcome wagon enthusiasm she'd hoped for, let alone expected.

Coming from a school filled with worshipers, she'd felt she had the world by the tail with a large following who would say or do just about anything she asked of them. They literally tripped over themselves just to walk beside her in the pack. At sixteen, she felt like 'Miss Universe,' and if she went up any higher, her already inflated ego would be blown to smithereens. She was cocky, arrogant and emphatic about her rein. Being the most popular girl, not only in her class but in the entire school, Keri knew she'd had full run of the place.

On her first day, at Kanyon Ridge High School, she saw him. He was the most gorgeous guy she had ever laid her eyes on. She didn't exactly stalk him, but she wanted to know who he was. Wanting him to notice her, she did everything possible to make it happen. Finding reasons to be near him, she went to all the places she knew he would be.

'How different this was from the boys back home,' she thought, and as her ego kicked in, she knew they would have fallen all over themselves to be with her, but she hadn't given them the time of day.

Being on the home team, he was next to the bleachers with a clipboard in his hand and chewing on a pencil.

Sidling over to him, she clasped her hands together while swaying back and forth several times. "Hi, I'm Keri Hamilton," she said, tilting her head sideways trying to impress him.

Looking up and unimpressed, he abruptly said, "Drew Greyson," and casually walked away.

That was all she got from him. *'Drew Greyson'* she swooned, *'he is everything!'* He was the typical poster boy for gorgeousness. He towered over her, standing at least six feet two to her five-six. He had the darkest, shiniest hair and the bluest eyes that mostly looked right through her. He had a perfect smile and an infectious laugh that was loud and carefree. He was the one who fit in no matter where or whatever the occasion, yet he wasn't quite the most popular boy in Kanyon Ridge. Everyone thought he was the greatest guy and he was friendly with everyone, except her, which drove her nuts and she wanted him even more. Focusing on ways to get his attention, she'd show up, uninvited, to school games and sit in the front row, but she couldn't hold his attention. She seated herself next to him in almost every class, but he didn't see her. School dances, noon hour sock-hops, home team games, but still nothing. The more he ignored her, the harder she fell, and the more it infuriated her. *'This would never have happened at her other school,'* she thought, emphatically. In fact, there was no comparison to her old gang. She had no fans here, nobody holding her in high regard and nobody tripping over themselves to walk by her side. *'This is horrible,'* she thought, *'just horrible!'* No one at Kanyon Ridge High liked or even wanted her around, and she felt it wherever she went. She got the full snub when she hopped on the school bus to attend a game.

The home team had an out-of-town game scheduled, and a couple of school bus drivers volunteered to drive them and the students who wanted to go for support. When Keri got on the bus, the only available seat was next to Drew. She could not believe her luck thinking he'd have no choice now but to talk to her. Sitting facing the window, he chatted with a few friends in the seat behind him as Keri quietly slipped into the seat. When the driver started up the bus, Drew turned around and saw her sitting in his seat.

"Oh... it's you," he frowned as if she was the last person he wanted to share his seat with.

"Hi, Drew," she said, trying to sound sexy even though she didn't really know how 'sexy' sounded.

Cocking an eyebrow, Drew scrunched up his face and without realizing it, '*pfft*' had escaped his lips. He'd tried to be nice, but there was something about this gal he just wasn't getting. '*Why me?*' he thought, '*why can't she just obsess over someone else?*' He had noticed though, when she first showed up at school, that she was a little thing about five-six maybe, medium brown hair with lighter blonde highlights. She had smoky blue-grey eyes that any guy in his right mind would get lost in, but not him. From the first day, all his friends wanted to know who the 'new chick' was. But something about her just made him want to run in the other direction, and he couldn't, for the life of him, figure out why. Out of curiosity, he turned from the window to look at her. '*There's that look again,*' he thought, '*all doe-eyed and smiling at him like he was a piece of chocolate cake.*' Every time he saw her, she was not only staring at him but actually looked as if she wanted to eat him up. At his age, he should have been flattered that the new girl in town had eyes only for him, but it creeped him out. She was everywhere! No matter where he went she was there like a watchdog. A slight shiver ran through him at the thought, but he went back to staring out the window annoyed at himself for allowing her to absorb even that much of his thoughts.

Taking a deep breath for courage, she touched his arm. Cringing at her touch, he yanked his arm inward. Seeing the repulsive look on his face, she yanked her hand back. She'd thought this would have been a perfect opportunity to get closer to Drew and maybe he might learn to like her a little bit but by his reaction, it was obvious that it wasn't going to happen.

She was sixteen, and he was seventeen, but she felt as though it didn't matter how old, or in their case, how young, they were, he was never going to like her back. Since she was not used to losing, rejection made her dig her heels in even deeper. This was beyond a game now; this was an all-out mission.

Sitting in silence, she stared at the back of the seat ahead of her. The seats were too tall to see anything else unless she leaned out into the aisle toward windshield. Desperately scouring the bus, she hoped to find an empty seat, but there were none. '*He acts like he hates me,*' she thought, as tears pooled in her eyes remembering his reaction to her touch. She swiped angrily at the tears as they crept out of her lids and rolled down her cheeks. The longer she thought about his rejection, the sadder she felt until she became overwhelmed with self-pity. Trying to hide her face from Drew, she hoped he wouldn't have the satisfaction of knowing he'd hurt her feeling, but he was quick to see her pain.

'*Oh geez,*' he thought, '*I was more than obvious when she touched me.*'

"Look, Keri," he began, "I'm sorry if I hurt your feelings. I didn't mean to, it's just that I didn't expect you to touch me, it startled me, is all," he lied, "please, don't cry."

6

As soon as he said the word 'cry' it seemed all eyes were on them and a hush fell over the bus. He did not want to be seen talking to her let alone be the center of attention. At seventeen he did not want or need the drama that came with this gal. When he opened his mouth to apologize, she noticed the attention it brought, and she wanted payback. She brought on the crocodile tears and the pitiful sobs, then out came the tissues.

"You were mean to me!" she wailed, as everyone gawked at the scene unfolding in their seat. Drew just looked at her in total disgust. He was young, but he was nobody's fool. He saw through her act the second she drew her audience in with her tears.

Sally Delaney, who was a friend of Drew's, saw the charade going on too. She also knew that Keri had been hell-bent on inserting herself into Drew's life since the day she set foot in their school. She had heard rumors and watched her from time to time as she worked her angles trying to get close to him. Sally didn't like her much either. She was 'that girl' who tried too hard to fit in where she wasn't wanted, and this was just another ploy to work on Drew's feelings for sympathy. Seeing the horrified look on Drew's face when she blurted out, *You were mean to me!'* it soon turned to a scowl when he caught on to what she was trying to pull off. He looked at Sally, and as they locked eyes, they both knew what her purpose was. Sally gave her head a 'come here' nod and relief flowed through him. Getting to his feet, he excused himself, moved past her and out into the aisle towards Sally's seat. Drew sat down while Sally wiggled in past Keri and occupied Drew's seat. Settling herself beside Keri, she leaned over and gave Drew a 'thumbs up.' Keri was horrified as the entire bus broke out in applause. Keri's eyes met Drew's but only briefly as he flung himself around to face the front of the bus.

After the disastrous bus trip, Keri was on the outs with just about everyone who had been on the bus, not to mention the entire school, once the story had made its rounds.

Realizing she was out of options to snag Drew, she tried to accept that it just wasn't going to happen.

Graduation was a couple of months away, and she was no closer to snagging him now than on her first attempt. Her first clue was his politely shunning her, and it should have been obvious to her to move on.

She had not found a single solitary friend since she'd enrolled in Kanyon Ridge High. Her life had changed drastically since leaving her old school where she had ruled and reined, had a following and was adored by everyone. Now, she couldn't have a conversation without them acting like she was just let off the Island of Leprosy. A prime example of being shunned by society and it was a culture shock being low man on the totem pole. She had always been on the top looking down on everybody, and it had been a much prettier place than where she was now... alone. Karma was rearing its ugly head.

2

Sitting alone and brooding in the cafeteria, Keri tucked her chin into her chest and was deeply entrenched in her own pity party. Raising her eyes to check the clock, she wondered how much time she had left before next class. Moving her eyes, she noticed someone she had never seen around the school before and he was looking straight at her. Her stomach churned with disgust as the unsavory character strolled over and uninvitedly plopped himself down across from her. As his scrawny frame hit the chair, it veered sideways and created a loud screeching sound on the tiled floor.

"Excuse me!" she roared, horrified that he'd have the audacity to sit down uninvited. She was in no mood for a rude intruder, and with every breath, she wished it had been Drew who had taken advantage of the seat. "What do you want?" she sneered, leaning into the table.

Raising a dirty palm, at the end of a ragged sleeve, as if to calm her down, he mumbled, "Easy there, Missy, I'm not here to harm you, just relax," he said bouncing his hand up and down.

"What do you want?" she enunciated as if he hadn't heard her the first time.

"Look, Missy, you might think you're better than me, and maybe you are," he said hitching a shoulder, "but I might be the only one here that can help you out."

"Pfft! Help me out!? I doubt that" she snorted, with a whole lot of sarcasm dripping from her curled-up lips. "How can *you* possibly help *me*?"

His mouth moved into a slow grin, "With Drewy-boy," he drawled.

Sneering the words 'Drewy-boy,' she saw filth behind his thin, bland lips. It made her skin crawl to look at the ugly greyish brown teeth that looked like they hadn't seen a toothbrush since he was in grade school.

"Drew! What do you know about Drew?" she scowled, throwing herself back against the chair.

"I know that you've been chasing his ass since you came to town and it's gotten you nowhere. You can't even get him to say 'hello' to you." He was extremely calm and soft-spoken, which was the complete opposite of what he appeared at the first meeting. His calmness annoyed her as did his knowing about her failure to capture Drew's heart.

"So?"

"So," he drawled, leaning in closer as if to share a big secret. "Quit lookin' at me like I'm a piece of shit under your shoe and I might help you with that." The words slipped from his lips like a well-rehearsed, slicked up salesman's pitch.

"Pfft! Ya right!" she smirked, cutting her eyes sharply at him. "I highly doubt that!" she said while thinking what a sleaze he was and wondered what he wanted from her.

Taking a quick scan around the cafeteria, he slipped a dirty hand into an equally filthy beige jacket pocket and came out with the tiniest vial she had ever seen. Holding it upright between his thumb and index finger, she sat up with interest and leaned in toward the middle of the table for a closer look. Just as she reached out for it, he dropped it into his palm as slick as a card shark and wrapped his fingers around it tightly and out of sight.

"What the...?" It was gone in a flash, and it only made her more curious. '*Oh, he is slick,*' she thought. Putting her elbows on the table, she locked her fingers as a resting place for her chin and stared at his hand. "What was that?" she asked, giving her chin a slight nod toward the vial while staring down his smug grin.

"I thought that would peak your interest," he said, showing his brown teeth in an even wider 'I gotcha' grin.

Glaring at him, she thought he was a worthless scuzzbucket, but she had to hear him out.

"It's just a little something that '*might*' get you past first base with 'ole Drewy-boy,' since he is playing hardball or in other words, hard to get."

"What do you know about Drew anyway?" she said, lifting her chin and squinting her eyes.

"I know enough that no matter what you do, you can't get his attention. Besides that, there isn't even competition," he said, with a '*tsk.*' "He doesn't have a girlfriend, and he still won't look at you sideways. How does that make you feel? And by the way," he said, sliding his thumb and forefinger over and down his top lip as if grooming an imaginary mustache, "I was on the school bus the day you made a complete ass of yourself."

She leaned back against the chair in defeat. '*Well, he's got me there,*' she thought.

"So," he drawled softly, "I can help you with that." Peeking over his jacket collar, scanning the room, he revealed the vial again.

This guy had the appearance of a rather hypnotic street thug but didn't quite seem to fit the conversation. *Which box did he belong in? The street thug or hypnotist?*'

"What is it?" she asked again, trying to act nonchalant.

"It's a little something that will render him," pausing, he rolled his eyes and made small air circles with his finger while searching for the right word, "shall we say, *unaware*, while you do your thing."

Squinting at him for several seconds, she popped her eyes and dropped her jaw, "Are you talking about... roofie?"

He sat back and grinned, knowing he had her full attention.

"Well, is it?" she insisted.

Dropping the corners of his mouth, he shrugged his shoulders offering no answer. He was slick and smooth, there was no doubt about it. He had the attitude of a gangster and was a little intimidating, but he didn't scare Keri. Taking her hands from under her chin, she slammed her palms against the table causing him to blink, but he kept eye contact.

"Who the hell are you anyway and what are you doing here? Are you a drug dealer?" she asked a little too loudly as she came up at him again. Taking a quick scan around the room, she noticed it brought no attention to her table.

"You can wipe that fake disgusted look off your face and keep your voice down, or you're on your own, Missy," he said through clenched teeth. His threatening words rolled smoothly and calmly while holding her stare. Except for the muscles flexing in his jaws, he remained calm, cool and collected.

"What is that?" she hissed again, barely in a whisper and feeling a bit desperate.

"That's better, now you're getting the idea, there's no need to raise your voice," he said slowly, giving his head a warning nod. His eyes never leaving hers, not even to see who else was in the room. His focus was totally on her, and when he began to speak, he could tell by the look on her face that, once again, he had her full attention. "Ok, here's the deal," he said leaning closer, "it's very potent, and a small amount can have a powerful effect, and all you need to know is that it works."

"Really? Where did you get it?"

"That's my business," he said, leaning back and poking himself on the chest, "and all you have to do is decide whether or not you want it and you'd better decide soon cuz I'm outta here," he said checking his watch.

"And if I do?"

"Then you come up with some cash and this transaction will be over."

"How much?"

"Fifty bucks for this vial and there is more in here than you'll ever use." Rolling the vial back and forth between his index finger and thumb, he taunted her, knowing for certain she wanted it. What he couldn't figure out was why Drewy-boy had no interest in this beauty sitting across the table from him. Everyone in the entire school knew that she only had eyes for him. '*Drew Greyson was either a damned fool, or he was gay; one or the other,*' he thought. No matter how hard she tried, he was noticeably oblivious to her attempts. "Well? Are you in or are you out?"

Glaring at him, her eyes darted back and forth from one of his eyes to the other, in thought.

Pushing his chair back, "I don't have all day, Missy," he sneered, in low tones, pretending he was about to walk away.

Reaching for her purse, she nervously took out her wallet. Taking out a few bills, she spread them apart and laid them on the table. Unzipping her change section, she dumped the contents out on the table too. Counting them as she pushed them around the table, she said, "I don't have fifty dollars."

"How much do you have?" he asked, pushing his chin toward the money. He knew exactly how much since it was his business to know. He might be considered a low-life in most people's eyes, but he did know how to count money since it looks the same in any direction. "Forty-four dollars and thirty-eight cents and I can throw in a coupon for a free twelve-inch pizza, your choice of toppings."

He squinted at her for a few seconds, "Okay, deal."

"Really?"

"Ya sure, I'm hungry, and pizza sounds good."

She pushed the money and coupon over to his side of the table. "Maybe you can use some of this money to buy yourself a personality," she snapped, glaring at him. Sneering, he showed stained teeth as he passed her the vial. Holding up a dirty finger again, he warned her, "I'm going to say this once more, and then I'm outta here. It takes only one drop in any unsuspecting fool's drink. Remember to put it in a dark liquid like cola or beer as it tends to make a clear drink cloudy, so again, one drop and don't panic. When you panic, you make mistakes which is why I am stressing 'one drop' because given too much can cause coma or even death as well as a long list of side effects, so use your common sense."

She'd read about the date rape drug, and that it was being used in bars and at parties. Rarely did the 'subject or victim' know or will even remember what happened. Supposedly, it becomes effective after only a few minutes and can last up to three or four hours. Bringing her attention back to him, he still had his dirty accusing finger pointed at her face as he wadded the money up in his grubby paw and stuffed it into his pocket. "Another important piece of information is this," he said, pointing at the vial and refusing to call it a drug, "it's pretty much untraceable since it doesn't stay in the bloodstream long so the longer he is out, the better off you'll be."

She heard his chair legs scrape on the tiles as he pushed it way. She felt the tiny vial in her hand, and for an instant, she felt a tinge of guilt, but it passed as quickly as it came. '*Whatever works,*' she said, under her breath, slipping the vial into the change section of her wallet. When she raised her head, he was gone. She didn't know who the guy was and right now, she didn't care. She looked around, and no one had noticed that she was even in the room. Pushing her chair softly away, she stood up, tucked it back under the table and left the cafeteria.

3

Kanyon Beach stretched across from Kanyon, Kanyon Creek, Kanyon Cove and Kanyon Ridge. All having the most popular places for their Friday night beach parties to kick off the weekend. Small groups of people, of all ages, used the beach and could be spotted all along the golden shores, distinguishable only by blazing fire pits. From the springtime, throughout the summer and into early fall, beach parties were a common occurrence by the very young to as 'old as it goes' for those wanting a beach gathering with friends. Many in the communities gathered around a fire pit on their own private spot and spent hours chatting about anything and everything just to stay involved. They used the yacht club facilities when needed, but they mostly stayed outside.

Drew and his friends had organized a beach party for the following Friday night. It had been designated as the teen spot for generations. A gorgeous golden sandy beach front with a brick barbeque built high on the shore so the tides couldn't reach it. They were a close bunch of friends who gathered together once a week to party and have some fun. They all agreed on a few simple rules and since they were all underage the first rule was, no drinking. Regular policing with curfews were enforced for the teens in Kanyon Ridge, and everyone knew that alcohol was off limits. Everybody brought whatever they wanted to eat and drink, and they all knew ahead of time what each one would bring to the potluck Friday night bash. The yacht club was used to store their supplies and other necessities, and weekly they'd take stock, and the group would pitch in and replenish as the weeks rolled around.

For his snack, Drew brought a large bottle of coke, chips, and pretzels that were put on a folding table and shared by everyone. They made a fire pit from a couple of old tire rims that were stacked on top of each other and pieces of driftwood were dragged close to the pit. They burned all the junk that drifted in with the tides, and it was their way of keeping the environment clean. Someone always brought a boombox, and those who had extra batteries brought them to keep the music going throughout the evening.

One of the perks after being uprooted was the waterfront property that her father's company had assigned him. Keri had gotten wind of a planned beach party close to where they lived on the Hope Point Road. She had never been invited to join in with the group, but she had seen the bonfires from the deck along with voices and music. Anger roiled in her gut as thoughts of her popularity at the other school surfaced. *'There wouldn't have been a beach party without her. They wouldn't dare have fun without her being front and center,'* she thought angrily. She had been the queen of the school, and everyone knew it.

Watching, from her deck, she thought she would wait until it was dark enough so she could arrive unnoticed. They all looked like cartoon mice on the sand as they scurried around the beach collecting firewood, setting up tables and unfolding beach chairs. Hoping for a chance at Drew, she tucked the vial into the tiny front pocket of her jeans. She had things to do, and it didn't include collecting wood.

Music blasted as she set off with only one person in mind, Andrew Greyson.

* * *

Drew became lost as sparks soared wildly into the air while the fire snapped and crackled in the darkness. Inhaling deeply, scents of salty wood wafted through the air and into his nostrils. A multitude of conversations buzzed around him while off in the distance he saw groups of three and four people scattered along the beach either strumming guitars, chatting amongst themselves or singing to the tunes from the boombox. Farther down the beach he saw red flames glowing from several fire pits where other groups had gathered. He loved these nights out with his friends.

The firelight created shapes of people, but no one distinguishable through the glow. The evening was dark and clear with the sound of waves crashing on the beach. An eerie feeling crept up his arms, neck and into his scalp causing him to look around. Out of nowhere, Keri Hamilton's face appeared in the firelight. *'Who the hell invited her,'* he wondered, thinking she must have arrived after dark, or he would have seen her approaching. He was instantly riled at the sight of her. There had never been anyone new invited unless all were aware and had agreed to the invitation. He knew for certain that nobody in his group would have asked her. It was their way of knowing who was there, for safety reasons. Bringing uninvited guests, unbeknownst to the group, was against the rules.

He was sitting on a log with a couple of his friends just out of the way of the fire. He had a white plastic glass of coke in his hand and a plate with a variety of snacks on it that he had been nibbling on. He set his plate down when he saw her walking toward him. Before he got up, he twisted his glass into the sand to keep it from tumbling over and headed off into the shadows to do his business. When he returned, Keri was sitting on the log, and his friends had wandered off.

"Hi, Drew."

"Hello, what brings you here?" he asked, out of curiosity.

"I saw the fire from my house and came to check it out. I live just over there," she pointed into the darkness.

"So, you came uninvited then?"

"Sort of, I guess," she said, unconcerned with his question. Lifting his glass from the sand, she passed it to him. "Is this yours?"

"Yes, it is," he said, taking it from her. He stood looking at her with one hand across his chest and tucked under his armpit and held his glass in the other. He sipped his drink and noticed that Keri was keeping a close eye on him as he drank. She eyed him up all the time anyway, so he was getting pretty used to it by now, but it didn't stop the shivers from running down his spine.

"Would you like a drink of coke?"

"Yes, please."

He went to the table, took a glass from the plastic sleeve and poured her a drink from his bottle and refilled his own. Walking back over, he leaned slightly to pass it down to her when he felt momentarily strange.

"Thank you."

Nodding his head, he stood up quickly, waiting for the dizziness to pass.

"You OK?" she asked, with fake concern.

"Phew!" he whispered, giving his head a shake. "Ya, I'm fine."

She patted the space next to her and invited him to sit down. Moving towards the log, he suddenly felt very calm and less annoyed that she'd come uninvited. She touched his arm, which strangley aroused him. Laying her head on his shoulder, he got a whiff of coconut in her hair, and as he put his arm around her waist, she snuggled in closer to him. Feeling warm and comfortable, he surprisingly became turned on by her presence. Gazing up at him, he noticed, in the firelight that she was quite beautiful and leaning in to kiss her, his only thought was to get her alone.

"Would you like to go for a walk?" he whispered into her hair.

"Yes," she smirked, "let's do that."

Stumbling to his feet, she caught him before he fell. "Steady there, Drewy-boy," she said softly, as an image of a grinning sleaze-ball occupied a space in her consciences. '*Let it go, Keri,*' she thought, '*this is what you've wanted all along.*'

'*Drewy-boy,*' he thought vaguely, '*where did that come from?*'

* * *

Waking up in a complete fog, on a cool sandy bed, Drew stared up into a black starry sky with just enough moonlight for him to get his bearings. Having no recollection of most of the party, he wondered why he was lying on the beach. Feeling as if he was about to jump out of his skin, his entire body vibrated uncontrollably bringing on nausea and profuse sweating. Remembering nothing, except the earlier part of the evening, he began to question what would make him feel edgy and uneasy.

'*What the hell happened?*' he winced, trying to push his forehead up into his hair. '*Whatever this was, it wasn't good.*' Shaking his head, he tried to think more clearly. Lifting himself up on his elbows, he looked around. The fire was out, the beach was empty, and he was lying in a patch of tall beach grass. Turning slightly, he stifled a gasp and closed his eyes in defeat. His stomach lurched at the sight of her lying next to him covered only with his shirt then noticed his belt unfastened and his jeans unzipped. Closing his eyes briefly, he swallowed hard. He had no memory of how he ended up in the bushes with Keri Hamilton. The beach was eerily quiet except for the waves rushing in. The fire pit was black with no sign of embers, and the only light was from the moon. Even in the moonlight, Keri looked beautiful but that hadn't stopped the tightening grip in his guts or the unanswered questions. '*How long had he been there? Better still, why was he there? Couldn't someone just shoot her to free him from this misery.*' he mused.

Keri looked as if she was sleeping soundly beside him, and he soundlessly rolled over onto his stomach. Getting to his knees, he dug the toes of his runners into the sand and swiftly lifted himself to his feet. Standing quietly for a second, she didn't move so taking one step at a time, he slowly backed away. A few more steps and she still hadn't moved, so he turned and walked away. As he got farther down the beach he mumbled while zipping up, "*And you can keep the shirt!*"

21

Pressing her lips together, Keri smugly smiled up at the starry sky.

Nearing the end of the beach, nausea rose wildly, and dropped to his knees in weakness. Retching into the sand, a stark, terrifying thought of dying there on the beach, alone in the darkness, crept over him. Once the queasiness had passed, he found the strength to stand and slowly make his way home.

Taking several days before he began to feel normal again, he still could not recall much about the beach party after Keri had arrived. Doubt began to form as to what had happened. Was it reality or a dream? He was a bit more than ashamed to ask anyone for details and he especially didn't want to know if anyone had seen him go into the bushes with Keri Hamilton!

* * *

The days of summer grew longer, and crowds gathered at the beach for a pre-graduation party. Drew looked forward to one of the last times they'd gather as classmates and friends. He was leery but relieved when there was no sign of Keri.

Watching the sun set slowly over the bay, Drew caught the movement of someone lurking in the shadows.

Seeing her edge her way toward him, stole the air from his lungs.

'*Dammit!*' he thought, '*why did she always have to show up?*' He felt contempt for her whenever he saw her around the school, in town or just anywhere in his peripheral vision. Giving him the creeps, he wished he'd never have to lay eyes on her again.

"Drew, I have to talk to you."

"Not now, OK?" he said, with frustration, "would you just... go away," he asked, cocking his head to one side hoping she'd take the hint but she stood her ground and stared him down.

"I need to speak to you, now!" she insisted, speaking through clenched teeth and hoping no one else could hear.

"Why are you here?" he asked, tilting his head in annoyance. "This is an invitation-only beach party so who invited you?"

"No one invited me, but I have to talk to you," she insisted.

"Can you not take a hint?" he said, trying not to be as ignorant as he knew it sounded. Arms folded across his chest, in obvious annoyance, he barked, "So, talk and then go, please," he said, annoyed, waiting for her to speak. Elbows digging into his sides, he spread his forearms wide with an exasperated look, as if to say, *'I'm listening!'*

"Drew..."

The word dropped off her tongue, and his stomach made an abrupt flip. Smug pleasure spread across her face as she watched him swallow hard and saw his Adam's apple bob up and down.

"What is it, Keri?" he said, with raised eyebrows.

It was her turn to swallow. Running her tongue across her lips, she opened her mouth. "I ... I ... um."

"Keri!?" he said, loudly, losing patience with her antics.

She flinched as he harshly spoke her name.

"I'm pregnant, Drew?"

"And...? Why are you telling me?"

"It's your baby, Drew," she said, in almost a whisper.

Blinking his eyes, her words penetrated his brain as he stood dumbfounded. "Mine?" he croaked, finding his voice, "how is that possible? What are you trying to pull?"

"It was here," she said, sweeping an arm out, "at the beach party, we... we... made love over there, several weeks ago," she stammered, pointing towards the grassy area, "don't you remember?"

"Are you being serious right now!?" he asked with a scowl when suddenly a vision of him waking up beside her whirled momentarily in his brain.

"Yes, I am. You asked me if I wanted to go for a walk and you lead me in there," she said, pointing to the spot again.

Running his hand through his hair, he pressed his hand tightly against his mouth while pinching his nostrils. '*What the hell was happening?* he thought as fragmented pieces from that night crept back into his memory... '*the fire, the two of them sitting on a log, his arm around her waist, her head on his shoulder... coconuts. Oh, my God! Why can't I remember anything more than that?*' he thought, '*then he remembered waking up with her wearing his shirt, it was real! Son of a bitch!*' Putting both arms out towards her, his hands waving back and forth but no words came as he stepped back away from her. Knowing she had him, she waited calmly, kept her mouth shut and for his benefit began wringing her hands while pretending to be nervous. Turning his back to her, he pressed both hands down hard on the top of his head wanting to push himself down into the sand and out of sight. He paced back and forth around the same spot until she thought she'd scream. Before she had a chance to open her mouth, he stopped and looked at her.

"What do you want me to do? Huh?" he asked, his shoulders nearly touching his ears and arms spread out from his side. He stared at her... she stared at him. Dropping his arms, his palms slapped loudly against his jeans causing her to flinch.

"I don't know! I think we should tell our parents."

His shoulders slumped, "Our... parents?" he repeated, closing his eyes in defeat. At that moment, all his hopes and dreams began floating away, out into the ocean waves. His dream of becoming an airline pilot and the freedom to fly was looking bleaker by the second. '*What was he going to do with a baby?*'

"I suppose we should think about getting married?" she said, more of a question than a statement.

"Married!?" he shrieked.

"Yes, for the baby's sake, it's the right thing to do, Drew," she said, holding the guilt card.

"The right thing to do?" he repeated, almost to himself. "You do realize that you are only sixteen and I am seventeen, and you want to get married, really?"

"Yes, I know how young we are, but we made a baby. We have to take care of it."

4

All eyes were on a very young and handsome seventeen-year-old groom standing in a church filled with family, friends, and neighbors, all waiting for the ceremony to begin. The organist played hideous music until she finally banged out the familiar, dum dum da dum, and everyone turned away from him and faced the door. A million thoughts ran through his head as he listened to that dreadful tune.

Drew's heart stopped or at least he was hoping it would, as the doors pulled open and Keri, on her dad's arm, stepped into view. Stopping just inside the archway as cameras flashed, videos rolled, Drew thought to himself, *'I look like a fool.'* Impatiently, he waited for this ridiculous ceremony to end. Nothing exploded inside him; she didn't take his breath away nor was she the prettiest bride he'd ever seen. His heart did not, could not or would not do a double-take from how stunning she looked. Although she was a good-looking gal, the opulence of the expensive gown that spilled out over the entire span of the aisle didn't make her beautiful... not to him. Even though he'd heard several oohs and aahs, it did nothing to lighten his heart or make him proud to be standing there. Knowing it was all done for this one day, she would never look this way again, so it didn't make it special for him. It was all an act put on by Keri and for Keri. The ceremony was for her benefit, but she was still, and always would be... the same Keri. He on the other hand was the sitting duck at the altar; her final prize.

Something inside him screamed, *'This would be a good time to run!'* But looking around the church, when his eyes should have been on his bride, he saw the work, the expense her parents had put into the wedding, he knew he couldn't run... oh, but he wanted to. Perspiration lay on his forehead, and his stomach knotted tighter... then there was the baby to think of, which was the only reason he was standing there.

Watching them slowly make their way toward him caused his stomach to tighten. Swallowing hard, he hoped the nausea would pass. Smiling brightly at him, he thought he was smiling too, but he couldn't muster one up. Mr. Hamilton reluctantly offered him his young daughter's hand but Drew just looked at it as if it was a foreign object. He didn't want to touch it, yet he knew he must. '*Oh God, now what*!? *Was he going to vomit right there on the altar?*'

Realizing that he was not happy to see her, the smile suddenly left her face but knowing he had to get it together for her sake, he swallowed hard and mustered up one of his gorgeous smiles. He saw the instant relief in her face... but thought, '*or is that her smug, self-satisfying look?*' He wasn't sure, or maybe he was since he wasn't clear on anything anymore.

The ceremony was a blur from the time Keri's father placed her hand in his until they walked back down the aisle, together, as husband and wife. Not remembering things was becoming far too frequent since he'd met Keri.

Feeling a panic attack coming on, he desperately needed air. Squeezing Keri's hand, he picked up the pace toward the double doors.

"Keri, I'll be right back," he gulped and headed off around the corner of the church. Pressing his back against the shingles, he closed his eyes and swallowed repeatedly, to no avail. Leaning forward into the rose bushes, he gagged several times, but nothing came up. Taking a handkerchief from his breast pocket, he wiped the perspiration from his forehead. Taking a few deep breathes, he wiped his mouth and returned to his bride.

"Drew, what's wrong with you? Are you feeling alright?"

"Yes, I'm fine," he lied, "I didn't eat today, and I'm feeling a little light-headed," was all he could come up with at the moment. He couldn't get back on track no matter how hard he tried. Standing in the reception line, he accepted handshakes, pats on the back, teasing winks from his closest buddies and endless congratulations. For a photo shoot, he was lead to a location he wasn't familiar with and hoped this day would come to an end. It did end, and so did a big part of him.

* * *

They had booked the dining room at The Kanyon Ridge Inn for the reception, and they were served a beautiful meal. Drew had no idea what he had eaten, he just knew it was food, and he was hungry.

Tables were cleared and as the band set up, Drew tried to get a grip. His father approached with two bottles of beer. Passing one to Drew, he said, "Son, I know you're not yet of legal drinking age, but I give you my permission to have a beer, you look as if you could use one." Accepting the beer, he tapped his father's bottle and took a slow drink and even though it was not what he expected, it felt good going down.

"Take your time with that my boy, make it last."

28

At the mere mention of the word 'boy,' a memory niggled at the back of his mind hearing Keri's words, '*Drewy-boy*,' *but from where?'* he thought.

Joining them, Mr. Hamilton gave his daughter a hug, shook Drew's hand and walked away.

"You're drinking beer?" Keri asked.

"Ya, my dad gave it to me," he said, as he sat it down on a table, "can you watch it for me, I'll be right back?"

"Sure," she said, eyeing up the dark colored bottle. Watching him go into the washroom, she reached into her bra, looked around the room and thought, '*Once more for old time's sake*,' she purred.

* * *

Barely remembering their wedding night, Drew woke the next morning, in a strange bed and naked. Opening his eyes, he saw Keri in the bathroom frantically rinsing a piece of clothing in the sink.

"What's wrong?" he asked, feeling a little nauseous when he rose up on his elbow.

"I'm sorry, Drew, there's blood..." she said a little sheepish. "I started my period this morning..."

"What!? You started your period! I thought you were pregnant? That's the reason why we are here, the only reason, Keri. What are you trying to pull?" Shaking the fog from his brain, he rummaged through the suitcase for some clothes.

"Drew, please, I am not trying to pull anything, I missed a couple of periods before we finished school and I thought I was pregnant but obviously I'm not."

Jamming his feet into a pair of socks, he glared at her knowing damned well she was lying. Self-consciously, he sat on the bed wanting to cover up his naked body. Putting both feet into the openings of his underwear, he yanked them up and snatched a pair of jeans. Angry at himself, he regretted not going with his gut knowing there was just something not believable when he saw her at the graduation party. With shaking hands, he hiked up his jeans and fastened them. He was livid beyond words and Keri saw the rage on his face knowing he'd married her for nothing. Thinking these past few weeks that they were expecting a baby had played on his consciousness to a point he could hardly think about anything else. Now watching blood swirl down the bathroom drain proved there wasn't one, and there never was.

Thoughts filled his mind in a dizzying flurry knowing it wasn't possible to dislike this woman any more than he already did. Before he could say or do something he would regret, he shoved his arms into the sleeves of his shirt. Giving her one last scowl, he grabbed his jacket, walked out slamming the door behind him. His entire body trembled as he headed out to the parking lot shakily buttoning his shirt. Wandering aimlessly down the street, he came to a restaurant, went in and ordered a cup of coffee. That's all he wanted. Coffee; hot and strong.

Alone in the booth, with nothing but time, scary thoughts began to form. Something had been happening to him since he'd met Keri. Mind-altering things that made him feel as though he might need to see a doctor. Surely, he wasn't losing his mind at such a young age! He was fine in all other areas except for when he was around her.

Saving face, he returned to the motel. After realizing how Keri had manipulated him all the way to the altar, he wouldn't have been able to look his family in the eyes if he'd left his bride the day after the wedding.

Waiting for him, she'd known all along that he'd be back. She offered no apology and was packed and ready to leave when he returned.

Someday, he hoped he'd be able to wipe that smug look off her face, once and for all.

5

Knowing how important being a pilot was to Drew, his dad had agreed to pay for his studies as a wedding gift.

Keri's parents had offered to pay their expenses for the apartment while they both worked toward their careers. It would serve no purpose for Keri to go out and work to pay bills while Drew carried on with his studies. It could be years down the road for Keri to even think about her career. So, for the next few years, the Greyson's and the Hamilton's agreed to foot their bills as part of their wedding gifts to them. Each parent gave them a credit card, trusting them to be fair with their spending. Knowing it would be scrutinized in the monthly statements, helped them to become conscious of their purchases.

Flight school was everything he had hoped it would be. He was actually glad that his classes kept him away from home much of the time.

Keri kept their small apartment clean and tidy, and she wasn't a bad cook for just learning her way around a kitchen.

Drew had hoped to find that special someone who'd add a bit of 'zing' in the relationship, but Keri had nothing that he found zing-worthy. He was sure there had to be something more than just coming home, eating dinner, watching TV and falling asleep on the couch where he woke from most mornings.

* * *

Keri's goal was to become a medical transcriptionist through a home study course. She had filled out and mailed all the appropriate applications needed to receive information on books and tuition to complete the course. In no time, she received a parcel in the mail with everything she needed to start her course. Thrilled and excited, she couldn't wait to tell Drew even though she knew, deep in her heart, he wouldn't be interested.

The information in the manual informed her that once the course was completed, she could send resumes out to hospitals, Medical Centers and other institutions who could benefit from her skills. She would then receive oral dictation, and her job would be to transfer it into text format, print off the assignment and courier it back. If one or more companies were to hire her, company policy was they would courier work to her home, she'd complete it in the allotted time and then courier it back to them at their expense. She would have to keep in mind that each company gave a certain amount of time to complete a task. Once the work was received, her pay cheque would arrive a few days later. Reading every word in the manual, she couldn't wait to get started. She'd spent the day reading over everything to be ready to begin the next day. It would take fifteen months to receive the two diplomas she'd need for a higher qualified position.

Advancing enough in his classes, Drew was finally able to sit in a plane and actually learn to fly it. Spending time in the classroom, he absorbed everything he could about flying. Spending extra time inside the plane, he learned and familiarized himself with the instrument panel and gears.

He was nervous on his first time flying out, but excitement mixed in knowing he had been waiting for this day for a long time. Sitting in the copilot's seat, he was instructed to describe the instrument panel and what every knob, button, and switch stood for before leaving the ground. Starting the engines, the pilot taxied to the runway. Drew felt goosebumps popping up on his skin as the engines roared and within seconds they were soaring higher and higher. In his headset, Drew heard the pilot's voice.

"Are you ready?"

Looking over at him, Drew smiled and nodded.

"Take the yoke," he said, pointing to the altimeter, "keep it as level and steady as you can, understand?"

Drew nodded his head and kept his eyes on the wide-open space. Being in the sky sent a rush of excitement through his body. This was his dream, this was where he longed to be, and he felt free. It wasn't a long flight, but it gave him a sense of how to control a plane, and once they were on the ground his instructor told him he was a natural. Finally, being in the sky had him literally flying high. Driving home was both sad and depressing knowing Keri was the only person he had to share his news with.

As fast as the thought grabbed him, he saw a phone booth. Thinking of his dad, he pulled over, stopped his car and called him.

6

Arriving home, Drew found Keri surrounded by mounds of books, papers, and equipment.

"What's all this?" he asked.

"I got the kit to begin my course," she said, excited to be able to share it with him.

"There is a lot of stuff here," he said, pointing at all the books, computer, and printer.

"Yes, it's all for my assignments."

It was obvious to him that she was anxious to start her course. They both were because the sooner they finished, the sooner they could reclaim their independence from their parents.

"I had my first flight today," he said, with a grin.

"That's nice, Drew," she said, as she went back to flipping through her books.

The smile quickly left his face as he shook his head and walked to the bathroom for a shower. '*Why be disappointed,*' he thought, '*she always was self-absorbed, why should now be any different? He didn't need her to validate his accomplishment.*'

Undressing, he turned the water on and stepped into the shower. While the water washed over him he thought about the flight and much to his chagrin, it turned him on. He blamed it mostly on the hot water rather than the flight for fear of admitting he loved flying that much. After drying off, he slipped into a tee shirt and jogging pants and went to the living room where Keri had a pot of tea and a couple of mugs on the coffee table.

"Would you like some tea, Drew?"

"Sure, sounds good to me."

Having a favorite mug, he'd used it always for tea and coffee, and as she passed it to him, he noticed that she hesitated but only briefly.

"Here you go, nice and hot, just like you like it."

"Thanks," he said, accepting the mug and taking a gulp. He was several mouthfuls into his tea when the episode he'd had in the shower resurfaced. Slipping his hand under her skirt and onto her bare leg, he leaned in to kiss her. Smugly, wrapping her arms around his neck, she pressed her body close to his causing him to lose control.

* * *

Time stopped there for him as far as memories of the evening were concerned. Waking up several hours later, he was still on the couch, nude and with an afghan thrown over him. A flash from the beach party greeted him in the dark silence in the middle of the night. He tried to bring the evening into focus, but the last thing that he remembered was Keri over top of him slipping his tee shirt over his head as he kicked off his jogging pants.

'What happened after that?' he thought, *'and why does everything come to a stop before he gets to enjoy the ride?'* Nothing was clear except the stirring in his stomach. Rolling off the couch, he pulled on his clothes and quietly left the apartment.

Driving himself to the emergency department, he pulled a number and waited to be triaged. Dizziness set in as he waited to be called in.

Describing his symptoms as clearly as he could, he waited while the nurse stepped outside. A few minutes later he was lead to the lab for blood work. The nurse took samples in several vials, asked him to wait, and someone would come for him. Waiting close to an hour, a doctor he'd never seen before, shook his hand and introduced himself.

"I have a few questions about your lab results."

Drew weakened at the tone in his voice.

"Please sit down, and I'll explain my findings."

"Am I sick?" Drew asked, nervously.

"No, it isn't a disease, Mr. Greyson but there is a drug in your system that we are quite concerned about. There was only a small trace, and if you hadn't come in when you did, we likely wouldn't have been able to detect it at all. It's a drug that doesn't linger in the body very long after it is ingested."

"What? I don't take drugs? What kind of drug?"

"This," he said, pointing to the sheet, "was used only a few hours ago. Have you been to a bar recently by any chance, Mr. Greyson?"

"No, I'm underage, I can't get into a bar! What are you talking about? Drugs?" Drew felt like he was popping out of his skin and he became flushed and nauseous. Swallowing hard, he knew he was going to vomit. The room whirled as he grabbed for a trash can and sunk to his knees. He felt faint and lifeless as he hurled into the can. He could hear the doctor talking to someone, but he was too weak to care. Someone came in with a gurney, and the doctor helped the attendant pick Drew up off the floor.

"Take this can and analyze the contents immediately," he heard the doctor giving stern instructions to someone in a green lab jacket, "there is no time to waste! And bring me the results STAT."

Feeling a cool, damp cloth on his face and neck, brought some relief from the nausea.

"Have you experienced these symptoms before, Mr. Greyson?"

"I have, yes, several times but not quite this violent," he said, trying to get up.

"Lie still and I will give you something for the nausea."

Drew remembered that he had mentioned drugs. "What drug were you talking about doc? I don't take drugs," he reiterated.

"This drug, you would not have taken on your own. It would have been slipped into a drink. Shorter term, it's called GHB, otherwise known as a date-rape drug."

"A what?"

"That's why I asked if you had been to a bar. This drug has surfaced recently at bars and nightclubs. It is slipped unknowingly into a drink and causes the victim to have memory loss for several hours and rendering them helpless and unable to remember much when they come around. This is what showed up in your lab results which is why we had you wait here so we could put a rush on the tests."

"It makes no sense, I haven't been anywhere for someone to drug me. How is that possible?"

"You've admitted that you've had these symptoms before so where were you at the time?" the doctor asked, with piercing eyes. "These are serious charges young man and whoever is slipping you this drug could be arrested."

"Arrested!? Are you serious?"

"I am very serious and to be honest, the police should be notified of this matter."

"Police? No, no police, please." Drew knew exactly who the culprit was, and he'd love to see her smug face peeking out from behind bars and out of his life forever. *'God, to what levels would she stoop? Was this as low as she could go? Was there more?'*

"Can I have a copy of the results, please?"

"Sure, it's your right, and I will get you one."

Waiting for the doctor to return, he sat up on the gurney. Feeling somewhat better, he felt that if he ate something, it might help. Whatever he gave him, to stop the nausea, worked wonders. He stepped down off the gurney, and the doctor returned with several sheets of paper.

"What's all this?" Drew asked.

"Copies of your blood work and the results of your stomach contents. It seems the drug was slipped into a cup of tea." The doctor eyed him for several seconds and said, "You know who did this, don't you?"

"Yes, I do." That was all he had to say as he folded the pages up neatly and put them in his pocket.

"Thanks, for everything Doc," he said, holding out his hand.

"Best of luck to you, son," he said, returning the handshake.

Drew left the hospital feeling a little brighter than when he went in. At least he knew what had been going on and that he wasn't losing his mind nor was he dying of some strange and dreadful disease. It became more than clear why he couldn't remember the beach party, his wedding night or last night.

It wasn't quite daylight when he slipped quietly into the apartment. Keri was still in bed and knew nothing about him being out, and he left it at that. He didn't want to look at her right then anyway. There was still too much to process, and he couldn't do it with her in the same room.

* * *

Several weeks later Drew arrived home from class to find Keri acting mysteriously. When he asked her about it, all she would say was, "You'll see."

He noticed, by looking at the table, that she had gone all out for dinner. She had a white tablecloth spread evenly across the table. The plates were centered around perfectly arranged silverware, the fork set on the napkin, wine glasses, and candles. *'Oh, God,'* he groaned to himself, *'nothing good can come from this.'* He went in to have a shower, and in the meanwhile, Keri had lit some candles. Delicious aromas invited him back to the kitchen and if nothing else, he was hungry. Serving a great pasta dinner with garlic bread, she poured him a glass of non-alcohol wine since they were still underage. Before he had a chance to put a fork full of food into his mouth, she raised her glass.

"I'd like to make a toast."

Laying his fork down he picked up his glass, held his breath, and waited for her to continue as déjà vu moment punched him in the gut.

"To you and me..." she said, as that familiar smug grin spread across her young face. Pausing, he thought she was finished, so he clinked the edge of his glass with hers.

"... and to our baby..."

Lifting his eyes to meet hers, he recognized that same smirk that he'd seen so many times. Closing his eyes in defeat, he breathed loudly through his nostrils and lowered his head. '*Son of a bitch.*' He couldn't remember if he had spoken the words aloud or to himself but either way, there it was. He was speechless. '*Could his life get any worse?*' he thought, as her words began to sink farther into his brain. "Wh... what?"

"We're having a baby, Drew!"

'*Ok,*' he thought, kicking his brain into gear, '*Show some emotion, smile, do something.*'

"Really? A... baby?" He wiped his mouth, his brow and laid his napkin down. '*Do something!*' his insides were screaming for some sort of a reaction to the news.

"I guess this does call for a toast then."

'*Oh God, man, come on!*' he thought, '*you can do better than that!*'

Watching him closely, her smile slowly faded. '*That same look was on his face on our wedding day! He doesn't want a child or at least not with me.*' she thought. Panic set in. "Drew?"

Looking at her face, he saw it. '*Get a grip!*' he scolded himself. "Yes?"

"We're having a baby, Drew, I thought you'd be more excited."

When his head stopped spinning, and his brain caught up, he began to breathe and fully absorb the news. Forcing a smile, he stood up from the table and took her hand. She stood up, and he folded her in his arms and felt her body relax. Closing his eyes, he tried to feel something, but there was nothing, no zing, no zip, no rapid heartbeats or excitement. His heart was sad, not only for himself but for Keri too, she deserved much more than what he had to offer her. He could not love her, and he knew he never would. There were so many things about her that he despised.

This pregnancy was just one of the many capers she's pulled on him. But now she was carrying his child. Some things would change, except her, she never would, she would always be Keri.

"A baby, huh? That's wonderful news."

"Are you OK with it, Drew? You looked shocked."

"I guess I am. I wasn't expecting this kind of news since it wasn't long ago that we found out that you weren't pregnant. It was sort of a reprieve for both of us to continue with our careers. When did you find out?"

"I took a pregnancy test this morning, and I could hardly wait for you to get home, so I could share it with you."

"This is um... very... um... good news. A baby!" He smiled while Keri squinted a questioning look at him.

"You really don't want a child, do you, Drew?"

Her blunt statement had caught him off guard as disappointment showed on her face, but he couldn't tell if it was real or not. He'd believed her at the beach party when she dropped a bomb on him then. How could he ever trust what she said or did since most times it was lies, trickery and deceit.

"No, Keri, it isn't that, I just wasn't expecting it. I mean we have been focusing on our careers, and I didn't think you were interested in getting pregnant."

"Since I wasn't pregnant when we got married..." Realizing what just came out of her mouth, she began to back paddle. "I mean, I thought I was, that's why we got married, and I certainly didn't expect my period to start the day after."

Squinting at her words, he wondered why her hands were flapping in time with her mouth as if she was covering something up.

"You were pregnant when we got married, right?"

She blinked several times at his question.

"Keri? Right?"

"I ... I don't know, I thought I was," she lied, "I'd missed my period, and when I went to you and told you, I really thought I was. But then my period started right after our wedding night.

"So... you were just late, you didn't miss one?"

It seemed she was fresh out of lies so, lowering her head, she said nothing so she didn't dig herself any deeper.

He knew at that moment he could have unloaded on her and been honest about everything. Maybe he would have if she had asked him before she dumped this on him. *'How could he possibly whine about being unhappy and wanting out of this marriage now that they were going to have his child!'* he thought, *'not going to happen.'* He knew he had to suck it up and continue to pretend to be happier than he actually felt.

"Talk to me, Drew."

"There's nothing to talk about, Keri, I'm just processing this news as best I can."

Thinking back to the evening a few weeks prior to when they had supposedly made love on the couch. *'That had to be the night that she'd gotten pregnant? Damn it,'* he thought, pressing his lips together and running his hand through his hair and down the back of his neck. He had to step away from her before he said something he'd regret. The entire episode at the emergency room was a direct result of her knowingly drugging him to have sex with her, and now she was pregnant. Entrapment, plain and simple. He would forever refer to his child as 'The Tea Baby.'

"Drew?"

Raising his hand to stop her from talking, he grabbed his jacket off the bench and left the apartment. Walking, with no destination in mind, he just needed to breathe, forget and walk until he couldn't find his way back home. Sucking in deep breaths of air, he kicked at a stone in his path.

'*Nothing was missing any longer?*' he thought, '*there were no blanks, no questions, and no changes, except one. Where would she get such a drug? Who was her dealer? Whoever it was, she was still Keri, and he was still married to her. All the times he had tried to recall certain things, but it had been obliterated from his brain. It was Keri's shenanigans the entire time. Always what she wanted and how she was going to get it. Tiny inklings of memory would trickle through his mind but nothing he could grab hold of or elaborate on. It was Keri, the burr in his side for almost a year. God how he hated that woman!*' The conversation was only one-sided, but it felt good to rant in his head. It would feel even better if and when he could speak those words to her. '*Someday,*' he promised himself.

* * *

Returning home, it was obvious that dinner had been ruined from the baby drama. The kitchen was left in a mess, and since the walk and the rant hadn't helped much so, he decided to clean up the dishes. Their one-bedroom apartment was too small for him to pace around in so when he heard water running he knew she was taking a bath. Once the kitchen was clean, he was happy to have a few minutes alone, so he turned on the TV and flopped down on the lumpy couch. Tucking his elbow behind his head, he propped himself up. Glancing down at the coffee table, he saw Keri's beach collection in a large, wide rimmed vase that she had brought with her from her parent's place. It had been on the table since they moved into the apartment. Tuning out the TV he became interested in the contents of the vase thinking it would help him understand Keri a little better by the types of things she'd thought were worth keeping. There were numerous beach rocks, colorful seashells, beach glass, bird feather, corks and everything imaginable was in the vase. Not knowing that part of Keri made him curious because she didn't seem to be the beachcomber type, yet she had quite a collection just the same. His eyes fell onto something that was totally unrelated to the other items. It looked like it didn't fit in the concoction and it certainly did not look like it was found on a beach. Something from deep inside his gut prompted his brain to react, and he immediately pushed himself to a sitting position. Planting both feet firmly on the floor, he took a closer look. It was tiny, but it looked out of place in the mix. If the vase had been turned at any other angle, he doubted he would have noticed it at all. He rooted around with his fingers carefully separating the rocks and shells until he got two fingers on each end and slowly pulled it out. As soon as he had it in his fingers, a shiver ran up his spine and into his scalp. A vial. Being in amongst beach paraphernalia, it didn't look like a stone or a shell. '*Handle it with care,*' he thought, holding it between his thumb and index finger only. It was smaller around than a drinking straw and barely a few inches long... if that. Noticing the bubble, it told him that it was a liquid of some sort. Holding the vial up towards the lamp lead him to a watershed moment. This had to be the drug!!!

The sound of water being sucked loudly down the drain broke his concentration. Giving the vase a quick shake, it settled the rock display, so there was no evidence of anything being disturbed. Having only a few minutes to spare, he dropped the small vial carefully into his pants pocket and laid back down and resumed his position. Coming out of the bathroom in her robe, Keri sat down on the edge of the couch next to him. Giving her a long, cold look, he swallowed hard to compose himself then got up before she had a chance to start a conversation. Not knowing what to expect from her, he became leery of everything.

"I'm going to take a shower," he said and left her sitting there alone. Once inside the bathroom, he reached carefully into his pocket and with his thumb and forefinger he brought the vial out again. Pulling a tissue from the box, he laid the vial on it, wrapped it carefully and stuffed it into a zippered compartment in his shaving kit. He turned the shower on full blast and leaned against the sink to compose himself. Feeling sick to his stomach, he felt certain of what he had just found. Making a mental plan, he needed someone he could trust to find out what he definitely needed to know.

* * *

The next morning, before leaving for class, he'd asked Keri for a few coins for the drink machine. Taking her wallet out, she rooted around until she found some. Four quarters were stacked between her thumb and finger as she handed them to him.

"Thanks," was all he said, heading down the hall to the bathroom. Taking the tissue out of his kit and laying it open, he put the top coin in the tissue next to the vial and put it into his jacket pocket. '*Perfect print,*' he thought.

Driving to the hospital, on his lunch hour, he searched out a friend of his father's. Walking up to the information desk, he asked if Don Hanson was in the hospital. Looking through the list, the volunteer said that he was in the lab and Drew asked if he could page him to the lobby. Anxiously waiting in the hallway, he saw Don walking toward him.

"Drew," Don said, reaching out his hand, "this is an unexpected surprise."

"Hello, Dr. Hanson," Drew said, shaking his hand.

"What can I do for you?"

"I need a favor, a big favor."

"Then let's go to my office."

"Dr. Hanson, I don't have much time, I'm here on my lunch hour and by asking this favor, I need complete and total discretion."

"It is always with discretion here in my lab, Drew, tell me what you need."

Looking at him for several seconds, he reached into his pocket, pulled out the tissue and passed it over.

Dr. Hanson looked curiously at the tissue then carefully unfolded it. "What do we have here?"

"I need those analyzed," Drew said, nodding towards the tissue, "and checked for fingerprints.

"Fingerprints? What is this, Drew? It sounds like a police matter."

Raising his hand, he said, "I came to you because I know you and I trust you, but I can't answer any questions that you might have. Can you still do this for me?"

Don had a few questions, but his instinct told him that if Drew was asking for his help, he could not turn him down. "Yes, Drew, I can do that. Come with me so we can have some privacy." Don led the way down the hall and into a private room.

Drew took the lab results from his pocket, unfolded them and passed them to Don.

"I need to know if the contents in this vial match what is in this report, and if the fingerprints on both the vial and the coin match. These results are from blood work I had done recently, and a drug called gamma-Hydroxybutyric acid showed up in my bloodstream and from a stomach sample. That's a date rape drug, isn't it?"

Slipping the vial and coin into a small envelope, he wrote Drew's name on it and slipped it into the pocket of his lab coat. Scanning the information from the lab results, he knitted his eyebrows. "Drew?" Don began, but Drew stood up and put his hand up to indicate that he couldn't answer his questions.

"Sorry," he said, "I know you asked me for discretion."

"Thank you, Dr. Hanson, I really appreciate it."

"Are you in any trouble, Drew? You can at least tell me that."

"No, Dr. Hanson, I am not in any trouble," he said, holding out his hand.

Shaking his hand, Drew thanked him again.

"When can I expect results?"

"Give me your phone number, and I'll give you a call when I have something."

"No, I can't do that, can I have your number, so I can call you in a few days?"

Scribbling down his lab number, he gave it to Drew. Taking the paper, he thanked him again and left the lab. Checking his watch, he still had time to make it to his next class.

Restlessly, Drew waited for the next few days to pass. Already knowing the results, he still needed clarification.

Calling him, Don said he had the results, and they planned to meet on Drew's break.

Don anxiously waited for Drew, and when he arrived, he led him directly to his private lab. He had a sheet of paper in his hand, and he sobered as he turned to Drew.

"This is not good, Drew."

The seriousness of Don's face caused Drew to sit up a little straighter. "What is it? What can you tell me?"

"This," Don said, passing the vial to Drew, "this *is* a date rape drug, and it matches perfectly with what was found in your bloodstream. Where did you get this stuff, Drew? This is an illegal substance and likely bought off a street dealer."

Sitting back in his chair, Drew closed his eyes for a few seconds not quite able to speak. Even knowing what the results proved, he was still shocked at the truth. Bringing his fingers up to his lips, he nervously twisted them while absorbing the information and realizing just how far Keri would go in her grand scheme to seduce him. He couldn't hate her more even if he tried.

"Drew, you can trust me with this. I am not permitted to discuss any of my lab findings with unrelated people. Please trust me."

Pressing his lips together, it felt as if his teeth would split through his skin. "My wife," he admitted, letting the words tumble right out of his mouth.

"Your wife! What the hell, Drew!"

"I can't say anything more about it, Don. Did you find anything out about the prints?"

"Reaching for another piece of paper, he said, "As a matter of fact, I did."

"And?"

"A perfect match."

7

Finishing up her assignments, Keri had done well. Passing in her final assignments, she waited patiently for her diplomas and was happy that she'd soon be contributing to the family income. Making several calls to local medical facilities, she announced she'd received her documentation and asked to be put on their list for services.

Receiving her first assignment a few days later, they informed her that it would be on a trial basis only to allow them time to deem if her work would be satisfactory.

Calling the appointed courier service, Keri sent off her first assignment. Going about her days, she waited for the results and her first pay cheque. Depending on her capabilities, she hoped it would lead to more work. Several days passed she felt excitement when the doorbell rang. Seeing the courier truck through the window, she quickened her steps to answer the door. A young man handed her a large padded package, asked for her signature and left. Opening the package, she saw a pay envelope, and through the cellophane, she spotted a cheque. Ripping it open, she pulled it out, gazed at it, closed her eyes and hugged it to her chest in satisfaction. Pleased with herself and her accomplishments she folded the cheque and tucked in the top of her bra. Reaching for the package again she pulled out more pages which included a contract for another assignment, a dictation recording and an instruction sheet that listed the specifics of the job. She had missed the top sheet completely in her haste to find more work, but then, there it was... the ego buster. A personal letter from the company informing her of the flawless job she had done for them and welcomed her to their company. She was floating on air as she re-read the page. Finally, she had done something that someone deemed worthy, approved of, and it felt great. With nothing but time, she began to work on her new assignment.

Slipping the small mini cassette tape into the recorder, she put the headphones on and pressed play. Her fingers flew across the keyboard as she paused only slightly to listen to the words. Reading it over and editing here and there, she was finished in no time.

As her due date approached, Drew accepted more classroom time than flight time, to be closer to home. Working in his garage, he heard her scream.

"Drew!"

Dashing into the house, he found Keri standing, legs apart, over a puddle of water. Sheer panic was noticeable on her face.

"My water broke! I'm in labor! We have to go!" she panted through quick sentences. "I have to go to the bedroom and change my clothes, please help me."

"Do we have time?" he asked.

"I'll make time, I'm dripping wet!" she hissed. Reaching frantically for Drew's hand, she doubled forward in pain and squeezed through the contraction. Flexing his fingers, he was hoping to regain blood flow.

"Sorry Drew, it hurts so bad!" she whined.

"It's OK, Keri, are you sure you should take the time to change?" he asked, trying not to sound anxious.

"I'll just be a few minutes if you'll help me."

"OK, what can I do?"

"I have a loose dress just inside the closet, white with pink flowers..." Spreading her legs and reaching for the bed, she began to breathe in tiny puffs while using the bed as a relief from standing.

"What are you doing? Are you OK?" he asked.

"Lamaze breathing through the contractions! If you'd have come to classes with me you'd know!" she snapped. Flushed and dripping in perspiration, she pointed to the closet. "The dress! Get the damned dress!"

Yanking the dress from the hanger he ducked into the bathroom for a hand towel then hurried to the bed. Raising her arms above her head, she said, "Take my dress off, pull it over my head."

Not ever having had the chance to undress a woman, he felt this wasn't a good time to ask for instructions. Taking the hem of her dress, he peeled it over her damp body. Reaching under her enormous stomach, she tucked a thumb in the elastic of her panties and tried to push them down, but she grabbed Drew's arm and bared through another pain. "Help me, Drew, we have to hurry!"

Yanking down her underwear, she stepped out of the soggy mess. "Pull the dress over my head," she panted. Taking a few seconds, he wiped her down with the towel before picking up the dress. Poking her arms through the sleeveless dress, it tumbled over her swollen belly, "Thanks," she said. "My suitcase," she gasped, licking her lips, "right there," she pointed.

"Do you want clean underwear?" he asked.

"No, don't bother, let's go," she said holding on to his arm for support.

Grabbing the handles, he took her arm and guided her across the house, outside and into the car as quickly as possible. A few tangled nerves and over-excited blunders, they made it to the hospital. She had been packed and ready for the hospital for weeks, but it didn't help with the nerves of two panicky teens about to become parents.

Pacing in the waiting room for hours, Drew waited for news. Finally, a nurse arrived carrying a blue bundle.

"Mr. Greyson?"

"Yes, I'm Drew Greyson," he said, stepping forward.

"You have a son," she cooed, tipping her arm and exposing a little face.

Looking at his baby boy, he felt something stir inside of him. "My son," he whispered. '*Finally, I have someone to love,*' he thought. Passing the bundle over to him, he clumsily took the baby from her arms.

"Your wife will likely be back in her room by now, I'll take you there."

Feeling proud, he could hardly take his eyes off his son. A rush of love engulfed him knowing this little guy was able to fill a void that had been missing in his life. Guilt crept in as he remembered the night Keri told him she was pregnant. '*Why is it that hindsight is always 20/20*', he thought, and wondered why he couldn't have felt these feelings months ago. He remembered her accusations earlier, and he realized now that he should have been more involved. He had just wanted to be as far away from her as he possibly could and avoid any contact with her and certainly making his own coffee and tea. Even though he had the vial, he still lacked trust. He never knew what she would be up to or what was coming next for him. Holding grudges toward Keri had kept him from bonding while she carried their child and he wasn't proud of that now.

Walking into Keri's room, she beamed with pride for giving him a son. He sat down on the edge of her bed, and something made him lean in and kiss her cheek.

"He is such a handsome boy," he said.

"Yes, I know he is," she said, touching his arm, "he looks just like his daddy."

Smiling at her, she realized it was genuine.

"How are you feeling, Keri?" He knew he couldn't harbor resentment toward her nor could he have negative thoughts. She was, after all, his baby's mother. He would never find it in his heart to trust her again, not that he ever had. He had tucked the vial away in a safe place along with the hospital records thinking he would never have to be reminded of them again. It was important that his son did not pick up negative vibes between his parents. Her voice brought him back to the moment.

"I'm fine, Drew, just tired. Do you mind if I just rest?"

"No, by all means, you worked hard today, close your eyes and rest. I can either just sit here with the baby or leave, it's up to you."

"You do whatever feels comfortable to you, Drew," she yawned.

"The 'baby' sounds weird," he frowned, looking down at the blue bundle. "Do we have a name for him yet?" Guilt crept in again and he silently scolded himself for not bothering to sit down with her and choose a name for his own son. Even though they hadn't known the sex of the child, they could have chosen names together.

"I was thinking," she yawned sleepily and pressed the back of her hand to her lips, "Noah Alexander, do you like it?"

"Noah," he said, speaking the name aloud while looking at the tiny face in his arms.

"I do like it, and it suits him, so, 'Noah' it is? I like that he also has my middle name."

"Yes, Noah, it is then, that was easy." Stifling another yawn, she smiled at how natural Drew seemed, holding their son.

Snuggling into a comfortable position, Keri said, "There's a lady in here, just down the hall," turning her thumb and pointing towards the door. "She had a baby girl yesterday, and she named her Sage. She visited me while I was in labor and brought her in. You must go see her, she is such a beauty."

"Sage? That's different, I've never heard of anyone named 'Sage' before."

"No, neither have I, but she is a sweet little thing."

Her voice trailing off, Drew knew she was fading fast and needed to sleep. As she settled into a well-deserved nap, Noah began to fuss, and he left the room. He quieted down as soon as Drew began to walk with him. Passing an open door, he heard a woman's voice.

"Hello?"

Stopping, he leaned back to see an attractive young woman sitting in a wooden rocking chair, holding a pink bundle. He hadn't seen her before, but he noticed that she was quite pretty. Even from the doorway, he sensed that she was petite with a mane of natural blonde hair and large bluish-green eyes.

"Hello," she said again, "come in so I can meet your baby."

"Hello, I'm Drew Greyson."

"Oh, you're Keri's husband."

"Yes, I am, and you are?"

"Lorraine Lawrence," she said, twisting around sideways exposing the gorgeous pink face in the blanket, "and this is Sage."

"My wife just told me about you and Sage," he said, "it's a beautiful name and it's the first time I've heard it called anything except an herb."

"There are reasons for all things, and some just can't be explained," she said, and Drew saw a glimmer of sadness in her face.

Propping him up, Drew introduced his son. "This is Noah," he said, with his own kind of sadness.

"They are beautiful babies, aren't they?"

"They certainly are, and neither one of us could ever claim to be biased."

"No, we would never be that!" she said, jokingly.

Taking one last look at Sage, he smiled and said, "She is a beauty!"

"Thanks," he heard her say as he made his way out the door and down the hall.

8

Settling back into the rocking chair, Lorraine softly hummed as she pushed back and forth moving the rocker. Practically a baby herself, she admired the bundle in her arms and quickly teared up, remembering how she came to hold this beautiful bundle.

Sage and a few trinkets were all that was left of those few days in her private and secret paradise.

She would never regret meeting the man who stole her heart the second she saw him. Although it didn't pan out well, she had this beautiful baby girl as a constant reminder of a time she would cherish forever.

Her mind wondered back to her first few days on the job. As a receptionist at Tanner Refineries in Kanyon Valley, she met several top officials in the oil business when they walked through the doors. Swinging open the heavy glass door, he walked up to her desk where she was busy on the phone with a client. Sensing someone's presence, she dutifully focused her attention on the customer she was speaking with. Ending the call, she locked eyes with the most handsome cowboy she'd ever seen walk through Tanner Refineries' doors. On that specific day, Lorraine knew that she had met the man she'd love forever. Standing before her, he looked like a god. Tall, slim, sizzling brown eyes and the sweetest smile that cracked into dimples. He had been surprised to see someone new at the front desk and curiosity peaked his interest. "Hello there, Darlin'," he drawled while touching the tip of his cowboy hat. "A new face at the main desk I see and a mighty purdy one at that."

Lorraine blushed and asked him what she could do for him.

"Well now, sweet thang, let's not be hasty. I'm kinda likin' it right here. The meetin' can wait another minute or two."

He had a drawl straight out of Texas and the devilish suave of J.R. Ewing, only younger. "Gage," he said, offering his hand, "Gage Holten, and you are?"

"Lorraine Lawrence," she said, accepting his handshake from across the counter. He took it but held on longer than necessary before lifting it to his lips to lightly kiss the top of her knuckles. She was floored, and her heart raced at the handsome gentleman standing before her.

She was all aflutter that he was openly flirting with her. He was everything she had only read about in love stories. *'The Tall Texas Stranger'* she could see the title now. She was seventeen, fresh out of business school and dumb as a post in dating skills.

"Well, Miss Lawrence, it surely is a pleasure," he nodded, curling a few fingers around the crown of his hat, he lifted it off his head. Exposing a neatly trimmed head of sandy blond hair, he laid his hat against his chest.

"And mine," she gushed.

The desk phone buzzed, breaking the spell that had fallen over them.

"Yes, Mr. Tanner?" she said, holding his stare.

"Lorraine, I'm expecting a client named Holten, from Texas, would you send him in as soon as he arrives, please."

"He's just arrived, Mr. Tanner, I'll show him right in."

"I'll be seeing you after the meetin' Darlin'," he said, with a broad grin and a wink.

"I'll be here," she said, a little flirty and with a satisfied smile. Flirting with clients was a rule breaker, and she has already broken it a few days into the job.

She was in another world when her boss came up to her desk.

"Miss Lawrence, are you free for dinner tonight?"

"I can be, Mr. Tanner."

"Mr. Holten and I are meeting for dinner at seven, and he is requesting that you join us."

"Is it a working dinner, Sir… or…?"

"No, just the four of us, my wife will be joining us, as well, so please call and make reservations for seven o'clock at Kanyon Valley Towers."

"I will do that right now, Mr. Tanner," she said, glancing behind him at Gage's wide, satisfied grinned while he tipped his cowboy hat and winked.

She lowered her head to hide her smile and lifted the phone.

Gage was expected to be in town for a four-day business trip, and from their first meeting and dinner with the Tanner's, they'd seen each other every night. She was lost in love and romance when he invited her back to his room after the dinner meeting, and from then on, she was a goner.

He showed up, one morning just before lunch hour and invited her to take a walk with him. It was a beautiful sunny day, and he asked her to walk on the beach with him. Not wanting to be noticed, she chose an area that was rarely traveled, in hopes they wouldn't be spotted. Knowing it was against the rules to fraternize with clients, she was taking an enormous risk. It was a rough area, and as they picked their way across the rocks, Lorraine saw something jammed between two small stones. It was a single, fairly large piece of dark blue beach glass and when she picked it up, it broke in half leaving a clear and distinct jagged edge.

"Look at this."

Two pieces lay in her palm, and he carefully picked them up and joined them perfectly. Looking into each other's eyes, they had the same thought. He slipped half into his pocket, and she kept the other piece already knowing where she'd keep it.

He showered her with compliments, beautiful red roses, heart-shaped boxes of chocolates and more love than she had ever known was possible. He had invited her to his room again on his last night in town. When she arrived, he was freshly showered and relaxed when he let her in.

Pulling her into his arms, he closed the door and whispered into her hair, "I have a gift for you."

"Gage, you shouldn't have, I don't need anything."

"You need this, Darlin'," he said, with his sideways grin. "Here, open it," he said, as he passed her a wrapped gift box.

Accepting it, she sat down, and he sat beside her.

"Go ahead, open it up," he said, nudging her elbow.

Gently untying the bow, she lifted the lid and gazed into a pink satin lined box at a beautiful silver chained locket.

"Gage, it's beautiful," she exclaimed, "but why?"

"Open it," he nudged his chin towards the locket.

Lifting the locket out of its clip, she studied the sides for the indent. Flipping it open, there was a picture of him on one side and a blank spot on the other.

"I want you to promise me that you will put your picture in here next to mine. Will you do that for me?"

She loved his Texas drawl, and she knew she would have done anything for him.

"I will, Gage, I promise."

"Turn it over and read the back," he said, nudging her again.

Looking up at him she read, 'G.H. & L.L.'. "Our initials, I love it, Gage, and I will cherish it always."

Holding out his hand, she gave him the locket, turned around and held up her hair. Feeling him hook the lobster claw clasp at the back of her neck, it dropped into place at the top of her cleavage.

"Perfect," he said, looking at it before he bent to kiss it and worked his way up her neck. This would be the fourth time they would make love and Lorraine would never regret her time with Gage.

"I promise I will be back in a couple of months and I would very much like to see you again, Darlin'."

"I would love that," she said, wanting to add *'as much as I love you,'* but she wasn't sure if that would have been the right thing to say after only four days. Until he surprised her.

"I love you, my Darlin' Lorraine, and when I come back I want to see your picture right there next to mine." he drawled, tapping the locket.

"I love you too, Gage, and it will be, I promise."

His hotel room was not far from her parent's place, and as they walked along the tree-lined sidewalk, they spoke in whispers as they made plans for his next trip. The night was clear and calm, and voices could be heard for a mile, and they wanted their plans to be their secret. He held her for a long moment before leaving her at the doorstep. Tears spilled down her cheeks as she watched him walk away from her. Missing him already, she held the locket between her fingers and slid the clasps to where she could see it. Unhooking it, she dropped the locket into her pocket so that her mother wouldn't ask questions.

Slipping off her heels at the door, she climbed quietly up the stairs unnoticed. When she reached her room, she laid the locket on her nightstand and scanned her albums for a properly sized picture. Tracing it and cutting it to fit, she pressed it into the empty heart-shaped frame next to his.

* * *

She had a shoe box on her closet shelf for sentimental items, like this. Taking the gift box out of her handbag, she put the locket back in it and added it to her collection knowing she would never show it to anyone. Rummaging in her coat pocket, she found her piece of blue glass. Putting it into the box, she closed the lid and put it back on the closet shelf.

She brushed out her long blonde hair, washed the bit of remaining makeup off her face and brushed her teeth. Staring at her features for a few minutes she thought how lucky she was to have met Gage. Her bluish-green eyes stared back at her as her gaze trailed down to her small, well-chiseled turned up nose and across her heart-shaped face. Taking a deep, satisfied breath, she ran her fingers through her hair and climbed into bed. Sweet thoughts of Gage's tender touches and romantic gestures clouded her brain and kept her from falling asleep. She tossed and turned for hours missing him, loving him and wishing to be with him. She couldn't wait to see him again and hoped the weeks would fly by.

She was tired and frazzled the next day at work. She wanted to lay her head down on the desk and go to sleep when the phone jarred her nerves.

"Tanner Refineries, this is Lorraine, how may I direct your call?" she said, stifling a yawn.

"Hello, Darlin'."

"Is this Conway Twitty?" she asked while giggling into the phone.

"I can be anybody you want me to be, Darlin'," he laughed into the phone.

"Gage, we have to be careful about calls, I could lose my job."

"You won't lose your job, baby girl, we'll be careful. Just hang up if someone comes by, I'll understand. I just wanted to say I love you, before heading back to Texas. I am just heading out to the airport and wanted to say goodbye."

"I love you too, Gage, more than you know and I miss you so much."

He could hear the sadness in her voice since he felt the same way. "I miss you too, Darlin', please wait for me, I'll call again soon."

Hearing voices behind her, she quickly replied into the receiver, "I'll wait for you Gage, I gotta go, bye," and hung up.

Hearing Mr. Tanner's voice, she raised her head and looked into his squinting eyes. "That Gage Holten is quite the businessman."

"Is that so, Mr. Tanner?"

"Um hum," he said, stifling a grin. Being fond of her, he was impressed by her abilities as a newbie.

She held a straight face and went about her duties.

* * *

Out of nowhere his calls stopped, no messages came for Tanner Refineries, and no one called or came to replace him. Days turned into weeks and weeks into a few months. Finally, Mr. Tanner informed her that he had lost the Holten Industries' account. There was no reasoning behind it, they were just done. Already heartbroken from not hearing from him, she knew there would likely be no further business meetings either.

Pride had kept her from calling him when everything inside her screamed to hear his voice. Many scenarios had crossed her mind, a woman answering, he'd hang up on her, hearing him say he didn't love her anymore. Rejection and the overwhelming feeling of being used by him, she could not bear it if any of these things were to happen. All that she had left was a shoebox filled with a few trinkets, but she still had her hopes and dreams, her fantasies, pride and dignity and nobody was taking that from her, nobody.

Stepping into the shower, she'd noticed her breasts were slightly swollen and tender. Shock ripped through her as she turned the water off, grabbed a towel and rushed out of the room to look at the calendar on the wall. Taking it off the nail, she flipped back a few pages to the previous months and scanned the days and weeks, several times, realizing she hadn't had a period in two months. Collapsing to the floor, she slumped against the side of the bed and covered her face with her palms in disbelief. *'What now*?' she thought, *'what am I going to do*?' Stumbling to her feet, she saw her reflection in a full-length mirror that hung on the back of the bedroom door. Lowering the towel, she turned sideways running her hand up and down her belly feeling a slight bulge. Being naturally slim and without an ounce of fat on her body, a baby bump would be noticed sooner rather than later. It became clear to her why her skirts and dress pants were suddenly fitting uncomfortably around her waist. Counting backward, it was evident she could possibly be two and a half months along. It had been that long since she'd last seen Gage, according to her entry. Thinking about the shoe box, she went to the closet and took it off the shelf. Opening the lid, she removed the locket and dug a fingernail into the slot. Popping it open, she revealed the pictures of her and Gage. Tears spilled down her cheeks as she gazed at the heart-shaped headshot of him. Lowering her hands, she pressed the opened locket against her stomach. "This is our baby, Gage, but you will never know about it. Nobody will ever know who my baby belongs to, nobody!" she whispered, adamantly. She had visions of him or his family ripping her baby from her arms. Perhaps even accusing her of being too young to raise a child and that perhaps they could offer he or she a better life, financially. Being in the oil business, she was sure they must be rich people, but their money would never buy her baby. She took the locket away from her belly, and with one last look at his handsome, smiling face, she returned it to its rightful place, in the shoe box.

'*Now for the hard part.*' she thought.

Pressing her lips together, she stared at her mother's expression as she told her she was pregnant. Waiting for her to speak, Lorraine stood in front of her still wet and wrapped in a towel.

"A baby, Lorraine? Who is the father?" she asked.

"I'm sorry mom, I can't tell you that."

"Why not, for Heaven's sake? You tell me right now!" she demanded.

Lowering her head, she shook it from side to side as she whispered, "I'm sorry, Mom, I can't tell you. I will tell you that he is not from Kanyon Valley or from anywhere near here, but that is all I will say."

"Why are you hiding his identity?"

"Because, mom, his family is probably rich, and I'm afraid if they know they will force me to give the baby to them and I won't do that."

Wrapping her in her arms, her mother held her close. "OK then, you've made your decision, and I will respect it, but you have to respect any decisions your father and I make regarding this. Agreed?"

"Yes, I agree."

Within weeks, the decision had been made. The Lawrence's were moving their daughter out of Kanyon Valley and agreed upon a place called Kanyon Ridge. In case the baby's father showed up looking for Lorraine, she wouldn't be easily tracked down. Her parents were certain that Lorraine had legitimate fears about losing her baby to strangers. Their plan was that their house would go silently on the market as they packed up their contents to leave town. The realtor had been instructed to list the house only after they were out of town and they could do business by courier, mail or phone and their information was to remain strictly confidential.

The Lawrence's kept a low profile for Lorraine's sake. Moving away seemed the safest option. Lorraine had gone to work at Tanner's Refinery as if nothing was different until the day they moved. She wasn't far enough along for anyone to notice a baby bump since she had replaced her wardrobe with looser pieces.

While Lorraine was at work, her parents were busy making calls to disconnect the utilities and packing up their car. Her father had asked for a transfer to another branch giving him a few days off to help with the move. Nothing was mentioned or seemed out of place when, at the end of her last day, Lorraine said her usual 'have a good night' to Mr. Tanner and left. When Lorraine got home that evening the Lawrence's got into their car, backed out of the garage and disappeared into the night.

9

The years passed quickly and before long Noah was off to kindergarten.

Noah adored his dad and waited patiently for him to come back from his flights. Having a few days off, Drew was happy to give some much-needed time and attention to Noah.

Puttering around in the garage, Drew cleaned up the lawn tractor and was sweeping the grass up off the floor when Noah wondered in.

"Hey, Dad!"

"Hi Buddy, how was your day?"

"OK, I guess."

"Just OK?"

Looking down at the floor, Noah kicked at nothing in particular.

"Something you'd like to share with me, son?"

"Maybe."

Smiling to himself, he noticed the shyness Noah was displaying. Propping the broom up against his workstation, he squatted down, to give Noah his full attention, hoping he'd open up to him.

"Noah, I hope you know you can talk to me about anything and it will always stay between us."

Although he was listening to his words carefully, Drew felt he was still uncomfortable. His first thought was that he was being bullied causing his defensive antennas to rear up. His first year in school, he didn't want his son to be a victim for years to come.

"Noah, are you being picked on at school?" Not certain he'd know what 'bullying' meant.

"No, Dad, I'm not being bullied," he said, looking at the floor again. Finally making eye contact, he said, "There's a girl at school…"

Turning his head to hide his smile, Drew pressed his lips together and then sobered up to give his attention to Noah's dilemma.

"Hmm, what about her?"

"She follows me around and tries to talk to me."

"You don't like that?" Drew asked, while flashes of Keri stalking haunted him.

"She said she wants to be my friend."

"So, what's wrong with that?"

"Nothing, but there are a lot of boys in our class that like her, but she wants me as her friend."

"You should be honored then. She's at least cute, right?" Drew said, teasingly.

Noah's eyes widened as a big gaping smile crossed his face. Raising his eyebrows, Drew smiled while loving the toothless grin.

"That cute, eh?" Drew asked, and when he saw his little cheeks flush, he touched his shoulder. Stepping between his dad's knees, Noah wrapped his arms around Drew's neck. Drew picked him up and hugged him for a long moment.

"Friends don't always have to be 'cute' you know, Noah, we are all unique in face and body, and we all want to be liked for who we are, not by what we look like."

"Thanks, dad."

"For what?"

"You know, girl talk and stuff," he said, looking up at Drew.

"No problem, Noah, anytime. Does this girl have a name?"

"Yeah, it's Sage."

"Sage?" asked Drew, as a memory of a little pink bundle came to mind. '*Sage Lawrence?*' he wondered.

* * *

Lorraine Lawrence sat reading the daily newspaper when she noticed a large ad spread across half a page, and it caught her interest.

'*Rockland Modelling Agency, looking for children ages five through eight, for a catalogue shoot. Interested parties should contact the local school. Auditions to be held in the gymnasium.*'

Lorraine jotted down the time and date on a notepad then scraped it, deciding, instead, to cut the ad out. Folding the ad, she put it aside and waited for the opportunity to talk to Sage. Lorraine knew that her daughter was beautiful, not only on the outside but she also had a beautiful spirit. She had always heard the phrase 'beautiful on the inside and the outside' and now she had a more profound understanding of it when she looked at her little girl. She had by-passed the clumsy, oafish stage and went straight into graceful and lady-like even as a little girl, giving Lorraine the confidence in knowing Sage might do well in modelling. She left the ad on the end table and waited for Sage to come home from school.

"Sage," she began and paused for thought. Leaning forward in her chair, she picked up the newspaper clipping before beginning again. "There is a modelling agency coming to Kanyon Ridge to do interviews for auditions, would you be interested in trying out?"

"What's an 'audition?" she asked.

"Well, it's to give an example of what you can do to show whether or not you can do a job, such as modelling."

"Modelling? I'm only five Mommy. Do you think I can do that?"

Lorraine thought it was a fair question, so she reached for a catalogue and flipped to the children's section. Finding it, she turned it around facing Sage. "These children are doing exactly what they are asking for in the audition ad. Do you think you can do that?"

Flipping through several pages, she studied the concept of the children's poses. Taking several minutes to digest what she was looking at, Sage responded to her mother's question. "I think I can do that," she said, nodding her head confidently.

"I believe you can too. Let's practice a bit and see how you do. Watch me, and then you can decide, OK?"

"OK," she said, shrugging her shoulders as if it were no big deal.

Getting up off her chair, Lorraine walked across the living room floor while keeping her back as straight as an arrow. On the other side of the room, she stopped, put her hand on her right hip and placed her left foot in front of the right foot. Moving slightly to the left and then the right, she pivoted on her right toes, dropped her hand to her side and walked back to Sage.

Sage excitedly clapped her hands at her mother's performance. "Mommy! You're a model!"

Lorraine laughed and said, "I modeled in a few school fashion shows in my day." Kneeling for a hug, she pulled away and rested her hands upon Sage's arms. "Would you show me if you can do what I just did?" she asked, pointing across the room.

Getting up, Lorraine could almost see the wheels turning in her daughter's head as if remembering the steps her mother had taken. Looking up at her mother, Lorraine nodded in confidence and indicated for her to begin. Sage began to move. Squaring her shoulders, toe poised, she began walking across the room. Holding her breath, Lorraine brought her hands up and rested them tent-like across her nose and mouth. Sage's hand came up to her hip, right toe poised over the left foot, pivoted, left and right movements, and before turning on the ball of her foot, she brought both feet into alignment. Dropping her hand to her side, she walked back to her mother.

Lorraine was impressed! Sage was the perfect little model! Crouching down, as Sage got closer, she gathered her up in her arms with pride.

"Did I do it right, Mommy?"

"You got it on the first try!" Releasing her, she raised her palm as Sage slapped it in a high five.

Making the call to the modelling agency, she requested Sage's name be put on the list. Taking only a few days, someone got back to her with specifics. Wanting to know Sage's age, what color was her hair and eyes, and weight was important. Did she have any experience? Did she have a recent photo that she could send to their office? Lorraine wrote down the address to mail out a photo.

Hanging up the phone, she began searching through boxes and albums for the perfect picture of Sage. Going through nearly every recent photo, she concluded that the head shot from her recent school pictures was the best choice. Taking the pictures out of the envelope, she cut a 5 X 7 off the sheet and wrote Sage's information on the back. Finding a greeting card envelope, she slid the picture inside, addressed and stamped it. She and Sage walked to the mailbox at the end of the street. Pulling down the handle, Lorraine watched as Sage dropped the envelope in.

Once Sage's appointment date arrived, it gave Lorraine more time to work with her. She didn't overwhelm her with poses, but they practiced walking, turning and posture while Lorraine encouraged grace and poise without being overbearing. She even went so far as to teach her to walk while balancing a few books on her head. She also encouraged her to imagine her head being pulled up by an imaginary string to keep her back straight, head back and chin up. She was a fast learner, and Lorraine was certain that she would be a natural. It made her feel she had done the right thing by submitting Sage's name.

On the day of the auditions, Lorraine turned into a total nervous wreck while Sage was calm, cool and collected and wondered why her mother was such a mess.

"Are you sure you aren't nervous, Sage?"

"No, Mom, I'm fine," she said, watching as her mother wrung her hands.

"Do you remember everything we've practiced? Your balance, turns, how to walk the runway?"

"Yes, Mom, I remember."

Lorraine was baffled at how relaxed Sage was while she nearly fell off her chair when she heard Sage's name being called.

"Honey, are you sure you're OK?"

Sage smiled and nodded at her mother who was seemingly coming apart at the seams.

"Mom," she said, at a frozen Lorraine. "Mommy? We have to go in now, it's my turn!" she squealed excitedly and anxiously waiting to begin.

"Are you Sage?" the interviewer asked, totally taken with her already.

"Yes, I am," Sage spoke up smiling broadly and proudly at the lady.

"My name is Ruby Rockland, Sage, you have a very pretty name."

"Thank you," she answered, still grinning from ear to ear.

"Are you using it as a stage name?"

Sage looked up at her mother in confusion.

"No, Sage Lawrence is her name," added Lorraine.

Nodding, Ruby began.

"So, Sage," she said, bringing her attention back to the child. "I have a few things I would like for you to do for me. It's just to show me what you can do so I can decide if you will move on to the next level."

Sage nodded to indicate she was ready.

"First," she pointed across the room, "do you see that red line over there?"

Sage followed her pointed finger. "Yes, I see it."

"Would you do a walk over to it and turn and walk back to this spot?" she pointed to another red line closest to them.

As far as Lorraine could tell it was red duct tape set up for the auditions. Watching the drill, Lorraine hoped she'd remember their rehearsals.

Sage looked beautiful in a pink, sleeveless, flowered blouse that hung out over a white knee-length skirt and wearing pink patent leather sandals with a small half inch heel. Her blonde hair, pulled back off her face with a pink and white striped hairband, fell loosely in waist length curls.

Nervously, Lorraine waited for Sage to begin.

Finally, when Ruby finished instructing Sage, she went behind her desk and said, "You may begin, Sage."

Sage, noticeably, went straight into serious mode as she held her head up and squared her shoulders. She didn't look left or right nor did she look at her mother for approval. Instead, she glided across the floor with elegance and ease and put one hand on her hip, paused, dropped her hand and glided back to the appointed spot.

Ruby just sat in awe watching this beautiful child do exactly as she had been instructed, but she certainly did not expect perfection. She broke out in applause and Lorraine, who had been holding her breath, joined in. She knew Ruby was impressed as soon as Sage began her walk. Her eyes darted from Sage to Ruby, and the look on Ruby's face was more than what Lorraine could ever have hoped for. Sage beamed with pride as they clapped for her. Sage knew at that moment that she was hit with the modelling bug.

"That was wonderful, Sage, great job!"

"Thank you, Miss Rockland."

"I have a few more requests for you if you're ready."

"I'm ready! she beamed."

Ruby asked her assistant to help Sage in the dressing room and in the meanwhile, she took a few minutes to explain the procedure to Lorraine.

"If we use Sage in our catalogue, I would like to see her in different outfits and scenarios, and the first will be beachwear."

Lorraine nodded her approval and waited for the show to begin.

Someone came along and lowered a curtain for the backdrop of a beach scene while another stagehand pushed in a floor that resembled sand on a beach. A bright light was turned on overhead resembling sunshine. The change artist worked with Sage and had her wear several bathing suits and hairstyles arranging from braids, ponytails, pigtails and wrapped in the back and held with a clip with wisps at the sides. They had her wear several styles of hats to accent the beachwear and of course sensibility for sun protection. She was a beauty and Lorraine could not have been prouder.

Ruby had called in a photographer to get an idea of how Sage could work a camera. She had them take dozens of pictures, including headshots of her in every outfit while doing exactly as Ruby asked. She smiled on command, was serious, joyful, playful and emotional at Ruby's request, and in her opinion as a professional, she was impressive for a five-year-old. Lorraine was in awe that her daughter had remained so calm. She never asked Ruby to repeat instructions, and she took direction without missing a beat. She was relaxed, calm and confident allowing the camera to catch it all. The photographer loved working with her.

There were no mistakes or retakes, and she never missed her mark.

"It's a wrap, people!" Ruby shouted from across the room. Being involved with Sage, they had totally forgotten the appointed time was up. Ruby's assistant escorted Sage back to the dressing room so she could get back into her street clothes. Lorraine silently eyed Ruby when she heard her cell phone ring.

"Ruby Rockland," she said after pressing the 'talk' button.

Lorraine knew it was rude to eavesdrop, so she pretended to be absorbed in a magazine article.

"Yes, we're done here." There was a pause. "No, that won't be necessary."

Lorraine only heard one side of the conversation, but she thought Ruby was talking to the gal who made the appointments.

"Please explain that the auditions are over and send everyone home." There was another brief pause, and Ruby uttered the words that floored Lorraine.

"Just tell them we will call them if we hold auditions here again." Pausing. "Yes, I understand they have been waiting, but as far as I'm concerned, we have found our model, so I won't waste time on the others." Another pause. "Yes, that's correct, we have our model." When she ended her call, she noticed Lorraine staring at her. She raised her hand and beckoned her over. Ruby stood when Sage came out of the dressing room and smiled as she very nonchalantly walked up to her mother as if nothing out of the ordinary had just happened. As far as Sage was concerned, she was only there to show Ruby what she could do, and that was all she expected. The fact that she had just spent the last hour 'working' meant very little to her. Smiling at Ruby, she took her mother's hand.

"Sage," Ruby said, leaning forward onto her desk, "I have some very good news for you."

Looking up at her mother, she looked back at Ruby and waited for her to continue.

"You did a fantastic job for us today, perfect in fact, and if it is OK with you and your mom, I would like to hire you for the job we are doing here in town."

"Really?" Sage dropped her mother's hand and clapped with excitement. "You mean… I have the job?"

"If you want it, Sage, we would love to work with you as our newest model."

Excitement showed on her face as she looked up at her mother again, "Mommy?"

Lorraine, showing pride in her, rendered her momentarily speechless.

"Are you ready for this, Sage?"

"Mommy, this is what we came here for. They picked me, and I want to do this."

"Well, OK then, you'd better tell Ms. Rockland that you accept her offer."

"Really?" Sage whispered.

Lorraine nodded her head towards Ruby indicating that she should deal with her. Ruby winked at Lorraine, appreciating her allowing Sage to be the grown-up for a few minutes.

"I'd love to!"

"Welcome aboard, Sage, and Ms. Lawrence, I will be forwarding you a portfolio of the pictures that were taken here today, along with my written permission to use them in the future for Sage's resumes." Ruby passed her a pad and pen, "Please provide me with your mailing address and a phone number for our files and if we need Sage again, we will certainly give you a call."

10

Over the years, Keri noticed new drivers for the courier service. Each one was friendly, courteous and professional while bringing her deliveries. She'd done numerous assignments until she could do the work with her eyes closed and it would still be perfect. She was proud of herself, and the home studies had paid off for her. Both she and Drew were established in their careers, and it had been ten years since they no longer needed their parents' credit cards. Since her very first pay cheque arrived, she never asked for their help or assistance in any way. She had money in a bank account, a fashionable wardrobe, a new car and she and Drew had long since moved to a new home. She loved her life but wished she'd gotten more than total disregard from her husband.

In one day, life took on a new meaning when she opened her front door to see a new courier driver standing on her step. As she swung open the door, anxious to receive her package, his face seemed to fall in disbelief as he slowly lifted his sunglasses to the top of his head.

"Hello," she smiled.

"Ma'am," he said, nodding his head while staring at her.

"You have something for me?" she asked.

"Oh, um, yeah, sorry," he stammered, passing her the package and the clipboard for a signature.

Taking it, she looked up at him and saw that he was smiling broadly. He was quite handsome, she noticed. Tall, blondish hair and noticeably intense brown and green hazel eyes that touched her soul. Passing the clipboard back, she raised her hand to the edge of the door and stepped inside.

"Um," he said, turning the board around to read her name, "Keri, I'm Jake, your new driver."

"It's nice to meet you," she said, extending her hand. "Jake?"

"Lansing, Jake Lansing," he said, taking her hand. He didn't realize it at the time, but he tugged on it enough to ease her out of the safety of the doorway and onto the step. He wasn't ready to let this beauty go.

Shuffling his feet nervously, Jake tried to make casual conversation. Keri, loving the attention, enjoyed watching him stammer and blush knowing he found her attractive at first glance. Running his hand up his sleeve, he looked at his watch.

"Do you have to be somewhere?"

"No! I'm done for the day, you were my last stop."

Not really knowing who Jake Lansing was, she took a chance. "Would you like a cup of coffee then?"

Shocked at the invitation or a lucky break, he raised his eyebrows in surprise. "Um, yes, I would, thank you."

Stepping inside, she closed the door and headed for the kitchen. "This way," she said, nodding her head. Following behind her, Jake was more nervous than he had ever been. "Are, um, you... alone?"

"Why? Do you want more than coffee?" she said, not intending to tease or flirt with him, but it brought something back to life.

Reaching for the coffee pot, Keri blushed to realize she was acting like a school girl. "Coffee would be a start," he teased back, putting them both a little more at ease.

Taking two full mugs from the counter, she put them on the table along with a sugar bowl and cream. He was standing close enough to her that she felt the heat from his body. She didn't move as her heart began to pound for this handsome stranger in her kitchen. He gently laid his hands on her shoulders and squeezed slightly. Closing her eyes, she relaxed under his touch. She couldn't remember her last tender touch, and she knew she wanted and needed more.

"I couldn't believe my eyes when you opened the door," he whispered, moving even closer. "You are the most beautiful woman I've ever seen," he said, breathing into her hair.

She didn't know if it was a line to get her into bed or if he was serious but either way she thought she might be ready. Bullshit baffles brains, and this was one of the times when those words had meaning. Turning slowly, she faced him. Raising her eyes to meet his she knew by his look that he was serious. Lowering his head, he stopped before his lips touched hers in case she wasn't interested. Lifting her lips to his, they melted into each other. He was fiercely into this gorgeous woman, and she was responding to his touch. He was the drink of water she had longed for and needed for so many years. It was Drew that she longed for or thought she did but now, right now, it was Jake who wanted her and was showing her just how much. She was feverishly hungry for human touch as she devoured his kisses. Tiny thrills flitted around inside her stomach as she came to like his touch, his kisses and the breathless feeling that has been lost to her since she was a young girl. Here was someone who genuinely wanted her and all she had to do was enjoy it. Her life flashing before her, she realized how many wasted years had sailed past.

"Are you OK with this," he whispered, placing his hands tenderly on the sides of her face, "are we alone?"

"Oh," she whispered, "we are, but I need to verify it to be certain, give me a second." Knowing Noah was at summer camp, Keri sent her first questioning text to Drew. *Where are you?* she typed and pressed send. Seconds later her phoned dinged, *I'm in the Caribbean, why? Is everything OK there?*

Yes, all OK, have a nice flight!

Dropping her shoulders in relief, she looked at Jake. Tilting his head in anticipation, he saw her smile.

"We are alone!" she said, excitedly and leaped to the front door to lock it and then rushed back into his arms.

Cradling her in his arms, he murmured into her ear, "Which way?"

Devouring his mouth, she began walking backward, and he followed. Reaching the bedroom door, Jake picked her up off her feet and carried her to the bed. Lowering her, he watched her chest rise and fall knowing she was ready for him.

Never in her wildest dreams did she ever think she would want anyone except Drew and now her mind was like... *'Drew who?'* as she gave herself totally and completely to Jake. His genuine feelings of tenderness, caring and a wanting that was like no other. It consumed her as she fell into an abyss of pleasure and longing that she had missed out on with Drew. His coldness toward her caused her to become accustomed to being alone as long as he kept coming home but being in Jake's arms confirmed she had needed more than Drew was capable of giving her. She clung to Jake as he made love to her, kissed her and held her tenderly. Nothing compared to this and she knew she needed more, and she didn't have to play dirty pool to get it. Jake was right here, willing and able to bring out the woman in her. A woman who had been deprived of love, passion and emotional connection. Jake had unlocked a fire in her that she never knew she had as she moaned, whimpered and bucked with pleasure while he ravished her body.

She lay happy, content and well satisfied in Jake's arms. He cuddled her close to him as if he never wanted to let her go and now he knew for sure that he didn't.

"So, where do we go from here, Keri?"

"Oh, do we have to talk about that right now, this feels so good," she said snuggling closer.

"I don't want you or me to end up in a world of hurt. That's not my intention and if this is just a one-time thing then I understand, just tell me now, but if it isn't, we need to talk about it."

"I know, but not now, OK?"

11

Noah had eyes only for Sage since his first day at school. He didn't remember talking about her to anyone except that one time with his dad. Even that had been difficult, but it felt great to talk about her with someone.

Throughout grade school, junior and senior high, they were always together. He respected that she was a model and he could certainly understand why. She was a beauty, and he had loved her as far back as first grade and when she first began her career. She was the talk of the school at times, but it didn't put her on a different level than the rest of them, it was just a job to her.

He played sports and had enjoyed the athletic side of his life. He wasn't an avid sportsman by any stretch, but he enjoyed the games, being outside and the camaraderie. He wasn't pushing for attention, scholarships or headhunters, he just wanted to play sports and pass his grades. Sage attended most of the games and rooted for their home team which gave him the joy of playing. In his mind though, he wanted her to be rooting only for him. She shared some of his classes, and he often met her in the hallways between classes. She was always ready with a smile for him, and he graciously accepted them with a nod of his head and a returned killer smile of his own. Their friendship meant everything to him, and he never thought of doing anything to ruin it for them. He had sexual fantasies about her and often wondered what it would be like to hold her in his arms. Not wanting to mess that up, he enjoyed just being her friend. The closest they came, was holding hands in the schoolyard and everyone in the class knew she belonged only to him. It had always been Noah and Sage. They hung out at the beach, took long walks in the sand and shared a burger and fries on Saturday afternoons. They just knew they would always be best friends and he couldn't risk scaring her off with love stuff, which could have gone either way. She would either run or stay, it could bring them even closer or drive them apart, and he took no chance on either. She seemed happy to be with him when she wasn't on the runway, and he cherished every minute he got to hang out with her. Her life was busy, and she seemed to like it that way.

* * *

In their senior year, his love for her only deepened as they matured. She had grown into a beautiful and graceful young woman, but he still didn't know how far their relationship had come. She stayed by his side and to everyone around them they were the perfect couple only they couldn't or wouldn't admit to it to themselves.

In a classroom, where she sat in front of him, he found himself staring at the back of her head. Adoring her long, silky, blonde hair, he became mesmerized as it fell off her shoulder when she'd bend sideways reaching for something in her school bag. Straightening up, she'd swing her head just right for it to flip over her shoulder and lay with the ends draped over his desk. Once, when she had done that flippy thing with her hair, it flew around and landed on his school work. It had captivated him and he couldn't resist touching it. Without anyone noticing, he slipped a couple fingers and a thumb around a section of it and moved his thumb back and forth across the silky-smooth strands. His mind went crazy with thoughts, and an overwhelming feeling of bravery swept over him as he slipped his hand farther under those silky locks and clasped his fingers tightly. Something stirred inside him as he held her hair in his palm. Going into a trance-like state, he imagined the two of them on a beautiful sandy beach, and he was gazing into her gorgeous eyes. Sliding his hand under her soft mop, he wrapped his fingers around it and drew her in to meet his lips. He was turned on by the imaginary kiss and what was meant to be a beautiful moment turned into an embarrassment when Sage tried to stand up, and he still had a solid grip on her hair. Caught off guard, Sage slipped back into her seat just as Noah tried to let go of her hair. The dampness from his palm caused her hair to matte and stick to his hand, and he had to literally lift the hair off his fingers. Turning around to face him, he managed to stammer out a ridiculous excuse which led to a lie. "I... I'm sorry, Sage," ahem, "I... um accidentally um... laid my books on your... um... hair."

"No problem, Noah, I'll try to keep my hair out of the way from now on." Giving him that smile again, she left the classroom, but Noah couldn't get up yet. Still turned on by his life-like fantasy, if he'd stood up, then everybody would have seen the obvious. Thank God it was the last class of the day, so he was in no hurry to go anywhere. He had to stop thinking about Sage and get his mind on another subject. He looked down at himself and thought, 'How can I go anywhere like this!' Shaking his head, he smiled anyway at the predicament he'd found himself in.

He had stacked and organized his homework, but when he reached down for his backpack, he saw a pair of shoes next to his desk. Running his eyes up a shapely pair of jean covered legs and a curvy body, he looked into a pair of gorgeous bluish-green eyes.

"What are you still doing here, Noah?" Sage asked, with a grin.

He inhaled deeply, trying to look calm and collected but he answered her with another fib. "Just going over work for tomorrow's classes, what about you?"

"I had a meeting with the yearbook club and saw that you were still here. Are you okay?"

"Yes, why?"

"Because," she said, getting right to the point, "I know you didn't have your books on my hair today in class, so... what's up?"

Dropping his head, he closed his eyes briefly knowing he had to come clean with her.

"I'm sorry," he said, raising both hands in front of his chest and spreading his fingers wide, "I lied... about the books. I... er... I... wanted to feel your hair, and I got carried away, okay?" Hunching his shoulders, he pushed his books into his backpack and stood up determined to forget this ever happened. Sage stepped closer as he stood up, bringing them almost nose to nose.

"You want to feel my hair, Noah?" she teased, tilting her head to the side while twirling a long lock around her finger. He became serious since he had never seen her openly flirt with him. Flames shot through his body as the raw image of the beach scene flashed through his mind. Without a single thought in his head except her, he dropped his backpack, and in a feverish moment, he was recreating that glorious moment. Gazing into her eyes, he curled his fingers around her silky hair and with a tug, drew her into him as the smell of strawberry shampoo teased his nostrils. Sliding his other hand around to the arch of her back, he leaned in closer. Lowering his eyes, he saw her shapely lips part and closing her eyes, she raised her lips towards his. A rush of passion surged through him as he closed his lips around hers tasting strawberry lip gloss. He had loved her since he was five years old and never once expected this moment to ever happen but here she was with her arms wrapped tightly around his back, the tips of her fingernails digging through his shirt and her body pressing against his. He was lost in an abyss as new, strange and wonderful sensations engulfed him. He was locked into a place he had never been before. Passionate sparks passed between them as their kiss deepened. His tongue searching for hers and when he found it, it took his breath away. He tasted it, tugged on it, pulled it playfully in and out of his mouth until he desperately wanted to swallow her up whole. Groping at each other he swung her around and just as her back hit the chalkboard it was as if someone had thrown a bucket of ice water over them.

"And what do we have here!?"

Springing apart breathlessly, the hall monitor, and spinster, Miss Edna Wilson, glared at them with a pair of close-set eyes and arched brows that made her look perpetually cross. Her hair pulled severely back into a tight bun and lips that were pursed into a wrinkled pucker. Peering at them through squinted ferocious eyes, she jammed her fists against her narrow and scrawny hips demanding authority. Sage's fingertips rushed up to touch her lips that were still moist from Noah's kiss, and she glared at her, in almost hatred, for interrupting their passionate and supposedly private moment. Miss Wilson's eyes fell to Noah's crotch as he grabbed his backpack and held it in front of him to cover up his more than obvious bulge as she stood there silently judging him.

"You are excused Miss Lawrence," she said, with lips puckered up like an apple doll and reeking with indignation while keeping her eyes on Noah. Sage picked up her school bag and gave Noah one last look before leaving the room.

"Would you care to explain yourself, Mr. Greyson?" she said sharply.

Noah ran the back of his hand across his lips where Sage's had just been. "I apologize, Miss Wilson," he said, raising one hand up in defense while holding the backpack in the other. "I know this is against school policies and if you don't report us I can promise it won't happen again."

Glaring at her with pleading eyes, he was asking for another chance to prove himself. She knew this was his first offense in all the years he'd been in school, and as they neared graduation, she saw no harm in letting it pass. After several seconds of scanning his face and watching him squirm, she relented.

"You are free to go Mr. Greyson, and I expect you to keep your word." Her eyes wanting to see behind his backpack, but she forced herself to hold his stare.

"Thank you, Miss Wilson, it won't happen again, you have my word."

She nodded her head, and he left the room without another word.

As she watched Noah leave the classroom a crooked grin spread across her face.

* * *

Sage was waiting for Noah to come out of the school with hopes of picking up where they left off, but when he appeared, he took one look at her and shot off in the opposite direction, binding himself to his word.

Knowing that going to her again, he would not be able to resist grabbing another handful of her hair, continuing from where they'd left off. Keeping Miss Wilson in mind, he didn't know what would happen if she found them in another compromising situation on the school grounds.

Her heart dropped like a stone as she watched him scurry away without a second glance. She was sure he'd come looking for her since they both had enjoyed the trip down 'passion lane' in the classroom. Knowing that sort of behavior was against school rules, she figured Miss 'Apple Doll' Wilson likely read him the riot act in no uncertain terms. Sage knew for certain she wanted to pursue this further. Noah is as hot as she had always imagined and finally getting a taste of him, she definitely wanted more.

Since kindergarten, she'd had a soft spot for Noah. He was shy and gorgeous even at five years old. They saw each other through missing teeth, chicken pox scars, measles, growth spurts, and puberty. He was always the sweetest kid in the class. He was her best friend, and even at the age of five, they knew what being a friend was all about. He protected her, defended her if anyone had been mean, and she knew, in his heart, that she was his 'girlfriend' from day one. The first time he smiled that toothless grin she was a goner. She tried covering her own gaps of missing teeth, but her smile was genuine, happy and friendly, making it difficult to cover up. It was obvious that it was love at first sight for the both of them. She felt quite special when he'd take her hand on the playground letting her know he cared. Every afternoon when school ended he'd give her a friendly hug with a promise of seeing her 'tomorrow.' They had twelve years of 'tomorrows' until everything fell apart.

Memories of Noah clouded her mind, and she longed for his touch. She was disappointed that he'd left her after the classroom incident. But as she watched him swiftly walk away from her, she followed him. She thought better of it, but she was determined to see where this attraction would lead. Only moments before she had been in his arms, so there was no doubt, she was tracking him down. Why hadn't she tried pursuing him before now? He had always been hot and sexy, but she didn't want to scare him off since she valued his friendship.

Running down the street, she was more determined than ever, to see how far this would go. It was 'make or break' time! She was certain she'd find him at the soda shop at the drugstore. It was one of the last shops of its kind in the area and teens loved to hang out there as if waiting for the next Fonzie to walk in and take over the joint.

He was at the jukebox reading labels and running his fingers nervously through his hair. Opening the door quietly, except for that stupid bell, to indicate a customer had entered, it still hadn't caught his attention. He didn't seem to care who came in, his mind was elsewhere. Hearing her say his name and touch him at the same time sent a jolt through his body.

"Sage!" he said, twisting around, "what are you doing here?"

"I wanted to see you, Noah," her voice was calm, cool and sexy.

He waited for her to speak again since, obviously, he was at a loss for words. Just looking at her made his brain foggy.

Leaning into the jukebox, she turned her face in to meet his eyes. When she opened her mouth, he nearly lost it. Those lips had been on his only minutes ago and were now only a mere few inches away.

"I thought we could pick up where we left off," she whispered softly into his ear, sending a thrill down her back at being this close to him again.

"We have no place to go, Sage," he whispered back, as a shivery tickle ran down his spine from her voice in his ear.

"Sure we do Noah," she said, with a sexy smile while her eyes roamed over his face and settled on his lips. Reaching down she looped her fingers around his hand and squeezed. Taking the lead, he followed her out the door and in the direction of the beach. Part way down the street he pulled her over so that her back was against a storefront and leaned in close to her. Searching her face, he knew, without a doubt, that she was the most beautiful creature he had ever seen and for as long as he could remember he'd loved her. Realizing at that moment, that he had loved her longer than he didn't. That sentence would only make sense to him because he hadn't loved her for the first five years of his life but that first day in kindergarten he knew he was a goner. She was the reason he wanted to go to school, and she made it fun. He loved the classes they had together where she had always sat in front of him, and whenever he inhaled, the smell of strawberries from her hair and lip gloss had set his nostrils on edge but never daring to go any farther.

Taking in her beauty, he pulled her firmly against him and inched his mouth to hers. Teasing her, he felt her tremble as she lifted her lips to his and he'd quickly pull away before they could touch. It was obvious that he was teasing himself too and their lips parted and came together. Passion took over their senses on the main street of Kanyon Ridge. If people saw them, they didn't care, and in between sane thoughts, Sage was non-verbally telling Miss Wilson to take a front-row seat because this was not her territory and Noah was all hers.

"Where are we going?" Noah breathed against her lips in between kisses.

"To the boathouse loft," she whispered, as she gasped for air.

He resisted taking her into an alley between the stores there in the middle of town, but that was just his hormonal instinct. Instead, he took her hand, and they began to run the rest of the way.

12

Running wildly down the street, Sage's thoughts flew back to their secret hide-a-way and how she'd stumbled across it. It was a place the school kids had taken over recently when the yacht club members left for a newer and larger space. It was a great place to hold teen dances, and it provided shelter at beach parties and afternoons at the beach in the summer. She had accidentally discovered the loft a few days before when she had been out for a walk and needed to use the facilities. Leaving the washroom, she stopped to take in the enormous great room. Nautical items were still on the mahognay stained wainscoting. Lobster traps were nailed onto the walls, and outdated life jackets hung on hooks. Fishnets hung loosely from the immense ceiling while buoys, shells and small pieces of driftwood laid inside the mesh. Across the room, a ladder stood against a wall causing her to wonder why it was there. *'There was no use for a ladder in the boathouse,'* she thought, walking over to it. Searching around the room for its purpose, she looked up and saw a trap door. The ceiling was high, and the ladder was long almost reaching the ceiling, so it seemed she had indeed, found the connection. Curiosity forced her to bravely climb up higher and higher. When she reached the trap door, she grabbed hold of the wooden handle, lifted and pushed simultaneously causing it to slide inward. She climbed higher to poke her head in to get a better look. Inquisitively, she surveyed the room. There were seven huge skylights across a dormer giving off a great amount of natural light in a beautiful loft. She couldn't help herself from climbing all the way up and inside for a better look. Once she was off the ladder, and inside she stood up full length. It looked as if it might have been a bachelor pad at one time and a perfect place for a tryst which gave her all kinds of new and exciting ideas. There was a small kitchenette with a fridge, stove, drop leaf table and two chairs. An L-shaped counter jutted out making a half wall and a view into the living room. A love seat was against the back of the half wall, and a matching chair sat on an angle with one of the arms resting snugly against the side of the love seat. A large white area rug made of soft fake fur that reached from under the coffee table and out into the living room. An older television sat in the opposite corner and underneath was a VCR with dozens of old taped movies. A bathroom was off the wall closest to the armchair and Sage went in curious to see if there was running water. Rusty colored water sputtered out of the old tap at first but in no time, ran clear with lots of pressure. Sink, toilet, shower stall, along with a stack of towels and wash clothes and even bars of packaged soap on a shelf. Circling the bathroom once more she backed out into the living area again. Along one stretch of wall, there was no furniture at all which caused her to become even more curious. Walking along and running her hand along the paneling, she felt a slight indent. Appling a bit of pressure, she heard a clicking sound and when she removed her hand a full double Murphy bed slowly lowered to the floor. She was in awe of the place. With one slight tug, it had automatically retracted into the wall. Excitement grabbed her since she was sure she was the only one in her crowd who knew about the loft. This room had had great meaning to someone back in the yacht club days, and she couldn't help but wonder who.

Wanting to get on with her walk, she made her way back to the ladder but when she looked down the opening, panic set in and she froze, paralyzed with fear. She had no idea how she was going to get down. It was steep, and when she looked at the ladder, she knew she could not turn around and get her feet on the top rung. Visions of the ladder sliding across the wall or falling backward, with her on it, sent her into hysteria. She dropped to the floor wide-eyed, seeing how far up she was and how far she had to go to get back down and knowing she couldn't do it. Fear tightened her throat, squeezing until she could hardly breathe. Her heart thumped rapidly inside her chest realizing no one knew where she was. Talking herself into at least trying to climb down, she stood up. She had to get her foot on the top rung, but she had to turn around backward to do it. She couldn't get her foot to leave the floor. Tears stung her eyes and began to pool as she looked at the blurred floor below. Wiping wildly at the tears, they flowed quickly down her cheeks. A surge of utter defeat caused an outright fit of bawling and howling sounds worse than an alley cat. She paced, panther-like, around the loft and ranted incoherently.

'Why had she come up here? What had she been thinking? How would she get down? Why couldn't she have minded her own business? How long would it be before someone found her body?' There was no end to the questions she fired at herself.

Wild panic washed over her as she cried and paced. She made several trips to the square hole in the floor but still couldn't muster up the courage to try again. She slumped to the floor again in total exhaustion. She'd begun to hear things that weren't there. When all else failed, now she was losing her mind too.

"Hello?"

She was hearing voices now. *'Great, just great! Was she that far gone?' Was she at the hallucination stage already?'*

"Hello? Anyone here?"

Her head shot up when she heard the voice again. She wasn't crazy after all.

"Noah!?" It was him! She couldn't believe her ears. "Noah!? I'm up here?"

"Sage?"

She cried fresh tears upon hearing his voice. She could hear him practically running up the rungs to get to her.

"Noah!" she whimpered as relief overcome her when his head popped up through the hatch. She raised her arms up to him as he raced across the floor. Seeing how upset she was, he fell to his knees and hugged her to his chest. She wrapped herself around him as close as she could get and still she couldn't control the vibration inside her body. He cupped the back of her head in one hand and held her with the other and rocked her back and forth to calm her.

"Noah, I'm so scared," she whimpered. Her teeth chattered, and her body shook as if she had fallen into a freezing pond and he was her warm blanket.

"Thank you for coming... I thought..."

"I know, Baby, just relax for a few minutes and then we'll talk, okay?" Realizing he had used the word 'baby' it seemed to fit in his vocabulary for her. He could feel her nodding her head against his chest as great sobs escaped her. Before long he felt her body begin to relax and the vibrations waned.

She gave a great shaky sigh and slowly lifted her head off his chest. She felt like a big mess, but she didn't care. She was so happy to be surrounded by his arms.

"Noah, I feel so foolish, how did you know I was here?"

"I saw the door was ajar and when I poked my head in I could hear sobbing and a voice."

Looking into her swollen red eyes, he took his fingertip and moved her matted hair off her damp cheek. "Wanna talk about it?" he asked, searching her face. In all the years he'd known her, he had never seen her quite this shaken and vulnerable.

"I can't get down," she said, with a shaken voice. "It's too high, I can't do it." Fresh tears rolled down her face as she said the words 'I can't' for the first time in her entire life.

Pulling her back into his arms, he said, "I'll get you down, Sage, we'll do it together." He felt another sigh rumble through her body. "Are you ready to try? I'm here, Sage, I'll help you down."

Looking up at him with huge sad and fear-filled eyes, she nodded.

"Before we go, why don't you tell me about this place," he said, trying to distract her for a few minutes.

She dropped her arms as he stood up and he held out a hand to help her to her feet. She started from the beginning, from her walk until he found her, then added that when she'd found the loft, she wanted it to be a place that maybe they could share, away from everyone and if they kept it a secret it would always be their special place.

"It's a beautiful loft, Sage."

"It is really nice, but I don't think I'll be able to come up here ever again."

He looked at her teasingly, "Not even for me?" he said, cocking his head to one side. *'He is such a good friend,'* she thought.

She smiled for the first time since he appeared.

"Let's get you down from here, okay?"

"Okay," she said while nodding her head and pushing her hair behind her ears.

Once they were at the opening, he began to instruct her. Putting his hand on the ladder, he turned enough to get one foot on the top rung then turned his body fully until he faced her. "Do exactly what I did, I'm right here, and I will not let you fall," he said, emphatically.

"Noah," she whispered, wanting to trust him but unable to trust herself.

"Sage, look at this," he said pointing to the top of the ladder.

Leaning forward, she moved her eyes to where he was pointing.

"The ladder is fastened to the board on the hatch, it won't move so turn around and put one foot on the top rung," he said firmly, from a few rungs down.

Knowing she had no choice, she had to get down the ladder. With shaky legs and very little fight left in her, she turned around, closed her eyes for a few seconds and took a deep, ragged breath. With one foot on the rung and both hands on the rails, she willed her other foot to follow.

"Don't look down," he said, softly, "one rung at a time and keep your eyes to the front. You're doing great. Just a few more rungs and you're done."

When she felt the floor beneath her feet, she let out the breath she didn't know she had been holding.

"Now that wasn't so bad, was it?" he said, a proud grin on his face while holding her close to him, protectively.

"It really wasn't, I guess I allowed fear to cripple me up there. I need to go back up!"

A slow smile crept across his face. "That's my girl. You go up, and I'll follow."

She made it to the top and into the loft with Noah behind her. Turning to face the opening, it didn't look as ominous as it did when she was alone.

"Ready?"

"Yes, I'm ready," she said, "I want to go first this time so you can close the hatch." Remembering the steps, she began her descent. Halfway down she stopped and watched as Noah pulled the trap door across the opening.

13

Racing through town toward the boathouse, Sage was more than anxious to climb that ladder again. Throwing open the door, Noah rushed across the floor while she closed and locked it. Taking the ladder rungs two at a time, he had the hatch open and the Murphy bed on its way down before she cleared the top. With no bedding, she improvised by spreading a couple of beach towels on the mattress. A dusty afghan from the back of the love seat would serve as a cover up if needed. Nervously, they stood looking at one other hoping the other would make the first move. Clearly, knowing what they wanted, both were anxious to get back to where it began, in the classroom. Noah bravely took the lead and stepped closer. Being their first time, he felt clumsy and awkward while Sage instantly began to breathe rapidly upon his approach. Pleasure swept over him as he watched her chest rise and fall. Slipping his hand under her hair, he knotted his fingers around it at the nape of her neck. Giving her a slight yank, he pulled her to his chest while gazing into her eyes.

"You are the most beautiful creature I have ever seen." And for the first time ever, he spoke the words, "I love you, Sage and I have for as long as I can remember."

Finally hearing the words she'd longed to hear made her heart race. Even though she always knew he loved her it was the first time he had ever said it.

"I love you too, Noah," she whispered.

Her words were music to his ears as he closed in on her lips. He was soft but powerful as their passion from the schoolroom returned with each tender touch. His kisses deepened, and as his tongue searched for hers, she volunteered it willingly. He tugged on it and played with it, sucked it in and out of his mouth until he lost it from desire. He paused, wanting the next move to be hers to be certain she was ready for him. After all the times he had wanted her, he could not believe the moment was finally here.

Pressing against him, she felt weak as a newborn lamb; quivering, she was more than ready. Unbuckling his belt, it swooshed from the loops and flew across the floor in the blink of an eye.

Travelling her neck with his tongue, kissing and suckling every crevice, he nearly lost his footing when he felt her hand slip into his freshly unzipped jeans. He was on fire as he reached the bottom of her sweater, pulling it over her head. Her breasts bounced as the sweater swept over them. Unhooking her bra, it rolled off her shoulders, down her arms. He could barely contain himself as she gasped and trembled when he touched her them for the first time. His hands were gentle, sending thrills to all the right places.

Closing her eyes, she arched her back, and her head dropped back exposing her long beautiful neck. She felt his lips, hot and moist against her throat covering every inch. Moaning at his touch, she pushed into his lips for more.

Cupping her face in his hands, he kissed her passionately; he was desperate for her. Moving her closer to the bed, he placed a hand on her back for support and lowered her down. Hovering, he memorized every curve, hoping the night would never end.

"Are you okay?" she whispered, "Have you changed your mind about this? If you have, I completely understand, this is a big step for both of..."

Before she could finish her sentence, he dropped down over her, holding himself up with his arms.

"Are you kidding me?" he whispered, gently rubbing her cheeks with his thumbs, "if it'd been legal, and I'd known what to do, we would have done this when we were five years old." Kissing her tenderly, he lay beside her. "Are you sure you want to do this? Are you ready?"

Widening her eyes, a smile crept over her face. "Oh, I'm ready, I was ready in the classroom until Miss Wilson interrupted us."

"Yeah, Miss Wilson," he said, widening his eyes in exasperation. "She practically threatened to turn me in if I hadn't promised to behave myself. I think she just trying to scare the crap out of me and shamelessly enjoyed every minute of it."

Laughing at the situation, she propped herself up on her elbow. She noticed that his eyelashes were long, thick and coal black as she gazed into his luscious blue eyes. Scanning his face, she couldn't remember when she hadn't loved him, and touching her lips to his, she had an overwhelming urge to devour him with kisses.

Pushing the hair off her face, he flipped her onto her back. Never taking his eyes off her, he hurriedly ripped off his clothes. Watching him undress, she twisted the button on her jeans and slid the zipper down. He was done talking. He wanted her right then and there. As he kissed her, he knew she was as ready as he was. Grabbing the waistband of her jeans and panties, she lifted off the bed enough for him to peel them off. Her eyes burned with lust and wild passion, and her lips shaped themselves into cries of ecstasy. Lying naked for the first time, she totally melted into his arms until she could no longer distinguish where his body stopped, and hers began. Making love was new, clumsy, yet magical. When she curled her body around his, he knew that he would love her forever.

14

With school finished and graduation behind them, suddenly he saw very little of Sage. The loneliness and the ache in his heart was a constant reminder of how much he missed her.

Noah had never quite gotten over that day in the classroom or the vivid memory of the afternoon in the yacht club loft. It had been the first time he'd admitted, aloud, that he had been in love since kindergarten. It was sweet music to his ears when he'd heard her say the words back to him. Whenever thoughts of that momentous afternoon in the loft crept in, it threw his world into a tailspin. The last he'd heard was that right after graduation, Sage went off on an extended modelling gig. Weeks passed, and there hadn't been a single, solitary word from her. He wondered why suddenly she'd gone off the radar. He'd heard only scattered bits and pieces of her success as a top model, but then, suddenly, it was as if the lights had gone out. There had been no mention of her, no magazine ads or cover spreads.

It had been a long time since they'd had contact and he was more than eager to see her. Taking a chance, he called her house. It was the one thing they'd never done, but he had to know. Not hearing a word from her in weeks, he had to call hoping she was back from a fashion show. He was baffled when the automated voice told him the number he had dialed was no longer in service, so he had driven over to her house. A 'for sale' sign sat as big as life on the front lawn surrounded by long grass, and the house was vacant. Dread hit his stomach, as thoughts of Sage being gone from his life, began to sink in. Cupping his eyes, he peeked in through the windows and saw nothing except empty rooms.

Rapping on the neighbor's door, Noah asked questions, but no one knew anything. Feeling panicked, he tried to sort out the confusion, but he couldn't seem to unravel the mystery surrounding her disappearance. He'd thought she was only away on a lengthy modelling gig, which at other times had lasted for several weeks, but this was different. She was gone, and not knowing where she was had left him horribly unsettled. He felt broken, sick with worry, had a hundred questions, and no one to answer them. She was just... gone. He waited with hope that she would contact him.

Weeks turned into months and still not a word from Sage. He missed her every day and never gave up hope of her walking back into his life someday with a perfectly good explanation.

As difficult as it was, Noah forced himself to take his concentration off Sage and move forward with his own career. It was time for him to decide on what he wanted out of life.

His parents had given him a time frame for either a job, college or the highway. He was old enough to start making choices, so he busied himself with a plan that he'd hoped his father would be on board with.

15

After their first time in the loft, Sage had been sent off on a gig, but it was taking longer than she'd anticipated. Finishing one job, she was called immediately for another. She chatted regularly with her mother, but she'd had no contact with Noah. She'd never think of calling his home and have his mother or father answer the phone. They had always found a way to see each other without calling, so that their parents couldn't ask any questions.

Traveling extensively, she worked long hours, put in long days and the demand for the runway seemed to be taking a toll on her. Taking her far from home, she missed her mom, her home, she missed Noah, and she was tired of feeling lonely and exhausted. At sixteen, she wondered if there shouldn't be more to life than just strutting down a runway.

Picking her head up off the pillow, she felt her stomach lurch. Pangs of fright caught her unaware as she fought nausea. Lying back down, she hoped she wasn't coming down with the same bug that had made its rounds among the girls. Flinging the covers off, she made a mad dash for the bathroom. Feeling alone and scared, she dry-heaved into the bowl and wished her mom was there to take care of her. Kneeling on the cold tiled floor of the hotel room, she felt weak, shaken and ragged from retching. Wiping her face and neck with a cold cloth helped with the nausea. Staggering back to the bed, she called her agent and told her she wasn't feeling well and asked for a bit of time off. Lying back down, she fell asleep, and when she woke up, she felt somewhat better. Calling downstairs, she ordered breakfast and hoped it would settle her shaking tummy. Dry toast and black coffee seemed to do the trick. Getting out of bed, she headed into the shower and hoped it would revive her like it usually did. Feeling somewhat calmer, she rooted through her bag for a clean pair of pajamas. A jolt shot through her body when she saw a full box of tampons under a layer of clothes. She'd always packed them for long trips to be prepared. *'When had she used them last?'* she thought. She really couldn't remember when she'd last had a period. Flashes of her and Noah caused her thoughts to drift back to the loft! Fear hit hard in her stomach as she held on to the bed until the dizziness passed. Taking a swipe at her damp forehead, she raked her fingers through her hair and dragged it back off her face. Trying to remember her last cycle, she thought, *'Surely, one time...'* she couldn't finish the thought. *'Would the information be in her calendar?'* she wondered, grabbing her over-sized bag. Dumping her entire life out on the bed, she rifled through make-up, a hairbrush, combs, hair accessories, a wallet and finally, her appointment book. Flipping through the pages of the small calendar, she saw a red circle around a date more than six weeks ago and none since. Panic and terror sent her into another fit of nausea. Heading back into the bathroom she bent forward on the vanity. Soaking a washcloth in the cold-water and wringing it out, she pressed it flat on her face with both hands. *'Breathe,'* she thought. Rinsing the cloth again, she moved it to the back of her neck. Sitting on the toilet cover, she brought the trash can closer just in case. Leaning forward, she covered her face again feeling the coolness. Deep breathing helped her stay relatively calm as she silently tried to make a plan.

Picking up the hotel phone, she shakenly called the only person she trusted.

"Amelia?"

"Sage? Are you OK?"

"I don't know what to do, I'm so scared."

"Sage, tell me what happened, why are you so upset? Is your mom okay?"

"Mom?" she sobbed, puzzled.

"Why are you crying?"

"Amelia, it's awful," she said again, sobbing and biting her lower lip as tears rolled down her cheeks.

"It can't be that bad, Sage."

"Oh, it's bad, Amelia," she said, wide-eyed and nodding slowly, "it's really bad." Bringing her hand up to her mouth, she covered it with her palm as another stream of tears fell.

"Sage, you're scaring me, tell me what's wrong."

"I'm... ah... I think I'm... I'm preg...nant," she stammered, with another outburst of crying.

Amelia sucked in her breath at what Sage had confided. "Pregnant? Oh my Gosh! Sage, your only sixteen! How can you be pregnant?"

"I've missed my period, and I never miss a period, Amelia, I never have," she said, in a rush of words that came out loud and nearing hysteria. "My career, as a model, will be over!" She flung one arm up in the air in desperation and then dropped it with a ringing slap to her thighs. "How do I tell my mother? She, of all people, knows how difficult it is to raise a child alone, I am that child," she said, poking at her chest. She knew Amelia couldn't see her, but as she gripped the phone tighter, she wished she was with her. "She was a child when she had me," she continued, "how could I have done this to her?"

"Does anyone else know about this, Sage?"

"No, nobody, I've only just figured it out, and you're the only one I've told. I had to call you, Amelia, you're my best friend, and I trust you."

She and Amelia's friendship had started as far back as the cradle. On their visits, it gave them bonding time with playdates, sleepovers and weekends. Living in different towns they were unable to share the same school or friends, but they were as close as most sisters.

* * *

Several days after breaking the news to her mother, Lorraine had called Amelia's parents, in a panic asking if they could visit.

Sitting around the Benton's dining room table, a plan was in its first stage. Lorraine had asked the Benton's to help her find a place for her and Sage to stay. Lorraine didn't care where it was or even how big, she just wanted a place to go as soon as humanly possible.

Hoping to make it a smooth transition, the Benton's offered Lorraine their basement which consisted of a bedroom, a den, a kitchenette and full bathroom. Recommending they bring personal items, the Benton's helped them arrange for their furnishing to be put into storage.

The Lawrence's and Benton's began sharing a house for as long as necessary. Amelia and Sage shared a bedroom during their stay, just like they had when they were young children. They each were the sister that the other never had.

Amelia was at Sage's side throughout the entire pregnancy. She was there during Lamaze classes, picking out baby clothes, a few pieces of furniture and eventually, into the delivery room.

Lying the baby on Sage's chest, she and Amelia teared up as he cooed and suckled on his tiny fists. At first glance, Sage saw immediately that he was the image of Noah. Her heart ached for him more, at that moment, than it had since running away. Wanting so badly to share this precious moment with him, it took everything inside her soul not to call and share the news with him. *'This little bundle is a piece of us,'* she thought. *'We created him from the loving moments that we shared together, and he should have been here to celebrate this new life with me.'*

A piece of him would always be with her now, and she had to be satisfied with that.

Lorraine made an appearance for her first look at her new grandson. Seeing the sadness on her daughter's face, she reiterated the choice she had made and how she feared the Greyson's could have decided to fight for custody of their grandchild, her grandchild. She had already proven how fierce she could be about her own child and how much she had been willing to sacrifice, then and now. The Greyson's could likely give the child a more stable home especially if a single parent issue was brought up in a custody battle. That same fear had driven Lorraine's parents to the same conclusion when Sage was conceived under similar circumstances.

"Having your child ripped from your arms is not an option," she said, trying to assure Sage they'd done the right thing. Since her mother had gone through it, she agreed with her mother's words. Back when Sage had shared her dilemma with her, Lorraine had remembered from as far back as Sage's birth who the Greyson's were. They were well-established people in the community, and they were likely financially secure.

Putting some distance between Sage and Noah, Lorraine followed the path of her parents and moved her daughter out of town, thinking it was the best thing to do.

Kanyon Creek was far enough away from Kanyon Ridge so there'd be a slim to no chance of meeting up with someone unexpectedly, and hopefully, they'd feel safer.

Sage was proud of her mom for wanting to protect her and her baby, and she had given up a lot to keep her family safe. Sage wondered now if her mom had made the right decision for her and her baby boy.

Once they had bathed him and bundled him up, they brought him back to Sage's arms. Her heart was heavy with loneliness and tears stung the backs of her lids. Forcing them away, she told herself that this is what she'd wanted. Looking at his tiny face, she saw Noah as plain as day. Lifting her arms, she brought his little head up to her lips for a kiss. He was precious and handsome, and he looked like his father. Thinking at seventeen, he probably wasn't ready to be a parent any more than she was. She wondered, *'if she hadn't had her mother, what would her choices have been. Barely seventeen, herself, would she...? No, she couldn't think that way... no what-ifs,'* she thought.

Knocking on her door, Amelia interrupted her thoughts. "Hey, there," she cooed, as she came closer to the bed. "He's a handsome boy, Sage," she said tipping her head to look at him. "I never had an opportunity to meet Noah, but if this little guy is any indication, then he must be the picture of handsomeness." She noticed tears in Sage's eyes for the second time since the birth. "Sage?"

Waving a hand, she tried to dismiss the tears, but they escaped anyway. "I just want so badly to talk to Noah, I miss him so much," she sniffed.

"I think that's a choice that only you can make, Sage," Amelia said, speaking softly and lightly touching her arm. "This is a very emotional time for you and being in here has given you lots of time to think about everything."

"I already made the choice when I left Kanyon Ridge, remember?" she said, sadly.

Changing the subject, Amelia asked, "Have you chosen a name yet?"

"Yes, I have," she said, quietly.

"Really?"

"His name is Grey... Greyson Alexander Lawrence," she answered, as a tear slipped down her cheek.

* * *

Moving from the Benton's, Sage rented a condo and had made arrangements for her mother's furniture to be brought out of storage. Becoming Sage's full-time nanny, gave Lorraine some much-needed independence and an income once again. Several months after Grey's birth, Sage saw an ad posted in the lobby, for an available apartment. Taking down the number, she made the call to the Super, arranged a lease and moved into the penthouse suite in the same building to be near her mother and Grey.

Eager to return to modelling, she contacted her agent hoping to pick up where she'd left off. Once the agency learned of her availability, bookings began filling up her appointment book. Being back in the spotlight again would expose her, though, and it made her feel vulnerable, so she had to come up with a plan. Needing a change, she pondered carefully and came up with the only reasonable thing to do. She'd decided to use another identity for the modelling industry. It had its family origins since Cassandra was Sage's middle name and Lucan came from her grandmother's lineage. 'Cassie Lucan...,' she thought, mulling the name over aloud. Hiding behind a new name excited her, and she became anxious to return to what she loved most. She was convinced it was the security she needed to go back out into the public again. Running it by her mother, Lorraine was fully on board with the name she had chosen.

When the day came for her to return to the runway, it was with her new name. Being off, for a little more than a year, Sage made her debut as 'Cassie Lucan.' She was on magazine covers, newspaper ads and even made the evening news as a newcomer to the fashion world. She was just grateful that she was introduced under her new identity and they had agreed to advertise her as 'newcomer.' *'Nobody will connect the dots or will know who I am,'* she thought, *'no one from school, no one from Kanyon Ridge... nobody, my past will be my secret.'* She reminded herself that is was for modelling and that she was, and always would be, Sage Lawrence. She'd never questioned where her name came from, and she didn't have to know. Her name, however, had enabled her to establish herself in her profession and had brought her to where she was in the industry. Changing her name would empower her to move on and disappear. Noah could never find her, and yet, for the umpteenth time, she wondered how he might feel about her as 'Cassie.'

The other models were aware of the change, but it was not a big deal to them since most were already modelling under an assumed name too. Unless her name appeared in magazines, Sage Lawrence had just vanished.

16

Noah and his mother had spent many hours planning and redecorating for the 'Grand Opening.' With his mother's help, he'd enjoyed the experience of choosing office furniture, paint colors and works of art for the walls.

Sitting in his newly decorated office, in a new leather chair and mounds of paperwork, Noah thought back to how he'd gotten to this point in the first place.

Prior to graduation, Drew and Keri put a limit of one year for Noah to come up with a plan for his chosen career. Once that time was up, plan or no plan, his free ride would end.

Against his parents' wishes, he had decided to forego college. They, themselves, did not have a college degree, so it only made sense to give him that same freedom of choice.

Noah had set out to make a plan and began by researching and jotting down several ideas on what he thought Kanyon Ridge could benefit from. A travel agency was a brief thought, and so was photography. Fleeting thoughts of opening a bookstore but took into consideration that most folks were keeping up with the times now and reading online. His interest dwindled after realizing there was a newer one in Kanyon Cove. He even pondered a catering service thinking he could probably pull it off since he loved cooking and by hiring a couple of helpers, he thought it might work. Instead, he tossed them all and concentrated fully on a business plan for a spa.

Finding a spot in the attic over his dad's garage, he diligently cleaned it up, made it into a proper workstation and began to secretly work hard on a plan without help or advice from anyone.

He'd purchased a second-hand drafting table, a clip-on lamp, a roll of architectural paper and a supply of mechanical pencils, erasers, and rulers. During weeks of intense concentration, he had worked on his plan to the smallest of detail. Leaving nothing out and no room for questions, he hoped he had them already answered. Going over them numerous times, he felt they were complete and ready for show. Calling a realtor, he asked about appropriate locations while explaining what he had in mind, what he thought he needed and asked them to call when they had a list of possibilities.

Making the call he'd been dreading, Noah had to pitch his plan to his father and get his reaction on the project. His father's opinion was all he needed, and he trusted him completely. If anyone were to tell him the truth, it would be him.

His latest text told him he'd be home in a few days and they made plans to have dinner together, just the two of them. Taking advantage of those few days, he tweaked his plans one more time hoping for perfection.

Getting a text from his realtor, he informed him of several locations that had recently come on the market and could possibly meet his needs. He was asked to let him know, at his earliest convenience, if he was interested in booking appointments for any of the listed viewings. Noah had set up a time for when his father was home on his scheduled days off.

* * *

Arriving at the airport early, he took some time to go over in his head the spiel he had rehearsed as he waited for his dad's plane to land. Pacing nervously in the waiting area, he stared at the tile floors sorting through his thoughts and trying to put them in order. '*Where do I start?*' he thought, as his confidence began to wane.

Hearing the announcement of the incoming flight, he felt nervous as butterflies danced in the pit of his stomach.

"Noah!"

Hearing his name, Noah's head shot up and saw his dad standing in front of him.

"Hey, Buddy, why so serious?" he asked, breaking Noah's stream of concentration.

"Hey Dad," he said, reaching out to hug him.

"You were quite serious when I walked up, what's up?"

"Mom is out, and the house is ours so let's go home and talk. There is something I'm anxious to run by you."

Smiling, he realized how suddenly grown up his son was. Putting his arm around his shoulders, he gave him a few quick tugs as they made their way to the revolving doors.

"Let's go, I can't wait to see what this is all about."

Noah was quiet on the way home but Drew filled in the empty spaces with talk about the flight until they got home.

"Would you please fire up the barbeque while I shower and change and then I'll start the salad. I'll leave you in charge of the steaks and then we'll talk, sound OK to you?"

"Sounds good, Dad."

Drew came out of the bathroom refreshed and dressed in a tee shirt and cargo shorts and looking relaxed. Pulling veggies from the crisper, he began to create a delightful garden salad. The aroma of grilled meat coming from the patio caused his stomach to growl. Bringing plates, silverware, and napkins to the patio table, he went back inside for salad bowls, dressing, and rolls.

"It smells great out here!" he said, returning from the kitchen.

"It's ready, let's eat!"

"You don't have to ask me twice, I'm starving!"

Enjoying their meal, it was extra special with just the two of them, for once. He noticed that Noah was not eating with the gusto he knew he was capable of, but he didn't say anything. Pushing away his plate and wiping his mouth, he saw that only part of his meal had been eaten.

"Noah, I believe we have circled this drain long enough, why don't you just tell me what is on your mind, son."

Noah, obviously nervous, looked at his father for several seconds before opening his mouth.

"Noah are you in trouble?"

"No, dad, I'm not in trouble," he said, smiling at the relief on his father's face. "I want to run a business plan by you and get your opinion on it, your *honest* opinion," he said, emphasizing the word 'honest.'

"A business plan? Whose? Yours?"

"Yes, mine, will you hear me out?"

"Of course!"

Gathering up their plates, Noah took them to the kitchen and came back with a tube. Setting it on the table, he grabbed the dressing and other items and ran them into the kitchen. Returning, he picked up the tube and said, "Come with me, Dad."

Frowning with curiosity, Drew got up from the table and followed him. Noah led him up a set of stairs to the attic of the garage and flipped the lights on. For a second, as Drew looked around, he thought Noah had plans to build an apartment.

"Wow! Noah, you've been busy, what is all this?"

"I've been working up here, Dad."

"I can see that but working on what, if I may ask?"

Walking further into the room, Noah stopped and laid the tube on the table.

"Nice job up here, son, and what's with the drafting table? Now you have my full attention!"

"Thanks, Dad," he grinned, seeing the pride in his dad's eyes. Pulling the cap off the tube, he began, "This is a project I've been working on since graduation." Pulling the pages from the tube and spreading them out on the table, using his desk objects to anchor them down, he switched on the lamp and said, "It's a plan for a spa."

"A spa?" Drew asked, leaning forward with interest. He had seen spas in other larger cities, but no one had come up with the concept to open one here in Kanyon Ridge. "Noah, this is amazing! Who did you hire to help you with the plans? This is excellent work."

"I did them."

Drew's head shot up, "You did these?"

"Yes, Dad, I did, and you are the first person to see or even know about them. I started right after graduation knowing you and Mom gave me a year to get my act together. I've been working on the plans every chance I had, and I wanted you to be the first to see them."

"Noah, I don't know what to say," he said, turning to face his son. "I am so proud of you! Where did you learn drafting?"

"We dabbled with it a bit in school and I liked it, so I wanted to see if I could create my own design for a business venture."

"Well, come on then! Tell me what this is about!" he said, slapping Noah on the back.

"I want it to be more or less a one-stop health spa. I know there are other separate businesses here in town, but I believe I can create the spa to meet everyone's needs. My intentions aren't to run other companies out of business, but times are changing, and I believe Kanyon Ridge needs to get in on the business of the future... spas."

"OK, go on," Drew said, impressed so far with his son looking forward to a future here in his hometown.

"Services will include facials, manicures, pedicures, waxing and/or electrolysis since hair removal is the in thing right now. Over here," he said, pointing to the plans, "are a couple of rooms for massages, one for aromatherapy, and over here will be for body wraps, exfoliations, and body scrubs. On the more expensive side of things, we will have hydrotherapy treatments such as sauna and steam baths. We will incorporate a beauty salon with all the latest in hairstyles, along with hair products for every hair type. Here," he pointed, "will be a nail salon which would only make sense, since we are offering manicure and pedicure services. We also need a space to set up a shop for nail technicians, aestheticians and provide in-store and mobile services. They can offer their knowledge on makeup application techniques, advice on nutrition and answer any questions that may arise from clients." He took a deep breath and continued while his father listened. "There is a spa treatment that is relatively new, Dad, and it's called a Salt Spa, and from what I've read, I believe it will be necessary to incorporate in this plan, a little farther down the road, of course. So, over here, I think would be the perfect location for it, when the time comes," he said, pointing to a spot on the page. "What do you think?"

Drew stood next to his son and shook his head back and forth seemingly at a loss for words.

"You don't like it, do you?" Noah said, in disappointment.

Rocking back on his heels a few times, Drew lifted his arms and dropped them to his side and continued to shake his head. Finally, he ran his hands over his hair and down the back of his neck. The corners of his mouth came down as he stared at the plans that were laid out in front of him. "I... um... I... I love it! I think this is an excellent plan, Noah!" he said, waving his hand above the pages.

"Really? Dad are you serious?"

"Yes, I am very serious, I think it's a great plan, and you've done a fantastic job here. I've heard all the ideas, but have you put together a business plan and a financial statement?"

"I have a proposed income statement, a cash flow projection, and a balance sheet," he said, moving papers around the table to expose them.

Drew scratched his head as he read them over. "This is very impressive, Noah, this is a great plan," he emphasized, knowing he had said it several other times.

Standing at the drafting table, papers scattered across the top, they both had grins on their faces. Drew's grin was for the pride he had in his son, and Noah's was for having his father's approval which meant everything to him.

"Thanks, Dad."

Drew pressed his lips together and looked at Noah again. "What's your plan, Son?"

Noah crossed his arms across his chest, the same stance as his father, and ran his tongue across his lips before answering. "I was hoping we could do it together, Dad."

"Together? Noah, I have a job."

"Yes, I know that, but you won't always be a pilot, Dad."

"What are you saying or trying to say, Son?"

'*It's now or never*,' he thought. "I was hoping you would finance my project, Dad, it could be ours. I'll look after the business until you retire and if you are interested in working afterward, then we can run it together as partners. Will you at least think about it before you say no?"

"Who said I was going to say no?"

"What?" Noah's face sobered at hearing the words.

"It's a great plan, Noah. I can't stress that enough. I've seen these spas all over the world, and you're right, they are becoming very popular. You have certainly done your research and put together a very convincing plan. This is a no-brainer and a foregone conclusion to success! Is there anything else?"

"Yes, as a matter of fact, there is. A realtor has found several locations that may work, and he set up an appointment for us to view them."

"You haven't looked at them?"

"No, I wanted to wait so we could look at them together. He wants us to meet at his office tomorrow morning if that's OK with you."

"Well then, we shall see what he has to offer before we go any farther."

"Thanks again, Dad," he said, reaching out for a handshake.

Taking his hand, Drew pulled him to his chest for a hug and gave him a few slaps on the back. "You've done an impressive job here, Son, I'm very proud of you."

"Thanks, I'm very excited to see what is out there for properties. It needs to be the right place and the right location for this to work. I'm sure I will know it when I see it. I have had it all pictured in my mind for weeks, I just hope there is something out there to match my vision."

* * *

Arriving at the Realtor's office a few minutes early, Noah introduced the agent, Phillip LeJeune, to his father. They were given several fact sheets describing the locations they were to look at. Drew noticed one sheet in particular that had caught Noah's eye. Peeking over his shoulder, Drew wanted to see which page he was fixated on so he could read up on it too. It was a lovely old Victorian home in the ritzier part of town, which wasn't a bad thing.

"I like this one, Noah," Drew said, hoping it was the response Noah was after.

"Me too, Dad, it looks like what I might be after."

"Then let's go over there and take a look!"

Smiling at his father, he non-verbally thanked him with a nod of his head.

Noah's eyes lit up when they pulled into the driveway. "Wow! This is a beauty!"

"It sure is," Drew said, getting out of the car.

They stood in the driveway and admired the massive structure. It was done in beige, trimmed in taupe and had a partially wrapped veranda and turrets with rounded window tops. The house itself was beautiful and had quite a number of intricacies of Victorian design, especially the eye-catching, painted roof over the top of the bay windows. The metal rails above the veranda would encourage anyone to at least take a look inside at the spectacular detail and lovely architecture.

Noah's mind was at full tilt imagining what he could do with the space. He could even imagine where he'd hang his shingle.

Phillip unlocked the door, pushed it open and waited for Drew and Noah to step inside. Noah just stood, for a few minutes, inhaling the amazing structure. After going through the house, Noah sadly admitted to his father that he thought it was much too elaborate for what he wanted. The rooms were spread too far apart and likely too small for some of the projects he had in mind.

Drew agreed with him but allowed him to make his own decisions, and he was doing OK so far.

The agent referred Noah to another sheet that became more realistic to him, and he consulted his father.

"Dad look at this one, it's the Medical Centre downtown. It's in an excellent location and has all the hookups and connections that I'll need already installed, which is huge in cost savings. This might be more beneficial in the long run. This house is beautiful," he said, waving his hand around the room, "but it could be too elaborate and too expensive to renovate it to what I will need."

"That makes sense, Noah, let's go and have a look at the Medical Centre."

As the agent locked up behind them, Drew and Noah looked over the sheet in detail.

"This does look like an ideal location, Noah. Look at the pictures, it has shelving for linens, cabinets for supplies and all the windows have blinds, which is another plus for you. Also, most Centers like this would likely already have a sound system for piped-in music. Each one of these offices has its own waiting area. So according to this sheet, each area has a reception desk, a waiting area and a dressing room at each of your reception areas. Meaning, each caller can be transferred to whichever service they are looking for. It isn't as elaborate as the Victorian, but I'll bet your mother can do a great job of making it inviting and relaxing."

"That's a great idea, Dad, we'll have a better idea after we take the tour."

* * *

Inside the empty building, they took their time looking around, and it seemed ideal and exactly what Noah was after.

"The sheet doesn't have an asking price on it. Why is that?" Noah asked Phillip.

"Would you be interested in this particular building? Does it meet your needs?" he asked, without answering Noah's question.

"Yes, it does, everything I'll need is right here, but I'm concerned that the price isn't listed."

Drew was impressed with Noah and he stood back and let him do his thing. He was negotiating with the agent, and as far as Drew was concerned, he was doing a great job by asking all the right questions. It was impressive to watch him take control of his future endeavor.

"There is a reason why there isn't a price listed for this property, Noah. When the building became vacant, it was turned over to the town, and Kanyon Ridge does not want or need the responsibility of it. So, when they listed it with us, it came with a few conditions. One was not to put a price on it and two, only let it go to someone who is interested in opening a business and not buying it to tear it down."

"I see, well I am certainly not interested in tearing it down, and I do want it for a business."

"Then let's go back to the office and talk," he said, glancing over at Drew.

Drew nodded his head slightly in agreement.

Sitting at his desk, Phillip pulled several papers from a filing cabinet. Looking at his new clients, he began his proposal. "This is the way it is," he said, "the property is on the market for offers only." Glancing between Noah and Drew, he asked, "Are you prepared to make an offer?"

Dropping his gaze from the agent, Noah looked at his father. "Dad?"

"What sort of offer are you looking for?" Drew asked. "We weren't prepared for a blank page, we were expecting to make an offer on something with a listed price."

"I understand, but these are the stipulations set up by Kanyon Ridge's town hall. Are you interested?"

"In my opinion, I don't think it is fair to expect a blind offer if we know nothing of what the value is on the property. For example, I could put an offer in for a thousand dollars and consider it a valid offer."

"Are you making an offer of a thousand dollars then?

"Sure," Drew said, with a shrug of his shoulder.

"Offer accepted then."

"What?" Drew said, leaning forward.

"They asked for an offer, and you made one, it's yours. Shall we draw up the paperwork?"

"I don't understand. Is the building condemned or something?"

"I can assure you the building is sound and in excellent condition. It meets with all of today's building codes, inspections, and our fire marshal's standards. It is safe and very sound. The town is going with offers only and using it for a business will generate some much-needed revenue in our community. So, it is, therefore, helping your son get established and start making money which the town will benefit from with taxes and revenue and it is also creating jobs for many people. Do we have a deal?"

Both Drew and Noah stood up and in turn offered him a handshake and accepted the terms as set by the town. They get rid of a vacant building, and Noah gets a decent start. It couldn't have been more perfect. It was as if it was waiting for Noah's plan to materialize. According to the listing sheet, the building had only been on the market for a few days, and the realtor hadn't put a sign up yet since he wanted Noah to have the right of first refusal.

Drew wrote out a cheque and handed it to Phillip.

"All that needs to be done is to change the deed," Phillip explained, "the town of Kanyon Ridge has already done all the

131

inspections and water tests. They just want the building to be used again."

* * *

For the next six years, Noah's business shot to the top with clients from far and wide. He had been the youngest entrepreneur, in the history of Kanyon Ridge, to establish such a wealth of clientele for repeat business. He'd earned his rightfully place as a businessman, and he was well respected in Kanyon Ridge.

17

Getting in from a flight, Drew decided to stop off at the Kanyon Ridge Bar and Grill for a beer and burger as an excuse not to go home. Standing at the bar, he ordered whatever was on tap and put his order in for the kitchen. Uneasiness crept in as his cell phone beeped from his jacket pocket. Muscles flexed in his jaws knowing full well who it was as he reluctantly reached in and pulled it out. Laying it on the bar in front of him for a few minutes, he was in no mood to deal with her drama. The bartender dropped a coaster in front of him and sat a glass of draft on it. *'Keri, who else would it be?'* he grumbled to himself. It was always Keri and always wanting to know where he was. He didn't have to look at the phone, he knew what it was going to say, but with a begrudging swipe, he opened the screen.

Where are you?

He wanted so badly to text back, *'None of your damned business'* but instead he closed the screen, laid the phone back onto the bar and took a long swallow. It had been a long flight, and he just wanted to relax without having to explain his every move to Keri every damned time he landed. A fire burned in his belly at the sight of her name. Before he got the glass away from his lips, his phone beeped again.

Drew, where are you?

He was five to ten minutes from home, depending on how heavy his foot was, but she didn't have to know that. Home was the last place he wanted to be. He thought about his answer for a few seconds, put his glass down and picked up his phone.

I'm taking another flight out, I won't be home

Hitting 'send,' he dropped the phone into his pocket. He was not one for lying, but she was getting on his last nerve with her relentless texts on his whereabouts. 'D*ammit!*' he mumbled, as his pocket vibrated.

When will you be home?

I don't know, tomorrow, at some point, maybe, I'll let you know. Holding the phone just above the bar, he let it drop, *'There, that should shut her up,'* he thought as the bartender slid his burger in front of him. Picking it up, he took a bite out of it. A switch turned on in his head as he stared at the screen for a few minutes. With not much else to do, he began to scroll up to read her messages. Almost every text had been the same. *'Why is she so concerned about where I am*?' he thought, after reading the messages again. *'She always has to know where I am, something is not right with this picture.'* He used to think it was out of concern but now he was beginning to wonder if there wasn't an ulterior motive. He didn't like it, and it wasn't sitting well in his craw. Still, he couldn't help but wonder if perhaps it was time he found out why she was dogging him for answers. *'So,'* he thought, knitting his brow, *'she thinks I'm not coming home, well... maybe I am,'* he thought. *'We'll see what all her curiosity is about.'* Finishing his burger, he dropped a few bills on the bar, gave a half-assed two finger salute to the bartender and left.

First, he had to decide where he was going to spend the night. The Kanyon Ridge Inn seemed like a decent choice since he'd need a place to lay his head until his next flight. He already knew it wouldn't be at home, regardless of how this trip went. Taking his bag from his car, he began walking down the lighted street towards the Inn. Stopping suddenly, thoughts... paranoid thoughts, began plaguing him and they were coming fast and furious. His mind spinning as her text messages ran through it, repeatedly. The same messages filling his brain, *Where are you? When will you be home? * she'd asked. '*Why? What was her point? What was she up to*?' Rationalizing his thoughts, he knew he'd only had a couple swigs of beer, and for the size of him, he figured that small amount was just enough to give him the artificial courage he needed. Courage, in any form, was better than none at all.

Becoming adamant now, he felt certain that Keri was playing him again and he had to know. Just once, that's all he wanted, just once, to have the upper hand. Knowing there wasn't a chance of being over the limit on a breathalyzer, he turned on his heels and headed back to his vehicle. The motel could wait. His stomach was aflutter with anticipation knowing there could be a mystery unfolding. The only way he could have felt any more like Detective Columbo was if he'd had a beige trench coat to put on. The headlights flashed as he hit the key fob to unlock his vehicle. Looking around, Columbo-like, he tossed his bag back in and slid onto the seat. Snatching his seatbelt forward, he buckled it up; in a few minutes, he'd be home. Concentrating heavily on his speed, he flipped the cruise button on the steering wheel to on just in case he got the urge to speed.

Trepidation followed him as he drove to their bungalow at 127 Shore Lake Drive. They lived on a street to street lot, and since their bedroom was located at the front of the house, he turned the corner on Willow Street. Turning the headlights off at their driveway, he pulled over onto the shoulder of the road. Quietly closing the car door, he walked softly on the grass to the deck and unlocked the door. He laid the keys on a planter to avoid any unnecessary jingling. Immediately, he heard soft voices coming from somewhere in the dimly lit house. Living there, for as long as he had, allowed him to move about as though he was blindfolded. Slipping off his shoes in the entry, he moved cat-like through the kitchen and into the living room. Sitting quietly on the arm of the couch, just inside the room, he listened to what sounded like, a lover's quarrel in the next room... their bedroom.

"How much longer are we going to do this, Keri?" a man's voice asked.

"My God, Jake!" he heard Keri say, "you ask me that same question every time you come here!"

"Keri, Honey, we've been doing this for fifteen years! How long do I have to wait for us to be together?"

Drew's back straightened. Holding his breath, he was stunned at what he was hearing. Reality engulfed him while realizing his freedom was even closer than he'd thought. He never expected to ever hear those words because, as naïve as he was, he had assumed that she had been as faithful as he'd been. The truth hit him in the face, sending a sense of relief to his soul. What he heard next made the hair stand up on the back of his neck, and he knew he'd made the right decision to come home.

"Look, Jake, I texted Drew earlier, so I'd know where he is. It gives us time, knowing how long he'll be away. Do you want to spend the time we have arguing, because if you do, there's no reason for you to be here, is there?"

Realizing his gut feelings had been spot on, Drew pressed his lips together, flared his nostrils and tried to get a grip. Continuing to eavesdrop, he couldn't determine whether he was relieved that their marriage was finally over or if he was pissed that he'd been blindsided, once again, by Keri, only this time with infidelity. Part of him wanted to do a happy dance, and the other part wanted to hit something because of the disgusting way she'd gone about this.

"You always know where he is, Keri, you have his schedule for Pete's sake. He told you that he was flying out again! Why didn't you just leave it alone? You didn't have to text him. What if that one text makes him suspicious?"

"Stop pointing your finger at me," she snapped, "it was one text? Are you serious? Pfft, it would take more than a text for Drew to be suspicious," she huffed.

Drew imagined her rolling her eyes at his being so naïve that even with the hundreds of clues she'd left, he still hadn't gotten it... until tonight... some Columbo he'd make.

"Look, Keri," Jake said, with a hint of frustration in his voice, "you have to tell him because this has been going on long enough! I can't see it being a big deal for either one of you at this point."

"I know, Jake, you're right. Meeting you was the best thing that has happened to me in a long time. Even when Drew is home, his heart isn't really here."

Drew felt his stomach lurch as he heard his name mentioned, again. *'How often had they talked about him?'* he wondered. What pissed him off, even more, was that she discussed their business with this guy, but she'd never talk to him. *'She was still the self-serving troll she'd been back in high school. She could've* been out of this marriage long ago,' he fumed, 'all she had to do was ask, and her wish would have been granted in a heartbeat. Instead, she chose to cheat and make a complete ass of him!'

"Drew hasn't really been part of this family since before Noah was born. I'm pretty sure he only stayed because of him. He was a great dad but a lousy husband."

'Oh, God! there it is, she's said the words aloud,' he thought. He knew she was right, but he had one thing going for him. 'He might have been a lousy husband, but at least he had been a faithful one!' he wanted to yell, as he silently defended himself.

Thinking about what he was hearing, he began to realize how selfish he'd been over the years. Focusing solely on his own unhappiness, he'd never given a single thought to her feelings, her frustrations or her sexual needs. He didn't really know what he had expected of her, but it certainly wasn't this. The truth cut a little deeper while he continued to listen.

"He said he'd be home in a day or two, so I will talk to him then."

"Are you sure this time, Keri? You've said these words to me a hundred times, and it has been long enough. If you don't love him, let him go! Why are you hanging on and accepting this crap? You deserve better. I want to give you something better," he said. Drew could picture him poking at his chest like a macho-man.

Hearing enough, he quietly stood up and made his way to the back door. Slipping into his shoes, he ever so lightly gripped the doorknob and gave it a silent twist and when he was sure it had cleared the latch he pulled it open. Pressing the lock, he stepped outside into the cool, clean air, closed the door and inhaled deeply. There was no one around for a high five, so he pumped

his fist a few times, then picked up his keys and made his way to
his car.

* * *

Pulling up under the canopy at The Kanyon Ridge Inn, he went
inside and booked a room. In the darkness, he tossed his satchel
onto the nearest chair and flopped down on top of the bed.
Slamming his head into the pillow a few times to find the right
spot, he clasped his fingers together behind his head and stared
out into the emptiness of the room. Running the conversation
over in his mind, a sudden shot of vile betrayal stuck in his throat.
He wasn't angry, he just thought about all those wasted years and
all this time they had both wanted their freedom, but neither one
had spoken up. There were so many '*whys*' floating around inside
his head. '*Why did he ever get married? Why couldn't he have
dealt with Keri in some other way? Why hadn't he grown a pair
back then and walked away when she told him she wasn't
pregnant.*' Knowing if he had done that, he wouldn't have Noah,
but then again, it was Noah who had kept him tied to Keri. Either
way, she made sure he was stuck. He knew he could never love
her and he never would. Although he had nothing to compare it
to, he had always felt there had to be something more. He wanted
to feel excitement, instead of dread, about going home. He
wanted to know what it would feel like to have that urge to just
drop his luggage by the front door and carry his woman off to the
bedroom and make mad, passionate love to her. Then afterward,
bathe in the feelings while holding her so close it felt like they
were breathing from the same lungs. He wanted it to feel like he

was in no hurry to go anywhere, except their bed. In all the years, he had slept with Keri, he never once had those feelings. '*Had he been watching too many romance movies in hotel rooms?*' he wondered. Thoughts taunted him as his mind went back there, to twenty-five years ago. Every time he'd ever gotten sexual with Keri, it was at her instigation and always after a meal or a drink. He never once went to her for anything, it was always her making the moves, and it seemed when she did, he couldn't resist even though he'd felt repulsed by her very presence. He'd figured it out years ago though, and he'd kept it a secret, but after tonight... her jig was up!

He could barely remember a time when Keri was not in his life. She had been a thorn in his side since high school. Twenty-five years of marriage and fifteen years of it were spent in betrayal. '*Fifteen years!*' he fumed. '*He could have been free before he reached thirty*' he thought counting backward. He was even furious with himself for not figuring it out sooner! Wanting to throw something, he yanked the pillow out from under his head, and he flung it across the room, knocking over a lamp. Realizing what he'd done, he laid in wait for someone to knock on his door, but no one came. Getting off the bed, he straightened up the mess, laid back down and resumed his position. He'd had no clue, she'd given no indication of an affair at least not until tonight's texts came in. Still, he didn't know why that set off alarm bells, but he was glad they had and even happier that he'd had the balls to act on them. '*How could he have been so dense? How dumb do you have to be to miss the obvious,*' he wondered. He had gotten that same feeling when he found the vial all those years ago. Intuition had been his friend that night too when he was led to examine the vase, and his answer had been there all along, hiding in plain sight. The answers had been on his cell phone this entire time too. He was more upset at himself right now that he was with Keri. *'How could he miss so many clues?'* he questioned.

Something always leads to a downfall and being too inquisitive had been hers. She had to know where he was so she could calculate her time with Jake. *'Who the hell is Jake, anyway?'* he asked himself. *'She had reasons upon reasons to ask for a divorce not to mention she had found someone years ago. Why hadn't she just come out and asked him? From what he'd heard back at the house, she'd known since day one how he'd felt about her. That was her first clue, yet she had hung in there and for what? What had she hoped to gain? Was she hoping his plane would go down, so she could collect his insurance? Was she disappointed that he was still alive? What!? Why!? Why hadn't he made a move long ago then he wouldn't be lying here in this motel room full of... what?... rage? ... no, hatred?... no, not really... relief?... yes, relief was the word he was looking for but not in such an unattractive way.'*

He could justify his procrastination because he had a son that he loved and didn't want to abandon, and he'd never met anyone who interested him enough to become a cheater. He'd never found anyone that he felt was worth the guilt of cheating and he never wanted to hurt Keri he just wanted to be rid of her. He unclasped his hand, sat up and ran a hand over his face and snorted. *'There it is! There's the irony'*, he thought, shaking his head. *He didn't want to hurt her, but she had no problem hurting him!'* He was hurting, but not because she'd found someone, but because he'd given up his freedom for her! Lying and sneaking around while he was out of town and bringing a man home to his bed! She hadn't had the decency to use the spare room or go to a motel. *'Noah had been a young boy of approximately ten years old when this affair started,'* he thought, *'how did she pull that off?...* It only took a second for him to answer that question! *'How did she pull it off? ... really?* he asked himself, *'she had more tricks up her sleeve than a magician!'*

Getting up off the bed, he went to the window, found the rod and parted the heavy, thick drapes. Silence, nothing was moving except for time... time marched on. He turned to look at the clock on the nightstand beside the bed. Bold red numbers stared back at him. 10:10. p.m. *'What a day this has been,'* he groaned. He hadn't slept in what seemed like three days, and it was likely going to be longer still. The adrenalin rush that he was on would probably last a good long while.

He felt an overwhelming urge to cry, but for what? Or for who? A dying marriage that had never been alive in the first place? The hurt of being betrayed? *'Hadn't he somehow betrayed her and their vows? Hadn't he promised to love, honor and cherish her always?'* He had done none of that except the 'remaining faithful' part, and he'd done that. She had obviously skipped right past that part of the vow and went directly to the first available man. *'Fifteen years she's been seeing this guy. How many before him?'* he wondered. *'What about the other ten years, who else had she been sleeping with before Jake?'* he seethed. *'OK,'* he thought, *'don't get ahead of yourself.'* Jake had pointed out that she deserved much better than what he was offering. Drew thought that just because she'd found somebody to fill the void that he refused to fill, it didn't make her a bad person just a hypocrite. He got back into bed at 11:11 and tried closing his eyes, turning off his mind and his heart, but his entire being felt vulnerable. He knew he didn't care that Keri had met someone, but she could have done the decent thing and come to him and been honest, so he could have moved on too. But that was Keri, always the manipulator, always the winner and now, there would always be animosity between them forever because of her actions. Years of her deceptions were hard to swallow, and he wished now that he had been a man-whore so when he confronted her, he'd have his own stories to throw back at her but all he had was, regrettably, a clean slate and a vial.

Taking his shaving kit from his satchel, he stripped off his clothes and padded into the bathroom. Turning the shower on, he brushed his teeth while it heated up. Stepping into the steaming hot tub and closing his eyes, he welcomed the water as it washed off the dirt of the day. Somewhat relaxed, he turned the bed down and slipped between the cool sheets but still, sleep wouldn't come. Relenting, he got up, unzipped his shaving kit and rummaging around until he found a bottle of pills that he kept for nights like this. Jet lag, time zones and other reasons that deprived him of sleep. Opening a bottle of water from the bar fridge, he washed down the bitter tasting pill. Putting the bottle back into his kit, his eyes fell upon it. *'That damned vial!'* He didn't pick it up or touch it, but as he looked at it, he got angrier by the second. As small as it was, it has haunted him for the past twenty-five years.

It was 12:12 a.m. when he checked the clock. Exhaustion filled him as his body relaxed from this horrible tension-filled day and he wondered why he kept seeing multiple numbers.

Hearing the incessant rapping on his door, he opened an eye. "Yes?"

"Cleaning staff."

Sitting on the side of the bed he buried his eyes in the heels of his palms as he heard another knock. Wiping his hands over his face and down the back of his neck, he hoped they'd go away.

"Sir? It's check-out time, I need to clean the room."

"I don't need the room clean; I'll be staying another night. I'll notify the front desk." Hearing the wheels of the cart rolling past his window, he laid back down and pulled the covers over him. Since the pill hadn't worn off, he was able to fall back to sleep.

Opening his eyes again, he checked on the time. 12:12 p.m. '*What is up with these multi numbers?*' he mumbled. He'd managed to get a bit more sleep but to get the effects of the pill out of his system, he decided on another quick shower. Regulating the water, he stepped in and allowed the hot water to consume him.

* * *

He had only one clean shirt left in his satchel. Shaking it out, he hung it on a hanger then gathered up a bunch of laundry to drop off at the cleaners. It was either that or wear his cleanest dirty clothes after his next shower.

Before leaving the room, he slipped the vial and a few pieces of paper into his jacket pocket, called the front desk and booked another night. Dropping off his laundry, he headed to a restaurant that served all day breakfasts. Choosing a window seat, he ordered scrambled eggs and bacon, whole grain toast, orange juice and coffee. He couldn't remember when he had eaten last, then the burger from last night crossed his mind. He hadn't realized how hungry he was until he smelled the plate of food and a freshly brewed mug of coffee. He savored every bite and forced himself not to gobble it down like a starving, homeless person. Pushing his plate to the center of the table, he wiped his mouth, and while lifting the mug to his lips, he froze. Keri walked by the window and Drew nearly lost his breakfast as his stomach churned at the sight of her. Lowering the mug to the table, he leaned into the window to see where she was headed. He caught the back of her going into a hair salon. *'There is no time for guilt in her life,'* he thought*, 'and keeping up appearances takes priority, so she'll be there for a while.'* He got up, paid his bill and headed for his vehicle, wondering if this hairdo was for his benefit.

* * *

Letting himself in the front door this time, he tossed his jacket on the arm of the couch and went to the bedroom. Taking a look at the bed, he wondered how many times he had slept on dirty sheets or laid his head where Jake's had been. All kinds of thoughts whirled inside his head, but there were no tell-tale signs that anything had gone on in there the night before or any other nights for fifteen years. He had walked into this room many times not knowing that another man had been in his bed, until last night. *'Keri must have thought she'd had pulled the ultimate scam,'* he thought. He could only imagine how proficient she'd become at washing and folding bedding with years of practice.

He went to the storage unit and got the biggest suitcase they owned, went back to the bedroom and tossed it heavily onto the bed. Unzipping it, he flung the top open and jammed pieces of clothing in by the fistfuls until it was filled to the brim. Stuffing as many items as possible into every available compartment and zippered pockets until it bulged at the seams. Struggling to zip it closed, he didn't want a reason to come back. Wheeling it into the living room, he tossed his jacket over it and left it behind a chair. Making his way to the kitchen, he brewed up a pot of coffee and waited for Keri.

When she arrived, the delicious aroma tickled her nostrils as soon as she unlocked the door. She waltzed into the kitchen, hair freshly done, but when she saw Drew she gasped as her eyes went to her watch. "Drew... um... you're back!"

"Yes, but you're looking as if you were expecting someone else when you walked in. Was there a coffee date happening here this afternoon?"

"No, don't be silly," she fidgeted, glancing again at her watch and hoping that Jake would see the car...

He was quite positive she'd made plans to meet Jake after her appointment.

"I'm not staying," he said, sharply.

"But you made coffee?"

"Ya, want a cup?"

"Sure, but you never make coffee," she said, with a frown.

"It doesn't mean I can't," he said, passing her a mug. "Besides, I learned to make my own coffee a long time ago." '...And *for good reason,*' he thought.

Taking it, she paused and peered into the cup. Raising her eyes, the smile faded from her face as vague memories crept into her brain.

Drew could almost read her mind and if she thought for one second that he would ever drug her coffee for sex, she was sadly mistaken.

"Go ahead, drink up," he said, nodding toward the mug and trying to sound smug for her sake. "Maybe it'll relax you a little," he added, "you look tense." Taking a long slow drink, he squinted at her through the steam.

Lowering the mug, he could see the wheels spinning as her eyes darted from one of his eyes to the other.

"Go ahead, it's drinkable," he gestured with his chin, "try it." Drew took another gulp from his mug and deliberately slurped rudely.

An uneasiness crept over her at his seriousness, and it showed.

Nervously, she sat the mug down, but he kept his eyes on her as he picked it up and passed it back to her.

"Don't be like that," he quipped and passed it back to her insistently, "I poured it for you and everything, so come on, drink up, and why are you so quiet all of a sudden?"

"Because you're scaring me," she said, sounding like a frightened child.

"With a cup of coffee? Seriously? You're afraid of a cup of coffee?" he said, as his voice pitched higher.

"What are you doing, Drew?"

"I'm having a cup of coffee, what are you doing?" he said, drawing his brows together. Just then his cell phone beeped, and as he read the screen, he saw her walk into the living room. Creeping over to the door, he peeked in and watched as she sat down on the couch and eyed the glass jug that still held all of her beach paraphernalia. She turned it back and forth while secretly scanning through the nooks and crannies made by the different sized stones and shells.

She nearly came unglued when he walked up behind her and spoke. "What are you looking for?"

"What?" she asked, yanking her hand back from the bowl.

"What are you looking for?" he asked again, glaring at her.

"OK, Drew, what's going on?"

Sitting his coffee cup down, he approached her while searching her face for a few seconds and realizing he'd never really known this woman. He had no residual feelings or guilty conscience after what he had overheard, so he just opened his mouth and let the words tumble out.

"When I said earlier that I wasn't staying, I'm not, and I want a divorce." A strange calm covered his body as relief flowed through him once he had spoken the words he had longed to say for years.

Rising up, she began to rant, "What? A divorce? Why?"

"I think you know why, Keri."

"How would I know if you don't tell me?"

"Because I don't ever want to look at you again and I'm leaving," he said, through clenched teeth. Just the sight of her was repulsive.

"Leaving!? Just like that?" she said, snapping her fingers and moving her head mockingly at him.

"Yes, just like that," he said, snapping his fingers back at her. Finally, he saw her for what she really was. A liar, manipulator, cheater and the selfish brat that he never liked back then, and he certainly didn't like her now. "Seriously? Are you shocked?"

"Yes, I'm shocked! You have the nerve to waltz in here and out of nowhere announce that you want a divorce! What about us? What about me? I'm your wife, and I have been for twenty-five years. I deserve better than this!"

"Better than what, Keri?" he said, tilting his head slightly and squinting at her. "To spend the rest of your life with someone who doesn't love you and never did?"

The look on her face was that of innocence so he ran with it to see where she would go next.

"But, Drew, you're preparing to retire, this is what we have been waiting for."

Narrowing his eyes in disbelief, he spat the words out, "Waiting for?" He was trying to grasp the fact that she had just heard him tell her he never loved her, and it meant nothing to her.

"Yes, our retirement, so we can travel and be together and now you want to spend *my* retirement with another woman!? I don't think so, Drew!" she yelled.

"When did I say I had another woman?"

She was ranting loudly and hadn't heard what he'd said. He could tell that she was nearing hysteria, while still hanging on to the innocent, wounded housewife act.

"Really, Keri, you think this is about retirement?"

"You're damned right it is, and it's going to happen! I don't plan on missing out on the life we have been waiting for! Are you out of your mind!?" she screamed.

"Are you?" he shot back, realizing how absolutely disgusted he was with her dramatics.

"Am I what?" she yelled.

"Out of *your* mind?" he snapped back.

"How dare you!" she screamed, raising her hand but he caught her wrist in mid swing before it made contact. Smacking against his hand, he gripped it and yanked her closer. Nose to nose they held their stare until she flinched. He glared at her for several long seconds realizing she had every intention of letting him take the rap for everything. If he hadn't come home to satisfy his own curiosity, he would still be under her conniving thumb.

"Don't you dare raise your hand to me, not now and not ever!" he hissed, and his nose crinkled into a snarl.

At that point, he wished he could have twisted the wrist right off her arm. Struggling hopelessly against his strength, his grip tightened.

"I'm sorry, Drew, I lost my temper. I don't know where all this is coming from. After all this time and you're leaving me? Why? I don't understand, we are so close to our goals."

"Goals? What the hell are you talking about, Keri? *Goals?* We have no *goals*," he sneered, "and you are being delusional if you think we ever had any. Maybe you did but I sure as hell didn't. My life's goal has been trying to get the balls to tell you that I'm done, and I have, so..." he let go of her wrist with a slight push, "... I'm done."

Stumbled slightly at his quick release, she began to whine. "No, Drew! We can't be over! Come on! You aren't being fair here!"

When he heard the word '*fair*' slip off her lips, he had to stuff his hands into his pockets for fear of slapping her. Not ever being a violent person, he was about ready to punch something.

"Oh, I'm not being '*fair*'!?" he said, eyes wide and nodding his head. "You have the nerve to tell me I'm not being fair!" he said, glaring at her with disdain.

"You aren't being fair, Drew, how is this fair? You come home and tell me you are having an affair, and you want a divorce, and you call that fair?"

"When did I say I was having an affair?"

Staring at him, she tried to backtrack to his statement, but she couldn't. "Didn't you say you were leaving me for someone else?"

"I said ... I am leaving. I said nothing about an affair or another woman. Why would you even say that?"

Blinking, she swallowed hard. "I just thought..."

"I know what you thought. Let me make myself perfectly clear. I will say this once and only once. I have *never* been unfaithful to you in the twenty-five years that we have been married, but right now, I wish I had."

"But..."

"But nothing," he barked, "that's the truth."

"Then why are you so angry? Why are we screaming at each other?"

"Because..."

"Because...?" she added, waving her hands around waiting for him to answer.

"When I told you I wanted a divorce, I guess I expected you to accept it. After all, we haven't had a real marriage for years, and I'm tired of going through the motions. I've had enough, and I thought you had too."

"Why would you say that, Drew? I love you, and I want our marriage to work."

Annoyed with her lies, he knew he had to end it once and for all. There wasn't a snowball's chance in hell that she would take responsibility or admit to anything. She never had and never would. The perfect wife act was getting really old since he already knew about the fifteen-year affair. She was the same conniving witch that she'd been back in high school.

"Keri, come on, you can't be serious. This can't be a total shock to you. I know you want out of this marriage as much as I do."

"This comes as a total surprise to me."

"Are you telling me that you have never once thought about asking me for a divorce?"

"No, I have not!" she roared.

Lying had become second nature to her, and she continued to lie since she walked through the door. Knowing he had had enough, he opened his mouth and let whatever was on his tongue, roll off.

"Well, I guess *Jake* will be disappointed to hear that now won't he," he said, calmly while watching her reaction. As he spoke the words, the fire left his belly.

First, she paled, then she stumbled backward and then silence.

"Jake? Ho..." she swallowed and cleared her throat, "how... um... do you know about Jake?"

"I was here last night and heard it all, so wanna tell me again how much you love me and how much you want this marriage? Hmmm? Poor Jake," he sneered, "well, he can have you! He's waited years for you, *fifteen* to be exact," he spat the words at her. "I wonder how he'd feel right now hearing you trying to protect this marriage," he said, narrowing his eyes before speaking again. "It took me a while to figure it out, but I did."

"Figure... what... out?" she faltered.

Glaring at her for several seconds he wondered if he should just let it go and walk out the door or let her have it with both barrels. Both barrels sounded pretty good, so he went with it.

"Drew?"

Narrowing his eyes, he made the decision. '*Screw you,*' he thought, '*you made your bed a long time ago.*' Walking over to the back of the chair, he wheeled his suitcase closer. Unzipping the breast pocket of his jacket, he rummaged around inside until his fingers touched it. Closing his fist around it, he brought it out. Looking at her again he extended his arm and slowly opened his fist. There in the palm of his hand was the tiny vial, from all those many years ago, coming back to bite her in the ass. He saw her gasp as she clamped her hand to her mouth. She stumbled backward as if seeing a tarantula crawling up his arm.

"Is this what you were looking for in the bowl?"

"How long have you had that?"

"How long have I had it? Is that all you care about?"

She was horrified. "Drew, I..."

"Save it!" he spat, "I've known from as far back as the beach party that something wasn't right. No one loses consciousness for no reason. If you knew that the only way you could ever have me was by drugging me that should have been your first damned clue. I've had this vial analyzed along with blood work, and when I got the results back, there was just enough trace left in my bloodstream to match the contents of this vial. GHB, Keri, a date rape drug," he clarified, glaring intensely at her.

"Drew, I... I..."

"I don't hear you denying it!"

"You can't prove anything," she sneered, defiantly bracing her shoulders back and cocking her head to one side.

"Oh really?" he said. Going back to the pocket of his jacket, he came back with two official-looking documents. Opening one, he never took his eyes off her face as he turned it around slowly. The snap of the paper caused her to flinch as he flipped it over. "Proof enough for ya?"

"Who...? What?" She was like a caged animal now as reality faced her.

"This is the analysis of the content from the vial proving it to be an illegal street drug."

"This... this..." she stammered, waving toward the page, "still proves nothing."

Unfolding the second page, he continued to glare at her. "Maybe not, but this does."

"What is that?" she sneered, with her chin stuck out.

"Your fingerprint."

She blinked as a spray of saliva hit her face as he spat the 't' off his tongue while enunciating *fingerprint.*

"Why did you stay, Drew?" her voice trembled.

"For Noah," he said, wishing he never had to speak to her again, "and I wish I hadn't. He was the only reason why I stayed."

"You could have left, Drew, we had nothing between us."

"We have always had nothing between us, and if weren't for your antics we never would have!"

"I'm sorry, Drew."

"Shut up, Keri, just shut up! 'Sorry' is when you make a mistake that you regret. This was deliberate, and it happened more than once, not to mention it is illegal. I don't want to hear that you are sorry because you're not. You are only sorry that you got caught and if you weren't Noah's mother I'd have your ass thrown in jail!"

"Jail? Drew!"

Drew knew that if she'd been a man standing in front of him, he would have laid her out. Rage filled him as he thought of all the years she had robbed him of, it would have felt great to get one good poke in. He knew that it was wrong to think in these terms, but she deserved these thoughts.

"Drew? Please unclench your fists, you're scaring me."

Once the fear in her voice kicked into his brain, he came out of his fit. He relaxed a bit, but Keri was still leery. She knew he was angry and with good reason. She thought her tricks were behind her, but here they were.

"What are you going to do about the vial, Drew?"

"If you behave yourself, then nothing. I want a divorce, no hassles and no antics from you, and if that sounds like blackmail, then it is, but this *is* going to happen. I just want this to be done. You will hear from my lawyer who, by the way, also has these same copies." Flipping them at her, he walked to the couch again. Stuffing the papers and the vial back into the pocket of his jacket, he zipped it back up and grabbed the handle of his suitcase. As he walked past her, she gripped his arm.

"Drew, please, don't go!"

Looking down at her hand, he snatched his arm away. "You will be hearing from my lawyer and remember," he said, leaning in close to her face, "no muss and no fuss, this *is* done." Cocking his head ever so slightly so that she knew it was a warning without him ever saying it again. Raising her fingers to her lips, tears streamed down her cheeks. Drew didn't know if they were real or crocodile, and for once he didn't care.

Gripping the handle of his suitcase he walked toward the front door. Stopping for one last look around, he leaned back as something caught his eye. Looking past Keri, he saw a man's shoe. Standing the suitcase up, he walked to the kitchen door. Leaning back against the counter, stood a stranger with the saddest and most pitiful look on his face that Drew had ever seen. It only took an educated guess as to who it was and when he saw Drew, he stood tall... embarrassed, but tall.

The two men stared at each other for several seconds both knowing who the other one was without an introduction.

"I'm Jake Lansing," Jake said, speaking first and manning up. "I'm not proud of what I've done, but I do apologize for the part I've played in what is going on here today. You're a bigger man than I am, Drew."

At the sound of Jake's voice, Keri walked over and stood behind Drew.

"I came in shortly after Keri, and the voices were so loud that when I knocked, no one heard me. I apologize for eavesdropping, but I'm not sorry I stayed to hear what was going on."

"Well, man, I've been there too. I sat on the arm of that couch," Drew said, pointing into the living room, "and listened to you and

156

my wife just last night and you didn't know I was listening either, and I am not sorry for hearing the truth. I gave her several chances for an out after hearing her tell you how much she wanted you and that our marriage was nonexistent, but there was nothing but lies coming out of her mouth. I'm sorry you wasted your time, but hey, she is all yours if you still want her and if you're here for your coffee date, there's some in the pot," he said, nodding towards the coffeepot.

"No thanks," he said. Glancing at Keri, he cocked his head, as if to say, *'you're on your own,'* and he walked out the back door.

Trying to feel a little bit sorry for her, Drew turned on his heels and walked out the front door.

18

Sitting alone in her living room, Keri was reliving the past. Bad memories plagued her as she relived more of the horrible times when she had been rejected by Drew and her pathetic antics to try and keep him. It had worked for twenty-five years, but now, when she really needed him, he was gone, and he holds the truth in his hands.

She had often wondered where the vial had gone, and since it had never reappeared, she had forgotten about it and hoped to never see it again. She shuddered when she thought about actually using it. It hadn't made her feel good about herself knowing that it was the only way she could get Drew's attention. She'd always had a difficult time with rejection, and it was Drew's rejection that had led her to extreme and illegal measures. Drew's refusal to like her had gotten the best of her. That hadn't been the greatest feeling in the world especially after the ego trips she'd been on every day at her previous school where she was the leader of the pack. If only she had been accepted in Kanyon Ridge High, maybe things would have been different. Instead of feeling on top of the world she felt as if she'd been sucked under by a current. Struggling to fit in somewhere amongst hundreds of students, but they'd all ignored her. Life had never been the same after that dreadful move.

She knew she'd never have had Noah if it weren't for the drug. It didn't make it right no matter how she spun it. The last time she dropped it into Drew's tea, though, she knew it was then that she had gotten pregnant. If she hadn't used it that last time, she would never have had her son. Snagging Drew had been her ultimate goal, but she lived a lonely and solitary life because of it. Then Jake showed up at her front door... gloating time was over. Common sense should have told her back then that Jake was the man for her. He loved her, and she loved and adored him. She didn't know why she couldn't let go of Drew. Was it because she'd worked too hard and schemed for too long to get him that it was impossible to let him go? Did she have abandonment issues because she wouldn't let go of Jake either. He made her feel like a woman and loved her with all his being. She should have taken it at the time. She'd had ample opportunities to walk away from Drew, reclaim her freedom and release him. *'Why does everything look clearer after the fact,'* she wondered. *'Why couldn't she have seen past Drew and her grand illusions and just walked away with Jake? All of this crap would never have happened,'* she thought sadly. Blaming her parents for moving her away and trapping Drew into a marriage he didn't want had been foolish. At sixteen, she hadn't wanted a marriage either, she just wanted Drew anyway she could have him.

The biggest deception of all had begun the night of the beach party when she drugged his drink. Once she and Drew were alone and away from the crowd... she remembered... "Would you like to go for a walk?" he whispered into her hair.

"Yes," she smirked, "let's do that."

Stumbling to his feet, she caught him before he fell. "Steady there, Drewy-boy," she'd said softly, as an image of a grinning sleaze-ball occupied a space in her consciences. *'Let it go, Keri,'* she remembered, *'this is what you've wanted all along.'*

Keri remembered as they headed off into the bushes, Drew began to drag his feet and he stumbled forward into the sand. He was passed out cold. The drug had been too strong for his system and worked the opposite of what she'd hope for. He was dead weight as she struggled to take off his shirt. She'd stripped down to her underwear, slipped his shirt on then reached over, unbuckled his belt and unzipped his jeans. She felt pretty cocky as she laid beside him pretending to be asleep. She remembered him sneaking away from her without a second thought for her safety. He just wanted to be away from her. She should have let it go then. Nobody with feelings would have left a young girl on the beach, alone and in the dark. Well, she'd show him!

Adding a drop to his beer on their wedding night he was passed out and useless, just like the first time on the beach. So, the morning after their sexless wedding night, when her period had started, she thought it was over. She thought that Drew would have picked up his stuff and walked away from her, but he had scruples. He'd sucked it up to save face with his parents and had settled down to a life of misery. They had both still been virgins, and he didn't know it. She'd claimed his virginity on the night he'd accepted his last cup of tea from her.

* * *

Once Drew was out of the house, in his car and on his way, he realized that he could have taken the high road back there. He could have been a pompous ass and blamed Keri for everything and walked out feeling pretty smug. Instead, he went there to tell her exactly what he had built himself up to say and do. Plain and simple. If she hadn't started with the lies and professing her undying love for him, he would have left it at that and pretended

160

to know nothing about Jake or the drug. But after listening to her ramble on and hoping for just an iota of truth to fall off her lips, he couldn't resist. Had he not known about her affair he would have come away feeling pretty much like a slug. She had tried guilting him into staying and hoping to continue having the best of both worlds including a beautiful home, a nice car, access to his bank account and a lover while he was away. She had taken full advantage of it all, even to poor unsuspecting Jake. '*As they say*,' he thought, '*all good things must come to an end.*' He just shook his head as the entire scene played out in his head again and again.

A priority stop was in order, and he headed for the bank. He took half of what was in his account and opened a new one and deposited his half into it. He canceled all credit cards that Keri's name was on and asked if they would send a new card to Noah. He wanted him to have a card for any incidentals for the spa which was his way of being involved in the business until he retired. Shredding his card, they replaced it with a new one. Feeling satisfied, he went back to the Kanyon Ridge Motel. He felt 'better'... not great but 'better.' He was 'free' for the first time since he was seventeen. Twenty-five long years tied to Keri and he walked away with his head up high and proud. Feeling as if he'd been let out of prison, he'd done his time.

He'd always thought there should have been important moments in relationships, but there hadn't been any with Keri. Racking his brain, he tried recalling even one but the only tender moment between them was Noah's birth. As far as he was concerned, she was and always would be a self-serving manipulator with her own agenda. He had to bring himself up on the carpet now and then and remind himself that she was the mother of their son, but that was all she would ever be to him. He didn't have to wonder anymore about why all the important things, he should have remembered, were wiped from his memory. At one point, he'd even thought that something might be wrong with him while believing he was actually developing early onset of dementia or Alzheimer's so soon in his young life. He agonized over and pictured his future in a ward somewhere not knowing anyone or even who he was, and it wreaked havoc with his mind until he found out the truth. Not only about Keri's antics, but the vial, Jake... all of it. He was done, and he was free!

19

Relief washed over Drew as the wheels of his plane met the runway. Staring through the tinted windscreen after parking at the ramp, he found himself absentmindedly rolling the tiny vial around in his fingers. As small as it was and despite the twenty-five years that had passed since finding it, he always knew where it was. Feeling it between his fingers brought back the painful memories yet again.

Being a pilot had its advantages. Except for the occasional scan, he was rarely selected for a customs search. Knowing where all those checkpoints were, he'd tuck the vial in his shaving kit, inside his tow along and out of sight. So far it had not been detected but he couldn't imagine what the consequences would be if an illegal substance had been found in his possession. Still, he felt that the only place safe enough was with him.

He would never forgive her, and he was more certain about that than he had ever been about anything in his entire life. Carrying the vial around for years still makes his skin crawl, but it served as a harsh reminder for the many wasted years and the disgust that he's felt for his soon to be ex-wife. His best day ever was when he finally got the chance to confront her and this past week was the first breath of freedom he's had in years.

Feeling jet-lagged from a long flight, he brought the plane to a stop at the assigned gate. The only downside to flying, for him, was the stale, stagnant and recycled air in the plane. Anxious to get off this bird, his lungs were begging for fresh air.

Loving his job, he worked long hours, and the simple fact was, it had kept him away from home. But since he was no longer tied to Keri, it was a simple pleasure to go back to the motel and just... be... something he had longed to be... free.

Until his recent separation, his days off were usually spent around his workshop, gardening or just being out in the sunshine for a jog as an excuse to be away from her. Anything that kept him from dealing with what was really going on in his head... Now finally, all the drama was behind him, and he was happy to have a second chance at a new life.

* * *

A pilot's uniform only added to Andrew Greyson's already handsomeness. Dressed in dark blue trousers and matching jacket while sporting gold wings on the breast, he headed off the plane. The gold braided stripes on the cuffs were offset by a crisp white shirt and dark tie. He turned many females into gushing messes whenever he strutted through the airports.

He was an easy six feet two, and his well-toned body alluded to the fact that he worked hard at keeping fit. Since he'd had no life beyond flying, he'd made good use of the hotel's gym no matter where he stayed. With eyes the color of cultivated blueberries, they were outlined with girl-like thick, black lashes while slivers of gray accented his short, dark brown hair. His smile lit up his entire face portraying the happy guy on the outside, but on the inside only he knew the true story.

Gripping the handle of his tow-along while rushing through the airport, his cell phone beeped. Pulling it from his jacket pocket, he swiped the screen with his thumb which displayed his next flight schedule along with several messages that had come in during the flight. Heading toward the revolving door, he scrolled with his free thumb to hurriedly read his new itinerary. Reaching the door, he saw that it was opening in his favor. Dropping his eyes momentarily, he quickly scanned the screen. Lifting them again to get his bearings, he saw her, but it was too late. In a split second, they collided almost chest to chest, expelling air from her lungs. Almost airborne, they became an entangled mess of arms, legs, and tow-along suitcases. As if in slow motion, his phone flew in one direction and hers went in another. As the handle of his suitcase hit the tiles, he desperately tried wrapping his arms around her as a cushion for their inevitable fall. Managing to go down first, she fell on top of him. Dumbstruck with horror, they both imagined what they must look like sprawled out full-bodied on a dirty airport floor. Once the world stopped spinning, and they realized what had happened, embarrassment set in as they laid in a twisted heap.

Catching a whiff of strawberry scented shampoo, his body relaxed slightly as pieces of her hair cascaded across his face.

Slowly, she brought her head up to see who the victim of her inattentiveness was. Wiping a few strands of her hair from his face, they gazed momentarily into each other's eyes rendering them both speechless. She was only a breath away, and his heart did a double take. For the first time in what seemed like a lifetime, he felt an embarrassing stir in his groin.

A surge of unfamiliar pleasure coursed through him as he lowered his gaze to her mouth. Watching her pull her bottom lip in with her teeth, strawberry lip gloss filled his senses.

'*Oh, my God, would you get a grip!*' he thought, scolding himself, shifting his body slightly to hide his apparent arousal.

Sputters was all that came out. "I... um... I'm so sorry," she whispered, "I should have been paying closer attention to where I was going."

Tiny puffs of air hit his face, as she spoke, causing him to blink.

"It's my fault," he butted in, taking total blame. "I wasn't paying full attention to where I was going either. Let me help you up," he said, shifting his body again to get out from under her and onto his feet. Reaching out a hand to help her up, the heel of her boot slipped on the tile before she was fully upright, and she dragged him down on top of her. Covering her eyes with one hand, her body began to shake.

"Are you okay? Are you hurt?" Getting no response, he asked again, "Miss, are you alright?"

"Yes, I'm okay," she said, bursting into giggles. It sent him into a fit of nervous laughter too along with relief that she wasn't injured.

"So, let's try this again, shall we?" he said, getting up. Standing above her head, he reached down, slid his hands under her armpits and lifted her up. Holding her steady until she was safely on her feet, a round of applause erupted from the crowd that had gathered to watch the calamity. Each was swiping at the dust on their clothing, and when she turned to face him, no words came out of her mouth. Slowly pushing the hair from her face, she could only stare at him. Just moments ago, she had been a hair's breadth away from him on the floor but standing in front of him, getting a more realistic look, made her heart beat a little faster. Familiarity leaped in after noticing, for the first time, how tall and handsome he was, and it took her breath away. He had the bluest eyes that she had seen on only one other person. A familiar smile and a nicely tanned face showed off his dazzling white teeth. He had a few laugh lines around his eyes, which told her that he smiled a lot and that was a good thing. Strikingly youthful looking, she guessed his age to be fortyish. Remembering the phrase, 'a twinkle in his eyes,' she saw that he actually had beautiful twinkling eyes. He appeared to be approximately six feet tall since she, herself, stood close to five feet seven and being in boots, with heels, she met his eyes with just a lift of her lids.

Someone handed him his cell phone and then offered the handle of his suitcase.

"Thank you, so much," he said, with a nod, "that's very kind of you."

Another stranger returned her strewn belongings, and she gracefully accepted them with a beautiful smile and a nod.

"Are you sure you're alright?" he asked again, looking for reasons to keep her there.

"Yes, I'm sure, just a little embarrassed is all," she said, nervously swiping more dust off her clothes and running her fingers through her blonde hair.

The sound of her voice quickened his heartbeat as his eyes roamed over her face in desperation. He couldn't just let her go, he needed more time with her. Blurting out the only thing that came to mind, he asked, "Would you have a cup of coffee with me?"

"Umm?" she faltered.

"Please?" he said, with pleading eyes while lifting his eyebrows for a ray of hope.

It was her turn to scan his handsome face. '*Why does he look so familiar*?' she thought. '*If she said 'no,' could she possibly go about her life never seeing him again? Did she want that? If she said 'yes,' then what?'*

"Please?" he asked again, as he tilted his head waiting for her to decide whether or not he was a pervert. He didn't want to sound desperate, but at that moment, he really was. If she refused, would he ever see her again? That wasn't an option he wanted to explore.

She smiled, and hope crossed his face.

"Yes, I'd like that."

Sheer relief escaped his lungs at her answer. "I would rather go anywhere other than this airport if that's OK with you? There's a restaurant just down the road."

Peeking at her watch, she said, "I have to be back in an hour."

"No problem, I'll have you back on time, I promise," he said, placing his palm on her back while steering her through the infamous revolving door and out to the parking garage. Opening the trunk, he depressed the handle of his suitcase and put it inside along with his carry-on. "I can put yours in here too, or in the back seat, it's up to you." He hadn't noticed her quick peek into the open trunk on her way to the passenger door.

Pausing, a look of panic washed over her face, as if to say, *'What am I doing, this guy is a total stranger! What if I'm never seen again!?'*

Immediately, sensing panic, he closed the trunk and moved around to the passenger's side.

"I'm sorry, I didn't mean to frighten you. I don't know what I was thinking. We can go back inside and have coffee at the commissary," he said, pointing towards the entry. "I can assure you that I am completely harmless, although, I suppose that is what most serial killers tell their prey." He tried to make light of it, but he clearly saw how rattled she was. Quickly scanning his face, she knew in her heart, he was harmless.

"Let's just put it in the back," she said, passing the handle toward him.

Relief washed over him again as he opened the passenger door for her. She likely had no idea how nervous and rattled he was as well. Putting her bag on the floor behind her seat, he went around to the driver's side and slid in beside her. Pressing the starter button, he asked again, "Are you sure you're okay? We can just go inside," he insisted, pointing again toward the airport doors.

"No, really, I'm OK, just a little nervous, which is understandable."

Seeing her glance quickly into the back seat, he hoped that duct tape and rope hadn't crossed her mind. "I have to admit that I am a little nervous too," he said. Smiling at her, he mentally pleaded with her to trust him as he put the car in drive and headed out of the garage.

The restaurant was only a kilometer down the road, and before they knew it, they were sitting across from each other ordering coffee.

He didn't have a clue who she was, but he was hoping to change that. Although he hadn't seen her before, he felt a complete sense of comfort around her and an overwhelming urge for a little more time before she disappeared across the skies.

He signaled the waitress for two coffees on their way to a booth. Looking deeply into her blueish-green eyes, her smile melted his heart. She seemed vaguely familiar. There was a noticeable resemblance to someone he'd met years ago... in the hospital maybe... Lorraine something or other. His thoughts were interrupted as the waitress sat two steaming cups down in front of them.

"Hi," he said, speaking softly from across the booth. The sound of his tender voice sent a weird and familiar excitement straight to her soul.

'Who was this handsome stranger anyway and why does he seem so familiar,' she thought again, *'I've never been this bold in my entire life, especially accepting a coffee date with a complete stranger. What am I thinking?'*

"Hi," she offered back.

"I'm Andrew Greyson," he said, reaching out his hand in introduction, "my friends call me Drew."

Her smile slackened, and the blood drained from her face. Her heart began to palpitate when she heard his name. *'Greyson?'* she thought, swallowing hard, *'Noah,'* her throat suddenly drying, she nervously reached for her coffee. *'Oh, please God, no, it can't be, it must be just a coincidence, I'm sure. But it was like looking at an older Noah.'*

"Cassie Lucan," she said, nervously offering her hand to him. Any thoughts or mention of Noah sent her over the edge of sanity.

Squeezing it, he laid his other hand on top, cupping it intimately.

Lowering her eyes to his hand, she was relieved at not seeing a wedding band but knew that didn't always mean anything.

"I see you're a pilot," she said, gently pulling her hands free and pointed to the wings on his uniform.

Pressing his lips together and smiling, he tilted his head to one side and raised his eyebrows, "Busted!" he said, teasingly and as they laughed, she couldn't help but feel a little embarrassed.

'*There's nothing like pointing out the obvious!*' she thought, '*he already knows he is a pilot!*' She could feel heat gathering on her cheeks, and it was refreshing for him to see someone blush, especially these days. He didn't know when he had felt this carefree with anyone.

"And you? Where are you off to?"

"Toronto, I have a modelling gig there this weekend.'

"I can see why you're a model, very impressive."

"Thank you, I only accept a few shows a year now. I work closely with younger models backstage along with my partner, Amelia, who is our designer."

"Younger models? But you are the perfect age for modelling."

"Thanks, but I've been at this a very long time. Actually, twenty years."

"What? You're just a baby!" he teased.

"Maybe so but I started when I was five years old, and I haven't stopped except for a break in my mid-teens," she said, not wanting to elaborate. "Mind you I'm not complaining, and I love being on the runway, but I also enjoy being backstage helping the up and coming models.

"It seems we have the 'runway' in common then," Drew joked, trying his best to make conversation with her. He noticed that even though she was a model, there was nothing fake about her. There were no gaudy looking fake nails, but instead, hers were clipped, filed and topped with a clear coat of polish. Her hair was real, beautiful, naturally blonde and long without extensions. He worked with many flight attendants, and he knew fake when he saw it.

"Yes, we do have that, but yours is far more dangerous and important than what I do. I walk it, and you fly off it, big difference. How long have you been a pilot?" she asked, passing it back to him.

"Long enough to retire soon," he said, "it's in progress." He did a quick calculation in his head. *'She's my son's age!'* he thought, with a feeling of discouragement. *'Surely this will be over before it begins.'*

"Retire? You're kind of young to be retiring?"

"I've been in the business for nearly twenty-five years, I think it's time for a change. I'm in a partnership, here in Kanyon Ridge, with my son and that should keep me busy after I retire." Smiling, he took a drink of coffee while thinking back to his flight courses before she and his son were even born.

A cell phone rang, and he recognized the ringtone as Cassie pulled it out of her pocket. She frowned when she looked at the screen. *'Keri'?*

He realized the mistake and pulled her phone from his pocket.

"I think we have each other's phone."

In the meanwhile, the call went to voice-mail as they switched phones. He didn't offer an explanation as to who *'Keri'* was, he just slipped the phone into his pocket without looking at it.

At that moment, no one mattered except Cassie... right here and right now. He saw her check her watch, but she didn't seem concerned.

"I don't mean to sound desperate, but every time you check your watch I know our time is limited so, I need to ask if I can have your phone number?"

Feeling relieved that he asked, she reached into her handbag for a pen. Writing it on her napkin, she slid it across the table with her fingertips. Reaching for it, she pressed her fingers down so he couldn't pick it up and he looked up at her curiously.

"If I give this to you, you'd better use it," she said, with a raised eyebrow and straight-faced but clearly teasing him.

"I promise," he said, raising his fingers in a Boy Scout gesture.

Smiling back at him, she said, "We'd better get going."

"Okay, let's go," he said, getting up and extending a hand to her.

Taking it, she stood up. They were facing each other, and without hesitation, he reached under her hair, bent his head slightly and pulled her in for a kiss. Time flew backward for Cassie to another time. She'd felt the same rush of passion as she did back then and to her surprise, she kissed him back and at that moment in time, they were the same age. A boy and a girl sharing an accelerating, heart pounding kiss and she felt as if she was back in that classroom with her back pressed against the chalkboard. 'Oh God... Noah,' she thought.

It wasn't a deep, tongue tangling passionate kiss but when their lips parted, and their eyes opened, smiles crossed their faces.

"I didn't get your number," she whispered.

"You will when I text you," he said, inhaling the strawberry scent in her hair. "Thank you for spending this time with me. You could have easily said 'no,' but I'm glad you didn't."

"Me too," she whispered.

She felt him tremble slightly and she reached up and placed her hands on each side of his head and brought his lips down to meet hers. He held her tightly as he kissed her a little longer and with much more passion this time. She welcomed his tongue with hers, and their kiss deepened. Drawing away from him, she laid her forehead against his chin. Spreading her fingers across his chest, she closed her eyes. Through his jacket, she could feel his heart beating. Opening her eyes, she lifted her head to look at him. "I hope I don't regret saying this, but I hope this doesn't end here."

Those were the sweetest words he had ever heard.

"I was thinking the same thing," he said, "but didn't dare to hope." Gazing into her eyes, he felt a sense of 'winning' that he had not felt in what seemed like a lifetime. He had never 'won' with Keri because she was always one step ahead. Right now though, there was no room for Keri in his mind.

"I have to go," she said softly.

He momentarily rested his chin on the top of her head and closed his eyes as if to hold the moment forever. *'What if I never see her again?'* he wondered. As if reading his thoughts, she looked up at him and said, "I'll be back in three days."

Loosening his grip on her, he slowly led her out of the restaurant. A few short minutes and they were back at the airport. He got her bag from the backseat, extended the handle and pulled it along behind him.

"I'll be fine from here," she said, reaching for the handle. "Text me," she said, leaning in to kiss him again. Taking her bag, she walked to the revolving door. Before going through, she blew him a kiss and disappeared into the crowd.

One short week ago, he would have been riddled with guilt at kissing someone. If their collision had happened back then, he would likely have just picked her up, apologized and left without stopping to get a name or see who his victim was.

Today was the first time in all his married years that he had ever done anything against his marriage vows, except this time, there was no guilt involved. It felt awesome to be free and to be who he had always wanted to be. Just Drew Greyson, guilt-free, at last.

Waiting in the parking garage until she was out of sight, he got into his car, laid his head back against the headrest and relived the last hour. He just wanted to feel what he was feeling, at the moment, which was remembering Cassie's heart beating against his chest and the strawberry scent in her hair and on her lips. That's all he was taking away with him, Cassie Lucan and beautiful thoughts.

* * *

A dingle on his phone caused him to lose focus on Cassie. Reaching into his breast pocket, he pulled out his phone, swiped the screen and pressed 'messages.'

We need to talk he read.

No, we don't, it's already done he typed back.

Please, Drew

Stop texting me!'

Blowing out the burst of air, that had built up in his lungs, he inhaled deeply drawing air back in. This was what freedom looks like and from where he sat, it was pretty sweet until thoughts of Keri threatened to ruin the beautiful feelings he was trying to hold on to. He was not going to let her get under his skin, not now and not ever. Smacking his palm on the steering wheel, he laid his head back against the headrest. Staring out at the concrete ceiling, he thought about Cassie. Keri would not take another moment from him, never again.

20

Cassie Lucan sat on the plane that would take her away from Drew. New and exciting feelings gripped her because of their chance meeting or rather their collision. She hadn't dated in recent years, and she'd never had a serious relationship since high school. Not that she couldn't have had one, it was just more important to concentrate on her career rather than a man. She didn't want to lose her focus, and she didn't have the time or the energy that it took to maintain a relationship. For now, she was comfortable in her own skin without pressure from anyone. She had her memories from the past, and she answered only to herself and her business partner. Meeting Drew though, hadn't taken away from the feelings she'd kept hidden about her first and only love. *'Did he bring out those hidden feelings? Was that the reason why she was excited? Was he a reminder of what she'd given up? Was she hoping to rekindle those feelings with a look-alike?'* she thought. *'No! She could never replace Noah! Never!'*

Now, here she was, thinking about someone she has known for a little more than an hour. Going over in her mind, their run-in and coffee introduction. Envisioning his face caused her heart to dance and beat a little faster. She felt an excitement that she hadn't felt in a long time. A permanent smile was plastered across her face that even she was aware of, but didn't care if anyone else noticed. It was the same smile she got when she'd read romance stories about young lovers' meeting and having a deep connection between them. This chance meeting with Drew gave her those same feelings, and she didn't want to lose them. Feelings of excitement and joy, along with wonderfully happy feelings, that could only be explained because of Drew, only Drew. She hoped it was for the right reasons and not just the familiarity of the past. Thinking about Noah, she wondered, again, how would he feel about her, as Cassie Lucan. '*Would she ever forget about him? Would his memory always be between her and a new start?*' she pondered. *Was he still in Kanyon Ridge? Did he still think about her or had he moved on?*'

A memory came back from something Drew had said. He was in a partnership with his son in Kanyon Ridge, which meant he was still there. She hadn't been to Kanyon Ridge for eight years except to drive along the outskirts to get to the airport.

* * *

Once Cassie was out of sight, he started his car and made his way back out of the parking garage. Sunlight splashed his face as he waved to the agent in the ticket booth. All airport personnel had windshield stickers allowing them to pass slowly but freely through the gate.

Things were different now, he admitted, weaving in and out of traffic heading towards the highway. Freedom was sweet even in the unsettling way it happened, he was over it, and he was finally moving on. Still, he berated himself for not manning up all those years ago, to set them both free. For years, he had been in a sham of a marriage, kick-started by Keri's manipulations. No matter how many times he'd thought about it, he knew he should never have taken that final step to the altar. There was never anything sweet and tender about Keri, and nothing ever came naturally with her, like it had today, with Cassie. Just thinking about her caused flutters in his stomach and suddenly, he longed to be with her. Habitually running his hand across his face and over his hair, he gripped the steering wheel. Searching his car mirrors for traffic, he eased safely into a lane and headed back to the motel.

He needed time to himself to think about things, go over the recent events and his fortunate run-in with Cassie. Meeting her briefly, he missed her already. He was elated to have had the good fortune to meet her just one week after he was finally free from Keri.

Wishing now that he'd been more inquisitive, he felt he should have asked for more about her trip. Like, where was she going? Where was she staying? He knew he could always text her, but he didn't want her to think of him as a desperate wimp and couldn't do without her for a few hours.

Arriving at the motel, he got another text from Keri asking where he was.

None of your business, stop texting me and get on with your life

Not having to answer her questions, he was moving on with his life and it felt great to be able to finally think in those terms. If she didn't stop harassing him, the next step would be to change his number.

He needed a place to live since the motel scene was getting old, fast, and he'd been there for a week already. It was OK for now, but in the meanwhile, he would search listings to see what was available. Thoughts of finding his own place was exciting, and for once he could see his future becoming a whole lot brighter.

His phone beeped. Opening the text, it asked if he could take a flight out to Toronto in a few hours.

Done

Wanting desperately to contact Cassie, he decided to wait until after he landed in Toronto.

21

Checking her watch, Cassie heard the pilot announce that the flight was on time and that he was preparing for descent. She had made the flight so many times she barely remembered leaving the ground and landing again. Now she wondered, how many times she might have flown with Drew in the cockpit, and had she ever heard his voice come over the intercom.

Making her way through the airport and outside, she hailed a cab. Giving the driver the address to the hotel she relaxed in the backseat while taking in the sights of the city and reliving the earlier afternoon's encounter. Reaching into her handbag, she took out her cell phone, no calls, and no texts. Feeling disappointed, she began to silently berate herself for being so impetuous. *'He's likely married, and since he had knocked me over at the airport he probably felt obligated to buy me a cup of coffee.'* The happy smile left her face as she thought that Drew Greyson might not even be his real name. Since he hadn't offered her his cell phone number, maybe he was just being a nice guy after all. But he'd seemed as into her as she was him. What was she thinking! Now she remembered why she didn't do relationships. Men! They were strictly a pain in the ass!

Then, again, there was that 'Greyson' issue bringing Noah's memory back to haunt her. Their relationship hadn't necessarily been a complete secret since they had become friends in kindergarten and she knew she had loved him since age five. They knew little to nothing about each other's family and never visited each other's homes or met the others' parents. They were school friends, doing school related things and hanging out. Cassie had

181

never mentioned Noah until she was sixteen and on the run. As far as she knew, Noah hadn't mentioned her to his parents either, and he never mentioned them to her. There was never a reason to since their time together was for them. Cassie and her mother were from the other side of town, and Noah was in a different category of the upper crust, so they kept 'family' out of their lives. Fear made them secretive. Afraid if their parents knew they were friends they might try to separate them. They knew they were in love and that was all that mattered.

* * *

Reaching over the seat, she dropped a few bills next to the driver as he pulled in front of the hotel. Insisting on him keeping the change, she knew it could likely feed his family, back home, for a month.

Stepping out onto the sidewalk with her suitcase, she pulled the handle up and walked inside to the reception desk.

"Hello, I'm Cassie Lucan, I have a reservation," she said, making herself busy scrolling her phone while the desk clerk scrolled through the computer looking for her name.

"Yes, Miss Lucan, welcome back, you'll be in room 443," he said, passing her the room card. Accepting it, she headed for the elevator.

Pushing the door open, she entered the decent sized suite, took her phone out again and flipped her bag onto the bed. Scrolling the list with her thumb, she stopped at Amelia's name and pressed call. Amelia Benton was her best friend, and she desperately needed to talk to her.

"Hey!" Amelia's pleasant voice rang out.

"Oh, hi Amelia! Where are you?"

"Why do you sound so desperate?"

"Sorry Amelia, but, where are you?"

"I'm just leaving the tanning salon, why?"

"Are you busy right now? I'm at the hotel."

"No, I'm not busy," she said.

"Then can you get your fake-tanned ass over here?"

Amelia laughed and said, "Yes Ma'am, I'll be there in fifteen."

"Thanks, Amelia."

"No, problem, see you in a few."

* * *

When she was a little girl, Amelia loved to spend time in her mother's closet. Whatever she chose to put on, she'd find several different ways to style it up by adding belts, scarves, vest or anything she could find to make that one simple dress look special. It impressed her mother to watch her do her magic. Her flaming red hair and deep emerald green eyes were as bold and beautiful as their owner.

In her teens, she still had a passion for fashion. While not acting like a typical teenager, Amelia had a flare and a style unmatched by anyone in her age group. She could be found in an array of colors that made her stand out in a crowd. She loved to wear brightly colored scarves with her 'out of fashion' outfits and usually chose a lovely knit sweater, a maxi skirt with an unusual print and an outlandish pair of granny boots or sandals laced halfway up her legs. She adored hats of various sizes and colors, which in turn kept her natural red hair from fading in the sun.

She loved roaming around in second-hand shops or vintage clothing stores rather than hanging out at a mall or a typical teenager's favorite burger joint. It was at these stores where her dream, to become a fashion designer, took flight. She decided to sew for herself and never once thought of anyone else becoming interested in her dream or her secret stash.

Certain items would catch her eye as she'd linger to feel the texture of silks, satins, brocades and other exotic material slip between her fingers. In her imagination, she could envision another more popular and fashionable design that would fit in perfectly with today's trends. After carefully selecting her pieces, she'd make her way to the dressing room. Once inside, she'd get a great view of her chosen items in the full-length mirror that hung on the back of the door. A wide, excited smile broke out across her face as she'd hold each piece up to her chest with the hanger under her chin. Already imprinted in her brain, she saw each piece in a different light. After paying for the clothes, she'd head home as excitement mounted knowing what she wanted to do with each carefully selected piece. First off, a trip to the laundry room to wash them and get the 'storage' smell off. She'd take them from the dryer to her sewing room where she'd slip the articles, one by one, over a headless mannequin. She'd twist it, turn it, move it around and shift it in several different directions until she was certain she had it right. Feeling satisfied with the position she'd take a picture for 'before and after' shots for the album. With pad and pencil in hand, she'd begin taking notes on ideas that came to her from just looking at the dress.

Once again, each piece went back on the mannequin where she'd rip seams, pull off sleeves, and stick pins here and there to totally redesign the dress to her liking. She'd spend hours behind the sewing machine. It didn't matter how many times she had to rip out a seam, she never got discouraged. In the end, she had taken something vintage and redesigned it into chic couture with a modern, classy yet vintage twist. After pressing the seams into place and ironing out the wrinkles, she'd carefully hang it on a rack alongside the other beautifully designed dresses and wondered if anyone would ever appreciate these works of art.

* * *

Cassie swiped the screen to turn the phone off and went to unpack. She was there for at least three days, four at the most and there were pieces of clothing that needed a hanger. Emptying her cosmetic bag, she had the items lined up on the vanity when the hotel phone rang.

"Hello?"

"It's the front desk. There's an Amelia Benton to see you, shall I send her up?"

"Yes, please do," she said. Hanging up the phone, she went to the door, waited in her entrance for the elevator to ding and saw Amelia step out into the hall.

"Hey!"

"Hi there!" Waving, she picked up her pace.

Cassie pulled her in for a welcoming hug. "Come on in. I'm going to order in, will you join me?"

"Sure, thanks, I'll eat whatever you're ordering."

"Nonsense!" she said, passing her the hotel menu, "order whatever you want."

Looking over the hotel choices, she glanced over at Cassie and saw that she was elsewhere in thought. "Okay spill, Cassie," she said. Realizing she hadn't heard a word, she tried again. "Um, Cassie?"

"Oh, sorry, have you decided?"

"Yes, I have. I'll have the veggie lasagna and garlic bread. You may as well order a carafe of coffee for us as well," she said, as Cassie called room service to place their meal orders.

"Where were you?" Amelia inquired. "Spill!"

Taking her hand off the phone, Cassie got up off the bed, walked over to the window and looked out over the city before speaking. "Amelia, do you believe in love at first sight?"

"I suppose so, why?"

"I met the most wonderful man today," she said, almost in a sigh.

"Oh, do tell!" Amelia said with interest and went to join her at the window.

"We bumped into each other this afternoon at the airport back home in Kanyon Ridge. I mean literally 'bumped' into and sprawled out on the floor," she said, with her fingers spread out and looking at the floor.

"What!?" Amelia laughed, her hand covering her mouth. She could envision two bodies sprawled out on a busy airport floor.

"You heard me the first time and yes, just like that," she grinned, knowing they shared the same image.

"Tell me what happened, Sa… I mean Cassie, geez, I have a hard time calling you Cassie."

Thoughts of Noah momentarily engulfing her as she thought about her name change and still longed to see him after years of living as Cassie. A new name did not wipe out her memory, just her existence. It was imperative that Amelia remembered to use her new name both in the fashion industry and their personal lives. Being known by two different names would only cause confusion with agents and clients alike. Shaking the thoughts away, she kindly reminded her that it had been many years since the name change and to let it go already. "Now, about this man, as I was saying," she said, rolling her eyes. "We met this afternoon when I went to the airport to fly here. He was coming out, and I was going in, and we rammed into each other and ended up on the floor. He is the most gorgeous thing I have ever laid my eyes on," she said, swooning, "well, for a long time anyway."

"Well, Cassie Lucan, I've never seen you quite so giddy. He must be pretty special for you to be swooning over him. Who is he?" Amelia asked, with curiosity.

Reluctant to say it aloud, she spoke his name. "Drew Greyson and he's a pilot," she said waiting for Amelia's response.

"Greyson?" Amelia's face sobered, "Oh Cassie, really?"

"Yes, my thoughts exactly. What are the odds of that? Running from one Greyson and meeting another one." Cassie said as her thoughts wandered briefly to Grey at home with his grandmother.

"A pilot! Wow! Isn't Noah's dad a pilot? Or is he maybe an uncle?"

"Noah and I never talked about our families, I know that seems strange, but it's true. I saw the name 'Keri' on his phone, but I never knew what his mother's name was either. How weird is that, I also never knew where he lived, and I never brought him to my place either. Maybe it's just me being paranoid," she said, giving her hand a swipe into the air, "but he is striking in that uniform."

"I'll just bet he is, but he seems young to be a pilot," Amelia said, with a furrowed brow.

"Well, that's just it, he isn't 'young' per se," she said, using air quotations.

"What? Is he 'old' then?" Amelia asked, also using air quotes.

"No, I mean, he's older than we are."

"By how much?" Amelia was quick to ask.

Glancing out the window again, she spoke thoughtfully, "A lot, I think."

"Oh, Lord, what do you call 'a lot'? I never met Noah, but you do have some old pictures so does he look old enough to be Noah's father?"

"I'm not really sure, I know he is older, and he looks a lot like Noah, but he seems very youthful, and he's in great shape. Actually, Amelia, I don't really care how old he is, and I can't stop thinking about him! It's driving me crazy that he hasn't texted me even though it has only been a few hours. I was sure he would have either called or texted by now."

"Well, get with the times, girlfriend and text him!"

She looked down at the floor, sighed in annoyance and said, "I can't, I don't have his number."

"He has your number, but you don't have his? Is there something you aren't saying here?"

Cassie pulled her bottom lip to the side and chewed on it.

"He's married, isn't he?" Amelia said doubtfully.

Cassie switched from the bottom lip to the top and continued to chew. "He might be, did I forget to mention that?" she said, wrenching her face sideways.

"Yes, you did! How old would you guess this guy could be?"

Sticking her bottom lip out in thought, she looked at Amelia. "I'd say... thirty-eight ... forty...ish...maybe?"

"That's not old!"

"No, not really but I'm nearly twenty-five so at least he isn't twice my age. Surely, he isn't fifty! What does it matter anyway," she said, shrugging her shoulders, "if he is married, and I think he is, then I don't have a hope in hell anyway?"

"Sage! ... oh shit!... I mean, Cassie! What are you thinking!?"

"I know!" she said, raising her arms in the air and not at all offended at her name slip.

"You can't be serious? Not with a married man."

"I know, Amelia, I've thought of nothing else. There isn't anything that you can say that I haven't already told myself so could you just not act like a mother and be my friend for a few minutes."

"I'm sorry Cassie, I can only imagine what you are going through," she said giving her a friendly hug.

"Besides," Cassie continued, "he said he would call or text and he hasn't so it's probably just as well that it's over before it begins."

Their food arrived, and they ate, although very little and drank coffee until the carafe was empty.

"I don't know about you, but I could use something a little stronger, couldn't you?" Cassie asked, "Wanna go to the bar for a glass of wine?"

"It's still early," Amelia said, looking at her watch. "How about we do the bar thing later tonight, I have some designs that I'd like to show you."

"OK, fine, later then. Show me what you have."

Opening her tablet, Amelia scrolled to her page and handed it over to Cassie for her approval. They made a great team.

* * *

Amelia and Cassie had been friends as far back as the crib. They'd usually meet up, like tonight, whenever Cassie was in town. It had been a few years since these two young entrepreneurs had taken flight. Amelia had Cassie to thank for getting her designing business up and running. They've been partners since the day Cassie walked into her sewing room. While Cassie was busy scrolling Amelia's designs, her thoughts wandered back there as she clearly remembered a specific day.

She had just turned the iron off when the doorbell rang. Greeting Cassie, she invited her in.

Cassie inhaled deeply and turned to her friend. "It smells like fresh laundry in here, what are you doing? Is there anything I can help you with?"

Amelia blushed and dropped her head. "How are things at home?"

"Things are fine. Thanks for asking but, what's up Amelia?" Cassie asked, touching her arm, "why are you blushing?"

"It's embarrassing I guess, I just haven't shared this part of me with anyone."

"Doing laundry? Really?"

Amelia giggled and said, "No, not really ... but yes ... I guess," she stammered, "just something I've been working on."

"Would you make sense, please," Cassie said, laughing with Amelia. "Seriously, what are you doing and why are you being so secretive?"

"Do you really want to see?" Amelia asked excitedly.

"Of course, show me!"

Slipping her arm through Cassie's, she led her to her bedroom/sewing room. Before opening the door, she turned and said, "Remember, I haven't shown these to anyone before so please don't be too critical." Chewing on her lip for a few seconds she changed her mind. "No, by all means, be as critical as you like, I need a second opinion."

"What do you have in here anyway?" she asked, as Amelia swung the door open to display several racks of beautiful dresses.

"Amelia!" Cassie inhaled deeply and clasped her hand to her chest in shock. "Wh..what is this? Where did you get this beautiful wardrobe?" she asked, walking over to the racks.

If anyone knew fashion, it was Cassie. She had been modelling for years, and her opinion meant a lot to Amelia.

Standing back from Cassie, she gave her the room to look around and judge the pieces. The expression on her face caused Amelia to smile, knowing Cassie liked them. Lifting hangers off the rack, she turned them back and forth, front to back, hung them up and moved on to the next dress. Cassie touched and fondled each piece as she pushed aside hanger after hanger displaying the most beautiful designs that she had ever seen.

"Incredible! Amelia! I love these! Look at this stuff! Where did you get these pieces?" she asked, still browsing the racks.

Blushing, Amelia had dropped her eyes as a memory took her back to another time when Cassie, known only as Sage back then, had called her, crying hysterically about being pregnant. Now she was Cassie Lucan, a top model again with a new beginning.

Cassie's voice brought her back to their conversation.

"Hey... where did you go?"

Amelia shook her head slightly, erasing the memory and shrugged her shoulders. She didn't want to bring up reminders of a painful time which, she was certain, was still in the process of healing.

"Amelia, I asked you what all this is about? I don't understand. Why did you bring me in here to show me this stuff? Where did you get these?" she asked, swiping her hand towards the clothing.

"I... um... I... made them," she said, shrugging her shoulders as if she was embarrassed to admit it or even take the credit. "You're the first person I've shown my work to because I don't know how they'd be received."

"Are you serious! You... made... these?" Cassie said slowly, almost in a breathy whisper.

"Yes, I did. I've always had a passion for fashion, and I wanted you to be the first to see them."

Tears filled Cassie's eyes as she brought her fingers up to her top lip.

"Amelia, I never knew this side of you. We practically grew up together, and yet you've managed to keep this a secret. These are positively and unbelievably beautiful!"

"You really think so?" she asked, raising up on her toes excitedly.

"Absolutely! I mean, we have to do something with these!" Cassie said, kick-starting the adrenalin.

"Like what?"

"Show them to my agent! Amelia, maybe we can get a fashion show together to give you some exposure. We can work together to show your work." Cassie's mind was in overdrive as Amelia listened to her ramble.

"You can design the clothes, and I'll model them or... we can both model them," she said, in a rush, "at fashion shows so we can get your name out there. A designer wearing her own creations on the runway will be huge!" she said spreading her arms wide. Cassie stopped short at what she was saying, and a crease formed on her forehead. "You do have a label, don't you?"

"A label?" Amelia asked, lost in the fashion lingo.

"Yes, your own label?"

"Ah, no, Cassie, all I do is choose the outfit I want and redesign it and this," she said, sweeping toward the racks, "is what I come up with. Here is an album that I've put together of before and after shots of each design. This is only a fraction of what I've done I have more racks upstairs and several more albums."

Flipping through the many pages of pictures, Cassie was in awe of Amelia's hidden talent.

"I can't believe you didn't tell me, but we can do this! We must get you established so your designs can stay as your own unique creations. We will need to come up with a company name or a label, register it with Joint Stocks and then we are in business!"

"Got a pencil?" she said sitting down. Cassie immediately began to plan.

"We need a name so let's try and come up with one."

Amelia was excited as her mind whirled trying to help Cassie brainstorm for a label name. Not knowing what to do, she was drawing a blank.

"Okay," Cassie said, "you take these old-style pieces, redesign them into something new, fun and gorgeous. So, we can call them 'retro' pieces, right?"

"Yes, I guess you can call them retro," Amelia said, "or restored pieces."

Amelia talked, and Cassie took notes as they brainstormed.

"You've just given these old pieces of clothing another chance with these designs, Amelia. I am so proud of you!" She stopped talking, and Amelia could imagine the wheels turning in Cassie's brain.

"What? Why that look?"

"I think I just came up with a name for your label!"

"Really!?" This was all new to Amelia, and she was stunned with all the dreams that Cassie was helping to make come true for her. "Tell me!"

"Remember when I said, you've given these another chance?'

"Yeah," Amelia nodded excitedly.

Scribbling her thoughts down on her notepad, she flipped it around to show Amelia. She moved her pencil across the pad as she explained her idea to Amelia. "We'll put 'Designed by Amelia Benton' across the top of the label and under the name in the right-hand corner we have several choices here, like 'New to You', '2nd Chance' or 'Passion 4 Fashion'," she looked at her and said, "your words, so which do you prefer? There will be an automatic front page splash," she said, spreading her fingers fan-like "with you and your clothing line, the process you go through for each

194

design and showing the uniqueness of each garment. There are no copycats, no cloning in bulk, just your original design so everyone will know, not only the label but, who Amelia Benton really is! This will be huge! What do you think?"

Amelia's eyes roamed quickly across the pad in front of her and with two fingers pressed against her lips, she gave Cassie's ideas some deep thought. "I think it's all pretty overwhelming, to say the least."

"I know, but you'll be famous one day, Amelia!"

Looking down at the scratch pad, Amelia pointed to the last choice, "I like this one."

"OK, 'Passion 4 Fashion' it is then. You know, Amelia, I believe we have our label! So... do you like it?"

"I do, I love your idea, and I'm so glad you stopped by today. This is going to make a huge difference in my life if this takes off. I have been out of school for a few years, doing menial jobs here and there with no real interest in doing anything except to sew. This is so exciting, and it makes me feel like I may finally have a start on a new career path."

"We have to run this by my agent right away, so what we'll do is take your albums with us and show her what it is that you've actually done and let her decide our next move."

Cassie assured her that she would be back in touch once she'd had a chance to speak to her agent. Amelia was on cloud nine with new hope that a career in the fashion industry was close at hand.

22

Landing the plane in Toronto, Drew thought about Cassie and wished he'd asked her where she was staying. Making his way out of the airport he turned on his cell to find yet another text from Keri along with a frantic voicemail.

Call me! it read, and from the seemingly frantic emphasis, he called her back.

"Drew, please come home, we have to talk about this, I have been calling all week."

"Is Noah OK?" he asked.

"Yes, Noah's fine, why?"

"Then there is nothing to talk about. It is done, Keri, stop texting me and stop calling my cell and leaving messages. Don't make me do something that you'll regret, I mean it Keri. When you hear from my lawyer, then we'll talk."

'But…"

Abruptly ending the conversation, he went outside and found a taxi to take him to his hotel. To rid himself of her constant calls and texts, he opened the settings on his phone and blocked her calls. *If that doesn't work I'll change my number, but one way or the other, she will get the message.'*

Walking into the lobby, he was greeted at the reception desk. "Welcome back to The Carleton, Mr. Greyson, we weren't expecting you back this soon."

"I wasn't expecting to be back either," he said, "is my room available by any chance?"

"It sure is!" he said as he programmed a key card. "Here you go, Sir, room 444, have a pleasant stay."

"Thank you," he nodded, but instead of taking the elevator up to his room he decided to go into the bar for a quick, well deserved drink before going up for a shower. Stepping away from the desk, he turned back to ask, "May I leave my bag here, with you, while I go into the bar?" he said, motioning with his thumb.

"Sure, Mr. Greyson, I'll set it here behind the desk," he said, taking the handle from Drew.

"Thanks a lot, I appreciate it," he said, strolling over to the bar.

* * *

Cassie and Amelia both ordered a glass of white wine, but not before the waiter asked for ID. Cassie was already defensive and annoyed that she hadn't heard from Drew and the waiter was testing her patience.

"You ask me for ID every time I come in here!" she said rifling through her wallet.

"Sorry, rules are rules, ID please."

They both opened their wallets to their driver's license and nodding, he walked away.

Amelia looked over towards the bar and raised an eyebrow. Cassie saw her reaction and asked out of curiosity. "What's that look for?"

"Speaking of handsome pilots," she said, nodding towards the bar with her chin.

"Well, the only handsome pilot I want to see is back in Kanyon Ridge," she said, not bothering to look around.

At the bar, Drew ordered a beer. Taking out his phone and the napkin that had Cassie's number on, he added it to his contact list. A coaster dropped on the counter, along with a beer and he began to text.

Cassie's felt her phone vibrate against her thigh and she reaches into her bag to check it. *Hi Cassie, it's Drew*

"Oh, my God! It's Drew!"

Hi there, I was hoping to hear from you she texted back.

His phone was lying on the bar when it beeped. Picking it up, he read the message and smiled.

Sorry for taking so long to contact you, long story

Her eyes peeled at the bar, Amelia noticed that every time he used his phone, Cassie's phone beeped and when Cassie sent a text, the pilot picked up his phone. She nudged Cassie under the table with her foot. When Cassie looked up, Amelia said, "Send him a reply."

I can't wait to hear it Cassie typed and pressed send.

As soon as she sent it, his phone screen lit up, and Amelia smiled like the cat that ate the canary.

"What are you smiling at?"

Amelia lifted her chin towards the bar again, and Cassie followed her stare. "That's your handsome pilot, isn't it?"

Cassie got up from her chair but nervously sat back down again. She began to type.

*would you like to join me for a drink? *

Pressing send, she got up and walked towards him while quickly typing.

turn around

Picking up his phone to read her message, he lowered his phone and turned to see Cassie walking towards him. Dropping his phone into his pocket, he went over to meet her. Opening her arms, he walked into them and held her tightly not believing his luck.

"What are you doing here? I thought you were back in Kanyon Ridge."

"I was, that's the long story."

"I can't wait to hear it then."

"So, what are you doing here?' he asked, pointing to nowhere in particular.

"This is where I stay during gigs."

Furrowing his brow and narrowing his eyes, he said, "So do I. I've stayed at The Carleton for years on my layovers, but I've never seen you."

"Same here. Sometimes I am here anywhere between two and five days depending on the shoot."

"And yet we bump into each other in Kanyon Ridge. Are you from there?"

"I grew up there during my school years. Then my mom and I moved to Kanyon Creek where I lease a condo." Somewhere in the back of her mind she reminded herself to shut up and not give out too much personal information.

"So, we are from the same town then," he said, "small world."

Taking the subject off herself and their hometown, she said, "I'm here with a friend."

A thousand thoughts swirled around in his brain when he heard those words. *'Of course, she would be here with someone!'* His heart sinking at her words, he didn't want to show his disappointment. *'Oh, God, she's here with someone, and I'm keeping her away from her table, you jackass! Did you really think this gorgeous creature would be in a bar alone!?'* "I'm sorry, I didn't mean to intrude. I'll let you get back..."

"No, no, it's fine, come, let me introduce you to my friend," she said, taking his hand.

"No, seriously, I don't want to intrude on your evening." The truth was, he didn't want to see her with another man.

She saw the look of embarrassment on his face, and she wanted to put him at ease. "Please, come and meet my friend," she said, with a wave towards a table.

The only table he saw, without a single man sitting at it, was one with a beautiful redhead about Cassie's age. Amelia lifted her hand and wiggled her fingers and relief filled his entire being. Moving his feet towards the table, he saw Amelia get up to bring a third chair to the table.

"Amelia, this is my friend, Drew Greyson. Drew, this is my closest friend in the world, Amelia Benton."

She reached out her hand while taking in his awesomeness. The word 'handsome' just wasn't cutting it for her. He was absolutely everything and more than Cassie had described, and she knew if she were in Cassie's shoes she would ignore any piece of advice she had given earlier.

"It's very nice to meet you, Drew, please join us," she said, pointing to the empty chair.

"Thank you, for inviting me."

"Thank you, for accepting." *'Okay!'* Amelia thought, *'stop being ridiculous, he is just a guy, Oh Lord, and what a guy!'*

Cassie smiled as she watched Amelia fall all over herself in Drew's presence. Drew didn't seem to pick up on it since he only had eyes for Cassie and he still couldn't believe he was actually with her!

'*How did this happen?*' he thought, '*he found her, or they found each other ... twice in one day.*'

"So, Amelia...?"

Her head shot up when she heard her name.

"Do you live here, in Toronto?"

"Yes, I do, I'm from Kanyon Creek though, but I moved here several years ago, when our business," she said, pointing to Cassie, "expanded considerably. It's great since I get to see Sa... ahem," she cleared her throat and swallowed hard... "um... Cassie almost every week. We work together, you know."

Cassie did a double take at Amelia's misstep, but she knew that she rambled when she was nervous, so she just sat there, watched and enjoyed.

"No, I didn't know," he said turning his attention to Cassie.

"Actually, I mentioned Amelia, my business partner, at the restaurant where we had coffee. It's a long story, perhaps for another time." She was elated to be with Drew and being able to share him with Amelia was an even bigger bonus. She knew her friend well enough to know that she was in awe of Drew and was not, in any way, in competition.

She and Amelia had many friends in common who were their age and older, but Drew was in a whole other category. He could have been 'King Andrew' sitting there and the only thing missing was the crown. His tall, lanky frame, the pilot's uniform, twinkling eyes even in the dim lights of the bar, a full head of dark brown hair speckled with grey. '*Oh, he was king alright,*' Cassie thought, '*and he can rule my castle any time!*'

Sitting back in his chair, he reached for his drink and for once in a million years he felt truly relaxed. They both thought he was pretty cool. Not wanting to leave either one out of the conversation, he talked to both, giving them equal attention.

"Well, it was very nice to meet you, Drew, but it's time for me to go home," Amelia said, sliding her chair out and standing up.

"It is a pleasure meeting you, Amelia," Drew said, getting to his feet, "do you have a ride home?"

"No, I'll just wait outside for a taxi."

"Um, no," he said, "that's not acceptable, wait here." He walked out of the bar and over to the reception desk. Cassie and Amelia watched curiously as he chatted with the desk clerk. They saw him pass a few bills and pointed into the bar then returned to their table.

"I've ordered a cab for you, and it'll be a few minutes, so sit down and relax with us while you wait."

The girls looked at each other, shrugged, and Amelia sat back down. They were impressed to have a gentleman at their table. Several minutes later, a loud voice resonated from the bar entrance.

"Amelia Benton! Taxi for Amelia Benton."

Raising her hand and sliding her chair back again, she stood up. "Thank you, Drew, I appreciate the ride," she said and reached out for a hug from each of them.

"It's taken care of, just be safe," said Drew.

"That was very kind of you to arrange for a taxi for Amelia and have them come inside to announce her! You never know how long a person can wait on the street for cabs to appear."

"It isn't anything I wouldn't do for my own."

Cassie left the conversation there in case it was something she didn't want to know or hear. If there was more to it, she was quite certain he'd tell her in his own time.

"It's getting late, I should be leaving too."

"May I walk you to your room?"

"Yes, I'd like that."

As they were passing the front desk, the manager got Drew's attention. "Excuse me, Mr. Greyson?"

"Yes?"

"Your bag, Sir?"

"Oh, yes, thank you, I totally forgot."

Glancing over at Cassie, he said, "I completely understand, Sir."

Taking the extended handle from the night clerk, he heard him whisper, "Have a good evening, Sir," nodding toward Cassie.

Looking at him, Drew squinted his eyes, tilted his head in Cassie's direction and softly said, "no, it's not like that."

"I see, well good night then Mr. Greyson, and thank you again for staying with us here at The Carleton."

Drew nodded his head and lead Cassie to the elevator. Once inside, he asked her which floor she was on.

"Fourth."

"Hmm."

When the elevator doors parted, they both stepped out into the hall. Cassie turned left and Drew followed.

"I'm right here," she said, pointing at 443 on her door.

"Seriously?"

"Yes, why?"

He turned slightly and gestured over his shoulder with his thumb, "I'm right here," he said, pointing to 444. '*And there were those triple numbers again,*' he noticed.

"No way!" she laughed.

"Well, since you are 'home' how about you go and get out of that uniform and into something a bit more comfortable while I'll order a carafe of coffee for us. Sound ok?"

"Awesome! I do need a quick shower though, do you mind?"

"No, not at all, take your time. I need to freshen up too."

"See you in a few then," he said, as they both slid their door cards into the locks and disappeared into their rooms.

23

Fresh coffee arrived shortly after she had freshened up and gotten into something less restrictive. Pajamas wouldn't be appropriate, which she longed for, but thankfully she had brought a pair of lounge pants and a matching silk tank top.

Asking the waiter to put the coffee on the table, she signed for it to go on her room tab. Drew appeared at the door as the waiter was leaving.

"Good timing," she said, "come on in."

"You look very nice," he said, as he did a quick scan, so she wouldn't think he was an ogre.

"You're looking more relaxed too," she said, running her eyes over him. Hair still damp and dressed in a pair of slightly wrinkled jeans, his white tee shirt showing off his lean frame. '*He smells so good!*' she thought.

"Thank you," he said, "but I'm afraid I look a bit wrinkled since my clothes have been packed in the suitcase for a while."

"You look fine."

"May I pour?" he asked, gesturing to the coffee.

"Yes, please, black for me."

He passed her a cup, and she watched as he added a spoon tip of sugar, a few drops of milk and stirred before speaking.

"How about that long story?" she asked, trying not to sound too inquisitive.

Drawing his lips into his teeth, he searched her face. Feeling nervous, she never wavered. '*What would he tell her? Why is he here?*' she wondered, '*The last she knew he was on his way home.'* Looking at him and giving him an understanding smile, she knew whatever it was she'd have to accept.

"Can we sit?" he asked.

"Sure," she said, making her way to the table. It was the only place in the room that had two chairs. The loveseat was too close and she sure as hell was not going to sit anywhere near a bed with him looking like that! '*No way*!'

Leaning forward, he put the flats of his arms on his knees, pressed his fingertips together and cleared his throat. "When I left you at the airport, I headed back to the motel."

"Motel?"

"Yes, I'm currently staying at the Kanyon Ridge Motel. Anyway, while I was driving, I saw my life playing out before my eyes. From high school to marriage, pilot school and to the birth of my son." He paused briefly giving her a chance to speak.

"So… you're married?"

"Yes, but recently separated and already on with the divorce."

Relief rolled off her. "Go on," she said tenderly, "what happened next? or … would you rather not…?"

"You made me realize how very lonely my life had been. I don't remember having moments like we had at the restaurant," he said, motioned between them then putting his fingertips together again. "I mean, tender moments, where you don't want to let go and happy to be where you are. I just wanted to head in the same direction as you and never once did I dream that I'd get a second chance but… God, I'm so glad I did. I didn't have the nerve or even felt I had the right to ask you questions, but then after you left, I wish I had"

"You had my number, you could have called and asked, Drew, so what aren't you saying?"

"What I am saying is, that after our coffee meeting, I finally know what I want and what I don't want."

'*Oh God*,' she thought, '*here comes rejection*.'

"Cassie, I am forty-two years old, and I can't remember being happy like I was today just having a cup of coffee with you, and now, here with you tonight. I know you are probably thinking I am just an old fool. You are likely the same age as my son which means I am old enough to be your father, yet I can't help how I feel about you."

Her heart quickened at his words, but she waited until he was finished.

"I can't begin to tell you what is in my heart, Cassie. I certainly don't want to make a fool of myself, but I feel as though I am falling in love with you."

He heard her gasp softly and tears pooled in her eyes.

"Cassie, I'm sorry, I shouldn't have said anything, now you really must think of me as an idiot!"

"Drew! No! It's just the opposite. I thought I was being the foolish one. I didn't know I could feel like this," she wanted to add 'again,' but she didn't think it was necessary. "I feel the same way as you. This has been such a crazy day!"

"Wh...what? Seriously? Cassie, I... um... I can't... um..." Standing up, he took her hands, tugged her off her chair and pulled her to him in a tight hug. He just wanted to feel her in his arms again. He loved how her hands clung to his back with passion. He knew she wanted to be in his arms as badly as he wanted her in his.

"This is the 'coming home' feeling I've never felt… until now," he said, whispering the words into her hair as his hand cupped the back of her neck.

Cassie couldn't help but wonder what kind of a home life he'd had but it sounded as though it had been a sad existence. Pulling away from him, she dropped her eyes to his mouth and sliding her hands behind his head, she drew his lips to hers. A moan escaped his body as passion began to build. Cupping her face in his hands, he pulled away from her, and his hands slid down to the top of her shoulders. Taking a step back, he kept his hands in place. Cassie's mind drifted to the cell phone at the restaurant.

"The lady on your cell phone? I must ask, is 'Keri' your wife?

"Yes, she is but also my soon-to-be ex-wife, we separated a week ago."

"What are we going to do now, Drew?"

"This is real, Cassie, and let me make myself perfectly clear. I did not bring this up to draw your feelings out in hopes of having someone to fall back on. I am not looking for a replacement. My son moved out several years ago and seriously, I should have too since there was absolutely no reason to stay. I am not looking for a fling or an affair. As unhappy as my life has been over the years, I can honestly say, with a clear conscience, that I have never been unfaithful. The closest I have come to cheating is with you and our kiss in the restaurant. Being free, for the first time in many years, I can't and won't refer to it as cheating."

He deliberately left out the part about Keri cheating on him. Right now, he felt it wasn't relevant, the important thing was that he was free to be with her.

Cassie's mind went back to another dimension in her life as he spoke. Interrupting him, she asked the dreaded question. "Your son?"

"Yes, Noah."

'*There it is,*' she thought, with a heavy heart, '*the past jumping into my present.*' Swallowing hard, she had to say it. "I... um... went to school with Noah." She hadn't spoken his name aloud in years to anyone except Amelia.

"I suspected you did since you look about the same age and you said you had spent your school years in Kanyon Ridge. So, does this change things for us now?"

"Not for me," she said... lying a little, "how about you?"

"Not at all."

Looking at him, she couldn't deny the stark resemblances between Drew and Noah. Their same color hair and those awesome, blue eyes. She began to question her judgment about Drew. 'The attraction she'd had for him at their first meeting... was it because he reminded her of Noah? The height, the build, those eyes and the smile. Was she looking for a safe replacement?' Not a day had passed that she that had not missed Noah. Since the day she and her mother left town, she knew she had to move on without him. The chance just wasn't worth the risk.

"I don't know why, but I never knew anything about Noah's family, but I do see a resemblance," she said, knowing it was a stretch since it may as well have been Noah standing there into the future being Drew's mini.

"This is a big step, Drew, are you sure you've taken enough time to think this through? This really isn't just a 'step' it's more of a leap."

"Yes, I know, but this is way overdue, Cassie, I just existed until I met you. Meeting you has made it quite clear that I have missed out on a lot of my life and it is time to start living again."

"I'm sorry you've had such a tough go of it, Drew, we only have one life, and all we can hope for is to eventually get it right."

"Hey, this isn't supposed to be a pity party, it's more of a celebration!" Drew said, trying to put a lighter tone to the conversation.

"What is your schedule like tomorrow?" he asked.

Reaching for her appointment book, she flipped a few pages then shrugged her shoulder. "I have an appointment around, elevenish. Then a fitting with the models at one o'clock, a run through before the fashion show begins," she said, hunching a shoulder, "around three thirty. That should run until four thirty, five at the latest."

"Would you like to meet up for dinner or coffee and if that doesn't work, we can have breakfast in the morning."

"Dinner sounds like you could be staying?" she asked tilting her head sideways hoping for a 'yes.'

"Oh, I'm staying," he said, nodding his head, "that's exactly what it sounds like," he grinned, knowing he had just made up his mind. He really didn't want to be anywhere else, and when Cassie smiled at him, he totally forgot where he was. "I'm glad you're staying," she said, throwing her arms around his neck and kissing him. He allowed himself to get lost in their moment knowing that he loved her already.

Pulling her close, she tingled from head to toe. A moan escaped from deep in her throat sending waves of passion coursing through his veins. There were no thoughts of guilt, no fear of someone finding them in a compromising situation, this was total freedom to do whatever he wanted to do, and with whomever he wanted to do it with. A luxury he had been denied since he was seventeen years old, and it felt strangely wonderful.

"Drew," she said through breathy whispers.

He moved her back towards the bed. There was nothing he wanted in this world more than to feel Cassie's body next to his. She followed him, freely. Breaking the kiss, he took a couple of deep breaths and searched her face hoping to bring his heart rate down. "Are you sure you are OK with this?" he asked, breathing like he had just run a marathon.

"More than I've ever been about anything," she said, reaching for his mouth again.

As he laid her down on the bed all thoughts of anything except Cassie, left his mind. Passion was at its peak, and they were a perfect fit. Slipping out of their clothes, Drew pulled Cassie close to his naked body. Skin to skin, Drew had never felt the sensation of holding a naked woman. This was a brand-new concept for him, and he had to learn how to make love to a woman at the age of forty-two. Trying not to seem pathetic, he was ready and waiting for her, and she felt his passion as she lay close to him. Cassie was as inexperienced as he was since she was not well versed in the act either. He seemed to instinctively know what to do when it counted, and it was the first time he would actually be conscious and able to enjoy this ride. He devoured her body with his hands and lips. Trying not to close her eyes, she struggled to keep her thoughts from going back to Noah. This was Drew, her time with Noah was over but... oh... the rush of memories...

Cassie, asleep in his arms, Drew was filled with many new emotions. *'This is the way love is supposed to be,'* he thought, pulling her tighter to kiss the top of her head. Relaxing a bit, he lay in the dimness of the room trying desperately to shake Keri and her antics from creep into his thoughts. But as he stared out into the darkness, he brought back the memory of where it all started. At the Kanyon Ridge yacht club beach party twenty-five years ago, to the very spot where his world went to pieces. It was when Keri pulled the ultimate deception with the drug, but that was all behind him now, and so was Keri. Traumatized by her for years, he tried, with everything in him, to leave that part of his world in the past and enjoy the freedom of life that he had longed for.

24

Cassie initiated the offer for Drew to move in with her several weeks after they met. Staying at the Kanyon Ridge Inn, it was only a bridge ride away between there and Kanyon Creek.

"Move in with me," she offered, when he decided it was definitely time to find an apartment.

"Seriously? We haven't known each other that long, Cassie."

Snuggling into his chest, "long enough for me to know I want you to move in," she said, softly. "We are far enough away from everyone so there will be no gossip and the private elevator opens up into my condo so that no one will see you in the halls and besides, I have all this space," she said, waving her hand around. "My mother lives on a lower floor, but we always check on each other before visits. She actually works for me, so she is pretty busy." Deliberately not mentioning her duties, she decided to leave that conversation for another time.

"I've been wanting a place of my own for a while now," he said, "living in a motel for close to a month is getting pretty lame."

"So...? Living here wouldn't be as lame..." she teased. "You can even have your own bathroom... bonus! You'll have to use the spare bedroom closet though because the master is taken." She was trying to make it as simple and convincing as possible, but the decision was totally up to him whether or not he was ready. Getting off the bed and walking toward the bathroom, she tilted her head, "The offer is still on the table," she said, "it's up to you, but I'll be right in here while you think about it." Teasingly, she looked over her shoulder, pulled her shirt over her head and tossed it at him, "totally your decision."

"That's a pretty fair offer, I'd say."

"It comes off the table, though, in about... oh... five minutes, so you'd better decide cuz you're definitely on the clock," she teased. Disappearing from his view, Drew knew she was teasing and leaped across the room behind her.

"OK, you win, I'm here if you want me," he said, taking her into his arms. He felt more at home in her condo than he ever felt in his own house. So many wasted years. But it took going through them to finally be home.

"Tomorrow," he said, "I'm going over to Kanyon Ridge to get my belongings from the motel, and it will give me a chance to clean up some loose ends while I'm there. I will likely be away for several hours."

"Sounds good to me and while you're gone, I'll give the closet in the spare room a good cleaning to make room for your stuff. This is exciting, I can't wait for you to get back." Reaching for her, he held her close while thinking how great it was that she wanted him here with her.

* * *

Driving to Kanyon Ridge alone, Drew decided to visit with Noah. It was a chance for him to relay the plan that he and Cassie had come up with before he'd left the condo. He and Noah had not had a talk about his leaving Keri, and he was uncertain as to how much he knew. He had to tread lightly and not divulge too much of the mess he and Keri had created in their lives. It wasn't fair to drag Noah into that unfortunate situation.

Once they discussed his leaving he would basically tell him that he was going to make a fresh start in Kanyon Creek. It was only a short drive across the bridge so while he was there, he was eager to begin to familiarize himself with the spa. He and Cassie had agreed, there would be no mention of another person in his life, he was simply just moving on with the rest of his life. It would be too soon to announce that he'd found someone new in just the short time he'd been away from Keri. He just needed a fresh start with his newly found freedom and Kanyon Ridge was just too close for comfort.

Happy, as always, to see his dad, Noah listened to his father respectfully and was quite happy that he was getting on with his life. He'd known from the tension in the house that neither of his parents had been happy. He was even more excited to hear that he was ready to learn more about the business and that a plan was in the works to retire. Offering him a set of keys, he was more than ready for his dad to join him.

* * *

Drew had arranged a meeting with his longtime friend and lawyer, Randy Kimble to give him the full version of his plan and thought it wise to hand the vial over to him for safekeeping. Not wanting to cause a conflict of interest, he'd asked his advice on a personal matter, and Randy gave him the name and number of a friend of his and the papers that Drew had asked for.

Without delay, Drew made an appointment to meet with Randy's friend, Matthew Conwell.

Scanning the motel room one more time, he dropped the card onto the desk and closing the door behind him, he headed out for his appointment.

Once in his office, Drew turned the file over with a list of what he wanted taken care. He'd added another page that he had written in the motel room when he'd gone in to clean the room out. He'd made it clear that it was for Cassie's eyes only. She had invited him into her home and loved him, his baggage, warts and all, so he had to make it right. He loved her, and he knew he would until he drew his last breath. She was the one who made him the happiest and had offered him a home, so she deserved what he had to give.

Thinking long and hard, about how he was going to pull it off, he could envision Keri's reaction, but he didn't care. Payback is a bitch, and she didn't deserve anywhere near what Cassie deserved. From the twenty-five years of her crap to the last several beautiful weeks with Cassie was no comparison. His mind was made up, and it was done.

Not an ounce of regret followed him as he left Matthew Conwell's office and headed back across the bridge… to Cassie and home…

Cassie had worked on the closet while Drew was away and decided that a few wicker baskets were in order for Drew's personal items. Making a list of possibilities, she stuck it on the fridge.

Stepping out of the elevator, he was welcomed by a smiling face and open arms; something he'd never experienced. It felt wonderful and he was satisfied with the decision he'd made earlier.

Helping him unpack, they arranged the closet to suit him. When she mentioned the baskets, he thought it was an excellent idea.

* * *

Meandering around The Emporium, Cassie looked for baskets while Drew hoped to find a few pieces of deck furniture, as a surprise for her. Suddenly, something pulled Cassie to another section. Stopping abruptly, a familiar scent filled her nostrils. *'Noah,'* her head shot up as a memory settled into her senses. A man was walking toward the exit. *'Noah! Had he been right here in the same store? Turn around, please turn around,'* she willed, wandering over as he moved closer to the exit doors. *'Noah, turn around,'* she hoped against hope, but to no avail. She never saw his face, but the lingering scent had told her it was him and her heart thumped rapidly as she watched him disappear from the store. *'So close!'* she thought.

"Cassie?"

Startled by his voice, she jumped after realizing she was there with Drew.

"Hi."

"Where were you?"

"I thought I saw someone I used to know, but I guess not, I couldn't get a good look," she said, looking defeated.

"Would you like to walk around the mall to take another look?"

Cassie slowly shook her head as if knowing this wasn't the time but then, ‘*when would there be a good time to run into Noah?*’ she thought. He had always been a permanent resident in her mind. Each time she'd think about him it was like a snapshot or a Kodak moment of their time in another life. She remembered, during their school years, while walking along the water's edge, he'd told her that his dad had met his mother on the same beach. Memories flooded her, filling her from a time she had longed to forget but they kept popping up in the most unlikely places and times. When she'd pass a men's shop and catch a slight whiff of the cologne he wore or a man in the distance that resembled him. A common gesture or a smile, the beach where the tide nibbled at their toes, so many things brought back pictures that she had captured in her mind's eye. They all had an enormous hold on her heart, and she could barely breathe when she'd think about their time together. Thoughts of the blackboard scene and the loft were indelibly imprinted in her brain, and they ran at full speed, like a film, drawing out old feelings that should have died a long time ago. The blackboard scene had nothing on the loft. The loft was everything she had ever hoped for.

“OK, then,” he said, bringing her out of her thoughts, “let's see if you like the selections I've made, come with me.”

Sliding her arm into his, she allowed him to lead her away... away from thoughts of Noah.

The white wicker deck furniture was a set made up of a rocker and glider stool, a comfy armchair and a round ottoman type loveseat. Included in the set were overstuffed cushions with dark green fern-like leaves on a white background. They had decided on a glass top table and two black wrought iron, cafe style chairs that would be perfect for intimate dinners and breakfasts. Cassie hadn't bothered with deck furniture since she rarely used the deck for anything other than a quick walk out with her morning coffee. This was absolutely perfect, choosing furniture with Drew. She had never shared this part of her life with anyone. It was Drew's first time too since he'd mentioned that Keri had been the shopper at their house. This was one more thing for them both to remember. Making memories that would last a lifetime. Cassie was surprised when at the checkout, Drew passed over his credit card.

"You didn't have to do that, Drew."

"It's my place too now, so I want to. Besides, I'll get the benefits of sharing some of our meals on it with you." Pulling her in close, he kissed her cheek and thought about all the days and years ahead they'd have to share with each other.

Once the furniture was delivered, they enjoyed putting it together and having their first meal on it that night. Even though it was only a delivered pizza and a glass of wine, they couldn't have been happier.

A few months later they were on the deck having brunch when Drew announced that he was going to Kanyon Ridge.

"It's time I took an active interest in the spa now that I have officially put my resignation in. It's time to retire," he said, "so I can spend time learning the business and having some quality time with you and Noah."

It was difficult hearing Drew speak about her and Noah in the same sentence, but she sucked it up, smiled and pretended it meant nothing. Noah was Drew's son, like it or not and she knew he would be saying his name from time to time. As long as she didn't have to see him or have any contact with him, she'd be fine. Even after nearly eight years, it still hurt her heart to hear his name aloud. She'd had years of avoiding saying it even though she had a constant reminder of him in Grey.

"Are you sure you want to go in today? It's Sunday and no one will be there."

"I'm OK with that for now. I won't be in anyone's way if I'm there alone. I'll see you when I get back, and maybe we can have a late supper on the deck," Drew offered.

"That would be wonderful, I'll wait until you get home before I prepare something, or you could pick up a pizza," she said, with a lusty pout.

"I'll see what I can do," he said, with a laugh. Holding her tightly for several minutes, he lovingly kissed her then pressed the elevator button. Stepping in, he waved as the doors closed, and he was gone.

25

Spending some time with her mother and Grey, Cassie stayed busy to avoid boredom. Knowing Drew would be away for hours, they did some necessary shopping, had a snack and then called it a day. She watched a movie on TV, had a shower and realized she was hungry again. She made an egg sandwich and drank a cup of herbal tea. Inevitably, boredom set in around ten-thirty and she wondered if Drew was on his way home. The place seemed empty without him in it, and it was strange that he hadn't called about dinner plans.

He had been accepting shorter flights recently so that he wasn't away for any great length of time. Cassie had taken an extended leave of absence from modelling so they could enjoy their time together. They loved each other's company, and since their love was still new and exciting, it mattered that they spend as much time together as possible. Wandering around the apartment, she cleaned up the bit of mess she'd made earlier and headed off to bed to wait for Drew.

Waking with a start, Cassie's heart pounded as if she'd had a bad dream. Glancing sleepily at the clock on the nightstand, it was 12:12. Her bed felt cold as she slipped back into a restless sleep. As the sun rose over the lake, Cassie slid her hand across the bed. It was empty and still neatly turned down as she had done for him every night for the last several months. Peering at the clock, it was 5:55 and an eerie feeling crept over her. Sliding her legs over the side of the bed, she pushed her arms into the sleeves of her robe. Tying it around her waist, she headed for the kitchen hoping to find him there. It wasn't like Drew to be away all night without calling and causing her to worry. Dialing his cellphone, she impatiently listened to it ring and then it went to voicemail. Hanging up before the message prompt ended, she slid the phone into her pocket and sauntered over to the deck windows. "Where are you, Drew?" she said into wide open space.

Fumbling with the coffee machine, she managed to get a cup of coffee. Watching the clock and pacing around the condo, she was at her wit's end.

Standing at the balcony door again, she gazed out over the lake and wondered again where he might be. Debating whether or not to call her mother, her cell phone rang cutting the silence. Grabbing her phone from her pocket, she saw a blocked caller on the screen. *'Maybe he's calling from the spa,'* she thought.

"Drew?"

"Cassie Lucan, please," said the unfamiliar voice.

"This is Cassie, who is this?"

"This is Doctor Wills at Kanyon Memorial Hospital, your phone number was located as a contact number for Andrew Greyson."

Feeling her legs go liquid, she stumbled to sit down. "I... don't understand," she stammered.

"Ms. Lucan, Mr. Greyson was brought in this morning."

Pressing the phone to her ear, she couldn't hear anything. Suddenly all she heard was the pounding of her own heartbeat swishing past her ears drums and feeling as if she was going to pass out.

"Are you there, Ms. Lucan? Hello?"

Gasping, she drew air into her lungs and closed her eyes, causing tears to escape.

"Ms. Lucan, are you alright?"

"No," she sniffed, "but go on, what happened? Is Drew OK?"

"I'm sorry to have to tell you this, but he died last night of sudden cardiac arrest."

"Died! No!!!" she shouted, "That can't be!" Barely able to hold the phone to her ear, her arm went limp and laid against her chest. Raising her eyes toward the ceiling, she blinked rapidly trying to take the words in. Slowly, she raised the phone to her ear. "Drew died of a heart attack? He was only forty-two years old!"

"No, Ms. Lucan, he did not have a heart attack per se, his heart stopped. There was no damage done to the heart, but since he was alone and with no one to perform CPR to restart his heart or call 911, there was no chance for survival."

"Where was he? Who brought him in?"

"He was at the Kanyon Ridge Spa, his son found him on the floor this morning when he went in, and he called 911. It seems likely that when he got up to leave, he went into cardiac arrest and collapsed. I'm very sorry for your loss and Ms. Lucan, you can pick up his personal items at your discretion. Er... um," she heard him clear his throat, "his family is still here, but I can arrange to meet you privately."

"Thank you... for calling," she said, tapping the 'off' button. Sitting there stunned and numb, she cried for Drew and for herself. She cried for all the time she thought they'd have, for the love they shared and how happy they had been over the last few months. She was sad for the so few memories they'd made and for their time that had ended all too soon that left her alone, again. Her heart sank as a sudden stirring in her stomach sent her bounding off to the bathroom as bile roiled up into her throat. She gagged into the bowl, but nothing came up except coffee. Giant waves of nausea washed over her as she dry-heaved into the toilet bowl. Sweat oozed from her pores until she was drenched. Knowing her legs wouldn't hold her up, she sat on the floor and turned on the cold water tap in the tub. Leaning weakly against it, she held a washcloth under the water and rung it out one-handedly and wiped at her mouth. Rinsing again she ran the cloth over her face and around to the back of her neck. It helped with the nausea, but it did nothing for the emptiness in her soul.

* * *

"Mom? I need you," she cried into the phone, "please come up."

Within seconds the elevator doors opened, and Lorraine saw her daughter curled into the fetal position on the couch, sobbing.

"Oh, my God, Sage, what happened?" Lorraine never got used to calling her daughter anything except 'Sage' no matter what she chose to call herself, she would always be 'Sage' to her.

"Drew is dead, Mom, he died last night at the spa."

"What!? Oh, Sage, Baby, I'm so, so sorry! What can I do?"

"Just take care of Grey until I get myself straightened out," she sobbed.

Lorraine held her and let her cry until she couldn't cry anymore. Between sobs, she told her mother what had happened, according to the doctor who called.

Lifting her head up off her shoulder, Lorraine looked into her daughter's swollen eyes. Her heartbreaking at the pain she saw there.

"Let me make you some tea, Sage," she said, softly. Sage just nodded. She was still weak from the bathroom incident, and her belly growled for food.

"Can you make a piece of toast too, please."

"Sure, Honey, no problem, I'll be right back."

* * *

Loneliness settled into her soul as thoughts of never seeing Drew again began to sink in. For the first time since she'd cleared out the spare room closet for Drew's clothes, she wandered in. Putting her hands on the closet doors, she closed her eyes and bowed her head. Taking a deep breath, she slowly lowered her hands to the knobs. Pausing slightly, she turned them and swung both doors wide open. Walking into the large closet, she reached up and touched one of his shirts. Wrapping her fingers around the body, she gave it a yank twirling the hanger wildly on the rod. She slipped her arms into the sleeves, brought the collar up to her nose, inhaled deeply and there he was, hugging her body. Moving in closer to his wardrobe, she lovingly touched each item one by one. His favorite cardigan, an old pair of washed out, faded jeans, Castaway dockers, his runners, dress shoes and slippers. His uniforms were lined up neatly, then the dress shirts, sweaters, vests and a dozen or more tee shirts, all hanging there waiting for him to choose an outfit. Leaning in closer, she could smell the freshness of clean laundry, and whiffs of his cologne lingered on his sweaters. Wrapping her arms around a cluster of clothes, she held them to her. Hanging the shirt back on the hanger she took his sweater down and put it on, closed the doors and left.

Emotions running high, she cried from missing him, a young life taken from family and friends and the thought of never seeing him again was more than she could possibly bare.

A long and endless day she had put in since early morning when she'd received the call. She'd snuggled with his sweater, laid with his robe wrapped around her and hugged his pillow. When naps wouldn't consume her, she got up and roamed around the apartment. She didn't know what to do with herself. She was lost and alone, and a gnawing feeling in the pit of her stomach told her she had to see him one last time.

Pulling herself together, she called the hospital and asked to speak to Dr. Wills. When he answered, she told him who she was and said that she was ready to pick up Drew's personal items and he gave her directions to his office. Before entering the hospital, she pulled her hoodie up over her head. Slipping past the waiting room, she turned her head in the opposite direction in case any family members were still there.

Noah thought he saw her pass the waiting room door but then again, he got that same feeling every time he saw someone resembling Sage. She was tall and slim like Sage, but so were many other women who entered his spa on a daily basis. *'It was just someone visiting at the hospital,'* he told himself and focused his attention back on his mother.

Dr. Wills' receptionist showed her to a small room that was cluttered with instruments and medical posters of skeletons and human innards. He startled her when he opened the door.

"Ms. Lucan?"

"Yes, I'm Cassie Lucan."

He was short and to the point as he passed her the plain brown, bulging envelope. Reaching out for it she had to ask, "Is he still here?"

"Yes, he is, would you like to see him?"

"I would if you can arrange it and if the room is empty. I wouldn't want to upset the family or intrude in any way."

"Come with me," he said, putting a hand on her back to lead her out into the corridor.

A few doors down from his office, he stopped, looked around and pulled back a curtain. It felt all cloak and daggerish as he pressed her back for her to go in. Drew was still on the gurney that he'd been brought in on. Tears streamed down her face as he pulled the sheet back. Putting her hand over her face, she pinched her nose to keep from causing a scene. Knowing she had no business there especially with the family close by, she couldn't cause a disturbance. The doctor put his hand on her shoulder and pointed to the curtain. She understood what he meant. He would stand guard in case someone came. She set the envelope on the bottom of the gurney and walked toward him.

Drew laid on the gurney as if he had just fallen asleep. He was devastatingly handsome, and when she touched his face, it was cold, making it even more real.

"Drew," she whispered, reaching under the sheet to bring his hand out. There were no words as he lay there lifeless, pale and still. He was young, gorgeous and very dead. Drawing in a heaving sob, her heart ached, and she felt sad, empty and alone. Laying her head on his chest, she stretched her arm across his body as tears silently flowed from her eyes onto the sheet. She wanted to scream and wail as loudly as she could to ease her pain, but she knew, for Drew's sake, she couldn't do it.

"I love you," she whispered, "you will always be with me. I wish we'd had more time," she said stroking his cheek. "We had so many plans and dreams for our future. I wish I had been at the spa with you, I wish, I wish, I wish," she said in frustration. She was beside herself with grief when suddenly she heard voices in the corridor. Standing up, she grabbed a bunch of tissues from the table and covered her face. Wiping her eyes and blowing softly she stood perfectly still and listened.

"I'm sorry, you can't go in at the moment. There is someone in there... um... preparing the body but I will let you know when the room is free."

Hearing footsteps, she thought it must be Noah and his mother. She breathed a sigh of relief when their steps disappeared into silence. Turning back to him, she kissed his lips, his cheek and his forehead. Lifting his hand, she cupped it to her cheek then kissed the inside of his palm.

"I have to go, my love," she whispered, "I know you understand why I can't stay longer. You will be in my heart forever, I love you so much, Drew." Lifting the sheet, she laid his hand back under, picked up the envelope and kissed his cold lips once more. Tiptoeing through the curtain, she forced herself not to look back.

"Thank you," she whispered, wiping at her eyes.

He nodded his head in acceptance.

"Is there another way out other than passing the waiting room?" she whispered.

Nodding his head sideways, she followed him to a side door. She mouthed the words, 'thank you' again and rushed off to her car.

Once she was home, and in the safety of her own space, she slipped the hoodie off her head. Clutching the envelope to her chest, she sat down. Thinking she might need something to calm her down she laid the envelope on the coffee table and went to the kitchen to make a cup of coffee. Popping a pod in the Keurig, she pressed the buttons. Staring at the envelope, she knew the last of Drew were in there.

Taking her mug into the living room, she sat it on the table next to the envelope. *'It is now or never,'* she thought, as she tore the flap open and dumped the contents out. The first thing she saw was his watch face down on the table. Picking it up, she turned it over and saw that the face was cracked, and it had stopped at 12:12. Suddenly, she remembered waking up and looking at the clock at 12:12. *'Drew must have cracked it when he fell,'* she thought, remembering that he'd always worn his watch with the face turned under his wrist and she guessed it must have broken when it hit the floor. Sadly, it made her feel a special connection to him knowing that she'd woken up the exact moment that his heart stopped beating. Suddenly, she felt the urge to call her mother.

Lorraine stepped out of the elevator and into Sage's waiting arms. Waiting patiently for her to calm down, Lorraine hugged her tightly.

"I went to see Drew today," she sobbed.

Lorraine saw that she was shaking and rattled. "How did that happen?" Lorraine asked curiously.

"A doctor helped me get in to see him, Mom."

"That had to be difficult, but a good thing… right?" she asked while moving her towards the couch.

Sitting there with such sad eyes, it broke Lorraine's heart that she couldn't fix this for her child.

"It was difficult, and it looked as if he had just fallen asleep. I miss him so much Mom, he was so young," she sobbed. Reaching for her mother again, she cried on her shoulder. *'Drew was her mother's age. What would she ever do if… no, no if's,'* she thought.

Rubbing her back, Lorraine tried soothing her by rocking back and forth.

Having her mother there was helpful. She was always there for her no matter what. She understood a mother's love now that she had Grey and knowing she would have done anything for him too.

26

Cassie found Drew's obituary in the local paper with details of the funeral and made plans to attend.

Hoping not to be noticed by anyone, she stood back from the other mourners. Hoovering above the grave, the mahogany coffin sat on straps waiting to be lowered at the end of the ceremony. Beside it, a heap of dirt lay covered with a green artificial carpet.

She'd pulled her hair back into a twist and covered her head with a thin black kerchief. Wearing large black-framed sunglasses, she nervously glanced around, incognito, at the family and friends who were gathered there. She was satisfied that she had come prepared. Standing across from her, she saw the man she had not laid eyes on in eight years. Clearly, it was Noah, the image of his father and also her son. She didn't know the woman next to him but guessed it to be his mother. She was certain he would not recognize her. No one would recognize her as Cassie Lucan, Sage Lawrence or anyone else for that matter. At that moment, she felt she had no identity. Who was she anyway? It was as if she had multiple personalities. Was she Cassie Lucan who loved Drew Greyson or was she Sage Lawrence who still loved, Noah? How could she love two men with such different fathoms of passion? Drew, whom she had just recently met and was learning to love him more every day and Noah, whom she has loved since they were in grade school and a connection that could not mentally or spiritually separate them.

It had been eight long, agonizing years and she had tried, with everything inside her, to forget about him.

Keeping her head bowed, she tried not to look over at Noah, but she could not resist. Slowly lifting her eyelids from behind her rose-colored sunglasses and from across the grave site, she met his stare. Her heart stopped. Surely, he didn't recognize her? From his stare, it left her feeling uncertain that coming here had been the right choice. Stepping sideways, she hid behind someone that had allowed her to escape his stare. Clutching her heart, she stood alone in pain for the man she was just learning to love and hoping she wouldn't come unglued in front of Noah. Holding a tissue over her mouth and nose, she sobbed into it. Closing her eyes caused tears to stream down past her sunglasses. It was impossible to hold back the flood or the ache she felt in her entire being. Opening her eyes, she saw that several people in front of her had moved closer to the service and exposed her again to Noah's stares. Not hearing a word of the Pastor's message, she doubted he knew the slightest bit of information about Drew except for what his family had provided.

Sparkling in the afternoon sun, her watch showed the time as 2:22.

Suddenly the coffin moved, and she drew in a long and jagged breath. Either a dry spot or a bug fetched up at the back of her throat sending her into a coughing spree. Covering her mouth, she tried to silence the barking sounds. Nausea rose from the pit of her stomach, and she struggled to steady herself from the dizziness while feeling her legs wobble beneath her. Trying to keep from gagging, she had the sudden urge to drop to her knees but held steady not wanting to draw attention to herself. '*When had she eaten last?*' she thought, wanting to vomit just thinking about food.

* * *

Watching from the other side of the spacious burial site, Noah stood with his mother. He'd noticed the tall, slim woman standing alone and wondered who she was. She had a strange resemblance to the woman he'd seen in the mall. He had nothing to go by except that she was tall, everything else was covered up.

Sharp wails were coming from his mother as he held her tightly against his side. He, too, wanted to weep for his dad but he had to be strong for her. She had seemed lost since the split with his father. He hadn't asked any questions but had listened to what they each had to say. It was pretty much the same story as if it had been rehearsed. They had basically grown apart over the years and wanted to go their separate ways. Noah had known his father had not been happy for as long as he could remember and felt he'd only stayed with his mother for his sake. So many times, he had wanted to tell him he didn't have to be unhappy because of him but he never wanted to embarrass him; only now he wished he had. *'How pathetically short his life had been and more than half if it had been spent in a life he hadn't wanted. Now that he was free to live, they were burying him,'* he thought. He couldn't help but feel the sting of irony. He had been dying to be free, and when he was, he died. Sadness gripped him as he felt a hot tear slip from his eye and down his cheek. He wished he had known he had been at the office, he wished he had called him to let him know he was there but all the wishes in the world would not bring him back. Wiping at his nose, his mother clung to his waist.

His thoughts strayed back across the gravesite to the woman in black. She'd wobbled unsteadily for few seconds but quickly regained her footing. His thoughts went to the mall again, and to the woman he'd seen there and thought it was Sage. He knew he should be listening to his father's final service, but he was distracted by this woman.

He remembered the mall was crazy busy with people scurrying about and children running wildly while their parents browsed. Noah wasn't comfortable in such chaos. His mother had usually kept the spa well stocked, so he rarely had reason to shop. Ducking into The Emporium with his list, he'd begun to do a visual scan for colorful baskets, to place towels in, for the rooms at the spa. His eyes went up to a higher shelf, and his heart nearly stopped. He'd seen a tall, blonde and beautiful woman browsing in the next aisle. For a moment, he'd thought it was Sage. His heart thumped inside his chest, and as thoughts of her came flooding back, he remembered things he had buried long ago. It had been years since he'd seen her, but he was sure it was her. Automatically his fingers curled in remembrance of the long blonde hair that he'd once had his fingers tangled in. Heat and longings rose in all the wrong places. She was tall, thin and gorgeous, exactly as she had been in high school. *'What happened to them? How did they lose each other after spending so many years as best friends and eventually, although briefly, lovers? She likely never knew the extent of how much he adored her although he had told her he loved her.'* He remembered being light-headed as he found himself being drawn in her direction with an uncontrollable urge to touch her shoulder. He was close enough that he could actually smell strawberries and he only had to reach out. He opened his mouth to say hello when a man's voice, from several rows over, spoke one word.

"Cassie?"

Looking up, she smiled at the sound of her name.

'*Dammit!*' Backing away, he felt a jolt of disappointment hit low in his gut. He had been sure it was Sage. 'Sage,' he loved her name, and he liked how, just thinking about it, made him reel. '*Sage, where are you now?*' All thoughts of shopping left him. Leaving the store, he'd felt torn between walking away and staying to lurk around shelves for sneak peeks at her look-alike. He'd opted to take his disappointment and leave.

'*Surely this wasn't the same woman?*' he thought, although he couldn't see her face or hair color, from behind dark glasses and the black vail-like scarf she wore but the build was the same. Cassie was her name. He would never forget it because just when he thought he'd found her; someone had called out the name 'Cassie' stopping him in his tracks. He never once thought to connect the unseen voice. '*Had it been his father's? Was this Cassie person connected to his father somehow?*' he wondered. '*Could this person be the same one he'd seen at the mall?*'

Suddenly, the coffin moved, and he thought his heart would stop. Focusing on the woman, he hadn't heard much of the ceremony.

As the coffin lowered into the ground, Keri lost her footing and went down to her knees. Guilt enveloped her as she wept for all the lonely years he had spent with her and more than half of those she had cheated on him, lied to him and never once offered to let him go. Feeling ashamed, she just wanted to hide her face from the world. Even though she knew that Drew would never tell another soul about what she had done, she felt as though everybody was staring at her and accusing her of his death. She knew at that moment that she would never forgive herself for all those years of selfishness that had bound Drew to her. The sweet and gentle man he'd been did not deserve to be lowered into the ground and she wished instead that it was her. She deserved to die, and it should be Drew standing there watching her being buried. It likely would have brought him some pleasure.

Richard Kimble stood sadly by watching Keri and knowing what she had done to his friend. He silently wished he was standing there with Drew watching her coffin disappear deep into the ground. His profound dislike for her grew even more and he wished that Drew had thrown her ass in jail just to prove a point.

Once the casket was lowered and people began to wander back to their vehicles, Cassie walked between a couple people and disappeared knowing Noah and his mother would be the last to leave.

By the time Noah got his mother calmed from her collapse, he noticed everyone had left, including the woman in black.

* * *

Matthew Conwell knew he had to make the call. He had met Andrew Greyson only a few weeks ago when he'd come to his office requesting several documents be taken care of. A young, handsome and intelligent man in his early forties, wanted him to set up his last requests, probably with no idea it would only be a matter of weeks until his will would be read. He had been somewhat shocked when he got a call from Randy Kimble informing him of Drew's death and to handle Drew's wishes on his end, and he would deal with the family.

His secretary had set up an appointment, and when Cassie Lucan walked into his office, he was more than stunned at her beauty even in her tear-stained appearance.

"Ms. Lucan, please have a seat."

"May I ask why I am here?" as if this was the last place she wanted to be.

"It's about Andrew Greyson's will, Ms. Lucan."

"OK, then, why am I the only one here? Why am I here at all?"

"Ms. Lucan, Mr. Greyson came to me only recently, requesting that I prepare a private will for him. Showing her to a seat, he went around to his chair. "May I continue?"

"Yes, please," she said, pressing her lips together.

"Mr. Greyson had asked that you read this letter, here in my office. I have a copy, but his wish was that you read it here," he said, passing her an envelope, "I will give you a few minutes," he said, getting up and walking to the window.

On the front of the envelope, it said, 'For your eyes only.' It was dated only a few weeks before. With shaking hands, she broke the seal and pulled the sheets out that began with:

My Dearest Cassie,

Only if I am gone will you be reading this letter and I hope that day is far into our future. I hope to have the opportunity to talk to you face to face about what I am writing about here, but for now this needs to be said. When we met several months ago at the airport, it was the best day of my life. My son, Noah, means everything to me but it was you who brought me the greatest joy.

I hope the next few lines will not make a difference in how you feel about me. Recently I took it upon myself, for no other reason than curiosity, to do an online search and was unable to locate a 'Cassie Lucan,' except for a modelling name, so I hired a PI to do a more thorough search which I could have done myself if I'd had access to Noah's yearbooks. I know, in my heart, if I had asked you outright, you would have been honest with me, but I needed to know more about the Cassie Lucan that I fell deeply in love with. The search brought me to Sage Lawrence. You must have had your own reasons for changing your identity, whether it was for your modelling career or other personal reasons, I don't care.

I have a birth record for a child named Greyson Alexander Lawrence plus pictures that were taken of him randomly, and at various locations. It wasn't difficult to put the pieces together since my son's name is Noah Alexander Greyson and that your Greyson is my grandson. He looks exactly like Noah did at that age. I expect that Noah is unaware of Greyson and it is not my place to tell him, but I hope one day he will come to know his son.

The name change happened at around the same time as Greyson was born, so I get the connection. I also came to the understanding that your mother is a single parent too. I remember meeting her once in the hospital when you were born. You are one day older than my son, and I knew when I saw you that you would become a beautiful woman one day. I don't know why, with so many people in this world, that we would bump into each other, but I am eternally thankful that we did.

Cassie/Sage (you will always be 'Cassie' to me) thank you for all the wonderful moments we've shared, and for giving me the most happiness that I've had in years.

In the manila envelope is everything that I have documented and pictures of Greyson for you to do with as you see fit. I had arranged this private meeting with my attorney in the event of my death, and everything will be explained at that time. Until then, I hope we have many wonderful years together and know that I will love you until my dying day and beyond.

Drew

No words were spoken until Cassie finished the letter. Still in shock from Drew's sudden death and now a letter from beyond the grave. It had only been written recently, and it felt eerie reading his words.

It had been deathly quiet when suddenly the lawyer cleared his throat, causing her to flinch. He waited for her to dry her eyes before speaking.

"There is more to be said, Ms. Lucan if you're ready."

"As I will ever be," she said, blowing into a tissue.

"Mr. Greyson hired me, only recently, to take care of his wishes set out before us today." He flipped through a few documents and passed one to her. Leaning in, she took it, wondering what it was. With a crinkled brow, she asked, "What is this? It looks like a deed."

"It is, in fact, a deed, to your condo. Mr. Greyson purchased it shortly after moving in with you, and in the event of his death, it goes to you." Shifting around a few more sheets of paper, he handed her another page. "This document shows that condo fees and content insurance will be paid for the duration of you living there. Ms. Lucan, Mr. Greyson had informed me that Sage Lawrence is your birth name which is why this next document is under that name to make it legal and binding."

"To make what legal and binding?" she said sobbing into a clean tissue.

"Mr. Greyson's life insurance policy is in your name."

"Wh...what? No! Drew's life insurance?"

"Yes, he named you as his sole beneficiary."

"I don't understand, Drew and I have only been together for a few months, there must be some mistake. His policy should go to his family."

"If he'd wanted it to go to his family he wouldn't have come to me to make the changes. I assure you this is a legal document which is why it is in your legal name, Sage Cassandra Lawrence."

He turned the document around and handed it to her. When she looked at it, she went limp in the chair. Pressing her fingers against her lips, she let the tears roll freely down her cheeks. "I don't believe this," she murmured, her voice barely audible.

"Oh, you can believe it, Ms. Luc... um... Ms. Lawrence. As a pilot, Mr. Greyson was heavily insured, as you can see and in the second paragraph, it is his wish for the inheritance to remain private. The family knows only that Mr. Greyson recently changed his will, but nothing else will be disclosed. Are you in agreement with that, Ms. Lawrence?"

Words would not come out of her opened mouth. She just stared at the man across the desk from her. He waited for her to speak but nothing came out. While chewing on a hangnail, she glanced from the paper to him, while the information sank in. Seeing blood oozing from her cuticle, she wrapped it in a tissue.

"Ms. Lawrence? I need your answer to the agreement."

"Yes, of course, but why? I had no idea," she whispered.

"Obviously, because he loved you very much and wanted to provide for you and your son, Greyson."

"He said that? He included my son in his will?" Pausing for thought, she felt as if her heart would explode with all she had taken in.

"Mr. Greyson hired me privately to do this will. The family's lawyer is dealing with the rest of it. I was also informed that his family knows nothing of your relationship so this meeting will remain private until you see fit to mention it."

"I doubt I ever will," she said, sadly.

"I'm certain Mr. Greyson would expect that." Clearing his throat again, he searched the file folder that laid open in front of him. "One more thing, Ms. Lawrence."

Hearing him call her 'Ms. Lawrence' sounded oddly familiar to her after being known as Cassie Lucan for the past, almost, decade.

"And what is that?"

"Your cheque," he said, flipping around an official-looking bank draft.

Reaching for it, she stared in disbelief. Skimming across the paper, she saw the day's date, pay to the order of, Sage Cassandra Lawrence and a total of five million dollars, staring back at her.

"My God," she croaked, looking up at him, "seriously?"

Tilting his head towards the cheque, he said, "The proof is in your hands, and I'm sorry we had to meet under these circumstances, but in most cases, it is because of the circumstance. It is a pleasure to have met you, Ms. Lawrence."

A slow grin crossed his face as he realized why Andrew Greyson had loved the woman sitting across from him. There wasn't a pretentious bone in her body and no sign of greed to be seen. She was just an honest young woman who would give the cheque back in a heartbeat for the man she loved. She gathered up her copies, folded them in half and slipped them inside her handbag. Carefully folding the cheque twice, she tucked it safely inside her wallet.

Getting up from his chair, he went around the desk and offered his hand. Rising from her chair, on wobbly legs, she took his hand.

Somewhere in the back of her mind, she tried to remember again when she'd had a decent meal.

* * *

Miles away, Noah and Keri sat in front of Randy Kimble, their family attorney. He laid it out as bluntly as he could since he had been a friend to Drew and not Keri. He'd had a rather distasteful attitude towards her since Drew came to him for advice. He had given him the name of a private lawyer so he could do his business without Keri knowing about it. He still had a visual of her on her knees at the funeral. Drew deserved better.

"Noah, your father's share in the business has been given to you, making you the sole proprietor of the spa. Along with that, he has given you one half of his work pension." Rifling through more papers, he turned to Keri. "Mrs. Greyson, the other half of Drew's work pension will go to you along with the home which in the event of his death, will be paid in full, if it isn't already and you are free and clear to do with it whatever you wish." Letting out a ragged breath, he continued. He still could not believe his friend was dead. Handing a bank draft to Noah, he shook his hand and told him he was sorry for his loss. Turning to Keri, he passed her the deed and a bank draft for her portion of his pension and politely nodded in her direction.

"And, I guess we're done," he said, closing the file and rising to his feet. He hoped he'd never have to look at her again.

Taking the papers, she looked at them in question.

"Done?" Keri said, "Are you serious?"

"You still have questions, Keri?" he asked, through clenched jaws. He detested the woman almost as much as Drew had. They weren't just on an 'attorney/client' basis, they were personal friends and often he and Drew shared confidences. The part that soured him towards Keri was when Drew confided in him about the drug incident all those years ago when he was still in law school. He'd never forgotten it, and he'd promised Drew he would keep it confidential. Drew had been desperate to talk to someone and said there were only two other people who knew the entire story, Dr. Don Hanson and himself. Drew had given him copies of all the lab results and the coins for safekeeping, but he had kept the vial until recently. When Drew came to him several months ago to share the news of a new woman in his life he had been on cloud nine. Randy had never seen him so full of life and finally happy. He had twenty-five years of misery and only several months of pure joy. There was just something about that that was unsettling, sad and just plain stunk.

"Where is Drew's life insurance policy?" she demanded.

"There is no policy, Keri, Drew dealt with that a few weeks ago with another attorney, so I have no information to give you on that particular subject," he lied, but he took great pleasure in watching her face drop. Besides, what he and Drew talked about in the privacy of his office would stay between them.

"He cashed in his policy? It was worth a few million dollars!" she shrieked.

"Yes, I know, five million to be exact," he smirked, "and I have no further knowledge about it, so, again, I think we are done here, Keri."

Taking Keri's arm, Noah led her towards the door to avoid a scene. Tension could be felt between his mother and their lawyer as he ushered her out. Her mouth still open in disbelief.

Following the appointment with the lawyer, Cassie spent the next several days alone. There was so much to absorb. Starting with the shock of suddenly losing Drew, the hospital, the lawyer and all that he had to tell her.

She owned her beautiful penthouse, strata fees paid up, and Drew's life insurance policy. That was the biggest shocker. What was she going to do with five million dollars? She couldn't fathom why Drew would make provisions for her and Grey in his will. They'd only had a few months together, and he'd never even met Grey, yet he had the heart of an angel.

She wished now that she had been honest with him about Grey. Knowing his heart as she did, she was one hundred percent certain that her fears had been for nothing. He would never have taken Grey from her, and she realized now that she had been living out her mother's fears. He had deserved to meet his grandson. Grey should have known Drew.

With that settled in her brain, she suddenly wondered why her mother had had such an extreme fear of her father's family. She was only slightly curious about who her father was, where he was from or if she had siblings, but she didn't dwell on it. Her mother must have had her reasons for running. Painful thoughts haunted her and plagued her with guilt for all the years she'd kept Grey away from Noah and Drew. Besides her mother, the Benton's and herself, he had been sheltered from what few family members he had.

Now that the funeral was over, she definitely had to make a plan. The first one was to stop modelling and take care of her son.

27

Lorraine loved her job as Grey's sitter and Nana. She and Sage had agreed that Lorraine would stay home and care for Grey while she went back to work. Babysitters were not an option, it had to be Lorraine since Sage trusted no one else. Although Lorraine had savings and money from the sale of the house, she still felt uncomfortable accepting money for taking care of her grandson. Sage convinced her that she'd have to pay somebody, so it may as well be her. She wanted a stable home for Grey and not be pushed from one babysitter to the next. When all was said and done, Lorraine went on her payroll. All this cloak and dagger stuff made them both feel like criminals on the run.

When Sage moved to her own penthouse on the top floor of the building, it gave them both more privacy. No one knew who Greyson belonged to since Lorraine was still young and Sage still looked seventeen. When Sage moved out, Greyson had stayed with Lorraine in the only home he had ever known. She was just a private elevator ride away whenever they needed a visit. Once he was old enough to visit on his own, it was with the understanding that he'd call first. It was only to keep them safe. Sage was in and out of town on jobs and so living with his grandmother had given Grey more stability, and Sage peace of mind.

Greyson's seventh birthday was approaching, and Lorraine had arranged a trip to the park with four of his school friends.

From the park bench, she watched them as they spent their energy on the playground equipment while she enjoyed the sun.

Closing her eyes every few seconds, she still paid close attention to the five boys.

Looking around the park, she noticed it wasn't very busy except for a man, with a cane, lurking in the distance. Glancing over at the boys she saw that two were taking turns on the slide, two were swinging side by side and chatting while the other boy was on the monkey bars. The sun felt glorious on her skin as she peacefully watched the boys.

She noticed the man with the cane had either gone or had moved on to another side of the park. Closing her eyes, she loved the feel of the warmth but soon opened them afraid of dozing off. Repositioning herself on the bench something shiny and blue laid on the bench beside her, catching her eye. Staring at it blankly, it took a couple of seconds for it to register. Something similar to an electric shock, coursed through her body. Straightening her back, she closed her eyes and willed it to go away, hoping it was only an illusion or heat stroke. Opening her eyes again, it was still there, and as she reached out for it, a voice spoke from behind her.

"Hello, Darlin."

Dropping her face into her palms, her face crinkled into a cry.

"No, no, it can't be," she whispered, reaching for the blue jagged edged glass.

"Gage?" she cried. Turning slowly, it was the man with a cane, standing behind her. Leaping from the bench, she looked into the eyes of the only man she had ever loved and had missed for the last twenty-five years.

"Wh…What are you doing here?"

"Lookin' for you, Darlin.'"

He was exactly as she had remembered. Those eyes, his smile, that Texas drawl. Everything she had ever loved about him.

"Why? After all this time?"

"It took me all this dang time to find you, girl!" he said, limping over to her. "You are still the purdiest dang thang I ever laid my eyes on," he whispered, wiping a tear from her cheek with his thumb.

"Gage," she whispered. It had been years since she'd been able to say his name aloud.

"Come here, Darlin'," he said, opening one arm.

Stepping forward and leaning into his chest, she wrapped her arms around his back. He leaned onto the bench for support so he could use both arms to hold her quivering body.

"Where did you go?" he asked.

"Where did I go? Gage, you left me, remember? I left because you never came back."

"I came back when I could, but you were gone. Nobody could tell me a dang thang except that you and your family up and moved away," he said while tossing his arm out into the air.

"It was months, Gage and with no word, I thought you had moved on."

"Let's sit down, Darlin', please, so I can explain some thangs to you." Settling on the bench, he laid his cane to one side and turned to face her.

"First off, I did not 'move on,' he said, using air quotes. "Thangs went to hell in a handbasket after we last talked," he drawled. "Shortly after I got back to Texas, the entire office went into a turmoil. Most of the accounts had been closed or redirected elsewhere, sections of the company had shut down, mine included, and chaos had taken over," he said, throwing his arms up in the air again. "After I called you that last time, every dang thang changed. My business phone was cancelled, my accounts were closed, and I was out of a job. My boss took the company phone right out of my hand and threw it into his desk drawer. I got a new phone, but I didn't have anybody's contact number, so I got on the highway and headed back to Kanyon Valley. I got no information from anybody, so after a few days, I headed back home. Somewhere, along the way, I was side-swiped by a semi and was pushed over a cliff in the middle of nowhere. Fortunately, the trucker stopped and called for help. I was at the bottom of a ravine, my car all tore up in pieces, and nobody knew if I was dead or alive."

"My God, Gage, I had no idea," she sobbed, as he continued.

"When they finally got me out of the wreck, I was airlifted to the nearest hospital, but I was out of it for weeks. I didn't know where I was or who I was, for a time. I had a busted leg, which they managed to save with rods and pins, but the other injuries took months to heal. They said yours was the first name I spoke when I woke up, but I had no contact information on me except for my parents. My phone was long gone in the wreck, but I had nothing stored in it anyway. When I was well enough to get around, I asked my parents to bring me another phone, so I could try and contact you again. Tanner Industries had no idea what happened.

Mr. Tanner said you just didn't come into work and he never heard from you again, not even to send your last pay cheque. The phone company had no listings under Lawrence, so I was out of options. I concentrated on my rehab to get back on my feet and out of the wheelchair. It took me a long time to adjust to this reconfigured leg," he said, giving it a couple slaps, "which I'm still working on."

"Gage, I wish I had known, I would have been with you."

"I know you would have, Darlin', I'm not on a pity trip here, I just want to explain why I didn't come back when I promised I would."

"How did you find me?"

"Well, after years of dead-end searches, I kinda gave up cuz it was lookin' like you had just vanished or didn't wanna be found. I didn't know if you were even still alive. That was the scariest dang thang about all this, was not knowin'. So, not long ago, I gave it another try. Ain't nuthin' worth havin' if you don't have to fight for it," he said, with a grin. "I did another online search, and there you were."

"Where? I'm not online."

"It showed you as the name listed on a lease, in a building, in Kanyon Creek."

Lorraine then realized that when Sage moved and signed a new lease, she had put her name on the older lease exposing Lorraine's name to public records.

"So, basically, I searched it out, found the building and waited to see if it was you. When I saw you leave the building today, with

251

the boys, I followed you. As soon as I saw you though, I knew it was you. I would have known you from anywhere, Darlin.'"

She loved his 'Conway Twitty' accent.

"I don't want to interrupt your life, Sweetheart, I just wanted to know that you were alright, and I can see that you are." He turned his thumb towards the playground, "Yours?"

"No, I'm his nanny, the one in the red striped tee-shirt. It's a birthday playdate with a few of his school chums."

"Are you married then?"

"Why do you ask?"

"Coz, if you aren't, you're gonna be. So, are ya?"

She searched his face before answering. "No, I'm not married and never have been."

"Is there a man in yer life?"

"Gage!"

"Darlin,' I'm just going to keep asking until you answer me so is there a man in yer life?"

"No, there is no man in my life,' she said, giggling like old times. "There was only one man in my life, and that was you, happy now?" she teased.

There were no words as he reached for her, drew her in and kissed her without a second thought. He felt her soften and a moan escaped her as their kiss deepened. Twenty-five years wiped away with a single kiss.

"Nana?"

Lorraine quickly broke away from Gage. "Grey!"

There were five little faces staring at them while they were kissing in public, on a park bench.

"Nana! You're bleeding, are you alright?

The beach glass had dug into her palm until it had drawn blood. Gage took a handkerchief from his pocket and wrapped it around the wound as he slipped the glass back into his pocket.

"We have to go, sorry Gage but I have to go."

"But…"

She was off the bench and herding the boys out of the park entrance before he could stand up.

On top of everything else, how was she going to tell Sage about Gage with all that she had on her plate? They had just recently buried Drew, how could she dump something else on her. She had to do something because she knew Gage wasn't going away.

Lorraine went up to Sage's penthouse unannounced, and when the elevator door opened, she called her name. "Sage?"

"Mom?"

"Yes, Honey, it's me, and I'm sorry I didn't call first, but I really need to talk to you."

"It's OK, I have to talk to you too, what's in the box? And what is up with the bandage?"

"Never mind the bandage," she said," patting the couch for Sage to sit, "it can wait, talk to me."

"I got a call from a lawyer's office a few days ago. He wanted to meet with me Mom, and you are not going to believe this."

"A lawyer? Really? What about, Sage?"

"I promised I would not disclose any information, so you have to promise too."

"Of course, Sage, that goes without saying."

Getting up from the couch, she went to her desk for the envelope and opened the flap. Sitting back down, she pulled out some of the pages, unfolded the penthouse deed and passed it to her mother.

"My God; what's all this?"

"I know, right!"

"Your penthouse is paid for?"

"Yes, Drew bought it when he moved in and look there," she said, pointing to another sheet, "the strata fees are paid up for as long as I live here."

"I don't know what to say."

"There are no words, Mom, believe me," she said tearing up, "but wait, there's more."

"What else can there be?"

Reaching for a tissue, Sage picked up another page and held it close to her heart.

"Mom," she said, her lips quivering, "Drew willed me his life insurance."

"You're not serious?"

"I am, and I got this from the lawyer," she said, flipping the page around showing Lorraine a photocopy of the cashier's cheque.

Lorraine's eyes widened, and her mouth fell open at the same time. She couldn't speak, and she could only stare at the paper.

"Mom? Mom?" Sage said, poking Lorraine on the shoulder, "are you breathing? Are you OK?" "I... I can't believe this Sage. Five million dollars!?" she said breathlessly. "What about his family?"

"I asked the lawyer the same thing, and he told me it was his wishes."

"I am so happy for you, Sweetheart, what a wonderful thing for him to do."

"It was, and I will likely never know the extent of the reason behind it."

"But... I am happy for you too, Mom."

"Me, why... me?"

"Because... you gave up your freedom for me back in the day, and when you were about to get it back, you gave it up again for Greyson. I'm so thankful to have you as my mom, so here," she said, passing her a cheque, "this is for you."

Lorraine took the cheque and turned it right side up and gasped. "Are you kidding me!? Two million dollars?... For me?"

"Yes, Mom, for you and you deserve it, and now that the funeral is over you are officially relieved of your babysitting duties. You need a life, Mom, you deserve to be set free, and I want to be a full-time mom," she said, spreading her arms wide.

"I can't believe this, Sage."

"Believe it but keep it to yourself, remember, 'mum's' the word. One more thing and then it's your turn. Passing Drew's note to her, she waited for her to finish reading it.

"Drew knew about Greyson, you and Noah and he still provided for you both?"

"Yes, he did, Mom, he was such a beautiful human being," she said, tearing up again.

Lorraine leafed through the few photos that had been taken by a P.I. and recognized the places in the background. She had been with him when the shots were taken. They had been careful to leave her out and only got shots of Greyson. "This is all, so mind-blowing."

"It sure is. So, you know what I know, but I still don't know what is in the box."

"The box," she whispered, "well, speaking of secrets, I guess your mother has a few of her own."
"Really? My Mom with secrets? Do tell," she teased, trying to lighten the mood set by Lorraine.

"Sage, nobody in my world," she said, spreading her hand across her chest, "has ever seen this box, nobody, but it's time that you did."

"Now I am curious."

Slowly she took the lid off the old shoe box and slid it under the bottom. Pausing, she took the gift box out and untied the ribbon. "This was given to me before you were born."

"From Grandma?"

Before speaking, she searched Sage's face. "No, Honey, from your father."

"Oh," Sage said softly.

Lifting the lid, Lorraine took the locket out. Sage was silent as she waited respectfully for her mother to continue. She had never mentioned her father before, and she thought something must be up. Finding the indent, Lorraine spread the locket open then passed it to Sage. Her first glimpse at the man responsible for her life. Running a finger over her father's face, she looked up at her mother, her face expressing questions.

"His name is Gage Holten, and he is from Texas."

"Oh Mom, he is such a handsome man."

"Yes, he is. We met shortly after I started working at Tanner Industries in Kanyon Valley. He was a client. We'd had four wonderful days before he had to return to Texas, promising to come back. He didn't, and shortly after that I found out that I was pregnant."

"Oh, Mom, you must have been devastated."

"I was heartbroken, to say the least."

Sage listened as she told her the entire story of her life on the run and to where Gage had come back for her, but they had already moved.

"Wait… What? He came back for you? How do you know that?"

"I saw him."

"When!?"

"Today."

"Well, tell me," she said, excitedly.

Lorraine told her about the afternoon at the park, his horrific story and the jagged blue glass. She held up her wounded hand and said, "hence the bandage."

"Where is he now?"

A blank look crossed Lorraine's face, "I don't know."

"What? What do you mean you don't know?"

"I left him at the park."

"Why?"

Greyson saw us kissing, and I was so embarrassed I rushed the kids out of the park. Sage, I freaked out, and I don't know how to reach him." She was sobbing softly, and while Sage tried to console her, her security phone rang.

"Hello? Oh hi," she said pausing, "yes, she's here," another pause, "who?" pause, "OK, send him up then, thanks."

"Who was that?"

"It was security, he said someone was looking for you, and since you weren't home, he sent him up here. I hope that's ok because he is on his way up."

They heard the ding from the elevator, and when it opened, relief spread through Lorraine's body.

"Gage!"

"Hello Darlin,' I hope you don't mind, but I convinced security to let me in. Dang, Girl, what do I have to do to keep you by my side?"

"Nothing anymore, Gage," she said, walking into his arms.

"… and who is this purdy lil thang?" he said, glancing over at Sage.

Sage was immediately in awe of her father; he was exactly as her mother had described. She was a little more than giddy with her mom and dad in the same room and meeting him for the first time.

"Um… Sage… this is… um…"

"I know who he is," Sage said, still holding onto the locket. Smiling broadly, she walked closer and passed it to him. He recognized it immediately and looked at Lorraine.

"Gage, this is… your daughter, Sage."

Sage finally got the relevance of her name… Gage and Sage.

"My… daughter?" he drawled softly, looking from Lorraine to Sage.

No one spoke until Sage wrapped her arms around him and spoke the word he never expected to hear. "Dad."

Reaching for Lorraine, they huddled in a three-way hug for several minutes letting the information sink in.

"Wow!" he said, "I found you and my daughter on the same day." He barely got the words out of his mouth when the elevator opened, and Greyson walked in.

"Hey Mom, hey Nana, we had fun at the park today, thanks for taking us."

Staring at each other, no one knew who should speak first. Feeling it was her place, Lorraine spoke up to introduce them.

"Grey, there is someone here I'd like you to meet."

"Hey, I saw you kissin' Nana in the park."

Sage pressed her lips together to stifle a grin waiting for her mom to continue.

"Grey, this is Gage, Gage Holten and he is your grandpa," she said, cutting right to the chase and determined there would be no more secrets.

"My grandpa, cool! I'm Greyson," he said holding out his hand. Gage picked him up off the floor and held him tightly while he giggled and kick to get down.

Gage was quiet for several seconds and kept glancing at the open box on the couch. Before saying anything, he turned to Lorraine. "I have a question for you Darlin',"

"Sure, Gage, anything."

"Is Sage the reason you disappeared all those years ago?"

"Yes, it was, Gage," she said and nodding without hesitating. "I was afraid if you knew about the pregnancy, your parents might take my baby from me. When I thought you had moved on, I panicked and couldn't imagine anyone taking my child from me."

"Darlin', I could have guaranteed that nobody would have ever taken your youngen from you. I wish I had known, but I am glad I do now."

"I wish I had been braver too Gage, but finding out I was pregnant at seventeen and becoming a mom at barely eighteen, I thought maybe your parents would have felt that they were more capable of raising a child than I was. My parents and I thought we were doing the right thing at the time."

Sage closed her eyes and suddenly realized that her story was exactly like her mother's. She felt certain now that she had, indeed, been living out her mother's fears.

"I understand," he said, "but you have to know I never forgot about you for a second."

"It has always been you, too."

He glanced into the old shoe box and reached in to pick up the glass. Reaching into his pocket, he pulled out his piece and joined the jagged edges, making a perfect fit.

"I can't believe you kept this stuff after all these years," he said. "Says the man carrying a twenty-five-year-old piece of broken glass in his pocket," she said, giggling like a school girl, "besides, it was all I had left of the man I loved."

"OK, you got me there. So, you're named after your daddy?" he said, grinning at Sage.

"I guess I am, and now I don't have to wonder anymore." She was torn between the joy of meeting her father and the heartache for the loss of the man she loved. An old saying crossed her mind, 'when one door closes, another one opens.'

28

Sage didn't know when it would be safe to revisit the grave. After several weeks, she couldn't wait any longer, she had to go.

Waiting in the car, endless minutes passed, or perhaps even hours, she couldn't remember. Gathering courage, she pulled the hoodie up over her head and put the sunglasses on again. Even though she was there alone, it made her feel secure and unsuspecting. Walking up the path, she saw a smaller mound of dirt in the distance, and suddenly her legs began to weaken. She had felt the same way at the service a few weeks before and also in recent days, only this time, spots formed before her eyes and she squinted to see past them.

She was relieved for the chance to sit down. Something felt wrong, she had never felt this weak and lifeless before. She'd blamed it on the grief she felt since Drew died. Her strength seemed zapped from her body, and she felt oddly strange. She'd had very little appetite since she'd gotten word of Drew's passing and she was beginning to feel the effects of it now. Letting the thought of food slide, she was there to spend time with Drew and then disappear before someone showed up. She tried to concentrate on why she came, but she couldn't focus. "Drew," she said aloud, but nothing else came out. She wanted to tell him how much she loved him, missed him and she wanted to thank him for loving her and for all he had done for her and Grey. Thoughts were there, but she couldn't form the words. Suddenly bile rose up in her throat causing her to gag, but nothing came up. Weakness caused her to fall over and rest her head on the mound. She didn't know how long she had been there, but she knew she had to find the strength to get up and go home. She began to cry, for Drew, for herself and for feeling so bad. Shivering, she wrapped her sweater tighter around her body and sat up. She just wanted to sit on the cold ground and indulge in self-pity for a few more minutes. Pulling out her phone, she wanted to call her mother in case she needed her, but she couldn't focus on the screen.

From a distance, he saw her sitting on the ground next to his father's grave. He had come to the cemetery every day to visit with his father hoping she'd be there. When he saw the strange car, parked on the roadway, his first thoughts were of her. Walking up behind her, the hoodie had slipped partially off her head exposing strands of long, blonde hair. It seemed to be the same woman that he'd seen at the mall.

"Cassie?" he said softly, remembering the name.

Her back straightened at the sound of his voice. The first she had heard it in so many years.

"Noah?" she said, without turning around. She would know his voice anywhere.

His brows crinkled, wondering how she knew his name. Stumbling to her feet, she timidly dragged the sunglasses slowly off her face. His heart skipped a beat when he saw her face. "Sage?"

"Noah," she whispered. Walking into his arms, relief flooded her body. Leaning on him for several minutes, fresh tears rolled down her cheeks.

He held on tightly not believing his luck.

All the sadness from losing Drew rolled off her and elation filled her soul at seeing Noah again. Pulling away, they looked at each other, neither one knowing what to say until she broke the ice.

"Why did you call me Cassie?" she asked, curiously.

"It doesn't matter at the moment but where have you been, Sage, and what are you doing here at my father's grave?"

"I... um," she dropped her eyes for a few seconds searching for words, "I... met your father, a few months ago, at the airport. I realized there was a connection as soon as he introduced himself, but we never spoke of our families except that you were his son. I saw the resemblance immediately and seeing you now, Noah, you look just like him."

"Are you the reason he left my mother?" he asked softly.

"No!" she said adamantly. "He would never have done that, he was an honorable man. He'd left her the week before and had already filed for divorce." She wobbled a bit and tried to steady herself, but there was nothing to hang on to. Noah reached for her, but she went to her knees. Her phone slipping from her hand and onto the ground.

"Are you alright?" he asked squatting beside her.

"No, I don't think I am, just let me be for a few minutes," she said waving a hand, "it might pass again."

"Again? What do you mean, again? What's going on? Are you ill?"

"I hadn't been, up until I'd gotten the news about Drew, that's when I started to feel weird. Then at the service, I got weak and..."

Noah remembered seeing her wobble during the service. "I know, I saw you."

"You did?"

"Yes, you were over there," he pointed, "and I was here with my mother, but I didn't know who you were except... well never mind," he couldn't bring up the mall incident now.

"This is so painful, Noah, I am so sorry about your dad."

"It was very sudden, and we are all pretty much still in shock," he said sadly.

She nodded, swallowed and tried not to gag.

"Are you sure you're alright, you're looking pretty green."

"Would you help me to my car, please, Noah, I should go home."

"You aren't in any shape to drive, let me take you."

"Really, you'd do that for me?"

"You are not well, Sage, of course, I'll drive you home."

"Thank you, Noah, I don't know why I have been feeling so rotten lately," she said, reaching for his hand. Once she was on her feet, the earth began to spin, blackness set in and Noah caught her before she went down. Sweeping her up in his arms, he grabbed her phone and dashed down the path to his car. Speeding towards the hospital, he tried not to break any laws. Stopping his car at the emergency entrance, he ran inside yelling for someone to help him. He didn't know if she was a doctor or a nurse, but she yelled for a gurney and followed him outside. Noah lifted her from the car and onto the gurney in one swoop, explaining that she had passed out. He was keeping up as they rolled through the doors and into a cubicle. Someone flashed a light in her eyes and another person pumped up a pressure cuff on her arm. Her eyes fluttered open and then closed again.

"What's your name, Miss, can you hear me?"

"Wh... where... am I?"

"I need you to tell me your name."

"Sage Lawrence," she said, barely audible.

Noah, she remembered Noah. She saw him through blurred eyes.

"Noah," she whispered, weakly.

"I'm right here," she heard him say.

"Where? I can't see you, Noah? I'm so scared."

Memories momentarily flooded his mind of the day at the loft when she panicked over the ladder. He saw that same fear in her eyes now.

"I'm here, I'll stay with you for as long as they'll let me."

"Husbands are allowed to stay," said the attendant, as she did her survey.

Noah opened his mouth to speak, but Sage squeezed his hand and begged him with her eyes.

"Yes, I'll stay."

Closing her eyes again, she breathed a sigh of relief.

"Do you know when she ate last?" someone asked.

He wanted to say that the last time he saw her eat was nearly a decade ago, but he knew he couldn't.

"Yesterday afternoon, I had toast and yogurt," Sage said, weakly, "what's wrong with me?"

"You seem dehydrated, we'll do some blood work to see if that will tell us anything. I'll be back with a tray."

Closing her eyes, she hoped the dizziness would stop.

"Sage," he whispered, "why do you call yourself Cassie?"

"I used Cassie Lucan for modelling purposes. No one knows me as Sage Lawrence anymore, but my medical insurance is still under Lawrence for my family's sake." Her voice was only a whisper, but he heard every word.

"I know you as Sage," he said unwaveringly. She was his Sage and always would be.

"I know you do, Noah, I changed it after I left school. I need to explain…"

"Explain what?"

"Why I left… please, no more lies."

He wondered if he wanted to hear it. The wound had opened when he saw her at the funeral. Not knowing for sure whether or not it was her but close enough to open it up again. For years, he'd searched endlessly for faces, shapes, and sizes, trying to find her in crowds, stores, and cars. He thought his search had ended when he'd seen her in the mall, but his dream died when someone called her Cassie. He'd been inches from her and didn't know it.

"I need to explain…" she whispered, but the nurse was back with the blood cart. Passing a clipboard to Noah, she asked him to fill it out. He looked at her and raised an eyebrow. Reaching into her pocket, she pulled out a small pouch and passed it to him. "My insurance is in the pink case; it's all in there."

'Of course, a pink case,' he thought, *'she loves pink.'*

"We'll put a rush on the blood work, but you need to stay here until we get the results. You get some rest, and I'll send your husband back in."

"Yes, please, send him back in," she said, waiting for him to return.

"Noah, please sit with me, I have something to tell you."

"Can't it wait until later, when you are rested and stronger."

"I'm so tired," she said, her eyes fluttering.

Noah smoothed her hair and ran his thumb over her cheek. "Get some rest, I'll be here when you wake up."

"Promise?"

"I promise."

His touch was soothing, and so was his voice, but she fought sleep. *'He has to know, I must tell him,'* she thought, as she felt herself drifting.

Soft voices brought her back around as she fought to open her eyes. Her hand stung when she raised it. As she stirred, someone pressed a button to raise the head of the bed, and she felt Noah's hand in hers. *'He did stay.'*

"Ms. Lawrence, welcome back, I am Dr. Morgan. We gave you an IV drip because you are slightly dehydrated, so in your condition, we started you on fluids. Let's see if you can sit up without the dizziness," he said, dropping a dish in front of her and sliding a hand under her back for support, "take it slowly, no need to rush."

Nausea began as soon as she lifted her head up off the pillow and she gagged into a kidney-shaped dish, but nothing came up.

"What is wrong with me? Why am I so dizzy and weak? Am I dying?" she whimpered.

A chuckle escaped the doctor, "No, my dear, I assure you that you are not dying, but I have some good news for you and your husband. You're pregnant and so comes the dizziness, weak feelings and all the rest of it because you haven't eaten or had anything to drink for more than a day. So, you must take better care of yourself for this baby's sake. Once the drip is finished, your husband can take you home."

Both she and Noah were in shock at the doctor's words.

"I'm pregnant? Oh, my God, not again!" *'Am I being punished. This just cannot be happening',* she ranted to herself.

"This is my dad's baby?" he whispered.

"Yes, Noah and nobody can know about this, you have to promise me!"

"Why can't anyone know?"

"Your mother, Noah, it would kill her. They've only been separated for a few months. Very few people knew about us."

Squinting his eyes, he asked, "What did you mean, before, when you said, 'not again'?"

Emotions were running high, and she became overwhelmed. Tears came but not only for herself and her condition but for all the wasted years of hiding and the lies... so many lies. Greyson should have known his father and his grandfather. She had deprived him of so much, exactly like her mother had done to her. Repeated mistakes and so many regrets, she couldn't do it anymore. Noah reached for her and drew her into his arms.

She clung to him with what little strength she had left. How could she love two men so passionately, Drew, whom she'd known for only months and Noah, the one she has loved for twenty years. She hadn't gotten him out of her system, she had just moved forward without him.

"I'm sorry, Noah, I'm so, so, sorry," she whimpered and drew in several exhausted breaths.

He felt her body tremble as she inhaled, "What are you sorry for?"

"For leaving you, for running away and for hiding the truth," she sobbed into his chest as he held her close.

"I don't understand anything you're saying except the 'leaving me' part. Can you be more specific, please," he urged, pulling far enough away to see her face.

"Do you have my phone? I dropped it somewhere."

"Yes, right here," he said, taking it out of his pocket.

Pulling her cell phone out, she pressed her thumb against the button to unlock it and scrolled to her pictures. Finding one of

Greyson, she hesitated for only a second before turning the screen towards him.

Noah looked at the picture and it was as if he was looking at a picture of himself at that age. Looking down at Sage, he furrowed his brows, then back at the picture.

"He's your son, Noah. I ran because I was pregnant. My mother thought it was the right thing to do. We thought, at the time, that your parents might take my baby away since I was only sixteen. I'm sorry, I'm so, so sorry. You both deserve to know each other, and neither one of you deserve to be separated any longer."

He looked at the smiling face, on the screen, and his heart melted. There was no reason to be upset for something that could not be undone. "My son?" Noah whispered, "Sage, I have a son?"

"Yes, you do, he is such a sweet boy, Noah and I can't wait for you to meet him, he needs to know you."

"He's beautiful, he's handsome, and he's mine?" he smiled broadly and proudly.

"Yes, he is, he turned seven a few days ago," she whispered.

Thinking back in time, it had been almost eight years, so given the time frame for pregnancy, he would be seven, and he definitely was his. He was mesmerized by the face he was staring at. "Look at him," he whispered back, "he looks just like me! I can't wait to meet him! What's his name?" Tears formed in his eyes when she said it.

"Greyson Alexander Lawrence," she whispered, "I changed my name, Noah so you wouldn't be able to find me. My mom and I moved shortly after I found out I was pregnant. We were so young, and I was scared, so we just ran. I allowed my mother's fear, from her past, to interfere with our future. I should have gone to you and told you, so we could have talked about our options. I was so worried about myself I wasn't thinking about how you would feel. Can you ever forgive me?"

He had the heart of his father and was overwhelmed with happiness and feeling grateful, not only for being with Sage again but also getting the news of his son.

Dropping the phone, he instinctively wrapped her in his arms. "Thank you, Sage, thank you for being honest with me, thank you for giving me a son." Drawing back from her, he looked at the misery in her eyes and without hesitation, he kissed her, and they both traveled back to the loft where Greyson had been conceived from their love.

Suddenly, he pulled away. "I'm sorry, Sage, I know you... we... are both still mourning my father, but this is a great moment for me. I never thought I would ever see you again and I find you and a son on the same day. I can't wait to get out of here and meet him." He eyed the drip at the quarter-full mark and knew that soon he would see Greyson. He watched her fall back to sleep, and he waited. Before falling asleep, she remembered hearing similar words from her father, just days ago. '*I found you and my daughter in the same day.*' Deja Vu all over again.

Once the bag was empty, Noah nudged Sage to wake her.

"Are we finally done here?" she asked, in a sleepy tone.

A nurse entered the room, with a clipboard. "I have your discharge papers Ms. Lawrence all I need is your signature, and you're free to go," she said, unhooking the tube and needle from Sage's hand.

Sitting up slowly, she was relieved that the dizziness had passed. Whatever was in the drip had done its job. Swinging her legs slowly over the side of the bed she heard a stern warning from the nurse.

"You must take things slowly at first. You are at a delicate stage in your pregnancy, and if you expect to carry to full term then you must do better than you have done these last few weeks, you hear me?" She playfully shook a finger at Sage then turned her attention to Noah. "I expect that you will be keeping a closer eye on your wife."

Noah wasn't certain if it was a statement, a question or an order. "Yes, ma'am, I will."

She blushed when he gave her that smile that would melt icicles.

"You do that, and I don't expect to see your wife in here again before the delivery."

"You can count on that," Noah said, looking at Sage.

Getting into the 'husband' role, Noah looked at Sage with the same smile he'd just given the nurse. "Well, wife, let's get you home," he said, with a wink.

"Yes, let's go home, Noah."

Once in the car, Noah began with small talk. "I'll have someone pick your car up and deliver it to you if that's ok."

"Yes, it's fine."

Silence came between them until Noah spoke again. "You'll have to tell me where you live, Sage."

"Kenyon Creek."

"What? You've lived just over the bridge all this time?"

Remembering his father's words, it made sense. He had said he was making a fresh start in Kenyon Creek. It was only a bridge ride away, but Sage never had to cross it after she left. Kenyon Creek had everything to offer that Kenyon Ridge had so there was no point in crossing over and taking a chance of an unnecessary run-in with Noah.

Lorraine never went back either, there was nothing left there for her either, so she basically stayed in Kenyon Creek or shopped in Kanyon Cove if she needed a broader selection.

"He knew," Sage said, softly," your father, he knew."

"He knew what?"

"About Greyson." Her answers were short and to the point, but he had to know.

"How did he know? How long had he known?" Noah was blown away by her sudden admission, and he had questions that needed to be answered.

"I'm not sure, Noah, I just know that he knew. He had information, pictures, he even knew that I was Sage Lawrence even though I introduced myself as Cassie Lucan. The hardest part was that he knew about us, 'us' being... you and me." Living a lie for so long, it felt good to be able to have an honest conversation with Noah. She had often wondered if she ever would since she'd had mental conversations with him all the time, almost daily but they were just in her thoughts and she never got any answers. Now was her chance as they drove across the bridge and into Kenyon Creek to her condo.

"He had tried to Google me, as Cassie Lucan and came up with nothing, so he hired a private detective to dig further. He was curious since he knew you and I went to school together. I guess all it took was an older yearbook from Kanyon Ridge High School and there we were. Obviously more digging lead to information on Greyson along with recent pictures and a birth certificate. I have all the information at home if you'd like to see it."

"It didn't bother him that you had a child by me?"

"I don't know, I don't think it did. He hadn't said anything or acted differently towards me."

"What do you mean?"

"Oh, I'm sorry, I should explain myself further, so that it will make more sense to you. I didn't know about it either until after he had ... you know... died."

"How was that possible?"

"I got a call from a lawyer several days after Drew died, asking me to meet him at his office. I was more than surprised, not to mention curious, as to why he wanted to see me. When I got there, he presented me with a letter from Drew. As hard as it was, I had no choice but to read it in his office. All the information was in an envelope. It had been written only recently since we had only known each other for four months. It could have been the day he

276

went to tell you he was moving to Kanyon Creek, that would make sense."

Tears welled up in her eyes, realizing it was only such a short time ago. Reaching across, Noah touched her arm, and without hesitating, she put her hand over his. Natural instincts returned between them even after the long separation. It was as easy as breathing to touch each other as if time hadn't passed.

"Turn left at the lights, first condo on the right," she said directing him.

As he drove in the parking lot, she pressed her fob to open the garage door.

"Drive underground to number seventeen."

Following her directions, he put the car in park. They unlatched their seat belts and turned to face each other.

"Now what?" he asked.

"Come on up, and I'll see if mom and Greyson are home, so you can meet them."

"I'm kind of nervous," he said, rubbing his hands together.

"Yes, I imagine you are, but this is long overdue, Noah and we need to do this. We are not sixteen anymore, we are grown-ups, so I have to do this not only for you and Greyson but for me and for your dad as well. He had written in his note that you should know your son. It has been such a struggle trying to keep this hidden, I don't want to any longer. Are you ready? Ready to meet your son?"

He let out a long, nervous and jagged breath through pursed lips before nodding. "OK! Let's go then, shall we?"

The elevator opened into her condo but was it quiet.

"Wow! This is quite the place? Is this yours, dad's or...?"

"Mine," she said, 'it's my place, he moved in with me. Make yourself comfortable, I'll be right back." She made her way to the bathroom to wash her face and brush her teeth, but the shower looked so inviting that she turned the tap on, stripped and got in. Leaning against the tiles, she welcomed the heat from the water. Closing her eyes, she let it run over her hair and body. Smiling, she placed her hands on each side of her flat belly recalling the doctors' words. *'They had thought the baby was Noah's and neither of us had corrected them,'* she thought. A baby was growing inside her... again. Thoughts of her first pregnancy flashed before her. Knowing that Noah was in her home, she felt the stress of the past several hours, wash away. Stepping out, she wrapped a bath towel around her body and squeezed the water from her hair with another. Flipping her hair forward, she ran her fingers through releasing any knots and then flipped it back. Opening the bathroom door, she smelled food and padded to the kitchen still in a towel.

"Something smells wonderful!"

Noah turned to speak to her but lost the words seeing her standing before him in a towel. He gazed at her wet hair and the beach fantasy gnawed at his stomach. Realizing the 'look' he was giving her, she raised her hand to her chest and grabbed the towel, and the other went to her hair. "I'm sorry, I smelled food and didn't realize how hungry I was. I'll go and get dressed."

"No, stay, I didn't mean to stare, it's just that you're so incredibly beautiful, Sage, come and sit. I hope you don't mind but I went through your fridge. I whipped up some scrambled eggs, toast, juice and a bowl of fruit," he said, not able to take his eyes off her. "I heard the shower running, so it gave me time to make you something to eat, the doctor said you had to take care of yourself."

"Thank you, it smells delicious," she said, taking a long inhale, as she sat on a stool at the counter.

Her hair hung in natural curls as she devoured her food. She laid the fork down and sipped on the juice, eyeing him for several seconds. "Noah, I have a favor to ask you."

"OK, what is it?"

Pressing her lips together, she paused. "Would you be Ok with packing up your dad's stuff and donating it? You should keep what you want though."

"Sure, I'll do that."

"I appreciate it, thank you, I can't go in there and do it," she said, swinging her long legs away from the counter and hopped off the stool."

"OK, with that settled, I'll go and slip on some decent clothes and be right back.

"OK, I'll clean up in here while you get dressed."

Coming back to the living room in a pair of lounge pants and tank top, she headed for the couch. "Come and sit with me," she said. Following her in, he didn't immediately sit down. He still felt comfortable around her, but it was weird being with her again after eight years.

"This is an awesome place," he said, looking around. Strolling over to the deck doors, he looked out at the lake. "Wow, you were lucky to find this treasure."

"Yes, I like it a lot, and there is a golf course just beyond the lake too. Come and sit with me," she said, again, patting the couch. Sitting down, she opened an album and flipped a few pages to when Grey was born.

"Here are some of Grey's baby pictures, I made this particular album after I brought him home. There are so many, but this one is special. It was his first months with Mom and me," she said, lovingly, then passed him the album. As he scanned the pictures, he smiled at the handsome baby boy.

"Grey? You call him Grey?"

Nodding she said, "I'm sorry, Noah, it was wrong of me to keep Grey's existence from you, I wish I could have a do-over."

Lightly, he touched her arm, "I know Sage, but you can't keep apologizing for a mistake just because it was a long time in the making. I understand. Really, I do. You've apologized already and I've accepted it, so stop; OK! I'm just happy to have the chance to meet my son." Gazing at her, he felt lucky to be there. This was something he never thought he would ever do again. He knew he had an unconditional love for this woman and he would do anything for her. Reaching for her, he pulled her into his arms, suddenly not caring about the time factor in his father's death. The years that had passed without her made him even more determined never to lose her again. She felt natural in his arms, and she clung to him too. She pulled away to say something, and before she got a word out, he slipped his hand under her still damp hair and pulled her in for a kiss. Lightly at first, waiting for a negative reaction but there was none except for an audible moan. The kiss deepened, and she clung to him with a hunger that hadn't been sated in a long, long time. Even her short time with Drew, she never lost her hunger for Noah. Time hadn't curbed the loss, years did nothing to ease the pain of leaving him. She had yearned for this moment for a very long time. Breaking the kiss, she inhaled deeply and wrapped her arms around his neck.

"This feels so right and yet so wrong," she whispered.

"I know, but can we maybe just concentrate on the moment and not think about anyone or anything for right now," he pleaded.

"Are you OK with everything that has gone on? Noah, I didn't set out to meet your father, it just happened. I don't want anything to come between us, again."

"It isn't 'real' to me, Sage, I never saw you with my dad, I didn't see you as a couple, and I'm not sorry or upset that you loved him, but I know whatever you felt for him it was not the same as what we had. Nothing will ever compare to that, and deep down in my soul, I know my dad would approve of what is happening here. He would want me to be here, and I know he would want me to be happy without guilt. I believe he would want this for us and for Greyson."

"I feel the same way, Noah. Your dad had a heart of gold, and so do you. I never stopped loving you or missing you, not even for a minute. You were always in my heart, and I had Grey to remind me, every day of the love we shared. He is our love."

"After hearing you say that," he said, softly, "I have a proposal, now that I know how you still feel," he paused then began again. "No one knows about the baby except for you and me, so how would you feel about raising this baby together as ours. No one ever has to know that he or she isn't mine. You are only a few weeks into this pregnancy, and I think we could make it believable. What do you think?"

"I'm stunned, I haven't had time to absorb the baby news after the day we've had. Would you really do that? You'd raise this baby with me?"

"Sage," he said, putting on a more serious expression, "I either have to begin my life with you or move on without you, it is totally up to you."

She saw the seriousness on his face, and it didn't seem as though he was giving her an ultimatum, but more of a choice.

"I... I... um, yes! I accept!" she said, throwing herself into his arms.

He breathed into her partly dried hair and inhaled the strawberry scent, and they were both sixteen again.

"Has anyone seen you, publicly, with my father?"

"Just Amelia and my mom, but they are both discrete and would never say anything. They both know how important it was not to tell people about our relationship. It wasn't only for you and Keri but for Grey too. He has never seen me with anybody, and we wanted to keep it that way."

"How did you manage that? He lived here."

"Yes, your father lived here briefly, but Grey has always lived with my mother. Since I traveled a lot, it only made sense for him to live with her than to move him back and forth around my trips. She has worked for me since he was born, and she has been his only babysitter."

"Then it makes sense not to involve my father in this pregnancy. You and I will always know that I am not the biological father and I'll be raising my half-sibling, but birth records will name us as the parent. We can do this, Sage, I know I want to, do you?" he asked again, giving her a chance to change her mind although he hoped she wouldn't.

"I do want to do this, Noah, I really do, but there is one thing I want to make clear."

He waited for her to continue.

"We know that Drew is this baby's father, but as of right now, as far as I am concerned, this baby is yours. I want you to be certain that you can accept that from this point forward."

"I definitely can, and I will raise this child as my own."

Taking his hands, she said, "OK," but, holding up one finger, "there is just one more thing, and I promise I'm done."

He gave her that adorable smile and nodded, "Go ahead."

"Whether or not we have a boy or a girl, I would like to name the baby after Drew. Are you OK with that?"

"I am, I am totally OK with that, do you have names already?"

"I do," she smiled. "Andy, if it's a boy, Andrew Alexander Noah Greyson," she said, "I'd like to carry on with the middle name into the third generation... well, it'll be third generation to the rest of the world."

"And if it is a girl?" he asked.

"That's something we must discuss further if you don't mind," she said.

"Sure, I'm willing to discuss anything with you at any time, and I hope we can make it a practice.

"Are you sure?"

"I am, go ahead," he insisted.

"If we have a girl, I was thinking I'd like to name her Andi, not short for anything, just Andi, with an I. I had been thinking along the lines of Andi Lorraine Keri Greyson."

"But...? You aren't OK with that now?"

"No, Noah, I'm not." Taking a deep breath, she continued, "You and I both know that this child is and always will be 'ours' but Drew is this baby's biological father, and we can't change that even if it doesn't have his name on the birth records."

"I get that," he nodded, "go on."

Taking his hands, she said, "From the conversations Drew and I had, I kinda read between the lines, and I don't think he liked Keri very much. Not that he ever said it aloud, but it was just a feeling I got. I'm not sure how he would feel about his child carrying her name if he had a choice," she said and left it there for him to absorb.

Noah searched her face and admired her perception. Nodding his head slowly, he pressed his lips together before speaking. "Sage, you are absolutely right," he said adamantly, "I agree with you on this one, my father did not like my mother, and he would not want her name attached to his child. Thank you though for thinking about her, but we can't do it. I love and respect my father, and I know he would want us to choose another name, so what will it be?"

"Are you sure, Noah? You're OK with a change?"

"I am totally fine with it, what else do you have in mind."

Smiling, she brought her hands up, prayer-like and touched her fingers to her lips for a pause. Dropping them into her lap, she said, "Since you, Drew and Greyson all have the same middle name, Alexander, what would you think about Alexandria? Andi Alexandria Lorraine... Greyson."

Drawing in a deeply emotional breath, he pursed his lips and slowly let it out. Nodding his head was all he was able to do while drawing her into his arms.

"I love it, Sage and I am totally OK with it and do you know what? If anybody isn't OK with our choice, then it's their problem, not ours."

Sage could only guess that it was his mother he was referring to.

"This day could not get any better," he said, and when he got his voice back, he said the words. "How do you feel about getting married?"

Her eyes widened and moistened, and she covered her face with her hands before speaking.

"When?"

"As soon as humanly possible," he grinned. He loved her so much, and he never wanted to leave her side again.

"OK!"

"Seriously?" he said, caressing the bare skin on her arms. They were like two teenagers plotting an elopement. Both filled with excitement, love and pure joy at finding their way back to each other. Sealing their agreement with a kiss the elevator dinged, startling them.

"Mom?"

"Over here, Grey," she answered, as he came into view.

"I'm sorry I didn't call first, I didn't know you had company, should I go back to Nana's?"

"No, sweetie, come here, I want you to meet someone."

Noah, seeing his son for the first time, felt the lump in his throat as Grey walked towards him. Inhaling deeply, he looked over at Sage.

"Grey, this is Noah, Noah Greyson."

"Greyson?" he asked, "cool, that's my name," he said, with the natural innocence of a child.

"Yes, it is," she said, "you were named after him, Grey. I know this is going to sound confusing to you since it has always been just you, me and Nana, but," she stopped, laid her hand on Noah's back, inhaled deeply and continued, "Grey, Noah is your dad."

Noah rose up from the couch as Grey's back straightened at the words and stared up at Noah while absorbing the announcement. A flurry of thoughts crowded his brain while taking in the resemblance, his height, the gentle man standing before him. Noah waited for him to speak hoping for good things and not a jealous tantrum or whatever kids might do.

"My... dad? I have a... dad?" he asked, looking up at Noah with tears in his eyes. "You're my ... dad?" he stammered, trying hard to keep his voice strong but it broke, every time, at the 'dad' word. Taking a few steps closer, he stood near the man he just learned is his father. The word slipped out as if he had been saying it his entire life, yet it was the first time. "Daddy?"

Noah went to his knees and scooped him up into a hug. Sage saw his shoulders heaving slightly as he teared up while holding his son for the first time. "Yes, I'm your daddy, Son," Noah said, through weepy eyes and not caring if he preferred to call him 'dad' or 'daddy' he was just happy to be here. He would have even been OK with 'Noah' until Grey got used to the news, but this was even better.

"This is all new to me too, so we can do this together, OK, Son?"

As he nodded in agreement, Sage had never seen such a genuine smile on her son's face. He looked at his father with pride and respect, and it was the perfect moment for her to tell him the news.

"Greyson, we have more news for you if you're ready."

He could hardly tear his eyes away from Noah to look at his mother.

"This *is* the best news, Mom!" he said, beaming at them both and wrapping his little fist inside his dad's hand. He was proud of his daddy already, and he wasn't about to let him get away.

"Well, this is good news too, Sweetheart, your Dad and I are getting married, is that OK with you? We are all going to live under the same roof if your dad will agree to move in."

29

Spending several days with Sage and Grey, Noah began to feel as though his life was finally becoming complete. The ugly and lonely hole that had settled inside his chest was, once again, filled with love, happiness, and contentment. He was at a place where he never thought he'd be again. Spending so many years alone, he'd been haunted by thoughts of Sage and unable to be with her, so he was in no big rush to go home. Everything he'd ever needed was in Kanyon Creek. Sage, the love of his life since childhood and someone he had longed for since he'd realized she'd gone missing. His precious son, Greyson, who had been an awesome surprise and someone he couldn't get enough time with. Loving this little person, who was his 'mini' was unfathomable from the first moment after seeing his picture. Bits and pieces of his father remained also. His clothes hung in the closet and his personal items were in the main bathroom where his razor still sat on the charger. They had been the same size in height and weight, and his dad had had great taste in fashion and fragrance. Wearing his father's clothes, it felt odd, but he was comforted. Sensing his approval, he felt close to him as a warmth emanated from his clothing.

Suddenly, his thoughts became a mental conversation with his dad. '*Who better to raise your child than me, Dad?*' he thought, '*the one person who knew how much you loved Sage*'. '*You know I will take care of your child, Dad and I will always love Sage. I know you loved her too and thank you for loving her and for giving us the chance to raise your child, my half-sibling and I promise to love this child with all my heart. Knowing it belongs to you will always be a reminder that you are with us.'* Hugging the arms of his father's shirt, he straightened himself up, drew in a few deep breaths and left the bedroom.

"I have a suggestion," Noah announced.

"What is it, I'm up for some excitement."

"There is something I'd like to show you if you will come with me to Kanyon Ridge."

"Sure, and while we are there perhaps, we can pick up some of your stuff and bring it here."

"Yes, we can do that too."

Driving through familiar streets, memories of this quaint little town flooded her thoughts. The few times she had gone back was only to see Drew at the hospital and again for her trips to the cemetery, but this trip was for a different and happier reason. Sitting beside Noah, it still felt like a dream, and if it was, then she didn't want to wake up.

"How did you sleep last night?" he asked.

"I had a wonderful sleep, thank you for asking. Having you in the house, I guess I am finally in a peaceful place."

"Good to hear," he said, reaching over to touch her.

"Thank you for both understanding and sleeping on the couch. Greyson hasn't spent many nights with me since 'his room,'" she said, using air quotes, "has always been at my mom's. The spare bedroom has always been just that, but now that things have changed, it will be Grey's room from now on. He's never seen me with anyone so, thanks again."

"No thanks needed, I am satisfied just being there, so thank you for letting me stay." They did a quick glance across at each other knowing they were in a good place.

"This looks very familiar," she said, straightening up and paying closer attention.

"Yeah?" He was grinning from ear to ear.

Making the turn toward the beach, he stopped in the parking area and turned off the car.

"Noah! The building has had some changes, why would they do that?"

"Want to see?"

"Yes! I do!"

Getting out, he went around to open the door for her. Walking on the beach brought back many happy times, and she suddenly became emotional. Tears rimmed her eyes, and she dabbed at them with a tissue.

"You sure you're ok?"

"Yes," she said, slipping her hand in his, "just good memories and hormones."

There was a set of stairs running up the side of the yacht club, leading to a large upper deck that overlooked the ocean.

"Wow! This is incredible! Did someone buy the yacht club?"

"Yes... I did."

"You did? Noah! That's... just... wow! I'm speechless."

Climbing the steps and onto the deck, Noah unlocked the loft door.

"This is not a ladder," he teased, "but it is the loft, a redesigned loft. Are you ready?"

"This is so exciting! Yes, I am ready."

Swinging the door open, she walked into the most beautiful space one could ever have imagined. Noah had added dormers with skylights which made the already huge loft look even more spacious.

"This place meant so much to me I had to buy it. You and I and the gang had a lot of great times here. I contacted the owner with an offer, and he accepted, so I decided to remodel the loft to live here. You remember how high the ceiling was downstairs?"

"Yes, I sure do, it's indelibly imprinted in my brain. I was never so scared in my life," she said recalling the ladder.

"Well, I lowered the ceiling but left plenty of space for the kids, of this new generation, to use as we did and those before us. As you remember, it hadn't been used as a yacht club for many years, so it didn't need the high ceiling downstairs anymore. The only other solution would have been to take the entire roof off and build up. But instead, I add dormers and skylights to widen the slopes and lowering the ceiling gave lots of room in the living space."

Sage walked slowly through the loft remembering the opening in the floor and the tiny bedsitting room and kitchenette with sloping walls. It had been replaced with a state of the art, modern kitchen and open concept spacious living room. Floor to ceiling windows had opened up the entire space for a great view of the water. The kitchen was built on the back wall with a six-foot, granite top island, with a sink that faced the dining room. A table sat in front of a set of sliding glass doors which ran across the entire length of the living room.

"How long have you been living here?" she asked, making her way farther through the apartment and into the spacious master bedroom, which also shared the same deck and view.

Walking up behind her, he rested his hands on her shoulders. Giving them a slight squeeze, they both suddenly became quiet and allowed the memories to rush in.

"It took me a while to complete this floor, but I've been here for a few years now," he said softly.

Sage leaned back onto his chest and closed her eyes remembering their first time here. He kissed the top of her head and slid his hands down her arms and flattened them across her tummy causing her to suddenly shiver.

"Noah," she whispered, placing her hands over his. "There are so many memories here, even though the space is different, the memories are still here and alive."

"Yes, they are," he whispered back, kissing her neck, "memories never die."

A moan softly escaped as she turned toward him. Lifting her eyes to meet his, she saw the same burning desire on his face that she was feeling. Raising his hand, he cupped her cheek while the other pressed her back pulling her closer. Her eyes closed as he brought his lips to her throat in tiny kisses. Tilting her head back her breathing became heavy with a deep longing. With his hand in the small of her back, he moved his foot hoping she would follow. Feeling the back of her knees touch the edge of the mattress, she stopped. Noah paused to give her the chance to stop him, but instead she began unbuttoning his shirt. His heart pounded as he gazed into her eyes. He saw that she wanted this as much as he did.

"Sage," he whispered.

Reaching up, she placed her hand on the back of his head and drew him in for a kiss. His insides exploded with passion for her. He couldn't hold her tight enough as he devoured her with his mouth.

"Oh, my God, baby," he murmured, "I have missed you every day," he said, breathlessly.

"Noah, I never forgot about you for a minute. I love you so much," she whispered in rapid breaths. She felt for his belt, but he wasn't wearing one, so she went for the button and zipper.

"You are way overdressed," he grinned, and swept her tee shirt over her head. Reaching behind to unhook her bra and whispered, "You are just as beautiful as you were back then." Sliding his hands inside her panties, he lifted her onto the bed and slipped her jeans down her slender legs.

"You still have too many clothes on," she teased, removing his shorts.

Gathering her up in his arms, it felt like an eternity since he'd last held her. Overcome by the scent of strawberry, he'd imagined lying with the woman he loved countless times. Now that he was where he had longed to be, he was in heaven.

"Are you sure we can do this? I mean…" he rested his hand on her tummy, "… you know."

"I don't think it'll be a problem," she said, bringing his lips down to hers.

He was lost in love, passion and overwhelming joy at being with her again.

Reaching down, he drew a fleeced throw over them as they lay in each other's arms, still with the same passion and hunger for each other. He held her close as if she were his life-line and closed his eyes and silently gave thanks.

Nothing was awkward, and everything was natural. It was as if they had been making love for years. Although he'd had very little practice, she was still a natural in his arms. Making love to the sound of the waves was about as beautiful as it got as they held on to each other.

Laying quietly and relishing in the moment, Noah posed a question. "How would you feel about using this as our summer house by the ocean?" he said, drawing her close to him. He'd been running a name around in his head for a few days and decided to say it aloud. "I think 'Grey-Law's Paradise,' is suitable, what do you think of that?"

"Pretty inventive of you, did you just come up with that?" she asked. "Even though this place has good and bad memories, the yacht club was our childhood hang out, the loft was also the beginning of an end for us. Grey was conceived here, and this is the only place we've ever made love. Both our first and last time, and now … our first time again. I think 'Lover's Loft' sounds about perfect, she giggled."

"That's why it has more meaning now because it's ours. I bought this with the hope that we'd share it one day and here we are."

His words moved her to tears. They had been so happy sharing this secret loft until it all went to hell causing her to run away from him. But lying there with him, it felt a little bit like coming back home.

Running a thumb over her cheek, he whispered, "No tears, Baby, this is our happy place."

"I know, I consider them happy tears… mixed with hormones."

* * *

"We have to make plans for our wedding before much more time goes by. I will soon be popping out here," she said, touching her tummy, "so what do you say?"

"I was ready yesterday! I mean, as far back as the hospital incident, I'm ready."

"So, when mom gets back from Texas…"

"Wait, what? Your mom is in Texas? What's going on down there?"

"Oh, my God! So much has happened, in such a short time, I forgot to tell you! My father is from Texas, and after all these years, he finally found my mom! His name is Gage, hence the name Sage," she smiled, doing a little pirouette in honor of her name.

"He is awesome, and Grey loves him so much. Wait until you hear his accent, it's like watching old episodes of Dallas," she giggled. "Seriously though, it's like a repeat of our lives," she said, sadly. Mom and her parents ran from him too when she was pregnant with me at seventeen, and he has spent the last twenty-five years looking for her. I think she believed it was best for us, her and I, to do the same thing when I became pregnant. How can four lives be so messed up under the same circumstances?"

"It does seem quite uncanny," he admitted. *'Even the situation with my dad is similar. He was seventeen too when my mom got pregnant,'* he thought but didn't want to bring up the past.

"It wouldn't surprise me, though, if they come back married. Gage, um… dad, is determined not to be without her and that, to me, is true love!" she swooned, and was happy to know that her mom was happy and content being with the love of her life.

"I can certainly understand that," he said. "It sounds like me trying to find you."

"You looked for me?"

"Ah, yeah!" he said wide-eyed. The fact that she had to ask surprised him. "When you left, at first, I thought you were just on an extended modelling gig but then when I tried to call, the line had been disconnected, so I went over to the house, and it was empty. I knew it hadn't been lived in for a while because the grass hadn't been cut for some time and it looked abandoned. Nobody knew anything. I asked the neighbors, the mailman, the flyer guy and nothing. So, I searched online for any clue, but Sage Lawrence just wasn't there. I even searched the website under models and couldn't find your name anywhere. I couldn't even find anything on Lorraine."

Sage went over to him, knelt down and laid her head in his lap, "I'm so sorry, Noah, I wish I could go back and do it right."

"I know Babe, but we can't circle that drain, we have to move forward. So, when your mom gets back… what? What's the plan?"

Getting to her feet, she wobbled a bit, and Noah grabbed her. "I'm OK, head rush, I just got up too quickly."

"Are you sure?"

"Yes, so… when my mom gets back, I want her to help me with …"

"Excuse me wife-to-be, who says we can't plan our own wedding? Do we look like two incompetent idiots here?" he said, with a cocky grin and sticking his thumbs into the sides of his shirt like a farmer with braces.

"We can do this," he stressed, "and… we will be ready for when Lorraine gets back, what do you have to say about that?" He was teasing her and was very entertaining in the process. "So, your dad will give you away, your mom will be by your side, Grey will carry the rings, and all we have to do is show up."

"I definitely must call Amelia, I can't possibly get married without my best friend!

Can we ask your mom to be our hostess and have her organize and oversee the reception?" Sage asked.

"That would be nice, but don't you think you should meet her first?"

"Oh, most definitely!"

They were both in agreement for Lorraine's part.

"Noah! I have an idea!"

"OK, ideas are good, and we need some, let's have it."

"What do you think about having our wedding at the loft and the reception downstairs in the yacht club? Can you picture us standing in front of the open doors with the water behind us and our family and friends joining us? Or we could have the ceremony on the beach!"

"Wow, I'm thinking a church, but that's even better. Where did all this come from? I love your idea, but don't we have to get permission from the owners?"

Playfully, she punched him in the arm and then hugging him she added, "Very funny, so do we have a plan going on here or what?"

They were like two teenagers planning a beach party like in the old days.

There was never any other choice for Noah than to ask his dad's best friend, Randy Kimble, to act as a stand-in for his dad.

Sage was somewhat disappointed that Amelia had gone overseas on a buyer's convention and couldn't attend, but they both knew she would come back with some pretty awesome ideas for her clothing line.

30

Lorraine, on cue, began her walk down the bridal path to stand and wait for Sage. Noah smiled, nodded and winked his approval. His heart beat a little faster when Sage come into view on the arm of her father. She was the most beautiful woman, bride, mother and best friend any man could ask for. Her hair had been swept up into a loose, French twist with long strands pulled out to hang loosely around her face and down her back. Tiny sprigs of baby's breath were pinned in several places around the twist and her veil. Looking radiant, she walked the carpet in a simple knee-length white strapless dress and a pair of three-inch heeled white sandals. Draping around her shoulders, the veil flowed down her back to the tip of her hemline and was held in place with a tiara. Her bouquet was done with pink baby roses with a mixture of tiny white chrysanthemums and accented with matching sprigs of baby's breath. She carried it in front of herself hiding the spot that was a secret only to them.

Proudly, Noah accepted when Gage offered him his daughter's hand. Overwhelmed, Noah felt blessed to have a second chance with the love of his life. Turning toward the Reverend, together they pledged their love, in front of family and friends. Greyson stood patiently waiting with the ring pillow and proud to be a part of his mom and dad's wedding. He carefully raised the pillow each time a band was required, and when the last ring was taken, he took his place with his grandpa, Gage.

Once the 'I dos' were spoken, and they were pronounced man and wife, the guests rose to their feet in applause as Noah kissed and held his beautiful bride.

Wandering over, Keri congratulated her new daughter-in-law and welcomed her into the family. Hugging Noah, she continued along to shake hands with Lorraine and Gage, she bent down and gave a hug to Grey and moved down the line.

Keri had had a sad look about her since the breakup with Drew. It played on her conscience every day with the hell she'd put him through. She'd held on to a man who never loved her and then watched the man who did love her walk away because of her selfishness and lies. Having no intentions of staying for the reception, she was not in the mood for festivities. Love and laughter were not on her agenda after the mess she'd created. Looking around the room one last time, she stepped out onto the deck. Pausing briefly, she took in the beautiful view and relaxed a bit as the breeze gave her some comfort. Her cell phone buzzed from her handbag.

"Hello?"

"Keri?"

"Jake?"

"Yes, it's me, I'd like to talk to you."

"OK, where and when?" she asked, looking out over the water and for the first time in months, her heart beat a little faster. She waited for him to answer, hoping he hadn't hung up on her.

"Jake? Are you there?"

"Yes, I am, I'm right here."

Glancing down over the beach, she saw him standing next to his car, waving up at her.

"Oh, my God! You are here!" she said, hurrying down the steps. He walked towards her watching her carefully and hoping she wouldn't stumble in her heels. He was at the bottom waiting for her.

"It's so good to see you, Jake."

"It's good to see you too, Keri. I was sorry to hear about Drew, it must be difficult."

"It is, but for the right reasons this time. I'm stunned, to say the least, that you even want to speak to me. I'm glad though for the opportunity to apologize for lying and hurting you, Jake. I know I lost the best thing that ever happened to me because of my stupidity and I hope you can forgive me. It is so wonderful to see you but why are you here?"

"I read the announcement that your son was getting married and I knew you'd be here, so I drove over hoping to gather the courage to call you. As soon as I saw that you were leaving, I knew I had to. I've been wanting to for a while but never got up the nerve until now."

"I can't imagine why you'd want to talk to me after the stunt I pulled."

"Regardless, I still love you, Keri, and I would like for us to have another chance."

Tears sprung to her eyes at his words. "Seriously? I … I don't know what to say," she said, her eyes pooling. Blinking from the sun, caused the pools to overflow.

Reaching out with his thumb, he wiped a streak away. Gently pulling her into his arms, she collapsed against his chest. Holding him tightly, she was relieved that he would even speak to her let alone want her back.

"Oh, Jake, I have missed you!"

"If my absence wasn't noticed, then my presence wouldn't have mattered," he whispered. "I read that somewhere," he said with a grin.

"Oh, you mattered, Jake and I love you so much. I will never forgive myself for hurting you."

"If you can try to forgive yourself, then I will too."

"Really? You can forgive me?"

"Hating yourself will only make you sick, Keri, you have to move on from this. You made a mistake, but it's done, let it go. If you can do that, then we can have a second chance at some happiness."

"I would love that, Jake, I still can't believe you're here. Would you like to meet my son and daughter-in-law?" she said, looking up at him.

"I sure would!"

"Then let's go inside."

EPILOGUE

While Sage slept, Noah sat in the hospital room holding Andi. She was his daughter, in every sense of the word, and he would love her as much as he loves her mother. He was still a bit overwhelmed knowing he's gained a wife, son and a daughter all in a span of eight months. *'Second chances are few and far between;'* he thought, *'this time we'll get it right.'*

While rocking his baby girl, he spotted a dime next to Sage's bed. Bending over to pick it up, he felt a tiny puff of air pass by him, and a thought quickly came to mind. He'd once heard that dimes appearing was a sign from Heaven.

"Dad?" he whispered, holding the dime in his palm. The room went slightly cool for just a few seconds, and he saw Andi's tiny fingers go into a curl as if she was holding onto someone's finger. She had a slightly cocked, and happy smile on her face and her eyes seemed to be following something around the room. Noah, letting himself go with the moment, felt his father's presence in the room. It was only seconds, but it felt longer. He looked down at Andi, and she seemed to be looking directly over her mother's head, and in an instant, Noah saw a piece of Sage's hair move, and he knew that his father was visiting to say goodbye. A slight press upon his shoulder told him he was there and that he approved. Andi's body was startled as her little arms flew into the air and she looked up towards Noah. It seemed he wanted to see his baby, kiss her forehead and know that everything was OK with his family.

"Rest in peace, Dad," he whispered, and he felt the room warm up again. He'd had a moment with his father, and he felt peaceful. Andi closed her eyes but kept the smile on her face as Sage woke up.

"I just had the weirdest dream. Drew was here, and it felt … real," she said, looking over at Noah.

He just stared at her dumbfounded.

"Noah, what's wrong? Are you OK?"

"Dad was just here, Sage, he made a brief visit," he said, holding his palm open to show her the dime. "I think he just wanted to be assured that we were OK and to let us know he is OK too. Is that weird?" He told her about the coolness of the room, Andi's expressions, her finger curl and even her hair moving and all of it happened before the room warmed up again.

"In my dream, he kissed me on the forehead, there were no words, but he told me he was OK and that we would be OK. It was peaceful and not scary at all, and it was wonderful to see him. We can't tell anybody about this, they'll think we've lost our marbles," she whispered, pointing a finger at her head, making circles and widening her eyes.

Noah smiled at her antics and said, "I agree, totally. This is between you, Andi and me because I know she saw him. She was watching him move around the room."

Sage teared up knowing how much Drew would have loved this little girl, his namesake. Noah went over and sat on the side of the bed having the same thoughts.

"He will always be with us, Noah, I think it is his way of letting us know he is watching over us and will always take care of us. I'm not sure if I ever believed in that stuff before but, I seriously do now."

Lorraine, Gage, and Grey came into the room to have a first peek at the baby girl. Grey, a proud big brother, smiled broadly when his dad squatted before his son to give him a better view of Andi.

"She is really cute, Daddy, she looks like Mommy! Wow! A baby sister. She has our middle name too, Daddy, I like that."

"Your grandfather and my dad; his name was Andrew, so Andi is named after all three of us."

"Awesome! May I hold her, Daddy?"

"Of course, you can!"

Noah settled him into the rocker and placed Andi in his arms explaining how to hold her head while the others looked on and smiled. Lorraine was busy taking pictures with her cell phone as Gage moved closer to the rocker.

"She's just about the purdiest thang I've ever seen," he boasted. "I thought my wife and daughter was just about perfect but this little thang right here … I'm sorry ladies, but this little one has got a big piece of my heart," he drawled while holding his hand to his chest.

Lorraine touched his arm and motioned that they should leave to allow some family time. She was pleased that Sage and Noah had found their way back to each other. Hers and Sage's lives had come full circle, from the same circumstances and both going about it all wrong and she was blessed that their lives had been corrected by two loving men. Going over to the bed, she kissed the top of Sage's head and held her for several minutes. Nodding her head, she silently told Sage that she was proud and happy that she'd found her love again.

Moving toward the chair, she hugged Noah, and her facial expression non-verbally told him she was sorry for his lost years without Sage. He held her tightly to assured her everything was OK. Hugging Gage's arm, he kissed her cheek as if knowing her thoughts.

Watching as Grey held his baby sister, no words were needed between Noah and Sage. Looking into each other's eyes, they knew that the secrets they shared would forever and always be only theirs.

Locking their fingers and taking a moment, they silently gave thanks to God for second chances.

The End

Other Titles by Dee

Timeless Love
Available Online & Print

The Grand Manor
Available Online & Print

Gypsy Heart
Available Online & Print

Gifted
Available Online & Print

Tidbits, Tips & Treasures
A Self Help Book
Available Online

Watch for Dee's upcoming books,
JOY
and
Then, Now & Forever

To remain in touch with Dee, contact her through
her website at
www.deelightfulreading.com

www.ingramcontent.com/pod-product-compliance
Lightning Source LLC
Chambersburg PA
CBHW070915260626
47162CB00007B/2682